FIRE
HORSE

FIRE
HORSE

Denis M. Way

W H ALLEN · LONDON
1988

Copyright © Denis M. Way, 1988

Set in Linotron Ehrhardt by Input Typesetting Ltd, London
Printed and bound by
Adlard and Son Limited,
Dorking, Surrey, and Letchworth, Hertfordshire
for the publishers, W. H. Allen & Co. Plc
44 Hill Street, London W1X 8LB

ISBN 0 491 03486 5

To Maurice Green –
thank you for the opportunity

Author's note

Hong Kong has had two phases in its history. The second began in 1949, when the curtain fell on Shanghai, and is still being lived out.

If it had not been Shanghai's fate to die when it did, it would not have been Hong Kong's fortune to rise from its ashes. And this story would never have been written.

Hong Kong is true. Shanghai was true. Many of the events in the story are based on fact. But the characters (apart from cameos by certain well-known personages), and the story itself, are not true.

And yet it could have been.

There never was a Royal Cumberland Regiment, nor a Cumberland China Limited, nor a John Stanford Huart, nor a Tu Chien, nor a Zagan family . . .

And I take refuge in 'poetic licence' in never having paid rent to the noble landlords of Connaught Centre, and in constructing, demolishing and reconstructing a skyscraper that never was, on a corner of that narrow thoroughfare that has *fung shui* galore: Ice House Street.

Denis M. Way
Hong Kong
July, 1987

The Legend of the Fire Horse

The Lord Buddha lay dying.

Intending one last magnanimous act before departing from earth, he summoned all the animals in creation to bid him farewell.

But only twelve came.

First to appear was the opportunistic Rat, followed by the resolute Ox, the rebellious Tiger, the gracious Rabbit, the aristocratic Dragon, the wily Snake. Seventh to present himself was the unpredictable Horse. After him followed the gentle Goat, the cunning Monkey, the argumentative Rooster, the loyal Dog. And last to arrive was the fortunate Pig.

True to his intention, the Lord Buddha rewarded the animals, regardless of their individual motives for attending. To each he granted a year in the order of their arrival, and assigned one of the five elements: Fire from Mars, Gold from Venus, Wood from Jupiter, Water from Mercury, or Earth from Saturn. And so each animal would rendezvous with its natural element once in every sixty year cycle.

And so the Year of the Fire Horse was created, as the element assigned to the Horse was Fire.

With this task done, the Lord Buddha died.

In time, the interaction of the unpredictable Horse with its Fire element and Mars, the God of War, produced a phenomenon – the Fire Horse in human form.

Men born in this one year in sixty were different. Their driving force, whether philanthropic or malevolent, was exaggerated. They possessed a penchant to destroy everything including their family and themselves, or an unquenchable passion to complete a great mission before their death.

The destiny of a Fire Horse was to be blessed with exceptional wealth and acclaim, or to be cursed with ruination by his own hand.

And it is so today.

Contents

Book I

IN THE EYE OF THE VORTEX

Shanghai: 14 August 1937 – 27 August 1940

1

The mid-August Saturday afternoon was sweaty hot. Off Shanghai a typhoon procrastinated. Its vanguard showers did nothing to alleviate the heat, and were fuel to the basting humidity. The spasmodic rain interrupted life and leisure in the International Settlement, in particular the cricket match in progress in the grounds of the Race Club.

The artillery fire was louder than the day before, the fighting closer. On the horizon, columns of black smoke pirouetted in the wind gusts, pinpointing death and destruction. Yet the cricketers paid it no heed.

Andrew Huart-Brent stood at the wicket. Just thirty, he was the youngest taipan of the China Trade, his *hong* the omnipresent, omnipotent Cumberland China Limited. Square of frame in tailored whites, scrubbed pads and gloves, he settled over his bat in a stance that was a carbon copy of the great Jack Hobbs, whom he had watched tame the Australians at the Oval in 1926. He moved forward into the drive as Stewart Barlow of Hardoons, a surly individual with the build of a publican, delivered the first ball after the third resumption of play. Sent with a grunt, it lobbed out of Barlow's unsupple fingers still moulded to the contours of the port glass he had nursed in the clubhouse. Andrew placed his shot neatly between the fieldsmen at extra cover and mid-off, and seeing the sodden turf would prevent the ball reaching the boundary, he called his partner through for the three runs that completed his half-century.

'Arse always beats class, Andrew,' Barlow muttered in ill humour as he passed the young taipan on the way back to his bowling mark. The Hardoon manager had not joined in the applause of spectators and fieldsmen, and the traditional calls of 'Well batted, sir!'

'I completely agree, Stewart,' Andrew responded brightly, eyes sparkling with mischief in his boyish suntanned face. 'But you

[1]

possess posterior enough for everyone in the game. Why is it you get so few wickets?'

Barlow glared. 'Up yours,' he growled and stomped away.

Andrew grinned to himself. The oaf fell into it every time. The next ball was sure to be an angry full toss and he wished he was at the striker's wicket to despatch it over the boundary. He winked down the pitch. His partner nodded and grinned back.

Suddenly a demonic roar erupted overhead and peaked in an ear-splitting crescendo. The heads of the cricketers jerked skywards in unison.

'Oh, bloody Christ!' Barlow swore, aborting his run-up. 'What now?'

A pair of camouflaged twin-engined bombers burst like messengers from Hell out of the layer of heavy rain cloud two thousand feet above the International Settlement. They levelled for a few seconds, then dropped their noses and dived at the harbour.

'Are they Jap?' someone asked carelessly.

'No, Chinese. Missimo's boys.' Andrew had seen the white sun markings. 'They're having a crack at the Jap navy in the harbour by the look of it.' He raised a gloved hand to shield his eyes from the light rain that had begun to fall again. 'Watch it, chaps!' he called to the sky. 'That nice fat cruiser you're aiming at's parked right outside my front door!'

The pom-pom-pom-pom of Japanese shore-based and naval ack-ack carried on the air from the harbour and untidy patches of flak blossomed around the two diving bombers like brown-black candy-floss. One veered off as if hit and wobbled towards the French Bund. Four small black objects dropped from it in an evenly spaced pattern.

'Oh my giddy aunt!' Andrew hissed, his eyes round and staring. 'No . . !'

A gust of wind was blowing the last two bombs backwards. It looked to Andrew as if they were falling right on the junction of Nanking Road and the Bund. It was certain to be bustling with a Saturday afternoon crowd.

'Brainless idiot!' Andrew smacked his bat against his pad in chagrin. 'He'll blow innocent people to hell and gone!' He watched, open-mouthed and helpless, as the bombs fell to earth with an agonising slowness.

Barlow let go an impatient snort. Arms akimbo, the cricket ball lost in his meaty paw, he bellowed from his bowling mark: 'So let 'em wipe out some o' their own no-account refugees. Get on with the game!'

'Play!' called the umpire, an independent merchant well laced with his own company's brand of imported scotch. 'This match'll finish today, by George. Come bloody rain, typhoon or bombs, we finish today. Play!'

Hidden from the eyes of the cricketers at the Race Club by the interposed buildings, the four bombs exploded anonymously in the distance, one after the other, as Barlow ran in and delivered his second ball.

Nanking Road was muddy, noisy, its bitumen jammed with automobiles and barrows and rickshaws. Pedestrians were imbued with an urgency bordering on mass hysteria as they charged into each other along the pavement that constricted and diverged. But the approaching typhoon was but one reason for this. Across the harbour in Pootung the column of dense black smoke billowing from the Asiatic Petroleum Company depot testified both to the reality of the sudden conflict without the International Settlement, and to the crass inaccuracy of the Nationalist Chinese Air Force.

Paulette Huart-Brent was caught up in the throng the instant she led her mother-in-law out of the Cathay Arcade of Sassoon House. In reflex she took one hand off the stack of parcels she had carried all the way from the clothing shops in the Avenue Joffre and Yates Road to whip her dress aside as an undisciplined Johnson cab obliterated an adjacent puddle.

Adelaide Huart-Brent caught the top parcel just as it started to fall. 'Do be careful, my dear,' the matriarch imparted in the headmistress tone she reserved for children, hired help and greenhorns. 'Andrew will be furious if we produce his tailor-made shirts covered in mud. You should have sent the *amah* home with them. In Shanghai the servants do what they are employed to do. Especially when one is in the family way.'

'Yes, Mother,' Paulette responded, clamping down on her quick Creole temper and conjuring a smile. 'I'm glad we took the extra time to pick out the best baby bonnets. I hope they're not crushed. Oh, watch out . . .'

A tram had clanked to a stop and a swarm of Chinese commuters unloaded and dispersed in all directions at a pace all except themselves would term reckless. Adelaide ducked a raised umbrella as the women were enveloped. 'Take that, you . . .' She used her own as a ram.

'Mother, why don't we cross over to the Palace Coffee House for some tea and scones and let this awful crowd go about its business without us.' She inclined her head towards the Palace Hotel directly opposite. Its coffee shop was a favourite rendezvous, ideal for catching up on the latest gossip in between sips of Darjeeling tea or barley water.

The suggestion produced a rare smile which gilded the matriarch's lined face. 'My dear, I have to take it all back. You're becoming more British every day . . . despite that colonial accent. It could even be that you'll pronounce "scones" correctly soon. You'll be a Shanghailander yet. Tea and scones – note the pronunciation – would be very nice indeed.'

Paulette knew her mother-in-law did not intend rudeness. Adelaide had run affairs all her life and it had tempered her. She had even managed Cumberland China for the two years between the death of her father, the *hong*'s founder, and Andrew's graduation from Cambridge.

The women paused on the Sassoon House steps before its revolving door and looked for a gap in the traffic. The grand building had been built seven years earlier by Sir Victor Sassoon to accommodate the offices of his vast financial and trading empire, which occupied the first three floors. It also incorporated the Cathay Hotel, its rooms from the fourth floor up to the eleventh where were the most luxurious suites in Shanghai. The Cathay ranked with the Hong Kong Hotel and the Peninsula, and the Raffles in Singapore as the best inn in Asia.

From atop these plutocratic steps Paulette had a better view of the refugees shuffling south along the Bund in a never-ending barefoot procession of hand-held carts and one-wheeled barrows piled with bundled possessions and crying, naked babies. Never had she known anything like Shanghai. The few months had dulled the novelty not at all. Her New Orleans upbringing had hardly been sheltered, but it had singularly failed to prepare her for this strange, exciting place on the other side of the world. And now there was a war approaching. She was not afraid. In fact she was excited at the prospect of witnessing it first-hand. The Huart-Brents and every Shanghailander she met assured her point-blank that the Settlement was inviolate. History proved it. Its neutrality had been respected during a succession of wars and rebellions. And this latest 'trouble' would likewise leave it untouched.

Adelaide was following Paulette's gaze in the direction of the refugees, her face folded in disapproval. She had ready a disparaging remark when the revolving door discharged a tall Englishman in white flannels. He stopped short and clasped the rim of his straw boater between thumb and forefinger. 'Mrs Huart-Brent, a good-day to you. Are you well?'

'Hello, Miles. Have you met my daughter-in-law, Paulette, Andrew's wife? My dear, this is Miles Gutteridge. He's with Glen Line. It's quite a large shipping company.' Not as large as it was, she added privately.

'Oh, yes,' Paulette smiled, extending her hand. 'The Glen Line Building on the Bund, isn't it? Weren't you taken over by Alfred Holt and Company two years ago? I'm happy to make your acquaintance, Mr Gutteridge.'

The Glen Line man held his approbation in check. Much was being said of the wife Andrew Huart-Brent had collared in the States and he could see most of it was true. An intelligent beauty stood before him, her large blue eyes framed by finely coiffured blonde hair. 'The pleasure is mine, Mrs Huart-Brent. A terrible day, I'm afraid. These typhoons are a nuisance, aren't they? Hullo, what's going on now . . . ?'

The women had also heard the foreboding sound from the direction of the harbour. Now others heard it too.

'More gunfire . . . ?' enquired Adelaide.

The sea of upturned oriental faces on Nanking Road had them instinctively looking at the sky. The bombers came out of nowhere, the scream of their engines drowning out the coughing of the Japanese guns on the warships in the Whangpoo and the shore batteries on the Hongkew wharves. The descant of war had stilled the junction.

The refugees, from personal experience, were first to break and run.

It was Miles Gutteridge who saw the bombs. 'God in heaven! Get inside, ladies!' They turned and pushed towards the revolving door, but it was jammed in a crush of bodies that attempted to barge in both directions at once. 'No time!' the Glen Line man yelled. 'Get down! Behind me . . !'

A chorus of screams erupted all around.

The first two bombs pitched into the Whangpoo. Twin spouts the colour and texture of nightsoil lifted nonchalantly into the air and flopped back into the harbour. The remaining ranks of refugees split in blind panic. Men, women, children ran madly into the alleys and roads leading off the Bund. Nanking Road was plugged solid with struggling humanity, half of whom seemed imbued with a fatal curiosity that rooted them to the spot whilst the rest desperately tried to escape around them, over the top of them, clean through them.

[5]

There came a high-pitched, shrieking, scraping noise and a flash of light as the roof of the Palace Hotel sheered off. Glass fragments fired down in a murderous cross-fire and a white cascade of plaster dust settled upon the crowded street. A thousand throats gave voice to raw terror. And then the fourth bomb exploded.

The crescent-shaped windows of the Palace Coffee House disintegrated in an eruption of needle-sharp splinters. Crouched together, gripping each other in panic, the Huart-Brent women felt their clothing torn by flying shards. A wave of wind and violent noise enveloped them. A heavy weight crashed down, skittling them, tumbling them like logs onto the pavement. There came a hollow supernatural quiet, broken by the crackle of things burning and a hideous screaming and wailing that was stereophonic, then more explosions as automobile fuel tanks erupted one by one. A nauseous wave of incinerating human flesh carried on a sudden wind gust.

Something hot and thick and wet was running over Paulette's leg. She looked down, but could not comprehend what she saw. Adelaide groaned behind her, so the thing was no part of her mother-in-law. Then Paulette Huart-Brent's inbred dignity dissolved and her abandoned screams were added to the cacophony of horror and pain that engulfed the junction.

The headless body of Miles Gutteridge lay half across her, its blood spurting over her legs in a regulated, intermittent stream like fluid from a pump. The blood ran into her shoes, overflowed to join the scarlet rivulet that was sloshing along the gutter.

Nanking Road was a scene of abject ruin. Torn bitumen, rock and earth was laid over with a hideous carpet of entangled bodies and disengaged limbs. A tram lay on its side, arms and legs jutting from its windows. Cars and trucks were aflame, their occupants jerking about inside like blackened puppets. The upper floors of the Palace Hotel were an inferno that spat out burning debris to fall spinning and crackling, bouncing about the gruesome coverlet of dismembered corpses.

Through the smoke and fumes the figures '1906', cut into the stone above the entrance of the Palace Hotel to record the year of its construction, were like a tally on some morbid scoreboard.

A wind gust fanned the scene of death. Rain came down in large drops that converged and ran pink into the gutter. Its procrastination over, the typhoon fell upon the wounded International Settlement of Shanghai.

*

[6]

The Chairman of the Shanghai Municipal Council counted heads again and found he at last had a quorum. His gavel cracked down once, twice and the heated voices delivering thirteen languages and even more accents were all quelled. Smoke from a variety of national brands of cigarettes, cigars and cheroots hung in suspended grey veils in the dim light of the chamber. Outside the massive Victorian stone building on the corner of Foochow and Honan Roads, the typhoon raged. Its winds swirled in squealing devil gusts, its rain drummed hard at the shuttered windows and ran from beneath the frames.

It took something exceptional to assemble the Shanghai Municipal Council at short notice on a Sunday morning in a storm such as this. And the Sabbath of August 15th, 1937, had it.

The members all sat facing the raised head table. They comprised every taipan and chief manager and the head of every administrative, public works and military arm in Shanghai. The Japanese delegation sat together near the main door in their customary station, notebooks out. Haiyama, the leader, was tight-lipped and hard of visage.

The side door opened and Andrew Huart-Brent entered. His eyes were red from lack of sleep, his face drawn and pale through his tan. His suit looked slept in, which it had been. Nevertheless, his ingrained spirit was intact. He skipped up the steps to the head table and took the seat beside the chairman that was reserved for the second most powerful man in Shanghai, the man next in line. A Chinese 'boy' hurried to the table bearing a teapot, bowed and poured.

'What we have here,' Andrew remarked drily as he lifted the Earl Grey to his lips, 'is a teacup in a storm.'

From anyone else the incongruous humour would have been disrespectful, but Andrew could get away with it. The chairman smiled sympathetically, and enquired *sotto voce*; 'How're your wife and mother, old chap?' On two occasions only was the fierce but generally ethical trading rivalry between Shanghai taipans shelved: whenever they found themselves on the same rugby or cricket team, and when Council business was conducted.

'They'll both be in hospital for a few days. I'm told Paulette will keep the baby, thank God.'

'Andrew, congratulations! I wasn't even aware she was pregnant.'

'I only found out myself a few days ago. She'll be fine. My two belles are toughies, but I can't say the same of Lorna Gutteridge. She collapsed on the spot when she was given the news, poor woman. She's in a coma. Miles saved Paulette's and my mother's lives, you know. He shielded them with his body. How can I ever repay . . . ?' His voice went the way of his manufactured cheeriness.

The chairman sighed. 'Glen Line have a fair deal for dependants of senior staff in cases like this. Still, it's a shocking affair.' He shook his head sadly, then lifted it to address the Council with the firm tone he employed to run its meetings. 'Gentlemen, the toll from the bombs that fell on the Nanking Road is over seven hundred dead.' He cocked an eye at the Commissioner of Police who confirmed the figure with a curt nod. 'And the Gendarmerie have put theirs – from those that later fell on the French Concession and destroyed the Great World Amusement Palace in the Avenue Edouard VII – at over a thousand.' He sipped from a glass of water, then continued, choosing his words with care as he watched the Japanese delegation transcribe every word. 'It seems the trouble in the north has arrived with a vengeance. The question is – is this violation of our neutrality an isolated incident, or can we expect recurrences . . ?'

Though the question was posed rhetorically, Haiyama was on his feet in an instant, his arms windmilling about. 'Chinese drop bombs on neutra'r r'and on purpose!' he shouted in staccato, almost comically accented English. 'Bombers on'ry preten' zey attack Japanese ships but drop bombs on neutra'r r'and on purpose!– You must protes'! Chiang Kai-shek want A'ries start fight on his side against Nipponese Imperia'r forces. Big trick! Chinese trick you, jus' r'ike they trick you ber'ieve Japanese Army start troub're firs'! Big trick. Chinese start troub're – '

As the tirade had turned into raw politics, the chairman had started tapping his gavel. 'An official protest to Nanking has been drafted, Mr Haiyama. We have received an unofficial apology from Madam Chiang who swears it was all a tragic mistake. But she has been unable to provide us with a guarantee against further mistakes.' He pursed his lips and fixed Haiyama with the look that was famous in Shanghai and the head of the Japanese delegation resumed his seat in bad grace. 'Gentlemen, this meeting has been convened to approve emergency measures. Firstly, the garrisons defending the Settlement must be reinforced. The Commander, British Forces has called for additional battalions and I have cabled the Prime Minister of England in support. Two battalions can probably be made available from Hong Kong, plus another from somewhere else in Asia. I understand we will be adorned with the presence of the Sixth US Marines and that the Italians are

[8]

endeavouring to uphold their obligations under the treaty by summoning troops from Abyssinia. I don't need to ask if the fourth country discharged with the duty of defending the perimeter of the International Settlement is calling for reinforcements, do I, Mr Haiyama?'

But the head of the Japanese delegation either ignored the provocation and the acerbic mutterings from all directions, or did not hear any of it, as he and each of his countrymen engaged themselves in feverish note-taking.

'The French are, it goes without saying, transferring their own units in from Indo-China,' the chairman added, referring to the *Conseil d'Administration Municipal*'s predilection for running their own concession in exclusively Gallic fashion. 'Now, may I have a proposer and a seconder to the emergency measures so far?'

'I so propose, sir!' called the chief manager of the Mercantile Bank. Andrew Huart-Brent seconded and the motion was carried with all voting in favour, except the Japanese delegation, who kept their heads down.

The chairman went on: 'I propose that evacuation of all women, children and non-essential personnel to Hong Kong be commenced forthwith. We have made the *Rajputana* available for British families and the *President Taft* for American. German evacuees may embark on the *Ottenburg* and Dutch on the *Tasman*. We are still trying to contact ships for all other national communities and I expect to receive more information after the meeting. We are preparing for a full evacuation, but let us pray this will not prove necessary. I advise all those living outside the Settlement to move in at once. It's getting dangerous out there.'

He surveyed the chamber, satisfied that the arrangements were the best possible at short notice. Despite the typhoon, he had worked through the night with the heads of each national community, except Haiyama, who had first proved difficult to contact, then had flatly refused to co-operate. The chairman knew the man was merely a puppet of the Japanese High Command in Hongkew. But what could he do about it?

'Curfew, Mister Chairman,' Andrew imparted. 'Sundown to sunrise.'

'Hear, hear,' agreed the chairman. 'To enforce it the Volunteer Corps is to be placed on readiness as of this moment. Colonel Hornby?'

'Here, sir! Yes, sir!'

A second vote ratified the evacuation measures and the curfew. Haiyama raised his fist. 'Chinese provoke you!' he shouted.

'Attack on Imperia'r Navy was on'ry excuse. Chiang try trick A'ries into joining him! No need reinforcements. This neutr'r territory! This – '

The chairman's gavel banged down. 'Meeting adjourned!' he cried. 'We've much to do. Contrary to Mr Haiyama's opinion, I fear greater trouble. I particularly fear the effect on our trade. I trust the measures we have agreed will restrict any disruption to it to a minimum. Thank you all for attending during this wretched storm. Good day, gentlemen!'

The Council chamber emptied with alacrity, each member anxious to return to home and wife and family, or to the mistress waiting in some downtown *pied à terre*. The Japanese representatives left exactly as they had sat through the meeting: as one. On Honan Road they parted with deep bows and scurried to their limousines. Haiyama rode through the typhoon to Hongkew, a private smile on his round face.

By August, 1937, the Second Battalion of the Royal Cumberland Regiment had completed its tour of duty in Rangoon. Its presence had been superfluous since April, when Burma had separated from British India and a local administration had taken responsibility for national defence. The Second Cumberlands were preparing to embark for home aboard the troop ship *Otranto*, when their commanding officer received a counter order.

Instead of heading west into the Andaman Sea towards the Suez Canal, Malta, Gibraltar and Portsmouth, the *Otranto* swung its bows east.

2

At the hottest time of the tropical day, in the steaming wardroom of the *Otranto* a birthday party of sorts was coming to an end.

'Cheers, John! Bottoms up!'

'This is one hell of a place for an infantryman to celebrate his thirty-first birthday,' Major John Stanford Huart, Commander, 'C' Company, Second Battalion, the Royal Cumberland Regiment, responded as he looked around at his fellow officers in feigned distaste. 'The irony of it! Courtesy of the RN. And on the high seas.' He picked up his glass with the double issue of rum. 'But what the hell.' And he tossed it down.

'Cheers!' A half dozen other glasses hit the narrow steel table and the inevitable song started up:

> 'Happy birthday to you.
> Happy birthday to you.
> Happy birthday, Man Mountain!
> Happy birthday to yooouuu!'

Huart winced at the nickname given him by the soldiers of 'C' Company. 'Party's over!' he declared. 'Drill for Seven Platoon on the foredeck, Grant. All pot bellies to be history by Shanghai. Ours and theirs.'

'Let's go then.' Lieutenant Grant Rodder pushed back his chair.

An hour later the two officers were together at the forward rail looking north whilst behind them the riflemen drilled in a circuit around the deck. The surface of the South China Sea was flat, monotonous, like a vast mirror reflecting the raw rays of the relentless sun as it bisected the ship's wake. The only cloud in the sky was an ineffectual bed of cirrus lazing on the western horizon. The day was scorching. South East Asia reserved its most oppressive weather for late August, when the typhoon season was in its final phase. At this time the great storms were most treacherous, springing out of nothing in the Pacific east of the Philippines and tearing hell-bent westwards to cast themselves upon the coasts of Indo and South China, there to abate back into nothing.

Major John Huart extended a straight seventy-seven inches towards the tropical sun. He looked the career officer he was. The creases of his khaki uniform were regimentally precise, the crown upon each epaulette gleamed golden. A thin line of perspiration fringed his temples, his sole concession to the extreme heat. His peaked cap was set square on his head, exactly half an inch above the top of each large, long ear. His massive shoulders were set as if carved from stone. Everything about the man was symmetrical, balanced. Even his voice, as he said to Rodder: 'I've been given a pass to step ashore in Hong Kong for a few hours, Grant. There's a spot of family business for me to attend to there. Something that goes back more than sixty years.'

Rodder, who had been watching his men with a wooden expression that belied the veracity of the criticism he would later deliver, peered back and up, eyes squinting in the searing sunlight. He welcomed exchanges with his company commander, a man who had filled his off-duty hours in Rangoon studying the

Burmese language and the basics of Buddhism. It had been an incongruous pastime for a man trained to kill. But John Huart, the subaltern suspected, had never embraced an idle moment in his life.

'Family business, sir? A relative in the garrison?'

Huart shook his head. 'Nothing military, Grant. Back in 1873 there was a split in the family. Both my great-grandfather and his younger brother, Charles, were serving in India with the Royal Cumberland Regiment. But Charles, it seems, fancied the ladies more than his commission. He was caught *flagrante delicto* aboard the wife of another officer and cashiered. He was a contrary individual and, instead of returning to England, he did just the opposite and trekked overland through Assam and Burma into south-west China. There he started trading in arms, operating out of Chungking and dealing with the mandarins along the central reaches of the Yangtse. His timing was superb. The Empress Dowager had reversed her prohibition on the formation of regional armies in the wake of the Taiping Rebellion, and every mandarin with one was in the market for munitions. He soon made a name for himself in what you might call the "legitimate" China Trade. He kept his hands clean of opium, you see. He died seven years ago at the grand old age of eighty-four. His company has survived him. Its head office is in Shanghai and it has branches all over China, including Hong Kong . . .'

'Which you will be visiting,' Rodder finished. 'How very interesting, sir. So you must have family in Shanghai.'

'Yes. I think it's my third cousin who runs the company now.'

'What company is it, sir?'

Though Huart's smile was hidden in the shade cast by his peaked cap, a chuckle confirmed his birthday humour. 'Charles named it Cumberland China Limited after the regiment. I think he did it to cock a snook at his brother, my great-grandfather: Brigadier-General Stanford Algernon Augustus Huart. Old Stanford was in command of the regiment when Charles was court martialled. I understand he endorsed the sentence handed down on his own brother with relish. There was no love lost between them.'

'Your ancestors sound like rare characters.'

'Charles Huart was certainly "rare". He built out of nothing a company that became one of the biggest in China. I'm looking forward to meeting his grandson, my third cousin. It'll be the first contact between the two branches of the family since 1873.'

'Get 'em up there!' A bellow split the air. 'Eff-Igh! Eff-Igh! Eff-Igh!'

Seven Platoon doubled by, Sergeant Dadds driving them like a merciless cowherd. Bare-chested, clad in cavernous knee-length khaki shorts, the soldiers stamped an angry beat upon the hot steel deck with their heavy boots. Their breath came in rhythmic snorts as they lifted their Lee Enfield rifles above their heads as they jogged, then lowered them to the NCO's commands. Sweat was streaming from their bodies softened by service in Rangoon, where the most strenuous duty had been an infrequent guard at the Governor's residence.

'So your side of the family carried on the military tradition, sir?' Rodder asked when the platoon had passed, though the answer was obvious.

'Unerringly, Grant.' Huart affirmed as his memory went to work. 'I can remember as a lad I used to stand and stare at my great-grandfather's portrait over our hearth with his stupendous moustache and his braid and his medals from the Indian Mutiny, Afghanistan, the Sudan. He survived them all. The strength of his character dictated that the men of subsequent generations would go into the army. His son – my grandfather – rose to the the rank of Major-General in the Great War . . .'

Huart fell silent as his thoughts moved chronologically on to his father who had not survived 1918, but had died terribly of mustard gas in the German counter-attack on the Fifth Army trenches outside Amiens. Huart would never forget the day the telegram had arrived. His mother's keening had brought him from the field, rugger ball in hand. That had been his first encounter with grief, and a long time had passed before he could accept that his life could continue with such an irreplaceable chunk torn out of it. His mother had passed on twelve years later, also very suddenly. But though he remembered her like a son, his recall of his father was still disproportionately associated with sadness.

'Yes,' he continued after long seconds. 'I followed family tradition. And here I am.' I didn't have to, he thought, but after the death of my father it would have been rank cowardice to have done otherwise.

He recalled how the family had been in a tight financial bind after the Armistice. His mother had supplemented her meagre widow's pension and handouts from the regimental welfare fund by taking a position as matron of a nearby college. She had worked all day whilst he and his younger sister, Claire, had attended school. Whereas Claire had done this under protest and was clearly destined for an early marriage, he had excelled and at thirteen had gone to Eton on a scholarship, graduated in 1925 and entered the Royal Military College, Sandhurst. Second Lieutenant John Stanford Huart's height had made him automatic choice as right-marker for the passing-out parade in January, 1927. The eighteen month infantry course had not taxed him and he had donned with pride the peaked cap with the badge that proclaimed 'Lead to Serve'. Doors into leading London banks, insurance companies and trading houses as a junior executive had opened before him, his career assured by the glowing reports in his Sandhurst file. But the military was sole option. Then he had ignored his entree to the Grenadier or Coldstream Guards in favour of family tradition. He had joined the infantry: the Royal Cumberland Regiment.

A pair of heels clicked together and snapped Huart back to the present.

'The men've completed drill . . . sah! Marginal improvement in my opinion. They're now merely slovenly . . . sah!' Sergeant Dadds' right hand was attached to his temple in a copybook salute.

The officers returned it and the NCO's arm whipped to his side. 'Very good, sergeant,' Rodder responded. 'Same tomorrow. 1400 hours.'

'Sahh!'

Dadds saluted again, flicked his eyes to Huart, turned on his heel and brought one boot against the other. He marched back to the assembled platoon, his arms swinging to shoulder level, fists palm down.

Huart watched him. He was wary of Sergeant Dadds. The man was an experienced NCO, but seemed to suppress an intrinsic sadism. Huart had been told that it had surfaced during the revolt of the Galons in the Tharrawaddy region north of Rangoon, when the followers of a crazed monk had been surprised to discover they were not immortal, that British bayonets could kill, that of Sergeant Dadds in particular.

'Bad luck your wife couldn't be with you on your birthday, sir.'

Huart turned back to Rodder with a rueful smile. He was missing Jennifer with a passion. 'You left your family in Rangoon, too, Grant.'

'True, sir. But being separated in the first year of marriage is hard to take. Especially with your first child due. When's it to be?'

'January. But such is a soldier's lot. It could be worse. The families will be joining us in Shanghai after a suitable period.' He looked to the northern horizon, towards which the bow of the

Otranto was cutting neatly through the blue glass surface of the South China Sea like the shears of a master draper. 'After all, it's not as if we're sailing into another Great War . . .'

3

The *Otranto* entered Victoria Harbour during the small hours of August 25th and dropped anchor between Stonecutters Island and Shamshuipo on the western shore of Kowloon Peninsula. She had made good time north through the South China Sea; there had not been a hint of bad weather.

Major John Huart disembarked at 0900 hours. Army transport carried him through streets crammed with refugees to Whitfield Barracks in Nathan Road. There he learned the address he sought was on Queen's Road in Victoria, on the island of Hong Kong itself. Despite the heat and humidity that had already claimed the day, and the coarse texture of his uniform, he decided to walk to the ferry down wide, tree-lined Nathan Road. He turned right at the Peninsula Hotel on the waterfront and saw ahead the 'Star' Ferry terminal on the very tip of the Kowloon promontory. He took a seat on the upper deck for the harbour crossing.

The sounds of a maritime confluence carried on a shimmering haze through the ferry's open sides. The shipping at anchor flew the flags of the world whilst less substantial local craft bobbed amongst it. To port Huart saw a tiny island, a bump upon the harbour amidst a flotilla of yachts and pleasure craft, and a duo of Royal Navy frigates in Admiralty grey berthed at the Naval Dockyard. He warmed to the sight.

The buildings of Victoria loomed sedately. One in particular captured his attention. It was a towering edifice, newly constructed of stately architecture, and standing three blocks inland from the Central Praya beyond a garden-embellished square spread about a traffic circus.

An imposing mountain reared above the building's shoulders, its face a sheer granite mask. Upon its spurs nestled garden terraces and colonial style mansions. Footpaths, roads, viaducts were chiselled into its contours, even at the summit. Through the heat haze Huart could see a funicular railcar being pulled by cable up an almost vertical track.

The ferry churned in to the pier on Hong Kong Island and he disembarked into the oven beneath the corrugated iron roof over the terminal. A white-bearded mariner with a cap emblazoned 'The "Star" Ferry Company' stood at the exit and mopped his brow as Huart plied him with questions.

'Island be Kellett Island, gen'ral. It be the home of our Yacht Club an' its commodore. That grand building be the Hongkong an' Shanghai Bank ... richest of 'em all. The mountain be Victoria Peak, an' the tramcar you see be owned by Peak Tram Company.'

'I thank you.' Huart took a card from his pocket. 'I'm seeking this address. Could you direct me?'

'Surely can. 'Tis the building on corner o' Queen's Road an' Ice House Street.' He pointed. 'Ice House Street be there. Follow it over two crossin's. The buildin' you seek be on next corner, lef' an' side.'

'I thank you again.'

'All part o' the service, gen'ral.'

The mariner saluted jauntily. Huart smiled, touched the peak of his cap with his forefinger and left the terminal.

He was upon the Central Praya. Hawkers abounded, calling out prices in guttural local dialect. Chicken vendors squatted, backs to the water, their produce spread before them, legs hobbled and protesting loudly. A duck merchant crossed Huart's path, bamboo cages crammed with squawking poultry hanging from each end of a long pole across his shoulders.

Huart crossed to Queen's Building, turned into Ice House Street and headed away from the harbour. This part of Victoria could have been an English provincial city but for the heat. And the Chinese. Uniformly short of stature; smooth skins shining with perspiration and hair with *char yau* oil and wax; wearing black trousers and white tunics of cotton or silk, or all black, or all white; they rent the torpid air with a harsh hawking, then spat fiercely upon the ground at their feet.

Ice House Street intersected first with Chater Road, then with Des Voeux Road, along which double-decker trams lumbered at pedestrian pace as though acknowledging the heat. To Huart's right the clock atop the Gloucester Hotel struck eleven, the chimes vibrating sonorously on the heavy air.

A burnished brass nameplate identified a three-storey building on the next corner as his destination:

He climbed the stairs to the second floor and saw an identical nameplate beside the first door he came to. From beyond it the clatter of a typewriter and the smell of ink, glue and burning wax came to him. Taking his cap from his head he pushed through the door to confront a gowned Chinese of advanced years sitting behind a counter sorting mail. The man looked up, his eyes expanding as his gaze rose slowly to Huart's face.

'Good morning. Is the manager in?'

The question was greeted with a violent grin, which Huart recognised as an oriental manifestation of embarrassment. Then the man nodded equally violently, and indicated a passageway around a high wooden partition.

'Misser Do' . . . Misser Bedlik all belong inside. You go inside, please.'

Huart smiled his thanks and went around the partition. There were a dozen staff in the office, all male, most of them Chinese flicking the beads of abacuses, one punching the keys of a bulky typewriter that had seen better days. A middle-aged Portuguese, a shade across his forehead and a worried expression on his face, studied a ledger through thick glasses. In a corner beside an open window a thin, young Englishman sat at a desk stacked with papers, each pile anchored with beach pebbles, supposedly against sudden summer gusts. Huart could see the stones were not needed because of the ceiling fan, which rasped ineffectually overhead.

'Good morning.'

The Englishman looked up in surprise. The shifting of the parquet flooring under Huart's feet had failed to disturb him. The noise of industry was interrupted as all eyes took in the newcomer.

'I am John Huart. Could I see the manager, please?'

The man's eyes rested briefly on the crown on one shoulder. He smiled easily and Huart liked him at once. 'I should think so, Major Huart. I believe Mr Dole is free at the moment.' He walked to a door in another partition, knocked and put his head through. A muffled exchange followed and a second man appeared. He was short, overweight, florid of face.

'John Huart?' The words came carefully, the eyes assessing. 'Surely you would not be related to our managing director, Andrew Huart-Brent . . . ?'

'My third cousin.' Huart shook his hand, felt it stiffen. 'My

[17]

battalion is en route to Shanghai so I thought I should pay you my respects.'

'We're pleased you have. Very pleased.' The manager introduced himself as Gilbert Dole; the younger man, Clive Bedrix, was assistant branch manager. The Portuguese with the shade was summoned. He was the accountant and his name was Roboza. 'Would you care for some tea, Major Huart?'

Huart followed Dole into his office, whilst Bedrix dutifully resumed his seat behind the wall of paper and Roboza returned to his ledger.

'Hong Kong is only an entrepot for South China,' Dole explained from a round-backed swivel chair behind his desk. 'Here we help to process the shipments through Canton. The branch there controls South China, you see. I report to the Canton manager and he to the director responsible for South China in the head office in Shanghai.' He wiped his brow with a handkerchief and lifted a critical eye to the copper-bladed fan that circulated slowly overhead. 'The summer here is pure hell. Between May and September the senior staff from Canton take leave. It adds to our workload as we must process their travel documents, luggage and the like. But this is only a temporary posting. I'm expecting a transfer to Canton . . . or even Shanghai. This is really a . . . er . . . training post.'

'How long have you served in Hong Kong, Mr Dole?' Huart sat beside the open window above Queen's Road, squeezed into a worn leather armchair.

'Er . . . six years, actually.'

'I see.' Dole's 'training' was prolonged. Huart recalled the state of Clive Bedrix's desk, the sweat sitting honestly on the young man's brow. Dole's desk was clear of any trapping of industry. 'Please tell me more of what you do here, relative to the rest of Cumberland China.'

The frown was quick, but not quick enough. 'We really do have a lot to do here. We provide warehousing and transportation services for the company's operations in South China. We are local agents for a number of insurance companies incorporated in Britain and America, and for many of the manufacturers the head office represents exclusively in China.'

'What sort of manufacturers?' Huart asked.

Dole spread his hands. 'Engineering equipment . . . machinery . . . package plants and mills for the processing of flour, sugar, soya bean, jute, etcetera – for the production of cement, steel, copper rod . . .' He ran off a list of company names, some of which Huart recognised as amongst the largest engineering enterprises in the United Kingdom.

'Is there much activity in Hong Kong for these companies?'

'Very little. Only government contracts.' Dole gave a wistful smile.

Huart was surprised. 'I would have thought with so many people coming in from China there would be new housing, sanitation, power and light . . .'

Dole's chuckle was indulgent. 'The Chinese you see coming into Hong Kong today, Major Huart, will not be here tomorrow. They are nothing but displaced peasants. As soon as Japan is brought to heel in China they will return there just as quickly as they left. China is their home.'

Huart was about to ask Dole who he thought was going to bring Japan to heel when the branch manager dug a thumb and forefinger into his waistcoat, withdrew a gold watch on a chain and announced: 'Why, it's lunchtime already. Would you care to join me, Major Huart? I suggest the restaurant at the St Francis Hotel. The walk is thankfully short in this abominable heat. I assure you the food is of an acceptable standard.'

'I'd be delighted, Mr Dole, thank you. But I regret it must be quick. I must be aboard my ship by mid afternoon. We sail for Shanghai at sunset.'

Dole smiled and nodded. 'A quick lunch it will be.'

'Will Mr Bedrix be joining us?'

'Ah . . . no,' Dole replied sharply. He gathered his coat and buttoned it with disguised difficulty. 'In any case, he will very likely be visiting his wife in hospital. She presented him with a son two days ago.'

As they left Dole's office Huart saw Clive Bedrix leaning over his desk, hard at it. He excused himself, crossed to the young man and bade him farewell. Bedrix winced at the strength of the handshake, then covered his discomfiture with a happy smile. 'May God be with you and your men, Major Huart. I hear it's getting dangerous up there.'

'And with you and your wife and baby boy, Clive. My congratulations. We are expecting our first in January. I envy you your son.'

'Thank you, sir.'

Huart nodded to the Portuguese accountant and descended the stairs to Ice House Street with Dole. 'You seem to have an asset there,' he said as they crossed onto Queen's Road.

'Roboza, you mean?'

'No, Clive Bedrix.'

'Oh, Bedrix. Yes. Ahh . . . very young, though. Needs more experience.'

'Could do with more training, Mr Dole, you think?'

'Definitely,' Dole agreed quickly, then frowned as he caught the satire.

The restaurant in the St Francis Hotel was half full. Its food, whilst hardly superb, was certainly palatable. Huart called for a light meal whilst noting his host showed less restraint, ordering four courses and a bottle of claret, the most expensive Bordeaux on the wine list.

Halfway through the main course, Huart asked: 'Does Cumberland China own the building where you have your office?'

'Oh, no. Neither do we own our office premises.' Dole forked a helping of corned beef and cabbage into his mouth. 'They're rented.'

'Rented from whom?'

Dole buried his face in his wine glass to hide another frown. He was thinking that for a member of His Majesty's Forces, the taipan's third cousin was showing an inordinate interest in matters unmilitary. 'The Victoria Land and Investment Company.'

'Who are they?'

'They own several buildings along Queen's Road. There is a strong rumour doing the rounds that they're in competition with another property company to purchase this very hotel next, demolish it and put up another office building. Now, who in their right mind would think of doing a thing like that? I say it'd be a crime against fine architecture. And a waste of money. Why, everyone knows Shanghai is the place to invest. If it wasn't for its harbour and its proximity to Canton, and to Macau, Hong Kong would be totally worthless.' Dole stroked his jaw. 'Yes, who would consider tearing down this lovely old hotel?'

'Businessmen perhaps?' Huart suggested and saw Dole blink. He finished his salad and sipped from his glass of tonic water. 'Please tell me more about this Victoria Land Company.'

The branch manager took another substantial draw of claret and swallowed it before replying. 'The Victoria Land and Investment Company is one of the oldest property concerns in Hong Kong. They have always concentrated on prime real estate in the Central District.'

'Do they have property interests in Shanghai?'

'None that I've heard about. And if they did, I'd certainly know of it. You see I'm a member of the Hong Kong Club and . . .'

'It seems they have faith in the future of Hong Kong. You do not agree with their policy, Mr Dole?'

The branch manager shrugged. 'I suppose owning land anywhere can't be bad, Major Huart. I've yet to see a poor landlord. But imagine the value of Victoria Land's holdings if they were in Shanghai instead of here.' He drained his glass and looked about. 'Boy!'

'Doesn't the company own any property here at all?' Huart pressed.

Dole killed this frown in time. 'None. We've extensive property interests in Shanghai, of course. We own our premises and godown on Shameen in Canton. We have holdings in Tientsin, Hankow, Foochow and Amoy, and a godown in Chungking – it was the company's birthplace, you know – and property in several other outposts in China. But here in Hong Kong we own nothing and I'm unaware of any plans to change the policy.' He saw his glass was still empty and clicked his teeth with impatience. 'Where is that waiter? They're never around when you need them. Boy!'

Huart caught the waiter's eye, inclined his head in the direction of the offending glass and watched as the bottle was picked from the rack at Dole's elbow and the last of the claret poured.

Half an hour later, the two men parted on the steps of the St Francis Hotel. The branch manager rolled back to his office, most of a bottle of Bordeaux swirling inside him, at peace with his world.

On a sudden whim Huart walked Queen's Road to the Hongkong and Shanghai Bank. Arching his back he admired the intricate mosaic that covered the ceiling of the banking hall at a height equivalent to several storeys. Everything about the building smelled new and rich. He exited onto Des Voeux Road between the crouching bronze lions and entered the square he had seen from the ferry. In the centre of the Chater Road traffic circus was a domed stone canopy under which sat a statue of Queen Victoria, and equidistant from it in each corner of the square were statues of other monarchs, plus one of Sir Thomas Jackson, chief manager of the Hongkong and Shanghai Bank in the nineties. The eminent banker had apparently possessed enough influence during his tenure to be mistaken for royalty.

Huart was deep in thought as the ferry carried him back to Kowloon. His visit to the Hong Kong branch office of Cumberland China had troubled him. His third cousin's business footing in the colony was inconsequential. A manager of superior intelligence, wider vision and greater energy than Gilbert Dole was needed here. But at no time did it occur to him that all of this was really none of his business.

As Kowloon Pier approached he looked up at the brawny mountains of the Nine Dragons, reclining on the horizon and shielding China with their mass. And his thoughts moved on. Awaiting him somewhere to the north, beyond them, was Shanghai.

4

First impressions of Shanghai invariably prove lasting, and for John Huart this was particularly so. Two dawns north of Hong Kong, he and all on board the *Otranto* stared in rapt fascination as the troop ship steamed from a blue China Sea into an ocean of agitated brown mud.

'Silt from the Yangtse,' announced a petty officer at the rail. 'It's something, isn't it? The river's more'n three thousand miles long and more'n twenty miles across at its mouth. We're in amongst the soil of China already, but we won't see the coastline for hours. We've a good fifty miles still to go before we pick up our pilot.'

True to the naval man's prediction, almost three hours later the coast of China pushed up the horizon. The first scavenger gulls appeared, swooping hungrily upon the fish scurrying away from the ship's bow.

The *Otranto* entered the Yangtse estuary, as wide as the horizon, and dropped anchor at the Fairway Buoy. A cutter of the Shanghai Licensed Pilots' Association came alongside and a barrel-chested seaman in a white uniform swung himself aboard and climbed to the bridge. The pilot steered the ship across the shallow swirling tidal flats to the Woosung Forts at the entrance to the Whangpoo River, its mouth braced by a long, curving breakwater. Then the twelve miles along the muddy, winding river were negotiated. The *Otranto* did this with relative ease as the Whangpoo was being sparsely used by river traffic. The reason was clear.

The ogre of undeclared war.

It had started the night of 'Triple Seventh' – July 7th, 1937 – at a little bridge named after Marco Polo a few miles south-west of Peking, which Chiang Kai-shek had myopically renamed Peiping – 'Northern Peace'. That it was the Year of the militant

Fire Ox was part of the reason; the rest had to be Japan, which considered North China to be Nipponese pie. It had cut its first slice in 1894, had been served up a second after the Great War, and had taken a bite the size of Manchuria in 1931. Now it had devoured Peking and Tientsin in a war it had honoured with the *nom de guerre* of 'The China Incident'. Shanghai was next on the menu.

But despite a military inferiority, the Chinese were defending its outskirts with a doggedness that was proving a rude surprise to the cocksure Japanese, whose warships and submarines ruled the river. Red-sunned fighter-bombers flew overhead, the morning rays glinting from the bombs slung underneath. Artillery fire reverberated from beyond both banks. Columns of black smoke danced on the horizon in a macabre chorus line.

The British soldiers lined the deck in a heavy silence as the awesome debris of battle passed by. Farmhouses were but ravaged shells, villages were smoking, half-submerged ruins, their protective bunds of earth and stone destroyed. Atop each cottage a Rising Sun flag flew. From a distance the derelict communities looked like wasted poppy fields.

And there were the corpses. Bodies of peasants drifted face down in the muddy water, skins like bloated, discoloured gourds, to be pushed aside by the ship's bow like so much effluent. Hundreds more were strewn about the countryside, some hideously dismembered.

'Christ almighty,' groaned Grant Rodder. 'That kid's my boy's age.' They were all staring at the body of an infant stretched across a wire fence, its abdomen torn open. 'Only a bayonet could have done that.'

Japanese soldiers stood in groups on the river bank and stared back at the Second Cumberlands with the expression of predators on a frayed leash. The air was charged with their contained belligerence.

'And they tell the world there's no war in China,' Huart muttered. 'What will it be like when it starts?'

'Bloody short-arsed butchers,' Rodder delivered grimly.

As the troop ship wound south, villages became suburbs of ramshackle dwellings and stone huts. There was diminishing evidence of the Japanese as the invaders had still to advance on the city proper where they knew stiff resistance awaited them. River craft began to appear. A smell like burnt sugar became discernible and grew stronger.

'Opium,' declared the petty officer. 'For certain the addicts'll

[23]

be last to leave. Opium divans and heroin dens're all along the river's edge.'

Unseen artillery gave out a continuous, stereophonic drum roll. Thick banks of smoke drifted across the *Otranto*'s path and hung over the muddy water. The bitter-sweet aroma from the clandestine divans tickled the nostrils. It all combined to produce a preternatural atmosphere. The ship was silent with an anticipation that was almost tangible.

The outline of factories and godowns appeared on the horizon. An hour later the *Otranto* slid into Holt's Wharf on the Pootung waterfront. Across the opposite bank the waterfront buildings presented a fairyland setting as they tilted at angles with the settlement of their foundations into the mudflats. They shimmered in a haze of brownness accentuated by the colour of the water. Although summer was ending, the temperature was in the eighties, and there was no breeze off the river.

Huart was instantly struck by the contrast between the horizontality of the legendary port city and the georama of the green mountains and blue water harbour of Hong Kong. Shanghai sprawled away on both banks of the Whangpoo over a flat terrain that boasted not a single hill. The highest points on the horizon were man-made, the nearest being the chimney of the Shanghai Power Company's generating station in Yangtsepoo.

The grey men-o'-war of the Nipponese Third Fleet intimidated the river. The largest, a three-funnelled cruiser, was berthed diagonally opposite at the wharf fronting Hongkew, the sector where 20,000 Japanese lived. Huart could see an American battleship, a French cruiser and a brace of Royal Navy destroyers further south in Battleship Row, where the Whangpoo bent to the left and widened into the harbour proper and the British sector of the International Settlement.

The *Otranto* dropped anchor. Huart had just turned away from the rail to supervise the disembarkation of 'C' Company when he heard a popping sound from somewhere in Pootung. He listened for the whine and when he heard it his training took over. 'Incoming rounds! Down!' His call was strong and his men threw themselves to the deck. He joined them as the shells passed overhead and looked up to see two spouts of silty mud lift from the river a hundred yards away. Then he heard the laughter.

'Send 'em back where they came from! They're a mob o' pansies!'

'Lyin' down on the job! Look at 'em all!'

'Infantrymen? Yer s'posed t'be on yer feet not yer bloody guts!'

[24]

Grinning deckhands were digging each other in the ribs and pointing at the prone infantrymen. There were two more pops from Pootung and another brace of shells flopped tiredly into the Whangpoo just twenty yards from the *Otranto*. The deck was sprayed with water and the derision ceased abruptly.

A Newcastle accent boomed through the air. ''Tis nowt but a peepot Chink field batt'ry, Major! Nowt t'worry about.' Huart looked up to see the pilot at the rail of the upper deck, his fists gripping it like the paws of a polar bear. 'The Chinks're aimin' at the *Idzumo* over there . . .' He nodded to the Japanese cruiser. 'They're at it all the time. Jap Naval HQ's aboard, y'see. Not even a Jap ship, neither. Stole 'er from the Russkies in 1905, they did. Chinks've ne'er 'it 'er yet and ne'er will, beejesus! Nowt but a bloody shower o' shit, the lot of 'em!'

His judgement delivered thus, the pilot pushed himself off the rail and disappeared. The Second Cumberlands climbed to their feet and looked at each other. 'Bloody 'ell,' said a rifleman. 'They shoot the real stuff 'ere, don't they? Who was it tol' us this was goin' t'be a cushy post?'

'Shut up and move!' called Huart. 'That battery may be small, but it's more nervous than a vestal virgin on her wedding night. It's firing from well out of range. The next round could fall smack on our heads. Move!'

The *Idzumo*'s guns came to life from across the river and delivered a salvo directly over the *Otranto*'s forecastle. The Second Cumberlands moved. The shells exploded deep in Pootung amongst a cluster of straw ice houses, starting new fires which quickly took hold. Except for the wharves, factories and cotton mills along the Whangpoo bank, Pootung was deserted. Not even a dog scavenged amongst its ruins.

But there were no further incoming rounds and the *Idzumo*'s guns fell silent. In the contrasting quiet the soldiers disembarked into their barges. From the open, more vulnerable craft the competition for room on the river was more apparent. Deep-sea junks with sails extended like great ribbed fans, smaller lorchas, lighters, tugs, barges, sampans, and rafts of lashed bamboo, those aboard riding with legs apart over the wash of more substantial vessels with adroit indifference, came and went in every possible direction. The barges rounded the bend at Pootung Point and they were in the harbour of Shanghai.

On the Hongkew bank stood an outstanding building, twenty-two storeys of large apartments with wide balconies, newly constructed of red brick that glowed in the midday sun. Huart knew this was Broadway Mansions, where his third cousin lived. Below it, like a rugged iron coat-hanger, Garden Bridge spanned Soochow Creek, a narrow, stinking waterway that was visually devoid of water, clogged as it was with a bank-to-bank mat of sampans and junks. In an unbroken line that could be seen stretching out of Hongkew but, in fact, started miles further north, the refugees were crossing over it into the British sector, whose famous waterfront rose ahead like an original masterpiece. Huart had seen pictures of it taken from several different angles, but this was the *chef-d'oeuvre*.

The barges carried the Second Cumberlands by the Bank of China and the spire and pointed green roof of the Cathay Hotel. Workmen swarmed over the bamboo scaffolding covering the Palace Hotel, repairing the damage wreaked by the bombs of a fortnight before. At the row of jetties in front of the Custom House with its clock tower and the adjacent domed headquarters of the Hongkong and Shanghai Bank, the barges squeezed between two rows of freighters, tramp steamers and trawlers and berthed.

'Everyone off, Mister Rodder! The pleasure cruise is over. We assemble on the wharf over there. Then we march to the barracks.'

'Yes, sir! Alright you landlubbers, kit on! Quick march!'

They disembarked for the second time that day, this time onto the Bund, the most famous thoroughfare in Asia: the waterfront and main street of Shanghai. On its eastern flank were the docks which handled the produce of the Yangtse Valley: silk, tea, tung and vegetable oil, peanuts, ham, smoked duck, textiles, garments, cotton goods; each contributing its smell. On its western stood shoulder-to-shoulder the humbling stone and granite buildings housing the great *hongs* and their basement godowns, the banks, shipping and insurance companies and businesses that ran the China Trade. One was the head office of Cumberland China Limited.

From the upper floors flew a profusion of the flags of countries and companies. Ground floor windows were sandbagged against the danger of more maverick bombs. The fortifications gave an incongruous, sinister touch: British led capitalism buttressed against an oriental war.

Upon the Bund travelled every manner of transport, and walked every nationality. English traders dressed as if for Regent Street. Turbaned Sikh money-changers jingled coins in the pockets of their long coats. Pom-pommed French sailors ogled superbly beautiful Russian damsels decked out in finery, noses at ultra-aristocratic altitudes. Robed Jewish merchants, Americans, Dutch, Germans, Poles, Portuguese; Shanghai Chinese, Cantonese, Fukienese all went about their business amidst hawkers, cobblers, coolies and beggars giving forth a babble of dialects; Ningpo, Kompo, Hangchow, Soochow, and all expectorating hard into the pavement.

Tramcars rocked on tracks through trucks, buses, taxicabs, limousines transporting the rich of all races. Bicycles with towers of cane baskets teetered around mule carts stacked with bales of cloth. Rickshaws rolled behind sweating pullers, carrying burdens contrastingly well-heeled.

And there were the refugees. The displaced of China flooded the Bund in their quest for sanctuary in this fearsome city of twelve square miles and 60,000 foreigners within a bigger city of four million Chinese built on the Yangtse mudflats. They came in family groups, their worldly goods piled on single-wheeled barrows or bundled on their backs. The accumulated brown dust of their journey clung to them. Their clothes were pieced together. Their skin shone with sweat. Their feet dragged. But their eyes were bright with residual life and hope, and when they saw the Second Cumberlands many smiled as if recognising their salvation.

'Cor, don't look like they've ha'penny 'mongst all of 'em.'

'Gimme minute alone wi' tha' one wi' turned-up nose an' soon will 'ave.'

'Ha'penny, Briscoe? Ain't you a gen'rous fucker an' all.'

'Gen'rous I'm not, fucker I am, Decker mate. Look – she smiled at me.'

'No s'prise. You standin' in broad daylight wi' dick in 'and an' all.'

Huart listened to his men's barrack room humour and said nothing. He was thinking a great deal, and he was thinking of them. This Shanghai posting was going to involve more than just guard duty on the perimeter of the British sector, spiced with off-duty sorties into the port city's infamous sin districts. He had studied Hongkew from the barge through his binoculars and had seen there the military might of Japan. He had seen the arrogant brutality of the guards on Garden Bridge, their white antiseptic masks a spooky insult, as they forced each and every refugee to bow and beg passage and rewarded with rifle butts any whose ceremony was adjudged faulty.

Major John Huart marched at the head of his company through the streets of the British sector, past its office buildings, emporiums, shops, stalls, restaurants and crowds of watching, garrulous Chinese whose faces registered a gamut of emotions: from grinning delight to impassive disapproval. As he marched his mind stayed on Hongkew. The Japanese sector had clearly been converted into a military base from which war was being waged on Chinese positions in Chapei to the north and to the west. So much for the neutrality of the International Settlement, he mused. A clash with Japan was inevitable. Sooner or later. He knew that. But he was not to know that his personal confrontation with the Rising Sun would be very soon indeed.

5

The Aichi dive-bomber came from the left. It flew out of Pootung, across the harbour, over Garden Bridge, the setting sun at its rear. It buzzed acrimoniously past the broad balcony on the twentieth floor of Broadway Mansions at a distance of fifty yards and followed Soochow Creek east.

'It's like having a loge seat in the theatre of history in the making,' said Andrew Huart-Brent as he watched the warplane climb into the sky above Chapei, drawing intermittent and ineffective ground fire.

The conflict had come within rifle range of the concessions' perimeter and the Huart-Brent balcony provided a panoramic view of it: the exploding artillery and mortar shells, the pyres that once had been buildings and now warmed and tainted the air of the neutral zone.

Andrew plucked his *stengah* off the tray proffered deferentially by his head houseboy. 'Thank you, Ling,' he acknowledged with a balance of commonality and patrician hauteur. The servant bowed himself from the balcony, leaving John Huart with the impression that his long white gown was the cleanest garment he had ever seen. He himself had come to dinner in his best dress uniform, his spit-polished toes glinting.

The setting mid-September sun flamed the red brick of the building. The view down the Bund was unobstructed. In the foreground the British Consulate nestled amidst impeccable lawns, and the English style flower beds, bushes and trees of the Public Gardens spread to the harbour wall. Freighters sounded off like farmyard geese. Barges ploughed along, joined bow and stern like caterpillar chains. The smell of bunker oil carried heavily on the evening air. Directly below, the sludge of Soochow Creek met the brown harbour in a bi-colour straddled by the black latticework of Garden Bridge, over which the flow of refugees was broken only by the obeisance to the Japanese guards, whereupon the humiliated scurried over the hump towards the benign squad of Seaforth Highlanders, then past them into the safety of the British sector.

'Many are of the opinion we brought all this on ourselves,' Andrew went on. He was one year his third cousin's junior, inside a well-cut tuxedo, cummerbund taut about his midriff. He was all but six feet, rugged and possessing the jet black hair of the Huarts. 'China and Japan have been at odds for over fifty years. But the Japs've really only taken a leaf from the British history book. The Manchus refused to take the western nations seriously and had to be forced to concede trading rights. But the Japs recognised our technological superiority and copied us. They went into China in the nineties after new colonies and took them. Now they're going a step further. They need North China as a buffer between themselves and Russia, and as a raw material source. I don't like their style, but I see it from their side.' He drank his *stengah* from the long glass. 'It's an irony of history, John. The Treaty of Nanking may have won us Shanghai, Canton and Hong Kong, but it also gave the Japs expansionist ideas that are now coming into the open with a vengeance.'

They watched the reappearance of the Aichi dive-bomber over Chapei, its nose down at forty-five degrees, swooping upon the spot from where the ground fire had come. The sound of the explosion reached them seconds after they saw its flash and a building collapse in a billow of dust.

John Huart felt strange. It was indeed as if he was viewing from a seat in some cinema the ravaging of an old, ostensibly inoffensive city by professional invaders. There were real people down there being killed, but he could not conjure up the outrage and revulsion he thought he ought to feel. It was all so . . . so unreal! Perhaps it was the distance that made it so. Or perhaps it was just because he was a soldier.

He sampled Andrew's Johnny Walker and suggested: 'They've done more than copy western military technology. In many ways they've surpassed it, as Russia discovered in 1905. And how much have they developed since then? China's a perfect testing ground for them, as Spain is for Germany.'

Andrew's shrug seemed to communicate that as long as Japan

conducted its war games outside the concessions it was within the rules. 'Japan has become a formidable nation,' he agreed. 'And not just militarily. Its factories can produce just about everything the country needs to survive.' He waved his free hand towards Chapei. 'This spot of trouble had better clear up fast. There're business opportunities going to waste.'

Huart frowned, but asked instead: 'How long do you think it will go on?'

'Around Shanghai? A month, two at the most, until the Japs win outright, or there's another negotiated truce as there was in '32 when they marched into Chapei in retaliation to a trade boycott imposed by Chiang Kai-shek. Chiang smartly removed it and the Japs marched back into Hongkew.'

'You think the Japanese objective for Shanghai is again so limited?'

Andrew assessed his cousin over the rim of his glass. In his experience soldiers handled subjects outside the basics of war with the depth of an empty cup of tea. But here was an exception. 'I do,' he admitted. 'But even if it isn't, it'll matter little to us. The concessions have been protected for nearly a century by international law. This settlement has been a bulwark against the constant troubles in China in that time: the Taipings in the fifties, the Boxers in 1899, the Sun Yat-sen Revolution in 1911, the '27 trouble when the Communists were double-crossed and driven out of Shanghai by Chiang and his Green Circle friends . . .'

'Green Circle?'

'The *Chin Pang* – our biggest triad society. Chiang rewarded its chief by making him chairman of the Opium Suppression Bureau. Imagine the hay he made out of that! The Frenchies went one better and gave him a seat on the *Conseil d'Administration Municipal*.' Andrew's expression told Huart such reciprocity was a way of life in Shanghai. 'And there was the trouble in '32 that I mentioned. We survived it all. It'll be the same this time. As soon as the Japs have occupied enough of North China to meet their needs, they'll call a halt to the hostilities. Then they'll consolidate, form an administrative government as they did in Manchuria with some Chinese puppet at the top, and it'll be business as usual.

'Thirteen countries have trading rights in China, and Japan is one. The others won't permit infringement. Particularly us – Britain. Even if the Japs did the impossible and occupied all of China – just consider the size of the place – the concessions would carry on trading. *Maskee!*'

[30]

'*Maskee?*'

Andrew grinned. 'It can mean a lot of things . . . such as: "that's the way it is". The French would use it instead of *c'est la vie*. An optimist would have it mean "at least it can't get any worse". It's from Portuguese – a catchphrase of the Shanghailander. You'll hear it everywhere.'

'But it can get worse.' Huart felt inclined to dissent. 'I believe Japan does aim to occupy all China. The military lobby in Tokyo is stronger all the time and with militarists in power the status quo is never safe. The very concessions you speak of were taken at gunpoint. You're here through military aggression. Do you think Japan, having already succeeded in thumbing its nose at the Allies, will settle for half measure?'

He sipped his scotch as Andrew, wearing almost a smile, waited for more.

'The concessions have survived profitably for you, the foreign masters, because China has had an unstable, corrupt administration. But Japan has a stable history. It has banned foreign interference and has backed up that ban with effective force. If Japan controls China it'll commandeer raw materials for its own factories and disallow purchase of non-Japanese goods. Foreign companies will no longer be able to profit from the China Trade, only Japanese. The days of the concessions will be over.'

Andrew completed his smile. It was patronising. 'Japan couldn't do it all on their tot. It's impossible. They'd need an infrastructure . . .'

'They'd establish one. And quickly. Look at Korea.'

Andrew shook his head. 'Why should they go to all that trouble when they can merely cooperate with the municipal councils? We've been trading in China longer than they have. Why should they reject our expertise?'

'Because they're more insular even than the Chinese. They're the most racially prejudiced people on earth. They're collectively mindless. Outside Japan, the world doesn't exist – except to serve Japan's needs.'

'You must have a lot of time for reading, Cousin John.' Andrew laughed suddenly. 'It's a pleasure to meet a man with conviction. But I'm afraid I disagree with yours. Certainly the Japs look down on the Chinese and regard them as an inferior race. But not so the foreign traders. They respect us. As an example, Morita-san from the Yokohama Specie Bank has been after me to open an account. And I've just decided to do it!'

'Isn't that a little treasonable, Andrew?'

'I'm a businessman. This place lives on business. The Municipal Council is apolitical. Business and politics don't mix.' Andrew pressed a button on the wall and Ling materialised, bowing. 'Another *stengah* for me. Scotch again, John? Or how about some of Paulette's best white wine? She selected a case at the Heublien wine auction in New Orleans last year. Yes? Good. Ling, a glass of Missee's special white wine for Major John.'

Ling bowed again and left. The diversion was accepted as a truce and the subject changed to family history. Andrew spoke of the 'China Huarts': 'Charles Huart married here in '81. My grandmother was a beauty, but fragile. She died bearing my mother, who inherited no frailty – as you will see when you meet her. I'm sorry she's not recovered enough to join us tonight. Even so, the doctor had to tie her down. Shame, really – we needed her to make up the number.' Andrew grinned to seal his humour and took a half inch of his fresh *stengah*. 'After his wife's death, Grandfather didn't stay in one place long enough to remarry. No son and heir was ever sired – at least not within the confines of matrimony . . .'

In the sudden silence John Huart glanced at his cousin and saw the far-away look on his face. Andrew wiped it away and quickly carried on.

'He was setting up the company's branch offices all over China and transferring the head office from Chungking to Shanghai. He decided the only way to produce an heir was to press my mother into a *mariage de convenance*. She married at eighteen to Alexander Brent, a London shipping magnate who divided his time between there, here and the west coast. I arrived on the scene, my parents divorced and my mother changed her surname to Huart-Brent. I was groomed to take over the company, but when Grandfather died in 1930 I was at Cambridge. Up to my return to Shanghai in 1932 my mother ran the company with Arthur Dennison, who started the Tientsin branch in '94. He and Agnes are coming to dinner. Arthur'll enjoy helping me shoot your theory on the Japanese to pieces.'

'I look forward to the skirmish,' Huart replied in good nature.

The sun descended into China, dropping the curtain on another Shanghai day of business and war. Lights came on along the Bund where the police could be seen imposing the curfew, ordering the refugees to the side of the road to live out the night. The kaleido-scope that was the port city by day slipped beneath the censoring wrap of darkness. The Custom House clock struck seven, its chimes ringing powerfully across the city.

[32]

' "Big Ching" says its time to go in, John.'

' "Big Ching?" '

'The Custom House clock. Come on inside. The guests'll be here at any minute – if they've managed to beat the curfew. I'm so glad you could get here early. There're six decades of family news to catch up on.'

They entered the living room as Ling ushered in two couples, the more elderly proving to be the Dennisons, the other surnamed Bloomfield; he was general manager of the Shanghai Waterworks and guest of honour. His wife said breathlessly: 'Your lifts are so efficient, Mr Huart-Brent.'

'Elevators, Doreen,' her husband corrected, smiling deprecatingly.

'What's that, dear?'

Andrew laughed. 'Well, I suppose they were made in the States.'

Agnes Dennison moved protectively to Doreen's side. 'Come, my dear, we can leave the men to their talk. Where's the lady of the house, Andrew?'

'Giving our new chef soufflé lessons. He was assistant *chef de cuisine* at the Palace Hotel until the bombing ruined his *crème brûlée* and he resigned in protest. Paulette lives dangerously – ' Mischief played in Andrew's eyes. 'He's made more soufflés than I've had dirty thoughts.'

Doreen blushed red as she hurried after Agnes, and Arthur Dennison took George Bloomfield out to the balcony. Ling bustled from lamp to lamp, from guest to guest as the last of the China sun slid below the horizon.

Andrew rested his head on a lace antimacassar and listened from one end of the chesterfield as his cousin told of the day when, as a small boy, he had first heard of the 'China Huarts' from his grandfather; how the old general had let go a nasal snort in prognostication of the explosion to come. ' "Uncle Charles and his brood cohabit with heathens! They're the offspring of a devil's strain that drove the family to the brink of scandal! My father – God rest him – fought his wars ten times over to erase the shame. China is welcome to the brood of Charlemagne Roland Huart!" Then the old boy stomped off and never spoke of it again. Such condemnation only made me more determined to find out about the "China Huarts". I searched for hours through the shelves of the library in Aldershot until I found a volume titled *Twentieth Century Impressions of the Great China Trading Companies*. 1908 edition, I think – '

'I have that volume in my office,' Andrew inserted. 'It was

published every five years or so. It was the forerunner of the *Hong* List.'

'It told me about the branches the company had all over China in places I'd never heard of – Tsingtao, Wuhu, Kiukiang, Newchwang, Ichang . . .'

'Had? Present continuous tense, John, please.'

Childhood fantasies of circumnavigating the world to find the 'China Huarts' rose out of memory. 'I kept my ambitions from Grandfather or he would have had me caned. But my father was not so dogmatic. Perhaps if he had been a harder man he might not have died so young. My mother also passed on too soon in life. She died of viral pneumonia in 1930. Before I went to Burma my brother-in-law – Claire's husband – advised us to sell the old home and invest on the London Stock Exchange. Values were rock bottom after 1929. "There's but one way they can go," he said. He was right. My investments have trebled. And in Rangoon I met Jennifer.'

'Ah, yes . . . Jennifer. And when will she be making the journey?'

'Our first child is due in January. Allowing the customary three months, then the sea voyage, I expect her to arrive in Shanghai in May.'

'Too long,' Andrew commiserated. 'We're expecting our first in March. Paulette was lucky to survive the bombing without a mark – physically.'

'I will be meeting her tonight, Andrew, won't I?'

'I shall fetch her at once, sir.' Andrew left and returned in a minute with, on his arm, the most striking woman Huart had seen since the day at the Governor's residence in Rangoon when he had first seen Jennifer.

Paulette Huart-Brent was the brand of woman for whom men sprang to their feet without thinking. This occasion proved no exception. Arthur Dennison, who had returned from the balcony, kissed her cheek. George Bloomfield took her hand, then abruptly dropped it as if it had suddenly occurred to him his fingers were trespassing on property above his station.

With a grin that failed to disguise his infatuation for the woman at his side, Andrew provided the introduction: 'Paulette, darling – this is John, my distant cousin from distant parts. And to save you asking the obvious question – he's six foot five. John – my wife, Paulette.'

In high heels she was slightly taller than her husband. Her snow blonde hair was cut in Harlow style. The black Mainbocher floor length evening gown was undeceiving, giving even the hint of pregnancy to her waist and hips. A single string of pearls of undisguised worth traced the contours of her fine bosom. Two gold rings, one projecting a substantial diamond, adorned the fingers of her right hand. Huart saw the left was devoid of a wedding band. She was almost ethereal, with an extrinsic cooling power that was in refreshing contrast to the men inside their dinner jackets and cummerbunds, and Huart within his obligatory dress uniform.

Andrew had met Paulette Charbadour in New Orleans in 1935. The courtship had lasted but three months. She was a year his senior, and a divorcee. He had thus broken convention and risked the censure of his Shanghai peers; and in so doing, had demonstrated the rebellious blood of Charles Huart flowed in his veins. Huart could see why. If the exterior was a guide to the woman within, Paulette Charbadour had been worth the risk.

He took her hand. It was metallic to the touch, like dry ice.

'So, John, what is your feeling for our "Paris of the East"?' Her voice, pliant with the tones of the American south, pronounced it 'Paree', as would a Parisian, giving the 'r' a resonant roll of the tongue.

'Some prefer "Whore of Asia", darling.' Andrew grinned as he exaggerated her diction, and Paulette's teeth flashed.

Huart said: 'Paulette, you are undoubtedly Andrew's finest import.'

Her husband's eyes widened as she laughed. 'Oh, *ma preux chevalier* . . .'

Agnes Dennison and Doreen Bloomfield reappeared just as Ling came from the dining room to announce the serving of the first course. Tipping his head surreptitiously towards the guest of honour, Andrew leaned to his wife's ear and whispered something Huart did not catch.

Paulette went to George Bloomfield and took him by the arm. She smiled at him as if there were no-one else in the room but the two of them. 'You look to me like a man who knows his wine, George. We're serving Chateau Lafite 1913 with the roast turkey. Please give us your opinion of it. We'll change it at once if it's not just right.'

'Oh, but I'm hardly. . . . Well, if you like.' The guest of honour appeared on the threshold of orgasm as they entered the dining room where awaited the smoked mackerel and three servants exuding collective efficiency. In the distance the Japanese howitzers delivered a concomitant obligato.

*
[35]

'Cannons!' Andrew called with innate satisfaction as his white kissed both red and black on the outside edge. He moved around the table into position for his next shot. 'Ling, pour Mr Bloomfield another port.'

The general manager of the Shanghai Waterworks took the proffered glass and grunted. 'So what is the Council doing about matters in Hongkew?' It was put with an aggressive frown. 'This patrolling by the Japanese Consular Police is nothing less than a blatant challenge to the SMP.'

'We meet Monday about it,' Andrew replied as he leaned over the table in shirtsleeves, one eye closed, the other squinting along his cue. 'In the meantime our police've been told not to be provoked into anything.'

'The Japs won't stop at just provoking.' Bloomfield grunted again. It was the caveat of his dissatisfaction. 'We ran into a patrol coming here from Yangtsepoo. It was twice the size of an SMP patrol and armed to the teeth. What's more, I've heard the Kempetai have begun something of an inquisition on the Chinese in Hongkew. Oh, another good'un, Andrew.' He turned and looked up. 'You've seen them on the Garden Bridge, Major Huart. Why won't the British Army do something instead of just looking?'

Despite the width of his shoulders, Huart's shrug was imperceptible. He was momentarily disarmed, not just by Bloomfield's challenge but by the inadequacy of the only reply he could make. 'We're under strict orders not to intervene outside our sector under any circumstances. Our hands are tied. Whilst the Kempetai stay in their own backyard . . .' He would see the Japanese secret police in action himself next week when the Second Cumberlands relieved the Seaforth Highlanders on Soochow Creek. But this evening he had been able to assess the Japanese soldier at close quarters. He had climbed out of his sidecar at the Garden Bridge checkpoint to dwarf a squad of them, but they had been unintimidated. The lieutenant who had inspected his pass had saluted him woodenly on his way.

'Eat, drink and be merry, for tomorrow we die!' Andrew cried as he played his third shot. '*Maskee!*' He puffed his cigar and watched his white clip the red and drop neatly into the corner pocket.

'*Maskee* it is,' Arthur Dennison concurred drily from a shadowy corner.

Andrew had won again. Ling racked up his score, then leaned under the lamp hanging over the table to set up the balls for the next frame as Bloomfield snickered. 'Did you hear Stewart Barlow had his best straw-boater stolen the other day? Right off his head. It happened as he was sitting on the tram at the stop in front of Whiteaway Laidlaws. He was holding court in the Long Bar after it happened and swore the scoundrel would've won the hundred yards at the Berlin Olympics.'

'It was Whiteaways' bailiff doing a repossession, no doubt.' Andrew's bland supposition brought smiles. 'You start this frame off, George.'

'Hardoons can't be doing as well as they make out if Stewart Barlow's taken to riding on trams,' Arthur Dennison observed.

'Hardoons are alright,' Andrew said through a cloud of cigar smoke. 'I have it on good authority that our Stewart is still using up the book of free tickets he was given by the Tramway Company during the strike in '25. Short arms and deep pockets has that man.'

'No blooming pockets at all,' Arthur muttered, thinking of the size of Barlow's unpaid account at the Country Club for which he was treasurer.

Huart, a rank beginner at billiards, was content to listen to the chat that switched from subject to subject. Finally, George Bloomfield justified his invitation by 'confidentially' revealing that a large order for cast iron water mains and valves would be mailed to Cumberland China by week's end. '*A votre santé*!' Andrew downed his port and conceded a frame at last. 'Good shot, George!' he acknowledged as the red hesitated on the lip of the pocket, then dropped in. 'That was a ball-grabber.'

'Shot of the night,' Arthur agreed.

'Grandfather could wield a cue,' said Andrew. 'He played billiards like he did business – took every chance imaginable. George, have you heard how he landed his first order – the order that started the company?'

Bloomfield shook his head. Arthur's subtle wink told Huart it was an oft related tale.

Andrew rested the base of the cue on his instep and placed his hands one upon the other on the tip. 'Charles Huart's arrival in Chungking was well timed. It was coincidental with the opening of six new ports along the Yangtse. It was the time when we British were pushing for trade to open between Burma and western China. This, as you know, resulted in the building of the Burma Road. Chungking became the centre of attention and all manner of "foreign ghosts" were descending on it looking for trade. Grandfather was one of them. The Grand Imperial Mandarin of Chungking needed artillery for his company of foreign mercenaries and Grandfather found himself up against a German flogging brand new Krupp field guns that could outshoot everything. Grandfather could only offer second-hand British guns from sources – doubtful sources, at that – in India. The Hun must have thought he had the order in the bag.' Andrew puffed his cheeks in imitation of a pompous Prussian general. He came to attention and presented arms with his cue. ' "My guns are Krupp! Der newest und der besten in der veldt! Dey vill outschoot your schrap metal by a mile, Englischer!" Says Grandfather: "You're full of bosh, Boche!" Says the Hun: "Ach! Insult! Ve fight duel. I vill have der sabre!" Says Grandfather: "Keep your bloody sabre, Boche. I'm going to use my field gun." Says the Hun: "Vaat? Field gon? In dot case, I vill use my Krupp! Englischer, you are not jost stupid, you are also dead und stupid!" '

The raconteur looked around to see only grinning faces urging him on.

'Grandfather stepped out the range directly into a strong wind and sent back a message by runner: "Now shoot me if you can, you Boche blowhard!" It made the Hun so mad he fired without checking the wind. Grandfather was shaking in his boots, praying for the wind not to drop. The round fell short – just. Well . . . the mandarin had witnessed all this and was so impressed he gave Grandfather the order on the spot, without asking him to return fire. It was a good thing, too, because his gun hadn't a snowball's chance in hell of making half the range of the Krupp piece.'

The appreciation of Andrew's rendition reached the balcony, to where the ladies had adjourned after dinner and where the night air was tangy with autumn's first chill and the smoky aroma of the suburban battlefield.

'That's Andrew telling the story of his grandfather's first order,' said Agnes Dennison. 'I've heard it so often I'm starting to believe it.'

Paulette watched the distant fires that winked and flared and was quiet.

'But the story doesn't end there,' they heard Andrew go on. 'When Grandfather was alone he collapsed from loss of blood. A piece of shrapnel had lodged in his side! Now – who's for some more of my vintage port?'

At 11:30 John Huart took his leave. The other guests were observing the curfew by staying overnight. 'Noblesse oblige,' he laughed when he was entreated to do the same. 'My pass expires at midnight.'

At the door Andrew repeated his invitation to visit Cumberland

Building. 'I think the floors might take the weight, but it'll be touch and go.'

'It'll not be possible for a few weeks. Perimeter duty starts Monday.'

'Be careful out there, Cousin. But always eat, drink and be merry – '

'For tomorrow we die. Goodnight, Andrew. Goodnight, Paulette. It's been a unique evening. It seems to have been successful for your business . . .'

'You mean George?' Andrew grinned. 'It's easy, really. No man can resist when I roll out my big guns.' He encircled his wife's waist and drew her to him and she laughed throatily and rubbed herself against him. Then she raised herself on tiptoe and cupped a palm under Huart's chin. With her lips against his cheek she said: 'Goodnight, *ma preux chevalier.*'

Jammed in the sidecar, Major John Huart rode to his quarters in pensive discomfort. Her perfume lingered in his nostrils, the impact of Andrew's relaxed power and *savoir faire* impinged upon his thoughts. And he acknowledged he was already looking forward to his next encounter with the Huart-Brents of Broadway Mansions, the unspeakable 'China Huarts'.

6

The wall of flame was eight miles in length. Chapei had been mutilated. The Japanese had bombed and shelled it until it was all but levelled; the Chinese had fired what was left as they pulled back. The spectacle imparted a message to those cloistered within the foreign concessions as sombre as the enveloping smoke was thick; so thick it eclipsed the sun.

The command bunker at the Yu Ya Ching Road bridge shook with the blasts from another salvo and debris rained all around. Factories, godowns, huts and hovels were blown in bits across Soochow Creek to litter the perimeter of the British sector. Sand streamed from rents in the sandbagged walls and roof and built miniature pyramids upon the floorboards.

'They've shortened range again,' Huart muttered, squinting through his binoculars. The line of vision was clear, apart from the smoke. The floating colony had evacuated Soochow Creek a month before. 'That lot hit a hundred yards in. They can't reduce any more without dropping in the creek – or on top of us.' He straightened his back and looked at Grant Rodder. 'We should be seeing the first Chinese any minute now.'

A machine gun rattled on the far bank; an errant burst stitched a tattoo across the bunker and all inside ducked in reflex. From somewhere to the rear a familiar rushing noise grew louder and another barrage charged overhead like a runaway express train. A string of brick godowns a block into Chapei received a direct hit and again the bunker was showered.

The guns of the Third Fleet were firing from the harbour directly over the International Settlement, their target the trapped remnant of the Nationalist Chinese Army. The 'Doomed Battalion', so dubbed by the world press, had withdrawn under fire along the banks of Soochow Creek. They were now fighting a last ditch stand with their backs to the waterway.

'C' Company had been manning the perimeter for six weeks. The hunched infantrymen, in battle dress with tin helmets pulled low, had witnessed the approach of war with a strange sense of detachment. Sweat traced black channels through the dusty stubble on Huart's face. He had been in the command bunker since midnight. It was now eleven. A gut feeling told him something was about to happen. And it was instantly verified.

'There they are!'

He lifted his binoculars again. 'I see them, Mister Rodder.'

The figures that darted into the shell of a building gave him his first sight of the 'Doomed Battalion'. The machine gun sprayed in a broad arc. There came the thump of grenades, then a brace of sharper explosions. 'Mortars,' he muttered. 'The Japs're closing in for the kill.'

'The barrage has lifted,' Rodder observed in confirmation.

Huart licked his lips. 'Mister Rodder, what's the standing order regarding armed personnel attempting to pass a perimeter checkpoint?'

The subaltern blinked. 'Order them to halt and about face . . .'

'And if they insist on coming through?'

'They can't, sir. This is neutral territory. No armed force can enter.'

'The operative word is "armed", Grant. What if they were unarmed?'

'We'd have to take them into custody pending orders from the C-in-C.'

'Right. And that's what we're to do if those poor devils try to swim for it. We disarm them and get them to the rear. Smartly.'

'Sir.' The smile on Rodder's tired face said much.

A bren gunner lifted his head. 'Here they come!'

Huart saw first two, then a half dozen, then a score with their wounded over their shoulders scramble to the water's edge directly across from the command bunker. Their uniforms were a mix of blue, olive drab and khaki hanging in tatters from their wasted bodies. They were streaked with blood. Few carried weapons. They splashed into the creek and waded towards a gap in the barbed wire that fenced in the British sector as a mortar shell tore into the north bank. A staccato machine gun burst sprayed the struggling figures in the water. One was hit and fell. He was hoisted between two comrades and carried forward.

'Pass the message, Grant.'

'Good news I'll take myself.' Rodder ducked out the rear of the command post and ran bent double to the next bunker. A shower of broken bricks fell about him and stray bullets kicked up dust at his feet. He pitched forward and somersaulted to the rear of the bunker. 'Let them through, corporal!' he shouted into it. 'Disarm every one, but let them through.'

Huart could hear the muffled cheer. He took the handset from his radio operator and called for transportation. Then he joined Rodder to take command of the rescue. The smell of war fell upon him, the din of it hit his ears as the Chinese rearguard turned and fired off their last rounds.

In ten minutes over a hundred made it across to the south bank. Exhausted, but visibly grateful for their deliverance, they were helped through the barbed wire, disarmed, then escorted to a staging area at the rear. Troop transports arrived and the survivors boarded. The trucks carried them grinning and waving through streets crammed with their shouting, dancing, laughing countrymen to an internment camp at Kiaichow Park. Word spread like a fireball through the Chinese community: the 'Doomed Battalion' had escaped the hated Nipponese dwarfs, the 'foreign ghost' soldiers with the red body hair, big noses and smelly feet had saved the heroes. It was the first item of good news for as long as anyone could remember, and it was received as if it represented ultimate victory.

As the procession of survivors thinned out and finally ended, so did the war in Chapei. In contrast to the thunder of battle that had continued since dawn, the silence was weird. And with it Huart saw the Japanese advance units appear on the north bank of Soochow Creek. They stood in a line to fix the Second Cumberlands with a murderous glare. The heat of their outrage supplemented the fiery breath of the furnace behind them.

Huart looked at them. They were like soldier dolls in stereotyped poses of aggression, each painted with the same malevolent face. He had ready the order for his men to cock their weapons and stand-to. He held it. It had come to him with a chilling psychic clarity that the next few minutes risked sucking Britain into the 'China Incident'.

An armoured car with a Rising Sun emblem drew up on the north bank. Its heavy-calibre machine gun pointed ominously across the creek. A troop carrier unloaded a platoon of fully armed infantry. Another armoured car appeared and took up position. Huart thought he could hear the metallic tread of tanks approaching from the bowels of Chapei. He said grimly to Rodder: 'If it's their plan to shoot at British soldiers today, Grant, they'll have to start with me. After all, I did start all this.'

And so there could be no doubt who was in charge, he stepped to the edge of the waterway. He stood, hands on hips, and glared across, fully conscious of the guns that seemed to traverse in slow-motion unison until all muzzles were pointed in his direction. And he ignored the reality of the tempting target his unprotected bulk was presenting.

A warped voice through a loud hailer broke the lethal silence. 'See you, Englishman! Imperial Nipponese Army demand return of Chinese bandits!'

Huart's eyes searched the Chapei bank for the origin of the voice.

'Hear me, Englishman? You must return our prisoners now!'

It occurred to Huart that the voice betrayed a stint at a British public school and the irony of it registered. Then he saw him: a diminutive company commander upon the bonnet of the second armoured car, his legs encased in polished knee-high boots and spread arrogantly. The thick rimless lenses of his spectacles obscured his eyes, giving him an alien, robotic appearance.

Huart squinted through the drifting smoke and swelled his chest. His voice would require no artificial aid. 'The Chinese soldiers have given themselves up to the forces of the International Settlement! They have been disarmed and placed under guard. And there they will stay!'

The Japanese officer's frame seemed to lift and expand in anger. 'They are no soldiers! They are bandits! They must be returned to us! They are prisoners-of-war! Do it now or we have no choice but using force!'

'Prisoners-of-war? What war? Has Japan declared war at last? Oh no, sir! The Chinese soldiers – soldiers, you hear – have been taken to a place of internment. If you attempt to cross this creek we are empowered by terms of treaty to defend our boundary. You will be in contravention of International Law! I suggest you reconsider your threat . . . sir!'

The officer lowered his loud hailer. He attempted murder with his eyes. He was only a captain. He barked a command and his men ran to take up offensive positions. Then he climbed down into his armoured car. Both vehicles backed away and machine gunners ran forward, set up tripods and sighted on Huart. A hundred Model 38 bolt-action rifles did the same.

'Nobody fires without my order!' Huart turned and walked with measured step to the command bunker. 'It's probably all a bluff,' he muttered as he passed Rodder. If so, he added to himself, it's a damn good one.

He radioed battalion headquarters for reinforcements and found himself talking to the commander, Lieutenant-Colonel Rae, who said with calm and precision: 'A company from the East Surreys should be with you in minutes thirty. Can you hold the situation until then? Over.'

Huart almost smiled. The next move was hardly his. He, too, spoke concisely, occupying the airwaves for the minimum. 'We are taking defensive action. I request an anti-tank unit. I anticipate that we will be facing armour in event of an assault. I request a sapper unit with enough explosive to bring down a two-lane road bridge. I request "Alabaster" be placed on standby. Over.' 'Alabaster' was the call-sign for Artillery.

'Anti-tank and sapper units will be despatched soonest. Confirm "Alabaster" is on standby and is monitoring. Over.'

With grim-faced satisfaction Huart heard Rae perpetrate the bluff. It was common knowledge that Japanese Intelligence eavesdropped on every radio message, and though they well knew the British garrison had no artillery detachment, the ruse cost nothing. 'Does "Alabaster" have the co-ordinates? Over.'

' "Alabaster" will be through to you at end of this transmission. Over.'

'Will keep our line open. Over and out.' Huart gave Rodder the handset. 'HQ will come back in a moment pretending to be "Alabaster". Give them the co-ordinates of Jap High Command in Hongkew. That will have our bowlegged friends choking on their raw fish.' He took his helmet from a nail. 'I'm going out to organise the deployment of the reinforcements.'

'Keep a weather-eye open, sir.' The subaltern gestured across the creek.

'You can count on that.'

For the next two hours the infantry of the British and Japanese armies confronted each other across Soochow Creek. For each second of those one hundred and twenty minutes Huart listened for the incoming naval barrage that would herald the assault. At 1330 hours two light tanks drew up on the Chapei bank, their steel skins covered in dust and soot. The nozzles of their 57mm cannon were threatening black orifices. Huart's throat was dry, but his brain was in turbulence. Would history record him as a military misfit whose interference in an oriental blood-letting started an international war? So be it then, he resigned himself. If I am judged thus, then life itself has gone irreparably awry. Then he looked across the creek and what he saw on the north bank told him it was already so.

He answered queries in monosyllables and spoke tersely into the radio every fifteen minutes. Headquarters informed him the Shanghai Municipal Council and the Japanese High Command were meeting to debate the fate of the survivors. Huart tried to visualise Andrew hastening to attend it.

On the Chapei bank the Japanese armour stayed real and oppressive, the infantry concealed and motionless. Though mute in the harbour to the east, the guns of the Third Fleet remained an object of intimidation.

How long now? Huart asked himself again and again.

The minutes dragged. Another hour passed. Then another. And, slowly, as time went by, Huart felt the warmth of a budding confidence. For, with time, he told himself, the situation must diffuse. The Council was standing its ground. It was supporting him. It was not capitulating to Japanese demands. It must be! Or else he would have been told to prepare a section of riflemen to escort the survivors back across the bridge.

Another hour on the knife's edge went by as the autumn sun descended to the horizon. If there was to be an assault, Huart knew it must be now.

The radio crackled loudly; startling the operator almost off his stool. It was 1749 hours, the update from battalion headquarters was not due for another eleven minutes. Then the call-sign of garrison headquarters was heard. Huart looked questioningly at Rodder and took the handset. The authoritative voice of the

[44]

Commander, British Forces, told of the Japanese High Command's ungracious acceptance of the Municipal Council's decision to intern the survivors. Hongkew was to telegraph an official protest via Tokyo to Whitehall. But, that apart, the incident was over.

Across Soochow Creek sudden activity banished the quiet that had prevailed for six hours. The engines of the tanks and armoured cars roared into life. The vehicles of war reversed into the burning smoking ruins of Chapei. Troop carriers returned and drove away full, leaving in position a single section in preservation of Japanese face.

The Second Cumberlands emerged from their bunkers and cheered to a man. They shook their fists and catcalled and whistled until Huart had to order them to desist. But he did so with a smile on his face. He was a happy man. The relentless Japanese Army had been made to back down.

The 'Soochow Creek Incident' was to make Major John Huart famous in the eyes of the free Chinese of the International Settlement. They pointed him out as he supervised the manning of checkpoints, as he patrolled the perimeter at the head of a detachment of his men, or as he sat squashed into his sidecar. To them he was a living symbol of Allied support, rendering decrepit by comparison the lip service that had been paid by the foreign powers since the evening of July 7th. He accepted the honour with mixed feelings. He found the pointing fingers, the wide admiring eyes disturbing. He was a big enough target for the Kempetai as it was.

7

Bubbling Well Road began at the fresh water spring where Nanking Road ended. A twisting avenue of imported plane trees, it housed the elite of Shanghai society, particularly the Chinese, who called it *Dai Ma Lu:* Great Horse Road, and whose degree of elitism was in direct proportion to their personal wealth. The origin of that wealth was quite immaterial.

Five hundred yards east of the junction of Bubbling Well and Jessfield Roads on the western boundary of the International Settlement, a three-storey mansion of marble and granite hid behind a high stone wall capped with barbed wire and shards of glass fixed in cement. A private Shangri-la was the landscaped garden laid about a three hundred year old gingko tree, with serpentine paths that twisted through bamboo grooves, willows, grottoes, pools bursting with carp and goldfish, pavilions and amorphous nodular rockeries like henges of grey coral. The pervading theme was one of unequivocal peace and longevity. The name of the residence was Great Horse Mansion. It was the home of the Tu family of Shanghai.

Late one afternoon in the week after the Japanese completed their occupation of the Chinese Municipality of Greater Shanghai, a sleek black Oldsmobile nosed from the driveway onto Bubbling Well Road and turned west. In front were a Chinese chauffeur and a hulking Russian bodyguard. In the rear, wrapped in an ermine coat against the late autumn chill, sat Tu Chien. Though but thirty-one, he ruled the family's vast enterprises and controlled its immense assets. His father was dead, his life taken by the followers of Chou En-lai in retribution for the role played by the family in the 1927 double-cross of the fledgling communists. At his side in *cheongsam* and silk stockings, her shoulders covered by a brocade jacket with a three inch collar, sat a lissom Soochow beauty: Tu Chien's favourite concubine, Yueh-ming, mother of the elder of his sons.

As the big American automobile cruised Bubbling Well Road, Tu Chien was deep in thought, stroking with his fingers the long black hairs that grew from a mole on the side of his jaw. Cogitation was his custom when approaching a business deal of magnitude, and this day the depth of it was extreme. For he intended returning to Great Horse Mansion having made a deal that would double the family's income overnight.

He felt the soft touch upon the back of his hand and stirred.

'Did I disturb your thoughts, Lord?' the exquisite voice murmured in Shanghai dialect. 'I am sorry. I did not mean to.'

Men who are fortunate know from experience that the lilt of a Soochow woman trained in elocution possesses the power of a subtle aphrodisiac. Tu Chien smiled abstractedly as his core warmed. 'Your touch is fated to disturb, Yueh-ming,' he breathed, and, as public affection risked the denigration of both giver and receiver, he replaced her hand delicately upon a silk-clad thigh. 'You give me enough difficulty controlling my thoughts under normal circumstances. Did you need to wear that perfume?'

'It is the French *Chanel* you gave me on our son's birthday.

[46]

Should not Ohara-san be distracted to the maximum? Fat intestined pig that he is.'

Tu Chien looked at her in admiration. 'Yueh-ming, you have the body of a goddess, the face of an imperial beauty, and the brain of a mogul. Hoi-nam will certainly be a brilliant, handsome and feared man.'

'There is little doubt of that, Lord. Even at five he was master of the abacus. Now at eight he understands most of the entries in the ledgers you select for him to study. And he will be handsome, like his father.'

Tu Chien's face remained stoic, but her words pleased him. 'It is the quality behind a face that matters, Yueh-ming, not the beauty upon it. Yet you are right. Hoi-nam grows into a fine youth.'

On Jessfield Road a large red-turbaned Sikh of the Shanghai Muncipal Police occupied the sandbagged traffic pagoda in the centre of the junction. The chauffeur slowed almost to a stop and made a hand signal with thumb perpendicular. The Sikh held up a white-gloved palm to the traffic on Jessfield Road and waved the Oldsmobile into its right turn.

'Smelly red-headed black orang-utan,' hissed Yueh-ming. 'I am so glad our son had the fortune not to be born into a race like that.'

'Ourselves, also.'

They followed Jessfield Road out of the International Settlement into the quarter known as the Badlands, a district of nightclubs, gambling houses and opium dens. Though outside neutral territory, it drew power and water from the concessions. The Badlands had been a Japanese playground before the hostilities. Now it nursed the scars of war.

Once over the Shanghai-Hangchow-Ningpo railway line they were in Chapei. The light faded as if a curtain had been dropped on the world. The late afternoon sun hid behind a fog of residual smoke. Tu Chien's face turned to slate, reflecting the new surroundings. His heartbeat quickened. They were no longer in safe territory. The chauffeur drove nervously through narrow streets riddled with craters and lined with ruins. There was no doubt who ruled here. Each pile of rubble supported a Japanese flag. Nipponese soldiers guarded every corner, standing beside rifles with fixed bayonets as long as they were tall. All that moved on the roads were military vehicles painted with red suns. The battle for Shanghai had taken half a million lives, only ten per cent of them Japanese. The gaunt faces of those whose *heung ha* had been made a battlefield held eyes dulled and desolate. Chapei was a wasted graveyard inhabited by ghosts of the living as well as the dead. It smelled like a crematorium.

In the rear of the Oldsmobile communication froze. Tu Chien forced his mind to close out the surroundings. He concentrated instead on the vital and dangerous task ahead: his meeting with Colonel Ryoku Ohara.

To control the occupied districts, the Japanese were installing a puppet administration called the Great Way Shanghai Government, *Ta Tao* for short. It was implementing a policy already effective in the north to sap the will of the population: the establishment of a comprehensive network of heroin and opium divans. The upshot would be a vast market for narcotics, for which the safest supply route would be via the undamaged docks of the foreign concessions. The *Ta Tao* ran a police force of collaborator-mercenaries commanded by Kempetai officers. Its head in Chapei was Colonel Ryoku Ohara, who, on his transfer from Tientsin, had instantly become tacit overlord of drug distribution for the district.

The Tu family owned a string of godowns on the Yangstepoo docks, one of which did not warehouse textile material. Tu Chien had lobbied Ohara in Tientsin. And if he negotiated well today, the *Ta Tao* police chief would sell the family the exclusive right to supply narcotics to Chapei.

But he knew it would not be easy. His opening bid must not be too low, nor too high. Ohara would demand fifty per cent for himself. His fat eyes would be ogling Yueh-ming. Tu Chien would bow and say: 'I know it is an honourable Japanese custom to present a true friend with any personal possession he desires, but I have a gift for you more appropriate to a man of your status than my worthless third wife who would be, after all, only a second-hand offering. Yueh-ming has a younger sister – almost a twin – not stretched by childbirth, nor touched by any man. I know you will find her a rare treasure, and one worthy of you.' And Ohara, whose obesity was matched only by his appetite for carnality and his inability to conduct business with a clear head once distracted onto that tangent, would shift his ground. Tu Chien would leave having relinquished but a quarter of the fortune-to-be plus a wench, albeit a choice one and perhaps even a virgin, from one of the family's brothels in Foochow Road.

After twenty minutes of the ordeal of Chapei the Oldsmobile stopped at a solid wooden gate in a high wall, on each corner of which concrete gargoyles convulsed. The bodyguard got out and pulled on a rope. Somewhere inside a bell rang. Bolts were thrown back and the gate opened to reveal a scowling *Ta Tao* police lieutenant in a khaki uniform with a Sam Browne belt and an automatic in a holster on his hip. He looked the Russian up and down menacingly, then peered into the interior of the Oldsmobile. At last he nodded and waved the car inside. They drove into the Chapei headquarters of the *Ta Tao* police force.

Yueh-ming touched Tu Chien's icy hand and shivered. The place was grey, cold, godless. A paved courtyard was dominated by a pagoda-like building with a roof of ribbed tiles supported by solid red-painted columns. A series of wooden steps led up to the entrance arch and upon them stood, arms akimbo, a warlike uniformed figure as wide as it was tall. The face of Colonel Ryoku Ohara was a melon of flesh that seemed to squash his eyes from existence. It wore an expression that was half smile, half evil impatience. 'I greet you, Tu-san,' it uttered. 'You are r'ate.'

'So sorry, Ohara-san,' Tu Chien answered in English, in which he pretended to be uncomfortable. 'The roads are bad.' He stood to one side. 'And my wife took very long to make herself more beauty in your honour.'

A slim white thigh extended from the Oldsmobile's dark interior. Ohara's eyes darted like startled fireflies behind their fleshy crevices to the apex of the slit in the *cheongsam*. Tu Chien took the long, curved fingers in his and Yueh-ming stepped elegantly, slowly, into the courtyard.

The *Ta Tao* commander caught his breath. His groin twitched. Such is what money can buy, he thought in furtive approbation. The flesh of his face wrapped into a smile. Yueh-ming shivered again, but managed to bow.

Out of the very earth beneath her feet, there came a scream. It was a curling, throaty scream that rose rapidly in pitch, then ended abruptly. It came again. It was as if something preternatural was meeting with horrible death immediately underground. She gasped. Tu Chien frowned.

Ohara chuckled. 'Zere are dungeons ber'ow. Wour'd you r'ike see zem?'

'Dungeons?' Tu Chien said uncertainly.

The Japanese gave a belly laugh. 'Yes. Dungeons. You r'ike see?'

Tu Chien glanced at Yueh-ming, whose eyes had widened in fear. But was there curiosity there also? He looked back at the *Ta Tao* commander and smiled. 'Third wife and I would like very much, Ohara-san. And could we talk our business whilst we make our ... ah ... inspection?'

Ohara's smile vanished. His bluff had been called. The dungeons were the last place he wanted to go just then. He was hungry and the evening meal awaited them. And he was impatient to fix his price with this Chinese viper. Would it include the woman? His scrotum tightened in speculation.

But Tu Chien was in no hurry for raw fish, dried seaweed and overcooked beef that made the skin smell for days. Indeed the eating habits of the invaders were despicable. No wonder they were stunted and bandy-legged. However, he would compensate on his return to Great Horse Mansion. Today began the six-week season of the 'hairy' crabs of the Yangcheng Lake. If the dwarfs knew how to appreciate such a delicacy, or the soft scales of hilsa herring, Nanchang steamed buns, fermented glutinous rice soup or sweet stuffed Ningpo dumplings they would surely be a better race. But what could you expect from a nation of degenerate island barbarians?

The screams continued unabated as they climbed the steps ahead of Ohara. They were giving Tu Chien a strange thrill that ran up his spine and filled his chest.

He looked again at Yueh-ming and she interpreted his message. '*Wen suo wei wen*,' she whispered, employing the lilt of the trained courtesan. 'We are about to experience something new, Lord.'

He glanced back at Ohara and saw the squinting eyes fixed on the slit of her *cheongsam* as it opened and closed at each step. He saw the fat lips slightly parted, heard the breath wheezing over the tip of the tongue with exertion and contained excitement. *Eeiiyah!* he exulted to himself. The prize is already secured!

8

It was mid-morning, Monday, December 13th. Nanking was suffering its gross violation two hundred miles up the Yangtse. The sky over Shanghai was joyless grey. A petrifying north wind blasted the Bund, howling between the buildings and bullying the trees. It tested the insulation of Major John Huart's British Army greatcoat as he walked to Cumberland Building, and bespoke the agony that was Nanking this portentous day.

With the transfer of the front line to the west, life in the concessions had quickly returned to normal. The harbour was once again a scene of relentless maritime industry with its mix of deep-sea ships from foreign lands and Chinese coastal vessels large and small. Huart watched it all as he walked. A Foochow junk drove its cargo of logs before the wind, trailing its long *yuloh* steering oar in its wake. A tow of a dozen barges passed, low in the water under a load of dried egg yolk, albumen, antimony ore, or bales of straw braid spirited down the Yangtse from Chinkiang, Hankow, Kiukiang, Ichang, or even from as far as Chungking.

Cumberland Building was a four-storey structure south of Nanking Road, between the headquarters of the North-China Daily News and the Custom House. Being a *hong* building with a Bund frontage, the freighters of the shipping lines for which Cumberland China were managers or agents docked directly before its basement godown to load and unload, instead of tying up bow and stern at the line of fifty or so mooring buoys in the centre of the harbour and doing battle with the currents.

Inside the headquarters of Cumberland China, Huart saw business making light of the conflict on the Yangtse. The staff seemed gripped by an industrious fever. Not a one was idle. The European managers sat behind corner desks befitting their rank, or in offices demarcated by half-height frosted glass partitions. They spoke with authority into telephones, read files with concentration, signed authorisations with long-stemmed pens. They had something else in common: all were in uniform.

'They all serve with the Shanghai Volunteer Corps,' Andrew explained as they moved through the Shipping Department on the first floor. 'Company rule. We all serve our master, Almighty Shanghai – how we love her – when there's trouble about. We're proud of our SVC. We've a British company, a kilted Scots company, and – there's no racial integration – a Eurasian company and a Chinese company. There's also a fully equipped White Russian battalion. Fearsome lot, they are. Professionals, you see. I'm with the Shanghai Light Horse, myself. I do love riding.'

A witness to the heart of a great *hong* at work, Huart was stimulated by the pervading atmosphere of raw commerce. He noted the unbridled respect afforded his cousin by the European staff, most of whom were his senior in years, none in rank. He detected wariness in every Chinese at the taipan's approach, though he could see no outward reason for such trepidation. He asked many questions, which Andrew answered readily and comprehensively, intrigued by their quality.

[51]

'The company dominates in banking and finance, property and utility management, insurance, shipping, engineering . . . import of machinery, locomotives, weaponry . . . export of cotton goods, silk, tea, tung oil – '

'Tung oil?'

'It comes from the seed of a tree that abounds in the Yangtse gorges. The Chinese use it to burnish and waterproof their boats. It's also used in the manufacture of varnish and paint. And therein lies a sorry tale.'

'Tung oil?'

'Paint. We can't get ours to sell. We've given it up as a lost cause.'

'What's wrong with your paint?'

'Nothing. Absolutely nothing. It's the tins. We had them made in Japan, you see – before the trouble – and the Chinese know it.'

Huart shrugged. 'A dollar Mex inside each tin should fix that. Welding it somehow to the bottom so they have to use up the paint first – '

Andrew was looking at his cousin with a twinkle in his eye. 'Now why couldn't our blasted compradore think of that?'

The tour of Cumberland Building continued into the Import-Export Department on the second floor, where Andrew excused himself for a few minutes for a short, earnest discourse with a willowy Englishman in an office with 'Distribution Manager' on its door. When he rejoined Huart he went right on with his commentary. 'The head office has fourteen departments and a thousand staff, seventy of whom are British, plus some Americans to handle our USA agencies. Our total staff, including the nineteen branch offices, is over three thousand. We are accused of exploiting poor, ignorant China. You almost did it yourself the first time we met. I didn't pick you up on it then. You'd only been here five minutes.'

Huart's view that the foreigners had long capitalised on Chinese shortcomings was unmodified. The truth cannot be hidden, he told himself. But he had also come to acknowledge the viewpoint of the Shanghai trader: business is born of opportunity. He anticipated the words to come.

'Of course we trade for profit. No profit, no survival. Survival's the crux of it in China – for the Chinese. We employ more than 2,300 of them who, without the wages we pay, would starve. We give work to delivery, installation, maintenance subcontractors and their scads of coolies, and umpteen companies whose manufactured goods or material we export and who, without us, would go out of business. Exploit China? Nay, John. We serve China!' Andrew took Huart's elbow. 'Let's go upstairs to my office and retrieve our overcoats. I'm standing you lunch in the Shanghai Club. There you can pretend to be a real businessman for a few hours, though you hardly look it. Have you more free ideas by any chance, Cousin?'

On the steps of Cumberland Building they turned up the collars of their coats against the icy wind and watched a man die.

Groove-shouldered 'bamboo coolies' formed a human conveyor belt from the basement godown across the Bund to a freighter registered in Melbourne. They were synchronising their exertion with their habitual chant.

'Yo-ho..! Oh-ho..! Yo-ho..! Oh-ho..! Yo-ho..! Oh-ho..!'

An aged coolie, stooped under a bale of animal hides, slipped and fell, tossing his load into the path of a bullock cart. The animal threw back its head and reared. The cart veered to one side and an iron-rimmed wheel skidded over the back of the prostrate coolie. A sound like the squashing of dried twigs carried to Huart's ears. The Cumberland China overseer ran forward and snatched up the bale from the roadway in strong forearms. 'Next!' he shouted at a group of unengaged coolies squatting at the roadside. One ran up. The bale was thrown at him, bowling him over. 'Pick it up and load it!' The line reformed. The chant resumed.

'Yo-ho..! Oh-ho..! Yo-ho..! Oh-ho..! Yo-ho..! Oh-ho..!'

Andrew stepped off towards the French Bund, the *Quai de France*, several blocks south beyond a maze of flags flapping in the wind. Huart cast a final look back at the remains of a dispassionate death and followed.

They walked with hands deep in their pockets, hunched against the swirling wind, and ignored the beggars. Tucked into the base of the buildings, a stagnant queue of refugees huddled under makeshift lean-tos. Letter writers, money changers, shoe-shine boys and hawkers broadcast their trade in sing-song repetition. Bitter-sweet aromas rose from the cooking stalls. Stench reached out from the nightsoil barges beside the jetties and the piles of garbage awaiting collection by Council carts. The tang of toilet water from the bodies en route to the Shanghai Club contrasted with the lingering stink of sickness and starvation along the walls. It all combined to form the Bund's unique unapologetic smell.

[53]

'Big Ching' struck noon overhead as Andrew inclined his head at the lane between the Custom House and the Hongkong and Shanghai Bank. 'It's no accident the Bank's cheek and jowl with the Imperial Chinese Customs Service. The duty passes through those doors down there into the vaults. East and West see one way where money is concerned.' He jerked his thumb at the statue of Sir Robert Hart betwixt the columns atop the Custom House steps. 'That Irishman was a businessman.' It was his supreme compliment.

Huart gave a wry smile. 'And a philospher. He once said: "The day will come when China will repay with interest all the injuries and insults she has suffered at the hands of the European powers." '

Andrew peered at his cousin. 'It has to be a misquote,' he told him.

Twin down-at-heel queues of Chinese led from the reclining bronze lions before the entrance of 'the finest building east of Suez': the Hongkong and Shanghai Bank. Identical cats had guarded the steps of the bank's new headquarters in Hong Kong, but they had not been so avidly attended.

'They believe touching one of the paws will bring luck – or work, which amounts to the same thing,' Andrew advised. 'Not to do so as you pass is to court disaster, to tempt fate. Chinese have a phobia about it.'

They crossed Kwangtung Road. 'Here we are,' Andrew announced. They were at the Shanghai Club, Number 3, the Bund. The Sikh doorman bowed.

The Club was one building removed from the Avenue Edouard VII which divided the British and French sectors. Its entrance epitomised what came within. Twin rows of kingly columns led from the Bund across a lofty marble hall furnished with dignified leather armchairs and ringed with a balcony onto which fronted lodgings for members. The hands of a round clock with Roman numerals were at 12:12. They checked their coats and Andrew enlisted the co-operation of another member in signing Huart into the guest register, saying: 'Now at least you're a "temporary member".' Across the hall was a door from behind which came the sonority of a male assemblage. Andrew pushed through it and they entered the Long Bar.

It was as good as its name. The bar counter ran the length of the south wall on which shelves were crammed high with bottles of every type and brand of drink, alcoholic or temperance. Men crowded every inch of it three deep, their combined body heat supplementing the open fireplace. All wore business suits or uniforms with insignia of the British Army, Royal Navy, RAF, the Merchant Marine, the Volunteer Corps or Municipal Police. Along the north wall games of liar dice were in progress, the players quaffing pints of draught Tsingtao. At the head of the bar where it did a right-angle before the windows over the Bund, a trio of river pilots drank together. The air was thick. Cigar and cigarette smoke filled the void beneath the ceiling. Huart sniffed the pervading smell of malt and money, thinking it must be the longest bar in the world.

'One hundred and eleven feet,' Andrew said and went on to explain how each member was allocated a spot at the bar in accordance with his place in the community pecking order, and that club rules prohibited women, except on the occasion of the annual ball, and Chinese and Eurasians under any circumstances, apart from the serving staff.

Huart removed his cap, but he was still recognised by the white-jacketed Chinese 'boys'. They whispered to each other, their wide eyes fixed on him. He felt uncomfortable, still unused to the attention.

The eyes of men sought Andrew Huart-Brent as he pushed his way to the corner at the head of the Long Bar where the taipans drank. To some he introduced his cousin, who was not once recognised as the man who had defied the Japanese Army at Soochow Creek. Huart acknowledged the irony. The Chinese knew him, the Kempetai would surely know him, but to his own countrymen he was a face in the crowd.

'Congratulations on the Chekiang Railways deal, Mr Huart-Brent,' called a Blue Funnel Line executive. 'You're the toast of British Locomotive, I wager. Ah, can we discuss the rolling stock, or will you ship in-house?'

'We just may share it around this time, old chap. Give Arthur a call. Tell him we've spoken.' Andrew moved on. The junior shipping man beamed hugely, too green to recognise professional palaver when he heard it.

'Andrew, about that 600,000 sterling guarantee on the Chungking Mill contract. Our guv'nors in London have agreed it's unnecessary. Bit o' good news, eh?' This came from the credit manager of the Oriental Bank.

'Good show, Thorold. That'll speed things up a bit.' He gave another man a playful punch on the shoulder. 'Hey, Humphrey! Why so glum, old chap?'

A Jardine director turned. 'Oh, hullo, Andrew. It's the blasted trouble. Our tea crop's ruined and we've orders up to here.' He drew a finger sharply across his throat. 'But you must be in the same boat . . . ?'

Andrew shook his head sympathetically. 'We saw it coming, old chap, and picked in a hurry. Could we look after your main customers for you until your next crop? Things'll be back to normal by then. *Maskee*.'

'Don't miss a piddling trick, do you Andrew? *Maskee* yourself.'

Andrew shrugged and made to move on but found a bear of a man in his way. 'You've entered Prince Unicorn in the Autumn Sweepstakes, Andrew, I hear. Sir Victor says it'll still be running when the next race starts.'

Delivering his disdain with a lengthy silence, Andrew ended it with: 'You know, Stewart, you don't quite make it as a superior being. You may see all. You may hear all. But you know fuck all. But please put your money on the Sassoon horse. It'll help Prince Unicorn's odds lengthen. Not that any wager of yours would carry much significance.'

Stewart Barlow belched. 'Up yours, too, Andrew.'

At last they reached the head of the bar. Here the Bund traffic and the horns on the harbour added to the din and Andrew had to raise his voice to introduce his cousin to his fellow taipans, utility heads and senior bankers, then to order a round of *stengahs*. Huart noted how Andrew's youthfulness, vitality and flamboyance shone amidst the group of richest and most ruthless money men in Asia.

'All of us sit on the Municipal Council, John,' Andrew explained. 'That day you were playing "Red Rover" with the Japs across the Soochow Creek, it was this soiree that was engaged in a war of words with their High Command. Thank God, old chap – ' he turned to the head of Arnhold and Company, the engineering arm of the Sassoon empire, ' – I didn't know at the time it was my own bloody family at the root of it, eh?'

Joining in the laughter, Huart's head contacted someone at his rear. He turned to apologise and recognised the pilot from the *Otranto* who gave forth in Tyneside brogue: ''Tis so nice t'see you on your feet for once, Major.' A tumbler of neat scotch disappeared in a single toss. The pilot turned, banged the glass upon the bar and called for a refill for himself and his contemporaries in a voice that split the room.

Andrew took Huart's arm. 'No trespassing there, John,' he whispered. 'That's hallowed ground – reserved for the pilots, crazy beggars that they are. Even a taipan carries no authority inside that ring.'

Later Huart was to learn it was the pilots' precursors who had earned them their privileged position at the Long Bar. In the last century each had competed with his own boat to board vessels coming into the Yangtse estuary and direct them from the Fairway Buoy through the channels over the bar at Tungsha, then the forty miles of turbulent shifting shallows at rise of tide, which could be as much as fifteen feet, to the Woosung Forts. Masters had gladly purchased the pilots' skill, and still did.

Huart returned his attention to the gathering of taipans. He sipped his *stengah* thoughtfully and listened to the banter of the supreme China hands, feeling a rank outsider in a bizarre world.

The smoke rings drifted lazily above the leather armchair in the smoking room opposite the Long Bar, matching the disposition of the man who was their creator. Even the youngest taipan of the China Trade was weighted by a sumptuous Shanghai Club lunch of roast beef and Yorkshire pudding, rhubarb pie, blancmange, cheddar and four glasses of club port.

The identity of the occupant of every other chair but one was hidden by spread copies of the *North-China Daily News*, the *Shanghai Evening Post and Mercury* or the London *Times*, which gave forth a symphony of snores. From that last chair John Huart asked suddenly: 'What plans have you for the Hong Kong branch, Andrew?'

It produced a cocked eyebrow. 'Hong Kong? Plans to visit, you mean?'

'No, not just to visit. I meant business plans.'

Andrew inspected the tip of his cheroot. 'Business in Hong Kong? Sleepy place. Not even China, really. Last place I'd visit on business. Canton? Now, that's different. But affairs're in order there. I've a good man running it. No need to go south just yet. No need.' His eyelids drooped.

Such indifference to a subject Huart considered important hit a nerve. 'But Andrew, what would be the consequences if the trouble – as you call it – spreads to the south and affects Canton? Hong Kong's importance would magnify and you'd need a sound operation there to handle it.'

Chin upon his chest, Andrew studied his cousin. 'What makes you think our current operation in Hong Kong is lacking?'

Huart told of his visit in August.

Andrew drew again on his cheroot. 'So our Mr Dole did not impress you?'

Huart hesitated, then shook his head. 'Chinese are flocking into

[57]

Hong Kong from China, like they are here. They'll need housing, sanitation, power, industries to employ them. Hong Kong has a sound British colonial administration, not one composed of businessmen as you have here – '

'Careful, John. Remember who you're talking to and where you are.'

'I'm saying that Hong Kong behoves itself to display more of a social conscience. . . .' Huart could see Andrew was not appeased, but he carried on. 'Very well, look at it from purely a business point of view. Parts of Hong Kong would have to be virtually rebuilt because of the trouble – as you insist on calling it – and what do you have in place there to take advantage? Nothing but a rented office run by a moribund clerk!' And with an emphasis that surprised himself, for it really was none of his concern, he thumped a palm hard upon the arm of his chair.

The snoring from beneath the *Times* broadsheet opposite choked off. A profusion of mutton chop whiskers appeared and bloodshot eyes glared at Huart. 'I say, old chap. . . .' The eyes went to Andrew and the expression of affront vanished, any protest stifled by the presence of a taipan in the smoking room. The man dug his watch from his waistcoat, squinted at it, grunted, hauled himself to his feet and strode from the room.

Andrew gazed with unseeing eyes at the chair that retained the imprint of a broad backside. He nursed his cheroot and remained silent for a full minute. I've been presumptuous, thought Huart. I've gone too far. He had his apology ready when Andrew spoke. 'Cousin John, how would you like to be the next director of Cumberland China Limited?'

Huart was certain his ears had played a trick, and when he failed to reply, the question was duplicated.

'You must be joking, Andrew. I'm a soldier, not a businessman.'

Turning his head slowly, Andrew looked his cousin in the eye and said: 'I never joke about business. And you're a businessman alright. You're misplaced in that uniform. I recognised that the first time we met. Oh, you're a damned fine soldier too. You've proved that. Think about it, John. There's a drop or two of Charles Huart's blood in you. What you detected during your visit to the Hong Kong branch is illuminating.'

'Thank you, Andrew. I – ' A raised palm cut him off.

'But as for this trouble – as we do insist on calling it – you're still wrong. You're too damned alarmist about Jap intentions in China. You're not alone in it, but you're wrong. The Japs affecting Canton? No, John. It's North China they want. Russia, remember?

Morita-san has personally assured me the Jap army will keep their enthusiasm within bounds. He and his cronies have warned Tokyo against endangering the China Trade – '

'Morita? He says one thing and Haiyama does another. As for your North China theory – is Shanghai in North China? Is Nanking?' Huart could see Andrew did not want to hear more, so he ended the debate by pointing to the *Times* headlines spread over the arm of the chair opposite.

US GUNBOAT *PANAY* SUNK IN DELIBERATE JAPANESE ATTACK

Neither the future scope of the 'China Incident' nor the composition of the board of directors of Cumberland China were discussed further that day. But Andrew's invitation remained in Huart's thoughts. It had been, he knew, an offer not lightly made.

9

The victory parade started out from Hongkew Park. It was led by officers on horseback, haughty and erect in pressed khaki uniforms with jackets buttoned at the neck, their heads topped with peaked cloth caps. They rode with one hand loosely on the reins, the other resting on the hilt of a *samurai* sword and they thrust their calf-high black leather boots out from the flanks of their mounts. Behind them the footsoldiers of the Rising Sun marched in tight-knit, high-stepping formation. They were proven killers, hand-picked from the ten divisions under General Matsui Iwane. They were the men who had taken Shanghai, eliminating sixty per cent of Chiang Kai-shek's modern Kuomintang Army in the process. They marched in full battle dress. Their tin helmets bobbed. Their stubby legs, encased in puttee strapping to the knee, kicked ahead in perfect unison. Hand-grenades, six per man, jiggled on their hips. Their Model 38 bolt-action rifles were carried over their shoulders; with bayonets fixed the weapons poked high above their heads, from butt to lethal tip at least a foot longer than their bearers were tall. Like those of their officers, the eyes of the footsoldiers bored ahead on an elevated plane of superiority, reflecting pride and sinister intent.

Out of Hongkew, across Soochow Creek over the Yu Ya Ching Road bridge the victory parade marched. Into the British sector.

The Shanghai Municipal Council had given its permission for the parade with reluctance and trepidation. That it had been given at all was a manifestation of the swelling power of Haiyama, whose backbone had been transformed to steel by the blatant fact that the concessions were completely surrounded by the Japanese military.

To say that trouble was anticipated was to state the obvious. The British garrison had cancelled all leave and detachments were positioned at strategic points along the route. The Municipal Police was deployed in force and the Volunteer Corps was mobilised and placed on standby.

High above Yu Ya Ching Road a captured Chinese barrage balloon, anchored somewhere in Chapei, hung in the cold grey December sky. It trailed a banner on which red ideograms lauded the victory and denigrated Chinese 'subhumans' in general, Chiang Kai-shek in particular. Japanese civilians had flocked into the British sector to line the route and each one waved a Rising Sun flag with vigour. The children watched open-mouthed as their heroes marched into their field of vision, then out again.

The free Chinese population looked on in abject disbelief. Their faith in the governors of the International Settlement was shattered. How could it be? Why were the bandy-legged dwarfs being permitted so to brandish their inhuman conduct through territory that had been deemed by the foreign powers as neutral and inviolate? The faces that peered at Huart and his men that morning exhibited incomprehension and betrayal.

The first incident occurred a block short of Nanking Road.

'*Chung . . . Kuo . . . wan . . . shui . . . aaahhh . . . !*'

The screaming man threw himself into space from a roof. He plummeted to earth in a swallow dive, his arms spinning wildly. His call of 'Long live China!' was cut off with his life as he hit Yu Ya Ching Road not a chain before the front rank of marching men. His head exploded with a 'Pop!' and the visual effect of a bursting water melon. The Japanese infantry, without losing step, marched over the remains and turned into Nanking Road, the blood of a wasted protest on the soles of their boots.

'Here they come. Just look at the cocky little shower.'

Huart looked up at the NCO's words. Through the cloth advertising banners that hung from the upper storeys of the shops on Nanking Road he could see the parade approaching. He watched the front rank grow larger, his breathing tight. He felt the hatred of the Chinese spectators rise around him like a heated, tangible mist. Something had to happen.

And did.

The home-made bomb came out of the crowd before the Sun Emporium. It detonated amidst the formation of soldiers, laying them and the nearest onlookers about like skittles. The crowd panicked. It tore its way in all directions. But it got nowhere. A wall of Japanese infantry was instantly in position as if precision drilled for just such an incident, bayonets projected at throat level. The crowd was surrounded in seconds.

'Corporal!' Huart shouted. 'Radio HQ for medical assistance! Tell them we have – ' He quickly counted the writhing, groaning bodies. 'Two dozen wounded civilians. Then bring your section and follow me!'

'Yessir!'

He shoved his way through to the armed cordon, his eyes searching for an officer. The Japanese soldiers were pressing in upon the crowd, using their rifles as rams and shouting wildly. The Chinese were cowering, wailing in terror, their eyes darting about. One or two saw Huart and screamed to him to enact another rescue. Others took up the call.

'*Banzaaaiiieeeh!*'

Huart froze as the bayonet jabbed into his throat and lifted him onto tip-toe. He looked down the length of the Model 38 rifle into a pair of slitted eyes that burnt into his with raw resolve. The lip of the midget on the other end curled and a hiss of stale breath issued from between his teeth. Though Huart's adversary was but half his size, the point that rested on his Adam's apple was razor-sharp and ready to be thrust upwards at his any move.

And in line behind the entire section of British riflemen were likewise neutralised; all but impaled.

Suddenly the Kempetai were there. They pushed their way into the crowd, slapping faces, kicking groins, screaming insults. They dragged away men, women, children, all protesting their innocence, kicking and screaming.

Trucks with red suns appeared and their tailgates crashed down. The civilians were thrown bodily inside until they filled the trucks, which then reversed and sped off in the direction of Hongkew.

From the wrong end of the bayonet, Huart watched it all happening only yards from him. His heart thumped in helpless despair. It was certain the hapless civilians would never be seen again. He choked on a curse, consumed by humiliation. The

[61]

bayonet tip went deeper. Blood flowed down his neck, under his collar, over it, over his uniform, streaking it red.

As suddenly as they had materialised the Kempetai were gone. At a shouted command the Japanese soldier pulled back his bayonet. He continued to aim his rifle at Huart's breastbone as he backed onto Nanking Road where the parade reformed its ranks. It stepped off in precise concert towards the harbour as if the violent interruption had never happened.

Huart wiped the blood from his throat and swore out loud. He should have fought back, he fumed inwardly, knowing full well that if he had done so he and a section of his men would very likely be lying on Nanking Road with their throats torn open.

'Where's the blasted medical unit?' he yelled. 'These people need help! Fast! Get on to it!'

'Yessir!' The corporal's voice was shaky, the red blood smeared across his larynx a stark contrast to the white skin of his face.

Huart's breath through his nostrils was burning, the beat of his pulse against his eardrums was an angry tom-tom as he strode away from the scene that would stay with him forever.

The next day Whitehall issued a long diplomatic protest. It was ignored by Tokyo. The Shanghai Municipal Council protested at greater length, and protested again. The Japanese High Command in Hongkew turned a deaf ear. With the plucking of the civilians from the heart of the British sector, revenge had been taken for the escape, six weeks earlier, of the survivors of the 'Doomed Battalion'.

Eyes that had once beheld Huart in admiration now avoided contact. Faces that hitherto had smiled warmly at him now delivered blank judgement. He was no longer a symbol of defiance and honour. Not only had the Japanese extracted a general retribution, they had squared their personal account with Major John Stanford Huart.

10

Shanghai's winter is a distinctive season. The petite scavenger gulls abandon the Whangpoo and migrate. The city sheds the coat of brown it has worn for the summer and slips on its winter grey. The deciduous plane trees lining the avenues of the French

Concession and Bubbling Well Road stand suddenly naked, boughs lifted in ghoulish supplication to the dulled sky which filters the sunlight into a grey ether. It can be bitterly cold but seldom vicious. Snowfalls of short duration occur from time to time. The rich acknowledge the Siberian wind by turning up fur collars; their womenfolk don mink stoles and gloves. But the most chilling aspect of the winter of 1937–38 was not the temperature.

From the day autumn gave in to winter's claim, a diabolical toll was extracted from the legions of starving refugees. They struggled through each day, begging, scrounging, stealing, dreading the approach of night. The fortunate survived each nocturnal ordeal beneath makeshift lean-tos, but those abandoned by fortune died anonymously of exposure and starvation. They froze to death by the thousand on the sidewalks. The rigid corpses, drained of all human colour, were collected each dawn by mule-driven death carts in something of a macabre medieval flashback.

The Second Cumberlands had been called back to duty in support of the Municipal Police. The *Ta Tao* police were patrolling their side of the British perimeter looking for trouble. Clashes had become commonplace.

Each morning Huart stepped over the bodies. Amongst the tangle of death, worst were the babies, abandoned by parents in a final heart-rending act of survival. He saw the infant beggars, eyes put out, limbs deformed. He saw the dying drug addicts. He saw the child streetwalkers in threadbare *cheongsams* and holed hosiery, casting about with oriental Greta Garbo eyes that hid a consuming desperation. He saw the refugees who had not yet died throwing themselves at passing carts, tearing at bags of rice or millet, bales of cotton wool to pack inside their rags against the cold. He saw the boat women in sampans all but swamped under offspring, waiting for the slop to be cast from the ships. But he could do nothing about it and soon he found he did not see any of it. The spectre of suffering and death became invisible, blended into the state of living.

At Christmas dinner in Broadway Mansions, Huart met Andrew's mother at last, and he could see how Charles Huart had succeeded in forging a new life and a thriving business in China against all odds. It was commonly acknowledged that Adelaide Huart-Brent was Charles' son in a woman's body. After ten seconds in her company, Huart subscribed to the theory.

'Andrew is too soft! He treats the Chinese staff as if suddenly they are his equal. A day's holiday a month indeed! I never heard anything like it. They'll only go and work it for the competition.

[63]

They won't think it dishonest, just that you're a fool, my boy. Silas Hardoon would turn in his grave. Andrew, I tell you – you take too much note of what happens in America. This is Shanghai. This is a special place. I tell you – '

'Yes, mother.' Andrew came over to kiss her lightly on the forehead.

'Yes what, my boy?'

'Yes, mother, you do tell me. All the time. Now, come to dinner before you remove what little face I have left in front of my very own cousin.'

They dined on stuffed aubergine, venison, pudding and stilton and washed it all down with Chateau La Mission Haut Brion 1912. After the meal they assembled on the balcony to breathe of the crisp, dry winter air and to toast the festive season with Taittinger *Comtes de Champagne*. They looked down on Soochow Creek, again crammed with boat people, its course hooped by road bridges; and at the harbour and the rump of the Whangpoo on its way south into the grey haze that hid the horizon; and the Bund and the luxurious sprawl of the concessions where, a few hours earlier in the streets bejewelled in the spirit of Christmas, the death carts had collected a thousand frozen corpses.

Something momentarily trespassed upon Huart's conscience. 'There but for fortune – ' he thought, then was distracted by a breath of French perfume. It was the hostess with a fresh glass of champagne.

'Merry Christmas, Paulette.' He kissed her on the cheek and they touched their glasses and drank.

'Merry Christmas, *ma preux chevalier*. It is beautiful, is it not?' She looked out over Shanghai, her eyes melancholy with the Taittinger.

'Not in the first and second dimension.' Huart saw her quick frown and knew Paulette did not like people to disagree, even on trivial matters. 'Shanghai as a city is basically ugly, but she dresses well. She wears her negligee of romance, adventure, challenge like the finest courtesan in the history of the East. And she has captured me.'

She looked at him. 'You paint with words. And yet you are a soldier?'

Huart shrugged.

She shivered. 'It is so cold here. Not like New Orleans in winter.' She drew her sable-lined coat around her developing midriff.

Andrew saw it and hurried over. 'The last thing I want is the mother-to-be catching a chill. Paulette, John, why don't we go inside?'

They returned to the apartment where Ling was stoking the fire in the hearth. Its flames licked and danced and the living room was filled with warmth and good cheer. Major John Huart looked back once, then closed the balcony door on Shanghai and its suffering humanity.

11

Early on New Year's morning, in an alley off Foochow Road, Jeremy Parrot stood with his back to a wall and willed the onset of ecstasy. The alley was deserted save two people: himself and the adolescent Chinese girl kneeling before him. The death carts had taken the corpses, and those who had lived through the night snuggled front to back along the walls like a chain of mandarin ducks had gone in search of continued survival.

The hair of Jeremy Parrot was unkempt. His eyes were bloodshot. His mouth was open, issuing a succession of moans. His overcoat lay where it had been discarded, a distance away. His jacket and shirt were in place, but his trousers were not: they were crumpled around his ankles. In his right hand he held a one CN dollar note, devalued to just a shilling, before the girl's eyes. His left alternately pushed her head into his groin then lifted as she drew back. She smacked her lips at each stroke and the incongruous rhythmic sucking noise carried along the alley.

'Faster, you bitch! And stop biting!'

The young man's brain was befuddled. He had been celebrating New Year's Eve and the lifting of the curfew at a Foochow Road cabaret where he had delivered up his cash, save the solitary dollar, to a Hungarian taxi dancer possessed of a cleavage arranged so as to put her clientele into a state of apoplectic extravagance. On Parrot it had worked a treat. But when his arrival at impecuniosity had become manifest, she had left with another. Ultimately he had found himself alone in the cold grey light of the new year being propositioned by this pixy in a faded *cheongsam*. 'What the hell,' he had slurred. 'I'll give it up next year.' The girl had giggled. She was a child, but hardened. 'Okay, I catchee you. One dollar buy stand up blow job. You likee number one.'

Now, oblivious to the world, Parrot built his climax. The alcohol was not helping and each time his concentration wavered, the cold air set about his scrotum with needles of ice. The girl pumped quicker. He moaned, marshalled himself and felt it coming deep down inside. He grasped the girl's head and pushed. She was ready for his thrust, accommodating it with an adjustment to the angle of her throat. Her teeth nibbled.

Parrot stiffened. 'Aaaaahhhh . . .' he crooned. Then, 'Uhh?!'

The steel-capped butt of a Lee Enfield rifle slammed upon his instep.

'What the – ? What are you doing? Oh, God – you!'

The girl looked up and squealed in fright. Like a crab she scuttled on her haunches to the opposite wall. She wiped her mouth with the back of her hand and looked on, her almond eyes wide. She had money to collect.

Parrot, instantly sober, looked pie-eyed into the leering features of Sergeant Dadds. Behind him a section of Seven Platoon stood amused.

One man put out a hand. 'Tol' you, Decker. Know that soun' anywhere.'

'Cor, Briscoe, you must 'ave one o' them pornographic memories!' Decker handed over a note.

Dadds sneered: ''Ul-lo Mistah Parrot! Fancy meetin' you 'ere. A lucky break, eh? Fer me, t'at is. Now p'raps y'can pay me t'at fookin' bet yer lost in Monk's Brass Rail. You ain't f'gotten, 'ave you? I been waitin'. Now 'ere I find yer blowin' yer funds – if yer'll excuse my choice o' words. 'Ope you've got some left. Funds, I mean. No, Parrot, don't pull up yer strides jus' yet. Need 'em down as evidence. Don't we, men?'

'We oughta dust 'im off fer fingerprints, Sarn't,' called Decker.

'Dust 'er off,' corrected Briscoe. 'Dust 'im for mouthprints.'

'Wouldn't touch 'im with yours,' Decker asserted. ''E's probably got the clap by now. Hey, 'e's goin' blue! Look at 'is family jools!'

They all laughed. The cold was indeed affecting the pigmentation of Parrot's genitals. His undischarged manhood had retreated into nothing.

'For Christ's sake, Dadds, have a heart, will you?' Parrot pleaded. The NCO's command had stilled him, half bent, hands reaching for his trousers. 'I don't have your money on me. I'm down to my last dollar and I owe that to the, er . . . young lady over there. You know how it is.'

'Dollar for gummy gobble?' whistled Decker. 'Chucks it abart, don't 'e?'

[66]

' "Young lady", Parrot? Don' see any o' them aroun' 'ere,' said Dadds.

Despite his situation, Parrot's breeding now tried to exert itself. He was a nephew of the owner of China Rice Exporters Corporation, sent east from Norfolk by his father and taken on by his uncle as a junior manager in a family scheme to make a businessman of him. But even Parrot himself would have to admit that, to date, the only 'business' he had conducted was to his financial detriment in the establishments of Blood Alley and Foochow Road. 'Do get it right, Dadds. My name's pronounced "Par-oh". I'm not some bird in a cage! It's French, you see. My family – '

'French, is it? So t'at's why you wus gettin' French kiss, eh? Nah. 'Tis "Parrot" alright. You been caught wi' fookin' pecker out, Pretty Polly.'

'Have a heart, man!' Parrot cried. 'It's jolly cold. Cold enough to – '

'Freeze yer fookin' balls orf,' finished Dadds. 'Always wondered abart t'at. Can a bloke's nuts really be freezed orf? Let's find art now, eh?'

''S'no balls to get froze off in first place, Sarge,' suggested Decker.

Dadds' smile was evil. 'Yus. They're disappearin' fast an' no mistake.'

Parrot went for bluster. 'Look here, you men! You . . . You should defend us civilians, not persecute us. I'll jolly well put in a complaint about the lot of you!' But this brought only laughter. He groaned. His eyes darted about in desperation and fixed on a large figure approaching from Foochow Road, swagger stick in his hand. 'Help! Help me, please!'

Dadds stiffened to attention, instantly into an immaculate salute, right arm executing a semi-circle like an automaton. 'Mornin' sahh!'

'Good morning, sergeant,' Huart said with uncertainty, perfunctorily returning it. 'At ease, men,' he told the riflemen who were stiffly at attention. Then he looked at Parrot. It was a pathetic sight. 'Pull up your trousers before you emasculate yourself!' He heard the snickers as the young man clawed at his belt. Nodding at Parrot, he asked the Chinese girl shivering in her *cheongsam*: 'How much you catchee this man?'

'Five dollar!' She enthusiastically held up extended fingers.

'You lying little slit-eyed bitch!' Parrot shot upright. 'We settled on one dollar. You – ' He stopped. 'Oh hell . . .'

[67]

'Hell, indeed, Mr Parrot,' said Huart. 'That's what I'll wager you'll get from your uncle when he hears about this.'

'You know my uncle? And me? Who are you? And it's "Par-oh". "Par-oh"!'

'Not according to your uncle.' Huart now knew the names of all captains of Shanghai industry, and their pronunciation. 'It appears to me you owe this girl five dollars for services rendered. I suggest you pay up.'

Parrot glared hard at Huart, then shrugged. 'I don't have enough on me. I'll sign a chit for her.'

Huart shook his head. 'She'll never collect. Give her your overcoat.'

'What?'

'Your overcoat, Mr Parrot.' He pointed his swagger stick at the garment on the ground. 'You don't seem to need it. She can pawn it for enough to adequately compensate herself.' And her entire sizeable family to boot, he thought. 'Give it to her at once or, by God, I'll file a report on you. You've a closet of coats at home, I'll wager.'

'What's it to you?' Parrot hissed. 'Who are you anyway? Who do you think you are . . . ordering me about? I'm a civilian. I've my rights. I'll – '

'You can certainly sound off once your fly buttons and your braces are in place, Mr Parrot. Shut up, please, and give the girl the overcoat. She's a civilian, too.'

Parrot made an attempt to stare Huart down. Then, with minimum grace, he scooped up his overcoat and threw it at the girl. She grabbed it and ran from the alley squealing her delight in shrill Shanghai dialect.

'On your way, Mr Parrot.' Huart jerked his thumb towards Foochow Road.

'I asked for your name, soldier,' Parrot issued through a curled lip.

'Huart. Major John Huart. H-U-A-R-T. Make sure you get it right when you make your complaint. Address it to Headquarters, Second Battalion, the Royal Cumberland Regiment. I'll certainly spell yours right when I reply to your uncle. I'll even pronounce it right. Now evaporate, Mr Par-oh.'

'Huart? I've heard of you. You're a blasted Chink lover. Yes, I'll make sure I remember you. H-U-A-R-T. Bank on it. I'll remember you. And I'll get even. That I promise.' Jeremy Parrot's frozen legs carried him with difficulty to Foochow Road. He looked back a final time to confirm the authenticity of his threat, and it registered with Huart how much the face had resembled that of a spiteful rat, then he disappeared.

Huart turned to Dadds, who still wore the scowl that had seen Parrot on his way. Lowering his voice, he said: 'This'll go no further, sergeant. I'll not put you on a charge this time, although intimidating a civilian as you did is an offence. You're a cruel man, Dadds. Keep your animal instincts in check in future or you'll answer to me. Now, on with your patrol. You're behind schedule. That's why I came looking for you.'

Dadds snapped to attention, his face a mask of stone. 'Sahh!' He turned on his men and barked a series of orders as Huart left the alley in search of the Nine Platoon patrol. The British Army had a job to do in Shanghai, he told himself, even if it was New Year's Day.

'Oh shit,' muttered Briscoe. 'Man Mountain's chewed 'im up again. He's been like bear wi' sore 'ed since that day 'e nilly got 'is throat cut.'

'Sooner 'is missus drops 'er bundle an' gets 'ere the better.'

'Better fer us an' no mistake, Decker mate. Them two 'ate each other's guts more n' more. Trouble's gotta come of it . . . I tell yer.'

12

'I'm afflicted! I tell you I'm damn-well afflicted!' Andrew Huart-Brent, youngest taipan of the China Trade, placed his elbows on the Long Bar. He rolled a half-empty tumbler of straight Johnny Walker between his palms; he had switched from the habitual but soda-diluted *stengahs* an hour before. He peered into the golden blend as if seeking the answer there, then shook his head, seemingly in confirmation of a decision made in the negative, and repeated in a tone of self-recrimination not wholly manufactured: 'I am damn-well afflicted! It must be so!'

At his side in pressed khaki, John Huart cocked an eyebrow. His cousin's discourse had developed in aimlessness with each double shot of scotch. In fact, their binge at the Long Bar was a repeat performance of the night of January 21st, six weeks earlier, the day when the Great Northern Telegraph Company had told him he was the father of a son. Jennifer had given birth two days before that, apparently with little difficulty despite the baby's size. At eleven pounds eleven ounces, James Sinclair Stanford Huart had proclaimed which side of the family he was physically to emulate. More recent letters had confirmed the mother was recovering speedily and the child developing with a purpose.

In the small hours of Tuesday, March 8th, 1938, Paulette had presented Andrew with a girl at the Country Hospital in Western District. She had insisted the child be named Vivienne. Andrew had wanted his daughter called Charlotte, but had given in with the justification that, after all, it was too close to 'Charles', the name reserved for his first son.

Once again the new fathers had met at the top corner of the Long Bar to 'wet the baby's head'. Andrew had started at five o'clock; Huart had not arrived until six. It was now after eleven. Remembering his unfortunate disposition on the morning of January 22nd, Huart was this night treating Johnny Walker with respect. Not so his cousin.

'I am afflicted,' Andrew admitted for a third time, lugubriously on this occasion. He downed his scotch and snapped his fingers at the bartender with an unnatural imperiousness. 'Like my grand-father – may God rest his soul and forgive me for speaking ill of the dear departed. Charles Huart took all that China threw at him and came up trumps. But even he could produce only females.'

Huart frowned. 'Females, Andrew? Plural? Did I hear you correctly? That was a slip of the tongue, wasn't it?'

Instead of dismissing it with customary jocularity, Andrew hesitated. He nodded, too decisively, and responded in a tone not unlike that used by a father to deflect a question posed by a child too soon in life: 'Yes, John. It was just that. It was just a slip of the tongue.'

Huart did not press. There was no need. He already knew. Charles Huart had fathered more than one daughter. Adelaide Huart-Brent had a sister.

Andrew went on quickly: 'Some people say a child's sex is determined by the father. What a cock-eyed theory. Look at me. I'm five feet eleven and three quarters. Almost made it . . . not quite. Well, as good as made it. I'm a first class athlete. I enjoy the company of women. The more the merrier. I have hair on my chest from my neck to my . . . No, it's got to be Paulette who's at fault. She's so much a woman she had to make a daughter.' He upended his refilled tumbler, exhaled forcibly as the liquor bit into his throat and drew the back of his hand across his mouth. He gestured for another, inclining his head at Huart.

'Not for me, thanks, Andrew.'

'We "China Huarts" make females. You "Military Huarts" make sons. And what about my long lost father? How do you reconcile that one? Alexander Brent was a small fry. How could he have made a son like me? Shoots that theory to pieces, doesn't it? Oh, no. I have my mother's genes. Everyone says that. Everyone. What do you think, Cousin?'

'I think we should call it a night, Andrew. It's been quite a day.'

Andrew thought about that, then nodded. 'Probably the best idea I've heard all day.' He snapped his fingers again. 'Boy! My chit!' A wad of forms was pushed across the counter and he laboriously signed each one, focusing with effort. 'I'll take no bets on the state of my head in the morning. If I could invent a pill that would bring on the hangover the night before and get it over and done with, I'd make a million.'

'You'd make more selling the formula to the distillers,' Huart pointed out. 'With a pill like that, nobody'd drink again.'

Andrew looked at his cousin. 'Alright, John,' he sighed wearily. 'It's obvious that I'm no match for you tonight. Let's be on our way.'

Even at midnight the Bund still lived. Dark figures moved upon it in a noctural microcosm: beggars, hawkers, touts, pimps. The buildings were in darkness, sleeping but possessing an abstract power. The refugees huddled side-by-side along the walls, wrapped for the night in sacks, strips of cardboard, newspapers or anything that could be made to hold together. The sky was clear, the stars winking pinpricks of silver upon a black canopy. There was not a breath of wind. A heavy frost was a certainty, perhaps even a late season snowfall. Along the Bund outside the Shanghai Club, the foreigners' sanctum of warmth, fellowship and sustenance, could be heard the stereophonic chorus of teeth chattering in wasted gums. Huart belted his greatcoat tightly about him, but the cold made short shrift of its thick wool.

The Huart-Brent Rolls-Royce was at the entrance as usual, the Sikh doorman holding open the rear door. Andrew remained heavily silent as they rode north into the traffic at the Nanking Road junction. Huart matched his solitude, believing he understood. He would have felt a dose of regret himself had Jennifer given him a girl. But this mood of Andrew's was excessive, no doubt fuelled by the fierce competitive spirit he had inherited. John Huart, British Army major, had fathered a son; Andrew Huart-Brent, no less than a Shanghai taipan, had come second, his prize a daughter. But was that all? That 'slip of the tongue' returned to Huart's thoughts. Did there exist a branch line of the family? Was Andrew competing in something that was more than merely inbred? Was he in fact in a race to sire an heir to Cumberland China?

The night ended on a subdued note. Andrew bid a dispassionate farewell at the British checkpoint at Garden Bridge where Huart alighted to radio for his own transportation. The Second Cumberlands had resumed perimeter duty and he returned the salutes of the guard detachment as he watched his cousin's Rolls-Royce cross Garden Bridge, pass through the Japanese barrier, then turn left into Broadway Mansions. The giant building loomed, its square shoulders silhouetted in series against the night sky, the lights from its apartments pinpointing havens of luxury.

The streets were dark and a cold mist was settling. The motorcycle's engine reverberated hollowly off the black hulks of the buildings. The night made Huart, shivering in the sidecar, feel quite alone in the world; even the rider in balaclava and tin helmet above and beside him was not really with him. There was only himself. And his thoughts.

Who really does control Cumberland China? Was Andrew only a figurehead concealing the true power? Was that power Adelaide Huart-Brent? Or was it the ghost of Charles Roland Huart?

Five months had passed since he had first met his third cousin. In that time his respect for Andrew had grown steadily; he was the mirror image of the man who had it all: youth, power, wealth, heritage, destiny, and the most beautiful and desirable wife in Shanghai. Later, John Huart would acknowledge that it was on the night of the birth of Andrew's first daughter that a crack, albeit one small enough to overlook by itself, appeared in the mirror.

13

The sunburst splayed phosphorescent out of the crack in the cloudbank that had blanketed Shanghai for weeks and in the foreign concessions the peach trees erupted into spring blossom like brightly painted parasols.

Brilliant morning light bathed Holt's Wharf and Pootung. It transformed the surface of the Whangpoo from silty brown to golden. Huart's senses raced, his anticipation accelerated as he lifted his face to the sky and smiled, The day, this marvellous day, smiled with him. The thrill of it welled within him. He had not felt this way since his wedding day. No, he decided. This was so much better. This was here and now.

He was standing on Holt's Wharf for the second time in his life. He had been there for two hours, occupying the same spot, x-raying the dung-coloured Whangpoo in the direction of the Yangtse until his eyes ached. He relaxed his aural muscles with a diversionary survey of Yangtsepoo across the river, then resumed his northward scrutiny.

Holt's Wharf was a broad slab of concrete laid over waterfront land that Alfred Holt and Company had bought from the Imperial Chinese in 1906. Although it was outside the International Settlement, it flew the Union Jack. It was self-sufficient, generating its own power and drawing water from its own well. Mobile steam cranes towered above its godowns and its administration building. It had come through the battle for Shanghai, fought in closest possible proximity, virtually unscathed. Not so the rest of Pootung which, like Chapei, had been flattened and torched. The straw ice houses, hitherto a characteristic of the area, had vanished from the face of the earth.

At long last a steel bow poked out of the Astrea Channel. The bow became a ship, and the ship became a merchantman. The bands on its smokestack designated it a vessel of the Blue Funnel Line. It was the vessel he had been waiting for. It waded south with ponderous caution through the narrow waterway, then hove towards Holt's Wharf. It came in slowly, ever so slowly. Huart bit his lower lip and shifted his weight from leg to leg, his impatience manifest.

'Nine months, eh?' The Lancastrian-born immigration man grinned nostalgically at his side. He was in his fifties and white of hair. 'What's second thing you're goin' t'do when you get her 'ome, lad?'

But Huart was not listening. He stood amongst the muster of short-legged, long-gowned clerks with ledgers in hand, officials from the customs service, a British officer and a red-turbaned Sikh constable in the uniform of the Municipal Police, and craned his neck as the ship docked. Coolie-stevedores, rags hanging from wiry frames, scurried forward to sling the hawsers over the bollards that were worn smooth and gleamed in the sunlight. The companionway came down with a rattling thud a few yards away.

He looked up and there she was.

Jennifer MacLurie Huart stood, slim and lovely, upon the top step, her cotton dress rippling in the breeze. One hand brushed from her face her long titian hair, shining almost vermilion in the sunlight. She held in the crook of her arm a white bundle and cast her eyes along the wharf.

Huart ran to the companionway, up the steps. For a brief blinding time he was oblivious to the fact he was a senior officer in the Shanghai garrison, in full uniform and in public. He crushed his wife in his arms and kissed her until the bundle he had overlooked gave forth a wail of protest. The coolie-stevedores paused in their labour, which was unusual in itself, to watch the display of affection with wooden disapproval.

'Darling, you look magnificent!' he exclaimed happily. 'It must be the Viking blood in you. How was the voyage? Not rough, I hope.'

She laughed, eyes dancing with the same sprinkling of lights that had captured him at first sight in Rangoon three years before. 'Please, John! The rigours of the voyage were nothing compared to that greeting. What's happened to you. You used to treat me like I was made of glass.'

'Crystal, darling. Plain glass is an insult to you.' They kissed again.

Huart held her at arm's length. 'So this is my son,' he breathed, eyes wide with a new father's tender unfamiliarity. He took the bundle with eager but unpractised hands and nearly dropped it over the side.

'Ah, excuse me, old chap,' came a plum voice from behind him. 'Could you kindly trot yourself to one side? The rest of the ship would like to get off, but you are rather large and the gangway is rather narrow. And I'd suggest the baby might also be a trifle safer on terra firma. Goodbye, Mrs Huart. Thank you for making the voyage such a distinct pleasure.'

'Goodbye, Captain Moore. And thank you, too.' Highly amused, Jennifer drew her husband aside and listened as he began to talk rapidly, gazing down at his son now safely cradled in his right arm.

'Look at his eyes roaming all over the place. Look how he takes everything in. Quiet, isn't he? Just like his father . . .' She rolled her eyes and he laughed. 'Let me help you with your luggage, darling. Do you have much? I have such good news. I have two days leave. And approval's come through for our married quarters in the Embankment Building. That's a residential block requisitioned by the garrison as an officers' mess. I hope you like it, darling. It has a balcony and an *amah*'s room and . . .'

'What room, John?'

'An *amah*'s room. A maid's room. A Chinese maid comes with the quarters. *Amah*'s the local word. You'll pick it up. There's so much to tell you about Shanghai. It's so big. So ugly and yet so beautiful. So full of life and . . . well . . . there's a horrific refugee problem. But it's quite safe. For us, I mean. There's so much I want to show you and – '

'John, slow down,' Jennifer gasped. 'You must be joking . . . James is not like you at all. Shanghai's turned you into a proper chatterbox.'

'Sorry, darling. Here, you take the baby. I'll carry the luggage. I give you my solemn promise not to say another word until after.'

'Until after what, John?' Then she smiled, gripped his arm and squeezed it when he winked. 'I was wrong. Shanghai hasn't changed you at all.'

They crossed the harbour aboard the floating pontoon that made an hourly connection between Holt's Wharf and the Customs Jetty on the Bund. Huart watched Jennifer's eyes darting about, taking in the same larger-than-life scenes that had confronted him on his arrival the previous August. She said little, fully entertained by it all.

The Embankment Building was on the south bank of Soochow Creek. Thankfully, the apartment allocated to them faced into the British sector and not north at the blackened ruins of Chapei. It was equipped with a brass bed, the largest the garrison quarter-master could find. Thirty minutes after carrying Jennifer over the threshold, Huart held her in his arms within it. He breathed the fragrance of her that had scented his dreams for nine long months. He caressed the post-natal swelling of her belly, the one physical change in her. Yet to his hungry eyes she was more beautiful and desirable than ever. He handled her with a gentleness that belied his size. He held himself in check, as he always did. She really had to be treated like a fragile crystal goddess; because it was her first time since the birth of James, and because he adored her above all else and treated her thus. He loved her with a veneration born of wonder that he had found a woman like this in his lifetime.

Captain John Stanford Huart had met Jennifer MacLurie, daughter of the chief manager of the Bank of India and Burma, in Rangoon in the spring of 1935. It had been the occasion of the Governor's birthday. She had alighted from a Bentley convertible in a frock of lilac chiffon. Watching her, Huart's world had contracted about him. He was hypnotised. In no time he had manipulated his position as guard commander to engage her in conversation, and for the rest of the afternoon he had heard not a word spoken, save those issued through the lips of Jennifer MacLurie. The feature he had loved most about her was her eyes, set below long curving lashes that fluttered as she laughed, and he had seen those lights for the first time. But what had intrigued him was her skin: it was a creamy white despite the strength of the Burma sun.

'It's a secret,' she had told him in a stage whisper. 'I apply *thanaka* bark to it.'

'The ointment Burmese women put on their faces?'

She had nodded. 'With Edinburgh hair and fair skin, I have to treat the sun with respect. I grow my hair long, wear hats – like this one – and rub on *thanaka* bark. But lightly, so the yellow pigment doesn't show.'

Huart had smiled down at her; she stopped a foot below him. 'What you might call absorbing the local colour.'

She had pulled a face. 'Captain Huart, how droll.' Then she had laughed richly, her eyelashes fanning the tropical air, and he had known there and then that no other woman would ever interest him again.

Rangoon, 1935, was the hub of a booming export trade. Burma was the rice paddy of the world. Export of tea, cotton, sugar cane, rubber, jute and teak lined the pockets of the Burma traders: the British merchants and the southern Indians who owned all the arable land on the Irrawaddy Delta. As the eldest daughter of the chief manager of the first bank in Burma, and a beauty, Jennifer MacLurie was in demand. She mingled with Rangoon's elite. At cocktail, dinner and garden parties a constantly reshuffling selection of eligible bachelors competed for her smile. She had taken none too seriously, until Captain John Huart.

She had quickly adjudged him out of place in the military, and decided he was destined to lead more than just soldiers. 'Not exactly a square peg,' she had told her parents. 'More a hexagonal one. A big wide wonderful hexagonal one.' They had exchanged looks and asked him to dinner.

Jennifer went out of her way to arrange for him to meet her father's business contacts and loved to listen to him prove himself their equal in debates on the developing and deteriorating international situation.

Sinclair MacLurie accepted his daughter's selection and quietly set about educating his future son-in-law in the banking business.

The two would dissertate often, energetically and long, analysing the world from the verandah of the MacLurie bungalow in the foothills of the Pega Yoma, or over tiffin in the British Club, or sitting late in the banker's private office on Strand Road. Sinclair would sprinkle his discourse with anecdotes from twenty-five years in the world of international finance. It was he who persuaded Huart to write to the 'rebel' branch of his family in Shanghai. 'No wee company, Cumberland China. Men who run the China Trade're no fools. Those that put Chinamen to work for them're guaranteed wealth. But, laddie, 'tis shaky wealth. Chinamen're the best workers on earth, but they work best for their own. Beyond the family, the world means nowt. It'll be over for men like your cousin once there comes a man to make China work as a collective. Could be Chiang Kai-shek. It weren't Sun Yat-sen, nor Yuan Shih-kai. Chinamen serve foreign masters for reason of pragmatism – survival. But 'neath those yellow skins they despise the white man. 'Tis like our smiling Burmans 'round us here.' The banker tapped out his pipe and peered at the sky as if reading the stars. 'Ne'er forget the words of Sir Robert Hart, laddie: "The day will come when China will repay with interest all the injuries and insults she has suffered at the hands of the European powers".'

Jennifer stirred at Huart's side. He bent and kissed her lightly on the neck. She murmured and awoke, graceful even at this most natural moment.

'How long have I been asleep?'

'Only twenty minutes, darling. You're tired. You've had a long trip.'

'But James ... where is he? I must ...'

'He's asleep, too. The *amah*'s with him. Relax, darling. Rest a while longer. You're going to need your energy.'

'Oh? Mother did warn me about men like you. You're not going to try catching up on nine whole months in one afternoon, are you?'

He chuckled. 'Of course not. I'm no satyr. It'll take at least until the end of the week.' He caught the haymaker in mid-swing. 'Didn't I just tell you to save your energy? Tonight we're going out on the town.'

And they did, ending up at the Cathay Hotel. They drank draught beer in the English pub atmosphere of the Horse and Hounds Bar. They sat over aperitifs at a window table in the Tower Restaurant. They dined, savouring each morsel, each drop of the 1929 Chateau Canon and danced, their bodies moulded into one, as the Filipino orchestra played Benny Goodman, the Dorsey brothers and Glenn Miller. They sat, heads together, and looked down on the restless Bund and the albescent strip cast by the spring moon rippling on the harbour. Shanghai was suddenly different for Huart, excitingly new for Jennifer. The romance of the port city, an experience hitherto only within the grasp of others, an illusion only tangible in the eyes of lovers, was now theirs to share.

But that night excitement was not unique to the Huart table. The eyes of the Chinese waiters were bright, there was a spring in their step and they held their heads high as they moved between the tables. 'Isn't it wonderful,' Jennifer commented. 'And a surprise. I'd heard the Chinese were inscrutable, that they kept all emotion from their faces.'

'Ordinarily I suppose that's true. But today they've reason to smile. Chiang Kai-shek's won a decisive battle.' The *North-China Daily News* had written up the counter-attack at Taierchwang which had trapped a Japanese force of 60,000 advancing on Hankow and killed a third of them. It was the Rising Sun's first major defeat in modern history. 'They've had no good news since . . .'

'Since when, John?'

'Nothing, darling.' Huart adeptly changed the subject. The 'Soochow Creek Incident' seemed insignificant now. He no longer felt a hero.

Between midnight and dawn they made slow, tender love whilst their son burbled in his crib. As Huart rested he listened to the novel sound in interested distraction. He drew Jennifer to him, gently, not waking her, and held her. He felt complete. His life was full again. When he dozed he would awaken immediately, refusing to waste any of this most wonderful of nights in sleep.

A steam train chugged into the North Station in Chapei, crammed full of Japanese troops returning from the battlefront. It wailed balefully into the night like a ghost rider. And Huart held Jennifer tighter still.

14

Turmoil is standard prognosis for the Year of the Tiger, but for that of the Earth Tiger it can be more temperate. Subsequent to the shock of Taierchwang, Japan regrouped its forces and reviewed its strategy. The 'China Incident' enjoyed an intermission.

John and Jennifer Huart set about recapturing the serene existence they had known in Rangoon, and surpassed it. They immersed themselves in a new life. They became Shanghailanders. They absorbed themselves in each other, and in their son. Huart detected every little change in James, no longer the semi-personal bundle of tender pink flesh, long spindly limbs and large head to which he had first been introduced. He watched the baby grow towards an individual character with his own smile and frown and unique body, duplicate of no other on earth. But though he could have smothered the child with an outpouring of his love, he did not. He held back. He was determined for his son to grow into a man of strong character, independent and afraid of nothing. He refused to pamper him and one night even scolded him for crying without any apparent reason.

'You're much too strict, John,' Jennifer chided. 'He's a baby, not one of your soldiers. Be a little softer with him, darling. Please.'

And Huart replied: 'James will be a man. Anything less would hurt me more than I can comprehend. I will not molly-coddle him, Jennifer.'

'Be too harsh on him and you'll only succeed in driving him closer to his mother's skirts,' she reasoned.

'We'll see, my dear.'

The demands on the garrison in its support of the Municipal Police grew, and Huart was transferred to battalion headquarters as adjutant. Though leave became harder and harder to come by, they went out together at every opportunity: plays at the Lyceum Theatre in Frenchtown, Russian ballet and opera at the Carlton Theatre, dinner dances at the *Cercle Sportif Français* – more commonly known as the French Club – in the Rue Cardinal Mercier. They sampled Parisian cuisine in the restaurants along the five miles of the Avenue Joffre that was Shanghai's Montmartre, the goulash at the *Hungaria*, reindeer steak at *Kafka*'s, fish and chips at the Metropole, mixed grills at Jimmy's Kitchen. And on their wedding anniversary they splurged on a dinner on the top floor of the new Park Hotel and looked down on the Race Club where once they had sat in the comfort of the Cumberland China box. Afterwards they called in at Del Monte's, one of the countless glittering casinos.

'Let's go, darling,' Huart soon suggested. 'I feel uncomfortable here. Most of these people look like they don't own the money they're throwing away, and I see more concealed sidearms than in the battalion armoury. If we get rich it'll not happen in a place like this, because of a lucky throw. No, it'll come with hard work plus luck of a different kind.'

She took his arm and squeezed it. 'We're rich already, John. We've got all we need. We've had our luck. Now we must hang on to what we've got.'

He bent and kissed her and led her out of the casino. The doorman, an enormous Russian in Cossack rigmarole, looked on imperiously. 'And if the world won't let us . . . ?'

'Then we'll fight it. We'll fight the whole world. Together.'

'The world has no chance.' He passed the doorman a note. 'Taxi, please.'

Jennifer hit it off with Andrew's mother, but less so with Paulette, and Huart took note. She accompanied the Huart-Brent women on their browsing expeditions through the Russian shops and the boutiques along the Avenue Joffre, and regularly went with them on summer evenings to the open air concerts in Jessfield Park. In July the three of them went by train to Peitaho for a long weekend, whilst Huart's duties kept him in Shanghai. Then in September Adelaide led the trio north to the beach resort at Tsingtao where they tried hard to appear relaxed whilst discussing the war-scarred country they had crossed to get there. Jennifer's reluctance to leave her husband behind was partially compensated by the certainty that her love for him would heighten during their time apart.

She would sit with the 'garrison widows' through the gossip sessions held across tables spread with spicy Shanghainese dishes, or with oily Pekinese, or tongue-scoring Szechuanese in the myriad restaurants along Soochow Road. She experimented with rubbery *biche de mer*, a speciality of Shantung, and recoiled in horror on learning it was also called 'sea slug'. And she washed down her rice with tiny cups of harsh brown-black Chiuchow *cha* at a teahouse in Swatow Road. But her favourite was the Cantonese fare at the Sun Ya Restaurant in Nanking Road.

She took English tea breaks in the repaired surroundings of the Palace Coffee House where she luxuriated under the high ceilings, surrounded by soft walnut panelling. Over barley water in the Renaissance Café between the Avenue du Roi Albert and the Rue Père Robert in Frenchtown she studied a contrasting Shanghai society: the sophisticated and the Bohemian.

It was the happiest season in the life of Jennifer MacLurie Huart, wife of the most lovingly protective husband in the world, a man of rock-like strength and good looks. A man, she knew with a passion that he drew out of her as soon as the lights were off, who was destined to do her proud.

'Paulette does not love Andrew,' Jennifer announced matter-of-factly one October evening over supper as a late summer storm broke upon Shanghai.

Huart frowned and placed his knife and fork on his plate. He glanced at James sleeping solidly in his crib despite the rumbling of thunder and the flashes of lightning. 'Why do you say that?' He looked quizzically at his wife and read the feminine communication in her shrug.

'She as much as told me so today. Not in as many words, of course, but in another way. I say she's more in love with his community status than with him for himself. I know they seem to go so well together, but with her so much is on the surface. I'm sorry to say it, John . . .'

'I've never noticed anything wrong between them.' Huart kept his tone devoid of argument. He had learnt never to dismiss Jennifer's intuition. 'It's a certainty Andrew is deeply in love with Paulette . . .'

'Andrew is still a little boy in so many ways.' She looked at him with eyes that suggested this judgement sometimes applied to all men. 'He inherited a great Shanghai *hong* and the fortune, power and prestige that goes with it. He needs a wife like Paulette on his arm to complete the image of the grand patrician couple. But I fear she seeks the amusement of a constantly changing scene. Oh, Andrew is her *bel esprit* now. Of that there is no doubt. But I hope the man in him takes charge before it's too late. I do like him so . . . despite his faults.'

Huart kept all trace of chauvinism from his smile. 'I'm sure Andrew's in control of his marriage, darling. It's true that all men have some weakness where women are concerned, but few of us will admit it.'

'So you admit you have a weakness for women.'

Huart's kiss was long and deep. 'Any weakness only comes afterwards.'

Later they lay in each other's arms and listened to the drumming of the rain punctuated by the intermittent thunder. The lightning flashes were weaker now, the storm moving inland. They savoured the tranquillity of that exquisite period that follows uninhibited, wholesome lovemaking.

Jennifer broke it. 'Darling, have you spoken any further with Andrew?'

'He's been away for a while visiting the branches. Including Hong Kong. He's transferred his top man from Nanking to take over there – '

'Then he's taken your advice!' She brimmed with happy enthusiasm. 'And you're not even on the payroll. Has he renewed his offer?'

'Yes. Often.'

'Well . . ?'

'It's too soon. I'd be a liability. Making offhand suggestions about the Hong Kong branch and a spot of indirect bribery to sell paint – '

'Which worked a wonder, didn't it?'

' – are one thing. Being a full-time businessman is another. Besides, the length of my military service doesn't yet give me licence to turn my back on the regiment. I'll not be branded a coward, Jennifer. There's big trouble coming. I have a feeling I'm to be needed most where I am.'

She sighed. 'It's your decision, darling. I'll not try to influence you. But you know how I feel. And Daddy agrees with me.'

A violent thunderclap wrenched James from the innocence of his slumber. Jennifer climbed from the bed and went to comfort him, just beating the *amah*. Lying alone, Huart read again in his mind an intelligence report he had seen that day. Japanese forces had made an amphibious landing on the South China coast a few miles north-east of Hong Kong and were closing on Canton and the Pearl River port of Whampoa through which the Nationalist Chinese Army was being provisioned. He wondered if Andrew had yet modified his theory on Japanese intentions south of the Yangtse.

Canton fell on October 21st. Four days later a fresh Japanese thrust took Hankow. Chiang Kai-shek moved his seat of government to Chungking.

In the Long Bar, Stewart Barlow did a rare thing and bought the chief editor of the *North-China Daily News* a drink. 'Today's editorial was spot on, ol' man! 'Course Chiang Kai-bloody-shek should sue for peace! An' bloody quick too, afore this country's nothin' left with which to bargain. An' – more's the importance – nothin' left for us, eh?'

The Shanghai taipans had a lot on their minds that autumn of 1938. The benign influence of the Earth Tiger was on the wane. The real 'war' in China was one thing, the slide towards war in Europe was another.

' "Peace in our time". For whom, I wonder?' Huart muttered as he leaned on the mantelpiece beside the wireless that crackled with the BBC news.

Jennifer looked up from folding the day's quota of rewashed nappies. She watched as her husband's finger reached up and abstractedly rubbed the scar on his throat, just above his Adam's apple: the scar that had not been there when he had left Rangoon in August, 1937; the scar he flatly refused to talk about.

'Darling,' Jennifer opened with significant emphasis at the appropriate moment one Sunday morning in March. 'I saw Doctor Watkins yesterday . . .' Huart heard the inflection loud and clear. He looked up from the *North-China Herald Weekly* and saw that her eyes confirmed the message. She nodded. 'He's soon going to have to find someone to replace me at the out-patient clinic in the afternoons. I'm pregnant again.'

From Huart's mind flew the week's review of the world and local disharmony: the German occupation of Bohemia and Moravia; the seizure by Japan of Hainan and the seaports of Foochow, Swatow, Changchow and Wenchow, the last of Chiang's supply routes save a narrow-gauge railway from Haiphong in French Indo-China and the Burma Road; the bloody demise on the Cathay Hotel steps of another prominent collaborator at the hands of General Tai Li's 'Chungking Underground'; the firefight on Penang Road in which the Second Cumberlands had lost a rifleman to a *Ta Tao* machine gun.

He lifted James off his knee, put him in his cot and went to her. 'What a marvellous surprise, darling. How many months is it?'

'I'm into my third.'

'Why didn't I notice? No morning sickness this time?'

'You've been busy. Going to the barracks before six each morning, coming back after ten each night. You've had enough to worry about without . . .'

He shook his head. 'It's no excuse. I should have seen it. I'm so sorry, darling. It's all this . . . all this . . .' He waved his arm helplessly.

'This trouble. I know. What do you want? Another boy . . . or a girl?'

'It's a dangerous world for any child to be born into. But James needs a playmate. You must be hoping for a girl, darling. Any mother would.'

'Perhaps. What about you?'

'Since you did ask, I'm the old-fashioned type. I'd be happy with half a dozen sons. One right after the other.' He kissed her before the words of protest could tumble out. 'Kidding, darling. I'd love a girl.'

James pulled himself to his feet and burbled as if he understood it all.

As the months of 1939 passed, international tension grew as surely as Jennifer's belly. Roosevelt stood up before the world for the first time and demanded that Japan withdraw from China, threatening trade restrictions, including an oil embargo, if it did not. The thunder was ignored. All foreign concessions in China now met blatant Japanese challenge. The British Concession in Tientsin was blockaded for sheltering fugitives from the Kempetai and its womenfolk, attempting to pass checkpoints, were stripped and searched at gunpoint. Whitehall ordered the fugitives to be handed over and the intimidation stopped. Chungking's protests, though loud, fell on deaf ears. British hearing as well as British face had been lost. Shanghailanders read of it with a mixture of feelings.

'Face? Bah!' Stewart Barlow scoffed two thirds along the Long Bar. 'What a load o' bull! In this country face comes with a full rice bowl. The whole o' China is starving 'cause they don't know how to fight their own bloody battles and somehow it's all our fault – we British. Face? Bah!'

There were nods all round. Despair was nigh. No country, even Britain, seemed to possess the backbone to draw a line across the path of the aggressors and stand to it with steel instead of words. Confidence was so low that even Stewart Barlow was heard to speak words of wisdom.

In July Roosevelt made good his threat and denounced the 1911 treaty that had placed trade with Japan on a 'most favoured nation' basis. It had no effect.

The British garrison was in a constant state of tension and it seemed to Jennifer that Huart carried it all on his lofty, broad shoulders. She watched him assume progressively greater responsibility and saw him less and less. She stoically accepted the change it wrought upon their marriage. She filled her mornings with James, her afternoons at the out-patients' clinic of the British Military Hospital. All the time she bloomed in her second pregnancy, harbouring a deep maternal happiness.

The crises were many. Wang Ching-wei, sheltered in the Badlands by the Japanese, created one when he called a press conference at 76 Jessfield Road, administrative HQ of the *Ta Tao*. The head of the puppet 'government' was a prime target. A raid by Madam Chiang's dive-bombers was rumoured, as was a suicide attack by Tai Li's men with satchel charges strapped to their bodies. Huart commanded the deployment of the two companies of Second Cumberlands that lined Jessfield Road.

'We're to kip out here for God knows how long because of some traitor?' Grant Rodder's question was rhetorical but loud enough for Huart to hear it. 'Give me a good line of sight and I'll do Tai Li's job for him.'

'Leave Chinese politics to the Chinese, Captain Rodder,' Huart advised.

'Yes, sir!' The newly promoted commander of 'C' Company threw a salute that was unnecessary and marched off in high dudgeon.

Huart let him go. They were all on edge.

They camped on Jessfield Road for three days. Wang Ching-wei delivered an ineffectual speech and returned to his Badlands sanctuary. There was no sign of Kuomintang aircraft nor insurgency, nor any protest, save Rodder's. As the British soldiers climbed aboard their transports on the last morning a shot rang out from across the road. The man beside Huart screamed and fell to the pavement, a bloody mess in place of his nose.

'You are not to retaliate, Major Huart!' ordered Rae. 'Over.'

'But we can see the sniper that shot down one of my men, sir. Over.'

'Is your man dead? Over.'

It made a difference? 'No. But his own mother won't know him. Over.'

'I repeat, Major Huart. No retaliation. Contain your men. There's nothing to be gained. Jap HQ will just say it was an accident and promise to punish the offender like the last time. Is the order understood? Over.'

Huart shook his head in angry frustration. It may very likely have been an accident: the sniper's target had probably been himself. Events had turned garrison duty in Shanghai into a highly dangerous farce.

'Is the order understood, Major Huart? Acknowledge! Over.'

Huart sighed and depressed the switch. 'Acknowledged.' But I'm damned if it's understood, he added under his breath. 'Over and out.'

He looked at Rodder and at his men with their faces and

weapons pointed across Jessfield Road. He shook his head and listened to the curses.

On September 1st the world exploded.

The British garrison in Shanghai went onto full alert. The Second Cumberlands drew double ammunition and combat rations and manned the perimeter facing Hongkew. For ten days Huart slept alternately on a camp stretcher in his office and on three planks in the command bunker.

The Huart-Brents moved out of Broadway Mansions into the Park Hotel. The adjoining suite was reserved for Adelaide but she refused to take it.

'Mother, you're cut off in Hungjiao. Will you listen to reason – '

'Your reason, Andrew! What an example you're asking me to set my staff! They're terrified enough without seeing me abandon ship.'

'But, Mother, how can we save you if – ?'

'I'll save myself. Andrew, you're a baby. What would your grandfather think of you if he were alive today? What would he say if he – ?'

Andrew hung up with tears stinging the back of his eyes.

The concessions held their collective breath. They waited, apprehensive and watchful, like rabbits crouched in warrens directly in the path of the tiger, which was an appropriate simile considering it was the Year of the placid Earth Rabbit. But it seemed that Japan did not intend to use its Anti-Comintern Pact with the Axis as a licence to expand its war in China. The Second Cumberlands cut their strength on the perimeter and Huart returned to the Embankment Building at nights.

Jennifer now spoke little of the Huart-Brents or Cumberland China, but in her mind she still dressed her husband in a business suit and sat him with the directors at the board room table on the top floor of Cumberland Building. She visited that room with Adelaide and Paulette and scanned the portraits of *hong* executives, past and present, hung along the wall in order of rank, spearheaded by an oil of Charles Huart that dwarfed the others. She saw her husband's dark eyes and large long ears. Andrew's cleancut likeness, done five years before, stood out fresh and youthful amongst the stern faces framed with beards.

Adelaide inspected her own portrait with critical gaze. 'Oh, the painter did a fine job,' she explained when Jennifer paused quizzically at her side. 'It's just that I wish I still looked like that.'

Jennifer intently studied the faces of the compradores, those Chinese middlemen without whose connections and dispensing of largesse no east-west trade could go on. She stood before a portrait of a robed official with watery Mongolian eyes and a white beard to his waist until Adelaide came over and said: 'The Grand Imperial Mandarin of Chungking. He who gave the opportunity. Painted in 1873, by Charles Roland Huart.'

'Your father was a painter, too? I mean, it's very good.'

'He was many things and excelled at all.' She glanced at the portrait of her son, then back at Paulette, and muttered something that sounded to Jennifer like: 'Except in making a direct male heir. I had to do that.'

Jennifer went to the windows over the Bund and gazed through them at the harbour where the freighters waited in line to exchange one cargo for another via the rotating chain of coolies that filed in and out of the godown beneath her feet. Yes, she confirmed to herself, this is where John belongs, not the British Army; but the war in Europe was capturing all attention, dominating all conversation. No, she acknowledged sadly, he won't leave the army now, not with things the way they are. But not a word on the subject would she utter in his hearing.

When Whitehall ordered the transfer of two battalions from Shanghai to Hong Kong and Singapore, prime targets for the Axis, the Second Cumberlands stayed put and shouldered an even greater burden in the maintenance of security and law and order in an increasingly lawless society.

The second Huart son was born on October 10th, 1939. He was christened Andrew John. His 'uncle' appreciated the gesture above all others and was his most ardent devotee. Andrew continued to employ the camouflage of humour to publicly bemoan the delayed arrival of his own male heir. In private, however, he discarded the humour like the false mask it was. 'I'm afflicted!' he would castigate his reflection in the mirror. 'I'm afflicted with a third cousin who won't take second place in anything – who's bigger, has a wife he can make sons with, and who seems to know what the Japs are going to do before the Japs know themselves!'

Christmas 1939 found the world in temporary repose. In Europe it was the time of the 'Phoney War'. In China, Japan postponed offensives and stood to its blockade of the Chungking supply routes. 1940 began quietly until March 31st when Major John Huart issued what should have been a routine order: at 0600 hours, April 1st, 'C' Company was to relieve the Municipal Police

[87]

at all checkpoints along Jessfield Road. Recalling his narrow escape outside Number 76, Huart decided to take personal charge of the handover. He could not know that this decision among decisions was to precipitate the first of a chain of events that would have a profound effect on the rest of his life. By Chinese logic the decision had actually been made at the instant of his birth: at the time known as the Limit of Heat, the beginning of autumn, in the Year of the Fire Horse.

15

Colonel Ryoku Ohara slammed a meaty paw upon his desk. He swore in the language of a Yokohama whorehouse as the inkwell shot into the air and coated his fist blue. Amidst end-to-end curses, with his other hand he fumbled a white paper napkin from a drawer. In a chair positioned so as to broadcast the inferior status of its occupant, Tu Chien thought of the silk handkerchief in his pocket, then cancelled the gesture. Let the uncouth baboon clean up his own mess, he decided, feeling hardly inferior as he watched the *Ta Tao* police chief furiously squash the sodden blue napkin in his fist and throw it at the waste paper basket, missing by a yard. Ohara swore afresh, turned on Tu Chien and hissed in English: 'I ask again, Tu-san, where is shipment of Indian opium?' He grimaced at the need to communicate in the *gaijin* language with this slippery eel whose service he had come to need ninety-nine percent for personal gain and one percent for the 'greater' cause of Dai Nippon.

'In Ningpo, Ohara-san,' Tu Chien answered flatly. 'It has been impounded there. It will take time and favours to have it released.'

'Time? How much time?'

Tu Chien pulled a lugubrious face.

'But I need it tomorrow! *Aaahhyiii!*' Ohara's cry exhibited a fragility born of panic. His eyes bulged bloodshot through the flesh around them.

Tu Chien, armed with the knowledge that the opium was actually stored in one of the Great Horse godowns on Soochow Creek after unloading from a Goan trawler at the French Bund, held back his answer. Indian opium drew top dollar. It was more powerful and of finer texture than the indigenous variety which was only an *ersatz* mixture of pork rind, dried pig's blood and sesame seed in opium dross. Demand for the Indian drug was so great that Tu Chien had been able to increase his mark-up a thousand per cent in the last six months through the supply channels he opened and closed at will. And now he was setting Ohara up for a further increase of no less than five hundred per cent. At last he poked a molar with a toothpick and sighed: 'Impossible. So sorry.'

Ohara swallowed. Fear squeezed his brain and bulged his eyes. Tu Chien could not believe it. The baboon was blind to the ploy. What ailed him? 'Ningpo?' It was a squeal. 'Why not r'and at British docks. Or French?'

'Security has become much too tight in the foreign areas.'

Ohara shook his head and his jowls rippled. 'Pay off French por'ice is easy. Dey r'ine pockets r'ike crazy men, 'speciar'y now is war at home and soon go in army. An' British por'ice are – how say? – short fist.'

'Short handed, Ohara-san.'

'Yes. Pr'enty British army gone Hong Kong, Sing'pore. Not un'stand what you say, Tu-san. Foreign docks now easy pr'ace.' Ohara leaned forward and a foot of his desk disappeared into the fold of his massive belly.

Tu Chien conjured a quick smile. What the *Ta Tao* police chief said was indeed accurate. 'So sorry,' he demurred. 'Not accurate. The frog eaters and the ones with smelly feet have tightened their security for business reasons. They can line their pockets, as you say, much quicker marketing their own opium. They make more as principal than taking my *kumshaw*. Landing this shipment at Ningpo was a risk, I agree. A calculated one. But I did not want it examined by men I control no longer. How could I know your customs officers have grown so greedy? You must call them . . .' He nodded at the telephone. 'And tell them that – '

'No!' The shout was spontaneous. Ohara glanced nervously at the door and lowered his voice. 'I cannot. Ah . . . commun'cations with Ningpo gone out. Sab'tage! Accursed agents of Tai R'i. May his borrs expr'ode!'

'His bowels, Ohara-san.'

'No! His borrs!' The *Ta Tao* police chief leapt to his feet, his vitals in both hands. 'These my borrs! Now you grabbem and you squeezem!'

Tu Chien kept delight off his face. So Ohara was playing a lone hand. Greed had induced him to break the rules. In that case, was five hundred per cent enough? He thought quickly on this.

When in control, exploit it! Ohara was on the run. He had been fed lies and was feasting on them.

'Tu-san,' the *Ta Tao* police chief pleaded, 'preeze do somet'ing!'

Lifting his right hand, Tu Chien rubbed his thumb and forefinger together in silent, unambiguous communication and said softly: 'It will cost a lot . . . a lot more than last time, Ohara-san. The risks increase – '

The fat torso shot forward. 'Of course. Of course, Tu-san. For me money no probr'em! Can you get opium here 'fore seven 'clock t'morrow – ?'

'Impossible! So sorry.' Tu Chien sat back as the fat face fell. 'But why the urgency? What is your problem?'

The fat hands spread in helpless supplication. They were sweating. The bulging eyes lifted to the ceiling, the capilliaries a mosiac upon the whites. Ohara was sleeping badly. 'Aiiih!' he cried, his voice rising to a piggish squeal to banish the dregs of his self-esteem. 'Genr'ar Obe visit to'morrow! Chapei have too much troub're. Chinese opium no more doing good. Too weak. Too weak by much. I mus' show Obe I have Indian opium! He must see I have sor'ution to probr'em and . . .' The voice died away, then Ohara thumped the desk with his fist as if grasping at a straw that had suddenly blown within his ken. The inkwell jumped and splashed again, but he ignored it, obsessed by the flash of logic. 'Tu-san! If Obe send me to Chungking front, that worm, Takahasu, take over Chapei. Your opium franchise go to Reds from Yerr'ow River!'

Tu Chien blanched imperceptibly. *Eeeeyahh!* It was true!

Ohara pressed his newly perceived advantage. 'What you t'ink zat? What you do zen? What – ?' He broke off in mid sentence as Tu Chien raised a hand, and in so doing unconsciously confirmed his novel inferiority.

'Do not put excrement on Buddha's head by repeating yourself. I will try to deliver the opium by seven. But, as I said, it will cost a lot.'

Ohara visibly deflated with relief as if a valve had opened. 'How much?' he asked, his decision made irrespective of the figure. Even so, his eyes bulged wider when he heard it. Then he nodded, took another paper napkin and wiped the ink from his fist, the cold sweat from his brow.

In the rear of the Oldsmobile as the chauffeur sped it through Chapei's sullen streets into the Badlands, Tu Chien's brain machinated fiercely, his emotions alternated between elation and fear.

[90]

But an observer would be fooled: none of it touched his face. Then came a flash of dissatisfaction. He should have asked for more! He had left money on the table!

They came to the sandbagged roadblock at the junction of Jessfield Road and Bubbling Well Road. Beside it stood an armoured car, its Municipal Police crew lazing on its fenders, smoking. The Sikh policeman on duty waved the Oldsmobile on and they re-entered the sanctuary of the International Settlement. Again the big car had not been stopped. Tu Chien smiled everywhere except upon his face. If the police discovered what a pittance was their *kumshaw* compared to the true value of the contraband the family slipped past their noses each day . . .

He extracted his gold watch from the fob of the waistcoat that had been hand-made for him by C. N. Gray, the Nanking Road tailor patronised by the elite. Both hands pointed down at six. It had a spontaneous centripetal effect on his thoughts. His asking price had indeed been too low!

'Take me to Factory Number Four!'

'Yes, Lord.' The Oldsmobile swung left off Bubbling Well Road.

Tu Chien's brain churned on fresh input. The *Ta Tao* pig with bloated intestines needed but a sample to fool his General Obe, and that could be delivered personally with the explanation that the rest remained impounded in Ningpo and only another one hundred percent price increase would pry it loose. The obese baboon would squirm and protest, but would eventually agree. It would take at most an hour: small sacrifice for double profit. And for the same old product, no less! The sample would be pure Indian grade, but the subsequent bulk delivery would be plain, ordinary Chinese *tu*, perhaps with the pork rind removed. The genuine article would fetch more sold piecemeal in the French Concession.

This was the Year of the Gold Dragon. This was the year when the gods shielded the bold, for dragons render the waters void of all poisons and protect believers from any and all disease. This was also the year when errands of great importance should not be entrusted to lesser hands.

Tu Chien agreed with all this and it decided him. He would have to leave for Chapei at dawn. But the Oldsmobile would attract attention leaving the International Settlement so early . . . unless it was transporting a family of believers to pray to the Jade Buddha ahead of the ten thousand peasants who flocked there every day. Yes, it would be an adequate ruse.

Then a familiar thought impinged upon him. He put it aside. But it came back at once. It loitered in his brain and gnawed at him like a mongrel at a bone. It puzzled him, but it did not alarm him. He was too elated, too confident to accommodate any competing emotion. But why should it come to him at this time? He knew the awesome risk he took every day of his life. He was a Fire Horse. And not just any Fire Horse – he had been born on the first day of its year, thirty-four before. Knowledge that any miscalculation would bring certain calamity, not only physically upon himself but also upon those he loved and cared for, was as much a grand challenge for Tu Chien as it was a caution.

The Oldsmobile drew up at an iron gate in front of a string of buildings in a compound facing Soochow Creek. This was the Great Horse Textile Mill and Spinning Factory, one of several owned by the Tu family. But a section of this factory processed something other than textiles and garments. The gate opened and the big car powered through. Tu Chien's eyes scanned the five buildings standing in juxtaposition. His ears heard the muffled tumult of the thousand machines. His nose sniffed at the odours of industry: the smells of fresh fabric, boiling dye and the sweat of two thousand unpaid children. It was the scent of money, more being made each and every second.

Above everything connected with his heritage and his destiny, he knew it was a converse truism that any fortune made by a Fire Horse must dwarf all others. This being so, it was certain he would become the richest man in Shanghai. No, not just Shanghai – China. All China! Yes, that was his destiny as a Fire Horse! Calamity was for others.

Tu Chien knew, and knew again, of the inevitability of the coming of the day when he would be the richest man in all China!

16

The Second Cumberlands had rebuilt the roadblock into a rough square of low sandbagged walls. In each wall there was a gap to admit vehicles for inspection within a smaller square contained by wooden traffic barriers and covered by a Bren gun fixed in an emplacement. All around, urban Shanghai was hushed: Bubbling Well Road to the east, the Badlands to the west, the French

Concession to the south, Western District to the north. The city was inert, locked in that lethargic state that comes with the dregs of slumber, before the first spark of wakefulness. The immature dawn coupled with an overcast sky to submerge the junction in a deep greyness streaked with shadows. The stillness of its periphery rendered the roadblock a focal point spectral in nature. All was still, except the soldiers moving about the square of sandbags.

In the gloom, Huart did not see the black shape of the Oldsmobile until it was a hundred yards away. It materialised out of the shadows like an ebony phantom. He watched it slow to a crawl and approach tentatively, like a jungle predator exposed before an unfamiliar prey. Then it stopped. The occupants of the front seat were just discernible. A Chinese chauffeur peered at the British soldiers. He seemed confused. Beside him a broad-shouldered Caucasian, a Russian by the outline of his vast head, was half turned to the rear where sat two other silhouettes. Huart could see the pointed collar of a jacket, the type worn by well-to-do Chinese women. A smaller shape moved about, then a small pale face appeared at the window. It belonged to a Chinese boy of about ten, peering out at Huart in wonder as he stood before the roadblock.

'Hul-lo,' came from Sergeant Dadds. 'Cop t'is lot. Check 'em out, sah?'

Huart nodded. 'Take two men with you. Approach with caution.'

'Sah! Briscoe! Decker! Front n' centah!' Dadds' eyes gleamed hungrily.

In the velvet upholstered interior of the Oldsmobile, surprise had become disbelief, followed by dismay. Now an air of indecision dominated.

'But where are the useless red-headed piles of horse dung?' Yueh-ming enquired in Shanghai dialect, her instinctive phraseology exposing the Soochow peasant girl beneath the veneer of acquired dignity. She pulled the brocade jacket about her and the collar dug into her neck. Her eyes were wide and she shivered with sudden fear.

'What do I do, Lord?' the chauffeur called plaintively.

'Look, Papa!' Hoi-nam's infant cry was enthusiastic. 'Look at all the foreign ghost soldiers!' Then, with childish awe: 'Look at that big one! He's a ghost giant! Will he bully us? Don't stop, Papa! Don't stop!'

The bodyguard withdrew his Mauser automatic from the holster under his armpit, laid it upon the seat beside him and awaited orders.

'What am I to do, Lord?' the chauffeur repeated. 'Shall we go back?'

Tu Chien stared through the windscreen, his brain meshing frantically. Questions ricocheted about the inside of his head. Why were British soldiers here instead of Sikhs? What had gone wrong? The horrifying truth came to him. They had fallen into a trap! Who had set it? Ohara, that fat intestined pig? No. He had too much to lose if the sample should fail to arrive. The Reds from the Yellow River? They had everything to gain. But one question kept recurring: What was he going to do?

'Lord?' The chauffeur turned and looked at him. 'What am I to do?'

Tu Chien's brain went into overdrive. There were three alternatives. They could submit to search – but there were twenty kilograms of Indian opium in the boot and the eyesight of these British soldiers was untreated by *kumshaw*. They could turn back – but then the sample would not reach Ohara in time and the family would lose the Chapei franchise. They could break through the roadblock – the opening in the wall was dead ahead, the barrier beyond it carelessly raised. He looked at the three soldiers approaching line abreast, Lee Enfield rifles held low. Then he looked past them to the giant officer standing erect, watching intently.

'Lord . . ?'

The eyes of Tu Chien and John Huart locked together. Through the greyness something passed between them. Each recognised the other, though prior to this moment each had not known of the other's existence. And Tu Chien knew then that there was only one choice. The giant would find the opium in the boot; he would not let them run. Tu Chien pried his eyes away from his enemy and looked again at the raised barrier. And made his decision.

The instant before the Oldsmobile lurched forward with a concerted roar from its six cylinders, a scream of scoring rubber and a fart of exhaust smoke, Huart shouted a warning. Dadds, eager for a confrontation, had broken a 'standing instruction'. Instead of approaching the vehicle at a tangent, he was advancing from directly in front, Briscoe and Decker on his right. But though the warning was loud, it drowned in the explosion of sound as the big car charged.

Dadds reacted instantly and threw himself out of the path.

Decker, on the far right, also dived sideways and rolled clear. But Briscoe was less alert. The powerful engine propelled the luxurious mass of metal straight at the paralysed soldier. It hit him dead centre and smashed him backwards. Arms flailing, he disappeared into the void beneath the Oldsmobile like the dinner of some prehistoric monster. His rifle was heard to discharge with a muffled cough and his scream to abort at its peak, lost in a sickening drawn-out crunching noise.

The long black barrel of a Mauser thrust out the front passenger window. It spat fire. The air beside Huart's head crackled. He ducked, dropped to one knee behind the sandbagged wall, his Webley in hand. 'Open fire!' he yelled and supported his elbow on the wall, aimed dead centre of the massive torso framed in the window and squeezed the trigger once, twice, three times. The bodyguard bucked back and up, his boulder-sized head impacted against the roof of the car as the bullets punctured his waistcoat. The Mauser flew from his fingers and spun across the bitumen. Huart jerked his head to the left and swore at what he saw. 'Aim at the tyres! Dadds! The tyres, blast you!'

Sergeant Dadds had completed his evasive action with an athletic flip into a prone firing position. Rifle at his shoulder, he was blasting a fusillade of .303 bullets into the cabin of the Oldsmobile.

'Dadds! Blast you . . !'

But the NCO kept firing.

The face of the boy was pressed against the rear window, eyes wide in wonderment as if watching a scene in an adventure movie. The glass in front of the face disintegrated. Blood spurted onto the roadway in a crooked stream. A high-pitched female scream erupted from within the car, then terminated abruptly in a grotesque gurgle. The Bren gun opened up. A tyre exploded. The Oldsmobile veered sharply and two wheels lifted into the air. It seemed to hang there for long seconds, balanced at an angle of forty-five degrees.

Tu Chien looked on entranced as his personal world was blown apart around him. It was all being done in slow motion. The gods were determined to prolong to the limit this torture of tortures. He saw the lurch of the bodyguard's frame as the giant's bullets drilled it. He felt the searing burning poker puncture his hip as one of those bullets deflected from the Russian's sternum, tore through him and then the back of the seat. He looked down at the limp body of Yueh-ming, tossed across him like a discarded doll, warm and sticky red from the blood gushing from a gaping hole in her slender neck. He looked up to see his elder son's head erupt and shower him with a mottled spray like regurgitated congee. He watched the chauffeur slump over the wheel, his foot hard upon the accelerator, sending the limousine of death on a blind surge towards the sandbagged wall. All around him the dire symphony went on and on: the shouting of the soldiers, the barking of their rifles, the crunch-crunch-crunch of their bullets puncturing the car's metal skin, the rat-tat-tat-tat of the Bren gun aimed low and being fired in precise short bursts, the 'pop' of a front tyre bursting, the screech of hubcaps across bitumen. Then the car tilted to the right. The left side began to lift slowly, deliberately off the ground.

The imprint of horror stitched itself upon the lens of Tu Chien's brain. The image began to rotate, slowly at first, then gathering speed like a centrifuge. Superimposed were the ugly, red-skinned foreign ghost faces, photographed in minute detail and filed forever: the large square mien of the officer giant with his eyes squinting along the barrel of his revolver, the long nose of the man behind the Bren gun, the cruel leer of the prone sergeant with his tongue poking out of the corner of his mouth as he emptied his magazine into the car.

The Oldsmobile crashed onto its hood, then rolled over again and again. Its boot flew open. It hit the sandbagged wall and somersaulted end over end across the enclosed square of the roadblock. It bounced on the far wall, flipped into the air, then crashed down upon the western carriageway of Jessfield Road, sending a shower of glass in all directions.

It shuddered to rest squarely upon its four wheels that were sprung from their mountings, in a lake of seeping petrol and blood that oozed from beneath buckled doors. It was a convoluted tangle of scored metal and twisted chromium. Its vacuous windows gaped, edges jagged with glass slivers like shark's teeth. Its suicidal charge had lasted but eight seconds. In jumbled heaps upon its floor lay five bullet-riddled bodies, only one of which still breathed.

Several more seconds were to pass before Huart caught sight of the trail of white powder that started on the eastern carriageway of Jessfield Road near the dead body of Private Briscoe. It followed the path of the Oldsmobile through the roadblock, over its walls and ended on the western carriageway in a small pyramid directly beneath the gaping boot of the demolished limousine. It explained a great deal.

'Sergeant Dadds! I want a word with you.'

'Sahh!' The NCO's face was an unrepentant mask of satisfaction as he reloaded ten rounds into the magazine of his Lee Enfield.

'You fired too high, Dadds. There's nobody left alive to interrogate, thanks to you. You've done a grand job . . . blast you.'

Dadds stood at attention and took Huart's burning gaze between the eyes. 'Thank you . . . sahh!' He saluted with parade ground precision and marched away to supervise the loading of Briscoe's body onto a stretcher.

Huart grimly admitted defeat to himself. Dadds would remain an animal no matter what anyone in this man's army tried to do about it. The papers that would initiate the platoon sergeant's repatriation had been filled out a long time ago. They would be put into the system before day's end.

But the fate of Sergeant Dadds had already been decided by somebody else. Huart was standing with his eyes drilling the back of a man who, in less than twenty-four hours, would also be dead.

Nobody knew where or when Sergeant Dadds met his end. His men were to recall that at 'lights out' he had been in his 'farter' in the platoon Nissen hut and had boasted on into the darkness about how he had 'rid th' world of a few fookin' Chinks an' put one over on t'at big fookin' Chink-lover into th' bargain'. It was the last utterance heard from him. Nobody had heard him leave the hut during the night. Not one of the guards at the main gate, nor any patrolling the grounds, had noted anything out of place. At first light, when the bugle sounded 'reveille', his bed was empty. No-one paid it much attention. It was likely he was out in the 'crapper', or giving the guards a hard time over some minor inadequacy as he was wont to do on unpredictable occasions.

Decker, first out of the door, found him. In fact, he tripped over him and fell full length, sending his shaving gear flying. He picked himself up, ready to fight, his humour at a nadir since his witnessing of his best mate's demise the morning before. He had spent a sleepless night, staring at the empty bed next to his, remembering their times together.

'What in 'ell d'yer t'ink yer doin' there! I oughta . . . Beejeeeezuzzz!'

Jaw locked open, heart jammed into his windpipe, Decker stared at the naked body of Sergeant Dadds. Or what was left of it. It sat on the hut steps, granitic with rigor mortis. It was headless, but the head was there, held in the lap in both hands as if it was an offering. The eyes were open. No longer scornful or truculent or cocky, they bulged like boiled eggs, the pupils dilated into pinpricks of abject terror.

'Ohhh Jezuz Keeeeriiist!'

The rest of the platoon came running. Within seconds thirty men stood around the neatly arranged remains of their sergeant. They all stared. Their mouths hung open. They looked at each other with eyes that sought an explanation. But it was beyond all of them.

Decker's stumbling upon the corpse of Sergeant Dadds coincided with one other discovery. The sole survivor of the Oldsmobile was found to have gone missing from the custodial ward of the British Military Hospital. Tu Chien had undergone an operation the previous afternoon to remove the Webley bullet from his hip. It had been unsuccessful: the bullet was wedged into the hip joint. Only BMH's specialist surgeon was deemed to have the skill to remove it, and he was on home leave. Incredibly, it was the only wound on Tu Chien's body save the abrasion to his skull that had knocked him unconscious when the vehicle had rolled. Nobody in the hospital could remember anything suspicious about the night before. Nobody could proffer an explanation for either incident.

But when the identically mutilated body of the Bren gunner was found outside the main barracks gate at dawn the next day, Huart had one. He knew then that the Second Cumberlands had tangled with the highest echelon of the Shanghai underworld and had been delivered a punishment, and a warning. Dadds and the gunner had been ritually executed: put to death in a macabre and horrific fashion Huart believed no man deserved. In addendum, their prized captive, whose survival he had heard of with elation, had been spirited from custody as if he had been a ghost.

Huart was staggered by the power of the phenomenon they had by chance encountered. A damning realisation hit him: it was likely he was the next target for the assassin henchmen of the Chinese drug-runner with the bullet in his hip. Had he known it was his own bullet, he would have replaced the likelihood with certainty. Had he been quartered in the barracks, he would probably already be dead. Security at the Embankment Building was tight since feuding between *Ta Tao* agents and the 'Chungking Underground' had intensified. Nevertheless, would Jennifer awaken one morning to find her husband dead beside her, his head in his lap?

He confided in no-one, certain that to do so risked having him dubbed a psychiatric casualty of the string of violent incidents and

smartly invalided home. Instead he responded to the conceived
threat by tightening his personal security, managing it so discreetly
that even his wife did not suspect that he considered a danger
threatened the family.

Weeks passed. Nothing happened. Gradually the events of April
1st and 2nd slipped into memory. Time painted them over,
submerged them under layers of new days during which two-year-
old James and baby Andrew filled Huart's hours at home. His
love for Jennifer broadened and rose to a higher plane where he
knew nothing in life could ever threaten it.

But Tu Chien, recovering in Great Horse Mansion, had not
forgotten Major John Huart. He sat in his chamber, a room as
silent as the graves of his third concubine and his first son. In the
beginning he had thought of joining them to live in perpetual
silence. After a week he began to plan his revenge. The giant had
earned a special death, nothing as routine as had been met by the
others. The ritual of clinically severing the head, layer by
epidermic layer, from the body tied to a block of ice before a
mirror placed to reflect one's own execution, was an end too plain.

'It will be a revenge so gradual ... so subtle ... so sweet – for
me,' Tu Chien promised himself. 'First I will investigate him. I
will learn more about him than he knows of himself. There is one
certainty. Such a man must have sons.'

17

'Whatever's to become of us?' Adelaide Huart-Brent demanded
halfway into the main course of the farewell dinner taking place
at the table along the south wall of the Tower Restaurant. 'Not a
battalion staying behind to protect us? Not one company? Not
even a ... ? a ... ?'

'A platoon, Mother,' Andrew helped out from Jennifer's right
elbow.

'Not even a single man jack in a British Army uniform?' she
carried on without a sign that her son had been heard, her eyes
upon John Huart in the host's chair. 'How can this Churchill
fellow expect us to defend ourselves on our own from the criminals
in the streets, and from those trigger happy spies who are supposed

to come from Chungking, and from the horrid Japanese? This Churchill! He . . . He must be a socialist!'

Sitting with his back to the harbour, Huart bit on a chuckle. The Tower Restaurant remained Shanghai's best, its standard maintained to that of Sir Victor Sassoon. A British Army major's ability to host a table for seven there was due more to the daily devaluation of the CN dollar, now not worth sixpence, than to generosity from the garrison paymaster. The monetarists rated China's worth as lowest of the low, though its war stayed undeclared whilst the six months of inert but declared war in Europe had met a rude end. Britain faced invasion. Lacking the means to protect remote outposts in China, Churchill had ordered the last of the Shanghai and Tientsin garrisons to Singapore. They would sail in a week.

In the aftermath of his mother's interpellation, Andrew chose to inject characteristic levity. 'You're forgetting the Shanghai Light Horse! I'll have Ling up at dawn pressing my uniform for the war games. Wait till the Kempetai sees us in action. It'll alter the course of world events!'

Nobody even half smiled. The sobriety was not unique. A third full, the restaurant was a quiet place. So much had changed, Huart thought sadly.

'Alter it in what direction?' Paulette asked without sparkle.

Andrew gave a half-hearted laugh. Had that been a criticism?

'This is time to be serious!' Adelaide cried. 'Shanghai is to be drowned in disorder and all you can do is make puerile fun of it! All we'll get from the Council is non-stop jokes if you ever get elected chairman!'

Andrew frowned hard and long. What was it coming to? How long had such public disrespect to a taipan been the form? He was about to mount an indignant defence when Arthur Dennison, ever reliable, called to the head of the table: 'Is Britain really giving up on us, John?'

Huart studied the network of wrinkles on the aging China trader's face, many of which had not been there last summer. Projecting an authority more second nature than specific, he replied: 'Japan has started building her so-called "Greater East Asia Co-Prosperity Sphere" by simply sailing into the undefended French Indo-China ports, occupying the airfields, cutting the Haiphong-Nanning rail link and forcing the closure of the Burma Road. Hong Kong and Singapore are next. They are strategic bases. Shanghai is not. The infantry units stationed here are considered to be reserves. It's as brutally simple as that, Arthur, I'm afraid.'

A heavy, almost bitter silence followed. Huart had given them more salt than salve. He sympathised with the Shanghailanders, acknowledged their justification for protest. But the fact was hard: Shanghai's value to Britain had shrunk to a dimension not worth protecting.

'What's to become of us?' Agnes Dennison took up Adelaide's cry. 'This has been our home all our lives. Does Churchill want us to leave?'

Huart could feel Paulette looking at him, her beautiful eyes delivering judgement. She had ceased calling him *ma preux chevalier*. 'The choice is yours,' he offered, grimacing inwardly. It was fine for him to make grand pronouncements, he told himself. He was leaving Shanghai, though it had not been his choice. Even so he put a hardness into his tone. It risked discourtesy, but something was needed to steel spirits this night. 'You have the choice whether to stay and support Andrew and the Municipal Council and the police. Or you can up and leave and make a present of the Settlement to the gangsters, the spies, the Japanese . . .'

A fork was being tapped against a glass. Heads turned to the foot of the table. 'Enough of this!' The taipan was back in Andrew. 'Of course we're staying! Enough of this defeatism! With the garrison away the Volunteer Corps will be fully mobilised and expanded. We're responsible for our own defence, and that's that! We'll all do what we have to do! To cover the higher defence budget, the Council meets tomorrow to raise taxes. All *hongs*, companies and individuals that have enjoyed the profits Shanghai has given them in time of plenty will be ordered to return a little of it until this spot of trouble is over and the garrison comes back. And hear this! It will apply equally to Jap enterprises – '

'You think your Mr Haiyama will sit still for that?' Adelaide enquired.

'Leave Haiyama to me, Mother. He'll squeal like a stuck pig, but he'll tell them to pay. He's a warmongering so-and-so, but he'll stop short of provoking the Americans on the Council.' Andrew looked at every face. 'Who says it's permanent? Even semi-permanent? Who's to say Germany'll invade England? Seems to me they're getting cleaned up in the air. Our fighter pilots are the finest in the world. Our traders are the smartest in the world. And here in Shanghai we have the smartest of the smart!'

But still there was silence. Jennifer saw the dinner had to be saved and announced: 'I can't believe we're going. After Shanghai,

[101]

Singapore will be so quiet. My parents live there now. You must all come and visit us.'

With a smile that looked forced, Paulette said: 'Singapore is so nice. Sundowners in the Raffles garden, tennis at the Tanglin Club . . .'

Jennifer gave back a smile of her own. Paulette had become more British than British, she was thinking. Even her accent had modified itself to its environs. The lifestyle given to the wife of a Shanghai taipan had moulded Paulette Charbadour into the shape that fitted it.

'Sounds dull.' Andrew lifted his glass aloft, missing Paulette's frown. 'John and Jenny will be back here before they know it. *Maskee*, I say!'

'*Maskee!*' echoed Jennifer. Adelaide gave a resigned sigh, drank up her wine and called: 'Eat! Drink! Be merry! For tomorrow we die!' Paulette said nothing. The Dennisons chorused '*Maskee*,' but without vigour and Huart looked at them with concern. They no longer wore the indomitable countenance of the Shanghailander. Their spirit had been sapped by age, and by chronic adversity in that, although they had not been deprived of material comforts as such, the serenity of life that foreigners of their station once took for granted was now a joy of the past.

'You two'd better look after those sons of yours,' Andrew demanded good naturedly. 'There'll be places on the board for them twenty or so years from now. And that reminds me – ' He raised his hand and snapped his fingers. 'Boy! Champagne! A magnum, no less! Make it *Florens Louis*.'

Glasses were charged and Andrew was on his feet. 'To Cousin John and his lovely wife, Jennifer – who is much too good for him, if that's humanly possible. May the very best of fortune travel with you. May this trouble that gave us rare joy by bringing you here, and now gives us deep sadness by taking you away, be shortlived. May you return to China, to Shanghai – not just as my cousin, but also as a director of Cumberland China!' On his face an unshakeable grin now glowed. '*A votre santé!*'

Huart stood. In his dress uniform he towered over the table. The sparse diners looked. Women pursed their lips in approval. Men frowned. Sight of a British Army uniform, hitherto a comfort, would soon be extinct.

The Dennisons straightened their hunched shoulders with effort. Adelaide waved her glass. The vintage champagne was swallowed with relish, its quality acknowledged. It was the first of several toasts that night.

From outside, the sounds of Shanghai punctuated the sequence of salutes to John and Jennifer Huart. A freighter grunted. A tramcar rattled east along Nanking Road, its bell jangling. A cab honked its horn to attract the attention of diners leaving the Palace Hotel opposite. A Bund silk hawker shouted in repetitious solicitation, a food vendor gave contest.

Jennifer's smile carried her love and a message along the table to her husband. They must return to Shanghai. Here he would find fulfilment. Here he would break the regimental bonds that contained him. One day. When the 'trouble' was over. She saw him smile back as he acknowledged the toasts to the future, and she knew her message had been read. He too was truly sorry to be leaving Shanghai, the Huart-Brents and the life they represented: a life that would make room for John Stanford Huart.

18

As strong as the building that contained the packed chamber in which it was heard, the voice of the Chairman of the Shanghai Municipal Council carried to all ears. In the seat reserved for the deputy chairman, the man next in line to lead, Andrew Huart-Brent listened with head lowered and felt the sadness of the mass of men: an enveloping sadness that it had come to this. In the old days it was the Chinese businesses that were taxed so, not theirs. And justifiably! If the Chinese chose to move into the sanctum of the concessions to trade, they would have expected to pay a premium for the privilege. This was not Chinese soil, after all! It was international turf, legally ceded to the foreign traders. It was so sad! So sad that events had relegated them to the status of upstart Chinese industrialists. Damn this prolonged trouble! Damn the blasted Japanese warmongers! Damn them to hell! They're ruining it all.

The chairman neared the end of his address, his eyes fixed on Haiyama, who sat with his countrymen in a group near the front of the chamber. As Japan had grabbed more and more of China and its noose around the necks of the foreign concessions had tightened, its delegation on the Shanghai Municipal Council had moved progressively forward.

' . . . And so the Supplementary Defence Tax will be imposed

[103]

forthwith! The necessity for its imposition is deeply regretted. Its prolongation will depend on the need for the Municipal Police and the Volunteer Corps to mount full-time emergency defence. This in turn will depend on the . . .'

The strong voice died away. Something unique had happened. The restraint of the chairman was famous, but it had just run out. His thoughts had flashed back over the halcyon years of success, profits and absolute power, then had projected forward to visualise just the opposite. And who was responsible for it? He was gripped by a sudden anger. He focused through a red haze and saw Haiyama sitting there before him – much too close. God in heaven! The man will be in this very chair next!

Every pair of non-Japanese eyes followed the damning glare to Haiyama, who was staring rigidly back up at the most powerful man in Shanghai with his jaw set, his lips contracted into a thin line. The skin on his face coloured and he began to quiver with suppressed rage.

A voice in the chairman's brain was telling him to calm down, to call a recess. He had always listened to that voice and had always obeyed it, but now other voices spoke louder and there were more of them. These new voices propelled him to his feet; they thrust his right arm forward and pointed his finger like a witch doctor's bone of condemnation directly between Haiyama's burning eyes. The voices combined into one and flowed from his mouth in a torrent. 'This in turn will depend on the good sense and common decency – basic human qualities thus far completely lacking – of our honourable . . . *Honourable*? Hah! It will depend on the qualities . . . *Qualities*? Such a contradiction! It will depend on the qualities of our *dis*honourable – yes, dishonourable – Japanese colleagues . . .'

Haiyama rose slowly, deliberately to his feet. His face was puce. His whole body vibrated like a volcano about to erupt. His right hand went inside his coat and out again in one swift movement. There was a pistol in his fist. He raised it until it was pointed straight at the man who stood in the centre of the dais.

Andrew Huart-Brent was first by a full second to anticipate what was going to happen because his brain did not reject it, absurd though it was: the head of the Japanese delegation shooting dead the Chairman of the Shanghai Municipal Council in its chamber packed with its members. Still standing fully exposed, the chairman had not moved. Colleagues at the head table, their actions weighted by years of council protocol, their reactions dulled by precedent or the absence of it, sat and stared during that full second between the instant the gun appeared in Haiyama's hand and the moment it fired.

With the propulsion of a rugby halfback Andrew threw himself to his left. His outstretched hands shoved the chairman sideways into the man beside him, knocking all seated that side of the table to the floor like dominoes. Chairs clattered in all directions, the legs of the oak table groaned as they gouged grooves across the floorboards.

The report from Haiyama's pistol filled the chamber. It crashed against Andrew's eardrums as his body speared horizontally; at the same instant he felt the bullet tear into his groin and a searing pain ate him whole. From a great distance he heard the gun jam as Haiyama pulled the trigger a second time. But he did not hear or feel his collarbone snap as he hit the floor. He had already fallen into a black, bottomless pit . . .

19

Three years to the day after his first sight of Shanghai, John Huart savoured his last. The port city wore its late summer coat of brown and the afternoon heat was thick as he and Jennifer took a final stroll east on Nanking Road towards the harbour. The Second Cumberlands were embarking at midnight. Their troop ship was to sail on the dawn tide.

They committed unforgettable Nanking Road to memory, peering into each side-street where vendors sang out, rang bells or rapped bamboo pieces together to bring business to the food stalls, kitchens and shops selling untold varieties of rice, grain, tea, herbal medicine or incense, or imitation money in the shape of the old Chinese *tael* or paper houses or boats or cradles to be burnt during the Festival of Hungry Ghosts . . .

Along the way, successive choruses of cicadas sounded off in the trees, giving forth in high-pitched whirring oratorios. It was a sound the Huarts had come to take for granted and would miss, a sound that was as common to summer Shanghai as was the breaking of surf to a beach.

On the Bund they thrilled as always to the incessant activity, the fight for pavement space amidst the potpourri of humanity. Lines of cooking stalls sizzled, coolies hawked and spat, hawkers sang their chorus. The money changers were more abundant now, dealing in every denomination of foreign currency as the CN dollar lost the last of its value like sand through an hourglass, jingling gold and silver coins in their pockets and calling out exchange rates in unfaltering contest.

A truck with a smoking exhaust rumbled past, its load of animal hides delivering a vile smell into the fumy air. A convoy of laden carts rolled by, the bullocks swishing their tails at hordes of persistent Whangpoo flies. There was a procession of English sedans, French saloons, low-slung American limousines, interspersed with and hindered by an undisciplined corps of rickshaws.

Huart saw a sleek black Cadillac pull in to the kerb in front of the Jardine Matheson building ahead, but he thought nothing of it.

On the harbour the tramp steamers lounged like pampered courtesans upon its rippling dung-coloured surface, surrounded by a network of attentive barges. A pair of grey frigates flew the white ensign on Battleship Row, waiting to escort the last of the Shanghai garrison to Singapore.

Arm-in-arm, the Huarts passed by the entrance of the Cathay Hotel, the Bank of China, the Yokohama Specie Bank, the Yangtse Insurance Building, their thick metal doors open for business. The girders of Garden Bridge rose over the trees ahead. Broadway Mansions grew taller with each step.

They came abreast of the Jardine Matheson building, and Huart stopped dead in his tracks.

Jennifer felt his hand stiffen in hers. She looked sharply up at him, then followed his gaze to a Chinese man in a long-gown tailored from hand-spun Soochow cotton. He was leaning on a walking stick pressed hard into his thigh as if he depended entirely upon it. At the kerb behind him was the Cadillac Huart had seen earlier, its rear door open. Another two Chinese were seated in the front, both looking malevolently over their shoulders. The man's face was drawn, as if he was holding on to an intense pain, and he studied Huart through ice-like, penetrating eyes.

'John?' Jennifer asked, her voice hushed. 'Who is he?'

'Stay close to me, darling.'

Huart inspected the man in the long-gown, unable to place him in memory. The walking stick triggered something: the man's hip was faulty. A hip wound? Then, like a replay of some scene in a horror movie, the spectre of the corpses of Sergeant Dadds and the Bren gunner rose up before his eyes. And he knew.

This was Tu Chien.

Huart drew Jennifer on. The man thrust his jaw forward as if about to speak. Although he was physically more than a foot shorter, something about him elevated his being and gave the impression that his eyes were somehow on the same plane as Huart's. Jennifer's head swivelled between her husband and the man. She could not speak. She was confused. A feeling of dread germinated in her. Suddenly, the man's mouth opened. He gave forth four words. Four separate monosyllables penetrated the air and hit Huart's ears as if they were charged with electricity.

'*Sze . . . Yiu . . . Yu . . . Gu!*'

Tu Chien waited for his words to impact fully. Then he turned and limped to the Cadillac. One of the bodyguards got out and helped him into its rear. The limousine pulled from the kerb and accelerated north. A pair of dark oriental eyes stared maliciously out the back window until the car and the eyes passed behind the British Consulate.

'John! Who was that?' Jennifer was tugging at his sleeve. He looked down into her large, round eyes. He gave a smile that he knew was weak and watched her long eyelashes flutter as she blinked. 'John . . ?'

He knew that dismissing it all with a fabrication would only insult her intelligence, so he said simply: 'He is a crook, darling.'

'A crook? But why was he waiting for you? What was it he said to you?'

'A few months ago – April Fools' Day to be exact – we stopped a car at a roadblock. He was in it with other civilians – members of his family, I think. They tried to run the roadblock. Later we found opium in the car's boot. There was shooting. Four people in the car were killed: the chauffeur, a bodyguard . . . and a woman and a small boy. I think they must have been his wife and child. He was shot in the hip. The bullet must be still in him. That's why he has to use a walking stick.'

Her hand was at her mouth. 'Oh, darling. How awful. But I don't understand. How can he be free if he was caught carrying drugs? How can he be driving around Shanghai large as life?'

'He disappeared from the hospital. The dead had no identification on them. The car mysteriously caught fire in the pound. Our file on the incident left my office for police headquarters and never got there.'

'But how . . ?'

'That's Shanghai, darling.'

'But you could testify . . .'

'He'd have a hundred witnesses to swear he was elsewhere that morning.'

'What's his name? Do you know that?'

'Yes. He is called Tu Chien.'

Jennifer's intuition was at work. 'Are you telling me everything, John?'

He hesitated a fraction too long. 'Yes, of course I am, darling.'

She wanted to extract the truth there and then, but instead she let her voice fall an octave and asked: 'Darling, are you afraid of that man?'

He blinked and thought a moment. 'Afraid? No . . . Yes. But not the way you might think. I'm a soldier. I'm not trained to combat men without guns who nevertheless deal in death. I know little about Tu Chien and his ilk. But here we soldiers have been thrust into a role supporting the police. I've learnt a lot, but still I don't know how the Tu Chiens of this world think or react to a given set of circumstances. They place no value on life – anybody's life – except their own and their family's. Darling – ' He grasped both her arms. 'Did you realise those two in the car were holding guns? One was pointed at me and the other at you.'

'Oh, John!' Jennifer gasped, then recovered herself. 'But what was it he said to you? You've studied Chinese.'

'I don't know.'

This was almost a lie. Huart had worked out the literal meaning of the four words, but it was nonsensical. Chinese dialects are a complexity of idioms and he knew he had been delivered one as some form of curse. But why the melodrama? Tu Chien could have had him murdered on the spot, on the Bund, right in front of his wife. The man had already demonstrated he could get away with anything in Shanghai.

Jennifer, as if reading his thoughts, mused: 'What an unusual little man. Why would he go through such a weird performance?'

'I don't know.' This time Huart lied properly. Perhaps Tu Chien wanted him to look death in the face, just as Dadds and the gunner had been made to do. 'Whatever the reason, it seems I've made a bad enemy here.'

Her grip tightened on his arm. 'Then, my darling, it's for the best that we're leaving tonight. He can't do us any harm in Singapore, can he.'

Huart smiled down at her. 'You're so right. Let's forget all about it. By the time we return to Shanghai, he's sure to have met with a sticky end. Now, we must hurry. We're late already. The boys'll be asking for us. I'm glad we could have this last little "tour".'

Jennifer sighed. 'Shanghai has become so dangerous. Look what happened to poor Andrew in his very own Council chamber. And what punishment for the brute that shot him? Sent home to Tokyo and received as a hero! I'm only surprised the other Japanese voted in favour of the defence tax.'

'They were too embarrassed to do anything less, darling.'

'Embarrassed? I doubt Japanese have such an emotion.' She sighed again. 'The Shanghailanders will need every prayer we can offer for them.'

'They'll need something more material than prayers. I see no end to the trouble.' Huart peered up at Broadway Mansions and picked out the balcony on the twentieth floor. 'He's up there, looking out over his Shanghai like the taipan he is. They won't beat him. He's his grandfather's progeny alright. They're bred tough out here, these "China Huarts".'

'God bless them and keep them.' Jennifer linked her arm in his and they walked onto Garden Bridge whilst Soochow Creek oozed sadly beneath them.

From his position of enforced horizontality upon the rattan lounge in the shade beneath the awning over the balcony, Andrew Huart-Brent watched the two-year-olds at play. James, a sturdy strong-willed infant, dominated the game; Vivienne, her blonde hair flying about, followed his every lead. From inside the apartment could be heard the lusty wail of Andrew John calling for his afternoon bottle.

The youngest taipan of the China Trade reached out gingerly for his *stengah*. He drew it to him and sucked through a long straw. He grimaced with the pain and swore beneath his breath. It was too weak. His gesture of defiance had gained him nothing. He was under medical orders not to drink more than a basic quantity of fluid, and no alcohol whatsoever; and he had been warned off making any movement at all. Beneath his dressing gown, from midriff to thigh, he was strapped in bandages. Haiyama's bullet had been a 'dum-dum'. It had torn a path through his groin an inch in diameter.

Andrew blinked on his tears. They stung his eyes. But they were not sent solely by the wretched never-ending pain at the base of his belly.

'It's bad news, I'm afraid, Mr Huart-Brent,' the specialist had said not an hour before. 'That bullet did more damage than we first thought. Give all your love to your daughter. She's the only child you'll have.'

The verdict had been received in bitter silence. Andrew had felt like a bystander pronounced guilty of murder. But he had known it all along. He had known it the moment he had awakened in the hospital bed to discover his manhood embalmed like an Egyptian mummy.

'This is to be kept strictly between the two of us, Doctor,' he had said at length in a tone subdued but firm. 'You are to tell no-one. No-one, you hear? If word of my . . . my affliction . . . God damn it! If word comes back to me from any source other than yourself, I'll have the Council revoke your licence. Do you hear and understand me?'

The specialist had frowned hard, then had nodded.

'Good. You are to tell my mother and my wife there are no complications. That I will recover fully. Tell them there is no reason why I should not be able to go on and produce a son after the wound has healed. I want you to go and tell them that now. Now, Doctor. Or else.'

The specialist had bitten back his professional protest, well knowing one man only carried more power on the Municipal Council than the taipan of Cumberland China. He had obeyed and five minutes later Adelaide and Paulette had come onto the balcony, their smiles brighter than the summer sunshine. Andrew had joked with them, had held Andrew John in his arms and tickled his belly. When they had left him alone again, he had shouted for Ling and had demanded the houseboy bring him the *stengah*.

Now, as he watched the children, the tears returned. Through them he did not see James' towering uniformed father and titian-haired mother walking arm-in-arm over the hump of Garden Bridge. In fact, he could not see anything. He did not care to. For Andrew Huart-Brent was immersed deep in a very personal misery.

The security guard at the entrance to the Embankment Building called to his colleague as soon as he caught sight of the two '*sing song*' girls in their tight *cheongsams*. ' "Number Threes",' he grinned in Shanghai dialect, referring to the charge of three dollars the highest quality girls used to impose upon their regular clients in the days of his youth.

'*Choi!*' the second guard scoffed. 'Your standards exceed your station in life, or you need glasses. "Number Fours" for sure, old friend!'

Right in front of them the girls stopped and began to argue. The guards listened, riveted by the gutter language, the flashing eyes, painted lips, gleaming teeth, narrow waists . . . They fantasised themselves copulating with the exquisite bodies hidden from their eyes by the thin layers of tight silk, and were oblivious to the two furtive figures that crossed the lobby behind them and disappeared up the stairs.

After a minute, the perpetrators of nocturnal joy ceased their argument and departed with theatrical acrimony in opposite directions, later to be reconciled in one of the Tu establishments in Foochow Road.

On the third floor of the Embankment Building, the leading assassin took a surgical scalpel from his shirt, tested the cutting edge with his thumb and held it up for the second man to see the weeping red line. They both grinned. The grins came easily for they were the closest of friends. They had graduated from medical college together, had gambled and whored together, had fallen deeper and deeper in debt together.

'This will be easy,' the leader said. 'An *amah*, an infant and a baby.'

'Shall we have the woman first?'

The leader laughed. 'It depends what she looks like. Servants of foreign ghosts are usually plain. I will gladly cut the unclean bitch's throat.'

They picked the lock of the Huart apartment with ease and entered. Immediately inside they stopped short, looked about and swore in unison.

'It's empty! They've all gone!'

The apartment had been stripped bare in preparation for the next tenant. They went from room to room, but it was the same in each. They stood in the empty kitchen and looked at each other. Their fear turned the air cold about them. Tu Chien's reward for failure was death. In the case of their failure, the death of each of them would be perpetrated by the hand of the other. The means needed no imagination.

The leader thought quickly. 'I have an idea,' he said. 'But first we must swear a pact of secrecy here and now. We must tell nobody what we are about to do. Do you agree, my friend?'

'If I do not . . . ?'

'You are dead. I am dead. We are horribly dead together, as we have been together in life.'

[111]

'Do I have any choice then? I swear, my friend. What is your idea?'

'Follow me.'

They left the building by the tradesmen's entrance and walked quickly along the bank of Soochow Creek to Honan Road. Three blocks south they stopped at the entrance to an alley out of which was issuing the chords of a choir of children singing a religious hymn in voices that were strident and tone-deaf. The two assassins looked at each other. The leader nodded. 'Remember our pact of secrecy,' he muttered.

'To the death.'

The leader slipped his scalpel up his sleeve and led the way to a flight of stairs into the nearest building. Above the lintel a sign read:

ORPHANAGE FOR THE CHILDREN OF OUR MOTHER OF MERCY

The Cadillac returned Tu Chien to Great Horse Mansion at four p.m. He was well satisfied with his confrontation with the giant on the Bund. It had served two purposes: he had delivered the curse, whilst simultaneously confirming the murderer was separated from his sons.

'You have something for me,' he demanded of his manservant as he levered himself into his chair with the aid of the walking stick made of ebony.

He lifted the two glass jars filled with formalin to the light and minutely inspected the contents. The human testicles floated anonymously. One pair looked the size to have been cut from a boy of two and a half years, which indeed it had; the other pair was like twin beach pebbles contained in a sac, ostensibly removed from a baby in its first year.

Every night Tu Chien shared his bed with pain that was twofold: mere physical pain from his hip, plus an impossible agony that infested his brain every waking minute, every tormenting dream. Despite the extremity of his discomfort he refused to resort to opium. Opium was his enemy. It had made him greedy. It had caused him to tempt fate with consequences so terrible he still could not believe them. It had blinded him to his destiny as a Fire Horse. And he had paid dearly for his blindness.

But this night Tu Chien put the jars beside his bed and slept content.

20

Eight hundred miles to the south-west a new life started. The boy child had a head of black hair, the dark eyes and proud forehead of his quite beautiful Eurasian mother. And the large ears of his grandfather.

'Look! Your son has two crowns, Mrs Zagan,' the sister on duty in the maternity ward at St Xavier's Hospital said, pointing at the twin whirls. She, too was Eurasian. She had paid close personal attention to Elizabeth Zagan since her admission, recognising another fighting the same battle as her own. 'Two crowns at birth is a sign of determination. In a boy it is good. He will be a fine son.'

'He will be a leader,' Elizabeth Zagan asserted. 'A righter of wrongs.' She looked up at her husband and smiled. It was a smile with two crowns, a determined smile. 'He will be first,' she told him. 'We will call him Matthew – first in the New Testament. Matthew will always be first.'

Jean-Baptiste Zagan knew it was useless to argue. She had had her way ever since their marriage, and before. He bent to kiss her forehead.

'I must go,' he whispered. 'I have my Paris editor to keep happy, and China National Aviation waits for no-one. And neither do Madam Chiang Kai-shek and T.V. Soong. I've been like a puppet master, pulling strings to get a seat on their flight to Chungking.'

'It will be dangerous. You will be flying over occupied territory.'

'If a slip of a girl like the Missimo is able to do it, then so must I. And, my precious, it is my job. Now I'm sounding like my editor.'

She touched the back of his hand. 'Be careful, Jean-Baptiste.'

'With a healthy son now added to a beautiful wife? I now have too many reasons for staying alive. Worry not for me. *Au revoir*, my precious.'

'You speak of health?' she called after him. 'Then cut down on your smoking if you mean it.' But he had already gone.

Elizabeth Zagan looked down at the child in her arms. A novel sensation crept over her. She tested it. It was good. She allowed the sensation to envelop her. She put a name to it: Fulfilment. She had attained a very special goal, one set for her long ago. Her mother's dying wish had been for a grandson, and she had always been a dutiful daughter.

Her mother had once told her: 'You may marry a foreigner, but only if he is white and tall and intelligent and has character. You may marry a Chinese, but only if he comes from north of Fukien. Should you marry a black man or a midget southerner from Kwangtung that squawks like a duck, my ghost will return to live in your womb and make it barren. Then you will be of no use to anyone and unworthy even to have memory of me.'

After her time of mourning, Elizabeth Jane Huart, a maiden, had sought out a husband. It had not taken long. It is an old rule but a true one that she who is born a beauty is born married. She had first met Jean-Baptiste Zagan at the Sorbonne. They had corresponded after her return to Hong Kong, and then he had secured a posting here. She had not loved him, but she had known she could not afford to be fussy.

She was Eurasian.

And now that he had done his duty by her, all the residual love left in her after her mother's death could be put to use. She would give it all to her son. She would direct his life. She would ensure that he learnt how to be first.

'My son, you have a special goal, too,' she told the new being in her arms. She looked out through her window up at the peaks of the Nine Dragons silhouetted against the South China sky. 'There exists a great wrong which only you can put right.'

Elizabeth Jane Zagan, née Huart, touched both crowns on her son's head with loving fingertips. Then she stroked the thick lobe of his ear. The ear of Matthew Zagan's grandfather.

Book II

MAMMON MOVES SOUTH

Hong Kong: 3 June 1949 – 30 November 1956

1

'*Aiiyah!* It is nothing more and nothing less than an overgrown rock!'

His judgement delivered, Tu Chien leaned against the main-mast of the big high-sterned junk and focused on the spectacle rising from the ocean ahead. The volcanic mountain-top bulged out of the horizon, hitherto a monotonous knife-cut demarcating the South China Sea below from the pastel blue sky over the Tropic of Cancer above. It was the flyspeck on the map of Asia that had been colonised 107 years before by the British, who had adulterated it with the name: Hong Kong.

The grey cotton long-gown flapped about Tu Chien's spare frame. He wore it habitually now. Western dress was a thing of his past; it restricted circulation in his mid-section and helped him to remember too well. He turned to peer through the stinging morning sunlight up at the afterdeck and flicked a driblet of perspiration from an eyebrow with his index finger. Though eighteen days short of Summer Solstice, the heat of the new season was already mature. 'An overgrown rock surrounded by the sea!' he repeated. 'Is that it? Is that what we have been seeking all these days?' His voice carried above the lapping of the red and white patched sails, the rush of water beneath the prow.

The captain of the junk nodded. The sun glistened from his bare muscular torso burnished deep brown by four decades of elements. He called back in his patron's Shanghai dialect, adulter-ating it with the Ningpo accent of the master mariner of the China coast. 'Ha! A useless rock it might appear to be, Lord. But it gives haven to no Communists. Not yet.' He spat emphatically to leeward, then threw a command in Ningpo dialect to his feet. The heavy *yuloh* oar pivoted under pressure of experienced hands and the big junk swung to starboard until the eyes painted starkly on its bow stared at the entrance to the East Lamma Channel.

The junk was indeed big. The Cantonese would categorise it *dai ngaan gai:* a 'big eyed chicken'. Designed to run steady in rough weather with a full load of Foochow logs, on this voyage it wallowed heavily, its timbers groaning with effort as if they were about to rupture. The running swell caught it and the flat prow lifted, then smacked down hard upon the sheet glass of the ocean. Tu Chien threw his arm around the mast and wedged the stick against his thigh. He held on as the junk shuddered, then settled, then ploughed ponderously on its new course, sails lapping in the capricious breeze. He faced forward and resumed the vigil he had maintained at the mast since Foochow, four days earlier.

The stark grey rock grew larger. Now the spurs of its mountain peaks were defined, digging into the South China Sea like the clawed toes of a colossal dragon cut from granite. *Hao!* Tu Chien thought. It is a dragon rock! A safe refuge. But for how long? Even as I breathe, the vanguard of the peasant army heads south for Canton, not a hundred miles to the north. Did we not abandon Shanghai, then Foochow, just in time?

The junk had made painstaking progress. To an experienced eye the reason was obvious: it was too low in the water, dangerously so. Yet though the weather gods had been sparing with sailing winds, they had benignly held back any impatient early summer typhoon. Even a moderate storm would have sent the junk to the bottom. Gold is the heaviest metal on earth. The Kuomintang had not sequestrated everything out of the Bank of China vaults to Taiwan. The hold of this *dai ngaan gai* was full of it.

The Communists had timed well their southern offensive. In the Year of the resolute Earth Ox it is decreed that ground captured will never be lost. On April 20th the end for Shanghai had changed from probable to inevitable. That night Mao's troops had crossed the Yangtse; the Royal Navy frigate *Amethyst* had been fired on and immobilised. The next day Tu Chien had ordered the family's gold and portable assets to Foochow.

Shanghai fell on May 26th. The Tus had quit the city a week beforehand.

Tu Huang, second eldest, had fled to Taiwan with his family, minus two of his sons, the third and sixth, who had been detailed to go with Tu Chien, his second-born son, his Number One Wife, three concubines and all other offspring. The two nephews were needed to assist the patriarch establish the family's enterprise anew in the British Crown Colony.

It had taken much gold to secure their escape. On the Yangtsepoo docks every face they saw was a potential communist assassin. The agonising journey north along the Whangpoo had been spent below the deck of a dilapidated Swatow coastal trawler.

It had been an exercise in spitting in the face of the communist tiger, one to test the temper of the hardest nerve. But the family had come through it well. After two and a half hours the Woosung Forts had passed to port and they had entered the expanse of the Yangtse Estuary. Two more hours and they were in the China Sea, plunging south into the anonymity of its oceanic wilderness.

Two days later they had reunited with their riches in Foochow. It had taken five days to find the junk's captain, who was a distant relative but not so distant as to abrogate filial bond. Three more days had been used up striking a bargain that would make him rich for the rest of his life. A last day had been needed to load the treasure. Those nine days in Foochow were the most tremulous of Tu Chien's forty-three years: the Communists were advancing south, coming ever closer every minute.

The family was under sentence of death anywhere in China. If the peasant army had its sights on Hong Kong, it would apply there, too. They were dead because of 1927. And they were dead for collaboration. Kuomintang amnesty had been bought in 1945, but communist memory was incorruptible.

'A great ship approaches, Lord!'

The captain's shout wrenched Tu Chien from his cogitation and his eyes followed the pointing finger to see a massive ocean liner steaming at great speed towards them out of the south.

'So much steel can sail so fast?' the mariner wondered aloud. 'But they cannot make a steel junk, these foreign ghosts.' He spat again, mopped his brow and squinted up at the sun as if chastising it for being there.

The liner passed by a hundred yards to port. Tu Chien squinted to read the letters painted across the liner's stern. 'Q-U-E-E-N-M-A-R-Y. It is a famous ship. It is a floating hotel for rich foreigners.'

The captain yelled an order and the junk swung to port directly into the great ship's wash. It burrowed into the man-made waves, shuddered and stopped dead in the water. Tu Chien grabbed at the mast and a sharp pain shot from his hip. It circumnavigated his body, then dissolved slowly, leaving beads of sweat to mingle on his forehead with those sent by the tropical heat as he looked north at the *Queen Mary*'s shrinking stern.

Unseen on the liner's after-deck a long gaunt face peered back at the insignificant junk, whose appearance had signalled the imminence of journey's end. The face turned away and its owner ambled to his cabin to pack his suitcase for the disembarkation at Hong Kong.

[119]

The *dai ngaan gai* steered back to starboard. Tu Chien turned and looked over the prow at the rock that now loomed, coated with a deep tropical green, out of the blue ocean.

A thin fine-boned youth in tailored *saamfoo* came on deck. He shielded his eyes from the sun with one hand as he stared about, then picked his way along the deck with difficulty, though the junk was steady in the water as it headed for the channel ahead. His skin was pallid; he had languished below for the entire voyage, racked with seasickness. Knowledge that all the family save his steel-cored father were faring no better had been small comfort.

'Hoi-sang!' Tu Chien commanded without turning his head to acknowledge his second-born son. 'Tell the family to come on deck now. Our new home is ahead. We shall land soon.'

'Yes, Papa.'

The patriarch turned now to observe the youth retrace his uncertain steps to the hatch leading to the stern cabin. In that fetid, comfortless habitat, the family had listlessly cocooned itself since Foochow.

Half an hour later the junk veered hard a'starboard round the tip of Ap Lei Chau Island and Aberdeen Harbour edged into view. A gaggle of smaller junks and sampans became a confluence as the *dai ngaan gai* headed into their midst, its sails now filled by a cooling breeze that dropped off the mountainside and rippled the surface of the water.

The smells of the new land carried to the family as they stood together on deck: the combined aroma of green vegetables, mushrooms, nuts, pork ribs, rice and noodles simmering in countless unseen *woks*. The rich refugees from Shanghai drooled. For days they had been able to eat so little, and then only fish, boiled Ningpo style and mixed with rice that grew more stale by the serving. Now the air told them they had arrived amidst the southern Chinese who were reputed to eat anything with four legs except a chair, anything with wings but an aeroplane, anything with scales save a dragon and that because that creature survived only in legend; and to eat every part of it all wriggling, blinking, heartbeating fresh.

Tu Chien knew he was looking at the country of tomorrow. The time for vicissitude in a man's life, it is said, comes within the 'six golden years' between thirty-six and forty-two. So what if he was just beyond them? There were so many adages, each contradicting another. It was a trial to be Chinese, but an honour to be Shanghai-born. The gormandisers from Kwangtung will soon witness the skill of a man from the City Above the Ocean.

[120]

He would grow richer amongst them and they would be unaware in their blissful gluttony of their personal contribution to his wealth.

But, as always happened when the peak of elation was scaled, Tu Chien sobered. Hoi-nam, his first-born, was not at his side to share this day. Neither was Yueh-ming, the only truly beloved of those ever admitted to his bed. The knowledge that this was due to his own greed stayed inexorably with him. The marasmus of it ate at his core, more lethal even than the real cancer that rotted his hip. He had learnt the most vicious lesson of his life at permanent cost. Not since that accursed day had he, nor would he ever again, deal in the white powder that produced dreams. For him it had produced a nightmare that refused to leave him be. And what was so damnably ironic was the fact that he had grown just as rich by other means. It had taken a little longer, that was all.

Yes, he had instituted revenge. But it had not been enough. The gods had plotted against him, granting his adversary flight before the admonition of full and just punishment. The making of eunuchs of the giant's sons was to have been only the beginning of a programme of revenge. But he had escaped. The defilement of his sons would have given such a man gross agony, but nothing to equal that which Tu Chien had suffered, and still suffered. Somehow he knew that the war had treated the giant grievously. Somehow he knew the curse had worked. But it was inadequate comfort. He had to know! He had to see it with his own eyes!

Tu Chien shut the door on the past and turned its faulty lock. He came back to the present: they were entering the harbour proper at Aberdeen; the family were staring at the thousands of lesser junks around them, tied in bobbing curving rows to each other, and listening to the din of the makeshift maritime community of the newly displaced from their *heung ha* in China. And they frowned on the tens of thousands who were grasping for the patronage of the dragon rock whose toenails they tickled with their impermanent presence. A life like that was not for them.

To Aberdeen Harbour had come a junk that was larger than them all; its stern was the highest, its *dai ngaan* the biggest. And stowed in its hold was enough gold to purchase every craft in the harbour. Or even to purchase the very harbour itself. And then some.

Tu Chien looked up. A hawk, black wings fully extended, hovered above a peak. It drifted in a slow, deliberate circuit on the summer breeze as if it had mastered the flow of time and destiny. It was an omen. 'Hoi-sang!' he called. 'Tomorrow we buy

[121]

a house and furniture. The next day we begin to consume new wealth. We have come to this dragon rock called Hong Kong. It will be the new Shanghai! We begin again! Bigger! Better!'

2

The proud steel bows of the *Queen Mary* bisected Lei Yue Mun Channel, and Victoria Harbour unrolled before the great liner like a seascape carpet. It produced a sensation of homecoming that was tainted with sadness. So much had changed in the world, but nothing more than John Stanford Huart, civilian of three months.

He saw the changes born of the crown colony's rapidly swollen and still swelling population. The mountains forming Hong Kong Island passed to port, slopes sewn in a matting of subtropical foliage ulcerated with brown scabs of squatter hamlets held together in a spontaneous jumble of wood, cardboard, wire and string. Grey buildings and godowns had been constructed on the foreshore, none in any way significant. Victoria's Central District and the point of Kowloon Peninsula called Tsimshatsui, literally 'Sharp Sandy Mouth', drew nearer through the heat haze. Huart saw they remained connected by the unflagging, criss-crossing ferries.

He stood with the crowd at the rail on 'C' Deck, an anonymous seventy-seven inches and one-ninety pounds. Since the start of the voyage he had acknowledged his fellow passengers as little as possible. In fact, he had given no time willingly to others for years. Ever since . . .

'What's that big building, Mummy?'

Huart peered along the small finger and saw that the Hongkong and Shanghai Bank continued to dominate its circumjacence. At least something hasn't changed, he thought, and savoured a small dose of comfort. But the harbour was unaltered too, with its swarm of junks, lorchas and wagtailed sampans, its international merchant navy. A floating metropolis clung to the Causeway Bay waterfront and spread like a bobbing jigsaw puzzle between it and the detached bump of Kellett Island. The land shimmered in the June heat. The smells peculiar to percolating Hong Kong transmitted to Huart fragile memories of his brief encounter with it a dozen years before. His senses rekindled as the *Queen Mary* churned through the harbour like the great white monarch it was. Holt's

[122]

Wharf grew out of the haze ahead to announce the Tsimshatsui waterfront.

Huart's memory stuck at the day in his first life when, standing on that other Holt's Wharf, eight hundred miles to the north-east, a million years ago, he had seen her ship come out of the Astrea Channel, bringing herself and his first son to him . . . He closed it all out with an effort.

The liner used an hour docking. Huart waited under his felt hat in the throng on the wharf before the customs shed. In his hand was the portmanteau that bulged with all his worldly possessions. He was concentrating on nothing and it must have been a minute before he heard the female voice calling his name from the middle distance. The voice was familiar. He shook himself from his melancholy and listened as it came again.

'John! John Huart! Here, John! Over here!'

He looked into the crowd waiting for the disembarking passengers in a compound beyond a wire-netting fence and saw a blonde woman in a floral summer frock and a wide-brimmed sun hat waving a pair of white gloves. He had last seen Paulette Huart-Brent nine years ago and she had hardly changed. At a distance of many yards he again felt the impact of her. 'Paulette! What are you doing in Hong Kong?' he called as he crossed to the fence. 'It's wonderful to see you so unexpectedly . . .' He broke off with the stab of alarm. 'But where is Andrew? Isn't he with you?'

Huart had been following the civil war via the *Times:* the communist victory in the Battle of the Huai-Hai in which four Kuomintang armies had left 200,000 dead on the Soochow Plains, Mao's occupation of Peking and Tientsin. Despite all this, a letter from Andrew had discounted it all in typical insouciant fashion. It had mollified him as he could not conceive that anyone, least of all his inured taipan cousin, could make the same mistake twice. Then came reports of Chiang Kai-shek's retirement, the transfer of power to his deputy, the convening of armistice talks in Peking and press predictions for a peace formula. So Huart had boarded the *Queen Mary* at Tilbury with confidence, though World War III would not have stopped his return to the East. He had opted to do it in style, Cunard's 'Four Oceans Cruise' being too convenient to pass up.

On April 22nd the *Queen Mary* had called at Gibraltar and he had heard the wireless reports on the shelling of the *Amethyst*. In Singapore it was announced the cruise would terminate in Hong Kong and Huart had decided to fly on to Shanghai from there. The 10,000 sterling he had remitted ahead out of his army gratuity and his liquidated investments was sitting suddenly precarious in the doomed Bund headquarters of the Hongkong and Shanghai Bank. The balance of his cash was in the wallet inside the tweed coat he already knew to be too coarse for the climate.

'Andrew's in Shanghai,' Paulette replied. 'He's as well as can be expected, considering what the internment did to him. He sent us here three weeks ago for safety. The Communists took Shanghai last week. Andrew will call us back there once things have settled down and he's come to terms with the new government. *Maskee*, as he would say. I have a letter for you from him.' She took an envelope from her handbag and poked it through the fence. 'Go and complete your procedures and we'll see you on this side. We're all here, except Andrew's mother. It's too hot for her. She's in the hotel. Vivienne has grown so much. She's eleven now. And you've yet to see our new baby daughter, Suzanne. Go on. Be quick!'

Huart smiled through the acidic pangs of childlessness and picked up the portmanteau. Waiting in line before the trestled table that served as the customs and immigration counter, he read Andrew's type-written note.

CUMBERLAND BUILDING, 4TH FLOOR, THE BUND, SHANGHAI, CHINA.
Wednesday, 18th May, 1949.

My Dear John,

Welcome back to China! Things don't change, they just continue to vary. It seems we are to have yet another government here and just as well as the Communists could not be any worse than the last shower.

All this must come as a shock and I'm sorry. We didn't know the extent of the Nationalist censorship on the press. It seems all the 'Great Kuomintang Victories' were thorough hidings. Only when we heard of the *Amethyst* incident did we realise the Communists were as close to Shanghai as they were.

I've sent Paulette, Mother and the children to Hong Kong for their well-being. They will meet you and entertain you there for a while. I've been surrounded by women so long that it'll be strange without them, but the shooting will soon start all over again and the last ships and flights out are leaving. You won't be able to get here until things settle down. I'm staying in Shanghai to ensure that, as far as Cumberland China is concerned, this happens with the minimum of delay.

Paulette will arrange a room in the Gloucester Hotel where the family is staying. I'll telephone at ten a.m. every Monday and Thursday, God willing. It's truly marvellous to have you back with us, John. I do apologise with all my heart for this quite temporary setback to the commencement of our partnership. I promise to have it sorted out with Mao as soon as I can.

By the way, if you have any more sterling, hold on to it. The Gold Yuan today is at 23,000,000 to the US dollar. Tomorrow it will likely be double that. Incredible! It was introduced only nine months ago at a parity of four. (The name is now a joke as there's no more gold in China. Chiang took it all.)

Maskee, John! We'll meet very soon. That's another promise.

Very best wishes, love and respect,

Your Devoted Cousin,

Andrew

P.S.: I hope you're not feeling too collar-proud, General!

The postscript was apt epitaph to Huart's two dozen years in a British Army uniform. In the words of the Bond Street tailor who had fitted him with six three-piece suits, it had been a 'tall order'.

'Why, it's true!' Paulette gasped as they embraced tentatively amidst the piles of luggage, the men in felt hats and double-breasted suits despite the heat, and women in summer dresses an inch below the knee. 'I thought my eyes were deceiving me. John, you've lost so much weight!'

'The war, Paulette . . .' he mumbled. It was the answer to much.

She appeared about to ask, but Huart pretended to look away at the straw-hatted coolies ferrying suitcases, boxes and sea chests to rows of black limousines, taxis and rickshaws on Salisbury Road. He saw instead a boy who matched his image of James at eleven. He lifted Vivienne aloft. She whined in disapproval and he quickly put her down. 'She loved her Uncle John doing that when she was small,' he excused himself.

'Our Vivienne's a big girl,' Paulette replied on her daughter's behalf. 'She was two when you last picked her up like that. She's eleven now.'

'Nearly twelve!' the girl pouted. 'Mama, can't we go now? It's so hot.'

Huart was introduced to three-year-old Suzanne, who was slung across an *amah*'s hip, looking up at him. The child's pure blonde hair and blatant prettiness was her mother's, the cherubic brown eyes and skin texture must have come from the genes that Andrew had once derided as inferior.

'John, now please meet Rex Wagoner. Rex owns Pan Atlantic Insurance.'

Huart shook the hand of a man who had gone unnoticed although he stood but an inch shorter, aware that it controlled an international insurance empire. Cumberland China was Pan Atlantic's agent. Wagoner's head office was in Chicago, his accent patently mid-western. Huart noted the assessing brown eyes, muscular frame and golf tan. But the greying, receding hairline gave the insurance mogul away. He was nearer fifty than forty. 'Have you also come down from Shanghai, Mr Wagoner?'

The American shook his head. 'I flew in from Los Angeles last week.'

'That must have been wearisome. Such a long journey.'

'No problem. I use my own kite and set my own schedule. I came by way of Hawaii, Guam and Formosa – Taiwan as Chiang calls it now. I'm setting up in Taipei. I like to keep ahead of the game and move in the minute any new government takes over. Like in China soon. That's why your boss is staying on the job in Shanghai. Too bad you can't be up there with him.'

The criticism hit home. Not yet firm upon his land legs, Huart felt at a disadvantage. Whilst he sweated in a tweed suit made for a London autumn the American stood at ease in a cream hand-tailored cotton outfit. 'I can hardly dictate Cunard's schedule to them . . .'

'Should've flown. Like me.'

Huart changed the subject. 'You must be in the box seat in Taiwan . . .'

'Why?'

'Well, America is "Most Favoured Nation" there isn't it? The press . . .'

Wagoner snorted. 'Save us from the goddam Limey press! No favouritism's goin' to be ours at all. Truman cut aid to Chiang, you know. Formosa – Taiwan – had a standard of living after fifty years under the Nips that made China medieval. When those KMT carpetbaggers invited themselves in, the locals revolted and Chiang had it put down with blood and guts – '

'Rex, the children,' Paulette interjected softly.

'Sorry. No, Big Fella – it's this that counts in Taiwan.' He rubbed his thumb and forefinger together and winked. 'My ol' man used to say: "It's not who you know or what you know that counts, it's knowing who to pay and what to pay him". My ol' man was a very successful businessman.'

Huart pulled a face. 'Shame. It seems basic human intelligence now counts for precious little.' Wagoner's eyebrows lifted. A battle line was drawn. Huart turned to Paulette. 'How is Adelaide? Well, I hope.'

'So-so, John. She hated leaving her *mahjong* cronies and the house. She feared the Kuomintang would requisition it and she was right.'

'Grandma's always so bad-tempered,' whined Vivienne. 'Mama, can we go?'

'Alright, dear. Rex, call a cab, please. Actually, we'll need two.'

'A taxi?' Huart asked. 'We're taking the vehicular ferry then?'

'Star Ferry. The Gloucester's straight across. In Des Voeux Road.'

'But the pier is only a few hundred yards away,' Huart laughed.

'John, it's too hot to walk,' Paulette told him. 'Just standing here is an ordeal. You must try to be a civilian now, *ma preux chevalier.*'

Wagoner, humming, 'Colonel Bogey', flagged down two taxis, pointed at the front of the first one then at Huart, opened the rear door for Paulette and slipped in beside her. Huart shrugged and squeezed in beside the portmanteau. The *amah* and the girls took the other taxi. They crossed the railway line onto Salisbury Road and tailed a pre-war single-decker bus past the Peninsula Hotel and the railway station. There were few people about and Huart found himself likening Tsimshatsui to Jessfield Park on a summer Sunday afternoon. As they boarded the Star Ferry, he studied Wagoner. The American walked like an impatient bantam, his chest and jaw thrust forward and rear end projected, as if challenging each and every obstacle to fall in his path. It was a certainty his road to success had been carved out with neither a meek nor a benevolent hand.

They sat on a bench on the upper deck. The ferry cast off with a belch of black smoke and Paulette set about updating Huart, whilst Wagoner lit up a Camel and read the *China Mail*. 'After the Japanese came, we – myself, Andrew's mother, Vivienne – were exchanged via the Red Cross for internees from Hawaii. I lived out the war in the states, but Andrew was interned, mostly

[127]

at Lung Hua. It took its toll on him. The rebellious idiot wouldn't follow the rules. The guards picked on him – he was bigger than they, you see. They took it out on all the English and American prisoners, and especially Andrew. In '44 the Japs found an old contract in Cumberland Building for a munitions sale to a Manchurian warlord who had resisted them in '31. With this "proof" that he was a traitor they tortured him. His weight fell to eighty pounds. He lost three toes from beri beri. All his hair fell out. Of course, he's much better now, but don't expect the Andrew of old when you see him.'

Huart nodded sadly, unable to come up with an adequate comment. Instead he directed an avuncular gaze at the beautiful child fast asleep on the *amah*'s lap. 'Well . . . there's proof he's back to normal in one respect.'

'What do you mean?' Paulette asked, then followed his eyes. 'Oh . . .' she murmured, then announced: 'Arthur Dennison died. He was too nice a man to survive Lung Hua. Agnes left with us in '42. She's still in London.'

'How very sad. Poor Agnes.' Huart's spirits fell further. He had been looking forward to renewing contact with the old China hand and drawing further from his wealth of experience. Could the news get worse?

'And now it looks like it's happening all over again,' Paulette sighed. 'Shanghai was a hard place when we left. Martial law. KMT soldiers were everywhere, bullying and stealing. Hundreds of thousands of them were living on the streets, unpaid, taking whatever they wanted. Refugees again. Horrendous – blocking roads, swarming across Garden Bridge. The traffic jams were so bad you had to walk everywhere. Worse than in '37! Dead bodies were all over the place. The Chinese mayor hadn't a clue what to even begin to do. It was unsafe for us to go out even in broad daylight with all the soldiers and the beggars and the criminals about. It was never like that when the Municipal Council was in control . . .'

She paused, shook her head and carried on. 'And the inflation! The paper money devalued by the minute! Basic commodity prices doubled over sixty times between our return to Shanghai in September '45 and August last year. Then T.V. Soong issued his wonderful Gold Yuan – and you know what happened to that! Andrew had to insist on his clients settling in greenbacks or sterling. Paying the local staff became a farce. They needed a wheelbarrow to take away the notes one month, two wheelbarrows the next. People were spending it as soon as they got it – it was

[128]

devaluing so fast. I went shopping with jars of jam, tins of sardines – anything! No shop wanted to take paper money. The whole country was bankrupt!'

Huart blinked in wonder. 'How did Andrew keep things going?'

'He didn't. There was nothing to keep going for. Ships stopped calling at the end of April. The staff would come in to the office and sit and look at each other. The Chinese would play *fantan* and the Europeans would go to the Shanghai Club at eleven and not bother to come back.'

'When did you decide it was time to get out?'

'When a bunch of KMT louts stormed into Broadway Mansions and set up a mortar on the roof and a machine gun post right on our balcony – '

'You're joking.'

'They could sight down the Bund, you see. The day before we left by RAF flying boat, the floating population disappeared from the Soochow Creek. We knew it was time to go. The Chinese were paying fortunes for exit permits, abandoning what they couldn't carry. I saw brand new Cadillacs and Rolls-Royces left in the street. One was chock full of fur coats!'

'But Andrew has stayed. He must believe the situation is not hopeless?'

'All the taipans have stayed. They say that it's inevitable the China Trade will go on even under a communist government.'

'If I'd known, I'd have sailed direct instead of indulging myself on the *Queen Mary*. I'd be with him now ...' Suddenly Huart felt he had let the side down. What was his worth in Hong Kong, sitting around in the branch office? What shape was it in? How could he justify his presence?

He was about to ask Paulette's opinion when, as if she had been reading his thoughts, she said in a voice totally cheerless: 'And what's to become of this place? The Communists are hell-bent for Canton. Refugees are swarming over the border like rats before a flood to live in squalor all over the hillsides. I hear the population is estimated at almost two million and rising every day. In 1945 there were only 600,000 here. This place – ' She waved her arm in an encompassing gesture. 'This place just won't be able to handle it! It'll be overrun if it keeps up. And already communist troublemakers have been inciting riots over some "Walled City" in Kowloon which for some reason still belongs to China.' She sighed again. 'And the local social life wouldn't excite a backward hillbilly. I do hope the Communists have the common sense to let Andrew and the taipans re-establish the Municipal Council and let them run things the way they were before the war. Then we can all go back to Shanghai.'

'That's totally against their basic ideology, Paulette,' Huart reasoned. 'The old days are gone. Times change. They must. That's progress. Shanghai changed after the war when it picked up with a Chinese mayor and a Chinese administration. It would still be so but for the civil war. Shanghai is a survivor. We must do what we can to help Andrew. And I'll start by seeing what I can do in the branch office here.'

But neither were convinced and the crossing was completed in silence, Huart thinking deeply. The possibility of Mao's Communists disregarding the border between the British leased New Territories and Kwangtung was real. There were the facts of HMS *Amethyst* and the subsequent firing on three separate Royal Navy rescue vessels. What respect the Communists would afford another British possession upon the rump of the country they were in the process of taking over by force was a subject for nervous speculation. British and Gurkha troops had been garrisoned in the New Territories after the Japanese surrender as a deterrent to Chiang Kai-shek, who had coveted the only treaty port unrestored to him in 1943. Would they soon be resisting not the Nationalist Chinese but the Communists? Huart's war was perhaps not over after all.

They walked onto the Central Praya through the rickshaws joined shaft to wheel. The waterfront was unchanged, except that billboards adulterated Queen's Building: COOK'S, MESSAGERIES MARITIMES, MOLLERS, THORESEN & COMPANY, THE EAST ASIATIC COMPANY, HONG-KONG & WHAMPOA DOCK, and from its roof flags flew. Automobiles with the sloping lines and hard tops of the post-war fashion were parked at forty-five degrees down the middle of the Central Praya and around the lawned square that was now stripped of its statues. The Bank stood facing with its symmetrical shoulders framed by the omnipresence of the Peak. The City Hall had gone, its site empty.

Again Wagoner hailed two taxis and Huart squeezed into the front of one. At the granite arch before Queen's Pier they wheeled off the Praya into the square, then rounded the circus on Chater Road with its empty baldachin. Wagoner pointed at the vacant site where the City Hall had been. 'Don't that say it all? That pile of nothing was going to be the Bank of China. Whether it's finished or not now is up to the Commies. It was T.V. Soong's baby and he used the same architect and same design as for the Bank of

China on the Bund. Its height was to be twenty feet over the Hongkong and Shanghai as a symbol of KMT superiority and Chiang's claim to Hong Kong. I bet he and his boys don't feel so superior now.'

'You seem well informed,' Huart commented over his shoulder.

Wagoner shrugged. 'It's a habit, Big Fella. Prerequisite for winning.'

'The trams aren't running,' Paulette observed. 'Another strike. The Communists are setting the place up. They won't stop at the border.'

The lobby of the Gloucester Hotel was cramped, but Paulette had cleared Huart's registration in advance. He was in 403, facing Pedder Street. Wagoner continued his commentary as they waited before the wire grille for the elevator. 'The Nips continued this place as a hotel. Now it's the only place in Victoria worth staying. The Hongkong Hotel's still next door – you can get to it through the arcade – but its days are numbered. And there's the Cecil a block away, but it's not for us.'

The elevator came and Paulette said: 'You go up and drop your case and wash up, John. Lunch at 12:30 in the restaurant. Adelaide will join us.'

'Grand,' he smiled. 'I'm looking forward to seeing her again.'

'And, John . . .' Paulette's voice and eyes dropped. Huart knew what was coming. He held his breath. 'It goes without saying that we're all very, very sorry about . . . about everything. Words are little comfort, I know. If there's anything we can do. Anything. Please ask. Please.'

Huart nodded. He attempted a smile. 'Lunch with the Huart-Brents will do the trick, Paulette. See you at 12:30.' He nodded again. 'Wagoner.'

'Big Fella. Don't get lost.'

The wire grille closed with a slap and the elevator jerked into the air. Huart waited for it to pass through the concrete slab of the first floor before he blinked hard to suppress the bitter tears that, even after seven long slow years, still rose up with the memory.

Rangoon, 1946.

It was a thoroughly tropical September day.

Colonel John Stanford Huart, DSO, did a rare thing on seeing an aged Sinclair MacLurie standing inside the door with CHIEF MILITARY ATTACHE – WAR CRIMINAL AFFAIRS painted on it. He smiled. Then he kicked back the British Army issue revolving chair and strode around the ironwood desk to grasp his father-in-law's outstretched hand.

MacLurie saw the transformation at once. Huart was a ghost, a walking residue of the man that had been. His eyes had dulled. He was a junk yard of tarnished brass: his belt buckle, his buttons, the crown and two pips on his epaulettes, his Distinguished Service Order and Burma Star at his breast, as askew as they had been for that morning's march-past on the anniversary of the signing of the Japanese surrender in Burma.

The two had last shaken hands an eternity ago: almost six years. It had been on Collyer Quay the day the Second Cumberland had sailed from Singapore back to Burma. Their ultimate destination had been Lashio, a town five hundred miles north-east of Rangoon. Jennifer and the boys had remained behind. Lashio was no place for a family; quarters there were basic tents and bunkers. It was the southern terminus of the Burma Road, which Churchill had re-opened after victory in the Battle of Britain. US arms and materiel for the Nationalist Chinese were unloaded there from the Rangoon-Mandalay supply train onto trucks, which set out on the circuitous, treacherous 720 mile course to Kunming and Chungking. The tour of duty had been reckoned to last six months. It had continued for eighteen before being rudely curtailed by the Japanese.

February 15th, 1942 was the first day in the Year of the Water Horse. It was the day for visits to relatives and for settling debts. Yamashita's XXV Army used it to visit Singapore with guns and to settle a debt that was conceived to be long overdue. It was the day Huart lost every member of his family and half his soul. It was the day his first life ended.

''Twas quick, laddie,' MacLurie said quietly, reverently. 'None of them would have felt any pain. 'Twas just past dawn. We were casting off. We should've got away during the night but with the infernal confusion and changes of orders . . . 'Twas a tub – the last thing afloat in Singapore Harbour. I was on the foredeck helping to secure the baggage. All the others – Jenny . . . wee Andrew was in her arms . . . James . . . and my Annie – they were all standing in a group by the rail on the rear deck. A Jap bomber came over. There was a delayed explosion. It must've been a torpedo. The rear deck went up in flames. And they were gone. No human being could've lived more'n a split second in an explosion like that one. Later that day Percival surrendered and I was a civilian prisoner. Oh, laddie . . . 'twas the worst day in a man's life . . .' He looked deeply into his son-in-law's eyes. ''Twas quick,' he repeated. 'They'd have not felt a thing. No pain. Not even a wee pain . . .' His voice trailed off.

Huart continued to look at the floorboards. 'Thank you, Sinclair. I did wonder how they died. If they died . . . If they died in pain. It . . . it haunted me . . .' The eyes dulled again. The ghost took over the man.

It took but an hour to put paid to Huart's stock of Chivas Regal and they adjourned to the officers' mess for more. Under its influence and MacLurie's probing the past was unlocked. Huart told his story. At no time did he slur. His capacity for scotch had become a Burma legend.

'For me the real war started in the spring of '42. I got this trinket in my very first action.' He touched the DSO on his chest. 'The General Staff was pinning on medals like they were going out of fashion. And it did just that – the metal was needed for more important things. We were pulling back from Lashio to link up with Stillwell's Chinese near Mandalay, then fight a delaying action to the Assam border to hold up the Jap invasion of India until the monsoon broke . . .' He held up his glass for a refill. 'Interesting combination: an American commanding a Chinese division in Burma where we British, Indians and Gurkhas were mixing it with the Japanese. A cosmopolitan war it certainly was. A world war . . .'

'Go on, laddie.'

'The Japs had smartly cut the Burma Road. Orders to withdraw from Lashio came at once – there was no reason to hang about with the Road gone. My company came upon a Jap advance unit that had surrounded a company of Stillwell's men. The Chinese were being cut out a section at a time. The Japs weren't looking over their shoulders and it was simple for us to hit them from behind and open an escape route. Fifty-odd Chinese escaped and headed north for Yunnan. It was over so fast. I remember a sensation of total confusion – gunfire echoed about the jungle and it sounded like we were completely surrounded when we weren't. I took a piece of grenade in the back, but I didn't know it until after. Funny . . .'

Huart took up his replenished glass. MacLurie waited for him to go on, certain his son-in-law had not talked about himself this way in years.

'Funny . . .' Huart repeated, 'that was actually the second time I found myself playing big brother for the Chinese . . .'

'The second time?'

Huart nodded. 'The first was in Shanghai. Not a shot was fired – by us.'

'Sounds like a tale worth hearing, laddie. Tell me about it.'

So Huart recounted the 'Soochow Creek Incident'. 'By then,' he concluded, 'the Kuomintang were getting such a thrashing that anything resembling a victory was played up. I even found out later that my role in the escape of the "Doomed Battalion" was reported to Chiang Kai-shek . . .'

MacLurie willed with his eyebrows for Huart to continue, and mellowed by the scotch and company of kin for the first time in six years, he did so. 'It was in Lashio, just after the invasion, when Chiang met Wavell for a conference. As adjutant I was present. As Chiang was climbing into his Dakota, he said to me – through his interpreter as he spoke no English – "I hope, Major Huart, when this war is over we will meet again so I can prove to you the esteem in which you are held by we Chinese. One of the brave men you saved at the Soochow Creek is now my aide in Chungking. It is an honour for me to thank you on his behalf, and China's." '

'How remarkable. So how do you plan to collect on that debt, laddie?' MacLurie whistled. 'Just think of the accrued interest!'

Huart pulled a face. 'Come on, Sinclair. You read too much into it. It was the passing comment of a master politician. Nothing more.'

'Pr'aps so, and pr'aps not. Anyhow, I recommend you not to forget what he said. A wee favour from on high can change the lives of men.'

Huart returned his father-in-law's gaze. 'Indeed, the lives of men . . .' He reclined until his head rested on the back of his chair and he closed his eyes and the words came out. 'My life ended a thousand times on that three hundred mile retreat to Assam. We fought the heat, the dust, the rains, the mud, the jungle, the mountains, the valleys, the rivers. We fought the Japs and the snakes and the scorpions and the great ugly poisonous red beetles and the leeches and the mosquitoes . . .'

His eyes opened and stared sightlessly up into the fan going round and round. 'And when I got to Imphal and they told me . . . I did die.' He upended his glass and swallowed hard. 'We got there as the monsoon broke – those of us who were still breathing. I'm told I arrived vertical, but totally exhausted, racked with malaria, the shrapnel in the small of my back, my uniform hanging in strips off what was left of me. But I'm damned if I remember a thing about it. My first recollection was of the hospital sheets with dull red patches where the blood hadn't been washed out properly. I thought the nurse was Jennifer and then they told me . . .'

'What did you do when you recovered, laddie?' MacLurie asked quickly.

'The frontier, as you know, is a chain of jungle-strewn mountains two hundred miles wide,' Huart went on as if reading from a reconnaissance report. 'Roads are few and far between and tracks are almost impassable. It gave the Japs a natural north-western frontier to their "Greater East Asia Co-Prosperity Sphere" and it allowed us to sit in Imphal and lick our wounds. I was put in charge of preparing it to be forward base for the re-invasion of Burma. The Cumberland Regiment was no more. Eighty per cent of the men were dead or prisoners. It was reformed in England and I was offered promotion to Lieutenant-Colonel and asked to lead it. But I insisted on staying where I was. If there was to be a re-invasion, I wanted to be in it. Then, at the end of '42, Orde Wingate formed his Chindits and I joined him. Our first sortie into Burma was touch and go. We were to be reprovisioned by Dakotas, but most of the parachute drops fell on the Japs. We blew railway points and took out a few of their frontier posts, but we had to withdraw prematurely or be cut off . . .'

'So the first sortie was a failure?'

Huart shook his head. 'Not at all. It put the wind up the Japs – showed them their Burma frontier wasn't as invincible as they thought. And it gave the Allies some heart. We'd been taking it till then. The Chindits dished a bit out.' He paused again and gazed into his scotch as if seeing it all replaying upon the meniscus. 'And it did me good – psychologically if not physically. I felt as if I'd made an effort to avenge them all . . . I killed men – Japs, I mean. I shot them and I saw them fall and bleed and die . . .' Again he paused. 'I came out with another dose of malaria. I was a scarecrow. I'd lived on bullock meat, python and rice for weeks. I swore then I'd never eat rice again – and I haven't.'

'That's the end of the story?' MacLurie asked when this pause extended.

Huart nodded. 'There was no more action for me after that. The doctors ordered me into a staff job in Delhi, supervising the training of Indian troops under Mountbatten and Stillwell. I saw the war out there.' The last of the scotch went down. 'Time to eat. You're still the world's best listener, Sinclair. I've not talked of it to anyone. Thank you.'

'We'll continue over dinner, laddie. You've told me but half the story.'

They walked to the dining room where Huart signed his father-in-law into the visitors' book, feeling stronger than he could remember. It was not the scotch. Common loss had forged an unbreakable bond between them.

The soup was tepid. As the half-empty bowls were taken away, MacLurie asked: 'What was it brought you back to Rangoon after the war, laddie?'

'I'm not sure really. I feared the memories. The wonderful memories. But London was unbearable. I couldn't stand the inactivity. So I decided to confront my ghosts. Something of an exorcism, I suppose. I speak Burmese and I know the country and its culture. I was a natural for this post.'

'You're a man hunter?'

Huart pushed his chin out. 'My job is to hunt down and prosecute war criminals, Sinclair. And I love it. Perhaps it's a continuation of my revenge.' He sat back. 'But that's enough about me. What're your plans?'

'My plans? Finish this wee sabbatical first, then retire to my cottage outside bonny Edinburgh.' He picked up his glass and winked. 'Where I just might start to distil my own brand of triple malt.'

'Retire? But there're years in you yet.'

'Not enough, laddie. Younger men're running the bank now. Men your age. What are you? Forty? Yes, young men like you.'

'Where will you go from here?'

'Saigon. Singapore. Hong Kong.'

'Shanghai?'

MacLurie looked up. 'No,' he said slowly. 'Why do you ask?'

'No reason. But I sometimes wonder how things are going with my cousin's company there. It must be all organised again. I did have a plan to quit the army and go to Shanghai ... He offered me a directorship, you know.'

'I know. Jenny told me.'

'But that was as much for her as for me.'

The old Scot was watching carefully, measuring the strength of his words to come. For him the conversation was nearing its crux. He had sought out his son-in-law for more than a family reunion. Disturbing reports had reached him. He had come to save John Huart before they both died.

'Laddie, Jenny is gone. Your sons have gone. They'll go on living forever in your memory, but physically they are gone ...'

'Sinclair . . .'

'Be quiet and listen. I lost my wife and my daughter and my wee grandsons to that same bomb. I consider myself entitled to speak to you on the subject. I'd forgive you for closing your ears to anyone else. But you must listen to me.' He placed a withered hand on Huart's wrist. It was cold, like the limb of a statue, but he gripped it hard and held it.

Seconds passed before Huart nodded. 'Alright, Sinclair. Go on.'

'Jenny always thought you should have left the army. She used to say you were misplaced in a uniform, that the world was being cheated . . .'

'Cheated? What did she mean by that?'

'That you were born to be in business. That you were born to write the rules, not follow them every minute of every day of your life. She saw that. Your cousin saw it too and offered you a seat on the board of his company – your family company. Not just because your name is Huart, but because you possess a keen brain and the ability to detect business in a situation. Laddie, it's a Scottish banker talking to you . . .'

A silence visited the table. Eventually Huart lifted his eyes from the empty glass in his free hand and asked: 'So what should I do, Sinclair?'

'Have you written to your cousin, laddie?'

Huart lowered his head again. 'No,' he replied too firmly.

'Why?'

'I fear he's dead.'

'Dead? How do you know, for the love of God!'

Huart's fist came down upon the table and the crockery and silverware jumped. Heads turned and, seeing the perpetrator was only Colonel Huart, the faces registered a singular lack of surprise and turned away again. But MacLurie knew he had struck the nerve for which he had been searching. He had penetrated the core of his son-in-law's torment.

'Why shouldn't he be dead?' Huart hissed, his eyes on fire. 'Everyone else is! All my family is dead! My father. My mother. My wife – your daughter. My sons – your grandsons. All of them dead and gone! So what's to save my cousin? Death seems to be in store for any member of the family that gets close to me. D'you know that? Is there some curse upon me? Tell me. What it is about me? You profess to know so much. Tell me!'

MacLurie shook his head lugubriously. 'I never thought I'd see the day when I heard John Huart taking excuse for himself from the supernatural. Laddie, you're sounding to me very much like a quitter – '

Huart snatched back his arm. 'Quitter? I suppose you think I'm wasting my time and the taxpayers' money here in Rangoon. There's a mountain of work to be done in Burma. The remnants of a foul war have to be cleared up. The country has to be rebuilt. Our brief is direct British rule until 1949, longer if the Burmese can't get themselves organised by then. Their army has to be trained. Their administration has to be taught how to manage the country to the point when it can take over itself . . .'

'And what will you do after that happens, John?' MacLurie put in. 'What will you do when Burma no longer wants you around?'

Huart's mouth clamped shut. The muscles of his neck quivered. Though pride, or fear, prevented him from admitting it, he had no answer.

That night they got rotten drunk together. They debated the post-war world in terms unintelligible to anyone else. They blacked out together in Huart's quarters and awoke late with duplicate heads. MacLurie stayed a fortnight. Each night they drank less and Huart listened more.

'I've still got a job to finish here, Sinclair. I'm no quitter.'

'Finish it fast, then laddie. And when it's done, write to your cousin.'

Sinclair MacLurie sailed away and the ghost resumed control of Huart's body. But his deterioration had arrested itself. He survived day to day.

At 4:20 a.m., January 4th, 1948, the time and date selected according to the lunar calendar, the Union of Burma became the first British colony to be granted the status of an independent nation. At 3:40 p.m. the same day, the time and date fixed by the Peninsular and Orient Steamship Company, the *Windsor Castle* cast off from the Strand Road docks. At the rail, swimming in a sadness that had no bottom, Huart watched his last sunset glint from the golden skin of the Shwedagon as it lowered behind the trees that lined the bank of the Rangoon River. The new Burma had no need of him. He stood looking back, feeling like a rejected parent.

The Gulf of Martaban became the Andaman Sea, which in turn opened into the breadth of the Indian Ocean. Huart's thoughts skated aimlessly into the future as he stood and stared over the forward horizon where awaited an ineffectual posting in London, and a promotion to major-general to go with it. The voice of Sinclair MacLurie continued to echo in his head as the liner

[138]

carried him further and further in the wrong direction. He listened to it, and he listened to his heart. Both told him the same thing: the covenant of his life, his third life, lay to the east.

He wrote the letter to Andrew Huart-Brent the second night out of Rangoon, and rewrote it every night until Bombay where he posted it.

England had changed irreparably. It was the time of the Health Act, and nationalisation as Attlee's socialists plucked the Bank of England, British Railways, the coal mining, gas and power industries from private enterprise and put them under control of the State. It was time, too, for the infamous Groundnuts Scheme with Whitehall throwing 36,000,000 sterling into East and Central Africa. England, it seemed, was no place for a businessman, nor a politician, and certainly not a soldier.

Andrew's reply took ten weeks, by which time Huart had convinced himself his cousin was indeed dead. The next day he resigned his commission. The British Army, though convinced his Burma ordeals had finally caught up with his sanity, maximized the delay before his demobilization.

Major-General John Stanford Huart became a civilian on 1st March, 1949.

The clock atop the Gloucester Hotel struck the half hour and jerked Huart from the greyness of his immediate past. He dug out his watch. It was ten minutes slow. They would be waiting for him in the restaurant.

The room was cool. The high ceiling and the copper-bladed fans revolving silently below it saw to that, and the teak-panelled walls gave it an old-world softness. The balcony admitted the bright mid-day light from Pedder Street and looked across it into contrasting offices in stylish, colonial Jardine House and the China Building, which seemed built out of converted tenements.

Huart swung his legs off the brass bed. It had been too comfortable. He had been accustomed to spartan accommodation for so long he found both the bed and the room commodious. Civilian life in the East was going to take pleasant adjustment, he told himself.

He collected his room key from the bureau and lifted his felt hat off the peg beside the door. He held on to the knob a few moments whilst he found his land legs again and listened to the subdued, genteel sounds of post-war Hong Kong coming in through the open balcony window.

He thought of Shanghai and an impatience filled him.

3

The ordinary black telephone upon the davenport in Paulette's suite was the focus of extraordinary attention for the three hours until it rang and she took it up. 'Yes, it's me. Yes, I'll accept the charges. Andrew? Is that you? I can hardly hear you, there's too much static. Why are you so late? We were about to give up and go down for lunch.' She talked at the top of her voice for a minute, then said: 'Yes – John's here,' gave Huart the receiver and went to report to Adelaide who was recovering in her suite from what she called 'a turn', a phenomenon she blamed on the 'barbarous and inhospitable equatorial weather they serve up down here'.

Andrew's voice indeed sounded like he was nearly a thousand miles away. It was forced through coursing static. Hearing his third cousin for the first time in nine years gave Huart a joy that was tainted with anxiety.

'Things don't look so bad here, John. The Communists are setting an unprecedented example in good manners. They've eliminated corruption overnight and there's no crime and no traffic jams. That's some achievement. They're polite to a fault. I haven't found the right man to talk to yet. In fact, it's difficult to find anyone to talk to at all. They say they don't recognise the British or US consulates. The quicker they declare the new government and the quicker Attlee and Truman recognise it, the better. But it's early days yet, John . . .' There was a surge of static. Huart grimaced and strained his ear until the voice returned. ' . . . first ship since the Communists took over docked yesterday – the *Shanking*. But they won't let anyone land. How the captain got through the wrecks in the river without a pilot I don't know – but if one can get through, so can others. It's the start, Cousin. You'll be up here trading in the "New China" before you know it. So how're things in Hong Kong?'

'Hot!' Huart shouted back. 'And quiet. I wasn't aware Gilbert Dole was still here and in such poor health. It seems he suffered similarly in Stanley to what Paulette tells me you went through in Lung Hua – '

'Poor devil, then.'

' – We're inundated with refugees, as you can imagine. The government has yet to work out a housing policy. And – Rex Wagoner is here.'

'Oh is he now? Is he alone? How are you getting along with him?'

'He's alone and I'm coping with him with extreme difficulty.'

'I know the feeling. Wagoner likes to think of himself as America's best export, flying that converted warplane around the world. He's always trying to get one up on his father – who is still the twentieth century Alexander the Great of the insurance world – from the way he talks to everything else he does. He has two redeeming features: he's one of our biggest principals, and his wife's a real doll – too good for him.'

'Andrew – ' Huart yelled over the static, 'how much time do you have?'

'Three minutes. Better go. I'll call Thursday if I can. The 'phone network is still operating. The workers have stayed on the job. But there's no guarantee it'll be that way on Thursday. The branch office has money – I transferred down half our liquid funds in time. It should see you through provided it doesn't take too long to get things going here. Look after affairs down there, John. You have full authority. Understand?'

'I understand, Andrew.'

'Good. Give my love to everyone. *Maskee*, John. *Maskee*. Cheerio!'

The line went dead without Andrew having made any reference to matters personal. Whether this had been due to his preoccupation with the situation in Shanghai, or to first-class perspicacity, Huart did not care. He was grateful in either case.

The next call was a day late. The static was worse. There had been no change in the situation, and that in itself was bad. Halfway through the call Andrew burst into a tirade at those he deemed culpable. Strangely, the Communists were not on his list. 'Blast Roosevelt and Truman and all the stupid Yanks! And Chiang Kai-shek and his brigands. And the Soongs and the Kungs. Between the lot o' them they've killed the richest, most progressive city in Asia. And who was it made it great? Not Roosevelt, not Truman, not Chiang who destroyed it. We did! We made it great! We businessmen, that's who! We who had the guts to get down amongst the mud of the Whangpoo and the silt of the Yangtse. Through the troubles – ' A pause for breath. 'And through the war – when Roosevelt gave it away to Chiang in '43 and we were eating dirty rice and gruel in Lung Hua and being beaten and humiliated by the rotten Japs. And he gave it away!'

Andrew's voice had risen to a shriek. He paused again for breath, but before Huart could interject he was off again. 'The place wasn't his to give in the first place! His flag was one of thirteen. So he didn't like imperialism . . . I tell you, John, it

wasn't only we foreigners who flocked to Shanghai to get rich –
the Chinese came, too. In their millions! Here they at least had a
chance to survive, whereas in the rest of the godforsaken country
they had no hope. And who gave them that chance? We did! We
businessmen. Not the blasted politicians! And he sat in his blasted
wheelchair and gave it away to Chiang so he'd fight the Japs. And
Chiang took it from him and fought the Communists. And now
look – '

A coughing fit punctuated Andrew's rambling, but not for long.
'Still they couldn't beat us. We rebuilt it! Our offices and factories
were turned upside-down, but the Swiss and the Swedes kept it
going and we picked it up as soon as the Japs were done. Even
when the Communists took over the Brit coal mines in Shansi –
ours, too – we bartered for the coal with rice and wheat, and the
oil the Yanks sent in, and we kept the power stations going and
the cotton mills running to make the stuff we needed to pay the
Yanks back. Britain has 400,000,000 sterling invested in China,
most of it in Shanghai? What do you . . . ?'

Huart had to cut in. 'Andrew! We're running out of time. If
nothing's happening in Shanghai, it is here. Our office lease
expires in three months. Dole doesn't have Power of Attorney to
negotiate an extension. Can you give me the necessary authority?'

There was a brief silence, then Andrew's voice returned, calmer.
'Sorry. I got carried away. But I feel better for it. Thanks for
taking it. Of course you have Power of Attorney. I'll get an authorisation down to you as fast as I can. The grapevine has it there's
another ship docking in a few days. I hear it's the *Anchises*. I'll
send the letter with it.'

'Good. Our tenancy's sound despite a shortage of Central
District space and a waiting list. We're protected by an edict called
"The Landlord and Tenant Ordinance" which fixes rents at 1941
levels with fifteen per cent maximum increase. I'll press Victoria
Land for a five-year extension.'

'Good, John. Go ahead. Let me know how you get on.'

'I'll do that, Andrew. Goodbye for now.'

'Cheerio. And *Maskee*. Always *Maskee*.'

Huart hung up and frowned at Paulette. 'Is he well, do you
think?'

'Well, his heart . . .' she began, then ran to the dressing table
to pull Suzanne's three-year-old fingers from a jar of face cream.

Ten days passed before Andrew's next call came with news that
was worse and delivered with more invective. 'That bastard Chiang
has bombed the *Anchises* and blockaded the Yangtse! Now nothing

[142]

can get into or out of Shanghai. Doesn't he know where he's not wanted? He's nothing but a damn opportunist who married Sun Yat-sen's sister-in-law. Him and his people-eating wife! And the Yanks prop them up. Don't they know the Chinese are ninety-nine per cent peasants who hate the rich, hate the Kuomintang and hate Chiang? To them communism is a step up! Truman wanted China united, but non-communist. But then his damn fool Yanks let the Japs surrender to Mao in Manchuria and give him an instant arsenal. With friends like that, Chiang didn't need the enemies he had. The Yanks lost every way: Chiang lost the war, the Yanks lost Mao, now we've all lost China!'

Huart stopped his cousin there. The calls, now not only infrequent, were also unproductive, and revealed a progressive deterioration in Andrew's thought processes. 'Andrew .. ! I want to send Gilbert Dole home.'

'Dole? Who's Dole?'

'Gilbert Dole, Andrew! Your Hong Kong branch manager.'

'Oh. Yes. Dole. Why? What's wrong with him?'

'He's very ill. I want to superannuate him. What's the company ruling?'

'There is no rule. It's never happened before. Take your own decision, man. You're the director in charge down there, aren't you?'

Huart frowned at his cousin's pique, but replied in a level voice: 'I suggest a month's pay for each year of service including the occupation years, plus one year's pay as gratuity and a first-class sea passage home. It'll bite into our bank account, but the man's done well to keep the office going since the war.'

'Sounds generous. Does it have to be first-class? What the hell, John! You're in charge. Who'll take over the office?'

'Roboza, the accountant. I'll promote him to office manager. He has the experience and seems competent enough.'

'How is the lease extension without my Power of Attorney?'

'We managed by substituting my Letter of Appointment signed by you and pleading special circumstances. I found a solicitor who was sufficiently enterprising. Victoria Land have granted us a new lease for three years at a fifteen per cent increase with an option for an additional two.'

'Fine. Is . . . Is Wagoner still there?'

'He flew out a week ago. He'll be back before long, though. Why?'

'Nothing. Oh, we owe him a quarterly report. Could you improvise?'

'It'll be the shortest report in history.'

'Can't be helped. I'd better go now. Could you put Paulette back on?'

When she hung up, her expression mirrored his concern. 'I'm getting more and more worried about him, John,' she said. 'He didn't even close with his usual *Maskee*. Can't we get him out of there?'

Huart shook his head. 'Nobody can get an entry visa and Andrew can't apply for an exit permit. He's the only non-Chinese left in the company. The Communists won't let him leave. They need him to sign the cheques!'

'God help us,' she breathed.

As more weeks passed, Andrew's calls became more widely-spaced. When they did come through they were more and more unenthusiastic, totally devoid of sanguine philosophy, and the object of increasing alarm. Huart watched the bank balance ebb with each debit. It was still impossible to plan his own passage to Shanghai, nor Andrew's withdrawal from it, which would be tantamount to closing eighty percent of the company but would halt the cash outflow from the all but defunct head office. The Hong Kong branch office had to be converted from a clearing station for South China to a profit centre in its own right. In a hurry. 'I'll not consider laying off staff,' he promised Francis Roboza. 'We need more business here. We need new business. We must go and get both.'

The Portuguese eyes of the newly-appointed office manager looked back across Gilbert Dole's desk at the new director who now more than occupied the chair behind it. 'Go where, Mr Huart?' he asked innocently.

Huart looked back at him. It was a good question.

4

Every table in the converted basement off Theatre Lane that was Jimmy's Kitchen was occupied, and Huart was glad he had taken the precaution of making a reservation. The air was heavy with a permeating humidity, from which wire-framed fans delivered only intermittent relief as they oscillated across bases fixed to the walls above the heads of the diners.

'Andrew said he spent the night of the typhoon bailing out the basement of Cumberland Building. It's a wonder the 'phone worked this morning.' Paulette shifted her bottom upon the straight-backed wooden chair. The heat of the summer of 1949 was proving a challenge even to her. 'Oh, this weather!' she complained, looking up critically at the nearest fan.

Adelaide released an unfeminine snort. 'Weather? It's more like a dawn to dusk Turkish bath, this Hong Kong. Even after dark it's impossible to concentrate on a game of *mahjong* without a block of ice under the chair.' She shook an ivory-backed fan for emphasis and squinted at the cardboard menu. 'Andrew bailing out the basement? In my day the local staff did things like that. What's the world coming to?'

Huart glanced at Paulette, but she made no move to defend her husband. He shrugged; it was convenient to accept that criticism had become the old lady's trademark and went largely unheard. But despite Adelaide's condemnation of the heat, she sat there in a high-collared, long-sleeved full length evening dress. Paulette had chosen something more sensible, and decidedly more fashionable, and wore her hair brushed back and tied to expose her slender neck. A man could adjudge her in her low thirties and still feel he risked insult. Paulette would soon be forty-three, but she radiated the benefit of having escaped the ravages and deprivation of internment, enhanced by her skill with modern cosmetics.

On July 24th, the eye of Typhoon Gloria had passed directly over Shanghai. Her skirts had swirled across the East China coast, up the Yangtse where they provided the necessary cover for HMS *Amethyst* to slip the communist trap south of Nanking and make it to the open sea. It had been the main topic of dinner conversation in Hong Kong for the past week. British 'face', a vague memory in China, had been partially restored.

'When are those communist fellows going to let my son go?' Adelaide went on, her gaze upon Huart as though she deemed him responsible for it all.

He spread his hands palm up on the white tablecloth in a gesture of helplessness. 'We still don't know. He's been told straight that he's not allowed to leave, that he has to stay put to authorise the payments of salary to the Chinese staff and the new taxes – '

'Taxes? What taxes?'

It was Paulette who replied. 'A new system of taxation – or extortion – has been levied on all foreign-owned companies. Every

[145]

single thing they have is now taxed, particularly items classified as "luxuries". The Communists are getting nowhere taxing profits – there's no business to generate any. Andrew now has to pay tax on Cumberland Building, on every room in our apartment including bathrooms and balcony, on servants' salaries, on our car . . . These taxes have already been increased twice.'

Adelaide snorted again. 'Imbeciles. What are they trying to achieve? Andrew must reduce his other overheads, then. Lay off staff . . .'

'He can't,' Huart inserted. 'No Chinese is allowed to be disemployed or even to have his salary reduced. And not only that, staff laid off in previous years are entitled to make retroactive claims through special tribunals. Andrew is in a vice. *We* are in a vice.'

'Poor Andrew.' Paulette's eyes skimmed the menu. 'He complains about the food. You know how he loves to eat, but all non-Chinese restaurants have closed except Russian. He's tired of borscht and rice and noodles. And there's a nine o'clock curfew – not that there's reason to go out.' She buttered a slice of French bread, then continued. 'Shanghai is running down. The Communists are bewildered by a westernised city of six million people. Andrew says doctrine has taken over and common sense has taken a holiday. Spies are everywhere, looking out for any sniff of capitalism. The workers are afraid of each other and of their supervisors, and the supervisors are afraid of each other and of the workers. Nobody takes even the most insignificant decision. Everything is referred upwards until it is out of sight and, of course, nothing ever gets done. Nobody is responsible to make anything happen. Everyone is terrified of making a mistake as they know what'll happen to them if they do. All documents must be written in Chinese, but no translator is allowed to work for a foreigner, and you must know the law even if you can't read Chinese. And still no mail is getting through the blockade. I suggested to Andrew that he take this opportunity to learn Chinese – he never had the time before – but he says none of the staff are brave enough to teach him.'

Adelaide was aghast. 'Good gracious! It sounds like Never-Never Land. They'll close the Country Club next. Then the Golf Club. Then the Race Club. And Andrew's Shanghai Club! Then you'll know it's all over.'

Paulette made a derisive noise. 'It's as good – or as bad – as that now. The police regularly carry out identity checks in the Long Bar. They took Stewart Barlow away the other night for not having his papers.'

'Couldn't happen to a nicer person,' Adelaide commented tartly. 'But imagine the nerve of those communist fellows entering the Shanghai Club! I'll bet they didn't even bother to take out "temporary membership".'

Huart curbed his laugh, unsure if the old lady was actually joking. He could now recognise the portent of it all. The Communists were extracting a retribution from those foreigners who chose to remain in Shanghai. Thinking aloud, he said *sotto voce*: ' "The day will come when China will repay with interest all the injuries and insults she has suffered at the hands of the European powers". Could it be that day has come?'

Both women were staring at him. 'What, John?' frowned Adelaide. 'That sounded like some sort of communist rubbish to me.'

'They were the words of Sir Robert Hart. Sinclair MacLurie told them to me in Rangoon. Funny how they've stuck in my memory over the years . . .'

'Sounded very much like a misquote,' Adelaide asserted.

Paulette's eyes were round. 'A prophesy. Will it happen here, John, do you think? The Communists will stop at the border, won't they?'

Adelaide got in first. 'Of course they will! This is British territory. And even if they don't, we have the British Army in the New Territories to stop them.' She glared at Huart with innate authority. 'And we have our very own army general right here to show them how it's done.'

Huart smiled good-naturedly. 'Don't worry, Paulette. Hong Kong's claim to its piece of China is legally quite different to Shanghai where no foreign country had any jurisdiction after 1943. Mao will stop at the border.' He lifted his head and surveyed the diners. Yes, there was a tinge of desperation in the air. People were talking too loudly, laughing too easily, trying too hard to appear relaxed. Hong Kong was indeed on edge. 'And to make sure of it, I've just heard that two squadrons of Spitfires and one of Sunderlands have just flown in.'

Adelaide examined the place, and frowned at a trio of Englishmen in a corner drinking San Miguel from dark green bottles and remembering the war years in voices that carried. At the next table four American Navy petty officers guffawed as a joke reached its punch line, then wiped curry from their mouths with white napkins and tucked them, streaked yellow-brown, back into their collars. 'What sort of a place have you brought us to, John?' she asked indignantly. 'Since when did you start frequenting doubtful establishments? Look at the menu – it's dog-eared! What on earth is mulligatawny soup? I've never heard of it.'

'It's an Indian dish, Mother,' answered Paulette. 'It's rather spicy.' She smiled to herself. 'It should suit you nicely.'

Adelaide either missed or ignored the jibe. 'Indian, you say? This is not even a British restaurant, John?'

'Adelaide . . .' Huart postulated with the appropriate mix of firmness and respect, 'it's time we looked to our resources. There's little income from Hong Kong and with the blockade there is even less from Shanghai. And Canton, the last branch office in China that is still operating, is scaling down as the Communists move south. If something doesn't change for the better – and very soon – we'll have to start doing something drastic about our overheads here. The first to be trimmed – by order of myself – will be certain luxuries, such as expensive dinners. This is really a fine restaurant at reasonable fare. It's one of my favourites. Now, why don't you try the stuffed trout? It's a house speciality. Or the port wine duck? We've kept the waiter hovering long enough.'

Adelaide pursed her lips and blinked. 'The waiter? Isn't it his job to wait?' She squinted up at the little man in a starched white coat who was standing patiently at her elbow with pencil and order pad in hand, then back at Huart. 'I'm not even the slightest bit convinced, John. Look over there – that woman just has to be a prostitute.'

Despite himself Huart found his eyes involuntarily following her stare to a couple ordering their meal two tables away. The man was elderly, Eurasian and impeccably dressed in evening wear. His head was large and round and topped with thinning, oiled hair. His *cheongsam*-clad female companion was pure Cantonese and much younger, but not young, her beauty over-accentuated with rouge and eyebrow pencil.

An amused half-smile found its way to Huart's face. 'That gentleman is none other than Sir Bartholomew Orr. The Orr family has owned the Cathay Electric Corporation – Hong Kong's power utility, no less – ever since its inception. He's the chairman of it. The lady with him is one of his wives, but I'm not sure which one. So you see, Adelaide, Sir Bartholomew Orr, knighted by King George for his services on behalf of the prisoners in Shamshuipo camp as their go-between throughout the Japanese occupation, does not regard this restaurant as beneath his taste.'

But this only made Adelaide release one more snort. 'His Majesty is able to make a mistake just like any other man.' She slapped the two-part menu closed and fixed the waiter with such a look that he backed off six inches. 'My good man, I desire a T-bone steak, if you please.'

'Oh yes, madam. How you like steak done?'

'In this heat? Rare, of course. How else?'

As usual, Huart found the food to his liking, and judging by the absence of criticism, so did the two ladies. Over coffee he chose to return to the subject of economy. 'Tomorrow I will be checking out of my room in the Gloucester and moving over to the Cecil – '

'The Cecil?' Adelaide grimaced. 'That dosshouse?'

Huart nodded. 'Yes, "that dosshouse". It's good enough for me, and it's also closer to the office.'

Paulette nodded uncertainly. 'I hear the tariff at the Gloucester is going up again . . .' She knew they should move also, but did not wish it.

Adelaide said nothing.

Huart changed the subject again whilst noting that disquiet continued to blemish Paulette's features as she wondered how much longer they could keep the suites in the Gloucester. He, himself, was thinking further ahead: wondering how much longer they could survive in Hong Kong at all.

5

The idea came to Huart only after he had been studying the agency files through the entire day. When it did, he stepped to the map of Asia that dressed the rear wall of his office and extended a tape measure from Hong Kong to Taipei, then from Hong Kong to Manila, then to Djakarta, Singapore, Saigon, Pnom Penh, Vientiane and Bangkok. 'It is so,' he affirmed to himself. 'Hong Kong is the hub of a wheel. Its spokes reach out to every capital city in South East Asia. Yes, it makes sense.'

He sat down and picked the top file from the stack on his desk. It was the agency file for Golden State Cement Corporation of California. He opened it and began to read it again, clause by detailed clause.

All company records had been lost in the Japanese occupation, but that had not stopped Francis Roboza. In 1945 he had set about painstakingly rewriting them all from memory. It had taken months. The new 'records' were imperfect, but provided a base on which the Hong Kong branch office could function. Huart acknowledged the situation would be impossible if not for the Portuguese accountant's diligence and excellent recall.

On the *Queen Mary* he had had visions of business deals, entre-preneurial triumphs, profits, the good life. But those visions had been lit by the glow of Andrew's magic and the hearth of the Broadway Mansions apartment. Now that glow flickered near death. Andrew was alone in Shanghai, fighting for survival, using every atom of his skill and experience. Huart was alone in Hong Kong, also fighting but with no experience upon which to draw, his skill untested.

From its base in Shanghai, Cumberland China had prospered from great and multifarious business. But in Hong Kong it was all but unemployed. Here it owned no property, no factories or mills, no mines and no silk or tea plantations. Here it managed no utilities, laundries, breweries or apartment blocks. Here it imported little and exported nothing. In Hong Kong there was a transportation industry of sorts, centred around one single-track twenty mile government-administered railway to the border. The harbour was busy, but Cumberland China's shipping agencies were confined to the 'territory' of China, with Hong Kong excluded. An agent called Male & Son and Company, Limited held the local franchise for most of the American and European lines for which Cumberland China had serviced the Yangtse Valley trade through Shanghai for over seven decades. Charles Huart must have considered his most southern outpost too insignificant an item for inclusion in his agency agreements.

Though keepers of a population of two million, the Hong Kong Government, convinced the bulk of it was transient and would return to China once the civil war ended, was not announcing any housing policy. But Huart was not so certain this was correct. Amongst the refugees were wealthy and capable businessmen from Shanghai, Ningpo, Foochow, Amoy, Swatow and Canton who would not return to a land controlled by communists. They would stay and seek to carry on the profession they had inherited from their fathers and their grandfathers. They would set up factories and employ workers. There would follow a demand for housing, a market for construction materials, engineering equipment, contracting services . . .

He had almost laughed out loud at himself. 'How the devil do I know? Who am I anyway – if not a retired infantry general landed on the bones of my behind in a place ceded from a country on whose own behind it sticks like a bug, praying it won't be sat upon and squashed out of existence.'

The idea, nevertheless, had been tangential to his original train of thought. It had taken root when he had opened the Golden State Cement file and read that the company made no cement itself, but designed and fabricated entire production plants. Its agency may thus be inapplicable to present day Hong Kong, Huart had told himself, but what about elsewhere? UN aided rebuilding programmes were in full swing all over the region: Taiwan, the Philippines, French Indo-China, Cambodia, Laos, Thailand, Malaya, all of which would need cement plants. And what other equipment could Cumberland China offer through its existing agencies?

Huart worked late that night, examining every engineering agency file in the office. By midnight he had shortlisted four others, all British: Rosefair and Benson of Leicester: soya bean and peanut oil processing plants, Lionel Hope and Sons of Belfast: jute and cotton mills, Harold Soames of Wigan: flour and sugar mills, and Frobisher-Cash of Leeds: textile machinery. Like Golden State Cement, each was an international leader in its respective field. Attached to the inside front cover of each file was a hand-written facsimile of the original Agency Agreement, reproduced as closely as Roboza's memory had been able. All had been 'signed' by Charles Roland Huart and by each principal's authorised representative between 1890 and 1910, seemingly an active period for the founder. Under the clause headed 'Territory', licence was limited to 'All the Provinces of China, and the Crown Colony of Hong Kong', except in two cases where the tiny Portuguese enclave of Macau had been added.

'Well, nothing ventured . . .' Huart drafted letters to each manufacturer seeking authority for Cumberland China to solicit business in other Asian countries and for those countries to be added to the Agency Agreement. He finished at three in the morning. Roboza came at nine to find Huart waiting for him with the drafts. 'Have all these typed, Francis, please, and deliver them to the GPO by close of business today.'

'Air mail, sir?'

Huart thought about it, then nodded. 'The urgency justifies the expense. This new air service between England and Hong Kong only takes a week.'

Later that morning, with the office filled with the clacking of the typewriters as two of the male clerks made heavy weather of his letters, Huart asked Roboza: 'Who ran the Insurance Department before the war?'

'Mr Daubney put Mr Bedrix in charge.'

Huart nodded. Colin Daubney, the director sent from Nanking in 1938 to take over in Hong Kong, had obviously shared the high opinion he had gained during his brief encounter with Gilbert Dole's young assistant in August, 1937. The ill-fated Daubney had died in action with the Hong Kong Volunteers on Christmas Eve, 1941. 'What happened to Mr Bedrix?'

Roboza shrugged. 'He went to England in 1940 and enlisted in the RAF. He flew Hurricanes. He only wrote to us once. Perhaps . . . he was killed.'

'Perhaps.' Probably, Huart corrected himself. 1940 RAF fighter pilots were a breed virtually extinct. 'Do you have his address in England?'

'I'll check, sir.'

Huart sat in his office and hoped until Roboza came in with a memo on which he had typed a Leicestershire address. He stared at it. If Bedrix was alive and willing to return, he was the man to recover the branch's insurance business. But could the company afford him? Gilbert Dole was no longer drawing salary, and he himself had only taken reimbursement for business-related expenses since August 1st and was now living on personal savings. He thought ruefully once again of the 10,000 sterling frozen in Shanghai, then scribbled sums on his desk-top blotter until he made it cost in. Minus Dole and himself, plus Bedrix, equalled a net 'saving' in the monthly payroll. He drafted a telegram.

POSITION HONGKONG BRANCH INSURANCE DEPARTMENT MANAGER STILL OPEN STOP SUGGEST YOU APPLY SOONEST STOP CONFIRM BY RETURN CABLE STOP

JOHN HUART — CUMBERLAND CHINA LTD — HONG KONG —
23.8.49

'Send this cable by runner to Electra House at once, please, Francis.'

Roboza read it. 'I will go to church tonight and pray, Mr Huart.'

The blue and white return envelope came a week later. Huart tore it open and his eyes took in the truncated message in one sweep.

YOURS 23RD INST STOP JERRY TOOK LEFT ARM IN 1941 STOP DO YOU WANT ONE-ARMED MANAGER? STOP

BEDRIX 26.8.49

[152]

Huart drafted an immediate reply.

IF RIGHT HAND CAN WRITE INSURANCE POLICIES YOU'RE
WANTED STOP AIRMAILING P AND O TICKET TODAY STOP
ACKNOWLEDGE SOONEST STOP

HUART 31.8.49

'It will be good to have Mr Bedrix back,' Roboza smiled happily.
'He was a good man. Very efficient. Oh, will it be a first class
ticket?'

Huart hesitated. 'I'd like nothing better than to have Clive
Bedrix return to Hong Kong in style. But the situation demands
economy.' He saw the office manager's sad nod. 'So buy a first
class ticket, Francis, and debit the premium over the second class
fare to my personal account.'

6

The brain of Andrew Huart-Brent was possessed by abstract
philosophies, the most prominent being a conviction that moods
had colours, that of despondency being deep grey with red pin
stripes.

If the third taipan of Cumberland China had been in control
of his faculties he would have been glad his office door was locked
and the world could not see him like this. He was sitting slumped
forward in the leather chair from which he had run his *hong*, given
interruptions, since 1932. His head drooped to hover inches above
his desk. His eyes tried to focus on the grain patterns in the wood,
but the lines merged until they disappeared and his brain reverted
to another world where dream figures from his memory floated
aimlessly before his eyes. The fingers of his right hand were
around the empty famille rose teacup that had contained the last
of his stock of Johnny Walker. It was the only item intact of his
mother's collection of Ching Dynasty porcelain which, too fragile
to carry out of Shanghai, had been assigned to his care. His left
hand hung on the end of his left arm somewhere below the chair.
He was like a decaying vegetable that was once the pick of the
crop.

It was almost eleven a.m., Friday, October 21st. Three weeks had gone by since the day the bombastic proclamation had been made before him by the representative of the 'Workers' Committee' that the People's Republic of China had been proclaimed in Peking by Comrade Chairman Mao Tse-tung.

Mao. Mao-Mao-Mao-Mao! The name threatened the last of Andrew's sanity. He would surely go stark raving mad if he was ever to hear it again.

Almost a week had passed since news had come of the fall of Canton.

And still Attlee refused to recognise the new government in China. Still he ignored the flow of telegrams from Shanghai, all sent from Cumberland Building. If Andrew knew the prime minister's aides laughed as loudly as they fed his protestations into the Downing Street shredder as the Chinese censors who reworded them, it would have put an end to him.

And still the white-sunned bombers dropped their loads on the Whangpoo docks. Still the blockade kept the trading ships from the Yangtse, and Whitehall protested the obstruction to commerce with chronic silence. Still the order of the day for Andrew Huart-Brent was – nothing.

His nostrils twitched as he smelled something bad. It was some time before he could accept that it was himself. Had he bathed this week? He screwed up his face at his foul breath and the gasses from his tortured bowel and lifted his head. Too quickly. His senses reeled. He grasped the edge of his desk with both hands in panic. His heart kicked and began to thump against his ribcage. Soon the palpitations subsided, as they always did. But then the nausea surged in his gut and he pushed himself to his feet and lurched to the bathroom.

After he had vomited into the toilet bowl until there was only bile in his stomach, he felt better. He pulled the chain. Nothing happened. He pulled it again and again. Still nothing happened. There was no flushing water. He picked up the bucket, placed it in the wash basin and spun the tap. Nothing happened. He twisted it to its limit, then more. It came off in his hand. A single drop fell into the basin. It was a rusty red-brown. They had turned off all the running water to the fourth floor.

Andrew Huart-Brent began to cry. He slid down the wall into a squatting position and put his head in his hands. His fingertips touched the cold, smooth, hairless skin. Oh God in heaven above! He was living in an alien moribund body. What had he done that was so bad that it warranted such penance? For the first time in his life the third taipan of Cumberland China admitted defeat. He looked to the ceiling, to the unseen heavens beyond and cried out for help. But it was not to the Almighty that he appealed. He staggered back to his office and looked up at the portrait.

'Grandfather! Tell them to ease up, for the love of Christ! Tell Chiang. Tell Attlee. Everyone listened when you were chairman of the Municipal Council. It can't end like this! I'll be remembered as a failure. Grandfather! I need more time! I have no son to take over. There can never be a son . . .' His voice broke into a chuckle that cracked into a laugh and ended in a coughing spasm. 'Ha, Grandfather – we're both failures there, aren't we! We're two . . . of a kind in that, aren't we! But rather you and me, than . . . poor John. To have two sons – and lose both. Oh, poor John!'

A sob surged in his throat. He bit down on it. 'You know I'm sorry about Ching-hsu, Grandfather. You know I'm sorry about Elizabeth Jane, too. I couldn't stop it. You know how Mother is. She's like you, Grandfather. You wanted a son so much she became a man for you. She sent them away! I wasn't even here! When I got back from England they'd gone. She sent them away before I came back. I didn't know! I don't know where they are. I can't find them! I failed at that, too, Grandfather . . .'

Suddenly it was quiet. In the absence of the pleading wail that had come from deep inside him to obliterate every other sound in the world, it was as if his life had ended and he was shut in his tomb. The Bund was quiet below. The harbour was silent; only sailing junks and sampans used it now and they made no noise. It was deathly, deadly quiet. Except for the hum in his ears that would tell him he was sick if he ever listened.

Then through the hum, from down below, came a stamping of feet that grew stronger. The floorboards began to vibrate. The walls seemed to sway in rhythm. STOMP-STOMP-STOMP-STOMP! Then came the chanting. Louder. They were coming closer. Louder still. They were coming up the stairs to the taipan's domain. Was nothing sacred any more? They were coming for him!

'No! No! No! Noooooooo . . . !'

Andrew Huart-Brent screamed at the top of his voice. But the stamping feet and the relentless chanting and the rattling of the furniture and the broken crockery like a dance of skeletons overpowered his utterance.

John Huart read with satisfaction the letter under the masthead of the Golden State Cement Corporation, written by Charles F.

Kreitzer, Vice President Marketing. It had been the last of the five replies to come in and it was the best. Rosefair and Benson and Harold Soames had agreed to include all Asian countries in Cumberland China's 'territory' for a trial period of two years. Lionel Hope and Frobisher-Cash had restricted approval to Taiwan, the Philippines and Indo-China as they already had agents for Singapore, Malaya and Thailand. But Kreitzer excluded only the Philippines where, he explained, Golden State Cement was already active. He, like Rex Wagoner, was interested in Taiwan (he still called it Formosa), and offered to fund a marketing report on the country to be compiled on a visit there of not more than two weeks, provided it was verified by a *bona fide* national purchasing authority.

'Grand stuff!' Huart cried aloud to his empty office. He reached out to call Air Asia-Pacific and check their flight schedule to Taipei. The telephone rang as his fingers made contact.

A call from Andrew was immediately identifiable by the plum voice of the public school educated operator employed by the Telephone Company to handle international connections. 'Is that Mr John Huart. H-U-A-R-T?'

'It is.'

'A call for you from Shanghai, Mr Huart. A Mr Huart-Brent. He wishes to reverse the charges. Will you accept?'

'Of course.' The patter was identical every time.

'Connecting you now. Hold on, please.' There followed a pause before: 'Go ahead, Mr Huart-Brent. Mr John Huart is on the line now.'

The static coursed down the landline. Huart listened hard for Andrew's voice. But this time there came a noise like a warped incantation, as if the line was connected to an undersea cable. Then there was an unintelligible whisper, followed by a hammering sound. 'Andrew? Hello? Hello? Andrew, is that you?' Huart listened harder. The warped noise was again broken by the hammering, and once he thought he heard laughter. 'Hello? Hello? Who is it? Hello?' He decided the line was out of order and was about to hang up when he heard the two words break the static.

'Send . . . Money . . . '

Huart pressed the receiver into his ear. 'Andrew? Andrew, is that you?'

'Yes.' The voice was weak, but now the warped sound had died away.

'Andrew, what's happening? What's all that noise?'

There was a pause. Then the whisper came back. 'Staff . . .

union. Hundred outside . . . door singing . . . Mao songs. Won't let . . . me go. Say . . . take me before . . . People's Court if . . . don't get what they want . . . today . . .'

'What is it they want, Andrew?' Huart shouted. 'What do . . . ?' There was coughing, then silence as if the line had gone dead. 'Hello? Hello?'

A crackle, then: 'John, please shut up and listen!' Andrew's voice was suddenly very clear. 'They're demanding a salary increase backdated to the Jap surrender. They want the arrears paid in a lump sum. Today.'

'But that's outrageous. Why? Why are they asking for that?'

'Don't use up time asking questions, John. Please. I'm . . . I'm at the end of my tether. I've been locked in my office for a week. A week, I said. They won't let me out until I accept their demands. I'm out of food. Now they've turned off the running water. Send money, John! Today!'

'How much do you need?'

'They've worked it out at forty-seven thousand pounds. I have it all here except twelve thousand. But it cleans me out. I want you to send up twenty thousand sterling. Telegraphic transfer. Today.'

Huart swallowed hard. 'But how can they force such a claim on you?'

'The arbitrator arrives in an hour. He's a bastard. He'd agree with their claim if it was forty-seven million! It's been going on for ten days now! Three days negotiating – then they locked me in my office. My own bloody office, I tell you! Send the money, John! Please. Today.'

Huart swallowed again. 'This afternoon. I'll send it this afternoon!'

'Thank you, John. I – ' There was a loud crackle.

'Andrew, are you alright?'

Silence.

'Andrew? Andrew! Are you alright? Andr . . .'

'Have you finished, sir?' the plum voice asked.

'What? No! I haven't finished. Why are you on the line?'

'Your party has rung off, sir.'

'Rung off? We were disconnected! Get him back for me quickly, please!'

'I'm sorry, sir. There's a waiting list for calls to Shanghai.'

'How long is the list?'

'At least a week, sir.'

Huart groaned. He hung up and went to look for Roboza, his

heart banging like a piston. He was not sure if there was twenty thousand pounds sterling in the accounts. He felt an intangible something closing about him, pushing down on him. The words of Sir Robert Hart came to him and he swore at them and tried to erase them from the blackboard of his mind.

7

The British Bank of Asia, Hong Kong Branch, handed down its judgement without saying a word. Seated beside Roboza on the bench outside the door stencilled with H.M.G. HARRISFORD-HOUSE – CREDIT MANAGER, Huart watched others come and go as the big hand on his pocket watch completed a full revolution past the appointed time.

'They give us no face,' Roboza said lugubriously. 'We've had an account with the BBA here in Des Voeux Road, Central as long as I can remember.'

Hector Harrisford-House finally proved to be a rotund florid Cornishman in his late forties. Though of average height he seemed taller than he was due to an accentuated wave in his hair that stood above his brow like a family crest. His eyes were less prominent, encased in twin rolls of flesh that gave him a porcine appearance. Huart disliked him on sight, yet berated himself for not having met his banker earlier, at a time when his cap had been on his head instead of in his hand.

The credit manager peered obtrusively at the clock as he seated himself behind his substantial desk, whilst Huart and Roboza took lesser chairs before it. The parquet floor seemed to slope towards the door and this, plus the crest, conferred upon Harrisford-House an illusion of superior elevation as he made a meal of studying the two who had come before him. Both seemed out of place to him. The letter that had precipitated the meeting, signed by someone called Huart – that had to be the big one – had revealed an innocence in matters financial. The other one – well, he was Portuguese, wasn't he? A meal Harrisford-House's appraisal certainly was, like that of a butcher faced with two sides of beef and uncertain which should first be selected for carving. 'Your letter applying for an overdraft facility, Mr Huart, prompted me to check the history of your company's account. As far as I

[158]

can see it goes back a long way – to well before the war. I've been unable to determine exactly when. Records lost in the darned occupation. You know how it is . . .'

'Since 1913, Mr Harrisford-House,' Huart injected emphatically. It was a reasonable guess, being the year Cumberland China had registered its Hong Kong branch office as a separate company.

The credit manager grunted. 'Indeed? As long ago as that, eh? Well . . .'

A silence came. Huart, confident in the guise of a client of long standing, was about to break it when Harrisford-House cleared his throat and continued: 'You seem to be suffering from an outflow of funds. In fact, you have a red mark against you. Very bad – a red mark. You see, we keep a graph of each account. It shows the trend. It's quite a good system, really. By extrapolating the graph we can look into the future and see what lies ahead. In your case, Mr Huart – ' He ran the tip of a finger over a file on his desk, then looked down his nose from his height.

Huart was incensed. What a pompous –

'In your case, we deduce from your graph that you will be overdrawn in a matter of weeks.' The eyebrows arched above the wrinkled flesh and the whites of the eyes poked out and gleamed.

'Then you can see why we have now applied for an overdraft.' Huart felt, rather than saw, Roboza's warning glance. It was well placed. His tone had been aggressive, but the banker had also been out of line. Then he remembered a Sinclair MacLurie adage: 'A banker is like a desirable woman. They both sit on a gold mine. Treat them one and the same.' He decided to change his approach. But he knew he was already too late.

Harrisford-House's eyes harboured a school-masterly lack of mercy as his head nodded slowly up and down. 'Indeed. A quarter of a million dollars. But you don't mention how long you require the facility.'

'Why . . . permanently.' Huart smiled politely. 'An oversight. Sorry.'

'You're applying for a standby facility, then?'

'That's correct.'

'I see. Hmmm.'

Harrisford-House pursed his lips and lowered his head as if studying the file again. Huart waited. Roboza clasped and unclasped his fingers. Finally the banker cleared his throat. 'What is the life expectancy of the cash outflow? In your letter you mention the expense of maintaining your head office in Shanghai. How long do you expect it to continue?'

[159]

Huart had his answer ready. 'Until trade resumes under the new Chinese government. The managing director has remained in Shanghai to be in a position to start business as soon as . . .' Was that raw scepticism on the banker's face? Pangs of alarm prodded his insides. He ignored them and carried on. ' . . . as soon as Britain recognises the new government in Peking and the Nationalist blockade on the Yangtse is lifted.'

'You have inside information on when all this might happen?'

'Of course not.'

Harrisford-House's smile was unmistakably indulgent. Huart's annoyance resurfaced. Who was the customer, anyway? He fought down his ire. In this office it was misplaced. He was losing fast.

'Mr Huart, this bank has half its assets still in Shanghai – and in Tientsin, and in Hankow . . . Shall I go on? It is unnecessary, surely. If you wish, I'll tell you what we think will happen up there. And when.' Huart could think of nothing suitable to say. Harrisford-House seized on his helplessness and added: 'Let's confine ourselves to Hong Kong this morning, shall we? What steps have you taken to expand your base here?'

Huart told of his rehiring of Clive Bedrix and how he expected him quickly to have a positive effect on the branch's insurance business, and of his plan to seek out engineering contracts in other Asian countries.

'When do you expect these steps to contribute to your cash position?'

'That's difficult to predict. With advance commissions, perhaps four months, perhaps six. We need the facility to carry us until then.'

'Two hundred and fifty thousand Hong Kong dollars. Right?'

'Correct.'

'Hmmm. How many contracts did you say you've secured?'

'Er . . . none, as yet. I'm travelling to Taiwan next week.'

'To sign a contract?'

'Er . . . no. To commence a market study. For the Golden State Cement Corporation of California. We are now their exclusive agents for Taiwan as well as for Hong Kong, you see. That's a recent development which – '

'They are paying you a retainer in advance?'

'Er . . . no. But they will reimburse us. They are a well-known American corporation. No doubt you have heard of them . . ?'

Harrisford-House ignored the question. 'To commence a market study? In Taiwan? You have not started any contract negotiations yet? At all?'

Huart tried unsuccessfully to hide his act of swallowing. 'No. Not yet.'

'Hmmmmmm.'

Another silence. The banker's eyebrows arched again; the whites of his eyes projected. 'What security will you put up to cover the facility?'

Huart frowned. He really had not expected this. 'Security? But we have banked with you for the past thirty-six years, Mr Harrisford-House. Surely you're not telling me you require a security against our first application for credit after all that time? Surely not – '

The credit manager leaned forward. He looked up at the clock. He sighed. He peered down at the legs of the two chairs. When he spoke it was as if he was telling a retarded child how to respond to the call of nature. 'We have held an account in the name – I repeat, in the name – of your company for some time, yes. But, Mr Huart, there has been a world war. Perhaps you read of it in the newspapers? Not only that, there has also been a revolution in China and the Communists seem to have won it. Very many companies who have been based in China for very many years have disappeared off the face of the earth leaving behind overdrafts showing very large sums in very bright red figures. Your company is – like every other company in your predicament – not the same as it was. If it was, you wouldn't be here, would you? Therefore, Mr Huart, your application for an overdraft facility is being processed by this bank as if we'd never heard of Cumberland China Limited. I'm sure you understand. The graph, remember? Now, what security . . ?'

Huart was tumbling head over heels in a maelstrom of impotence and he was disliking the unprecedented sensation intensely. He chastised himself again. Too late another of his father-in-law's gems came to mind: 'A banker is only too happy to offer you credit the moment you produce solid evidence that it is not really needed.' He could think of nothing better to ask than: 'What would constitute an acceptable security, Mr Harrisford-House?' But he knew what the answer had to be and wondered why he was even bothering to prolong the interview.

'Does your company own any property in Hong Kong?'

That part of Huart's 1937 interrogation of Gilbert Dole came back to him like a prophecy of doom. 'No, we do not.'

'Your office is still leased after thirty-six years?'

'It is. And the rent is paid on time. Every month. You may check that with Victoria Land. I'm sure they'll attest to our punctu-

[161]

ality.' Huart knew his tone was testy and that he was being petulant, but he was past caring. He was rudely aware that he had
failed miserably in his gambit to buy vital time for Cumberland
China from the British Bank of Asia.

The sterility of the banker's half-smile confirmed it. 'That won't
be necessary, Mr Huart. You, yourself, also live in rented
accommodation?'

'I, myself, live in the Hotel Cecil.'

'Oh, I see. Hmmm. Your company holds certificates of stock?
Or bonds . . ?'

Huart looked at Roboza who shook his head.

'Any assets or merchandise that could be mortgaged?'

Huart sighed. 'Mr Harrisford-House, I think any further extension of this audience will only prove an insult to all involved in
it.' With thumb and forefinger he picked his felt hat from his knee
and stood up. 'Thank you for your time. No doubt you will be
sending your official reply to our application in due course.'

The Credit Manager, British Bank of Asia watched the backs
of the big Englishman with the military bearing and his unfortunate
Portuguese accountant exit through the side door. Then he picked
up the file on his desk and fingered the blob of red wax at the
top right hand corner. 'Hmmmmm,' he breathed. 'Official reply
coming up, Mr Huart.' He held the file between thumb and
forefinger over his wastepaper basket. And dropped it. 'Next!' he
shouted at the door in the facing wall.

The small wraith-like man in long-gown and cloth slippers had
been resting in the shade of the entrance to Lane Crawford on Des
Voeux Road, Central for several minutes. He supported himself by
propping a shoulder against a marble-clad wall and by tucking a
walking stick into one hip. The autumn sunshine was sharp and
clean and hurt his eyes as he squinted up and down the pavement
at the procession of foreign devils who paid him no heed. He did
not like being in Central District; it was an alien place. But the
banks were here and they would not come to him.

From this day on that would be different. He had just bought
one.

Despite the glare of the sunlight, the man with the walking stick
caught sight of the tall, broad-shouldered Englishman coming
towards him from a distance. He saw the business suit of thick
yarn and the felt hat square on the large head. He took note of
the long strides that brought the oversized foreign devil towards

him at speed. He glanced at the shorter, thinner Portuguese scurrying to keep pace. Then he looked back and up.

And Tu Chien grabbed hold of the handle of his walking stick with both hands to prevent himself from keeling over upon the pavement of Des Voeux Road, Central in shock. And he pushed himself against the wall to stop himself from stumbling into the path of the execrable foreign devil giant who had ordered the death of his first-born son and his third concubine, and who had fired the bullet that still festered in his hip.

The Kompo man further back in the shadows and dressed like a banking executive took a half step towards his *dai lo baan*, then stopped himself and looked out to the pavement.

Tu Chien willed his enemy to pass right on by. He need not have worried. The giant strode past the Lane Crawford doorway with an aggressive step, as if a consuming anger lived within him. Tu Chien read the map of vexation on the hated face as it passed and looked into the hated eyes that seemed to stare ahead without focus.

When the giant and his companion had gone twenty yards, Tu Chien stepped onto Des Voeux Road and hobbled after them. In contrast to his quarry's telegraphic mien, he tightened his facial muscles and gave no hint of the extent of the pain his hip was generating with each hurried step.

Huart and Roboza turned right into Ice House Street. By the time Tu Chien reached the corner they were climbing the steps into the three-storey building on the corner of Queen's Road, Central. He stopped, panting, and nodded to the building as the Kompo man went past him. He watched the man run up the steps as he leaned upon his stick and wiped the sweat from his brow with a silk handkerchief. The pain gradually dissipated, leaving behind it a smile that almost reached his face as he effusively thanked his gods.

8

'Taiwan sure is my private playground, Big Fella! Oh, Yessirree!' Rex Wagoner had to shout to be heard over the twin engines of the DC3, despite being jammed against Huart two rows from the front of the cabin. 'I been payin' quite a bit of attention to the place lately. It's sure the spot right now. Money galore. All lifted out o' China and lookin' for a pocket to slip into.' He fished out a pack of Camels and lit one.

Huart peered out at the uneven cloud and estimated that they would reach the coast of southern Taiwan in ten minutes. News of the defection of eleven China National Aviation Company aircraft had persuaded Wagoner to leave his Lockheed F5 in Hong Kong; the Kuomintang airforce would be skittish enough to take an unscheduled aircraft as communist. Having vital business in Taipei, he found himself beside Huart on the Air Asia-Pacific mail run to Kaohsiung, from where they were to take the train to Taipei.

Conversation had been stilted at first. But after several slugs of Jack Daniel's from a hip flask, and given the opportunity to expound on a subject dear to him, Wagoner was quickly into his stride. 'In Taiwan, Big Fella, money talks loudest. Find the right KMT general and you'll settle it all quick fast. Try to do it the conventional way and you'll beat your brains out against a brick wall and get nowhere slow. Savvy?'

Huart gave a perfunctory nod.

'You want to flog cement plants, eh? General Wen Wei-tung's your man.'

'You know him?'

'Sure do.'

Huart closed his eyes and listened to the roar of the engines beating against his eardrums. A full minute passed this way.

'Okay?' Wagoner demanded.

Huart opened one eye. 'Okay what?'

'General Wen Wei-tung. D'ya wanna meet him or no?'

'Sounds like a good idea, Wagoner. What's in it for you?'

'Learnin', ain'tcha. General Wen'll pay me a slice of his cut. And Pan Atlantic gets the insurance on any contract you land in Taiwan.' The American raised the unstoppered hip flask. 'Deal?' He took a swallow.

Huart opened the other eye. 'Deal, Wagoner.' What was there to lose? He peered out the window, seeking a glimpse of the Taiwan coast through gaps in the cloud, and saw it the instant the P51 with the white sun insignia opened fire with a burst of tracer that skimmed the port wing.

There was a full second of nothingness, then the DC3 lunged into a dive.

'What the . . !' Wagoner's head was everywhere until he saw the P51 climbing to attack again. 'Oh sweet Jesus!' he yelled, then followed Huart in grabbing at his seat belt. 'What kinda KMT kites was it defected? C47s?'

'DC3s!' Huart gritted his teeth and hung on as they plummeted to earth with engines screaming and superstructure groaning in a babel of shouts, banging baggage, rattling trays and cutlery and smashing crockery.

'Same fuckin' difference!' Wagoner rolled his eyes. 'That Mustang jockey thinks this is a Commie spy plane! What odds we get out of this one?'

Huart's head banged against the fuselage as the DC3 weaved and dived, then pulled up short and climbed, then dived again. The fighter fired in short bursts on every pass. The twenty passengers, all male, cursed and looked about with wide, staring eyes. The man in front of Huart babbled unintelligibly and buried his head between his knees.

'Thank our lucky stars he's a poor shot!' Huart shouted with his face pressed to the window. 'Odds, Wagoner? Your insurance fully paid up?'

Wagoner snorted. 'Good joke, Big Fella! No worries! That Mustang'll be out o' ammo soon. Our Aussie flyboy's standin' this kite on its ass.'

For what seemed an age, but was in actuality only a few minutes, the DC3 continued to outmanoeuvre the fighter. It dived to the sea and levelled out with its propellers skimming the waves. It weaved violently, throwing the passengers about in their seats. Huart heard another burst of firing from behind and saw the tracer fly wide and kick up spray as the bullets hit the waves. The sea was rough, uninviting, but waiting for them. He heard the man in front vomit wretchedly over his feet.

Wagoner gave a brutal laugh. 'I say he's got about three seconds of ammo left! I been countin'. No worries. No goddamn worries!'

Huart could not believe it. Wagoner was enjoying himself. In the war he had known men like that and had wanted to be like them. Then they had told him about his family and he had not thought on it any more; he had become like them without realising it, with revenge the incentive to go on living. Life became an automatic process: breathing, eating, defecating, sleeping – day after day after day. He was alone and unafraid in a world gone mad. So what has changed? he asked himself as the DC3 wrenched to starboard and his head cracked painfully against the window. He thought of Andrew imprisoned in Shanghai, of the importance of this mission and how the survival of Cumberland China depended on it. And he knew he belonged again. He had some-

[165]

thing to live for. For the first time in seven years the icy fingertips of fear prodded his gut.

He glanced sideways at Wagoner trying to light a fresh Camel and thought of the quirks of fate that twist life in and out of shape. The American took this flight because of the risk of his own aeroplane being attacked. And what had happened? The Air Asia-Pacific DC3 had been set upon!

'Here he comes again!' someone shouted.

'Look out!' screamed someone else.

'Get yer bloody 'eads down!' It was the purser at the rear of the cabin.

'Not another goddamn Aussie!' Wagoner laughed, his cigarette now alight. 'This's his last shot. What odds he don't make it, Big Fella?'

Huart knew instinctively the sharp crack in his ear was the sound of a bullet with his name mis-spelt. He felt a cold draught on his face and saw the small round hole in the fuselage an inch from his nose. He looked again at Wagoner, and choked off a laugh. The cigarette was scattered over the American's lap with only the butt still between his lips. His eyes were round as he cried 'Shit!' and beat his crotch with his hands. Huart sniffed the smoke in the cabin and knew it was not burning cotton.

An anonymous voice cried: 'The engine's hit!'

'Sweet fuckin' Jesus!' Wagoner cursed, his eyes now exceedingly large.

Huart peered out the window to see the port engine trailing white smoke. The propeller came to a full stop as it was feathered and the DC3 lurched and dropped like a stone. The cabin echoed with wild shouts. The man in front was slumped forward. The P51 attached itself to the port wing tip. Wagoner had been correct. It was apparently out of ammunition.

'He's a double idiot,' Huart muttered. 'Fires on an innocent plane – ' His eyes searched the smoking engine for the flicker of flame that would spell the end. ' – now he wants to blow himself out of the sky.'

Their pilot was somehow keeping the DC3 steady, just above the ground. Green and brown fields flashed past. The door to the cockpit opened and the co-pilot poked his head out. 'Why 'aven't ya got ya parachutes on? If ya all 'ad one brain between ya it'd be bloody lonely! They're under ya seats. Get 'em out! Get 'em on!'

'Who the fuck's left in Australia?' Wagoner groaned.

Frantic hands searched for bundles beneath cramped seats. 'I say, how does one put one on one?' implored a voice made in Oxbridge.

The purser was on his feet assisting frantic passengers into parachutes. He fell on Wagoner as the DC3 suddenly dropped sideways towards the fields that looked so close. It lifted again and steadied and the purser pushed himself upright. 'Parachute, mate.' He pointed under the seat.

'Waste o' goddamn time. This kite'll never get altitude enough for anyone to bail out and live. Who d'you think you're kiddin', Aussie?'

The purser shrugged. 'Suit yourself, Yank.' He moved on to the seat in front and shook the slumped figure several times, then gave up.

Smoke was pouring from the port engine. The door to the cockpit opened again and the head of the co-pilot reappeared. 'Landin' strip ahead! 'Ave ya down in 'alf a mo'! She'll be jake!' A chorus of cheers fired back at him and he grinned and pulled his head back into the cockpit.

Huart pressed his face against the window. They were flying over what looked to him to be farms. Up ahead he could make out the brown furrow that was the only thing that could have been a landing strip. But it was far too narrow and far too short. 'Hang on!' he yelled, mostly to hear the sound of his own voice.

There was a whirring and a thud as the landing gear came down and locked into position. The DC3 dipped forward and seemed to hang just above the ground for an eternity. Then its wheels hit and it shuddered as if it might fall to pieces. Huart was thrown forward into his seat belt, then was jerked up and down as everything bounced, hit down, then bounced again. He saw the end of the runway loom and the DC3 was hauled into a sharp turn. Its wheels tore into long grass and he saw the propeller churn it up and throw it into the air like a thresher. Finally the DC3 slowed and at last came to a complete stop.

'Everybody out!' The purser leapt to the rear, yanked the lever down and shoved the door open.

Wagoner was into the aisle in an instant, his hands upon the backs of seats, pulling himself towards the rear. He shouldered men aside, his bulk projecting him onwards, the downward slope of the resting aircraft and the absence of the hindering parachute assisting his passage.

'Look out you b –' a man cursed as Wagoner cannoned into him.

'Outta my way, short ass!'

He was first out of the DC3, brushing past the purser who had stationed himself beside the open exit. He jumped to the ground and rolled through the grass, then sprang to his feet and sprinted away from the smoking aeroplane with long strides.

Huart was last out. He appeared with, in his arms, the unconscious form of the passenger from the seat in front. The man had only fainted. He handed him down, then jumped himself.

He found Wagoner sitting astride a bund of stones, a fresh Camel between the fingers of one hand, the hip flask grasped in the other. He held his head to one side as he peered up at the sky where the P51 circled.

'Welcome to Taiwan, Big Fella.'

'You Chicago chaps don't hang around,' Huart observed flatly.

Wagoner took a swig of Jack Daniels and a deep draw on his cigarette. 'My ol' man told me: "Always look out for Number One. No-one else's ever gonna do it for you". My ol' man taught me a lotta things, but there's one thing I learnt for myself.' He peered up at Huart through narrowed eyelids. 'Heroes rate a goddamn heavy insurance premium, Big Fella.'

The close darkness with its heady incense fell upon Huart the instant he followed Wagoner through the semi-circular wooden door with its dragonhead bronze hinges. For several seconds he tried to work out how the door had opened inwards, until he felt the soft fingers on his forearm and he looked down a long way into a pair of almond eyes that glistened in the flickering of a lantern which was giving some belated illumination. He took a step and his head connected with a beam. Whatever this place was, it had not been built to accommodate seventy-seven inch men.

'General Wen?' Wagoner called out. 'Are you in here somewhere?'

A bamboo curtain parted and two silhouettes stood in the glow of another lantern hanging in a cubicle. Huart heard Wagoner's intake of breath. Then he blinked himself and looked again at the outlines of the twin long haired nymphs: very petite, very smoothly curved, very naked.

They were holding the curtain open and beckoning with fingers tipped in stiletto nails. Wagoner went between them, and Huart followed into the cubicle where the incense was even headier. There, reclining on cushions and smoking a long pipe, was a high-ranking Kuomintang officer. Huart's eyes went instinctively to the epaulette where the three stars glinted.

'I welcome you back to Taipei, Mr Wagoner. It is excellent to see you again. And this must be Major-General Huart.' The voice was immediately notable for its exaggerated aspiration of its 't's. The head was slicked with oiled hair which shone as it nodded to cushions on each side. 'Please sit.'

Wagoner hesitated and glanced back at Huart, surprised. 'General Wen,' he acknowledged as he sat down. 'Interesting little club you have here.'

Wen Wei-tung smiled quickly and Huart detected his ease with foreigners plus an assumed sophistication. 'I call this my private "business club", Mr Wagoner. It is distant enough from my office to ensure discretion.'

'Business club is it? Then these must be your secretaries, I reckon.' Wagoner grinned wolfishly up and down each of the two nymphs who stood either side of the entrance. They lowered their eyes before him, but at the corners of their lotus bud mouths experience gestured fleetingly.

'What do you wish to drink, gentlemen?' Wen asked.

'Jack Daniels,' replied Wagoner. 'On the rocks.'

The Kuomintang general put aside his pipe and turned to look at Huart with his eyebrows slightly raised. This made his eyes, already narrow, more elliptical, and his mien became thoroughly oriental.

'Jasmine tea, please, General Wen.' Huart spoke for the first time. 'I thank you very much for your hospitality.'

Wen nodded, seemingly quite satisfied with it, and spoke in rapid lilting Mandarin. The nymphs bowed and slipped away. Wagoner's eyes flicked from one derrière to the other and made their choice. Wen saw it.

'It is an honour to meet you, Major-General Huart,' Wen said, and Huart saw out of the corner of his eye the surprise return to Wagoner's face, this time competing with a subdued annoyance.

'The honour is mine, General Wen. But how do you know my army rank?'

'You are too modest.' Wen smiled. 'You do not remember – or I must have changed too much. Indeed, it has been over seven years.'

'We have met before?'

Wen nodded. 'In Burma. I was Generalissimo Chiang's *aide-de-camp* at the conference in Lashio with General Wavell and General Stillwell. You were present. You seemed to have much on your mind at the time.'

Huart lowered his head. 'Yes . . . I do remember – ' He looked up. 'I do remember you, General Wen. You had no moustache then.'

Wen laughed. 'Your memory is excellent.' The aspiration cut the air like a dart. 'The Generalissimo told me all about you. Indeed he spoke of you to all on his personal staff. He was of the opinion you were the only British officer in Shanghai with any real courage. I have no doubt he retains that opinion. Having now met you, I share it.'

Huart's mouth opened. 'General Wen . . . Please.'

'The Generalissimo has never forgotten the promise he made: the promise China has yet to fulfil – that your bravery should be recognised.' Wen's eyes were cool, so cool Huart could not fathom the sincerity in them. 'It is difficult to forget an officer so tall in a land full of men so short. Generalissimo Chiang is on retirement in Chungking. He would want me to extend to you his very best regards. And to renew his promise.'

'Ah, General Wen . . . Please?' This time Wagoner asserted the fact of his presence. 'This is really damned interestin', but I'm not sure if it has much to do with the business we're here to discuss – '

Wen's eyes quivered. 'It has much to do with it, Mr Wagoner.' The tone was clipped. 'It helps you to be associated with a hero of China like Major-General Huart. In such circumstances, how could I refuse you the insurance franchise for all shipments of military cargo between the US and Taiwan? And not promise you that claims will be kept to a minimum, even if some cargo does, er, turn up missing? Do you see what I mean?'

Wagoner blinked, but quickly recovered. He glanced conspiratorially at Huart, leaned closer to Wen and asked quietly: 'And the commission?'

'There is no need to whisper, Mr Wagoner. As I told you, this is my private club. The commission will be as we discussed. An advance of a quarter of a million US dollars – to be paid into my personal account in San Francisco. And ten per cent of annual turnover thereafter.'

'Agreed.' Wagoner sat back, well satisfied.

'Excellent!' The aspiration was heavier than ever.

Huart was stunned by the abruptness of the deal, the sums and percentages so casually tossed about.

Wagoner smiled at him as does a man whose superiority has been restored, then looked up expectantly as the curtain parted and one of the naked nymphs re-entered carrying a tray with a glass of bourbon and ice, a teapot and two cups. She squatted to set the tray on a low rosewood table and her hair fell forward to cover her tiny breasts. She poured the tea adroitly, her nails extended like porcupine quills. The cool smoothness of her thigh brushed Huart's hand. An aroma of musk mixed with the incense and infiltrated his nostrils. He knew the smell for what it was and guiltily took his hand away. Wen saw that too.

When she was gone, Wen passed a half-filled cup to Huart and the bourbon to Wagoner who grabbed it and raised it in toast. 'We'll be filthy rich together, General,' he grinned. 'We're both in the know, aren't we? There's another war comin'. In Korea, and damn soon. The stuff that'll be passin' through here and through Japan'll make the Berlin Airlift look like a teddy bears' picnic.' He swallowed half the bourbon.

Wen sipped his tea. 'You have left the British Army,' he said to Huart.

'Yes. I am now working with my family company in Hong Kong.'

'A trading company?'

'Yes. Cumberland China. You have perhaps heard of it?'

Wen nodded. 'I have. It is a very large company in China. Especially in Shanghai. I fear for the future of companies like that.'

'So do I.'

Wen looked directly at Huart. 'You have come to Taipei to do business.'

'Yes.'

'What sort of business?'

'Cement plants.'

General Wen Wei-tung nodded slowly. 'It is a most excellent choice. We have need of cement plants in Taiwan, General Huart.'

The warm scent of musk blended with the pervading incense and the perfume of sunflowers. It tickled Huart's nostrils until he breathed it in and, declaring it welcome, allowed it to penetrate his brain and enter his dream where his memory classified it in an instant.

'Jennifer . . .'

He breathed the beloved name again, then again, whilst his eyes remained shuttered under the weight of heavy sleep. He was unconscious, the state induced by the excess of syrupy rice wine he had consumed only hours before in the company of General Wen Wei-tung and Rex Wagoner.

The touch of cool, satiny, pliant skin against his was familiar, yet somehow different. The mouth on his was smaller, the lips parted wider, more experienced in the art of raw love: searching, probing, the tongue darting like a sensual asp. The fingertips on his back were softer, pressing into points that gave forth a soothing sensation such as he had never known. The nails were longer, sharper, stroking him, setting his nerve-endings afire. The thighs were narrower, not able to accommodate his girth, wriggling like . . . like . . . No. Not like –

'Jennifer!'

Huart awoke. The girl beneath him moaned. A slim hand slipped to his groin. He felt his rigid, throbbing member grasped by strange fingers.

He lifted his head and forced his brain to function, to pull out of the deep, deep dream in which he had been submerged, back to reality. The succession of recollections that flashed before his eyes included that part of the conversation over dinner when General Wen had insisted that Wagoner and he move out of their hotel into his 'private villa'.

The room was in darkness, the shadows streaked by brilliant moonlight cascading through an arched window. The light illuminated a shiny garment laid across the arm of a chair. It had a high collar. Silk brocade. It was a *cheongsam*, unfastened, laid open.

The girl moaned again. She was so small her hot breath cooled against the centre of his chest. She spread her thighs, drew him towards the apex. She pushed her pelvis high. Her fur-covered mound rubbed into his groin. She drew him closer, closer until he touched and something went through him like an electric charge.

'Stop . . ! Stop!'

He pushed himself off her and, with his arms fully extended, looked down at her in the darkness. He twisted himself across to the edge of the four-poster bed, his head impacting the canopy in the process. He sat there and insisted: 'What are you doing here?' then realised the absurdity of the question and the fact she would not understand. He stood up and searched about with his hands for his bathrobe. He found it and slipped it around his shoulders. 'General Wen? Did he send you? Wen Wei-tung? He sent you to me?'

The girl looked at him nonplussed. Her eyes dropped to his groin and she smiled invitingly, an obvious question in her young eyes.

Huart shook his head. 'No, my dear. Very sorry. It's been a

[172]

long time. And you're beautiful. But you're second best. You'd better go now.'

He pointed at her dress on the chair and then at the door. She looked back at him, uncomprehending. He did it again, more forcefully.

This time all expression slipped from her face and she sprang from the bed, picked up the *cheongsam* and, naked, flicked through the moonlight to the door and was gone.

Huart walked to a stone inlaid table and poured himself a cup of whatever was in the pitcher upon it. It was cold tea. He swilled it around his mouth to neutralise the acrid after-taste of the rice wine and, seeing nowhere to spit it out, he swallowed. He grimaced in the darkness. His gut churned. His head throbbed. He went back to the four-poster and lay down, now wide awake. The girl's scent lingered and her warmth reposed in the bed beside him. He rolled onto his stomach and groaned. His member was still rock hard.

He willed himself to sleep, but failed. Jennifer was fully revived in his brain, vivid and warm. He was defeated, and he acknowledged the truth of it. He surrendered to the temptation of sweet memory, ignoring the certainty of the pain that the consequential, inevitable withdrawal from its embrace would inflict upon him.

He still could not picture his sons. They were so small when he had last seen them. He tried to imagine what they would look like today, had they lived. James would have been eleven years ten months, Andrew John just turned ten. They would both be big, strong boys, dark hair, deep brown eyes, fit and healthy . . . No. They were both dead. Long dead.

It occurred again to John Huart that he was cursed.

The grin that possessed Wagoner's face the next morning said it all. He held up four fingers. 'So how did you bat last night, Big Fella?'

'Lucky seven,' Huart responded flatly.

Wagoner frowned. 'What? You came seven times? Come on, Limey – '

'Not just seven times, Wagoner. Seven women. One after the other. I'm a Hero of China, remember?'

9

In the Year of the Earth Ox, December 8th gave grist to the chroniclers of Asian history yet again with the exit from China of Generalissimo Chiang Kai-shek and his retinue. Of less worldly significance, but of extreme importance to Cumberland China, it also returned Clive Bedrix to Hong Kong. Huart was at Holt's Wharf to greet his insurance manager, then saw him installed in the Cecil on the floor below himself.

The next day Charles F. Kreitzer, Vice President Marketing, Golden State Cement Corporation of California, and his chief engineer stepped off a Pan Am DC6 onto the Kai Tak tarmac. Their first sight of Hong Kong was Lion Rock with strips of autumn cloud draped over its ridges like discarded wedding veils, their second the big smile and hand of John Huart.

That night Huart, Bedrix and the Americans, who had checked into the Peninsula, dined at Jimmy's Kitchen. They bit into the tangy pickled onions, cut into thick T-bone steaks and quaffed a full-blooded Rhone red. The conversation was loud, enthusiastic, led by Kreitzer, a bluff and robust individual. Huart joined in, certain luck had turned for him.

The next night, leaving Bedrix and his sea legs in Hong Kong, they ate in a Szechuan restaurant off Chung Hsiao Road in Taipei, where General Wen Wei-tung again proved a consumate host. Huart called for a second dish of the spiced *daofu* bean curd and minced meat that scored the tongue until doused with a cold local lager, and this time took the rice wine sparingly, whilst chiding the Americans for ignoring his warnings.

Negotiations with Wen were so smooth Huart could not believe it, and neither could Kreitzer and his chief engineer. Besides fixing the format for a contract to build two cement plants, one near Taipei, the other in the south, Wen invited Huart and executives of Lionel Hope and Sons to Taiwan as a string of cotton mills was needed across the country. Over dinner Wen made great play of Huart's 'relationship' with Generalissimo, now President, Chiang Kai-shek. The Americans were even more impressed.

'You're a killer-diller, John!' Kreitzer cried. 'You're the best that's happened to us since Joseph Aspdin went and invented Portland cement.'

Again there was the invitation to stay in the Wen villa. For Huart the format was different, in that his sleep was not interrupted. But next morning neither of the Americans seemed able to look him in the eye.

'Had the best wet dream o' my life . . .' the chief engineer whispered at last. 'But this mornin' I wus damned if I could find the goddamn stain.'

Kreitzer broke up. Huart looked away to hide his grin. They joked all the way back to Hong Kong where the Americans reconnected with Pan Am.

On Christmas Day, Huart hosted dinner at the Repulse Bay Hotel for Bedrix and the Huart-Brents. The temperature of the grey day was too low for the verandah, so they took a table in the main restaurant from which they could look out on the bay. They had not received a Christmas call from Andrew. Knowledge that his yuletide would be an austere one, amidst whatever hopeful or importuned friends remained in Shanghai, dampened spirits. Huart tried to liven the meal with a toast: 'May we be sitting here at this very table next Christmas – Andrew with us, fit and well.'

'Hear, hear!' Bedrix, though he had not met his taipan, raised a glass in his right hand. It was one of a sequence. The Hurricane pilot could handle his drink. The left sleeve of his dinner jacket was pinned with regimental precision. Suzanne could not keep her big little eyes off it.

Adelaide nodded sadly, whilst Paulette persisted with the distant look that, it seemed to Huart, had prevailed since he had last seen Wagoner's back. It had been a welcome sight. The American had returned from Taipei full of himself plus tales of his latest business 'coup' and his thwarting of the Kuomintang Airforce. Huart had rated not a mention.

'Not here, Uncle John. Not here in Hong Kong,' pleaded Vivienne. 'We'll be having Christmas in Shanghai. Grandma said so. Didn't you, Grandma?'

'Perhaps we will, my dear,' agreed Huart. 'But it's not important where we have it – just so long as your papa is with us.'

'I 'member Papa,' announced Suzanne brightly. 'Is his head grown back?'

'His hair, Suzie,' smiled her grandmother. She glanced a criticism at Paulette, who remained seemingly absented from the conversation.

'Sorry.' Paulette had sensed the silence. 'I was just thinking that next Christmas we won't be in Shanghai . . . or here. Shanghai's lost isn't it? The Communists are almost at the border. Attlee won't recognise that Mao exists. The company's virtually bankrupt.

My husband's as good as in jail. Not a very encouraging formula for the next twelve months is it?'

Adelaide bristled audibly. 'An end to such talk! We will persevere. We will stay here because we have to. We are Huarts. China is Huart country and this is China – or the closest to it. We stay. We support John, who's doing his damnedest to save the company. We stay. And we pray.'

Huart toasted this with Chablis Grand Cru, the thrill of Taiwan overruling austerity. Andrew would have done it with Dom Perignon.

Two days later the advent of a winter monsoon coincided with a call from Shanghai. Huart accepted the charges, his heart thumping. God willing Andrew did not need more cash! The account at the British Bank of Asia continued to dwindle, despite Bedrix showing the loss of an arm was a minor handicap by already landing insurance contracts and collecting premiums. Another remittance to the head office would need the sanction of Hector Harrisford-House. Huart knew he would find no sympathy there.

'I need the audited accounts!' Andrew's voice was unusually strong.

'Last year's?'

'This year's. 1949.'

'But there're still four days before the end of the financial year – '

'I'm looking at the same calendar you are, Cousin.'

'The auditors will want at least a month after that – '

'Pressure them. I must have a certified copy of the accounts latest 15th January. My money will run out about then and I need proof of bankruptcy to show that we're bled dry and staff must be laid off. They'll say I'm lying if I can't produce the latest accounts. You must do nothing to make the balance sheet look worse than it is. Don't transfer anything. They're as sharp as hawks and they'll fasten onto any withdrawals.'

'As you wish, Andrew. But there's little left to transfer anyway.' Huart was thinking the line may be monitored. He added: 'You're sounding fit.'

'I'm feeling fit. Rumour has it Attlee is to recognise Peking at last. The procrastinating no-hoper hasn't answered one of my telegrams. As soon as Britain recognises the People's Republic of China the Communists will let trade recommence. My ordeal here will have been well worth it.'

After Andrew had rung off, Huart dialled Bedrix on the internal line. 'How are things coming along with the Godown Company, Clive?'

'Swimmingly. We sign a three-year contract tomorrow.'

'Why, that's grand. Male & Son have held that account for decades. GLU won't be at all happy at losing it.' Greater London Underwriters, GLU for short, were Pan Atlantic's foremost rivals. 'When's the premium to be paid?'

'As soon as the policy is signed. I've given Francis the draft.'

'How've you been able to do it, Clive?'

'Their financial controller and I are old drinking mates, John. Blood, particularly that contaminated with San Miguel, is thicker than water.'

'Obviously. But hear this: ask him to postdate the cheque. It'll start the new decade off right.' Huart said no more. In the army it had been called The Need to Know. Bedrix need not know the all of it. Yet.

'I follow. Make '49 look as bad as possible and then '50 looks so much better by comparison. Then we go back to "Three H" for an overdraft.'

Huart grimaced at the credit manager's nickname. 'Something like that, but not quite. By the way, do you know Percy Landers of the H and K?'

'Yes. Why?'

'When our account with BBA is into the black and getting blacker, first thing I'm going to do is personally call on our friend "Three H", and close it right to his face. But before that, we need another banker.'

'I'll fix lunch at the Hong Kong Club with Landers tomorrow, John.'

'Grand.'

'Bring along that membership application. I'll have Percy second you.'

'Grand. One good turn deserves another. I've told Francis to cable tickets to your wife for the next ship out. No, don't thank me. You're getting back to the hotel too late at night. I feel responsible for you.'

Andrew's new-found strength supplemented Huart's enthusiasm and steeled his conviction that Cumberland China's luck had indeed changed. Taiwan offered untold opportunities, and Bedrix's undoubted ability instilled in him great visions of the future.

The year ended with the newspapers announcing Britain's recognition of the People's Republic of China, and the downgrading of its diplomatic post in Taipei to consul level. The Shanghai rumour was proved accurate.

Huart was enthused. 'All we need now is for Chiang to admit defeat and lift his blockade on the Yangtse,' he told Paulette as they dallied in Statue Square on New Year's Eve. 'Then the ships will go back in to Shanghai. Then the China Trade will have a chance of living on.'

He was feeling more confident than ever. Bedrix, good as his word, had sealed the Godown Company contract and the premium cheque was in hand. Despite the holiday next day, the auditors were coming in to begin an accelerated examination of the accounts. It would cost extra, but was necessary.

Orchestra music emanated from the Hong Kong Club as the New Year's Eve ball gathered momentum. Clive Bedrix would be there, thought Huart. Percy Landers from the H and K would be there, as would every European who was anybody in Hong Kong. It's time I was there. He looked about the empty square. Chinese avoided this domain of the westerner after dark, especially this night when they knew it was not uncommon for foreign devils to go mad. They celebrated their lunar new year in a fashion more sedate, receiving family in their homes, then paying return visits. Seven weeks were still to pass before it. It was an event overlooked by the European community. But, Huart wondered, can we go on ignoring it?

1949 had been the last year in a decade of turmoil and radical change in China, and in Hong Kong, for which 1950 boded fresh danger. The reality of the People's Liberation Army intimidated the flimsy border as communism gripped the Middle Kingdom. How could Andrew be proved right? How could the *hongs* stay in Shanghai? Their survival was inconsistent with the fanatical ideology that was sweeping the vast land twenty miles north, driving hundreds of thousands across the border before it was closed tight, to convert quiet colonial Hong Kong with its deep blue-water harbour and its green-sloped mountains into an incestuous haven.

'The last decade saw the destruction of Asia . . .' Huart thought out loud.

Unsure if he had been addressing her, Paulette looked up at him and saw his eyes focused across the harbour, where the slopes of the Nine Dragons shone in the bright moonlight like giant waves in a dark sea. 'John?'

He looked down at her and smelled again the perfume of their first meeting. But she had changed. They had all survived a dire period, and none of them was unmarked by it. 'The next decade

[178]

will see the region rebuilt,' he told her, his eyes clear. 'I intend to participate in it.'

He walked to the fence around the stone baldachin that once had covered the statue of Queen Victoria. The empty throne was a symbol. Britain had given up its Asian colonies: India, Burma, the treaty ports of China. But not Hong Kong. Not yet. 'Look at it. The war has changed the British Empire forever. This is Asia, Paulette – not England. Look around when you walk the Praya. The population is ninety-nine percent Chinese – '

'Yes, John,' Paulette agreed, bemused. 'Refugees.'

'Refugees for now. Citizens tomorrow. Hong Kong citizens. People fled from communism and never wanting to go back.'

She took his arm. *'Ma preux chevalier,* you wish to launch a crusade?'

He did not smile even a little. 'If I intend to participate in the rebuilding of Asia, I must think differently. I must think Asian!'

'I have suspected it for some time, John. You're a hopeless romantic!'

He ignored her again and threw out his arm in a gesture that encompassed Statue Square. 'All these anachronisms must go! These buildings – forty-five years old. Only four storeys. Too uncommercial!'

Paulette looked at Prince's Building and Queen's Building. They were like sleeping twins, their arched Italianate balconies in shadow like closed edificial eyes, their helmeted corner towers bathed in moonlight.

Huart turned to the dormant construction site that waited to give birth to the new Bank of China. It was still unclear if the Communists planned to complete it. Then he pointed up at the Hongkong and Shanghai Bank. 'There's the future. Buildings built for Hong Kong – for the people of Hong Kong: European and Chinese. Tall and modern. No more three and four storeys. Now we need ten, fifteen, even twenty storeys. And what do people need to get up that high – ?' He looked at her, his eyes alight.

She was engrossed despite herself. 'Elevators, John?' she asked softly.

He nodded. 'Elevators. But only those of the most modern design. Fast, automatic elevators.' He gripped her arm. 'I must go back to the hotel and leave Clive a message. I'm going to America.' And he strode away.

The clock above the Star Ferry pier chimed midnight. It was joined by the clock in the Gloucester Hotel tower. The chords of 'Auld Lang Syne' floated from the balconies of the Hong Kong

Club. The horns of the ships on Victoria Harbour saluted the new year. The opening seconds of the new decade told Paulette something significant. Even if the *hong* survived, her husband's crown would be loose upon his head. For in the southern outpost of Hong Kong a pretender to the throne had emerged. She looked back at the empty, dead baldachin and shivered, then hurried after John Huart – a man of vision whom she knew she must take very seriously.

10

The seven weeks between the western and lunar new years were hyperactive for Huart. He delegated the day-to-day tussle with the bank balance to Bedrix and travelled. In the Philippines he tracked down a soya bean processing plant for Rosefair and Benson and a flour mill for Harold Soames, both to be built near Manila. In Saigon he heard of a 10,000 bag-per-day jute mill that was pending financial approval from Paris and lodged a prequalification with Société le Indo-Chine on behalf of Lionel Hope and Sons. He manipulated passage as a guest of the USAAF and fulfilled his new year pledge to visit America. He returned with an Agency Agreement signed by the president of Haig Denver Elevator Corporation in his attache case and quipped: 'Clive, we're going up in the world!'

'You've got a head start, John,' Bedrix returned, saving for later his report on that morning's confrontation with Hector Harrisford-House after Cumberland China's account had slipped marginally into the red.

Huart flew twice to Taipei, the first time to settle with General Wen Wei-tung, who staked a personal claim on half of Golden State Cement's twenty per cent deposit. The plan was for Wen to collect the 'commission' from his San Francisco account during his 'inspection tour' after the ratification of the contract. The second visit, in company with Chuck Kreitzer, was to attend the official signing ceremony at the headquarters of the New Productivity Corporation. They flew back to Hong Kong on February 16th, the last day of the old lunar year, each with a copy of the contract in his pocket. Huart was content, any personal misgivings about the morality of the deal diffused by the reality of

[180]

Cumberland China's five per cent commission, one per cent of which would be remitted by Golden State Cement on receipt of the deposit from Taipei. It would be enough to cover the overheads of the branch office for the rest of the year. The cash problem was as good as beaten.

But the Year of the Gold Tiger introduced itself with sombre grey skies, cold drizzle, and a wintry call from Shanghai.

'It didn't work, John.' Andrew was cheerless. 'I can't convince them the accounts are not doctored. And now I've been ordered to pay all staff a double Chinese New Year bonus. It comes to six thousand pounds.'

'What happens if you refuse to pay it?'

'I'll be hauled before the People's Court. From what I've heard of the way it's conducted, I may not be able to handle it. What can be done?'

Huart thought fast. Noises on the line indicated it was being monitored. It was time for Andrew to get out. 'It's impossible! We've paid staff their thirteenth month here, too. The bank balance is zero. The BBA have given us two days to put it back in funds. The situation is critical.' He did not mention the Taipei contract, revelation of which would only exacerbate his cousin's plight. But it did present a possible solution.

Andrew's voice was fragile. 'It's worse than merely critical here, John. Please do something. I must give them my reply within the hour.'

'Alright, Andrew. Hold on. I'll arrange something.'

'Can you promise me that you will?'

Huart hesitated for only a moment. 'Yes, Andrew. I can promise.'

'Thank you. Thank you.' Andrew rang off without preamble. 'Cheerio' and *Maskee* were parting shots of the past.

It was time to call Percy Landers. The credit manager of the Hongkong and Kwangtung Bank agreed to see Huart at once. The H and K's Queen's Road head office was five minutes walk. Landers was impressed with the contract documents bearing the masthead of the New Productivity Corporation of the Republic of China. 'When is the deposit to be paid, John?'

'Clause 17. Within one hundred days of contract signature. We'll have our one per cent in our hands by – ' Huart decided to build in a month's leeway. 'June 26th. I'll sign a personal guarantee if you require it.'

'Oh, I don't think anything that drastic will be necessary. Golden State Cement Corporation of California, eh? Sounds solid enough.

We'll check them out, nevertheless. Your Agency Agreement seems in order. I'll call the Trade Department of the US Consulate. It'll only take a minute.'

In an hour Cumberland China had been granted a loan equal to ten thousand pounds sterling. Huart remitted six thousand by telegraphic transfer to Shanghai, then cabled Andrew that the money was on the way.

That afternoon, twenty miles north, the People's Liberation Army came upon the border fence between Kwangtung Province and the New Territories. And stopped. Mao's victorious push south was over. The flood of refugees into Hong Kong dried as if a giant valve had been closed.

The *Hong Kong and Oriental Daily* and the *South China Morning Post* began giving space to the ideological dispute between North and South Korea. Huart looked ahead and tried to assess the effect on Hong Kong should the war of words develop into outright conflict, as Wagoner had predicted. In April he received a call from Andrew that was more encouraging than any in the ten months and ten days since the fall of Shanghai. It did not include a plea for more cash, just news. Trading ships were now penetrating the Yangtse blockade and one had loaded an order for tea that had been placed on Cumberland China in January, 1949 and had made it back to Hong Kong. The Communists seemed to be adopting a more conciliatory attitude towards the foreign traders and an air of optimism lifted Andrew's voice. 'There's a ship in next week with a consignment of Loughborough valves for the Waterworks. Remember George Bloomfield? He ordered them in '48. He's told the Chinese unless he gets them the water supply system will completely pack up. Last winter they made him install valves made in Wuhan. Every last one of them split in the first freeze. The shipment's worth four thousand pounds. I've been promised payment in thirty days. They seem quite certain of it. Things look like they're on the move again here. *Maskee!*'

'*Maskee*, Andrew,' agreed Huart and hung up.

The old byword had injected warmth. But it cooled when Huart called Landers and heard him announce the commission from Golden State Cement had yet to arrive. More than seven weeks had passed since the contract had been signed in Taipei. A termite of unease took its first bite.

On May 1st Bedrix was made general manager and celebrated

with Huart over a Hong Kong Club lunch at which the subject was business and more business. 'We have a good mechanical engineering package,' Huart affirmed, 'but we must extend our electrical range and look at telecommunications. Cathay Electric and the Telephone Company will need new plant if Hong Kong develops. More people live here now than ever before. More people mean more electricity and more telephones. I've even heard a whisper that this new "television" phenomenon could come here soon.'

Bedrix nodded over his ham steak. 'Yes. Cement plants, cotton mills, soya bean factories, etcetera, are fine for now. But the region needs only so many. The market is finite. We'll work ourselves out of business in a few years.' He inclined his head towards two senior club members in conversation at a corner table. 'See the old gent with the whiskers?'

'Ivor Male? The man with Owen Catchpole, you mean?'

'They lunch here twice a week. I've overheard snippets of conversation and they're never about the weather.' Owen Catchpole was general manager of the Telephone Company and known to run his utility with an autocratic hand, taking all major decisions himself. 'Male & Son are agents for AXE Communications. They're talking about the Telephone Company's next order for crossbar exchange equipment. That's pretty expensive stuff, John.'

'Who's the competitor that's losing out to AXE?'

Bedrix smiled. He had anticipated the question. 'Mercury. I've compiled a report on them. I'll bring it into your office after lunch.'

Huart nodded. 'But exchange equipment is only one item on my list. We also want products that are needed on a continuous basis. Like cable and telephone sets and switchboards . . .' His eyes returned to the two men with their heads together in the corner. 'And I must turn myself into the best friend Owen Catchpole ever had in his life.'

The deadline for receipt by Golden State Cement of the deposit from the New Productivity Corporation of the Republic of China was May 25th. The day came and went. Huart estimated the banking process would use a week in the transfer of his commission across the Pacific. He waited the full seven days before cabling San Francisco. Four more days went by and he could sit and wait no longer. He placed a long distance call, person-to-person. His fears were confirmed by Kreitzer's opening sentence. No deposit had been received and General Wen was not answering telegrams.

A Mandarin-speaking clerk telephoned Taipei for him. After four hours of wrong numbers and cut lines he got Wen's aide who proved reluctant, saying only: 'Gen' Wen go 'spec'shun tour.'

'Inspection tour? In Taiwan?' Huart demanded.

'*Wo bu tze dao*. I not know.'

'Overseas? Is General Wen overseas?'

'*Bu tze dao!* Not know.'

'Where then? Where is General Wen?'

'*Bu tze dao!*' The line went dead.

Huart sat in a cold sweat. Something had gone seriously wrong. But what? What had happened to Wen? Was he away for a short time? Or a long time? Had he been purged? The questions rang in his head. A hole was burning in the pit of his stomach. He had never experienced anything like it before, not even during the war. He hated the sensation and detested his helplessness. He really did not know what to do next. It was June 5th. The H and K loan had to be repaid by close of business on June 26th. He had three weeks to find General Wen Wei-tung. But where to even start?

'God! God! God!' he cried to his office.

That day, payment of monthly salaries, office rental, utility costs, and accommodation expenses at the Gloucester and the Cecil, plus deposit and advance rental on a house in Repulse Bay for the reunited Bedrix family sent Cumberland China's account at the British Bank of Asia plunging into the red. The H and K loan was already fully used. Huart spent the next day sitting by his telephone, willing its next ring to herald positive news. He sent Roboza to Electra House every second hour to check on incoming telegrams. But each time the office manager returned his face was longer. The tide of debilitating indecision crept higher, until Huart could feel it around his neck. Not even Bedrix's announcement of a contract with South China Motors to insure all their future imports of new British-built automobiles could produce any positive reaction.

When the phone did ring it was Hector Harrisford-House. 'I'll give you twenty-four hours, Mr Huart. One second after that we will close your account and let loose our legal people. Twenty-four hours. Hear?'

Exasperated, infuriated, Huart called Landers, who hesitated, then parted with enough to cancel out the BBA account, deeming it repayable also on June 26th. Cumberland China had bought itself three weeks. Huart carried the bank draft between thumb and forefinger along Des Voeux Road, Central, marched into Harrisford-House's office without knocking and threw it across his desk, ignoring the elderly man seated in one of the guest chairs. Placing both his large fists upon the rosewood surface, he looked the credit manager in the eye and hissed: 'There's your money, sir, with interest included. Invest it well, because you'll not see another red cent of ours, not as long as either of us live. That I promise with all my heart.'

Harrisford-House's face turned livid. He stood and glared back. 'And in my humble opinion, sir, neither will any other bank. Landers must have gone stark raving mad. Now kindly take your leave. You are interrupting my meeting with a most important customer. A real customer. One who does business with our money – plus a lot of his own. Good day . . . sir!'

Ivor Male cleared his throat. 'Now, Hector – watch your hypertension.'

Huart returned to his office aflame with bitter resolve. He attempted to connect with General Wen's office again, this time to be told the line was disconnected. He called San Francisco, scouring the panic from his voice lest Kreitzer suspect his agent was losing his equilibrium. By the time he replaced the receiver his spirits had slipped closer to despair.

The following week provided a diversion as Huart accompanied Angus Grey, Export Director of Rosefair and Benson, to Manila to open negotiations on the soya bean processing plant. It became instantly clear it was only the first of several more bargaining sessions to come as the Filipinos made manifest their love of haggling.

One look at Bedrix's face on his return to Ice House Street told Huart there was still no news from either Taipei or San Francisco.

11

Doomsday.

Monday, June 26th, 1950 dawned hot and still. By nine the humidity had already risen to the high nineties. The raw sun of the first summer of the decade burnt through sparse cloud and fell upon the ample brow of John Huart as he stood hatless on the steps of the building in Ice House Street in which his company rented its tenuous turf. He had decided not to prolong the inevitable. The distance along Queen's Road, Central to the Hongkong and Kwangtung Bank was short, but it was a psychological trek. British Army boots had never felt as leaden as the soft leather shoes Huart was wearing this morning. Despondency and the acceptance of failure shortened his step, lowered his jaw, narrowed his vision.

He passed the spot where once had stood the St Francis Hotel. Now it was an anonymous construction site enclosed in a honeycombed trelliswork of bamboo poles lashed together at right angles and covered with straw mats in the age-old fashion of Chinese scaffolding. A ten-storey building to be named Edinburgh House would rise over the grave of the hotel in whose restaurant he and Gilbert Dole had lunched that day a lifetime ago. He saw ahead, beyond the Hong Kong Hotel and across Pedder Street, the squat building that housed the H and K waiting for him. He looked into the faces on Queen's Road. They ignored him, fixed as they were on their own thoughts, intent on their own objectives. On this day, Cumberland China and John Stanford Huart, newest director of the once great *hong*, would be declared mutually bankrupt. Not a soul on Queen's Road would even hear of it, nor would care a damn if they did.

He concentrated on the Chinese faces, trying to decipher them. He could detect nothing. Were any of them, as he was, en route to their banker or money-lender to declare insolvency? It was impossible to tell what they were doing on Queen's Road, or what they were: borrowers or lenders or neither. Yet anyone looking at him could see at once that this day had brought with it the sad end to something of immense personal importance. The Chinese must be able to read us like books, he decided. What a disadvantage we create for ourselves! And then he recalled his resolution made to Paulette on New Year's Eve: Think Asian! Act Asian!

And with the resurrection of this thought his face turned neutral, his chest filled, his spine straightened, his vision broadened. He stepped across the Pedder Street intersection and entered the building that was his destination, his demeanour now that of a man on a routine errand.

Percy Landers looked preoccupied as he showed Huart to his usual chair and omitted to proffer his customary sherry. Huart interpreted these as very bad signs and his new-found bravado faltered.

'Well, John, what is it you want?'

[186]

Huart's eyebrows arched in surprise. 'Why . . . Today's the day, Percy.'

'Today? Yes, today's one hell of a day. But how does it affect you?'

Huart could see Landers was quite serious. The banker's eyes were never still for an instant, constantly flicking to the door.

'Today is June 26th, Percy. Our loans are due. You haven't forgotten?'

'Your loans? Ah, yes . . . your loans.' Then, to Huart's bewilderment, Landers started to chuckle. The humour aborted with a polite knock at the door. 'Enter!' The interruption had been expected.

A Chinese messenger boy in a starched half-jacket bearing the H and K crest hastened in, put a sealed envelope in a wooden tray and turned on his heel. Landers snapped it up and slit one end with one stroke of a silver letter opener. He withdrew a folded telegram and shook it open, beetle-browed. 'Please excuse me, old chap. This is rather important.'

'Of course, Percy.'

The banker read for several seconds. Then he threw back his head to gaze up at the ceiling with a distant expression and expelled his breath with a prolonged sigh. 'Your loans, John? Would a thirty day extension help?'

Huart blinked. 'Help, Percy? Of course it would help. But . . . ?'

Landers' face broke up in an avuncular smile. Huart could not help but reciprocate it without knowing why, and liking Landers more and more. 'My dear friend, on this day your loans are low down on the H and K's list of potential bad debts.' He waved the telegram at Huart and sighed again. 'Three weeks ago, after long deliberation, I personally approved a large loan to Donn Line. They agreed to place three of their vessels under lien to us as collateral. Last week two of those ships docked at Nampo. They were being loaded with ginseng root, fish, rice, barley, wheat – you know – to deliver to Nagoya, Keelung, Hong Kong . . .' He stood wearily and dragged his feet to the sherry decanter, where he took up two glasses and filled them to the brim. He gave one to Huart, then picked up the telegram again. 'I have just received confirmation from Seoul that the two ships are impounded in Nampo by the North Koreans.'

'Impounded for what reason, Percy?' Huart innocently sipped his sherry.

The banker's face reflected incredulity. 'My dear chap! You

must start getting up earlier in the morning. Do you mean you have not heard?'

Huart shook his head. 'I've had a lot on my mind of late, Percy.'

Landers put down his sherry and sighed yet again. 'Yesterday the North Korean army crossed the 38th Parallel and invaded South Korea. China has declared its support for the North. Truman has ordered the Seventh Fleet to Taiwan. The United Nations is convening a special meeting of the Security Council. I tell you, John – Mao's Communists will be landing in Taipei in a week. World War III started yesterday, you mark my words.'

12

The ensign of the British Merchant Marine had died at the mast of the freighter tied up apart in the muddy harbour. Its superstructure was a study in rust – it was as if fortune had defecated on it physically as well as metaphorically – and barnacles thrived along its chains. It had been there for weeks, ever since June 25th, its crew detained below deck. In its holds were the valves that had been ordered by the Shanghai Waterworks in 1948 and now corroded in wooden crates, pending payment of a landing tax that totalled twice their value and would never be paid.

Andrew Huart-Brent stood on the brown patch of land between the Bund and the harbour wall, where the green lawn and the technicolor flowers used to grow and which was once called the Public Gardens. He looked out at the miserable ship and he knew again that it was all over.

Whilst outbreak of war on the Korean Peninsula was the catalyst in an unlikely reprieve for John Huart and Cumberland China in Hong Kong, in Shanghai it was the event that brought to an end any and all indecision in the minds of the Chinese Communists as to the continued existence of the foreign trading companies. They were suddenly, irrevocably doomed.

China, in siding with North Korea, became the enemy behind the enemy in the eyes of the United Nations. The USA took up the UN spearhead and committed itself to the cause of South Korea. Truman warned Peking off Taiwan and then hastened to defend it. He imposed ostensible balance by ordering Chiang Kai-shek to cease air attacks on the Chinese mainland and lift the

Yangtse blockade, and by making the Seventh Fleet available to escort any non-belligerent trading vessel passing into or out of the Yangtse Estuary.

In Shanghai, reprisals fell hard and fast upon the few foreign traders who persevered. The new laws were devoid of common logic in the fashion of those made by the bloody-minded, designed as they were to eradicate this last capitalist legacy. The trading companies had been drained by wholesale taxation, maintenance of full salaries and claims levied via a People's Court sympathetic to any plaintiff that was Chinese; now taxes were doubled and doubled again; new taxes were invented. Upon capitalist Shanghai the final curtain fell. It was made of bamboo.

Andrew reviewed in his mind yesterday's telephone call to Hong Kong. It had only been permitted after he had written his application in thirteen copies. The quality of the line was worse than ever and he had hoped that those he knew were monitoring it were getting an earful of static. He had smiled wearily when he had heard John play his part with exaggerated dismay over the landing tax on the valves, and then pronounce what amounted to his invitation out of Shanghai, the birthplace he had almost grown to hate. 'We're in one hell of a fix down here ourselves. Under no circumstances can we help with cash from Hong Kong anymore. You'll just have to leave the valves on board. We're in one hell of a fix.'

Andrew had sighed lugubriously for his audience. 'That's it then. It's over. We're finished. There's nothing more to do but apply for my exit permit. They've bled the company dry both in Shanghai and in Hong Kong. They've done the impossible – they've got blood from stone.'

'What will happen to the staff, Andrew?'

'I suppose they'll be resettled in communes someplace. It's a terrible shame. Some worked for my grandfather, others have been with the company since they had their first pee. Tell Paulette and the children and my mother that I'm applying to come out. I'm admitting defeat, Cousin.'

'Don't say that, Andrew. The difficulties have been insurmountable. You did everything you could. How long do you think it will take?'

'A month, perhaps two. The procedure's tedious. I have to queue up for hours, perhaps days, for an application form, then advertise on two successive days in both English and Chinese newspapers – yes, we still have an English language press of sorts – inviting anyone with claims against me to come forward. Then

I have to front up to the appropriate department at the appropriate time with my application, copies of the advertisement, all personal papers and articles of value that I want to take with me. Even after all that there's no guarantee they'll let me go.'

'Stick with it Andrew,' John had encouraged. 'The worst is over.'

'I hope so. D'you know I've been evicted from Broadway Mansions? It was last Sunday when I was out walking. Seems the old fellow who owned the apartment – we only leased it, you see – is the great uncle of a Kuomintang admiral. The Communists have turned it into a rehabilitation centre for ex-Foochow Road "sing-song" girls. I'm staying in the Shanghai Club on credit at present. The club has been requisitioned, too. They try to make me feel like a intruder in my own club. Bloody communist bas – '

At that point the line had been disconnected. Andrew had forgotten himself. He knew his outburst had risked provoking maximum delay in the granting of his exit permit. But to hell with them – communist bastards!

The defrocked Shanghai taipan stood in the gardens that used to be and sniffed. He seemed to suffer from one cold after another now. He wiped first his nose, then the sweat from his face with a patchwork handkerchief and watched the tiny scavenger gulls skip and skim over the surface of the water, jabbing into it with their sharp beaks. At least the birds are still free, he thought to himself.

Two green-uniformed policemen watched him from a distance, just close enough to be able to prevent him from throwing himself into the harbour. The previous week Stewart Barlow had attempted suicide in that fashion, stones weighting his pockets. The Hardoon man had failed at that, too. It took four of them to fish him out. He, too, had taxes still to pay.

Andrew had been standing there a long time. The Chinese who dared to push close and glare at him took his tears as a manifestation of weakness. They began to jeer at him. He did not hear the derisive noises at first and he turned and looked back at the buildings along the Bund.

The roof of the Bank of China, the green spire of the Cathay Hotel atop mighty Sassoon House, the Custom House clock tower and the dome of the Hongkong and Shanghai Bank pushed proudly into the sky, landmarks of an era Andrew now numbly acknowledged had passed into history. The buildings may stand for another fifty, a hundred years – God knows they were built to dominate this waterfront for ever! He saw the washing hanging from the windows of the suites of the Cathay Hotel, the soldiers

[190]

with their red-starred caps in a group outside the Bank of China, the banners of propaganda in large scarlet ideograms hanging from the Custom House, the signboard above the entrance to the Hongkong and Shanghai Bank declaring the identities of its new owner-tenants: the People's Municipal Government, the Revolutionary Committee of the Chinese Communist Party and the Committee for Military Control of the People's Liberation Army. The hands of 'Big Ching' joined at midday, but no sound came from the tower. The chimes had been silenced.

Andrew saddened tangibly. His body seemed to slump in upon itself. The bitter tears welled. Then he heard the jeers. He looked up at the crowd gathered around him. They were pointing at him and cat-calling in base Shanghai dialect, making gutter accusations of his incestuous relationship with his mother and with animals and pointing out that he walked with a limp like a pox-riddled Manchu whore with bound feet. The chorus of derision was punctuated by loud hawking and spittle was cast at him. The police and the PLA soldiers hung back and grinned at his plight.

He turned his back on the crowd and stood proudly. He was dressed in a plain cloth suit made by the Chinese tailor in Yates Road, whom he had always patronised. The tailor had remained in business somehow. When it became unwise for Andrew to be seen in his shop, he worked from measurements in his records and sent the garments to Cumberland Building by messenger. Andrew paid with items from the office: jade or ivory ornaments that he had managed to retain as personal property, a typewriter, chair, canned fruit from the pantry. That morning he had received a note from the tailor stating in the colourless prose of the Revolution that he would no longer take orders from foreign capitalists.

Suddenly Andrew sensed the silence behind him. He turned. Three feet from him was a face he instantly recognised.

'Ling! Oh, Ling! How are you? It's a year since I last saw you!'

The former head houseboy, in plain tunic and silk pants instead of the long white gown he had been required to wear at all times in Broadway Mansions, stared back and did not return the greeting.

'Ling!' Andrew repeated. 'Oh, Ling!' He reached out his hands to his loyal servant, a solitary friend amongst a warlike throng. 'Where have you been? Are you well? Where do you live now? Ling . . ?'

The ex-servant's eyes flinted with distaste. Then his right arm raised above his shoulder. Andrew saw the bamboo stick clasped in the fist but his brain refused to acknowledge that it represented a danger to him.

'Want Ling bling 'nother *stengah*, master, ah? Or mebbe Missee' special wine? Mebbe Ling bling for you this instead – capitalist pig!'

The stick cracked down hard upon Andrew's forehead. Red flecks flew across his retina. He brought his hands to his face to protect himself as the stick came down again, and again. He tried to run. A foot tripped him. He crashed to the ground. He tried to crawl to the low wall at the water's edge, intending to throw himself over it and swim for one of the jetties. He felt the feet upon him. Sandaled toes sank into his ribs and heels smacked down upon his neck. His face was forced into the dirt of the Public Gardens until he could taste it in his mouth. He tried to spit it out, to scream, to hit out, to die fighting. He failed all.

Just before his left collarbone was dislocated a second time by a well-aimed kick, it registered with him that this was the spot in the gardens where he and Paulette and the girls used to come on fine Sunday afternoons. They would look up at Broadway Mansions looming majestically over Garden Bridge on the far bank of Soochow Creek and pick out their very own balcony. Often they would see Ling up there in his long white gown cleaning the French windows or watering the pot plants on the ledge.

Andrew Huart-Brent's last vision before he lost consciousness was Ling's kindly old face scored with hatred as he brought the bamboo stick down with both hands for one final killing blow. It hit across the bridge of Andrew's nose and a loud crack resounded through his body. A wave of pain lanced through him and a deep-rooted fire caught alight dead centre in his chest. His last sensation was a detached awareness with which came remote acceptance of the significance of the contrast between the bitter taste of the animal sweat on the bodies that pressed down on him, the dirt on the soles of the feet that stood on his face, and the sweetness and freshness of the green grass of the gardens where the Huart-Brents used to stroll.

But that had been another time, long ago. That had been another life.

13

The mosquito net was a coffin. Huart thought it was an apt similitude as he lived out another hot sleepless night tossing and turning within its confines. Then the knock came at the door. It was too tentative to belong to Bedrix. He called out. No answer came, instead the knock was repeated. He pulled aside the net and swung his long legs to the floor. One hand went to the table lamp, the fingers of the other searched for his pocket watch. It took several seconds for his eyes to adjust enough for him to see it was ten minutes past midnight. The knock at the door sounded a third time, more insistent this time.

'Coming!'

Tying a light robe about his naked frame, he crossed to the door and opened it with caution. A short figure stood in shadow in the corridor. He peered at it. He saw light reflect from the oiled hair, then noticed the moustache, but still recognition came slowly. 'Good evening, General Huart. It is so nice to see you again. You seem to have lost weight.'

It was the exaggerated aspiration of the 't's that finally delivered it to Huart's brain, addled by a succession of tortuous nights, that his visitor was indeed General Wen Wei-tung. 'Good heavens! Gen –'

Wen gestured for silence. 'May I come in?' he whispered.

'Why, of course.' Huart closed the door, switched on the room light and looked down at the vexing smile. 'Would you like a brandy? Or scotch?'

Wen extended his hand in something of a non sequitur. Huart took it perfunctorily, noting that though his visitor's face was fixed in that smile, the eyes were dull. This was a tired man. 'Scotch would be most excellent.' The aspiration pierced the air. Huart found it annoyed him.

Wen seated himself in a rattan chair near the open balcony window. Huart gave him a tumbler of Chivas and sat opposite, taking in the ivory toned cotton suit and the calf leather shoes with their shiny white uppers. A three star Kuomintang general could not look more unmilitary. Outside and below, the intersecting man-made canyons of Des Voeux Road, Central and Ice House Street were dark and hushed in the July night. In the half minute that passed before Wen spoke again, Huart kept face by holding tight to the questions that burned his innards.

'I apologise for the lateness and the clandestine nature of my visit, General Huart. But I should not be in Hong Kong at all. Your Special Branch would be most displeased to learn of my presence in the colony.'

'Special Branch?'

'Yes. It is a unit within your police force dedicated to keeping track of communist and Nationalist agents in Hong Kong. There are many of us.'

Though he had begun to suspect it, Huart's brows lifted. 'You're a spy?'

Wen continued the smooth smile. 'Perhaps you should close the balcony window. Voices carry far on such a night.'

Huart stood and slid the folding glass panels together. Stung by an urge to provoke, he asked: 'For which side do you spy, General Wen?'

Apart from a quick frown that killed the smile, the irascible question went unacknowledged. Wen announced instead: 'You have not been able to contact me lately as I have been travelling.' He sipped his Chivas.

'Travelling where, General Wen?'

'Washington. Seoul. And Hong Kong.' Wen paused, then went on, picking his words as if they were needles he was extracting from a box of pins. 'We knew in advance the North Koreans planned to cross the 38th Parallel on Sunday, June 25th, and we knew they would be supported by the Chinese Communists. It is inevitable that the PLA will become openly involved in the fighting soon, General Huart. My task is to stop the Korean conflict being used by Mao as a momentum to invade Taiwan. We are not yet ready to resist. Our navy is depleted – our flagship and several destroyers defected last autumn. We need the help of the Seventh Fleet for now.' The smile reformed. 'May I have some more Chivas, please?'

Wen took the refilled tumbler. 'Taiwan is legally Chinese territory, but "China" should be defined. Britain has granted Mao the full recognition it has removed from Taipei. Does that mean your country considers Taiwan should come under Mao's jurisdiction? If so, any invasion of it might be seen as a civil matter and not an act for the UN to denounce. We had to know what President Truman thought of it. We had to be sure the UN would protect us once war broke out in Korea. That is why the Generalissimo's aides, myself included, have been on highly secret diplomatic missions. It was I who told Chiang to accept Truman's demand to lift the blockade. It would, in any case, have been superfluous once hostilities broke out as Mao would have had to cancel any plans to reopen trade with the West. And isn't that what has happened? I regret your company has been a victim of it, General Huart, but there are much bigger things at stake. Now do you understand why you have been unable to contact me? All this was unforeseen when we last met in Taipei in . . . When was it?'

'February. February 15th.'

'Yes. Five months and four days ago. It seems longer.'

Huart used the ensuing silence to contemplate how to manipulate the subject onto cement plants. 'Of course I understand, General Wen,' he said with studied politeness. 'But I'm certain a man in your high position has not risked it to come and see me in Hong Kong at this hour of the night to discuss merely politics and war. I am now, as you know well from our dealings together, a businessman.'

Wen produced an easy smile. 'Indeed. My renewed apologies. Then we will revert to business. The contract which we have signed is null and void.'

Alarm stabbed Huart until he saw it was only an opening move. 'Go on.'

'I speak technically, of course. I hope it will be possible to find a way to reinstate the contract.' Wen raised his insignificant eyebrows.

Huart felt his own brows quiver, his palms sweat. 'Can you suggest one?'

Wen now smiled with confidence. He was on familiar ground, enjoying the game. 'The "Terms of Payment" clause has been broken. The deposit was not paid by due date. General Huart, you are legally justified in suing the New Productivity Corporation.'

'I'm sure that won't be necessary.' Huart knew that any claim would not even reach a Taipei court, let alone have a chance of being upheld.

'Excellent. Then we can agree to amend the clause by adding an appendix to the contract. It will naturally involve an expense.'

Huart quietly expelled his breath with relief. So it was only a question of money. 'How much . . . "expense"?'

'Oh, nothing visible, of course.' The smile expanded. It was like a lens that opened and closed by remote control. 'Madam Chiang has told me that the Generalissimo wishes the contract to go ahead. She was educated in the States and is his adviser on that country. She visits often, as everybody knows. Mr Kreitzer is a close friend of General Mark Clark, and through him has access to General Eisenhower, the next President of the United States. The contract has important political implications.'

Huart's heart lifted. After the weeks of anguish that throbbed in recent memory like an open wound, Wen's melodious diction was sweet balm. But he wished the man would get to the point. 'I see.'

The smile grew hard. 'President Chiang has put full responsibility in my hands. The decision whether the contract is to proceed or not is mine.'

'I see,' Huart repeated thoughtfully, knowing he was up against a master negotiator. 'You did mention an "invisible" penalty, General Wen.'

'Correct. An adjustment in my personal... er... commission.'

'It was ten per cent.'

'Yes.'

'And now?'

'Fifteen.'

Huart thought quickly. It was most probable Wen was dealing for himself. The deposit was still twenty per cent, of which he now wanted to grab three-quarters. Golden State Cement would be unable to give Cumberland China anything out of the meagre five per cent balance. This left Huart two choices: accept that there was no advance commission for him to clear his slate with the H and K, or negotiate Wen down.

He stood and crossed to the decanter of Chivas. He did it slowly, deliberating en route. One fact dominated: Wen was a greedy man. One question followed: How greedy? He knew the answer to that. It was clear they had dire need of each other. Their negotiating positions were equal.

As if he had been reading Huart's thoughts, Wen tipped the balance in his favour by saying: 'I do not wish to cause my business friends hardship, General Huart. Especially you. I know you are in financial difficulties and your head office in Shanghai is folding. But business is business. When in a position like yours, a reduced commission is better than none at all.'

Huart paused, decanter in hand and attempted to redress the imbalance. 'You forget the debt I am owed by China. The General-issimo's promise – '

The derisive laugh came instantly, as if the gambit had been expected. 'General Huart, you only have my word that Chiang remembers you at all. How do you know the flattering little story I told to everyone in Taipei was not made up by me entirely for my own amusement? Tell me, did the president invite you for an audience on either of your February visits?'

Huart could not stop the frown in time. It was true! He thought quickly, seeking the elusive solution, chasing the string tied to it that flew madly about his questing brain. 'What is the procedure for reinstating the contract?' he asked to break the long silence.

Wen's smile turned comfortable and he visibly relaxed as if the inevitability of his victory had loomed before him. 'A simple telephone call from me to Taipei will suffice. I can do it tonight, but you must first agree to my terms. And you must agree to them right now.'

The arrogance, whether real or imagined, was the turning point. It fired Huart's anger and he looked up sharply. 'I cannot, sir!' The surprise that trespassed upon Wen's face exposed a patch of shaky ground and Huart saw it. 'No, General Wen, I will not decide now. I will report on our discussion to Mr Kreitzer. It is his decision.'

Now the smile was forced. 'But you will lose vital time!' It was a cross between an entreaty and a warning. 'Your loans fall due in one week. On July 26th. Oh, do not be concerned with the integrity of your staff. It is not from them I get my information. Hong Kong gossips, you know.'

Huart said nothing, convinced he had prised open a crack in the oriental façade of General Wen, who made as if to say more, then nodded as if he had decided instead that the parley was ended. Huart held his breath. Would Wen back down? Would he reduce or even withdraw his claim for more commission? Wen stood up and, cocking an eye at his reflection in the cheval glass, took the time to smooth with his palms every single crease out of his suit. A smile that could have been one of resignation appeared on his face. 'Very well, then . . .' There came the briefest silence in which, for a fraction of a second, Huart even believed he had won. ' . . . I shall return here in forty-eight hours. I can give you no longer than that. It is too dangerous for me here in Hong Kong. If you do not, at that time, accept my request for fifteen per cent commission, I will have no choice but to instruct Taipei to cancel the contract outright.'

Huart willed his features to be faithful. Wen was no master at negotiation. He was a maestro. He had feigned weakness to give false encouragement, then had reinforced his original demand with even greater sway.

'In forty-eight hours, then,' Huart mustered, his words barely audible. 'I will have Mr Kreitzer's decision then.' He extended his hand like a gentleman in business. 'I promise nothing, General Wen.'

'So.' The hand disappeared into the clasp, but despite the power of it, the smile stayed intact. 'Thank you for the whisky, General Huart. It was most excellent.' And Wen was gone, leaving his last sequence of aspirations piercing the night air.

Huart went into the bathroom to wash the sweat from his body, out of his hair and stretched out under the mosquito net to think. The whisky had revived his senses and reverberations of the battle of wits just ended rang in his brain. He reviewed every word of it, and his ears picked up every sound in the sleeping Hotel Cecil and in Central District outside. He was excited, uncertain, apprehensive.

After several minutes he got up and checked the time. It was 1:30. In San Francisco it would be 9:30 a.m. yesterday. He dialled the operator and placed a call to Chuck Kreitzer. He sat and waited for his connection, listening to his head as something that Wen had said repeated itself over and over: 'When in a position like yours, a reduced commission is better than none at all.'

The soft tap at the door two nights later came well before midnight. Wen was identically attired; indeed his clothes did not look as if they had been off his body in the meantime. It was evident something other than eagerness had driven him to pre-empt the appointment. His grip was more inconsequential than usual, the flesh of his palm was clammy and a vapour of fear seemed to exude from his skin. The Kuomintang general had Huart wondering if he had the power to rescue the contract after all.

But the misgivings were dispelled when Wen accepted with minimum demur the counter-offer authorised by Kreitzer of twelve and a half per cent. 'General Huart, I will leave you now and make the telephone call to Taipei as promised. You will find I am a man of my word.'

Huart nodded, privately happy enough to believe almost anything. 'Thank you, General Wen. Mr Kreitzer expects the deposit to be remitted to San Francisco by telegraphic transfer immediately. It is Friday morning on the West Coast. He must receive it on Monday.' So he can transfer my three-quarters of a per cent back to me by next Wednesday when my loans fall due, he added to himself. 'And please – I'm not "General" Huart any more. Just "Mister" Huart: civilian and businessman.'

'Very well, Mister Huart. Fear not. Mr Kreitzer will not be

disappointed. The money will be sent in time for him – and for your bankers. July 26th will be a fine day for you.' The smile was shrewd, but fleeting.

They shook hands again. At the door Wen turned to look up at Huart with a strange fraternal expression and whispered: 'Everything I told you and the others about President Chiang's feeling for you was the truth. He remembers you and would be honoured to meet you again. Can you forgive me for my attempt to mislead you the other night?'

'We were negotiating, General Wen.'

Wen nodded. 'You learn fast, Mr Huart.' Then the face that had smiled through those negotiations two nights before drew into a frown. 'You do have friends in high places in Taipei. But you also have enemies: men who would have you ruined, degraded to the lowest depths imaginable – '

'Whatever do you mean?' Huart protested. 'Enemies in Taipei – ?'

'You also have enemies in Hong Kong.'

'In Hong Kong? Me? Don't be ridiculous, General Wen.'

'Examine your past, Mr Huart. Examine it thoroughly. You have crossed a highly dangerous man. A venomous man. You must beware. You must beware the man with the walking stick.'

Huart opened his mouth, but Wen was gone, evaporated as if he had never been, into the shadows that filled the stairwell. Puzzled, he went to the balcony and looked down into Ice House Street. There was no movement to be seen. The midnight darkness concealed all. It was as if General Wen Wei-tung had never left the Hotel Cecil, as if he had never been in Huart's room. Except for the smell of fear he had left behind him.

Wen's departing words stayed with Huart, too. Gradually a vision formed of the Bund . . . Jennifer on his arm . . . a black Cadillac . . . a man in a long-gown. Yes, the man was leaning on a walking stick. He was speaking to Huart. Four words . . .

The vision faded and left him with only the painful memory of her, and the two infant sons she had given him. He looked down and saw that the decanter of Chivas was in his hand. And he knew that although he might be a man reprieved, he was still a man cursed.

Midnight chimed upon Central District. Saturday, July 22nd, 1950, the worst day of the third life of John Stanford Huart, began.

[199]

14

Ng Yap the newspaper hawker rented thirty square feet of the wall of the building on the corner of Ice House Street and Queen's Road, Central from the Wo Hop Wo triad society. Every morning he collected on his bicycle his quota of the three English and dozen or so Chinese language dailies and arranged them along the patch of wall that was his. He took care not to encroach more than four feet onto the footpath or the police would book him. He was never late with his 'squeeze' or the Wo Hop Wo would hack the third and fourth fingers from his right hand. To date the police had let him be, and the Wo Hop Wo had ensured no competition dared set up within a hundred yards of his spot.

Ng Yap minded his own business. Never in his life had he cooperated with the police. He shunned them like the plague he considered them to be. At dawn on Saturday, July 22nd he arrived at his spot, leaned his bicycle against 'his' wall, glanced up at the adjacent steps. And quit a lifelong habit.

'*Gau meng! Ging chaat! Gau meng ahhh! Ging chaat!*' Save life! Police!

Realising his error, Ng Yap shut his mouth tight. He shook his head hard to agitate his grey matter. Why had the body been put there like that in the very place he was sure to see it before anyone else? It had to be a warning from the Wo Hop Wo! They had found him out! For three months he had been fiddling his 'returns': taking a sheet from inside each paper and folding them together to look like one extra. Ng Yap's brain stopped operating beyond this point. He was guilty! He stared with stark eyes at the naked corpse sitting with its red raw severed neck with the white bone showing, the head with the eyes of horror clasped between its hands in its lap, the garments folded in a neat pile beside it with the shoes placed on top. Then he heard the running footsteps and looked up to see the khaki uniform coming across Des Voeux Road towards him.

The police constable stopped in his tracks when he saw the corpse on the steps. '*Aiiiyah!*' he breathed. He could not tear his eyes from it for many seconds. By the time he did so and got his legs to give chase to the Queen's Road corner, Ng Yap the newspaper hawker was long gone.

'Come on in, Clive!'
But the knock came again. It was officious. It had to be Bedrix.

'It's open, Clive! You're early. I've great news! Come to the balcony and join me in some bacon and eggs and hear all about – Who are you?'

'Mornin', sir. Sorry to interrupt your breakfast. I'm Detective Inspector Peay. Spelt P-E-A-Y. Not P-E-A or even P-E-E. This's Sergeant Wong.'

Knife and fork in hand, Huart looked blankly across the room at the man in the rumpled suit who was framed in the doorway, a uniformed sergeant behind him. Peay was a caricature of the expatriate policeman, complete with West End accent. He came forward, stepping over the rug like it was a minefield, whilst the sergeant waited just inside the door.

Huart stood up and extended a hand as Peay came onto the balcony. 'John Huart. H-U-A-R-T. Not H-E-W-I-T-T. How can I help you, Inspector?'

'We're from Wa'erfront Branch, sir. We wonder if we might ask you some questions. Routine is all, sir.' Peay produced his identification card.

Huart glanced at it before nodding. 'Some tea?'

Peay nodded and spoke in heavily accented Cantonese to the sergeant who nodded and left the room, positioning himself outside in the corridor. 'Black wi' one sugar, sir. Sergeant Wong's strictly a *ching cha* man.'

Huart poured a fresh cup. 'May I finish breakfast? It's getting cold.'

'Go ahead, sir. Prob'ly nowt to do wi' you any'ow. But you know 'ow it is. We 'ave to check all leads. 'Specially when it's murder.' Peay dropped into a rattan chair which protested with a loud creak, and took up his cup. Huart looked up from his bacon and eggs to see the eyes of the Law probing him like a finger seeking a pulse. 'Body of a Chinese male was found at dawn on steps of a buildin' on corner of Ice House Street and Queen's Road. Jus' up there . . .' Peay nodded over the balcony.

'The building in which my company has its office?' Huart wondered aloud.

'If you say so, sir.' Peay extracted a creased notebook and flicked the pages. 'Eastern corner?' He saw Huart's nod. 'Quite a coincidence then, sir. I mean – that bein' your buildin' an' body havin' a card from this 'otel. You know, a card like you'd show a taxi driver.'

Huart frowned. 'The card brought you here?'

'We 'ad t'be quick off mark b'fore people went and checked out, sir.'

Huart placed his knife and fork on his plate parallel to the last slice of bacon. His appetite had left. 'You said it was murder, Inspector?'

'Yes.' Peay crossed his legs and the rattan protested again. 'S'no doubt 'bout that. He was murdered alright, poor chap. Good n' proper.'

'Oh? How?'

The roll of the eyes gave a theatrical emphasis. 'A terrible end, sir. Poor chap was done-in like I never seen b'fore – and I seen ev'ry kinda triad killin'. Be'eaded, sir. Neat an' clean like it was done by surgeon up at Matilda. 'Ead surgeon. Sorry, sir – bad joke. But this chap's 'ead was put in 'is lap, 'eld b'tween 'is 'ands. Body was stark bollick naked – sittin' on steps o' your buildin', sir. Found by a constable, it was. Lucky, too. Cause a right stir when office workers – yours included – start to arrive. I mean, no clothes, no 'ead an' all, sir.'

Despite himself, Huart's jaw dropped. 'How . . . How terrible.'

'Yes, sir. Terrible. Strange, too. Y'see, there was no blood. No blood anywhere. 'E'd been done-in someplace else and put on those steps. Queer it is. 'Nother funny thing. We can't fix time of death . . .'

Huart's eyes had fallen to the floor as if reading there some sinister but indefinable memory. He looked up. 'Oh? Why?'

'Well, though blood was fresh-like, rigor mortis 'ad set in, 'adn't it? It 'ad to or else body wouldn't sit there like it did, would it? Stone bloody cold it was, sir – 'scuse me French. T'was like it 'ad been deep froze in shape we found it. Like a bloomin' statue it was, sir. Oh, 'tis a ritual murder t'beat all ritual murders, so 'elp me.'

The tea in Huart's cup had no taste. 'How . . . How can I help, Inspector?'

'Well, sir, bellboy says at midnight last night 'e saw a Chinese male fittin' description of deceased descendin' stairs from this floor. Your room's next to stairs. You 'ave a visitor last night, sir?'

'No.' Huart's reply came so quickly he surprised himself with it. 'Er . . . could you describe the man that was murdered, Inspector.'

Peay squinted down at his notebook. 'Chinese. Five foot four. Fifties. Short n' stocky. 'Ead 'ad been dipped in Brylcreem – 'scuse me, sir. And it 'ad a moustache. Clothes piled beside 'im were cotton suit, kinda off-white in colour . . . That card I told you about was in pocket –'

'What shoes . . ? What were the shoes?'

Peay glanced up quizzically, then down again at his notebook. 'American leather casuals. New and expensive . . .' He looked up. Huart held his breath.

' . . . with white uppers.'

Huart's hands flew to his head, fingers outstretched, raking backwards through his hair. He coughed and the tea rose into his throat.

'Sir?'

Huart smiled dumbly. 'Tea . . . It . . . It went down the wrong way. Sorry.' He rallied himself. 'White uppers? No. That's not correct. I did see a Chinese man fitting the description in the lobby a few days ago, but he wore sandals. I thought it incongruous: business suit and sandals . . .'

Peay frowned. 'I see.'

Huart watched the detective writing in the notebook whilst a typhoon blew about the inside of his head. It couldn't be! It just couldn't be!

'Could you give me a report on your activities last night, sir?'

'Yes, of course. I worked in my office to about 8:30, then dined alone in the hotel restaurant until ten. The serving staff could confirm that. Then I wrote a letter to my sister in England here in my room. You can see the envelope on the dressing table. I went to bed at 11:30 or so.'

'Slept well?'

'Like a log. Awoke at 6:30.'

'Didn't get up durin' night at all, sir?'

'No, Inspector. Does someone say I did?'

'Well, sir . . . yes. Bellboy says 'e 'eard voices in your room as 'e went by five minutes b'fore midnight t'douse corridor lamps. When 'e came back 'e saw a man goin' down stairs.'

'He's mistaken. Or perhaps I talk in my sleep.'

Peay nodded and stood up. 'Wife says I do. That's all f'now, sir. Thanks f'your patience. These triad killin's are impossible t'solve. But we 'ave t'go through motions, you understand. Goodbye, sir.' He turned to go, then looked back. 'You sleep wi' your light on, sir?'

'I do. I've done so ever since Burma in '42. Goodbye, Inspector.'

Peay nodded and joined the sergeant in the corridor and they moved to the next room. Bedrix appeared at the door. Huart looked up at his general manager and tried to smile through the greyness that grew on his face like a fungus. He tried to push up the weight that bore down on him, driving him through the floor. All the way down. Right to Hell!

*

At 11:15 a Special Branch investigator was shown into Huart's office.

He had been stuck to his chair for three hours, staring out the window at the small-leafed banyans along Battery Path above Queen's Road. The black 'air roots' hung perpendicularly from their angular boughs like ropes from a gallows, their convoluted trunks epitomised his wretchedness. The Chinese staff knew that disaster had struck and kept away from his door. Roboza was at the Hongkong and Kwangtung Bank and Bedrix was discussing insurance with Cathay Electric Corporation. The office was like the grave this bad, bad, bad Saturday morning.

'Fender.' The introduction was as economical as the handshake.

Huart nodded. His eyes scanned the ID card and registered nothing.

'I'm from Special Branch, Mr Huart. You've heard of us?'

'Yes. You're colonial security.' His voice was so soft he could hardly hear it himself. 'What do you want with me? I'm no spy.'

Fender cleared his throat. Huart stared at him like a drunk attempting to focus on a single object. 'The Chinese male who was murdered last night and put on the steps of this building . . . You're aware of it?'

Huart nodded inanimately.

'We know who he is – was. He was a three-star Kuomintang general. He was here under cover. It would be convenient to deduce he was executed by communist agents, but they never go to such extremes and they keep away from Central District. The mode of execution is more in keeping with the style of a *tong*, or triad society. Strangely enough, this particular form of assassination was popular in Shanghai with one that backed the Kuomintang. It was called *Chin Pang* – the Green Circle Society.'

'Perhaps the man was defecting.'

'We have thought of that.'

Huart swallowed hard. He had to ask. 'What was his name?'

'Wen Wei-tung.'

The axe fell. Huart's head lolled as though his neck was broken. A numbness claimed him as he accepted the ultimate confirmation.

'You know him?'

Huart willed his faculties back together. The last thing he needed right now was an interrogation from Special Branch that could lead anywhere. He wanted Fender to go. He wanted to be alone. He had to think! What to do? What to do now there was no contract, no deposit from the New Productivity Corporation of the Republic of China, no commission from Golden State Cement.

And now that the H and K loans fell due in just three working days and had not the remotest chance of being paid.

He looked up and shook his head.

Fender cleared his throat again. 'Visited Taiwan recently, Mr Huart?'

'One look at my passport will show you I go to Taipei quite often on business. And so do many other Hong Kong trading company executives.'

'Are you sure that you have never met a General Wen Wei-tung in Taipei?'

'Quite sure.'

Fender smiled thinly and stood up. 'Very well. That's all for now.' He made to move to the door, then turned. 'Would you happen to know what this might mean?' He took a folded piece of paper out of his pocket and flicked it across the desk. Huart opened it to see four complicated Chinese ideograms drawn vertically in dark red.

'Sorry. Can't read Chinese. One of the staff can translate it for you.'

'I wouldn't ask your staff if I were you, Mr Huart.'

'Why?'

'You wouldn't see them for dust. I don't actually need a translation. I know what the characters mean. You see, I'm a student of the language – written and spoken. Not only Cantonese, I'm fluent in the Shanghai dialect, too. I spent several years in the Shanghai Municipal Police. Were you ever in Shanghai, Mr Huart?'

'Three years. '37 to '40. British Army.'

'Perhaps we've met before, then.' Fender plucked the paper from Huart's fingers and pointed to it. 'The Cantonese pronounce that *Say Yau Yiu Gu*. In Shanghai it would be *Sze Yiu Yu Gu*. The literal meaning is: "Your destiny is a fate worse than death". Have you seen or heard that message before, Mr Huart? Look at it again. It was in a pocket of the coat that was beside the corpse of General Wen Wei-tung.' Fender watched Huart's eyes. He saw the reaction there, subdued with effort, but there.

'I don't remember,' Huart breathed. 'I'm not a student of the dialects.'

Fender leaned across the desk and held the four ideograms in front of Huart's face. 'That's not ink, you know.'

'What?' Huart was only half listening.

'Those Chinese characters – they were not written in ink. It's human blood. Most likely the blood of General Wen.'

'Oh. So?'

'It's a warning – a warning in blood. I wonder who it's for?' Fender turned the paper around until the reverse was facing Huart and watched his eyes widen spontaneously. 'It is one of your company's credit notes, is it not? Now that is interesting. Somebody really does believe that you, or your company, owes them something.'

15

EXIT PERMIT GRANTED STOP TRAIN LEAVING SHANGHAI MONDAY JULY 24TH ETA HONG KONG BORDER NOON JULY 26TH STOP LOOK FORWARD TO SEEING ALL STOP

ANDREW

The telegram was waiting on Huart's desk for his return from a lunch with Bedrix in the Red Room of the Hong Kong Club during which he had singularly failed to pass himself off as good company. At least not all news was bad, he pointed out to himself. But the irony did not escape him. July 26th. Andrew's arrival would coincide with ownership of his company passing to the Hongkong and Kwangtung Bank. Huart reviewed his pre-lunch call to Percy Landers in which he had confessed the loans could not be repaid on time.

'I'm exceedingly sorry, John. There can be no extension. My star in the bank is tarnished enough over the Donn Line deal. I'm so sorry.'

'Tell me what will happen, Percy. What's the procedure?'

The banker hesitated. 'We'll have our auditors go through your books. They'll decide if the company should be liquidated or sold.'

'Sold?'

'You know the score, John. Male & Son is a likely buyer. They would, I'm sure, consider many of your agencies complementary to theirs. You might consider approaching Ivor Male yourself before the 26th.'

What a welcoming present for Andrew, Huart thought sadly. Driven from his home after an extended ordeal made worse by periods of false hope cruelly terminated, to find that what remained

[206]

of his *hong* was passing to a competitor for just enough to clear its debts. I hope he's up to the shock. 'I'll think about it, Percy,' Huart had muttered and hung up.

It was too much. A man of logic, he was neutralised by the notion that a curse delivered in Shanghai a decade before could now put an end to him in Hong Kong. He had revealed something of his predicament over lunch.

'You're suffering from a case of bad *fung shui*, John,' Bedrix had observed phlegmatically despite sight of the fact that if the company went belly-up on Wednesday, his personal future went with it.

'What?'

'*Fung shui*. The Cantonese believe it is the embodiment of the effects on life of wind and water. They believe these elements greatly influence a person's, a family's or a company's share of good or bad fortune.'

'I've heard something of it. What does it all mean?'

'Most foreigners dismiss it as superstition. Personally I don't. I feel it tempts fate to reject the principles of *fung shui*, which actually tend to follow the laws of basic physics. The Chinese position items in their homes so as not to obstruct the flow of good fortune, but to block off the bad. Mirrors are hung facing the door to reflect bad spirits and furniture must be in the right place. For example a bed must not face a door or a mirror. There must be light, fresh air, water, an aquarium or two. It has credence when you consider the earth's magnetic field and the effect of environment on health.' Bedrix had proffered a tentative smile. 'John, your office is dark with that blind half down. And the glass on your desk is cracked. That's bad. It gives a fractured image of yourself. To the Chinese that means death. You should replace it.'

Huart, feeling uncomfortable, had changed the subject. But immediately after lunch he had quietly asked Roboza to employ the services of a geomancer. The office manager had looked up at him in astonishment, then had smiled respectfully and nodded. 'You are very wise, sir.'

'It's Mr Bedrix who's wise. I have a great deal to learn.'

Huart fingered Andrew's telegram. What to do next? he asked himself over and over. He should telephone Kreitzer with the tragic news. He would do it tomorrow. Rather than sit in the office infecting the staff with his mood he decided to deliver the telegram to the Gloucester in person.

'Missee take nap,' whispered the floor boy as he pointed to the

DO NOT DISTURB sign hanging from the knob on the door to Paulette's bedroom.

'I'll not wake her, Ah Gun. But I'd like to put the telegram where she's sure to see it when she gets up. Could you let me into the lounge?'

The floor boy hesitated, then grinned. For only the tall-big foreign devil would he break a hotel rule and put his family's ricebowl at risk. He cautiously unlocked the second door of the two-room suite with his utility key. 'Missee want have master come Hong Kong chop-chop,' he said sagely to himself as he returned to his desk beside the elevator.

Huart moved to the davenport, intending to put the telegram beside the telephone. He heard a sound from the bedroom and stopped. It was muffled conversation. He recognised Paulette's voice and was about to knock at the adjoining door when he heard the male voice. A moan and a gasp of passion rooted him to the spot. He listened like a common eavesdropper.

'Why didn't you write this time? Oh, darling.'

'I like to surprise people.'

'Come here. God, I've missed you so much. Oh, the bed's a mess.'

'Who cares? Don't take your stockings off, Paulette. Just lie back.'

Back in his office, Huart employed himself staring at his telephone until it rang.

'Is that Mr John Huart?' It was the plum voice of the international operator.

'It is.' It must be Chuck Kreitzer. The time to announce the disaster had come. No, that couldn't be. It would be midnight in San Francisco.

'A call for you from Shanghai – '

'Shanghai? You must be mistaken.' Andrew was boarding the train today.

'No mistake, sir. A Mr Huart-Brent calling. He wishes to reverse the charges. Will you accept?'

'Er . . . yes. Yes!' My God, what had gone wrong?

'Connecting you now. Hold on, please. Go ahead Mr Huart-Brent. Mr John Huart is on the line now.'

'Andrew? Andrew, are you there?'

'Yes, John. I'm still here.' The voice was remote. 'I'm sure as hell still here.'

[208]

'Whatever's happened? I thought you were boarding the train today.'

'I did. I did board it. But they took me off just before it pulled out of the station. They came to me and grabbed hold of me and hauled me off the train. Like a bloody criminal. They hauled me off. They – '

'Andrew! But why?'

A haggard laugh came down the line, followed by a muffled silence in which Huart thought he could hear his cousin coughing uncontrollably. 'They have unfinished business with me – and with you, John. Oh, I feel so ashamed. I've let you down, John. I've – '

'Andrew, stop that! You're talking to family. What unfinished business?'

There was more coughing, then: 'Cumberland Building. They say taxes are outstanding on it. No foreigner can own property in China. It's a new rule. I must sell Cumberland Building to them before I can go – ' Huart waited helplessly for another coughing spasm to subside. ' – I said they could have it for nothing. No, they said. It has to be legal and above board. I have to sell it to them. So I said its cost was equal to the taxes due on it. No, they said. That's no good. The building's not worth that much, they said. John, can you believe it? Can you just bloody-well believe it!' Andrew was screaming now. 'The value of Cumberland Building according to their cockeyed assessment falls short of the tax due by . . . Guess how much. Guess how bloody much, Cousin!'

Huart had guessed. 'Ten thousand pounds.'

'Almost, Cousin. Almost. They're very ethical up here. Ten thousand pounds plus interest. Your personal ten thousand pounds plus interest, John. Frozen in the bank since the bloody Liberation! Liberation they call it now. Whose "liberation"? Not mine! Your life's savings, John. They want to clear their slate of it. They want you to authorise me to instruct the bank to pay the money to this thing they call "The State". Or they'll tear up my exit permit. John, I don't know what . . . I . . .'

'Andrew! Listen to me . . .' Huart's personal emergency suddenly seemed unimportant. He had to get his cousin out! His heart went down the landline, his compassion multiplied by what he had overheard an hour before. 'Andrew, the money's yours! If it buys you out of there it's worth every penny. I'll cable the authorisation at once. Hang on, Andrew. Hang on!'

Sobbing his thanks, Andrew hung up. His last word had been: 'Hurry!'

My God, thought Huart, what have they done to him? Andrew Huart-Brent, once the youngest taipan of the China Trade, now sounded like a broken old man. Again the words of Sir Robert Hart rang in his head, and this time he could not reject them as they rang with indisputable truth:

> 'The day will come when China will repay with interest all the injuries and insults she has suffered at the hands of the European powers.'

16

Every man in his short time on this earth is given a handful of days that contain a vicissitude of worth. For John Stanford Huart, Wednesday, July 26th, 1950 was such a day.

He arrived in his office later than usual: after nine. Again he had not slept, anticipating the cut of the H and K's knife a thousand times. He had placed a call to Kreitzer for the mid morning. Bad as the past week had been, this was surely going to be the worst day of his third life.

He had accepted the rationale that General Wen was seized at midnight on leaving the Cecil. Detective Inspector Peay had conjectured that the corpse had been frozen into its macabre configuration. There was an ice storage depot at the top of Ice House Street, indeed the thoroughfare had been named after it. Central District had been the scene of a crime most hideous, but Huart had still to fully accept it had been staged for him personally, its objective his financial and moral destruction. Even so, whether by design or happenstance, the assassins of General Wen Wei-tung had simultaneously put an end to the fledgling business career of one John Stanford Huart. For what was left to him? No family. No funds. Not even a reputation on which to rebuild his life.

And not only was he destroyed, so were the Huart-Brents. Andrew would find he had escaped from one ruinous situation only to be confronted with another: his *hong* gone, his finances used, his wife unfaithful. Shanghai had all but killed him. Hong Kong would finish the job. Now Huart knew the awful truth. He was indeed cursed.

When he had slept it had been superficial and invaded by

dreams that had no beginning and no end. The face of the man with the walking stick had floated upon the screen of his subconscious. What was the name that belonged to the face? Huart's memory had delved deeper, deeper. Then . . .

Tu Chien.

Tu Chien was in Hong Kong, too! Jennifer's lovely face, fringed with her shining titian hair, her eyes round with fear, had appeared.

'Darling, are you afraid of that man?'

He had sat bolt upright, wrenching himself from the dream. His forehead had scraped against the mosquito net and his sweat had adhered to the fabric then had dripped upon the back of his neck. He had slept no more.

On his arrival in his office he saw the changes at once: his desk faced east, the cracked glass top had been replaced by an octagonal blotter bound in red leather, the two wall paintings had been repositioned and in one corner there was a round aquarium with a half dozen goldfish. The geomancer had done his work. Huart smiled ruefully to himself. No longer could he be accused by Bedrix of tempting fate. The smile died fast.

July 26th was not only the day the H and K would call in its loans, it was payday. Or it should have been. But Cumberland China did not have the cash to pay monthly salaries, nor operating expenses. Bedrix would take in some insurance premiums and commission was due on a British Tube and Pipe contract with the Water Authority, but it would not be enough. The spectre of debtors' prison reared and Huart was momentarily gripped by panic. He grabbed for the arms of his chair and collapsed into it.

It was at that instant the telephone chose to ring. Huart started, then realised it was his call to San Francisco. It occurred to him he would be unable to settle the account for it as he picked up the receiver and made to deliver his well-rehearsed opening line, and was cut short by an effusive Californian voice that boomed down the line. 'Hey, John! Hey, John, baby! What a killer-diller you are! Jolly good show old man, old chap, old bean – as you Brits would say.'

Huart was thrown. 'Wait up, Chuck. Not so fast. There's been a disas – '

'What? Speak up, John! I can't hear you!'

Huart leaned closer to the mouthpiece and took a deep breath. He shouted his news across the Pacific Ocean: 'I said there's been a disaster!'

'A disaster? Whattaya talkin' about? Hey, John, whatta sense o' humour you've got. Oh boy, do you Brits really slay me.' Then, to Huart's utter astonishment, Kreitzer's booming laugh roared down the line.

'What's so funny, Chuck? I really don't think – '

'A disaster? Are you kiddin'? Half a million dollars is a disaster?'

Huart frowned. 'What? What did you say about a half a million dollars?'

'Hey, come on, John. This call is too expensive to use up on jokes. The deposit, boy! Are you hung over or somethin'?'

Huart stifled his response. What was Kreitzer talking about? Half a million US dollars, or slightly more, did equate to twenty percent of the contract. He was chasing for it, of course. But, no – his tone was wrong. Kreitzer was happy, deliriously happy. What was going on?

'Chuck, are you calling me or am I calling you?'

'I'm callin' you o'course! It came in this afternoon. Bank's closed now. It's after six. We'll transfer your share first thing in the mornin'.'

It took several seconds for Huart to digest what he had just heard and convert it back to words. 'What? Say that again, Chuck, please.'

'Great news, eh? That General Wen of yours is a killer-diller, too. Hey, John, we're drinkin' champagne here. French o'course. Hear the corks?'

Now Huart's mouth was open, his lips were moving, but there was no sound coming. His brain careered in all directions as it tried to make sense of Kreitzer's words. Had he heard them correctly? He had to be sure. He had to ask one more time. It was so important. So vital. 'Chuck – ' He spoke with his words spaced like a grammar school beginner. 'Are – you – saying – you – have – the – deposit? – You – have – got – the – cash?'

'Hey, what's wrong with you? I told you already we got the cash!'

'In – full – Chuck?'

'Half a million lovely greenbacks! The twenty percent deposit! Half a million smackeroonies! Hey, John – you sure you're okay?'

Huart pulled the receiver from his ear and held it away from him and looked at it as if it was the most beautiful thing he had ever seen in his life. He shook his head slowly from side to side in wholesale disbelief. Then, slowly, gradually, elation budded simultaneously with illumination. Somehow General Wen had telephoned from the Cecil, or had passed word to an aide before he had been set upon. Or he had authorised the reinstatement of the contract in anticipation of the decision on his commission, in which case it would have proceeded regardless of what the decision had been. But it was all irrelevant. The deposit was paid! The contract was saved! Cumberland China and the Huart-Brents and John Stanford Huart had all been saved! The world was back in one piece!

Then, like a shifting of gears, Huart's thought processes changed up, to be interrupted by a synthetic sound that was coming from the end of his right arm: 'Hey, John! What's up? You still there? Hey, John!?'

Huart brought the telephone back to his ear, and spoke into it in a matter-of-fact tone of voice: 'Chuck, General Wen is dead.'

'Huh? How's that? Dead? Dead, you said?'

'Yes.'

'How? When? Where?'

'Murdered. Last Friday night. Here in Hong Kong.'

'Murdered? In Hong Kong? What in hell was he doin' in Hong Kong?'

Too late, Huart thought of Special Branch and the possibility that his line was being tapped. 'It seems he was killed by communist agents.'

'Goddamn! That's heavy. How does it affect us?'

Huart found that he was suddenly thinking very clearly and Fender and his Special Branch mattered little. 'Chuck, listen. Wen is not important any more. But his commission is still in your bank account . . . isn't it?'

'Hey, it sure is. We're in no hurry for his sake after the way he went and screwed us around like . . .' Kreitzer's voice trailed off as his brain switched onto Huart's wavelength. Then: 'What should we do, John?'

'Chuck, do you trust me?'

'Hey, the money's in the bank, John. Sure I trust you.'

'Good. Then don't remit the twelve-and-a-half percent into Wen's account for the time being. Wait till you hear further from me. Clear?'

'Clear, John. How long'll it be, d'you think?'

'You'll have my instructions before the end of the week.'

'Hey, you're a killer-diller, John,' chuckled Kreitzer and rang off.

Huart put down the receiver a changed man. He sat in cogitation and listened to the tempo of his heart return to normal. Then he called Landers with the news and pleaded for a forty-eight hour reprieve.

[213]

'I'll stonewall as long as I can, John. I believe you, but the other two on the loan committee probably won't. It'll take two days to produce the documentation anyway. But I didn't tell you that, you hear?'

'Loud and clear, Percy!' Huart hung up and left the office. He headed for the Central Praya and the Star Ferry. The solitude of the leisurely ride across the harbour and back again was what he needed. He had to give clear, uninterrupted thought to his next move.

From the Praya he saw the black bellied clouds, swollen with rain, piled upon each other behind Lei Yue Mun. He saw the flashes of lightning and heard the belated distant rumbling of thunder. Fishing junks scuttled to the Causeway Bay shelter over the heavy swell that pulsated through the harbour. The humidity ahead of the tropical storm was oppressive.

Hawkers called out prices, discounting them at each call as they pushed for business before the storm hit. A junk drew up to the Praya as Huart passed and a deck hand cried out in harsh Tangar dialect, his attention divided between the berthing and the intimidating clouds that tumbled closer by the second. A coolie ran forward carrying a bamboo pole with a sling tied to one end, almost colliding with Huart in his desperation to collect the first bale of duck feathers and lug it to one of the godowns for the cash he needed to secure his daily bowl of rice. More coolies converged at the run, jostling for position, cursing the anatomy and the families of the others in base monosyllabic Cantonese slang. Huart looked at it all through eyes that, it seemed, could suddenly see again.

Swept up in the noisy activity he could now acknowledge he loved, he paid his fare at the ferry terminal, stepped onto the ramp and up into the bobbing craft. He grimaced at the discomfort of his three-piece suit and felt hat, required dress for a company director in Hong Kong. His trousers hung loose at his waist, held there by braces. His torso moved inside his waistcoat, not with it. Now, at last, he could seek out a good tailor. His elation uplifted him and his smile was a joy to see.

The ferry rolled as it ploughed across to Kowloon. In the middle of the harbour on the return trip the first gusts of the storm hit. Rain in large drops splattered the windows. The Praya ahead, Queen's Building and its billboards, the Hongkong and Shanghai Bank, the Peak beyond, all disappeared from view one by one behind a closing curtain of grey rain.

Huart noticed none of it. He was thinking of Rex Wagoner. The Chicago insurance tycoon was indeed a 'character': flying in and flying out with only a co-pilot cum navigator for company. Yes, he was just the sort of character Paulette would find appealing. But it was not Wagoner's idiosyncracies nor his morals that Huart was thinking about. The man was no fool when it came to raw business and he had instantly hit the bullseye when the subject of Wen Wei-tung had been raised during a brief, cool encounter in the lobby of the Gloucester the evening before.

'So Wen came to a sloppy end, eh? Too bad. Anyway, he'd become superfluous as far as I was concerned. Pan Atlantic's contract's signed and valid for another eighteen months. Wen was a lone wolf in the Taipei system, y'know, Big Fella. Seems he made enemies. He shoulda cut a few of his offsiders into his deals. Might've stayed alive then. Now I'll have to find out whose palm to grease to have the contract renewed. It won't be a problem. This war in Korea'll go on for years.' Wagoner had looked wistful. 'But it's too bad we paid Wen's graft already. That's the real crime. Terrible waste – paying live money to a dead man.'

The ferry docked at the Hong Kong pier. It pitched back and forth and up and down as the storm whipped up the waves and the piles churned them into white water. The ramp banged down and Huart's foot was the first upon it. He negotiated the steep, slippery surface with ease, his body balanced, his mind relaxed in the satisfying state that comes after a decision moulded under pressure of deep thought. The monsoon rain on the corrugated iron roof of the terminal was deafening. Huart was oblivious to that, too. His course of action was decided, and it entailed outright rejection of the warning drawn in the blood of General Wen Wei-tung.

He stepped onto the Central Praya and strode through the deluge towards Ice House Street, defying the wall of rain to slow him down.

17

The third taipan of Cumberland China quit the Middle Kingdom in the mid afternoon of Monday, August 21st, 1950. He exited from Shum Chun, Kwangtung Province, across the narrow bridge at Lo Wu, watched all the way to the edge of the New Territories of Hong Kong, British Crown Colony, by PLA border guards whose hard eyes bid him good riddance. It was a hot, humid, baking day. Wisps of cirrus suspended in the pastel blue sky were no screen to the raw heat cast down from the sun over China.

It took Huart time to accept that the figure coming towards him was his cousin. A decade less six days ago a different body had housed the soul of Andrew Huart-Brent. In 1940 a young, virile leader had lived in it, looking to the challenges ahead, eyes aflame with an inbred conviction that Shanghai, Cumberland China and the Huarts would surmount every hardship. This body weighed not eight stone. Its head was completely bald, its eyes stood out like half inserted glass marbles either side of a squashed, twisted nose. Its left arm was tucked in a sling. In its right hand it carried a sagging burlap bag holding all that China had allowed it to keep. It dragged itself along with a pronounced limp, its face grimacing with pain at each step. But it held its taipan head high: the intrinsic Huart pride was intact, seemingly the only thing that was.

The family stood with Huart in heavy silence. Andrew's mother, his wife, his two daughters looked at their man coming slowly, painfully to them. Tears strained at the backs of their eyes. Huart bit his lip and moved forward. He reached out for his cousin's right hand and a shock went through him as he felt the feeble grip, the brittle bones and joints. He looked into the hollow eyes and read the chronicle of frustration and humiliation written there. He drew Andrew by the arm to his family.

Paulette embraced him wordlessly. Huart looked on, his emotions confused by too much knowledge. Adelaide hugged her son. The girls reached up to their father who squeezed their hands with all his meagre strength. Suzanne was not old enough to have her joy over the reunion diluted by anything, but Vivienne's eyes pressed closed then opened wide to give forth the tears that represented the shock which had assailed them all.

Andrew murmured: 'John, the sun shines here. Does it shine back there?'

Huart looked north through the high wire fence with its rolls of barbed wire. 'Yes, Andrew. The sun still shines in China, too. God willing, one day you'll be able to see it again yourself.' He helped his cousin down the path to the rented Buick and into the passenger seat, then assisted the women and children into the rear. He took the wheel and, as they negotiated the narrow army track that was barely wide enough even to accommodate the lumbering bullock carts they came upon, the small talk began.

'What have you done to yourself, son?' Adelaide asked.

The Andrew of old would have laughed and said: 'I walked into a door.'

But all humour had been squeezed from him like juice from a lemon and only a residue of sarcasm was left. 'I had a settling up with disgruntled staff who had a good try at rearranging me.' And they listened in disbelief as he recounted the assault in the Public Gardens.

'Thank God you're safe here with us,' Huart breathed. 'We'll have the hotel doctor examine you. He'll likely want you to rest up for a – '

'Go to hell,' Andrew muttered defiantly. He stifled a cough and clasped his right hand to his chest. 'D'you think after . . . coming all this way to be with my family I'm . . . going to let some quack take over my life?'

Only Huart had seen Andrew's discomfort. He kept his concern to himself and said instead: 'Then I prescribe a world cruise at company expense.'

'Don't joke so, John,' Adelaide chided. 'You talk like we were back in Shanghai and . . .' She hesitated, then finished: ' . . . and rich again.'

It made Huart's smile wider. 'No joke, Adelaide. I've bought tickets for you all. The company can afford it. No-one is to worry about Cumberland China again. *Maskee!* We can truly say it again, Andrew. *Maskee!*'

Andrew looked at him. 'Where have I heard that lie before?'

Huart said no more on it. He had just read the telegram from Edinburgh with Sinclair MacLurie's abbreviated congratulations on his reaching forty-four when Percy Landers had called to say: 'It's come in, John.'

'How much?'

'155,000 US dollars. What do you want us to do with it?'

Huart had smiled with sweet satisfaction. It was his share of General Wen's vagrant commission. 'I'll be around after we collect my cousin from Lo Wu. The money's to buy him and his family a holiday, and to finance the rebirth of Cumberland China. I'll be seeking advice, Percy.'

'I'll have my people ready,' Landers had said, and rang off.

The Buick pulled over the hot dry mountains until the gradient dropped away and ahead they saw Kowloon and the harbour and the Peak strong and green through the heat haze. They passed by squatter hamlets, then wound through the industrial village of Tsuen Wan. Kowloon was busy with roadside hawkers, vendors and craftsmen. One-room factories and clay godowns fronted the road. Rows of two and three-storey tenements were garlanded with washing hanging from bamboo poles that were pulled in ahead of the cloud of dust raised by the Buick's white-walled tyres. Huart braked and accelerated and braked as men, women and children, barrows and rickshaws, and a dog or a chicken violated his path. The air crackled with a babble of dialects and the noise of cottage industry, and was heavy with the out-and-out smell of fish drying, noodles cooking and joss burning. Then they were motoring past the villas and houses of Kowloon Tong. Here birds flew, flowers grew and paintwork was fresh. They drove down tree-lined Nathan Road, turned at Jordan Road to the vehicular ferry pier and waited in the stifling heat for it to arrive and discharge its load. The Buick was quiet. Andrew had fallen asleep. Huart turned to look at his lolling head, his mouth hanging open, his painful breathing. It occurred to him that his cousin was a year his junior, but there he was – slumped at his side, an object of premature aging, exhaustion and power lost.

'Make sure you don't come back till the spring,' Huart commanded in good humour as they stood together beneath the granite arch on Queen's Pier. 'But there's an executive decision you have to take before you go.'

'And that is?' A hint of the old sparkle had returned to Andrew's eyes. In the month of relative inactivity broken by infrequent visits to the branch office – now the head office of Cumberland China by process of elimination – he had put on a stone and a half. His nose had been reset, his broken ribs had mended, but his left arm was still in a sling.

'I want to appoint Clive Bedrix a director, provided you agree.'

'I do agree. A good man. One of the best I've seen and I've seen plenty. But he's bogged down with insurance paperwork. He needs a deputy. I'll think of some names and put them in a letter.' He picked up the burlap bag that he had carried out of China. 'Take care of yourself, Cousin.'

'I give you the same advice,' Huart said quietly. 'Promise me you'll see a doctor in San Francisco. A good one.'

Andrew shook his head. 'A man only needs one mother, John. And I'm taking mine with me. But I know you mean well. Thank you. *Au revoir.*'

'Farewell, Andrew.'

The pinnace pulled away and headed towards the centre of the harbour, where the flagship of the American President Line was moored to a buoy. Huart caught Paulette's eye and saw her turn

[218]

away too quickly. She knew he knew. Indeed he had found it hard to pretend he did not. He also knew that Rex Wagoner would likely be in San Francisco when the liner docked. He had debated hard with himself before deciding not to tell Andrew. His cousin was still too weak, physically and psychologically. Perhaps his marriage would repair itself on the cruise. Perhaps time would be kind and oblige the secret to be kept for ever. But he knew that this was only a compromise of mind and it nagged at him. It was as if, by some redistribution of filial responsibility, Andrew had become his baby brother.

For the rest of the Year of the Gold Tiger, South East Asia continued to rebuild, Cumberland China consolidated, and Huart covered the region with zest. He landed contracts in Manila for Rosefair and Benson, and in Saigon, where he learned about extended credits offered by international banks and guaranteed by governments. A five year 'supplier credit' at discounted interest coaxed Andrew Rochetet, President of Société le Indo-Chine, into signing the contract for his largest jute mill yet with Hugh Dunlop, Sales Director of Lionel Hope and Sons of Belfast. Huart signed as witness on behalf of Cumberland China, sole agent.

In October China annexed Tibet and rumours grew of impending escalation of the Korean conflict. Hong Kong perfected its entrepot role with South China, its population stabilised and its industry adjusted to serve it. Huart asked Bedrix to seek out local opportunities and the new director opened negotiations for a Harold Soames flour mill with Nanyang Bakeries in Kowloon. New buildings sprang up and the first Haig Denver contracts were secured: two freight elevators for Boilincold Bottle Company's factory-godown in Kennedy Town, three sets of passenger elevators for the new headquarters for Kang Shipping under construction in Queen's Road, Central and two for the luxury Pine Apartments on the Peak. Then in December Cumberland China took the prize contract for the twelve-storey Intercontinental Building rising on the Praya west of the G.P.O.

That same month Peking openly committed its troops to the Korean War, and Truman immediately placed a complete embargo on trade with China.

Huart decided to form an engineering department and inserted advertisements for a qualified manager in newspapers in London, San Francisco and New York. Andrew wrote recommending a man called Julian Younghusband who had made a name for himself in the Canton branch. He was located in Kent and recalled as manager of the recreated Insurance Department. Roboza was given a budget to redecorate the office and came up with a functional design, befitting an accountant. Teak wood partitions were to be erected around the desks of the directors, providing small but effective offices, Andrew's slightly more spacious than the others. Three desks for the department managers were placed in each corner of the general office, their staff grouped before them. They were for Roboza himself, Julian Younghusband, and the yet-to-be-hired engineering manager. At the end of 1950, Cumberland China had a staff of thirteen who comfortably filled out the eight hundred square feet of office space.

The Year of the Gold Rabbit began on Tuesday, February 6th, 1951. The first telegram of the new year contained Andrew's announcement that, as Paulette was keen to see the Festival of Britain, they were sailing to London and would not return to Hong Kong until the summer. Huart suspected Paulette's whims had more to do with the international movements of Rex Wagoner, but he cabled Andrew an acknowledgement and mailed him résumés of the best UK applicants for the post of engineering manager.

Hong Kong newspapers were full of Korea, where China and the US were in conflict for the first time in history. Truman talked the UN into a unilateral trade embargo, and the Hong Kong Government had no option but to support it. The colony's entrepot role with China ceased overnight.

The wet season introduced itself, as it invariably does, in May. In the Year of the Gold Rabbit it descended upon the South China coast with rolling black clouds that dumped tropical rain on Hong Kong for four straight days. It was on the fourth day, a Saturday, with the rain still coming down, that the life of John Stanford Huart connected with that of Lennie Cosgrove the Fifth.

18

The Bowling Alley Bar of the Hong Kong Club was packed with its regulars who, by by-law, were all male. That it was so at 4:00 p.m. on the first Saturday afternoon in May could only be because the Happy Valley races had been cancelled, and that could only happen if the track was under a foot of water. Outside, the rain kept up its bombardment, corralling all within the building and submerging the world in grey. Lamps hung from the high kalso-mined ceiling, casting down quiet light to be absorbed by the walnut panelling. The atmosphere was slow, but light-hearted.

Huart stood at the bar with his fist around a tumbler of straight Chivas listening to the loud liar dice schools and watching the half-dozen red-faced bowlers amuse themselves sending the ball down the single lane to smash into the skittles a half-second before the hapless *foki* could withdraw his fingers after setting them up. He nodded to men from Taikoo Dockyard, Mardens and the Godown Company and felt his senses rejuvenate after those five courses with Owen Catchpole in the Jackson Room. The Tele-phone Company head showed little restraint when entertained at Saturday lunch. But it was worth it. Huart was gaining on Ivor Male in taking up Catchpole's time and he was confident business would soon follow.

'Double pink gin chop-chop, Lancelot, you indolent miscreant!'

It had come from Huart's left. He turned to see a man whose name he did not know but whom he had seen often around Central and in the Club.

The bartender served the drink with alacrity. 'How many, Lancelot?'

'Thirteen now, Mr Cosglow. *Sup saam gaw.*'

'Lancelot, either you can't count, or you're getting a fat gin drinker's commission. Let me see my chit, you slubberdegullion.'

The man took the proffered wad of vouchers in fingers capped with nails bitten to the quick and squinted at each one. Huart studied him. He was short, thickset and his posterior bulged over the stool. A mop of white hair sat on a round head and a ruddy complexion belied the impression of an indoors man. He had a Havana cigar in his mouth, a red bowtie at his Adam's apple, and a copy of the *Hong Kong and Oriental Daily* at his elbow. Huart read the headlines.

IS UN EMBARGO HONG KONG'S DEATH SENTENCE?

'Thirteen it is.' The man clicked his teeth. 'How gin goes by.'

The bartender took the chits. 'You been here all af'noon, Mr Cosglow. Good thing races not cancel ev'ry Sat'day, ah? Why you drink so much?'

'Cosglow' laughed. 'A wise man once replied to that very ques-tion: "I drink to make other people interesting".'

'Then I be pretty int'rest to you by now, ah?'

Huart joined in the chuckles and when they both looked up at him, he stated: 'George Jean Nathan.'

'Cosglow' extended his hand. 'Lennie Cosgrove. Very pleased to meet you, George. Hope you don't mind me borrowing your quote.'

The grip was firm and warm and Huart found that he liked the little man at once. 'Mr Cosgrove. In fact, the name's John Huart.'

'You're more a George than a John, John. But anyway, what's your drink? And call me Lennie. I detest formality.'

'Perhaps another scotch is in order. It is Saturday afternoon. Chivas.'

Cosgrove nodded to the bartender. 'On my chit, Lancelot.' He turned back to Huart. 'You look like a man in business, John. What's your line?'

'Trading: insurance and engineering. And you?'

Cosgrove raised his fresh glass and drank half. 'Supposedly, textiles.'

'Supposedly?'

The ruddy face twisted into a grimace. 'Have you ever heard of something called the Generation Principle, John? You shouldn't have as I just made it up. It goes: the first generation starts the business and makes the fortune; the second sits on the pot and can't decide to crap or get off; the third pisses the fortune against the wall; the fourth sells the business and clears off. I'm fifth generation Leonard Cosgrove.'

The voice had thickened with self-recrimination. Huart sipped his Chivas and wondered at an apt rejoinder, but Cosgrove solved the problem by continuing. 'My trouble is that I'm rich. Even after Maud takes half in the divorce settlement I'll still be rich. Now, what d'you think of a thirteen year marriage? Thirteen unlucky? Not for me. But then everything's lucky for Lennie the Fifth.' He grinned to himself. 'We didn't see each other from '41 to '46, so it hasn't really been thirteen years, I s'pose. I was interned in Stanley, and where was she? Safe 'n' sound in Geneva. I had to beg her to come out after the war. She hates tropical summers, you see. Even when she did come she went back every April, I hardly saw her long enough to give her one, let alone make a kid with her. Then somebody wrote her about Loretta Delgardo and me. That's what did it.' He looked up. 'Am I boring you, John?'

Huart shook his head. 'On the contrary. Father Ramon Delgardo's wife?'

'His daughter. Lancelot! Double pink gin chop-chop! Yours, John . . ?'

[222]

'I'm fine. Anyway, it's my buy.'

Cosgrove waved his hand. 'This here's my domain. You be my guest.'

Huart shrugged. 'You mentioned something about textiles, Lennie.'

'Textiles, indeed. Cosgroves were in it afore the Industrial Revolution. We're Yorkshire, you see. Hong Kong started with my great great grandfather – Lennie the First. He was sent east by his father in the 1830s to negotiate a bigger cotton quota from the East India Company and ended up here as an independent merchant. One day he went to an auction and bought one of the original marine lots on the Queen's Road waterfront. Then he went right ahead and reclaimed for himself the land all the way out to the Old Praya, which is now Des Voeux Road. Then my great grandfather – Lennie the Second – and Sir Paul Chater twisted William Des Voeux's arm in the nineties for another reclamation, which gave us the praya we have now. You won't believe it, John, but at the turn of the century we Cosgroves owned a strip of land that ran from the foot of Victoria Peak to the harbour's edge.'

Huart was intrigued. 'What happened to it?'

'My grandfather – Lennie the Third – sold all of it in '22 to Victoria Land. It filled the family coffers at the time, and from what I recall, we needed it. The Generation Principle, remember? Now all we own – all I own – is a house on the Peak and a factory over in Shamshuipo in Wai Wai Road. My father – Lennie the Fourth – was a harder-boiled egg. He ran things like Franco to the day he died. That was three months ago. Unfortunately he omitted to pass on his expertise to me before he went, even though I got to his bedside a good five minutes before the end . . .' But the black humour did not fool anybody. Cosgrove attacked his drink and lapsed into silence.

'I'm sure it doesn't end there,' Huart prompted.

'It does. It ends with me.' It came out a lugubrious mutter, and Huart remembered that gin was a depressant. Cosgrove shook his head as if to shuffle his thoughts and went on: 'As a young man I hobnobbed around Europe and the States. My father made the money. I spent it. He was paying me to keep shy of the business, but I didn't care. I was having fun. Then the war trapped me here. I hadn't been long married at the time, but I was here on my own asking my father for money, as usual. Then came Stanley. I survived it because I still managed not to take life seriously. I adjusted to the place and befriended a very enterprising chap who set up a brokerage business with the Jap guards. Jewellery, heirlooms, rings, watches, cigarettes, and so on. I was his salesman. We even sold shares in it to other prisoners and paid annual dividends. I might have been born with a crystal thermometer up my bum and wore my hair parted in the middle – ' He took a breath. ' – but I beat Stanley, John.'

Huart had listened well and could now label Cosgrove an inveterate survivor and one of life's beneficiaries. 'So now you run the show,' he said, tipping his head to the north-west in the direction of Shamshuipo.

'Yes. No. I mean, the factory runs itself. The production manager knows how to produce, he's from Shanghai, you see. The general manager knows how to export. He's Portuguese-Cantonese, named Ezuelo. His family have been the Cosgrove compradores since the Ezuelo clan moved here from Macau in the nineties. His eldest son'll take over from him.'

Huart nodded. It was a familiar story. 'So what are you worried about?'

'Why do I drink and bite my nails, you mean?' Cosgrove seized his glass for emphasis. 'I'll tell you . . . You seem trustworthy and rather down-to-earth, not like most 'round here – ' He swept an arm to encompass all in the bar. 'I drink because I'm bloody-well scared, that's why.' He picked up the newspaper and rapped a knuckle upon the headline. 'That scares the hell outta me. "Dying City" they're calling this place now. Are they right? No more trade with China. How're we going to survive?'

Huart gave him a hard look. 'By manufacturing and exporting to countries other than China as fast as we can. You own a textile factory. You're in the box seat to cash in on a new era. Shanghai's biggest industry was textiles: spinning, weaving, knitting, finishing. All the mill operators are either in Taiwan or have come here, and some brought their whole factories with them piecemeal. There's a vast labour pool in Hong Kong, many of them textile workers with experience. Tell me, what is there for you to be afraid of? You own a potential gold mine!'

Lennie the Fifth stared into his glass. 'It seems all my life I've been scared of something or other. How I wish I was a big blighter like you. No-one puts you down when there's a chance their face could get altered. Or when you've got money. It's because of money I've survived. Nothing else. I've had it all my life and it's always come easy. I've always been able to buy the life that suited me – to buy companionship. Oh, I don't just mean ladies of the night – I mean I've been able to buy my ticket in society. And I bought my marriage. I met Maud when she was on the committee of some charity or other in London. I walked up and gave her a cheque for ten thousand pounds and we were married a fortnight later. She was beautiful then. Lovely body. A lovely pair of . . . But, never mind – Loretta's are better.' Cosgrove smiled to himself as he ground the butt of his cigar into a glass ashtray.

Huart waited for the confession to continue, idly wondering why he had been selected to receive it.

'But the money I was spending had been made by someone else,' Cosgrove went on. 'My father broke the Generation Principle. In fact, he started it all over again. Now I've got to make the money all by myself. I've got to crap or get off the pot – ' He looked up and grinned like a truant schoolboy. 'You don't happen to be in textiles at all, John?'

'The company was big in it in Shanghai. Here we're only trading in textile machinery.' Huart was thinking of the agency with Frobisher-Cash.

'So, what words of wisdom have you for the fifth generation?'

'You've risen over adversity before,' Huart pointed out. 'In Stanley.'

'It was life or death. I had no easy way out then. I do now.'

Huart nodded, understanding this little man very well. 'You have three choices. One: pull yourself together and take charge of the business. Two: sell out at the best price – though those headlines have cut your worth in half. Three: merge.' He tossed down his Chivas. 'Merge with someone who is ready, willing and able to take over management of your factory and its exports. And share the profits with him.'

The grin was slow to reform, but when it did it stayed. 'I like number three most.' Cosgrove's head was nodding. 'You have somebody in mind?'

'Perhaps. Where can I find you?'

'It's not difficult. I'm known to drop in here on the odd occasion.' He chuckled at his own understatement.

Huart left Lennie the Fifth reaching for his fifteenth double pink gin and climbed the steps to Jackson Road. The rain had stopped and the cloud had lifted. The air was cleansed and a cool breeze was visiting Central District. European couples began to appear for their Saturday evening walk, despite the puddles that carpeted Statue Square.

He walked along Chater Road around the traffic circus towards Ice House Street. Bedrix should have returned after his own lunch

[225]

in Gaddi's across the harbour with the owners of the Nanyang Bakeries. Huart had much to discuss with him.

Why not textiles? he mused repetitively as he negotiated the puddles.

19

When Percy Landers delivered his opinion on the prospects for a merger with Cosgrove Textiles Limited, it was mixed. 'The company's history is solid,' he read from a file. 'The Cosgroves have banked for decades with BBA – ' He looked over the top of his reading glasses.

Seated in front of the credit manager's desk, sipping a sherry, Huart experienced a fleeting perverse delight at the thought of closing one more account on Hector Harrisford-House, but kept it off his face.

' – who are concerned that Lennie will sell out lock, stock and barrel to the Cheohs who, being Malayan, bank only with the Offshore Chinese.' Landers looked back to the file. 'BBA have tried to introduce management consultants, but Lennie trusts none of them. They're a new breed, after all. Yes – Cosgrove Textiles are solid. The machinery's in good order, the line management's experienced, the land on which the factory stands is their own.' He closed the file and removed his glasses. 'But – '

'But what, Percy?'

'Production will stop as soon as current orders are filled. Our estimate is that work in progress will last just ninety days. Not a single order has been booked since Lennie's father died. The problem is Lennie. He's a . . . a playboy . . . a dilettante. And a lush. I cannot recommend that you consider any merger or joint venture where he has any control, John.'

Huart did not seem surprised. 'Who owns the shares?'

'As sole surviving family member, Lennie does. One hundred percent.'

'Isn't that grand!' Huart exclaimed with a grin. 'Your report confirms what I suspected. Percy, I want to buy into Cosgrove Textiles. Would you fix the financial side of it if I can persuade Lennie to go along?'

'Er . . . certainly.' Landers opened his palms upon his desk.

'But your cash position – good as it is by comparison to a year ago – is still not positive enough for a reasonable purchase of stock in any company...'

Huart was ready for that. 'Lennie Cosgrove is not after cash, Percy. He's looking for a big brother. We'll do it with an exchange of shares.'

'You'll need your managing director's approval.'

'That won't be a problem. Andrew'll be thrilled to be getting back into textiles. We'll have the papers ready for him to countersign when he gets back – ' He glanced up at the wall calendar. ' – In six weeks.'

Huart caught sight of the white mop and red bowtie boarding a rickshaw in Jackson Road, right outside the Hong Kong Club. It was after three and a Friday; no doubt Cosgrove had lunched long in the Bowling Alley Bar on double pink gins and steak and kidney pie, in that order. The rickshaw moved off towards Chater Road before Huart could call out. He looked for a taxi, but there were none in sight on the Praya, nor in Chater Road. He saw the rickshaw wheel left before the Cricket Club.

'Taxi!' he yelled, but still there were none.

He cursed to himself. He had to confront Cosgrove before the prodigal passed up his merger proposal without even hearing it. A trio of rickshaws rested to the right of the Club entrance with their shafts upon the ground, their pullers squatting in the gutter. There was no choice but to take one. It would be his first ever submission to the indignity of being hauled about by another human being, but there was little choice. He strode to the leading rickshaw. The boy's eyes went very round as the seventy-seven inch frame blotted out the sun. He was wiry and fit, but this was the biggest foreign devil he had ever seen.

'*Ai yah!*' he muttered. '*Gau chaw ahh!*'

Huart used gestures to convince the boy he would be well rewarded, then climbed with some difficulty into the rickshaw. Pointing at the corner around which Cosgrove had disappeared, he shouted: 'Go! Quickly!'

The boy's feet pushed down hard. The muscles and sinews of his calves stood out, his back bent double in the effort to gain purchase upon the bitumen. Finally the wheels moved. Slowly, gradually, Huart was drawn forward. He heard voices and looked up. A group of members had appeared on the Club steps, their faces matching the pigmentation of the vintage port with which they had sealed their lunches. He groaned, but it was too late. He was pulled directly into their line of sight.

'Pick on someone your own size, sir!' sang Herbert Jarvis from Victoria Land, Cumberland China's landlord. The others laughed.

'Giddy-up, Dobbin!' called a manager in the Godown Company.

Huart waved over his shoulder, his face as red as theirs, then hung on as the rickshaw rounded the corner. Traffic was sparse on Chater Road and the boy got into stride on the flat bitumen. Huart saw Cosgrove's wheels turn right at Murray Road and disappear again towards Queensway.

'Follow that rickshaw!' Huart pointed ahead and at once felt ridiculous.

They rolled past the Cricket Club, its grass a lush green after the monsoon rains, then the New Oriental Building, then they turned into Murray Road before the Naval Dockyard. Cosgrove was out of sight. On Queensway Huart picked out the white mop a hundred yards ahead. A rocking tramcar passed by, heading into Wanchai. Its passengers looked down on the spectacle of a massive foreign devil sitting behind a struggling, sweating Cantonese youth half his age and one third his weight. Their expressions remained dispassionate, as if they saw it every day.

Huart knew that once Cosgrove got into the rabbit warren of Wanchai, he stood a good chance of losing him. He urged the boy on. The rickshaw ahead slowed behind a stalled Austin A40 and the gap closed. But Cosgrove was soon off again and in a few minutes they were into Wanchai. Here was a different world: a Chinese community adjacent to the Victorian and Edwardian buildings and wide roads of Central District, but, in reality, very distant from it.

On both sides of the narrow streets and lanes hung vertical signs painted with the ideograms of countless small businesses, and bamboo poles supported the ubiquitous laundry. The air sizzled with a stereophonic babble of Cantonese, the calls of children, the clatter of *mahjong* tiles, the chirping of birds in cages on window ledges, the gabble of poultry. The pungent bitter-sweet aroma of joss wafted from doorways and mixed with all the Chinese smells of Wanchai. Old men propped themselves on sticks and looked out from behind timeless eyes; letter-writers, barbers, seamstresses, shoemakers, artisans carving chops from ivory, all looked up indifferently, then reverted to their craft as the rickshaws raced by: dodging pedestrians in cotton *saamfoo*, mothers with infants in hand and more in red slings on their backs, hawker stalls spread with chicken wings, squid, bean curd, nuts, dried pork, *saygwah* melon sliced open juicy and red, cones of gleaming oranges . . .

Fifty yards separated the rickshaws, when Cosgrove stopped on a corner before a building with a corrugated iron awning held up by two pillars off which faded paintwork was peeling in strips. Huart saw him leap out between the pillars and disappear through a door. As his rickshaw drew up, Huart looked up at a sign that contained the only English amidst a constellation of ideograms. It read: OCEAN BAR – COME IN SAILOR.

As he discharged his debt to the panting rickshaw boy and mopped his brow, Huart could hear Louis Jordan and Ella Fitzgerald singing, 'Baby, It's Cold Outside'. He pushed through a double door and found himself confronted by a dimly lit bar room with a red tiled floor and a ceiling fan that stirred the cigarette smoke and sent to him the smell of cheap perfume, stale tobacco and burning joss. The doors closed behind him with a squeak. A dozen faces with eyes transformed by false lashes and American mascara lifted to him from chairs at tables with beer-stained tops scarred with cigarette burns. A trio of Royal Navy matelots sat on stools at the bar with their San Migs. On the wall behind the bar, a selection of half empty bottles stood on shelves constructed about the head of a hideous dragon with red electric light bulbs for eyes. A merchant seaman thumbed coins into a jukebox, his hand directed by a thin arm projecting from a *cheongsam* unzipped to heights unchaste. The Meltones led in Artie Shaw's band with 'What Is This Thing Called Love?'

Huart saw one of the faces rise and move towards him. He was saved by a call from a shadowy alcove to his right. 'Why if it isn't George Jean Nathan! Come and sit, George. Have a drink. Do you come here often?'

Drawing back a chair, Huart nodded to a very middle-aged Chinese woman and raised an eyebrow to the man he had chased from Central District.

'I know what you're going to say, George. You're going to say something profound like: "A hero is one who believes that all women are ladies, a villain one who believes that all ladies are women". Well, today I'm a villain on holiday. Have a drink! Have a woman – or a lady. Have both at once. This's the place for it, by Jesus. Meet Spring Blossom. She's the mama-san here. She's also the missee of the senior sergeant of Wanchai police station – and she's the well when it comes to the good oil on the horses that're "on" at Happy Valley. The jockeys come here for their fun, you see, and pass the word to the girls who pass it to Spring Blossom who passes it on to me every Friday afternoon. Sounds like a social disease, doesn't it? Spring Blossom, meet my friend, George.'

The woman, who had been coldly assessing Huart, lit up and gold-filled back teeth glinted. 'Please mee' you, George. Frien' of Lennie the Pig welcome. You like drin', or mebbe gir' join you?'

Huart shook his head politely. 'Scotch and water, please. Chivas if you have it. Thank you, but no girl today. I have a business matter to discuss with Mr Cosgrove. That's if he's interested.'

'Okay,' she conceded and stood up. Huart saw that her *cheongsam* was thankfully more demure than those of her charges. 'Bus'ness come firs'. I get drin'. You finish bus'ness then mebbe change min'. Okay?' She crossed to the bar where she put a foot on the rail, pushed a toothpick into her back teeth, called: '*Siu ga laan soei!*' and watched the bartender reach for a bottle of Bell's.

Artie Shaw gave over to the Inkspots as Cosgrove said in a stage whisper: 'The tale goes that Spring Blossom was the courtesan of a northern warlord in the days of the Wild Wild East. I can believe it, too. A certain class lies beneath that gold diggin' exterior, don't you think?'

Huart watched Spring Blossom bringing his scotch in a glass that looked like it had been used to fingerprint everyone in Wanchai and could see only the exterior. He took a tentative sip and cancelled a grimace.

Spring Blossom hovered. 'You lucky like Lennie, George? He born Year of Gold Pig, you know. That Year of Lucky Pig. Pig lucky so much, but not so smar'. You know wha' girl here call him? *Meen Foot Hau Jaak*. Tha' he Chinee name, you know. It mean: "Wide Face Narrow Back". Lennie Lucky Pig can talk abou' whole lotta thing. But only ten secon' each one.'

'Thank you, Spring Blossom,' Cosgrove said as he reached for a Havana. 'Having just divested myself of a nagging wife I now find myself landed with a nagging mama-san.' He waved his hand in dismissal. 'Now run along and get me another drink like a good girl. And none of your watered down gin, neither.'

She tossed her head and walked off.

Huart leaned on the table. 'I have a proposition for you, Lennie. And for the life of me, I can't think of a worse place to put it across.'

'Shoot, George,' said Lennie the Fifth, his eyes twinkling with boyish mischief. 'But keep it under ten seconds. Don't forget, the *Meen Foot Hau Jaak* ain't supposed to be too smart.'

20

'Cousin John, you're a chip off the Huart block and no mistake.'
Andrew Huart-Brent placed both feet upon the rattan table, leaned
back in the chair and clasped both hands behind his head. He
was quite at home on the balcony of the higher floor of the Cecil
that Huart had moved up to last November to be closer to the
balsamic autumn sunshine. On their return from Europe the
Huart-Brents had moved into a rented house on the Peak, but
Andrew found it too remote. He looked at his cousin relaxing,
legs crossed, in the chair opposite, and chuckled again. 'Yes,
Grandfather would've been proud of you. He started the company
in China, all on his tot, flogging guns to Yangtse mandarins. Now,
seventy-seven years later, you save it all on your tot, by grabbing
a kickback that would have gone begging. Even William Jardine
would have approved of it. Chinese graft is so much cleaner than
"foreign mud". Yes, the great Charles Huart would be proud of
you if he was alive today . . .' Andrew's voice trailed off with a
trace of envy as he looked across Ice House Street into the arched
balconies of Prince's Building with distant eyes.

It was the warm evening of a hot day and the red sunset bespoke
hotter days to come. The trams clanked and clanged as they ran
along Des Voeux Road before the banks, and across the harbour
the tugs hooted as they hip-and-shouldered a liner into Holt's
Wharf. The sounds carried up to the balcony where Huart listened
to them and found them reassuring. They were a signal that Hong
Kong was running to order.

Suddenly Andrew clamped a fist over his mouth. His chest
heaved and his body shook until the coughing fit subsided. It had
happened regularly since his return. Although he had regained
weight, it was fat instead of muscle and his face had assumed the
floridness of steady alcohol intake. Huart averted his eyes. It was
not the time to express the disappointment he felt over his cousin's
abandonment of vital self-disciplines. 'When do you think you'll
feel up to coming into the office, Andrew?'

'Oh, in a day or so . . . I suppose. Though I can't . . . see I'm
needed.'

'Why say that?' Huart protested sharply. 'Certainly you're
needed.'

Andrew's smile was wistful. 'Every dog has his day and this
one's had his. It's your turn now, John. Without me being around
you've rescued the company, scoured Asia for business, rebuilt

the Insurance Department, recreated the Engineering Department – and that chap Nigel Print, the one I interviewed in London, seems the right man to head it. And now you've put us back into textiles with a neat little share swop – '

'The Cosgrove Textiles deal will only be ratified if you agree, Andrew,' Huart injected. 'I would appreciate your study of the documentation. However, we are losing time. There's only a month's production left – '

'Damn it, John, the documentation's fine!' Andrew interrupted, stung by the unconscious criticism. 'The whole deal's fine. I couldn't have done it better myself, considering the cash restraints on the company. We're starting out all over again from scratch and we need a modern approach and fresh blood – you, that is. I'm manacled by memories of the way it used to be. I couldn't be as objective as you are now. No, John, you're running the company and doing it well. What role is there for me?'

Huart looked at his cousin. 'Andrew, I was lucky. The company seems to be on its feet and we have a direction now, but I'm not yet accepted as a member of Hong Kong society. I've not been here long enough. With you it's different. Your identity has preceded you. You're of a dynasty born in old China. You're first and foremost a taipan – a deputy chairman of the Shanghai Municipal Council. You're respected. You'll be able to open doors that will remain closed to Clive and me for a long time. Look at the reception given to you at every factory you visited in the UK. They were all delighted to see you and to hear that Cumberland China is continuing in Hong Kong. You cemented our agency links with them all.'

Andrew snorted. 'Except Loughborough. They still haven't been paid for those valves in Shanghai. First person I saw was the finance director.'

'How long have we been their sole agent in China and Hong Kong?'

'Since 1890.'

'Then surely we can work out some form of compromise with them to ensure we retain the agency here, don't you think?'

'No problem, cousin,' Andrew asserted with his grin. 'Their chairman and I are old friends. Whenever he used to visit Shanghai I would lay on a cricket match for him. He couldn't bat to save his life, but he could produce a reasonable off-break. I remember once he – '

'You see, Andrew! That's exactly what I mean! You have the long-standing relationships at the top that are vital for us to keep what we've got, and to create new opportunities, new business, new agencies . . .'

'Ah, yes. Agencies.' Andrew sighed and his eyes went distant again. Then he nodded. 'Do you know what I call a good agency, John? A Licence to Print Money, I call it. Yes. New agencies. We need lots of 'em.' He looked back with eyes that were clear and with the old shrewdness almost there. 'You're speaking of a chairman's role for me then, Cousin?'

'It would avoid the risk of duplication in your work and mine.'

Andrew nodded slowly. 'Not only are you the businessman I knew you would become, you have developed an undoubted tact. There's a "Chineseness" in you, John. Cultivate it. It will prove to be a powerful weapon for you.' He rose with difficulty and limped into the darkness of Huart's room. When he returned he had a tumbler in each hand, half filled with Chivas. 'The best thing that happened to me in England was the Harley Street specialist who prescribed a shot of whisky a day to stimulate my circulation.' He handed one to his cousin. 'Chairman it is. *A votre santé!*'

The four men sat with suit coats on, separated by the knotted hardwood desk that was so old it had split in several places along its grain. Protocol dictated that coats be worn to board meetings, particularly an annual general meeting. The temperature was rising from a crisp winter, but not quickly enough for the 'Glacier' wall airconditioner from Cody Refrigeration of Houston to be put to use. The Engineering Department was moving the line for which Huart had signed the Agency Agreement on his last visit to the States; the first shipment had reached Hong Kong in good time for the summer. But for the AGM of Friday, 26th April, 1952, open windows provided the ventilation, and the inlet to the chairman's compact pentagonal corner office for the sounds of Central District that were a background to Clive Bedrix's monologue.

' . . . in accordance with our decision to close the financial year on 31st March instead of 31st December, the figures thus cover a fifteen month period. Consolidated into them are those of Cosgrove Textiles, which . . .'

Andrew looked up from the typewritten sheet. The windows were in three of the walls and gave views to the south and to the west. The Chinese would say the *fung shui* of his office was supreme as no dragon could approach it unseen from any quarter. He looked down and listened on.

' . . . invoiced sales at $8,800,000 up to 120 percent, and net profit at $197,000 up 88 percent, thanks to the contribution from Wai Wai Road. Orders for textiles and garments have been strong and include the annual underwear contract from Hollingwoods of Manchester. In 1952–53, these revenues, plus a modest projected increase in insurance turnover – which has been affected by falling exports of manufactured goods due to the embargo on trade with China – plus a projected 75 percent increase in invoiced sales in engineering trading and contracting, plus the elevator and air-conditioning servicing operation under Nigel Print – give an estimated increase in net profit of 40 per cent . . .'

Lennie Cosgrove lit a Havana and looked ahead five hours to see himself aboard Cathay Pacific Flight 88 to Singapore, Loretta Delgardo beside him, drinking champagne on the first leg of their Riviera holiday. Ahhh, summer in the south of France – the management of Cosgrove Textiles left in the capable hands of Clive Bedrix and the Ezuelos. He looked further ahead and saw her in that swimsuit. Was modern fashion a ball-tearing delight or wasn't it? Cut low, off the shoulder, the leg horizontal to the crotch. Ahhh, the secrets it held – secrets thus far denied him. But the Riviera would fix that! Was he Lennie the Lucky Pig or was he not? Hot ash fell on the back of his hand and jerked him back to reality.

' . . . the results of financial year 1951/52 are considered satisfactory. It is recommended forty per cent of net profit be paid to the shareholders at a dividend of $3.10 per share.' Bedrix looked up, and rubbed his throbbing stump through the pinned sleeve of his cotton shirt. The first darned monsoon must be on its way, he told himself.

'My instructions are to leave my share in the company as an interest-free loan,' Huart reminded them all. 'It will be put to better use there than lying idle in my bank account drawing minuscule interest from the H and K.'

'It's against my philosophy to be so noble, John,' Cosgrove pointed out. 'This little holiday is going to put a large hole in my kitty.'

Bedrix smiled to himself. He knew Lennie the Fifth had agreed to the merger for the good of no-one but himself. 'I'll split mine down the middle,' he said. 'The company keeps half on loan and I'll take half.'

Andrew said nothing. Paulette had already spent most of the Huart-Brent dividend. He took off his reading glasses. 'Any objections? Fine. Pass it to our auditors, Clive. What's next? "Other Business". Is there any?'

'Two items, Mr Chairman,' Bedrix announced. 'Number one: conversion of the company's authorised capital into Hong Kong dollars from the present value in taels of gold. The matter has been referred to our solicitors. It seems the process will be rather involved due to the loss of certain vital documents in Shanghai. You will be required to make a number of Statutory Declarations attesting to historical aspects of the company.'

'So be it,' Andrew stated. 'The second item?'

'Our lease. It expires end July. We must take up the two year option at an increase in rental of 7.5 per cent, or vacate. We need another four hundred square feet to accommodate our new engineering operation. The adjacent office falls vacant in August and it's just what we need. Victoria Land will draw up a new lease for it at our current rental of 52 cents per square foot plus fifteen per cent. I propose we take up the option on these premises and sign the supplementary lease at the higher rental.'

Andrew sighed. 'Oh, to be a landlord.'

Cosgrove topped it with a wry laugh. 'To think that my own family used to own the very land on which this building stands.'

'Seconded,' said Huart. 'Do we agree to the new lease?'

When all heads nodded, Andrew asked: 'Any other "Other Business"?'

'Yes. I have an item.' Huart leaned forward. 'During my recent visit to the UK with Nigel Print we opened agency discussions with Anglo-Saxon Turbines. I'm confident they will appoint us. In addition, they are bidding to take over Sheepbridge and Slough, who have supplied the switch-gear and transformers for all Cathay Electric power station extensions since 1945 – and who are represented by Male & Son – '

'So if the bid is successful,' Andrew injected, 'Ivor Male will be made a present of the Anglo-Saxon agency, not us.'

'Not so. For the past thirty years, Male & Son have represented CEI, who are Anglo-Saxon's arch competitor in the manufacture of power turbines. I dined with Sir Reynard Armstrong in London. He's confident his bid for S & S will succeed. If it does, his Anglo-Saxon Electric Group becomes the largest conglomerate in the UK electrical industry. He's coming to Asia in June. A week in Malaya, a week in Singapore, and then here. Andrew, he told me he remembers you well, and also your grandfather's kindness, when he visited Shanghai as a youth.'

'He should,' chuckled Andrew. 'If I remember correctly,

Charles fixed it so Reynard lost his cherry in the most delightful circumstances.'

Huart went on: 'We must again make a fuss of him when he gets here – '

'I'll arrange some local stuff for him,' volunteered Cosgrove, grinning.

'Please, joking aside,' Huart said, smiling despite himself. 'We've been presented with what I consider to be a grand opportunity. If Armstrong awards us the agency for Anglo-Saxon Turbines, we can lobby for him to transfer Sheepbridge and Slough from Male & Son. Then, gentlemen, Cumberland China will represent the entire Anglo-Saxon Electric Group.'

Andrew leaned forward. 'John, I know you've been dealing personally with Reynard Armstrong. But, he's a Freemason, you know. He and Ivor Male will be as thick as thieves. Ivor's head of the local lodge. Reynard would never do him in the eye.'

Huart shook his head. 'My assessment is that business comes first with that man. And he's our age, Andrew. Ivor Male is over sixty – '

'Ivor will start to hand over to his eldest son on his graduation from Harvard,' Andrew interrupted. 'Abraham Male will be in Hong Kong soon for his summer vacation. From what I hear about him, he's a fire-eater.'

'Reynard is sure to be more impressed by your close personal friendship with Sir Bartholomew Orr than Abraham Male's ability to consume fire.'

Andrew frowned. 'What "close personal friendship" are you talking about? I hardly know Sir Bart.'

'Then you have six weeks to convince him you're the greatest chap in the whole world.' Huart winked. 'That should be easy.'

'But . . . But he's Eurasian!' Andrew protested.

'He's chairman of Cathay Electric Corporation as far as I'm concerned. He's your opposite number – your target. We must show Armstrong we have better relationships at the top in Cathay Electric than do Male & Son. We must convince him that appointing a sole agent for all his plant – his turbines, his transformers, his switchgear – is a more beneficial arrangement for him than to have his agencies split between two companies, one of whom represents his main competitor. We must ensure that he opts for us in this in favour of the Males.'

The skin on Andrew's face creased. Long seconds passed before a smile reluctantly emerged. 'Thank you for teaching me how to suck eggs, John. And what will you be doing whilst I'm off courting Sir Bart?'

'The financial and administrative power in Cathay Electric is with the general manager, Patrick O'Harah. I'm lunching with him today.'

Andrew nodded slowly. 'The general manager for you, the chairman for me. And what about Sir Bart's stepson, Kingston?'

It was Bedrix who replied. 'At Harvard with Abraham Male. Ivor pulled strings for Sir Bart to have him accepted. The link between the Males and the Orrs is a strong one. We've a hard task cut out for us.'

Huart asked: 'What more do you know of Kingston Orr, Clive?' The heir to the largest power company in Asia was something of an enigma.

Bedrix rubbed his stump harder and pursed his lips. 'He's not of Sir Bart's blood, but he's the only heir he has. The old man has always kept him in the background, whilst he has taken the decisions for the family and for Cathay Electric. You're right about Pat O'Harah, however. He's a highly effective general manager with considerable influence on Sir Bart. Much more influence, I would say, than Kingston.'

Andrew drew a deep breath. 'It's decided then. Into battle we go. Can I write to Reynard before he leaves England, John? Or am I too late?'

'An airmail letter will make it in time.' Huart leaned forward again. 'To reinforce the urgency of this – Cathay Electric will soon order two 30 megawatt turbo-alternators with boilers, transformers and switchgear. They plan to increase generating capacity from 45 to 100 megawatts by 1957. So far, all plant has been supplied through Male & Son, including the turbo-alternators from CEI. Our task is as clear as it is hard. We're going after business worth several million pounds – more than five times our projected turnover for the next two years. I think you will agree, gentlemen, that is an objective worth aiming at.' He sat back, then added to Andrew: 'Why not have Sir Bart meet Reynard in your box at Happy Valley? They both have a deep love for horse-racing. Ivor Male may have wonderful contacts in Harvard, but I have it on good authority that he detests any form of gambling.'

The chairman seemed to think on it for long seconds. Then he lifted his head and merely said: 'Thank you, John.'

21

The restaurant on the verandah of the Repulse Bay Hotel was fully booked, as it was every night of the autumn season when cool breezes wafted down from the mountains or drifted in off the bay across the beach of white sand. The air was dry, and held a sharpness that attested to the beginning of the end of the annual contest with the summer that had rested upon the South China coast like a sweaty palm since May.

The six men in tuxedos and five women in evening wear were the focus of attention as they moved to the end table overlooking the garden. All but one of the men were seen regularly in Central District; the sixth was a stranger: six foot three, brown hair streaked with silver, sporting a trim moustache and speaking with an accent originating anywhere from the Mid-West to the Pacific coast. Rex Wagoner had flown in for the weekend.

But it was the women who were responsible for the attention lingering upon the group. At least, three of them; for Olive Catchpole's figure cancelled all effort to adorn it, and Ruby Bedrix had still to master the cultural transition back to Hong Kong from Market Harborough.

Loretta Delgardo transmitted her existence with ebony eyes and high cheekbones that hinted at Latin blood, and with raven hair in a chignon and a Norell fandango outfit of fuchsia taffeta that confirmed it.

Paulette Huart-Brent's shining blonde hair had been cut and styled in a dove's tail. She remained faithful to Mainbocher and wore one of his embroidered chartreuse satin creations to her ankles. She had looped a white mink stole over her arms to ward off the open air of the November night, and had confined her jewellery to a broad green jade bracelet and matching necklace. She radiated a new womanhood, and John Huart, whose stag appearances no longer drew comment, knew why. He looked across the table at her and saw in her eyes the intensity that had been there ever since Rex Wagoner had turned up in his habitual unexpected fashion.

Then he switched his gaze back to the fifth woman at the table. And he looked again upon Jennifer's ghost.

Virginia Wagoner was a beauty among beauties. She was twelve years her husband's junior, and formed from a mould so different as to abrogate belief that they could be married. She spoke rarely, preferring to let her eyes that were as blue as the ocean depths speak for her. Her lips, her nose, her shoulder-length hair – if it had been titian instead of auburn – could indeed have belonged to Jennifer, but the rest of her was her own. She wore an ermine-lined herringbone ensemble that was in itself unspectacular, but anything she may have lost in couture to the women about her, she more than recovered with her magical facial beauty.

Huart picked up the complimentary pack of Craven 'A's from the starched white tablecloth and asked: 'Do you smoke, Mrs Wagoner?'

She looked up and met his eyes for the first time. There was a tiredness at the back of hers which was replaced by the hint of an invitation that itself evaporated as she replied: 'Not in public thanks, Mr Huart.' She turned to listen to a voice from her left and he heard Andrew saying: 'I hear tell the Communists've now requisitioned the Shanghai Waterworks and the gas and tramway companies as well as the Shell Company, British-American Tobacco and the dockyards.'

'So that's where Clement Attlee went to,' Cosgrove quipped. 'He must've emigrated to Peking as soon as Churchill turfed him out of Number Ten.'

Everybody laughed. There was not a socialist sitting at the table.

Andrew went on to lead a confabulation with Owen Catchpole, with Bedrix listening in, when Huart saw Ivor Male, his wife and twenty-four year old son come onto the verandah. That Abraham Male was the son of his father was plain to see: he had been awarded with Ivor's long nose and liquid eyes set wide on a symmetrical face that was capped with his mother's sand-blonde hair. His solid frame was squared off by a dinner jacket, and shrouded in a young buck's mantle of certitude.

Wagoner had been surveying the other tables and it was inevitable that he should see the Males. His eyes lingered upon them as if they were known to him, then flicked back to connect with Paulette's. Both were saying little and seemed impatient for the dinner to be ended.

Huart was saying least. He was confused. He was experiencing a sensation both exhilarating and hellish. He felt as if he had met his wife all over again, and was in the grip of that weird, wonderful hypnosis.

Virginia Wagoner returned her menu to the waiter and placed her order in a refined Vermont accent that rang on the clean night air. Then she said to Andrew: 'I know it's understating the obvious, but it must have been dreadful being held a prisoner in Shanghai twice over. You must have forgotten how freedom felt. I cried for you when Rex told me about it.'

Andrew produced a boyish smile, happy to be the centre of such sophisticated attention and comfortable with it. 'Oh, I don't know, Virginia. It enabled me to re-assess life's values and emerge a better person. One does not quite realise how much small things are worth until they're taken away. Things like Johnny Walker, Ritmeester, Sandeman's port . . .'

Sympathetic laughter circled the table.

'How fortunate for you to have your cousin arrive in Hong Kong at just the right time,' Owen Catchpole suggested.

'I may have been fortunate, but I'm not so sure John was. He faced a difficult time here – and lost his entire army gratuity in Shanghai.'

'All's well that ends well,' said Huart, taking refuge in the cliché.

'Has everyone ordered?' Andrew counted the nods, selected the poached turbot for himself and called for the wine list.

'Well, it looks like Hong Kong will survive the trade embargo,' Clive Bedrix announced cheerily. 'Exports are on the way up at last.'

'If it's not embargoes, it's something else,' Paulette injected sourly. 'By no means is it ended. The Communists have not finished with us yet. Look at Macau – forced to sign a co-operation agreement with Peking to keep it from being overrun by immigrants from Kwangtung. What next?'

'When did this happen?' asked Virginia.

'Earlier in the year,' Huart replied. 'There was some trouble here as well, after a particularly bad squatter fire – '

' "Squatter fire"? What is that?'

Huart swept his eyes around the table as if to demonstrate his audience was not confined to one. 'We call the refugees "squatters". Their camps are tinderboxes in the dry season. A large one caught fire and burnt to the ground, leaving thousands homeless. A communist mission from Canton applied for permission to come in to give comfort to the victims. The government refused and riots broke out in Kowloon. It certainly showed the communist movement is fermenting here, particularly in Kowloon.'

'Small wonder when the Walled City dead centre of it is still run by Peking,' Paulette pointed out. 'Andrew, have you decided on the wine?'

'Patience, darling.' A mixture of beef, chicken and seafood had been ordered for the main course. Andrew compromised with a Provence rosé.

Wagoner broke his brooding silence with a sudden laugh. 'Squatters? In Australia they have 'em – but at the opposite end of the social scale.'

'Well, Rex, in Australia it's normal for things to be upside down – '

Laughter again acknowledged Andrew's wit. Yet Huart detected a hardness in his cousin towards Wagoner. Could it be that he knew?

' – and down there a "taipan" is no merchant prince, but a snake with a deadly multiple bite that clots the blood and kills in minutes.'

Huart saw Wagoner's eyes narrow a fraction. 'Well, at least the Aussies copy you Limeys here in one way – they drive on the left, don't they?'

Andrew was in top form. 'In Shanghai we also drove on the left before the war and we were fine. After the war the Kuomintang switched us over to the right to copy the Yanks – and look what happened to us.'

That was enough for Wagoner. He put an end to the banter by turning on Owen Catchpole and asking: 'Who handles your insurance . . . ah . . . Owen?'

Whilst the directors of Cumberland China exchanged glances, the head of the Telephone Company matched Wagoner's veracity. 'Greater London Underwriters, Mr Wagoner. Their agents are Male & Son, whose owner, and son, happen to be sitting two tables behind you. Sorry about that, but you did ask.'

Wagoner turned in his chair. Ivor Male looked up, nodded to the Catchpoles, then proffered a smile that enveloped the end table.

There's one of the old school, Huart thought with admiration. But then his eyes intersected with those of Abraham Male and he saw something different. A warning registered. The young man listened as his father resumed their conversation, but his eyes continued to dissect every person at the end table, paying special attention to Huart and Wagoner, as if he considered them most likely to feature in his future.

Wagoner turned back. 'Must be a big account for them and GLU, right?'

'I suppose so, Mr Wagoner,' answered Catchpole, now embarrassed for his hosts. 'But your agents are negotiating part of our business, you know.'

[241]

'Part? I settle for part of nothin'. It's all for me – or forget it!' Wagoner downed his Jack Daniels and lapsed into an ominous silence.

Andrew forced himself to wait out the uncomfortable quiet until all were served their *hors d'oeuvre*. Then his intrinsic Huart defiance had him demonstrate to all that Cumberland China did other business besides insurance. 'John, when will Rochetet start negotiations in Saigon?'

'I'm calling him tomorrow. I expect he'll want me to go down soon to – '

'No, John, I'll go this time.' Andrew had interrupted and Paulette looked at him. 'My French is better than yours. You know how jolly arrogant Rochetet is, and how he insists on all negotiations being in French.'

'As you wish, Andrew,' Huart acceded. It was not the place to argue.

Virginia looked up from her avocado. 'Isn't it dangerous in Saigon with all this fighting between the French and the *Viet Minh?*'

'The French have the area close to Saigon – where our mill is – under control,' Andrew replied. 'It's quite safe. There's nothing to worry about. Rochetet is the one who should be worried. He thinks he's going to get a discount off his last price. Has he a surprise coming his way!' He sampled the wine that came with the main course and approved it. 'A toast!' he cried. 'After three and a half years, Cousin John has decided finally to emerge from that hotel and live like a normal human being. But only because the Cecil has been sold and is to be knocked down. In fact, that entire block is to be redeveloped. This place is getting just a little like Shanghai. A toast to John's return to the living!'

Virginia sipped her rosé and smiled. 'Where are you moving to, John?'

'A flat in Garden Terrace, at the top of Garden Road. It has a harbour view that's grand.' He stopped himself before he invited her to see it.

'What's the rental, John?' Cosgrove asked with his eyes squashed into Loretta's cleavage.

'One thousand, three hundred dollars a month.'

'Three bedrooms?'

'Four.'

'Servants?' Paulette enquired. 'A man on his own must have servants.'

Huart nodded. 'A manservant and an *amah* come with the flat.

It's walking distance to the office. I'm very pleased with it.' And he talked on, driven by some pleasurable challenge, and increasingly concentrating on Virginia as a result of it. It failed to escape notice. When coffee was served, Andrew excused himself and followed his cousin to the washroom.

'John, my grandfather once gave me some good advice when he saw me closing in on our compradore's eldest daughter. I was sixteen at the time and a virgin. She was eighteen with her cherry long lost. If I had got in there and donated mine, there would've been trouble. Grandfather took me aside and said: "Andrew, my boy, never – but never – put your meat where you get your bread and butter". I now pass that advice on to you, Cousin. You're old enough to know better. Virginia's a magnificent lady, but, for God's sake, she's married to our most important principal. Get on down to Wanchai if you want to get it up. Go talk to Lennie. He'll fix it so you won't catch anything.'

Huart set his jaw and finished fastening his fly buttons. Then he turned and looked his cousin in the eye. 'For a man who is so observant in one direction, Andrew,' he breathed, 'you seem to be amazingly blind in another. Don't you see what's going on between Wagoner and Paulette?'

Andrew blanched. His mouth opened. He stared back at Huart for a second, then his face fell. 'I . . . I've known about it for a long time.' He shut his eyes through the silence that followed, then broke it with: 'And not only that – I know Suzanne is not my daughter.'

'What? What do you mean?'

'You remember that time I was shot in the Municipal Council chambers? The bullet tore up my reproductive workshop. The doctor kept it quiet.'

Huart pulled a face. 'Oh, Andrew! Then . . . You think Wagoner . . ?'

'He's the most likely candidate, don't you think?'

It required no answer. 'What are you going to do about it?'

'I don't know. I carry the knowledge of it around with me like a deformed third leg that trips me up whenever I start thinking that I've got things under control again. Yes – a deformed third leg to go with my deformed foot. I really am afflicted. I must have been born that way. I don't know what to do, John. Pan Atlantic is vital to our survival – '

Huart grabbed his cousin by the shoulders. 'For heaven's sake! Do you put a little insurance business ahead of your self-respect?'

Andrew was saved from answering by Bedrix entering the washroom, but as they returned to the verandah he grasped his cousin's arm and whispered: 'John, please don't say anything to anybody. And it's not just "a little insurance business". We need Pan Atlantic. Without it the company would start to collapse. If that happened, I'd lose Paulette. I know it. She'd go to Wagoner without any hesitation. I don't know what I'd do then . . .'

Huart looked ahead to their guests seated around the end table. The men held cigars and glasses of port, the women sipped liqueurs. Conversation was easy. The dinner was a success – on the surface. He noticed Paulette and Wagoner see them coming and stiffen. And the deep sadness that he felt for his cousin fell on him.

As they passed the Male table, Abraham stood up and put out his hand. 'I'm not really interested in meeting you, Mr Huart.' The young man's voice was as hard as his smile. 'I just wanted to find out if your hand is bruised after breaking my father's ricebowl. We received a letter today informing us our electric power agencies are now transferred to you. Reynard Armstrong was not even man enough to sign it himself.'

Huart let his hand fall. 'You could have given up the CEI agency – '

'We honour our agreements, Mr Huart. And our promises. You can expect me to get even on my father's behalf for this.'

'That's no promise, that's a threat.'

'Damn right, Mr Huart. Check your ricebowl for cracks in future.'

It was after one a.m. when Lennie the Fifth, his tuxedo stained, his dress shirt hanging open, his bowtie askew, stumbled through the door of the Ocean Bar. He was tight with Repulse Bay Hotel scotch, rosé wine and port, plus half a dozen double pink gins downed in quick succession in the Bowling Alley Bar before it closed. He was thoroughly stewed.

He was also stewing mad. Loretta had turned cold on him again. It was all an act with her: all her sexuality, all her come-on. What more did the woman want? He had set her up in business, hadn't he? He had bought her that bloody Central boutique, hadn't he? He had taken her around the world, hadn't he? He had even promised to marry her – something he had sworn he would never, never do. Hadn't he? But still she pulled his hands off her knockers. Still she backed away when he pressed his thigh between her legs. Hell, a Latin broad should turn on, shouldn't she? Oh, no – not Loretta Delgardo, the bloody priest's bloody frigid virgin bloody daughter!

'Lennie, stop pleeeeze! I must save myself for our wedding night and you must go home. My flatmate will come home any time. It would not be right for her to see us like this. She wouldn't respect me. I wouldn't respect myself, or you. Please go. You're drunk again. Our first time mustn't be like this. Don't slam the door. The landlady will call the police like the last time we had a fight about this. Lennie, go now! Pleeeeze!'

She had torn his hands off her, fled to the bedroom and locked him out. Again. He had stormed from the apartment in Rednaxela Terrace, leaving the front door wide open. Don't slam it, she'd said, so he hadn't.

When the Club had closed, his anger and his burning scrotum had led him to the last rickshaw waiting in Jackson Road. The boy had never seen a bigger tip and ran into Wanchai in record time whilst Cosgrove had sat and nursed his lust, giving his head no space for thought of his inevitable awakening halfway through the next day on a cot in one of the cubicles above the Ocean Bar: alone and naked, his head raging, his throat like used sandpaper. It was as if everything in his world was condensed into his next act and nothing except that act was worth a damn.

Now he sat at the bar beside a matelot who had two heads – one of them with long black Chinese hair, and two bodies – one wrapped around the other like a convolvulus. He looked into the bulging eyes of the scaly red dragon that lunged its stiletto fangs at him out of the wall behind the bar. He heard the tinny voice of Guy Mitchell singing something about some girl that wore red feathers and the crackling of worn shellac coming from the jukebox. He smelled the air, heavy with a residue of smoke and burnt joss, stale beer, *heung peen* tea, and with that special scent: the smell of oriental sex, available for a price.

'Spring Blossom! Get 'ere chop-chop! Spring Blossom! Where are you?'

He felt the touch on the back of his hand and the voice seemed to come from a long way off. *'Ai yah, Meen Foot Hau Jaak.* What happen you? Why you come so late? Where you been? You not come here long time.'

'S'right,' he slurred. 'Long time. Been on holiday. Been busy, too.'

'Busy? You no sell bus'ness, ha?'

'S'right, Spring Blossom. No sell business after all. Ev'rythin' fine.'

'Tha' big guy George come here fin' you. He make you good deal, ha?'

'What "big guy George"? Oh, yeah. He make good deal. Any girls here . . ?' He twisted on the stool to peer about the bar and almost fell off.

'What' las' name tha' big guy George, ha?'

'George? His name's not George. There any girls here? I asked.'

'You relax. Lily come back soon. She been gone one hours a'ready. Betcha 'member Lily? You like her b'fore. She nice up here . . .' Spring Blossom cupped her hands under her own non-existent bosom and grinned horribly.

'Nice? Yeh, I remember. Big knockers. Big down here, too.' He made a grab for her crotch as she backed away expertly. 'I like big knockers.'

'Tha' big guy George – wha' his las' name?' she asked again.

'Bring Lily chop-chop, then I tell. But it's a waste of time with him, I tell you. His name's not George an' he don't like girls.'

'Ha? Don' like gir'? Why? He queer, ha?'

'Could be. He was in the army. He was a general, an' they're all queer.'

'Army? Gen'ral, ha?'

He nodded clumsily. 'Yeh. A general. Now go get Lily chop-bloody-chop!'

'Okay, I go. You write down big guy not George name b'fore go upstair, okay?' She passed him a pad and a chewed-up pencil and went out the door onto the street. Fifteen minutes later she returned with a girl in tow who looked much like any other girl in any other Wanchai bar and shook him awake. 'Lily come now, *Meen Foot Hau Jaak*. You wan' buy her drin' and dance firs', ha? Lily say she like dance – '

'She can bloody-well dance on her back!' He grabbed the girl's hand and headed for the stairs that led to the cubicles.

Minutes later Lennie the Lucky Pig was thrusting in semi-conscious bliss into a half-naked Lily who was writhing and groaning beneath him as she counted dollar notes behind his back. In the bar below, Spring Blossom was talking on the telephone, using Shanghai dialect except for the name that she spelt in English off the pad the *Meen Foot Hau Jaak* had left on the bar counter beside his untouched double gin.

'*Hai!* H – U – A – R – T. *Hai!*'

22

The Year of the Water Snake is prone to bring storms. Hong Kong battened down one August night under the wet and windy assault of Typhoon Susan. The scene was of man's temporary hibernation in deference to nature as families blessed with stone dwellings shut themselves within to sit out the tempest and the clatter of *mahjong* tiles competed with the howling wind gusts, the staccato attack of the angry rain and the rattle of windows. But the squatters were cast into a sudden and wretched struggle to survive as the typhoon flattened their makeshift dwellings as an open palm does a paper bag and swamped what was left with avalanches of mud.

Ten-year-old Mak-cheung failed to beat the typhoon back to the shack of wooden planks and forty-four gallon drums that the Wong family called home on the hillside above Shamshuipo. He lived out the storm cringing in the side doorway of a textile factory in Wai Wai Road. He was not really afraid, as the doorway was in a narrow alley and well protected. He was more apprehensive of the beating he knew awaited him at home. He was not to know his home was no longer there and that, himself apart, the Wong family no longer existed. He crouched there on the step, stiff and bored through the long night, with his arms wrapped about his knees as the rain water swirled around his feet.

Just before dawn, as the storm was weakening and the rain stopped, Wong Mak-cheung's boredom was broken. A Morris van drew up before the main entrance to the textile factory. Three Chinese men got out and pulled what appeared to the boy to be a life-size statue from the back of the van and placed it before the main entrance, then drove away. Mak-cheung watched the statue for several minutes until his curiosity overcame his fear of the unknown and he stepped out from the doorway. As he did so a devil gust swept down Wai Wai Road like a wall of hard air and slammed him into the side of the building. A ball-like object detached itself from the statue and rolled and splashed along the footpath, coming to a stop a few feet from the alley. The boy looked at it with globular eyes. The wind died momentarily. He ran to it and bent to look more closely. And recoiled in petrified terror and cried out for his father to come and save him when he saw the eyes staring at him from the severed head.

Fender of Special Branch paid a return visit to Cumberland China at the end of August. 'I see you've grown, Mr Huart,' he observed, studying the rows of new desks and the teak wood partitions that demarcated the offices of the directors. 'Hong Kong seems to be treating you well.'

'We have few complaints,' Huart lied. He was aware the unwelcome visit was connected with the murder, three weeks earlier, of Chiu Sing-man, Production Manager of Cosgrove Textiles Limited.

The factory had been at a standstill ever since. Many of its workers were from Shanghai and had recognised the style of the manager's demise. The next day not one worker had shown up, and a recruitment drive had proved a complete failure. Huart was at a loss. He could think of no solution to the dilemma, employing faculties that were affected by knowledge that the real target of the killers of Chiu Sing-man was himself.

'You continue to interest us,' Fender announced when tea and biscuits were served. He used a mildly intimidatory tone as if Huart was a petty nuisance that he had been lumbered with. 'We opened a file on you three years ago when General Wen Wei-tung's head turned up in his lap. Naturally it was the first one we took out when CID called us in again on this one.' He bit into a biscuit. 'We've investigated the two murders – assassinations, executions, whatever they were – both here and in Taipei – and we've come up with some interesting parallels.'

Huart gave a look of distaste. He was as defensive on this day as he had been three years before. Fender was like a poisonous spider, spinning a web, his eyes fixed on his prey. 'Interesting for you, perhaps.'

The man from Special Branch took time to finish his biscuit and wash it down with tea before continuing. 'The deceased came from Shanghai. But you would know that, of course. There is a large clan of Chius in Taipei who also fled from Shanghai. Some of them have disappeared recently.'

'So?'

'To cut it short, we have concluded that both General Wen and your production manager were eliminated by the *Chin Pang*. The *modus operandi* was – is – their trademark.' Fender paused to watch for a reaction that failed to materialise. 'You don't seem to be surprised, Mr Huart.'

'I was also in Shanghai. Remember?'

Fender nodded. 'British Army. It's possible you were in contact with the *Chin Pang* there? Several army officers were on their payroll.'

[248]

'No different from the Shanghai Municipal Police, then.'

Fender shrugged. 'Did you ever make contact with the *Chin Pang* in Shanghai, Mr Huart?' he repeated. 'Please answer me. It's important.'

Huart shook his head. 'It can't have been them,' he asserted.

'Why not?'

'They backed the Kuomintang. General Wen was a KMT general, you said.'

'Yes. That is an anomaly. We were hoping you could explain it for us.'

'What do you mean?'

'Come now, Mr Huart. We know you were doing business with General Wen. We've not been able to find evidence of any illegality so far. But just after his death there was a transfer into your company's bank account from a Californian corporation which you still represent, and which was engaged at the time in a contract in Taiwan. The sum transferred was far in excess of a normal agency commission for a contract of that size.'

'You give little credit to our ability to negotiate favourable terms.'

Fender took up a second biscuit. He leaned forward, his eyelids narrowed and pointed it accusingly. 'I think you profited directly from Wen's death, Mr Huart. I think you had the *Chin Pang* kill him for you.'

Huart gaped. His mouth opened and hung there as his memory reproduced that catatonic, macabre morning when Fender had confirmed the death of the only man he had believed could save him and the company. Slowly he unwound back to the present and he saw Fender's face there before him, three years older, equally dangerous as the investigator spun his web. But now also ridiculous. Huart threw back his head and laughed for several seconds. Then he asked: 'What equally preposterous theory will you try out on me next, Mister Fender?'

During the laughter Fender's expression had reverted to deadpan; Huart's reaction had told him much. 'So, Mr Huart, if you are truly as white as you pretend to be, it must be that whoever had General Wen and your production manager executed is really out to get you.'

'Get me? You mean kill me?' Huart put it as evenly as he could.

Fender shook his head. 'No. Not kill you. Ruin you. Disgrace you. For example: by trying to stop Wen completing his deal with you. According to the BBA you were facing bankruptcy at the time . . . ?'

Huart frowned. Hector Harrisford-House. May all his chickens die.

'. . . But it seems the *Chin Pang*'s scheme was foiled somehow. The deal was completed. Your money from San Francisco proves that. But the *Chin Pang* never give up. Never. And now they've removed your production manager after intimidating his family in Taipei. I understand that your factory's somewhat idle at the moment? I wouldn't be surprised if you find some of the workers you hired prior to the murder have *Chin Pang* connections. They'll be ensuring your machines stay switched off.'

Of course, Huart affirmed to himself. It follows.

'You're in serious trouble, Mr Huart. You crossed the *Chin Pang* in Shanghai.' Fender's tone had become salted with a mild sympathy. 'If I were you, I'd be looking over my shoulder. Ever consider a bodyguard? But, if they hit – when they hit – it won't be you to suffer physically. It will be your staff. We won't be able to look after all of them at once, you know. But, perhaps the *Chin Pang* won't need to do anything more. Perhaps they've done enough. Because, if your staff get wind of the danger they're in – including those educated clerks sitting outside your door – they'll be gone and they'll never come back. If I were you I wouldn't think of offering any shares to the public right now.' He picked up a third biscuit and looked thoughtfully at it, then also pointed it at Huart. 'They'd not be worth a single solitary crumb.' He popped the biscuit into his mouth and left the office, munching noisily.

Huart remained at his desk, locked in strenuous cogitation. His position was not just dangerous -- it was perilous! The textile factory generated the bulk of the company's consolidated revenue, and it had stopped dead. He looked at the telegrams on his desk that threatened cancellation of vital export orders. And he knew that only bold action would eradicate the influence of the *Chin Pang* over the workers and send them back to the production line.

He called the typing pool and summoned the best of the three Cantonese secretaries. They were soon to be joined by a fourth: Imelda, the eldest daughter of Francis Roboza. 'Take a letter, please, Betty,' he commanded as the thin girl, surnamed Pun, seated herself, shorthand notebook and sharpened pencil in hand. He took a deep breath and formed the opening paragraph in his mind. 'To His Excellency, President Chiang Kai-shek . . .'

23

Power hung in the air as thick as fog, and it thickened the nearer Huart came to the stateroom where the President of the Republic of China was to receive him. Though he felt conspicuous beside the dapper aide, who escorted him through the marble corridors that criss-crossed the mansion surrounded by manicured lawns, coiffured flora and gnarled rockeries, his step was positive and his bearing was erect. He felt quite at home inside this bastion of martial suzerainty. He remembered his first visit to Taipei, four years before. Now he had come again at a time when the future of Cumberland China was in the balance. And himself with it.

A large door of carved blackwood featuring centrally the ideogram for Longevity opened ahead. Huart found himself in a large room bisected by a narrow table, also of blackwood, that shone to hit the eye. It was lined with high-backed chairs, each engraved with Longevity, and upon it Huart saw the gift he had sent ahead from Hong Kong: a miniature gold-plated cannon cut with: 'CHUNGKING 1873'. It had sat on Charles Huart's desk and Andrew had hidden it under the floorboards of the office so the Japanese would not find it. In 1950 he had smuggled it out of China with characteristic audacity. No wonder the burlap bag had sagged so.

Andrew would not have believed the truth behind Huart's mission to Taipei; he was sceptical enough of the authenticity of the invitation with the wax presidential seal of Chiang Kai-shek. Yet it had been he who had suggested the cannon. 'The warmongering old basket'll love a gift like that,' he had said, then had frowned. 'But I still don't know why you're going over there with the strike at Wai Wai Road going into its third month.' Then he had sighed. 'But, knowing you, it must be important.'

Huart had been grateful to Andrew beyond words for sacrificing the heirloom to the mission. They both knew its value, never assessed, could not exceed the salvation of Cumberland China. The cannon had been polished to a shine and affixed with a second gold plate with the inscription:

TO HIS EXCELLENCY, PRESIDENT CHIANG KAI-SHEK —
A SYMBOL OF VICTORY AGAINST THE ODDS
JOHN HUART, OCTOBER 1953

A carpet so thick that Huart's feet twisted in his shoes as he walked on it lay upon the marble floor, the ubiquitous ideogram woven into it as large as any human hand could make it. Someone living here has every intention of living the fullest possible life, Huart told himself.

From a chair at the head of the table, Chiang Kai-shek rose to his feet.

It was impossible for Huart to distinguish the President's features in the shadow cast by the natural light from the floor-to-ceiling windows behind him. A second petite frame rose to stand at his side and Huart knew this had to be Madam Chiang Soong Mei-ling.

The aide moved ahead to initiate the introductions. Chiang's uniform was pressed so the creases stood out. Rows of medals crossed his chest and a golden tassel hung from each epaulette. He was hatless, his small egg-shaped bald head gleamed and his pencil-thin moustache was a line drawn across his lip. His hand lost itself in Huart's, but he smiled. His eyes were clear and put the lie to reports that senility was claiming him. Huart thought the light of leadership in Chiang's eyes had not dimmed in the eleven years since he had met him in Burma. 'Your Excellency, it is my extreme pleasure to meet you again in a time of peace . . .' he opened.

The aide started to translate, but was cut off as Madam Chiang usurped the task. Her Mandarin flowed like a mountain stream and she seemed to be supplementing Huart's greeting with words of her own. He hoped they were embellishments and was pleased to see the President's smile widen and to hear him respond in cooing Mandarin, which his wife translated simultaneously. 'I could never forget meeting a soldier of your bearing, General Huart. I regret our forces could not help prevent your initial withdrawal in Burma. I thank you on behalf of my country for your brave rescue of our soldiers north of Mandalay – for which you were justly decorated by your own country – and, in 1937, in Shanghai where, if not for you, our gallant patriotic survivors would have perished dreadfully at the hands of the Japanese invaders. It seems so many years ago . . .'

Chiang paused and Huart, his embarrassment showing, was grateful. Then he introduced Madam Chiang. With no ostensible humility, she presented herself in way that brought into question the accuracy of other reports of a rift in the marriage. ' . . . my wife, who is my most faithful servant, most ardent admirer and greatest supporter . . .' And, feeling a little strange, Huart took the hand of the woman seen by the West as the female power

[252]

behind the Kuomintang throne. Madam Chiang Soong Mei-ling was a blend of two cultures. Her hair was cut and pinned in the style of the Shanghai debutante she had once been, and her face had received the latest cosmetics. She wore an Adrian outfit that must have been collected during her most recent New York shopping trip. It adorned her small frame in a manner befitting the third in the line of Soong offspring who had for decades dominated the Chinese political and financial scene.

'Next, General Huart, it will be my greater pleasure to indulge myself in the task of proving the gratitude China holds for you.'

Out of the corner of his eye Huart saw Chiang Kai-shek remove something from a velvet case and hold it reverently in his right hand. When he turned, the President of the Republic of China, with unsteady fingers, pinned to his lapel a gold cross inlaid with white jade.

It was seconds before Huart could speak. 'Your Excellency, I'm honoured above my achievements. I thank you with all my heart . . .'

Chiang smiled disarmingly. 'Come, General Huart, sit down now and tell me of your business in Hong Kong. The plants which your company helped to supply are, I am told, operating to our complete satisfaction and assisting greatly in the reconstruction of our country. No doubt it is just the beginning of our co-operation.' He led the way to the table and for the first time Huart noticed the guards in the ceremonial uniform of the Kuomintang on the verandah outside, carbines across their chests.

The aide was dismissed. Tea was served. The three of them chatted on, Madam Chiang switching from Mandarin to fluent English back to Mandarin at will. Though Huart could have exchanged views with the Chiangs for hours, at no time did he lose sight of the objective of his visit.

At noon lunch was served in the presidential dining room. Conversation continued to flow during the meal, the topic moving from America to the armistice in Korea, to life in China before, during and after the Second World War, to China today. Though Chiang made no effort to disguise his emotions when speaking of the current regime in Peking, his wife honed his words to remain in keeping with the sociality of the occasion.

Finally, the fruit was served, signifying the end of the repast. Huart's time had come. He cleared his throat and said quietly: 'Your Excellency, there is some advice I seek from you . . .'

'I am at your service, General Huart,' Chiang responded with the earnestness of a well-meaning host.

Proceeding with care, for he was still unsure as to the lie of the land into which he was stepping with both his large feet, Huart went on: 'I have a particular problem at my textile plant in Hong Kong. I believe it originated because of an unfortunate incident in Shanghai in 1940 in which I was involved. The injured party was . . . the *Chin Pang*.'

Madam Chiang frowned. She hesitated before translating. When she did so, the President's eyebrows arched. Though certain he was already guilty of a gross breach of protocol, Huart was committed to it. He continued with the salient excerpts of his story, concluding with the demise of his production manager. 'My factory remains on strike today. If it continues it will ruin me. I believe the *Chin Pang* intends that should happen. I have reason to believe the instructions to bring it about may have come from Taipei. I had hoped Your Excellency could bring some pressure to bear to have them withdrawn. I seek your favour, hoping my request is considered neither ridiculous nor impossible. And I apologise most sincerely for my presumptuousness and my poor etiquette in making such a request, being your honoured guest on such an unforgettable occasion.'

Chiang Kai-shek's eyes now registered zero emotion as he listened to the simultaneous translation until it had finished. Then he nodded his head a fraction and issued a handful of Mandarin syllables. As Madam Chiang turned back to him to convey the decision of the President of the Republic of China, her face just as impassive, Huart held his breath.

'General Huart, you risked your life for our soldiers when you did not have to and have been presented with China's highest award for bravery. I regret it is not enough. I can only supplement it by promising you any instruction from the *Chin Pang* that affects you will be reversed.'

The words were what Huart had come to Taipei to hear, but they held a deeper meaning. He read it in Madam Chiang's face. He had asked for too much, but in such a way that her husband could not refuse. China's debt to John Stanford Huart had been repaid. It had been overpaid. Now the debt was on his account, and debtors were not welcome in Taipei.

[254]

24

On Christmas Eve, 1953, a spark ignited amidst the ramshackle jumble that was the squatter community of Shek Kip Mei. The fire tore through the hovels desiccated by the dry season. The entire place burnt to the ground in hours and 53,000 refugees suddenly had nowhere to live.

The directors of Cumberland China and their families gathered at midday for Christmas dinner. The occasion was becoming a tradition, as it had been in Shanghai, with Huart hosting this year in his new rented apartment on Garden Terrace. After the meal the men faced north from the balcony and looked down steep Garden Road and across the harbour to Kowloon at the pall of smoke that was once Shek Kip Mei, as it rose in sobering cynosure above the peninsula. With bellies full and blood running warm, they sipped their after-dinner drinks and talked in the cool of the dying afternoon. They discussed Eisenhower and confidently forecast a period of growth in world trade in the wake of the Korean War, and they reviewed Huart's proposal to open a branch office in Taipei.

'Clive should be responsible,' Huart said. 'I've seen enough of Taipei. There's nothing new I can do there.' What he saw was Madam Chiang's face and he read its message again. No, there was nothing more he could do there, except open an office to oversee the ongoing contracts and pay the local taxes and, in that small way, repay something of the 'debt'.

'I don't know how you can say that with a straight face, John,' Bedrix disagreed. 'You've got some magic over there that we should exploit to the fullest.' And he went on to express renewed admiration at the way the strike at Wai Wai Road had ended promptly after Huart's return from Taipei, with the workers appearing at the production lines and setting about their tasks with an energy designed, it seemed, to assuage an accumulation of guilt. 'You must have some sort of Taipei card up your sleeve, John. And the little you say on it, one could be forgiven for suspecting it comes from the bottom of the pack. You agree, Andrew?'

But Andrew did not reply. He still thought it all much too mysterious. There was more to this massive cousin of his, with his incongruous military background, than met the eye.

Huart diverted the attack with: 'It's settled then! We open in Taipei at Chinese New Year for good *fung shui*. Then I'll be able to sleep. It worries me when I find Chuck Kreitzer has been visiting Taiwan and not informing us. Soon he'll be deciding he doesn't need us.'

'Come, John,' Andrew spoke up. 'Our link with Kreitzer is protected by an Agency Agreement, which is a sacrosanct document – like a marriage licence.' He glanced back to see if Paulette was listening from the living room. 'A good Agency Agreement's a Licence to Print Money. If you doubt Kreitzer's integrity, then the agreement's no good any more and we should find another principal. There're plenty of other designers and fabricators of cement plants in this world.'

Huart groaned beneath his breath. How different a line this was to the one Andrew had taken that night at the Repulse Bay Hotel when he had stressed the indispensability of Pan Atlantic Insurance to the company's existence. 'It would be easier to set Kreitzer straight than to hunt for a competitor who isn't half as good,' he suggested. 'He's been prompting us to establish a base in Taipei, and now we're doing it. I think I can keep Chuck under control.'

He saw his cousin's quick frown. Andrew was starting to think that business was as easy as it had been when the foreign *hongs* had ruled the China Trade. It was having an effect on Bedrix and on the engineering manager, Nigel Print. Whilst Huart had been in Taiwan, Abraham Male had gone to Kowloon and Canton Cement and taken a contract for a plant extension from under Cumberland China's nose.

Andrew switched the subject to Saigon Phase Two. It was a bad choice. They disagreed on this, too. Huart wanted the contract for the extension to Rochetet's jute mill to be handled identically to Phase One, when the company had acted as agents for Lionel Hope on five percent commission. There had been no technical or commercial hiccup and the commission had been collected on time. Andrew wanted Cumberland China to take the role of principal on the next phase and accept the risks this entailed.

'The company is sound enough for us to finance some of these contracts ourselves,' Andrew expounded, 'and make a greater profit – rather than an agency commission that gets paid at the discretion of the people we represent. I'm tired of going cap in hand to people like Hugh Dunlop. At the rate we're growing we'll be bigger than Lionel Hope in a few years.'

The houseboy brought a round of port. 'Thank you, Ah Keung,' Huart said, and opened his mouth to give his money's worth on Saigon Phase Two.

[256]

Andrew gave him no chance. He was onto his favourite theme and there was no slowing him down. The smallness of the company in Hong Kong, compared with the great *hong* he had ruled, frustrated him, and he was driven to make it grow in the shortest time. 'Saigon Phase Two is the perfect size for us. It's not too big, not too small. And we won't finance it at all. Rochetet has not been terribly smart this time. Neither has Hugh Dunlop. Société le Indo-Chine will pay us twenty per cent deposit, only half of which we will pass on to Lionel Hope, the balance payable by DA ninety days from sight of Bill of Lading. We pay Dunlop at 120 days Letter of Credit, opened at sight. We will have our ten per cent profit right up front, instead of five per cent agency commission at the end of the contract, and we'll have $1,280,000 of Rochetet's money to play with for a full month before Dunlop draws on the LC. We are covered all the way.'

'Sounds neat,' Huart agreed. 'There's just one thing that can go wrong.'

'One thing? What thing?' Andrew protested.

'Yes, John,' Bedrix joined in. 'What can go wrong? I think Andrew has set up a sound deal. I think with Phase One going off so well – '

'Exactly my point,' Huart interrupted. 'Why change a proven formula?'

'For increased profit, John!' Andrew insisted. 'For Christ's sake!'

Bedrix nodded, but said no more. Cosgrove sat in a balcony chair watching them benignly out of one eye, whilst he surveyed the world out of the other via a snifter half filled with armagnac.

'Certainly return should be proportional to risk,' Huart conceded. 'If the mill was being built in Hong Kong I would agree the deal is fine. But there's one thing that could go very wrong.' He turned from Bedrix to Andrew and saw him bristle, ready to interject. 'Documents against Acceptance are not an irrevocable security like a Letter of Credit. When the shipping documents pass through the bank our money is committed to Lionel Hope in 120 days. That is irrevocable. The H and K would not let us renege on a Letter of Credit, even if we wanted to. That's the banking system, God bless it. But Rochetet can revoke payment to us ninety days after his sight of our document by refusing to honour our DA.'

'And why would he do that?' Andrew asked sceptically.

'Andrew – a full scale war is raging in Vietnam! The French are getting cleaned up and the only ones who don't seem to realise it are the French themselves and, by the sound of it, the board of Cumberland China! Tell me, Andrew – ' He heard the voice that told him he was going too far, but it was too late. 'What's French for *maskee?*'

It was a stinging comment on history. Andrew had twice failed to interpret the portents of the internal schisms that had erupted into war in China. Now, according to Huart, he was risking repetition in Vietnam.

'*C'est la guerre?*' Cosgrove suggested from the balcony chair.

Andrew stared back at his cousin, his lips tightened into twin colourless lines and his complexion turned from florid to puce as he held on to his temper with difficulty. Huart groaned silently again, seeing he had only succeeded in driving Andrew further along his chosen path.

'I'm the one who's been travelling to Vietnam, not you,' Andrew pointed out in a voice that sounded as if it was being forced through a wringer. 'The French hold on the areas around Saigon and Hanoi remains sound. The mill is in Cholon – within secure territory that happens to extend a hundred miles north of Saigon. Phase Two will be completed by May. By the end of June our money will be in the bank. After that Ho Chi Minh and his rebels can do what they damn-well wish. The war in Vietnam's been going on since '46. The French are backed up by the Americans in no uncertain way. Eisenhower's not going to let the *Viet Minh* overrun all of Vietnam – and certainly not in the next six months – cousin of mine!' He spun on his heel and left the balcony. Minutes later he returned with his overcoat across an arm and his family in line behind him, dressed to leave and all looking confused.

Adelaide appeared, holding a balloon of cognac. She looked at her son and clicked her teeth in disapproval. 'Petulant,' she announced to no-one in particular. 'Like his father.' Then she went back into the living room and resumed her chat with Loretta Delgardo, whose time she rated.

Andrew was not finished with Huart. 'Any comparison between Vietnam and Shanghai is simplistic. Shanghai was our home and we were blinded by our hopes and our dreams for its perpetuation. With Vietnam it's strictly business. Unemotional business. Cousin John, don't get too big for your boots – if that's possible. And don't delude yourself you're the only one who can pull off big contracts. I was doing it every day of the week when you had nought else to do but spit on the toes of your boots down there in Rangoon!' His angry eyes swept the balcony, and then he

[258]

produced a smile that stopped short of his eyes. 'I bid a good-day and a merry Christmas to you all!'

And the Huart-Brents were gone.

From his balcony Huart watched them descend the stone steps that led to his front gate, then the steep path to Garden Road. Andrew managed all this with difficulty, his limp pronounced. A Mercedes taxi responded to his impatient wave and the family climbed in. The cab started north in the direction of Central District, landmarked by the Hongkong and Shanghai Bank and the adjacent, slightly taller Bank of China, which the Communists had completed in 1951, then U-turned onto the lane that climbed to the Peak.

It was strange to see the Huart-Brents take a taxi. Their chauffeur had been told to bring the Ford Customline at six. It was only 4:30. It was stranger to see Andrew in such high dudgeon. Huart took it as a sign that much had changed. He chastised himself for precipitating the scene, but his apprehension over Saigon Phase Two was real. It had brought to the surface something bad. He had been unaware of the potency of the bitterness that had been brewing in Andrew and his confrontation with it had alarmed him. For he knew from personal experience that bitterness could be a self-destructive emotion, even an internecine one.

Huart decided then and there to back off and let Andrew have his way. In six months the contract would be completed. Most probably nothing at all would have gone wrong. In six months Andrew would have won the victory that seemed so important to him. 'Who's for another drink?' he called in good cheer. 'Armagnac, Lennie? Port, Clive? Merry Christmas to us all!'

25

Huart had not laid eyes on the man with the walking stick since the day before he left Shanghai in August, 1940. But his ghost had come to him often. He next saw him in the flesh the day Andrew Huart-Brent died.

It happened at Kai Tak on Wednesday, May 10th, 1954. The man was receiving the deference due to a patriarch from a well-to-do Chinese family whom he had met off a flight from Taipei.

Was it him? The form fit the ghost. It was him. A vice of indecision closed on Huart. Had his Chiang gambit the previous October won the war? Or only a battle? There was his enemy, right in front of his eyes. So what should he do about it?

The dilemma was thrust from him by Paulette's gasp of alarm. He spun to follow her gaze and saw two male nurses lifting a stretcher down the steps of Air Asia-Pacific Flight 44 from Saigon. An oxygen mask obscured the patient's face, but the head was plain to see. It was quite bald.

'It's Andrew!' she cried. 'Oh my God! Let me through!'

The man with the walking stick was forgotten.

Bedrix ran down the steps of the DC3 after the stretcher. Huart vaulted the railing, lifted Paulette over it and together they ran towards the door with the blood red cross above it. Officials moved to intercept but stopped when they saw that Huart's face brooked no interference. Minutes later they all watched helplessly as Andrew was slid into an ambulance. Paulette climbed in with him. There was no room for anyone else.

Huart took Bedrix's arm. 'Tell me all about it on the way to hospital.'

They ran to the Huart-Brent Customline parked before the terminal building and piled into the rear, jerking the chauffeur from his nap. Huart rapid-fired: 'Kowloon Hospital! Master is sick. Follow that ambulance! Quick!' The chauffeur crunched the Ford into first gear and flattened the accelerator, throwing Huart and Bedrix back into the seat.

'It's been absolute hell!' the general manager began through clenched teeth as they fastened onto the tail of the ambulance and sped into Kowloon. 'We hit an air pocket a half hour out of Hong Kong. Andrew grabbed his chest. He couldn't breathe. Thank the Lord a doctor was on board. But it really began yesterday on the *rue Catinat*.' His shoulder hit against the window as the Customline took a corner at speed. He dug in his pocket with his one hand and produced a squashed pack of Capstans.

'How long've you been smoking?' Huart asked. God, what had happened?

Bedrix lit a bent cigarette with a Zippo lighter. Inhaling deeply, he gasped: 'I used to smoke two packs a day in the war. Sometimes three. I gave it up in '45. Until yesterday. Christ, what a sight! I thought I'd left that sort of thing behind when the war ended.'

'What sort of thing, Clive?' Huart studied the bloodshot eyes, saw the pallor of the sagging skin, the cigarette shaking between the fingers.

'We were sitting at a sidewalk café. Andrew had just bought a copy of the *Journal de Saigon*. I still have it with me. Here – '

Huart peered at the headlines with difficulty as the car swerved, braked and accelerated along Prince Edward Road. Kowloon Hospital was a mile ahead. He fixed on the words 'Dien Bien Phu'.

'The French've been annihilated in the north,' Bedrix breathed. 'Their days in Vietnam are numbered. But for us it's worse than that! Look at the bottom left hand corner – ' He jabbed his finger. 'Société le Indo-Chine's Cholon jute mill was blown to smithereens two days ago by a bunch of religious extremists. Vietnam's over for us, John. The mill's gone. So has our $1,280,000 come June 16th.'

Huart was frowning hard in disbelief, refusing to allow his general manager's alarm to transmit to him. 'Rochetet won't honour our DA?'

Bedrix sighed and drew deeply on his cigarette. 'Rochetet went up with everything else at the mill – '

'No!'

'Yes, John.'

'But . . . insurance, then – '

This brought a bitter snort. 'With the civil war no insurance company would touch it. Not even Pan Atlantic. Didn't Andrew tell you . . ?'

Huart's face emptied. He sat there, disembowelled. Bedrix continued but he heard only parts of it.

' . . . so we were sitting at this café. There was not a thing we could do. Société le Indo-Chine was finished – its owner dead. Their bankers had frozen all funds. I'd persuaded Andrew to return to Hong Kong. He could do nothing in Saigon. I was staying to register our claim with the bank. Andrew ordered champagne – you know what he's like – flamboyant even in the face of disaster. As we drank it a class of schoolkids came down the *rue Catinat* led by two teachers. They were teenagers fresh from school themselves probably. So pretty they were in their *ao dai*. The kids were happy. They were all laughing. A car went by. An object was thrown into the middle of the kids. It was a satchel charge. It went off . . .'

Bedrix shook his head slowly. Tears welled in his eyes. He stabbed the half-smoked remains of his Capstan into the ashtray and slammed it shut.

'I saw it all in the war, John. I lost an arm. But I never saw anything like this. Those kids and young girls. In war – you know as well as I do – you grow inured to all the killing and the bodies. But it should be peacetime! There we were sitting under a tree outside a little French café drinking champagne, watching little schoolkids and . . . John, a child's arm fell on the table between us . . .' His voice trailed off.

After several seconds he went on. 'I think they were all killed. There was blood and bits of bodies all over the place. Enough explosive to kill an army. I think Andrew had the first heart attack right then. He was gasping for breath. His face was blue. But he insisted he was alright. Neither of us slept at all last night. Andrew was very ill this morning. He insisted on making it to Tan Son Nhut under his own steam. He refused to see a doctor in Saigon. Didn't trust them. He was in pain during the entire flight. It was the air pocket that finally did it.'

The ambulance pulled up at the emergency entrance of Kowloon Hospital and the Customline peeled off into a parking space. A stretcher was wheeled to the rear of the ambulance and Andrew was passed into the care of a chain of white coats along an antiseptic corridor. Huart gripped Paulette by both shoulders. 'He's in the best of hands now,' he said softly. 'Let's find the place where we should wait.'

An hour and a half later, Adelaide joined them in the waiting room that faced a door with the sign 'Intensive Care'. She merely nodded and sat down. Another hour went by in silence before a doctor appeared.

'Your husband's had a massive coronary,' he told Paulette. 'In fact he's had several in succession. He would probably be in better shape had he received treatment after the first attack. But now, I'm afraid . . .'

She bit her lip. 'Can we see him, doctor?'

'He's barely conscious.' A perplexed frown crossed his face. 'But he is asking for his cousin . . .'

'That's me.' Huart came forward.

The doctor nodded. 'Normally I wouldn't allow visitors, but he's quite insistent. So much so that I fear a further attack if I don't allow you in.' He gave a weak smile which said: 'He'll be gone in an hour anyway.'

'He's a stubborn man alright,' Huart agreed.

'Come with me, please.' The doctor turned.

'You, too, ladies.' Huart took both their arms.

Paulette hung back. 'But he only asked for you. I don't understand . . .'

'Come on, girl,' snapped Adelaide. 'You're his wife, aren't you?'

'Wait here, Clive, please,' Huart called over his shoulder.

Bedrix nodded dumbly and sat down on the bench again.

They went through two doors into a private ward with pastel blue walls that shrieked silence at them. A white-sheeted bed was half enclosed by an oxygen tent. Andrew was inside it, connected by tubes to a machine that bleeped loudly in the heavy quiet. The starched uniform of an English nurse crackled as she made room for them beside the bed. 'Only five minutes,' the doctor whispered. The nurse followed him out.

Andrew's skin was bloodless and Huart had a fleeting sensation he was already looking at a corpse. One of the eyes half opened and the left side of the face twisted in what may have been an attempt at a smile.

'Cousin . . . if you say . . . "I told you so" . . . I swear I'll have a . . . a heart attack.' Andrew's voice was pathetic, his words slurred, broken.

'Andrew . . .' Paulette began, but the eyes flashed at her and she stopped.

'Son . . .' Adelaide breathed. Again the flash, but less accusatory.

'Quiet.' The voice was unexpectedly strong. 'No time. I'm dying. It's been coming a long time. It's my due. But . . . before I go I've important business to discuss with John. Paulette . . . Mother . . . Kiss me. Leave me with him . . . a few minutes. Sorry . . .'

They were stunned, hurt, but did his bidding. They kissed the hand he pushed under the oxygen tent and left silently with glances at Huart.

'Andrew,' he began. 'What rotten luck . . .'

The hand moved sharply, cutting him off. 'Listen to me. What I have to say is vital to the future of . . . the company. I only have time to say it once. Listen carefully . . . please. There's much for you to do.'

Huart steeled himself to heed with both his large, long ears. His heart embraced his cousin, who was proclaiming himself dead at forty-seven after a life that had blossomed and flowed, then turned barren and futile. Twice imprisoned in his home, evicted from the country of his birth, his family fortune taken from him; mentally crippled by the truth of his wife's infidelity, the siring of his second daughter by another man. But despite all this, Huart knew Andrew's severest demon was fear of judgement as a failed taipan by his grandfather's example. The ghost of Charles Huart still lived within him. Its presence could be felt now.

[263]

'When I am dead . . . ask Francis Roboza to give you the key to my safe. In there you will find my will . . . also a letter in an envelope addressed to Arthur Dennison. Read it. It . . . was written by my grandfather. Arthur was to show it to me upon my becoming taipan . . . which he did. The letter tells how Charles had a . . . a mistress . . . a Shanghai woman of high birth called . . . Lin Ching-hsu. Lin had a daughter by my grandfather in 1911. He was sixty-five at the time, the virile old . . . When his will was read, it mentioned Lin and the existence of . . . of a child. My mother had them both sent away from . . . Shanghai. They came to . . . to Hong Kong in 1931 . . . and disappeared. The daughter, my half-aunt, would be in her forties now. She must have married . . . probably has children of . . . her own. Her maiden name was . . . Elizabeth Jane Huart. Remember it, John. Arthur told me both mother and daughter were great beauties. Elizabeth studied at . . . the Sorbonne. I've looked for her for three years. The letter instructed Arthur to care for Lin and his daughter and any children she may have. That charge was passed on to me. I now pass it to you . . .'

Andrew paused and breathed heavily. Huart made as if to speak, but the hand moved again.

'Any male progeny of . . . of Elizabeth Huart carries a direct blood link to Charles Huart . . . stronger even . . . than your own. Find her . . . John. Your sons are gone. I have daughters. One daughter . . .' Andrew choked off with a sob. It was a long time before he could go on. 'Eliz . . . Elizabeth Huart may have the family heritage . . . in her hands. She . . . She may have control of the company's future . . .'

Andrew stopped. He was breathing heavily. The nurse entered the ward and moved quickly to check one of the instruments.

'I'll find her, Andrew. I promise you that.'

The nurse looked at Huart and motioned for him to leave.

'Don't go!' Andrew cried out. 'One more thing! John . . . John, you must lead the company back to China. Cumberland . . . We must . . . must return to Shanghai, John. Promise me . . . you won't miss any . . . any opportunity for bus . . . for business there. You can do it. Promise me . . . John . . .'

Huart took the hand and felt the papery skin and the coldness of death. 'I promise you that, too, Andrew. I pledge that the company's future lies north. I shall not rest until it regains its birthright.'

Andrew nodded, then his eyes went wide and his fingernails dug into Huart's palm. He tried to sit up. 'Number One!' he shouted. 'We must be Number One again! You can be Number One, John. Not me – Mister Ninety-Nine Percent! Five foot eleven and three-quarters. Deputy Chairman of the Shanghai Municipal Council. Charles Huart's grandson. You can be Number One, John. You can do it. You can do . . . it . . . You . . . can . . .'

The mouth closed. The eyes rolled. The hand let go. The head fell back on the pillow. The silence flooded back. Huart's ears rang with it. He could hear his heart thumping in his chest as he looked at his cousin with his heart about to beat its last. He turned to the nurse. 'Get the doctor, please. And ask the ladies to come back. He's nearly gone.'

She accepted his authority without demur and left, her uniform rustling.

They sat around the bed and watched with silent acceptance as death inexorably claimed its prize. A full hour passed before the third taipan of Cumberland China gave a cry of anguish in terminal comment upon his unfulfilled life. And passed away.

Huart closed his cousin's eyes with his fingertips and drew the sheet over his head. He was last to leave the bedside. He continued to sit, looking at the sheet that covered the remains of his last known blood relative in the East. His head was full of the pledges he had made, and something else: the man with the walking stick. He had seen the look in the man's eyes that told him he had won this battle, or this war; but he had also seen the same eyes that had cursed him on the Bund fourteen years before. And he looked at the shape under the sheet and he knew that, though he may have won, that curse was still upon him.

And so the Year of the Wood Horse bequeathed John Stanford Huart the taipan's chair – such as it was.

26

Had Andrew Huart-Brent died in pre-1949 Shanghai, his funeral would have been a command performance. Not only would it have been attended by all members of the Municipal Council, all taipans, all chief managers of the banks, all general managers of utilities, all *hong* compradores, all ambassadors and consuls of the foreign powers; but also condolences would have been cabled by the Prime Minister of England, the President of the United States of America, the President of France, plus each chief executive of every multi-national corporation in the China Trade.

But he died in Hong Kong. There his company survived, a miniature of the *hong* he had ruled from the fourth floor of Cumberland Building on the Bund. Actual attendance at his funeral service was a measure of his fall from grace. No telegrams came from Downing Street, the White House, the Elysée Palace. No ambassadors or consuls attended, though some trade commissioners did appear; as did such personages as Sir Bartholomew Orr, Owen Catchpole and the Right Honourable Frederick Lloyd Oberon, OBE, Chairman of the Hongkong and Kwangtung Bank.

Lennie Cosgrove left Loretta in Monaco to end the honeymoon on her own, and flew back to be a pallbearer with Huart, Owen Catchpole, Percy Landers, Herbert Jarvis and seniors from the Government, Mardens and the Godown Company. Bedrix's disability kept him from any physical role.

By coincidence, Rex Wagoner also flew in on TWA in time for the funeral. But instead of bringing a respectful sadness with him, he wore more of a predatory mien than usual. Huart gave no time to ponder on it as, to his secretly shameless delight, Virginia came too. He found her beside him often during the long, sombre day. Gradually he fathomed why. Her eyes carried a message. It was as if she had taken a decision.

At last the day ended with Huart and Wagoner together in the American's Peninsula suite. Though it had been more a summons than an invitation, Huart had accepted, but had discovered with regret that Virginia was not joining them. He soon found out why.

'I've just wrapped up the purchase of Greater London Underwriters . . .' Wagoner slopped a Chivas into one glass, a Jack Daniels into another and saluted his image in the wall mirror. He turned on Huart, his eyes cold, the predatory glint undiminished. 'And so I'm transferrin' the Pan Atlantic agency to Male & Son.'

In the septic silence that followed, Huart could say nothing. It had to be a joke. Cumberland China had been doing well for Pan Atlantic.

Wagoner went on: 'I reckon they can best expand business for me in these modern times. Young Abe Male's damned impressive. Got balls, that guy. He fronted me cold in Chicago last month. He knew I was after GLU and what he proposed made sense. You know, Big Fella, you made a bad enemy when you took his

ol' man's electric power agencies. Seems now he's got even.'
Wagoner refilled his own glass without offering to Huart, who had
in any case yet to take any as he stood cast in stone, lips drawn
taut, jaw thrust forward, his eyes burning into the American's like
coals.

'You're in a mess,' Wagoner laughed. 'Lost your chairman. In
deep shit over that Saigon deal. You're for the high jump, Big
Fella. I'm pullin' out now – before it's too late. If you were in my
position, chances are you'd do the same. But you're not, and so
you're stuck.'

Huart slowly put down his glass. He straightened and pushed
both hands through his black hair until they clasped behind his
head. He inhaled deeply, audibly. He shook his head to stir up
his senses.

'What are you, Wagoner? You play around with Andrew's wife
right under his nose, then as soon as he's gone, you do something
like this. What are you – a man or an animal?'

Wagoner seemed surprised. 'I thought we'd been cagey enough
about it. Not like you. A moron can see the thing you've got for
my wife. It's stickin' out in front o' you every time you get near
her. Okay, go to it. Give it to her. I give you my permission. A
sorta trade, okay?'

'You're an immoral b – ' Huart took a half step then stopped.
He owed it to Andrew to keep his anger under wraps. Perhaps
the agency was gone, perhaps not. Losing his temper would only
clinch it for Male & Son.

'Immoral?' Wagoner swirled his bourbon in his glass and
laughed again. 'Lennie says you're a good 'un on quotes. Heard
the old Greek proverb that goes: "First secure an independent
income, then practise virtue"?'

A fire ignited in Huart that began to burn into inbred restraints.
He took another deep breath that squared his shoulders, and
smiled a smile that stopped short of his eyes. He saw the doubt
flicker across Wagoner's pupils. The voice, when it came, was
pitched low. 'Mark Twain said something apt. "An ethical man is
a Christian holding four aces".'

'Four aces?' Wagoner snorted. 'Limey, you don't have shit in
your mitt. You're done in Hong Kong. You never belonged here
anyway. I never liked you. Overgrown army general tradin' off
your family – '

'Shut up and look at me . . . sir.' The voice was lower still. 'I
happen to be a Christian – and in my hand I'm holding not four
aces, but five.'

'What the hell are you talkin' about, Limey? The only thing you hold on to is your cock every time you see my wife!'

Prior to that moment of his life, a rigid code of ethics had controlled the personal conduct of John Stanford Huart. It was a product of his heritage, his military training, his love for his family gone and the well of his self-respect. But Wagoner lived to a vastly different code, one that had crossed Huart and now delivered him a blatant challenge. Face to face with it, his lifelong code was tested to the limit.

And broke.

Huart's clenched right fist was suddenly an inanimate weapon at the end of a spring connected to a part of his brain that had lain dormant since boyhood. It swung upwards with power and speed through an arc that terminated on Wagoner's left cheekbone and hit with a crunch that testified to its accuracy and timing. The American was a big man, but the punch was a perfect one and he went over backwards like a redwood pine felled by lightning, his glass flying from his hand across the suite.

Huart stood over him, willing him to take up the fight. Wagoner was stunned. He moved slowly, raised himself on one elbow and rubbed his face. He grimaced. There was a touch of amusement in it, as if he considered it a victory to have provoked Huart over the edge. 'That was a punch, Big Fella,' he muttered. 'Savour it. It's finished you for sure.'

Huart gave Wagoner room to get up, but the American gave no indication that he wished to carry the fight. 'Hemingway said: "What is moral is what you feel good after".' He turned and walked to the door.

'You may feel goddamn good now,' Wagoner sang out, still rubbing his face. 'But you won't come Monday mornin' when you read in the paper that three months hence Male & Son'll be sole agents for both GLU and Pan Atlantic Insurance. You'll feel a right moron then!'

'Talk to our solicitors about it, Wagoner.' Huart turned at the door. 'And I never did like you calling me "Big Fella". It always made me want to call you "Big Shit".' A room boy appeared in the corridor with an armful of towels. Huart jerked a thumb over his shoulder. 'Take an icepack to the man in 620. He ran into a truck.'

He rode in the empty elevator to the lobby and stood there amidst the high-columned elegance. He looked about at the sophisticated of Asia and rubbed the fist that had committed so unsophisticated an act. He smiled hard to squash his anger. And the anxiety that welled inside him.

His taipan was dead. Cumberland China's net loss on Saigon Phase Two was $1,120,000. It would rip the heart out of the H and K account the moment Lionel Hope and Sons drew down their Letter of Credit. It would eliminate the profits of the past four years in an instant. All the work, the sweat, the anguish, the pain; all the luck, the brilliance, the skilful negotiations, the manoeuvring, the surviving – it all would have been for nothing. Cumberland China was back on the edge of the precipice. And he, its taipan designate, had just guaranteed the loss of its largest single revenue-producing agency. And what was an agency? Huart heard in his brain Andrew's voice answer that one: 'An agency, Cousin John? Why, a good agency is a Licence to Print Money'.

Virginia Wagoner stepped into the Peninsula lobby. Huart studied her outline in the light reflected from the fountain behind her. Her eyes raised to his with a hungry surprise when she saw him coming towards her. He took her arm, and she left the hotel with him without a word.

Upon the window ledge of room 202 of the Repulse Bay Hotel, Huart sat with just a bath towel tucked around his waist. He gazed down at the lawns and flower beds without seeing them through the half-light of pre-dawn, and out to the bay at the foot of the mountain against which the hotel nestled. The beach was deserted. Stringy waves drew lines in its white sand. He traced with a fingertip the contours of the scar at the base of his back that was a memento of Burma, when he had contributed to the longest retreat in British military history. Then he touched the one on his neck left by the Japanese bayonet on Nanking Road that day he had not fought back. His fingertip felt neither scar, but his brain felt both. So much has happened since then, he acknowledged. So much has changed. Now I have changed. No more retreats, no more defeats for me!

He looked back into the room. The dawn light divided the darkness into shadows and caused the white sheets on the bed to illuminate dully. They were rumpled and twisted. Two pillows lay discarded on the floor.

Virginia was a sculpture. Her lovely face was framed by her auburn hair splashed across the sheets. She looked up as he admired her and made no move to cover herself, but stretched her arms like a domesticated animal uncoiling from a deep sleep on a warm hearth. Her firm round breasts quivered. She smiled

[269]

and beckoned to him. He stood up. The towel fell to the floor, unfastened by the spontaneous resurrection of his manhood.

'If you are typical of a man kept in celibacy for fourteen years, John Huart,' she breathed, 'I'll give priests my profound respect in future.'

'I don't believe it myself,' he murmured, positioning himself over her.

She guided him with both hands. 'Believe it, John. Believe it.'

And again he drove himself into her, using a force that was strong yet kind, a determination unyielding yet considerate, a passion uninhibited yet not abandoned. She received him with an aching willingness, her arms grasping his girth as if only he could save her from whatever threatened her happiness. She wrapped her body about his like it was a main-mast in a typhoon and gripped her ankles together above his buttocks. Her flesh welded to his as she moved in tempo with him, accelerating as they squeezed, rubbed, willed each other towards some vortex that drew them deeper deeper deeper, enveloping them in an ecstasy that cloistered their bodies and their minds and banished the world.

Huart broke from her hungry mouth and threw back his head. He ground into her. His body quivered. He groaned a long deep monotone as fourteen years of imprisoned, subjugated virility let go in a hot salving seminal flow. She felt it explode over her abdominal nerve-endings and she wrapped her thighs about his and dug her fingernails into his buttocks. A scream burst from her abdomen into her lungs. She muffled it against his shoulder, oblivious to the blood her teeth drew from him.

They lay expended, arms thrown out, bodies together but unclasped. When at last he moved to withdraw from her, she tightened her loins, gripping him again. 'Don't leave,' she whispered, kissing the blood from his shoulder. 'Stay as you are, John. Sleep . . . just as you are. Inside me.'

'I can't stay,' Huart breathed, his face in the sheets. 'I have to get through that connecting door before the room boy does his rounds.'

'Your reputation is so pure, John? We've hours yet. Stay.'

They slept deeply until the sun's brightness at the window awakened her. He was still upon her, his torso at an angle so that his weight was to one side. 'Wake up, John. Wake up. Time to go.' She tickled his ear.

'What time is it?' he responded sleepily.

'I don't know. But I can hear movement in the corridor.'

[270]

Huart got up and stood looking down at her as she lay there with eyes lightly closed and a serene smile reposing upon her lovely face. Her skin glowed with the warmth of inner embers, and she whispered: 'The lady is sated, John. I feel like I'm floating in a tropical lagoon.'

He bent and kissed her on the mouth, then brushed each nipple with his lips and felt them harden. 'See you at breakfast.' He moved to the door to 204, picking his robe from a chair as he passed.

Over mid-morning tea and toast on the verandah, Virginia asked: 'It's rather dangerous, isn't it. What we've done, I mean.' She looked about the verandah, suddenly thankful it was half empty this Sunday morning.

Huart's nod was more sagacious than he felt. 'Very dangerous. Hong Kong is a village. There'll certainly be talk . . . if we make a habit of it.'

'Would you like to?'

He considered his answer for long seconds before delivering it. 'I'm not sure, Virginia . . . yet. I'm sorry. I'd like to let things readjust for a while. A lot has happened this week. Andrew's death. One or two problems in the company . . .' A punch-up in the Peninsula and an act of passionate adultery in the Repulse Bay Hotel, he added to himself. Yes, it had been quite a week. 'And you. I may have just ruined your marriage.'

She shook her head. 'It was already a wreck. We were both looking for a reason, or an excuse, to make the break, I guess. I hope that Andrew's death – and you – have provided both. Oh – !' Her hand flew up to her mouth. 'I'm so sorry – that must have sounded awful.'

He shrugged. 'The world's been an awful place for such a long time. Your husband's been having a protracted affair with Paulette, you know.'

'I know.'

He shook his head in wonder. 'How could a couple like you two happen?'

'Rex wasn't always the way he is.'

Huart grimaced. 'Forgive me, but . . . he's the lowest bastard I've met in my life. No, he's the lowest business bastard I've met in my business life. And that's rather short. There must be worse to come.'

'Sure to be. Watch out for them.'

'My solution to my problem with Rex was to punch him in the face.'

'Good for you. Did he hit you back?'

'As a matter of fact, he didn't.'

She pulled a disparaging face. 'He wouldn't. It's not his style. He's not a physical man . . . like you.' She looked at him in a way that brought the musky scent of the sheets on the bed of room 202 back to him and he stirred. 'But what provoked you to hit him?'

'He's transferring the agency to Male & Son.'

'Oh, John . . . I'll speak to him.'

'You'll say nothing. It's done. The best thing you can do is to initiate divorce proceedings. I'm sure he'll co-operate. He can hardly cite me as co-respondent with what I know of his adultery with Andrew's widow.'

'You have proof? Anyway, I never thought of you as vindictive, John.'

He thought about it. 'This week has done a lot to me. From now on this world will be seeing a different John Huart. There's something I owe to Andrew. And to the company. And to myself.' He folded his napkin and called for the bill. Within an hour he was at his desk, studying the fine print of the Agency Agreement with Pan Atlantic Insurance and drafting a letter to the company solicitors, Jackson, Sloan and Butler.

Then he focused his thoughts on his second Crisis: how to shore up the cave-in that was Saigon Phase Two.

On the other side of Victoria Habour, Virginia unlocked the door of suite 620 of the Peninsula Hotel and gave it a determined push. But the only item left of Rex Wagoner was a hand-written note that told her amongst the sarcasm that by the time she read it he would already be on his way to Taipei. She called reception and reserved a first-class seat on the TWA flight leaving that afternoon for Los Angeles, via Manila, Guam and Honolulu.

Virginia left Hong Kong without calling Huart. She had decided the next move was his.

27

True to the Wagoner threat, the pronouncement of his sacking of Cumberland China and Male & Son's substitution as sole agent was carried within a thick black border on the business pages of the *Hong Kong and Oriental Daily* and the *South China Morning Post* on Monday, May 17th, and every day that week. The Males were roundly congratulated in the Hong Kong Club by the same hitherto cordial faces that were averted from Huart after a curt nod. It was not altogether intentional rudeness. The community automatically embraced a winner, and discarded a loser like a summer suit the day the first winter monsoon blew down from the north.

With bile burning in his throat, Huart stepped west along Queen's Road to the H and K to confront his banker before Landers could get in first.

'Percy, the company is now me. You're looking at it. In his will, Andrew appointed me as trustee of his stock until his daughters come of age and that gives me control of the largest block of shares. I have a pledge of support from both Lennie and Adelaide. I hope you will also have faith in me – faith that I will continue to discharge any and all debts and lead Cumberland China back to profitability.'

Huart was perched on the edge of a store-fresh chesterfield. The credit manager had recently received a promotion and a new set of furniture to go with it, his favourite item being the leather easy-chair from which he was listening. He had taken to smoking a pipe, and was making a meal of filling it. 'You're instituting legal action against Wagoner, John?'

Huart shrugged. 'I'd like nothing better. Jackson, Sloan and Butler tell me I can sue for loss of projected profits due to misapplication of the "Unsatisfactory Performance" clause in our Agency Agreement. They also tell me that litigation will be extended and expensive. As neither time nor money is on my side, I've decided the expedient thing to do is to find, as quickly as possible, an insurance agency that can compete with Wagoner's empire and then start to take the bastard's business back.'

Furrowed with concentration, Landers poked a wad of tobacco into the bowl of his pipe with the end of a 'Double Happiness' match. He lit up and muttered: 'There's little room in business for your emotions, John.'

Huart said nothing. His decision had been taken after wrestling with those emotions for an entire night. Business sense had finally won out over spite and humiliation. Yet had it been base emotion that had thrust him into a delightfully physical interlude with Wagoner's wife? What did he really feel for Virginia? Was it love? Infatuation? Or was she only the instrument of his ignoble revenge? Remarriage was not even a remote consideration. He well knew that the inexhaustible demands of Cumberland China would render him a wholly unsuitable partner. Particularly now.

Landers brought him back to where he was by asking: 'How long will it take to find such an alternative agency and have it producing revenue?'

Huart shrugged again. 'I have just started looking.'

The banker dropped the blackened match into an ashtray monogramed with the H and K crest and peered out from under a beetled brow. 'John, your company's in a spot of bother again – my apologies for the understatement. You've a heavy debt, and you've lost your insurance business. Pan Atlantic accounted for a third of your consolidated revenue. Correct?'

Huart nodded unceremoniously.

'Of course, John, I've a great deal of personal faith in you, yourself,' Landers went on. 'But the loan you need to replace the value of Lionel Hope's Letter of Credit will require equal faith from two other loan managers, and then our board. It's over a million dollars, you see. If you still had the Pan Atlantic agency, or had already secured an alternative of equal stature, I would think there would be little problem – '

'Percy, Cosgrove Textiles is growing fast,' Huart cut in. 'Hollingwoods have just renewed their annual contract for the fourth year running. Our engineering activities are expanding. We are in final negotiation with Cathay Electric for a contract to manufacture and supply two 30 megawatt turbo-alternators, plus all the associated boilers, transformers and switchgear. Sir Reynard Armstrong, chief executive of the Ango-Saxon Group – you must have heard of him – will personally come out to Hong Kong to sign it. Our success is virtually assured – '

'Virtually, John? What does that mean? You have a Letter of Intent?'

'Not yet.' Here we go all over again, Huart thought, his mind reversing five years and seeing Hector Harrisford-House's piggish face before him.

Lander's brow furrowed deeper. 'Hmmm.' Huart groaned to himself. 'Three H' had enjoyed making that noise. 'What's the value of this contract?'

'Two and three quarter million pounds. We have had to give discounts.'

'And Cumberland China's commission?'

'Three and three quarter per cent.'

'Part in advance?'

'No.'

[274]

'That's too bad.' Landers puffed hard on his pipe to keep it alight. 'You're quite certain this Anglo-Saxon company will win the business?'

'Yes.'

'Your position is secured by a formal Agency Agreement?'

'Signed by Sir Reynard and Andrew. I'll send you a copy this afternoon.'

Landers took the pipe from his mouth and peered into the bowl. He studied whatever was in there for the best part of a minute, drumming the fingers of his other hand on the arm of his chair. Huart sat impatiently through the performance, aware his banker's next words would decide the future of Cumberland China. Finally, Landers clamped his dentures upon the stem of his pipe, lifted his head and looked at the man sitting on his brand new chesterfield. 'If it was Andrew asking me for a fresh loan under these circumstances, John, I'd have to turn him down. But as it's you, it's different. He must have been mad to go in as principal on that Saigon project – and totally uninsured into the bargain with a civil war going on all around it. Why did he do something like that?'

Huart shook his head sadly. 'I suppose Andrew was trying to prove something, Percy,' he sighed. 'He was unlucky. So unlucky.'

'He paid for his mistake with his life,' Landers stated. 'And that's a fact.' He took his pipe from his mouth and tapped the bowl into the ash tray. 'The profitability of your company will be seriously affected for many years because of what he did.' He looked up again. 'We'll want the loan repaid within five years, John. Can you manage that?'

Huart blinked once. 'You're approving my application, Percy?'

The banker gave a cautious smile. 'Now hold on. I'll make a favourable recommendation. That's all I can do. The board's decision is up to the board. Can you pay it back in five? 1,280,000 dollars is a sizeable sum for a trading company of your size. Sorry, another understatement.'

Huart took a deep, silent breath. 'Five years it is, Percy. I'll sign all the guarantees you need, personal or otherwise. So will Lennie.'

Landers stood up and extended his hand. 'Guarantees may not be enough. We may ask for Wai Wai Road as security. I'll call you in a day or so.'

Paulette Huart-Brent tossed her head in a gesture of defiance and glared around the Kai Tak Airport departure lounge. She lifted her eyes and said to Huart: 'I'm so glad to be leaving Hong Kong for ever. I've never felt at home here after Shanghai. In a way, it's a blessing Andrew left me nothing. Not that there was much to leave. He was such a – '

'Paulette . . .' Huart cut in and she heard the warning.

'The girls are welcome to the company stock,' she went on. 'You'll protect their interests better than anyone, John. Above all, you're a man to give others confidence. I hope you find Virginia can share your life. You'd make a good pair. I'm sorry if I've said something I shouldn't . . .'

'I'm married to the company, Paulette. It won't allow me a concubine,' Huart replied, willing the Tannoy to call her flight and terminate the strained farewell. Andrew's widow was a bitter and confused woman. He was glad her daughters were out of earshot. He glanced at them as they pored over the magazine stall, selecting reading material for the sequence of flights across the Pacific and the three overnight stops.

She shrugged. 'Still the moralist, John, aren't you. I guess you feel I treated Andrew badly. Maybe I did. But we were separated so long and Rex was there when I was in need of a real man.' She had over-emphasised the adjective. 'I'm going to him. We're to be married as soon as he's free. Virginia has agreed that he will be divorcing her, you know.'

'That will suit his ego right down to his flying boots,' Huart muttered. 'I wish you luck, Paulette. I think you'll need it,' he added, as a loud metallic voice announced the departure of her flight and countermanded any compulsion she may have had to respond. 'You'd better hurry if you want a good seat for the three of you,' he advised as the girls ran up, each carrying a stack of comic books. 'I hear the flight's very full.'

Vivienne pulled at her mother's arm. At sixteen she remained a child who seemed to have rejected her parents' sophistication. She made no secret of the fact that she was also happy to be leaving Hong Kong.

Suzanne came to Huart and he bent and kissed her on the forehead. Her eyes were big and red from days of tears. She had dearly loved the man she thought was her father. Life can be so strange, and so cruel, Huart thought. At eight, Suzanne was giving advance notice of great beauty and a rare dignity. Her pure blonde hair was her mother's, but Wagoner's colouring was unmistakable. How cruel indeed, Huart affirmed to himself.

'Goodbye, *ma preux chevalier*,' Paulette said uncertainly. 'I remember that night we first met in Shanghai. You were such an innocent then, but a lovely man. You came to Hong Kong by accident. You were a man half-empty, half-removed from reality.

Losing Jennifer and the boys had cut you in two. I see you changing now. You must complete the change fast, or this business world you're in will eat you alive. I'm sorry about what Rex did. I had no idea he was planning it . . .' She broke off, conscious that Huart was not paying attention. 'Well then . . . goodbye, John. I don't think *au revoir* is appropriate, do you?'

But Huart had heard it all. He watched as the last generation of Huart-Brents left Asia around the partition to Immigration. Suzanne turned and blew a kiss. He returned it, she disappeared, and he walked out of the terminal. He took a Mercedes taxi to the Star Ferry, and reviewed Paulette's words as he watched the crowded streets of Kowloon become the road around the Tsimshatsui waterfront. He concentrated on one, repeating it over and over to himself in time to the beat of the drum aboard the racing dragon boat that had the ferry cutting speed to give it way.

'Jen – ni – fer . . . Jen – ni – fer . . . Jen – ni – fer . . .'

The beloved name no longer came with the sting of remorse. Nor did it condemn his infidelity to its memory. It was a name – a beloved name. That was all. Yes, Huart told himself, the change in me is complete.

The two pledges given to his cousin on his deathbed were twin weights on Huart's mind. He felt he could handle the first: Find Elizabeth Huart.

But new international disharmony rendered remote any hope of fulfilment of the second. The Korean War was over, but Communist China's reservoir of belligerence was far from tapped. Artillery batteries on the mainland began a bombardment of Nationalist Quemoy and Matsu. The USA signed a defence pact with Taiwan, and John Foster Dulles snubbed Chou En-lai in Geneva. Huart had to accept that his reception by Chiang Kai-shek and his subsequent opening of a branch office in Taipei would have branded him an enemy of Peking. He had no choice but to put the second pledge out of his mind for the time being, and concentrate on the first.

He commissioned a private investigator, who drew a blank; few official records had survived the Japanese occupation. He placed messages in all the newspapers except the afternoon tabloid, *The Register*, because of its limited readership. But it seemed they were only read by hoaxers.

One morning in the second week of June, Landers came through to Ice House Street on Huart's direct line. 'The board's approved the loan, John. Sorry for the delay. However, there's a condition – '

'Wai Wai Road. I'll talk to Lennie – '

'Not Wai Wai Road, John. We require a director of our choice to sit on your board in a non-executive capacity to look after our interests.'

'Whom do you have in mind, Percy?'

'Yours truly.'

'I accept.'

'Come to my office at nine-ish tomorrow and we'll sign the papers.'

Huart hung up and released his breath. So it was to be Landers on his board. His Board. It had become second nature for him to think of it thus. He had accepted the H and K's condition without thought of obtaining prior approval from Cosgrove, Bedrix or Adelaide. They would accept it in any case, he knew. Indeed, there was little choice.

Once again, Cumberland China had been saved by the Hongkong and Kwangtung Bank. But this time its independence had been shaved; it was to have a string attached to it by one of the colony's best established and fastest growing financial institutions. Huart massaged this development in his mind. Was it a string that could be pulled in both directions?

28

'Here the *fung shui* – as the southern pygmies call it – is the most propitious I have known,' Tu Chien told his second-born son. 'Hoi-sang, we not only live in peace with the elements, we can at any time look upon the land we will soon own completely.' He pointed down at North Point, spreading from the foot of Mount Butler to the harbour's edge.

The young man did not venture a reply; he knew his father was not listening for one. The patriarch turned and surveyed the grounds that were his, with their spikey-trunked 'long-life' pines, leafy banyans with foliage like marquees, and border of thick brown bamboo where lived frisky grey squirrels, clicking geckos and whirring cicadas, and where butterflies rested between sorties amongst the flower beds. Rather no meat for dinner than no bamboo around the home, the old proverb said.

Tu Chien looked up at the colonial-style mansion that was also his. It sat opulently atop the main spur of Mount Butler; the spur ran north towards the harbour and gave rise to the salient known as Jardine's Lookout. He had bought the place for spot cash because of the location. The geomancer had told him the *fung shui* was indeed the best, matching that which followed the dragon's spine down through Mid Levels from the Peak to the Star Ferry pier, with Garden Road constructed along its spine. The Tu family had moved in on the first day of the second month of the year of the Wood Horse, the best day for such a great event, in the opinion of the geomancer. Tu Chien had christened his family's new home 'Dai Ma Dai Ha': Great Horse Mansion. It was a declaration of his intention for the family's good life in Shanghai to carry right on here.

The mansion was also the headquarters in Hong Kong of Great Horse Enterprises, and Tu Chien referred to it as he led his son into its wide marble foyer. 'The *fung shui* of our home serves our business well in this land of southerners and their foreign devil masters, does it not?'

'It does, Father. You were most wise, as always.'

The patriarch nodded. Business was indeed good, and growing better every day. The industries of Great Horse Enterprises encompassed its own Daima Bank, property, trading in diamonds and gemstones, textile and garment manufacture, and entertainment. But it was the family's clandestine businesses that were the most profitable. These comprised trade in the gold that was smuggled in from Macau each night, and a vast prostitution network which was fed, *à la* Foochow Road, via the plethora of Tu night clubs, cabarets, ballrooms and bars.

To keep on top of it all, Tu Chien sacrificed himself to a rigorous schedule that he was convinced was also keeping him alive. It began at dawn, when he invested half an hour in *tai chi kuen*, the slow motion exercise ritual which the foreign devils discounted with the malapropism of 'shadow boxing'. It promoted Longevity, one of the three gods of Everlasting Life, the others being Wealth and Happiness.

After that, at 7:30, he would go to his ground-floor office-study, and it was almost that now. 'Yes, our business goes very well, Hoi-sang,' he concluded, 'but it is only the beginning of a new beginning. In thirty minutes we meet with Wai-ming and Wai-tsun. This morning I have a matter of importance to discuss with you all. Be on time.'

'Yes, Father. None of us will be late, as always.'

Alone in his office-study, Tu Chien lowered himself into the hand-carved blackwood chair. The matching desk, from behind which he ran everything, was enormous. Its size was amplified by the fact that there were but two items upon it. One of these was only a telephone.

But the second was the possession of all Tu Chien's possessions. It was an eighteen inch Ch'in Dynasty ceramic horse with an elongated head, dragon-like body, and flowing tail, and was the only one of its kind ever made. Nevertheless, it was a copy. The full-size bronze original had been destroyed by fire 2,000 years ago along with the Sian palace of the sovereign emperor. Tu Chien had taken the historic animal as the coat of arms of Great Horse Enterprises. And to satisfy a whim, he had imported from Burma two pigeon-blood red rubies which he had inserted in the horse's eye sockets, and which glowed iridescent like an immortal fire.

Covering the facing wall from floor to ceiling was a magnificent tapestry of cut silk on which a scene depicting the capture of Peking by the Manchus in 1644 had been woven in metal thread. In one corner stood a statue of *Kwan Dai*, the God of War. Like the horse and the tapestry, this statue was also extraordinary. Its ferocious face and belligerent stance had been carved from a three foot block of albescent jade.

Tu Chien felt at ease in the company of these objects of aggression and inestimable worth. They kept any and all irresolution from him. And they confirmed to him that he was already the richest man in Hong Kong, just as he had been the richest man in Shanghai.

Windows opened onto a verandah, beyond which was a fountain where angel fish and red carp swam beneath broad lotus pads. The morning air carried the sounds of the garden into the office-study, which was airy and cool despite the heat rising outside. The *fung shui* of Tu Chien's business domain was in harmony with that of the mansion and the prevailing felicity of Jardine's Lookout. And the unseen Kompo men stationed on the verandah either side of the window guaranteed it would stay that way.

The door opened. 'I bring your breakfast, Lord.' The servant placed a tray on the desk, took up a porcelain teapot and poured black, pungent one hundred year vintage *bo lay* tea into one of the four cups. Then he brought the stack of morning newspapers. 'You require more of me, Lord?'

Tu Chien dismissed him with a wave of the hand, drank from the cup and expirated hard to clear any poison air from his lungs. 'Aaaaah . . .'

The diet of the patriarch was as strict as his daily schedule. It had been fixed by his *wah taw* doctor-herbalist to further ensure his longevity. At forty-eight by western reckoning, he could feel himself aging, and his fight against it was an obsession. The diet started on rising with a concoction of sliced deer horn that had been boiled overnight in the watery essence of chicken. It stimulated the circulation and rejuvenated the nervous system ready for the day ahead. Breakfast was a bowl of swallow's nest and vegetable soup, and the midday meal was another soup, this of boiled ginseng root that had been picked wild in Manchuria from the slopes of Cheung Bak Mountain. Only in the evening would Tu Chien partake of a full meal. And through every hour he was awake he took the bitter *bo lay* tea as a supplement to the painstaking diet.

And it worked. Despite the agony of his hip, Tu Chien had never failed to start or finish a day. He could feel the cancer feeding on itself, eating him away from the inside. And he knew it could be checked only by the quality of his diet and the stimulation of his dawn exercises.

He poured more tea and drank it down. 'Aaaaaaah!'

He always read the English papers first. It forced him to keep up with the unwieldy foreign devil language. He scanned the business page of the *Hong Kong and Oriental Daily* and saw that the announcement was missing. It had first appeared the week after he had seen the giant at Kai Tak. He had thought for a moment there was to be a confrontation that day. That would have been a test. He had been almost sorry when he had suddenly charged off through the door with the red cross above it.

Enquiries had uncovered the saga of Saigon Phase Two. Tu Chien's first reaction had been pleasure that the giant should confront his ruin at the posthumous hands of his stupid cousin after having avoided all the traps that had been set for him. The pleasure had changed to disappointment. Revenge could not be delegated, especially not to fate, he had reminded himself. Then the frustration had set in. For no longer was he able to lift a hand to direct that revenge.

The giant was a worthy enemy. Tu Chien had to acknowledge that. It had been proved. Beware the strong man pretending weakness; beware the courageous one feigning fear. He had underestimated him as mere soldier stock. He possessed great good fortune in matters of business, and he was intelligent, resourceful and bold. His manipulation of the President of the Republic of China into declaring sanctuary for him, a foreigner, confirmed all that. Tu Chien had cursed Chiang Kai-shek for the first time in his life, but he had obeyed the presidential decree. The giant's ploy had been one he would have been proud to claim as his own.

And this from a man whose sons had been made eunuchs, then taken from him as innocents in war. Tu Chien knew well the grief of a man who has lost a son. But to lose two! To lose all! He marvelled again at the power of the curse he had inflicted that day on the Bund. But why should it be a surprise to him? Had he not been born a special man? Had he not rare powers? Was he not extraordinary? Was he not a Fire Horse!

His rumination was ended by the return of the servant, who filled the other three cups with black, black tea and placed them on the low table before the three guest chairs. Ten seconds after he had gone with the empty soup bowl there was a respectful tapping at the door. Tu Chien opened his drawer and looked at the watch he kept there. He waited the few seconds to eight o'clock. 'Enter!' he commanded in Shanghai dialect.

The three young men came into the office-study and bowed in unison.

'Good morning, Father,' said Hoi-sang.

'Good morning, Hoi-sang, my son.'

'Good morning, Uncle,' greeted the other two in unison.

'Good morning, Wai-ming – third nephew. Good morning, Wai-tsun – sixth nephew. Come, all of you, be seated here. Join me for tea.'

They were all in their twenties, with Hoi-sang the youngest. He nominally managed all the legitimate operations except the Daima Bank, which was in Wai-ming's charge. The covert activities of the family were Wai-tsun's speciality. Tu Chien watched them, noting their daily development which, in his son's case, was much too slow. Hoi-sang and Wai-ming wore *saamfoo* and sipped the bitter tea with etiquette. Wai-tsun, as usual, took a token swallow, then replaced the cup upon its saucer and left it. He wore a western sports coat and slacks in the fashion of the Hollywood actor from whom he had taken his English nickname. The patriarch acknowledged the changing times, but of the three Errol Tu Wai-tsun was most fated to succeed. A wave of regret closed in. If his elder son had lived he would be Wai-tsun's age. Together they would have formed an unbeatable pair, and he would have no qualms about succession. And the family's future. 'Speak then, Wai-ming. What have you learnt?'

Third Nephew shifted his rear on the hard chair and cleared his throat. 'The Hongkong and Kwangtung Bank has loaned enough to offset the loss, Uncle. The repayment period is five years.'

Tu Chien leaned to one side and hawked and spat into the spittoon at his feet. He swallowed a mouthful of *bo lay* and expirated vigorously. His hand reached up and stroked the hairs that grew from the mole on his jaw. And he thought. He was neither surprised nor disappointed. It proved again the giant's worth. Patience was required; time was needed to evolve a plan equally worthy. He resolved to recruit time into his service, instead of succumbing to the temptation to regard it as his foe. His eyes focused upon the fierce visage of *Kwan Dai*, and the God of War glared loudly back at him from his corner.

'Your sister's eldest son, Wai-ming. What is his name again?'

'Wai-kit, Uncle. He has taken the English name of Alain.'

'He is eleven years of age this year?'

'Yes, Uncle. He was born in the Year of the Wood Monkey.'

'Then he will be intuitive and progressive in his thinking. Tell your sister I will see him. It is time for me to take a hand in his education. Does his father – the man, To – still run with the *Wo Hop Wo*?'

'Yes, Uncle.'

'Then I must take over this boy's life before it is too late.'

29

'Mother, there it is in the classified again. Your name's Elizabeth Jane, but your maiden name wasn't Huart, was it?'

She was looking down at the expurgated words of D.H. Lawrence, and said without lifting her eyes: 'You ask too many silly questions, Matthew.'

'Why would anyone be looking for an Elizabeth Jane Huart anyway? I know – I bet she ran off with the gardener and her husband wants her back. I bet he'd like to get that gardener, take his shears and cut off his – '

'Matthew!'

' – roses. What's wrong, Mother? That's a good book, isn't it?'

'You've read it? Really, Matthew, for a boy of thirteen . . .'

'Fourteen in two months and twenty-three days. Mother, can I invite Lana Cheung to my birthday party? She's a big help to me in biology.'

'Biology? But it's not a subject you're taking.'

'Not officially.'

Elizabeth Zagan frowned as a car drove along Braga Circuit and a cloud of dust rose past the window. Kowloon Tong was baking in the June heat. The pedestal fan squeaked as it oscillated. 'Lana Cheung is Chinese?'

'Four times more than I am, Mother. But only twice as much as you.'

She sighed, admitting defeat before they got into that again. 'Your father still hasn't written from Geneva,' she reminded him instead.

'But he does write,' Matthew pointed out, 'for the newspapers. It's an odd peace conference. The French are trying to beat the *Viet Minh* with words now. It must be all they have left after failing with guns.'

'You're as cynical as your father.'

He went out to the telephone in the hall. 'I'm calling Lana Cheung about a biology matter I can't quite grasp, Mother. She really is very good on the subject. But don't worry, she's only good in theory.'

Elizabeth Zagan sighed again. He was growing up too fast. She put her son out of her mind as she took up the *Hong Kong and Oriental Daily* and found the message. Oh no, she said to herself. You won't get me to fall for that one, Mr John Huart. I'm not so naive as my poor mother.

Her son's voice, speaking Cantonese, came to her from the hall. 'Lana? It's Matthew Zagan. Would you like to come over? Bring your big sister.'

30

Hong Kong's autumn is an annual reward, particularly for those who have endured the trial of its tropical summer. In November, 1954, there was for Huart and Cumberland China a double reward, but in receiving the second, he kept on the fringe of the limelight, as a good agent should.

'Signing a contract is a gift of life,' Sir Reynard Armstrong declared, a proud smile on his glowing face. 'But signing the biggest single export contract ever won by the Anglo-Saxon Group, and on such a superlative day as this . . . Why, it's . . . it's . . .'

Sir Bartholomew Orr came to his rescue. 'The Chinese would probably call it a Double Happiness, Reynard. It's a red letter day for Cathay Electric, too. May there be many more like it.'

A mix of wealth, dignity and history pervaded the power company boardroom. The maroon carpet was broadloom, the white ceiling freshly painted, and the oak table varnished so heavily the grain seemed to be encased in glass. The panelled walls were hung with portraits of Orr precursors. Some were English, hirsute of face, stern of mien; the rest Cantonese from Whampoa with long sparse white beards, liquid eyes and drawn inscrutability in full length robes with cavernous sleeves. Huart compared them with Sir Bart's aging features and saw the flat nose and flared nostrils of Whampoa, plus the reddish tinge to hair and eyebrows of the other race involved in the siring of the Orr dynasty a century before.

Then he looked at Kingston Orr. Born to Sir Bart's second wife from her previous marriage to his cousin, the power company heir appeared one hundred per cent oriental. Sir Bart had taken the proven dam into his bed in his quest for an heir. That Sir Bart was as barren as the Gobi in drought had not occurred to him until after years of trying to procreate an improvement on his stepson.

Right now, Kingston Orr was the only one not smiling, and when Patrick O'Harah called them all to the three copies of the contract document open upon the table, Huart noted he was the last to sit. After the signing ceremony they posed for photographs shaking hands, and Huart thought Kingston's was like a cold face towel. The stepson-heir looked askance and seemed separated from the proceedings.

'Sir Bart, I'd be honoured to have your permission to feature this in our annual report.' Armstrong's smile was now blatantly triumphant. 'Do you think I could take some of the prints back to England with me?'

'By all means, my dear Reynard.' Sir Bart turned to his general manager. 'Patrick, please give Sir Reynard the data on our growth since the war.'

'Of course, Sir Bart.' O'Harah stepped forward, inadvertently taking Kingston Orr's light. 'We have 80,000 consumers – a 150 per cent increase since '45. We've had to raise transmission voltage from 22kV to 33kV – '

'I meant in writing, Patrick. Reynard, you must come next door and view my private collection of seashells. It is a source of joy to me. I so love to share it with dear friends on special occasions such as this.'

'Sir Bart, there's nothing I'd rather do more,' Armstrong responded, his smile now extending from ear to ear, 'except to sign another contract with you.' He was teetering on the edge of euphoria. His choice of Cumberland China had been made over the objections of directors faithful to Ivor Male, and it had been vindicated in fine style. He visualised himself casting Anglo-Saxon's copy of the group's largest ever export order onto the table before the eyes of his Bond Street board with a flourish to suit the occasion, and almost walked into the wall.

'If you'll excuse me, Sir Bart,' said Huart, 'there's a matter concerning the contract that I'd like to go over with Pat. I've already had the pleasure of seeing your seashell collection. Reynard, you can take it from me it's something not to be missed.'

The power company owner gave a knowing smile. 'Of course, John. Business first, always. Thank you for everything. You've worked hard for Anglo-Saxon and deserve your success. You both do. We were impressed with the bid's technical content. And the price was right, too – in the end.'

All chuckled at the oblique reference to the long, hard negotiation. All except Kingston Orr. What an unhappy young man, thought Huart. But why? He was heir apparent to Asia's fastest growing power company. The world was at his feet. But he left the boardroom without a farewell to anyone.

Bending under the heel of age, Sir Bart took Armstong's arm, chattering amiably. They're no longer made from that mould, Huart told himself, and turned to Patrick O'Harah, who sat at the table jotting notes on a pad.

'What's on your mind, John?' The general manager looked up and smiled. Their relationship, initially one of business, had become a friendship.

'It's the down-payment under the extended finance, Pat. There seems to be some confusion on the effective date. The bank says one thing and ECGD another. My understanding is – ' He broke off as he saw that O'Harah was looking past him to the door, and turned to see the general manager's Portuguese secretary standing there, ill at ease.

'What is it, Maria?' O'Harah enquired.

'I'm so sorry to interrupt you, sir,' she said uncertainly. 'A Japanese gentleman is asking to see you.' She looked down at a card. 'He's Mr Tetsuo Hondo from Matamoto Electric. He insists he has an appointment with you, but I don't have it in your diary. Have I made a mistake?'

O'Harah smiled. 'No mistake, Maria. He wrote me from Japan. I forgot to tell you about it, I'm sorry. I'll see him here. Show him in will you?'

Relieved, the girl nodded and left, then returned with the visitor.

'Shall I wait outside, Pat?'

The general manager shook his head. 'This won't take long, John. I can promise you that.' His smile had gone strange. He called: 'Come forward, Mr Hondo. It's me you're looking for. I'm Patrick O'Harah.'

Tetsuo Hondo stood there in a dark blue business suit, staring at the general manager, nonplussed. 'You?' he began, wearing a confused frown. 'You Mister Ohara . . ?' It was spoken uncertainly with a heavy accent.

'Yes.'

'You not Jap'nese?'

'Do I look Japanese, Mr Hondo?'

'But – so sor-ry – Ohara Jap'nese name. Very common my country.'

'I see why you were confused,' O'Harah conceded. 'But this is not Japan. This happens to be Hong Kong. There are not many Japanese here – these days.' Though amused himself, Huart saw O'Harah's expression was humourless. He did not invite his visitor to sit, and when he spoke again, his voice held an unrestrained brittleness. 'What is it that you want?'

Hondo visibly recovered himself and bowed, proffering his business card. 'Sank you for see me today, Mr Ohara. I so sor-ry for stupid mistake. My company Matamoto E'rectric. Ver-ry rarge in Japan. We un'stan' you need new power p'ran' for gen'ration station. We, Matamoto E'rectric, hope we can have opportun'ty quote. Have here, Mr Ohara – ' He looked from the general manager to Huart, obviously thinking both were in the employ of Cathay Electric, dived into his briefcase and extracted a Japan Airlines ticket voucher. 'Have here one airp'rane ticket for you, Mr Ohara. For you come visit our factory. So sor-ry, gent'man – ' He bowed again to Huart, lower than last time. 'Can bring your tomorrow.' He turned back to O'Harah. 'Our factory in ver-ry nice prace in Japan. Our factory ver-ry modern. Have rarge capac'ty. Many dif'rent standard can do. British standard can do.

[287]

My company ver-ry honour if you accep' visit Japan come see our factory. I hope you – '

Patrick O'Harah could delay his interruption no longer. 'Actually, Mr Hondo, I have already had the opportunity of visiting your country.'

'Ah so.' Hondo smiled widely and bowed again, deeper than ever. 'Ah so. My country is so honour. When that, Mr Ohara?'

Huart saw the general manager's fists clench on top of the table and his knuckles turn white as he said: 'From 1942 to 1945. I was a prisoner, Mr Hondo. A civilian prisoner. I was forced to work like a slave. I was starved, beaten and humiliated every single day. I nearly died. I have no wish to pay a return visit to fucking Japan under any circumstances.'

Tetsuo Hondo blinked. He appeared not to comprehend. Then his manners, ingrained by tradition, asserted themselves. His face went neutral. He bowed again. 'Ah . . . so. So sor-ry, Mr Ohara. So ver-ry sor-ry.'

'So am I, Mr Hondo. So am I. Now, be advised that this company will not spend a single Hong Kong dollar on any item of Japanese equipment whilst I remain general manager. Not even a paper clip. Our order for the power plant has just been placed elsewhere. With Mr Huart here, as a matter of fact. For British plant. Do you hear? British plant. Don't waste your time trying to see me again, Mr Hondo. I don't want to see anybody from a Japanese company, or any agent of a Japanese company. If I do . . . If I do, I'll probably kill that person with my bare hands. Now, get out.'

Hondo quivered as if he had been struck between the eyes. But again he recovered himself and put the smile back on his face. He bowed again. 'So sor-ry.' He took one pace back and bowed once more to O'Harah and Huart in turn. 'So ver-ry sor-ry. Goodbye.' He bent and picked up his briefcase, straightened his back and marched to the door with head held high. At the door he turned, bowed a final time, and left.

'Did that make you feel better, Pat?' Huart enquired.

O'Harah's face was saturated with bitterness. 'Every fucking second of it.' He rose slowly to his feet as if the weight of memory was on him, then went to the liquor cabinet and poured two shots of Jameson's.

'You said some hard things there,' Huart pointed out, taking his.

'And I meant every single word,' O'Harah affirmed. He tossed down the Irish whiskey and grimaced. 'The stupid Yanks're committing commercial suicide financing those little bastards as they rebuild Japan. They'll use all those licensing agreements to learn it all, then they'll be out in the export markets competing with everybody. It'll be British firms that'll lose out. Firms like Anglo-Saxon need all the business they can get – what with rationing at home. I'll remain British first and British last. Always. And, John, no remarks about we Irish not knowing if it's Great Britain or the United Kingdom we're part of. We're the same blood, whatever you call it.' He replaced his glass in the cabinet and walked to the door. 'Expect a lot of business from us in future, John. Just keep your price increases within bounds. I meant what I said to that little Jap sod. There'll be no order placed with any Jap company whilst I'm general manager. And I intend to be around for a good long while yet. I lost a teenage son to those bastards in Malaya . . .' He looked hard at Huart. 'And you lost family, too. Or have you forgotten?'

Kingston Orr pulled a Turf from its pack, pushed it between his lips and lit up with a gold lighter. He glanced sideways at his office door as a passing shadow crossed the frosted glass with EXECUTIVE MANAGER showing in reverse. He laughed inwardly at the absurdity of the title. His stepfather lived in senile bliss. What was the purpose of trying to convince anyone that the heir apparent was starting from the bottom rung of the management ladder? The old man believed that people would believe anything. He even believed the British respected him. Sir Bartholomew Orr had been a collaborator in disguise, and they had knighted him for it!
  'O'Harah really said he would kill you if he saw you again, Hondo-san?' he enquired of the blue-suited oriental gentleman sitting before him.
  Hondo nodded. 'His accen' terrib're, Orr-san. But my English good. He say it and he mean it. He hate Japan. He have bad mem'ry make him sick.'
  'He's not sick, he's British,' Orr snorted. 'But tell me about Yumiko.'
  Hondo beamed and bowed from the sitting position. 'Sank you, Orr-san. My daughter good. She give good wish to you and hope see you soon.'
  A rare half-smile touched Orr's face with the memory of Yumiko Hondo and the weekends they had spent together away from Harvard. Had he really thought of marrying her? It would have given his stepfather a heart attack, and that was just why he had considered it. 'She promised to take me to Nikko and to

[289]

Kyoto. Tell her I will do my best to take her up on it very soon.'
He waited for Hondo to regain the vertical, then went on: 'Back
to business. Matamoto needs an agent in Hong Kong. Without
the right one you'll get nowhere. You need one who can work
with the British, but is not British and is therefore reliable.'

'So sor-ry – can rec'men' so rare agen', Orr-san?'

'Yes. A company called Male & Son. Abraham Male graduated
from Harvard with me. I consider us friends. The Males are not
British, but everyone thinks they are. They're Russian, but they
changed their name long ago. Abraham has his own score to settle
with John Huart, the man who was with O'Harah when you walked
into their trap. He's keen to meet you.'

'Sank you, Orr-san. When zat be?'

'Tonight. At dinner in my apartment. I have hired the best
kaiseki chef in Hong Kong for the occasion. I believe you like it,
Hondo-san?'

'Oh, yes. Ver-ry much. *Kaiseki* is so specia'rty. Ver-ry pop'rar
Japan. Seven course and two soup. Yumiko-san is good cook, too.
She – '

A shadow fell on the frosted glass. 'Come!' Orr's call beat the knock.

A spindly European in his late thirties entered. His hair was
fair but thinning, his nose narrow and hooked. He sported a mien
not unlike a rat, the impression accentuated by a wispy moustache
that hung past the corners of his mouth. His narrow shoulders
were tucked forward as if they were connected by a wire that had
been twisted too tight. He stood just inside the door and peered
at Kingston Orr in a manner that was neither subservient nor
superior, but a little of both.

Hondo stood, ready to deliver another of his bows.

'I apologise for the interruption, Hondo-san, but I asked this
man to come here at this time so that you may meet. He has just
joined Cathay Electric and will be acting as my commercial
assistant. His name is Mr Jeremy Parrot.'

He had pronounced it 'Par-oh'.

31

Auditors are but score-keepers, and Cumberland China's certified
their loss for financial year 1954–55. It was the ransom for Saigon
Phase Two, exacerbated by the falling off in insurance revenue;

Julian Younghusband had followed the Pan Atlantic agency to Male & Son. But there was a silver lining. Orders in progress with the loyal divisions guaranteed, barring further catastrophe, the return of profits in 1955–56. The Cathay Electric contract put the Engineering Division's projected revenue at a record. Export orders for Cosgrove Textiles rose again, and Wai Wai Road was in full production for Indonesia, Singapore, Malaya, and new clients in the USA and Europe. However, it would be some years before the slate would show no trace of the disaster that had been 1954–55.

At the AGM in May, the fourth month of the Year of the placid Wood Goat, the board heard Clive Bedrix present the annual report, end it with a succinct but enthusiastic forecast, then pronounce zero dividend. It was accepted with cheerful pragmatism as but a temporary penalty.

In attendance on behalf of the H and K in his capacity as non-executive director, Percy Landers sat and looked to the future with a cautious optimism, plus a stirring of personal pride. His bank had piggy-backed the company over another bad patch. But he had needed to resort to something of a personal crusade to have the loan approved. His contemporaries had demanded Wai Wai Road as collateral until he had volunteered himself as substitute. Now, if Cumberland China should go under, so would the banking career of one Percival Davenport Landers.

From the chair at the head of the table, Huart reported under 'Other Business' the lack of progress in the search for a replacement insurance agency. It hurt him publicly to admit it. Yet, as he gave the negative news, his brain moved on to fine-tune a compensatory plan that had been sparked in the Hong Kong Club a week ago by a quip from Herbert Jarvis.

'Our lease is due for renewal, Bert,' Huart had reminded his landlord unnecessarily. 'No doubt Victoria Land will want its usual fifteen per cent increase. You must think it money for old rope. Is there any chance your management service might improve fifteen per cent to make it up?'

Jarvis had looked at his tenant and friend in a way that announced the jibe had been as lightly received as it had been delivered. 'There's only one way for you to beat the system, John.'

'And that is?'

'Buy the godforsaken building and be bloody landlord yourself.' But then Jarvis had taken up his glass of claret and turned serious. 'Truth is, the return isn't worth putting up with the bitching we

get from tenants like you. Fat chance of you doing anything about,
it though, eh?'

'The bitching or the return?'

'Either. Both.'

Huart had not answered straight away. He had walked to Ice
House Street in thought, oblivious to the dust that was thick in
the air as Statue Square was levelled about him to accommodate
the Grand Fair being organised by the Chinese Manufacturers'
Union. The Chater Road traffic circus, the disused baldachin and
its attendant pedestals had all gone. In addition, a third land
reclamation had started, designed to remove the waterfront and
the Star Ferry pier towards Kowloon by a city block and provide
a plot on which would rise the new City Hall.

Cosgrove had chuckled on hearing the skeleton of Huart's plan,
but had reserved judgement. 'Ten out of ten for nerve,' was all
Lennie the Fifth would commit. Huart looked at him now as he
brought the AGM to a close. The little man tugged his bowtie,
drew on his Havana. And nodded.

Huart stood. 'Gentlemen . . . and lady. Lunch awaits us. A
table is booked at Jimmy's Kitchen. I hope that you can all join
me there.' He looked for Landers' gesture of affirmation. The
plan required his attendance.

Adelaide cleared her throat. 'I regret my opinion of that place
is unchanged. If it's alright with you gentlemen, I'll decline this
time. In fact, I have a *mahjong* game arranged. Thank you, anyway,
John, dear.'

'*Mahjong* will probably be more exciting than what we have to
talk about.' Huart's smile was regretful, but he had anticipated
the refusal, and indeed had selected Jimmy's Kitchen to ensure
it. He respected the old lady, but she did not feature in his plan.

'Oh, I've heard all your men's tales,' she scoffed. 'Enjoy your
lunch despite them. And make sure next year we have a dividend
to celebrate. Perhaps then you'll see fit to reserve at a decent
restaurant.'

It was in the plan to take an indirect route to Theatre Lane.
On the Des Voeux Road corner, Huart halted. 'Look there,
gentlemen – ' His eyes were on Landers as he pointed at the vast
triangular construction site where a thirteen-storey office block
was replacing the Hotel Cecil, Chung Ting Building and the
Alexandra Building. 'We are witnesses to the opening of a new
era. Central District is being transformed. I desire that we should
stake our claim in it.' His memory reversed to the eve of the

[292]

decade when he had made a similar resolution to Paulette Huart-Brent.

Landers' return gaze was shrewd. 'What is it you're suggesting, John?'

'Let's save it for over lunch, Percy.'

Bedrix gave Huart a quizzical look.

It was not until after a round of drinks and the arrival of the Muscadet and the lobster thermidor that Huart turned the ignition on his plan. 'Gentlemen, it's Lease Renewal Time again.' He heard Cosgrove groan on cue. 'I've taken a decision. I've decided that I'm sick and tired of dancing to the beat of a landlord's drum, especially now that we're growing and are in need of extra office space. Victoria Land will take advantage of our situation again, like they did two years ago . . .'

'Nothing surer,' Bedrix agreed. 'But there's nothing available in Ice House Street. We'll have to move out. Or break the company in two.'

'I have no intention of breaking the company in two,' Huart asserted.

'Then you've decided that we have to move?' Bedrix asked innocently.

'I have not. We move, and in another two years we double again and have no space to expand into . . . What do we do then? Move again?'

Bedrix looked flummoxed. 'You've decided not to divide the company into separate offices. And you've decided not to move. Correct?'

'Correct.'

'So you've decided the company is big enough for you. You've decided there is to be no further growth?'

'I have not. We will continue growing for many years to come. But the cost of moving office at the end of every lease will stunt our growth.'

Bedrix put down his knife and fork. 'I don't understand you, John.'

Huart said nothing. He sipped his wine and forked a slice of lobster, whilst Cosgrove tucked into his helping and tried not to grin.

Finally, Landers suggested: 'Growing pains are a fact of business – '

And Huart struck. 'Pains, Percy? You'll help us find the panacea?'

[293]

'Panacea?' Landers frowned. 'The only panacea I can see is for you to bite the bullet and – '

' – And buy the Ice House Street building out from under Victoria Land's feet,' Huart finished.

In the ensuing silence Bedrix looked from face to face and knew he was not party to something important. Huart took note of his disapproval, but there had been no point in confiding in him until Cosgrove had agreed to his part of the plan. And that had only come at the end of the AGM.

Landers had frozen in mid chew. 'I do believe you're serious,' he said through a mouthful of lobster spiced with paprika, mustard and white pepper.

Huart nodded. 'I am. And there's a good chance Victoria Land will sell. The site's a restricted corner, too small for them to redevelop in their own grandiose fashion, unless they buy the adjacent plot and develop both together. Ice House Street's rent-able floor area is only 36,000 square feet. At the going rate that's a paltry $30,000 a month. It has to be Victoria Land's least profitable building – the lame duck of Central District.'

Landers resumed chewing. 'It's no revenue generator,' he conceded, smiling like one who has inside information. 'By the way, I heard Victoria Land's negotiations with the Hsus for the neighbouring site of which you speak fell through two weeks ago. I heard that Billson Hsu told them to their face that he would never sell out to *gwailos*.'

'Please say that again, Percy,' Huart requested, and when Landers did so he nodded to himself. It explained the quip that had sparked the plan.

Cosgrove chuckled. 'Billson's a man of principle, alright.' He signalled to the head waiter and a bottle of champagne appeared with alacrity, already chilled. It had to have been pre-ordered. He studied the label with an exaggerated frown and Huart looked on amused. 'That's the stuff. Let's have it now, shall we?' Lennie the Fifth winked at Landers. 'So it means Victoria Land's ripe for an offer on Ice House Street, right?'

The banker ran his napkin across his lips and looked up with his brow beetled in the way Huart knew well. 'Very well – out with it, you lot.'

'It's quite simple, Percy,' Huart explained. 'We wish to make Victoria Land an offer for our very own building. A reverse take-over of sorts. We need your backing. We see advantages in the project for a bank.'

'What sort of . . . "advantages"?'

Huart took up his glass of champagne. 'We'll redevelop, of course. I've had a quantity surveyor and an architect look at the plans. They say an eighteen-storey structure is possible, albeit a narrow one, including a penthouse apartment for my use. Total floor area will be 300,000 square feet. Cumberland China will take two floors and the rest will be leased. Estimating new office rental in 1958 – when I expect the redevelopment to be completed – at $1.50 a square foot, with a premium for street frontage, revenue will be half a million dollars a month.'

'You've obviously done your sums, John,' Landers acknowledged matter-of-factly. 'So how much do you plan to offer Victoria Land?'

'Ten point eight million.'

'So little?'

Huart shook his head. 'Not so little. At the rental they're currently getting, it's thirty years income in cash. I think it's a good offer.'

Landers returned to his lobster. 'I ask again: What sort of advantages?'

'You're expanding, too. There'll be room for you in the building.'

'I see. What rental would you charge for ground floor street frontage?'

'Three dollars a square foot.'

'For us?' Landers pressed. 'Let's say we wanted the entire ground floor as our second Central branch? What would you charge us then?'

Huart looked at Cosgrove who gestured that the floor was his. 'Two dollars to the H and K and a five year lease with an option for five more.'

Landers swallowed the last of his lobster and washed it down with champagne. 'So you're looking for another loan to cover the ten point eight million plus the development costs.' He looked at Huart. 'Correct?'

'Correct. We estimate sixteen and a quarter million all up. We estimate also that we'll repay the loan plus interest out of rental revenue within three years of the building opening. You will have your money back, and your profit, by the end of 1961.'

Landers nodded, then pursed his lips and said flatly: 'Collateral?'

They all looked at Cosgrove this time. Lennie the Fifth pushed a Havana between his lips, called a waiter to light it for him, then grinned through the smoke. 'Wai Wai Road?' He shrugged. 'Why why not?'

Landers thoughtfully placed his knife and fork together on his plate. 'We'll think about it, gentlemen. We'll think about it very carefully.'

Huart could not resist it. 'Don't think too long, Percy. Land values are rising. You have first option till Monday, then we contact other banks.'

Landers' lobster almost made a reappearance. 'What in devil's name are you talking about, John? What other banks? How can you think of – '

'I'm for the baked alaska,' Huart announced. 'Anyone with me?'

'Bread and butter pudding for me,' said Cosgrove. 'Double helping.'

'Just coffee, thanks,' Bedrix demurred quietly. Though still put out, he was himself excited with the new development, and the scope of it.

Huart, accepting that it was the Bedrix's for dinner at Garden Terrace on Saturday night, and hoping that Ruby was over her bronchitis and could talk about something else, took up the bottle of champagne by the neck and refilled each glass, finishing with his own. 'Eat, drink and be merry . . .' he called, leaving the cry of Shanghai unfinished.

' – For tomorrow we buy!' Lennie the Fifth inserted and Huart laughed.

Landers' grin stayed put. He had not minded playing the pawn in Huart's plan. It could benefit them all. The best laid plans are the simplest, and this was simple in the extreme. What did the rulebook say? 'There is no co-operation without mutual advantage'. It fitted the plan perfectly.

That afternoon Sir Frederick Lloyd Oberon was to chair a meeting of the H and K board. Top of the agenda was a review of sites for the bank's second Central branch. Landers sipped his champagne in silent intrigue. The agenda was confidential. How had Huart known what was on it?

The truth was as uncomplicated as the plan: Huart had known nothing of it. The Year of the Wood Goat was the one for revolutionary ideas. His timing had been perfect, that was all.

32

The Fire Monkey started out from Sunday, February 12th, 1956, bringing progress to Hong Kong and business to Cumberland China, as it ought to do. The aggression engendered by its fire element would come later.

Huart corresponded with Virginia, flew to New York at the height of the summer and loved her in her Manhattan apartment over a long weekend. They discussed his business and hers over hamburgers and a Napa Valley red as the Hudson flowed below. With her settlement she had bought into a small cosmetics operation and was directing its marketing and distribution. The multi-faceted task was the focal point of her new life.

'I'm happy at last, John,' she admitted gaily. 'Our night in the Repulse Bay Hotel was the turning point. I don't know if my venture will succeed or fail. But somehow I know my timing's right. Cosmetics is taking off.'

'Good timing is the best type of good luck,' Huart told her. 'You have the brain for business, and the face for this one in particular. Could we co-operate some day, I wonder?'

She laughed throatily. 'We're sleeping partners. I like it like that.'

'So do I, Virginia.' Huart bent down to kiss her. 'Very, very much.'

Rex Wagoner and Paulette had married a day after his divorce was final. She had converted to Judaism to please him, and they had been travelling the world ever since.

Vivienne was at university in Chicago; Suzanne had insisted on a school of her own choice in New York State. Huart visited both and saw anew the difference between them. Vivienne had discovered boys and lost interest in all else. Suzanne had made up her mind to be top of her class and, despite the hours she spent with a school book in her hands, Huart could see she was destined to be as physically superb as her mother. He hoped the similarity would end there.

Cumberland China completed its purchase of the Ice House Street building from Victoria Land. To clinch it, Huart had to raise his cash offer to the equivalent of forty-one years' rental. It was his introduction to the significance of 1997. The extra money proved no problem; the H and K instantly came up with it. The bank's board had decided the site was not to be the second Central branch after all, but its new headquarters. They were impressed with the architect's blueprint for the tower to be built upon the prestigious corner, and had already approved their own design for a deluxe ground floor banking hall and mezzanine, and plush offices throughout the first four floors.

'It'll just mean nine months extra to pay it off,' Huart rationalised to Landers over roast beef in the Blue Room of the Hong Kong Club.

The banker smiled. 'We've done our sums, too, John. The board loves the project. We observe Chinese customs by policy. A corner site has good *fung shui*, and yours has the best. It'll add to depositors' confidence. We do love it – particularly now you've upped our option to ten years.'

The Fire Monkey ushered in a new era. 'Manufactures', just over 1,000 ten years before, grew to three times that, all but a few being small family enterprises. Export trade, virtually stagnant since 1950, began to happen. A Commonwealth Preference Scheme made Hong Kong goods more competitive, and membership of the sterling area stabilised the currency. Textiles and garments led the way, and toys. Then a plastics industry suddenly came to the surface to serve a world fad for imitation flowers.

As orders flowed in, Huart ordered an extension to Wai Wai Road.

A property boom resulted. Pre-war low-rise structures made way for new high-rise. Bamboo and matting scaffolding was strapped in place to enshroud buildings whose value had fallen behind the time. Central District's transformation continued: Alexandra House opened on its prime triangular site, the building beside the Hongkong and Shanghai Bank made way for rival Chartered Bank's new headquarters, Jardine House went and Central Building opened where the Hongkong Hotel was but a memory.

The reclamation for Kai Tak International Airport grew out of Kowloon Peninsula like Pinocchio's nose.

Estoril Court and its 3,000 square foot balconied apartments with panoramic harbour views rose atop Garden Road. In October the Cosgroves moved in and celebrated their first night with an explosive row. He spent the night on the other side of Garden Road in Huart's spare bedroom.

'On the Peak it was fog. Down here it's noise. The woman's never happy.'

'Perhaps she wants a baby and doesn't know it,' Huart suggested lamely.

'Even if I was to take that seriously, I couldn't keep the wench still long enough to start one. I created a monster when I bought her that boutique! Now she's talking of opening another – with her own money!'

Huart consoled him with a double pink gin, turned on the new Rediffusion black and white cable television service, and watched a newsreel of the attempt by British, French and Israeli troops to impress on Gamal Abdul Nasser that his nationalisation of the Suez Canal was not appreciated.

The British Crown Colony of Hong Kong was spawning a sequence of anomalies. Progress was manifest, but life for the Chinese working class remained arduous. Survival meant seven days toil for low wages, but competition for places on the non-stop production lines was bitter. It was a hard place, but in the communes of Kwangtung Province it was dubbed 'Teen Tong': Paradise. And Paradise was only a short distance away.

Immigrants began to pour across the border and the population climbed past 2,600,000. 'New' squatter communities appeared upon the hillsides like leprous eruptions that further scarred the landscape.

Hong Kong's colonial façade became akin to the anodised skin of a cracked pressure-cooker. It ruptured on October 10th, 'Double Tenth', anniversary of the 1911 outbreak of the revolution against the Manchus.

Huart found himself outside the entrance to the factory on Wai Wai Road, at the head of his Auxiliary Defence Service unit, watching one mob waving flags with white suns charge into another holding aloft a banner on which had been painted a large red five-pointed star. Behind him the production lines stood idle. They remained that way for several days until the 'Kowloon Disturbances' died down, and Hong Kong metaphorically stuck an anodised plaster over the crack and everyone went back to work.

Demolition of the Ice House Street building commenced as soon as the thirty-three Central District employees of Cumberland China had moved to temporary leased accommodation in York Building on Chater Road.

They were to remain there for two and a half years before returning to the corner of Ice House Street and Queen's Road, Central where they were greeted by the sight of their very own corporate headquarters rising sheer into the heavens over Hong Kong. And above its entrance arch they read, carved up there, the new building's name:

CUMBERLAND HOUSE

Book III

THE BORN AGAIN *HONG*

Hong Kong: 16 May 1961 – 30 April 1968

1

It occurred to the fourth taipan of Cumberland China, as he listened to Clive Bedrix intoning the 1960–61 annual report one May morning, that he was in danger of becoming a very rich man; it had been another record year. He put his T-bone steaks of palms upon the varnished pinewood surface of the Long Table and looked down its length. He had christened it thus because of its twenty-eight feet, and in some evocation of the famous Shanghai Club bar.

He studied the faces: Cosgrove's, embedded with a fat Havana; Bedrix's, grimacing as he rubbed his stump in a caveat to the rise in humidity; Landers', twisted around his favourite meerschaum; Nigel Print's, eager and alert as it always was at a board meeting (too eager?); Adelaide's, with its creamy soft wrinkles and hard clear eyes.

The seventh face belonged to Francis Roboza, who sat closest to the foot of the table and the world map with China in dead centre upon the walnut panelled north wall. He was taking the minutes in a 'shorthand' which only his daughter, Imelda, could decipher. Huart had a generous retirement package ready for the aging accountant, and on his impending UK trip, amongst a full programme of business appointments and a weekend in Edinburgh with Sinclair MacLurie, he would interview the shortlisted CAs and select his replacement.

Each was following a copy of Bedrix's report as he told them what they already knew: that in 1960–61 the 'manufactory' which had been Cosgrove Textiles was absorbed into the holding company as the Textiles and Garments Division; that the Property Department had been formed under Mr Daniel Vail who brought five years' experience with Victoria Land; that the staff had grown to 175; that Vivienne Huart-Brent's decision to marry and cash in her shares had precipitated a recapitalisation, a redistribution of shares and a reorganisation . . .

Not for long could it entertain Cosgrove, who now owned a

shareholding equal to Huart's, the title of Deputy Managing Director, and a responsibility for 'projects'. He tuned Bedrix down and peered out of the windows in the south wall. The curtains were hooked back, and from the boardroom seventeen storeys above Central District a spectacular view was revealed west over the tops of the buildings as far as Kennedy Town and beyond, almost across to Lantao Island. The sea was blue and beckoning. It was Tuesday, and Lennie the Fifth always went sailing on Tuesdays.

'... to summarise, our engineering trading operations have grown well, contracting and servicing less so, but acceptably. Textiles and garments were ahead of target. The Property Department cannot make a contribution until 1962–63 when the H and K loan is paid off, but a profit of five million is projected in 1963–64 – when we will have not only the best looking building in Hong Kong but also the most profitable per square foot.' Bedrix paused to rub his stump. 'The 1960–61 results shows an increase in sales of 36 per cent to $79,000,000 and an increase in profit of 52 per cent to $8,900,000. For 1961–62 we have targeted for a similar growth: sales up by a third and profit before tax by 40 per cent.' He blessed the Hong Kong Government for its modest stipend of 12.5 per cent. 'In accordance with our policy of rewarding shareholders with forty per cent of profit, a dividend of $9.00 per new share is proposed. Half the retained profit will be allocated to a third extension to Wai Wai Road.'

There were smiles, nods and humorous asides all around. Landers joined in on behalf of the H and K, which now enjoyed a minority shareholding.

Bedrix listened. From his side of the table, he had a different view. An unusual one. Upon the east wall, which was the longest of the five, three portraits hung in four panels either side of the main door. The first was of Adelaide, the second of Andrew, and the third was a new oil above a plate engraved with: JOHN STANFORD HUART. The fourth panel was vacant. Like the portraits, it was spotlighted. Bedrix knew the significance of it, as he had accompanied Huart back to Garden Terrace the day of Andrew's death and had heard him talk of 'succession'. He had thought it fatalistic at the time, and now knew the panel was kept vacant as a challenge to the fates. Something had happened to John Huart in 1954, and the shareholders of Cumberland China should be grateful for it.

His duty discharged, Bedrix looked to the head of the Long Table where the great silhouette in the light from the window in

the south wall sat framed by the mighty broadside of the Peak.
'The floor's yours, John.'

'Thank you, Clive. It was a grand report.' Huart checked that
Roboza was ready, then, as if seeking permission to begin his
oration, he cast a glance over his left shoulder. The fifth wall, the
south-west, was a chamfer at his elbow just wide enough to accept
the huge framed portrait that hung upon it. Charles Roland Huart
still intimidated the boardroom of the company he had founded
eighty-eight years ago. He had been repainted in his forties,
resplendent in black frock coat with red velvet lining and wing
collar. He sported dark wavy hair, his cheeks were pinked, his jaw
was square, and his ears were large and long. His eyes owned a
mischief, and were intense, cast slightly to the right at the illuminated void, as if he was impatient to espy the face of the fifth
taipan, and expected it to belong to no less a man than one of his
own progeny.

'I'll go straight into "New Business",' Huart opened. 'In
1961–62 the Textile and Garments Division will commence shirt
production: casual shirts, business shirts, formal dress shirts for
the American and British markets, plus the Continental market,
which will be a new one. I expect restrictions to be imposed under
the Lancashire Pact, and we must be ready to switch from the
UK to the Continent. Lennie, I would like you and Tony Ezuelo
to fly to Paris, Milan, Rome and Brussels. Take a designer with
you. You know the sort of people to see and what to do.'

Cosgrove nodded without comment. They had already
discussed it.

'Our shirts will carry the brand name "Golden Century". It is
a reverse derivation from our Chinese name, *Gum Bak Leen*, which
was selected as it embodies wealth and longevity – good stuff for
our *fung shui*. Our aim is for *Gum Bak Leen* to become a household
name in Hong Kong and "Golden Century" to become an international password for quality at reasonable price.' He paused, then
looked at the engineering director. 'Nigel, trading goes well, but
contracting and servicing are below target.'

Print cleared his throat. 'I . . . I plan to cover the trouble spots
myself and hire a man to run the trading department under my
direction, sir.'

'You've selected the man?'

'Yes, sir. Byron Browning. Deputy engineering manager at the
Dockyard.'

'I know him,' Bedrix revealed. 'Ex REME, isn't he?'

'That's right.'

[305]

Bedrix frowned. 'Isn't he a trifle old to be changing jobs?'

Print cleared his throat again and looked uncomfortable.

'Nigel,' Huart intervened, 'if you've screened and selected the man, go ahead and hire him. We'll be looking for continued growth in trading as a result, and a turnaround in the other engineering areas this year.'

'Thank you, sir. I'm quite confident of achieving the new targets.'

'Grand. Next . . .' Huart gave a quiet smile. 'Insurance.'

'Insurance?' Landers piped up from his chair next to Roboza.

Huart nodded. 'Over to you, Clive. I'll not steal your thunder.'

Bedrix smiled less quietly and hunched forward with his elbow upon the table as if his news was weighty. 'Gentlemen and Adelaide, I'm happy to announce our return to the insurance game. During my recent visit to Zurich I initialled an agreement with Ensurete Suisse. We are now their agent for Hong Kong, Singapore, Malaya, the Philippines and Taiwan.'

'Ensurete Suisse?' Cosgrove mused. 'Make chocolates, don't they?'

'They are new,' Bedrix conceded. 'The company was formed in 1955. But it's by whom it was formed that's significant. The owner is Prince Gino Lugano Androne. His family owns the Lugano Androne Bank. He was majority shareholder of Greater London Underwriters until the others got together and sold out to Pan Atlantic. Then he had no option but to sell, too, and set up Ensurete Suisse. It is a pure Swiss enterprise. Its objective is to insure the export drive that country is mounting. Trade with the Swiss is almost here, and we'll be ready to capitalise when it starts.'

Huart took over: 'The Agency Agreement is effective immediately. Accordingly, the Insurance Department is reopened. To manage it, Clive has put forward his son, Glynn. Tell us why, Clive.'

'Well, this is a little embarrassing . . .' Bedrix pulled a face. 'But you just have to look at his father to see the pedigree.' They all laughed richly. 'Glynn is twenty-four and has just come back to Hong Kong with his degree from Oxford in his pocket. He's had first-hand tutoring in the insurance business over the dinner table for years. Apart from that, he's got two arms to my one, and he's currently unemployed and becoming a bloody nuisance around the house.'

Adelaide led the laughter, then said deadpan, looking from her son's portrait to the man at the head of the table: 'I'm in favour of it. But in the past this company has never been one to condone nepotism.'

Huart chuckled with the others, then straightened his face. 'My final subject concerns our staff. Last year would not have been the great success that it was if not for them and I would like them to be rewarded. The customary way of doing it is with cash. I suggest we set up a bonus fund, into which a percentage of the retained profit is paid. It will be invested by the company and drawn upon when the results justify it. This year I propose a special bonus at Christmas of one month's salary, as well as the usual "thirteenth month" at Chinese New Year.'

'That's certainly sharing it around, John,' Cosgrove observed drily.

'I believe in sharing,' Huart told them all. 'If we don't reward the staff in good times, don't expect them to dig in with us when times go bad. We have no right to expect profits to go on rising like they are without taking out a little insurance.' He saw Bedrix smile at this.

'I'm sure you're right, John,' Cosgrove agreed with measured enthusiasm.

'I know I'm right.' Huart looked at the Rococo long-case clock that stood in the corner. 'This AGM is now closed. At Adelaide's behest, a table has been reserved for us all in the Jackson Room – on my chit.'

There was an hour to go before lunch and Huart filled it in his office, attacking the papers that had accumulated in the ninety minutes that he had been occupied in the boardroom adjacent to his office. His world had become the seventeenth and eighteenth floors of Cumberland House, which were connected by the spiral staircase between the office and his penthouse apartment. His world was carpeted in golden merino wool – indeed, he had chosen gold for the company colour – and furnished in rosewood. He enjoyed his world and he enjoyed the work he performed in it. There were just two nagging imperfections.

The vacant panel on the east wall of the boardroom, and the map on the north wall with China staring him in the face, served to remind him each time he took his seat at the head of the Long Table of those two pledges that remained unfulfilled after seven years.

2

The Eurasian woman caught Huart's eye as he descended the Cumberland House steps from the banking hall of the H and K at the end of the June business day. He watched her as he waited for the policeman to halt the traffic on Queen's Road. She was standing under the small-leafed banyan at the foot of Battery Path next to the stall that was famous for its hand-made lamp shades and its outdoor telephone. Dignified and finely dressed, with her black hair pinned and her skin a light tan, she was a head above the Cantonese around her. She could have been thirty or fifty, or any age in between. And he admired, not for the first time, how Eurasian women so projected the finest feminine qualities of both races.

The red sun was beginning its resplendent fall into China beyond Castle Peak. The air was light, cleansed by a week of persistent rain which had only ended after a twelve hour deluge had dumped twenty inches of water on the colony. Landslips had torn chunks out of mountainsides, mudslides had churned through squatter hamlets, tenements had collapsed, taking a toll in life and property. Flooding had been wholesale. Cumberland House had not been spared; its basement was still being pumped out and Huart had to park his Wolseley in upper Ice House Street outside the Club Lusitano, rendezvous for the elite of the Portuguese community.

He checked his watch. It was 5:15. He would just be able to make Middle Island in time to be aboard Scott Overbeck's pleasure junk by six.

'Playing nine holes at Deep Water Bay this p.m., John boy,' the Shearman Electronics chief executive had explained on issuing his telephone invitation that morning. 'I'll be on the junk by five myself. We need to cast off six latest if we're to get in an hour's swimming and catch the sunset from the beach at Lamma. She'll be a bobby-dazzler tonight.'

'I'll be there, Scott,' Huart had affirmed, delighted to be asked by the man from Silicon Valley. 'But is a job with Shearman such a soft touch, or is the electronics industry not as active as the press make out?'

Overbeck had laughed. 'John boy, when you pay a management team as much as we do to mind the store, you should be allowed to goof off once in a while. But don't you believe it – I'll be working. I'm testing a new-fangled walkie-talkie on the course, and a ship-to-shore radio we've started putting together out at Kwun Tong. Hush-hush, you know.'

Huart had been envious. He must get in on the electronics boom! It was to that end that he had struck up a friendship with Scott Overbeck. 'I hope you lower your handicap and put yourself in the mood to talk business.'

'Always ready to talk business, John boy. So long. See you before six.'

Whenever he was on Queen's Road, Huart studied the fashions. Young Chinese males had taken to modern western dress. Shirt collars pulled in by half-inch wide black ties, stovepipe cuffless trousers and pointed-toe slip-ons were everywhere. 'This place is getting full of yellow-skinned slant-eyed Brits!' a jaundiced expatriate had expounded within Huart's hearing one night in Jimmy's Kitchen. 'The population's pushing three million, only two per cent is non-Chinese, and yet they're aping us!' It had started Huart thinking, and looking at the fashions on Queen's Road.

The new production line at Wai Wai Road was at full speed. In a week the first batch of 'Golden Century' shirts would be passed to Tony Ezuelo's distribution department. Overseas orders had to be given priority, but the local market would not be ignored. Export quality shirts would be available in Central stores at discounted prices in a fortnight.

He had visualised opening a chain of 'Golden Century' fashion stores in Hong Kong, then extending it across Asia. He had exchanged views on it with Loretta Cosgrove, who was proving herself an astute businesswoman. She had herself financed her second 'Ming' boutique in Pedder Street and followed it up with a third in the Peninsula arcade; the fourth, on the mezzanine floor of the Mandarin, would open with the hotel next summer. It was European women who came in to buy the European designer creations at the 'Ming' boutiques. Chinese women on Queen's Road still wore the high collared silk *cheongsam*, its hem cut below the knee and slit to a height that was in reverse proportion to the wearer's age. But its traditional design was an inertia in the path of relentlessly changing fashion. Huart knew that Loretta had her timing right, too. It seemed some of Lennie the Lucky Pig had rubbed off on his second wife.

He was jolted from his rumination as a Chinese man in the pin-stripes of the legal profession hawked from deep in his throat, leaned forward and nonchalantly spat into the gutter six inches from Huart's toe. It was a commonplace ceremony. The Chinese regarded phlegm as the excreta of a throat devil that had to be evicted with loudest possible force. Huart smiled to himself. It was only the clothes that were western.

The policeman was taking his time. Huart peered at his watch. He looked at the Eurasian woman again, appraising her as she arched her back to look up at Cumberland House. Then she dropped her head and looked right at him. She held his gaze. She recognises me from somewhere, he thought. The policeman raised his hand and Huart stepped across Queen's Road with the after-office crowd. The woman had not moved. He stopped before her, his eyebrows politely questioning. Up close, her quality was confirmed.

'Such a fine building,' she said in English that bespoke a finishing school. 'There was one on the Shanghai Bund by the same name.'

Huart was impressed. 'The same company owned it. You are from Shanghai?'

She seemed to think on her answer, or whether to answer at all. Then her eyes seemed to glint with a challenging light. 'I was born there,' she finally said, and looked past him up at Cumberland House again.

'When did you leave?'

'Oh, long before 1949. I came to Hong Kong before the war. I left here seven years ago to join my husband in Europe. We have just returned.'

'Where did you live in Europe?' he asked conversationally, glancing at the gold wedding ring. The twinge of disappointment amused him.

'In Geneva. And Paris.'

'Paris is a beautiful place,' he said easily. 'It is my favourite city in all Europe, but I don't manage to visit it often enough.'

She smiled slowly, uncertainly, as if it was forming on her face against her better judgement. Again she looked across Queen's Road. 'Your company must be doing very well in Hong Kong to be able to put up such a fine building. I congratulate you.'

He turned and looked. He could not help it. He was so proud of it. The press had started out calling it 'that ultra-modern skinny tower stuck like a flagstaff on the corner of Ice House Street and Queen's Road, Central'. More recently this had been shortened to just 'The Flagstaff'. He cared little. Cumberland House was ultra-modern. It was skinny. It might well look like a flagstaff. But it was His!

He had virtually designed it himself, so unimpressed had he

been with the edifices going up all over Central District. Everything about them was square: their fronts were square; their sides were square; all their windows were square; every entrance was square. He had decided from the beginning that Cumberland House would combine the most up-to-date engineering with the best of pre-war architecture. Consequently, a new look in construction had come to Central District, coincidental with those grand old structures, Queen's Building and Prince's Building, receiving their death sentences.

Above all, the design of Cumberland House was functional. Its surface was bleached stone in a hot climate. Its windows were recessed at an angle to avoid the direct rays of the tropical sun and so draw optimum economy from the Cody Refrigeration central airconditioning plant. Its bank of elevators were Haig Denver 'Autovator', programmed to serve six floors each and minimise waiting time. But the architectural feature was the Roman arches. They rose from the street to the fourth floor and behind them the H and K's banking hall, mezzanine and offices were open to public view through solid glass walls. The unprecedented sight of raw money being processed in Central District had brought customers in off the street to line up before the H and K tellers, and had made *Gum Bak Leen* a household name faster than Huart could have dared hope.

He turned back and nodded. 'Thank you. We've been extremely fortunate.'

'What I don't understand – forgive me for asking – is why did Victoria Land not redevelop the site and build a Cumberland House themselves?'

It was much too good a question from a perfect stranger. Something told Huart to be wary, but he felt he could answer honestly. 'It was too small for them. Every company has its policy and they decided a building like that was outside theirs. Victoria Land's balance sheet makes our return on Cumberland House look like petty cash. But for my company it was a big step up.' He gave a half-frown. 'Are you from the press?'

'Indirectly. But I'm not a journalist. If I were, it's possible I would find your company an interesting story, and give it a title something like . . . "The Born Again *Hong*".' The light challenged again.

This had gone far enough, Huart decided. 'Do we know each other?'

She blinked, as if realising she had crossed a line she had drawn for herself. 'No. No, I'm very sorry. I must go now. I'm already late. My husband's waiting for me.' She deftly sidestepped and slipped by him.

'Wait!' He reached for her arm but she evaded him and ran across Queen's Road one second before the traffic accelerated over the intersection. The policeman shouted at him and he jumped back onto the pavement, from which he watched helplessly as the woman hurried around the corner into the narrow confines of Ice House Street. Cursing to himself, he looked up at Cumberland House as if it might somehow tell him what to do.

'Hello, John,' came a familiar voice behind him. 'You still have time to spend admiring your toy, I see.' It was Herbert Jarvis, of all people.

'Oh, good evening, Bert. No, I was just . . .'

'Beautiful weather.'

'Er, yes.'

'About time, too. Far too much rain this year. It's cost us the earth in repairs. Being a landlord's not all beer and skittles – as I can see you're finding out.' He nodded across Queen's Road to the six inch diameter rubber hoses running from the gutter to disappear into the basement of Cumberland House. 'Well, sorry, John. Can't chat now. Cheerio.'

When Huart turned back the Eurasian woman had been swallowed up by the crowd in Ice House Street. The last he had seen of her had been a behind of considerable quality. The realisation was already with him. He had found, and lost, Elizabeth Jane Huart.

3

'So nice to see you again, John.' The Jardine taipan stood in ownership of the doorway to the Hong Kong Club ballroom. 'So pleased you could come. But where are Lennie and Clive? They will be along, won't they?'

'Nice of you to invite us all,' Huart returned, firmly shaking the Hand of Plutocracy. 'I regret Clive's still on home leave, and Lennie may have to miss it, too. His flight was scheduled to land at Kai Tak at five, but BOAC's always late, you know, and then there's the ferry . . .'

'Jolly bad luck. At least you're here. You've met my wife, I think?' The elegant lady switched on a radiant smile as her husband looked away over Huart's shoulder and gave forth: 'Hello, old chap. So nice to see you again. So pleased you could come. So when're B and S going public, eh?'

'What? And be accused of tagging along after you lot?'

Huart excused himself and edged sideways through the throng crammed into the ballroom. The cocktail reception was one of an annual spate spanning the pre-Christmas period and extending up to the New Year's Eve ball. It was being thrown by Jardines to celebrate the unqualified success of their first public stock offering. It had been the paramount business event of 1961. Accordingly, every member of the Hong Kong Establishment was present. The directors of Cumberland China had been added to the roll two years before. The actuality of Cumberland House had done it. The identity of John Huart as owner of 'The Flagstaff' was now known.

He did a scan from his height, a Chivas and water between his fingers, and saw that, although space was at a premium, guests were still being admitted. There came a buzz, followed by a hush as Sir Robert and Lady Black appeared at the entrance. The Jardine taipan and his wife exchanged brief pleasantries with the viceregal couple, then escorted them into the ballroom through the human passage that had somehow opened.

Huart noticed Abraham Male moving from group to group, seeking out those whose goodwill might benefit him and engaging them in chat. His charm coated over a drive to make Male & Son a major *hong* in the shortest possible time. He took aside the company secretary of Cathay Electric, a man rarely seen in public, a man Huart knew from somewhere. Their heads stayed close together for minutes, then the two parted with gestures that bespoke an association of common interest. A danger signal sounded in Huart's brain. Where had he met the man with the face like a rat?

Male & Son, like Cumberland China, was growing. It dominated in shipping and insurance, but its engineering activities had been dealt a body blow a decade ago by the transfer of its electrical agencies and the consequent loss of Cathay Electric's business. Huart recalled how Ivor Male's son had shown his ability to strike back then, and now knew better than to ignore the rumours of Abraham Male's courtship with Japan.

He looked about for Sir Bart, whom he had seen arrive ten minutes ago, minus his stepson. Kingston Orr shunned the Club as, in his mind, the committee had offered him membership

[313]

because of his stepfather, not in his own right. Then he saw Cosgrove push his way into the ballroom. The little man stood on tiptoe, tugging at his bowtie as he cast his eyes about, then grinned as he saw the large figure forging a path towards him. As if by sleight of hand, a cigar appeared between his lips.

'I didn't think you'd make it.' Huart had to speak loudly over the noise of conversation as he pumped his partner's hand. Cosgrove had been in Europe for over a month. 'What happened? Was the flight early?'

'Not really. The new international airport makes the difference. I was through immigration and customs in a flash. The Armstong Siddeley was waiting and we caught the vehicular ferry just as it was leaving.'

'It's grand to have you back. How was London? Successful negotiation?'

Cosgrove snapped his fingers. 'Boy! Double pink gin if you please! Yes, London was a breeze. Tony Ezuelo did all the talking. I sat back and let him have his head. He's developed into a top class bargainer. I signed the '62–'63 contract with Hollingwoods, plus one with Marks and Spencer. Then in Paris we landed a trial shirt order from Galleries Lafayette . . .'

'Well done. How do you think we should reward him?'

'Give him more independence. It would leave me free to do new things. I've some ideas I'd like to discuss with you. Tomorrow morning?'

'Sounds like a good time to listen to ideas.' Huart raised his glass in a casual toast, then gestured with it. 'What do you think of all this?'

Cosgrove grimaced as if he actually disapproved. 'Jardines do nothing in half measure. I see even the Governor is here.' Then he shrugged. 'I suppose they deserve it. A successful public issue it was. Most timely.'

'Timely for you, from what I hear.'

The eyes of Lennie the Fifth danced. 'I heard about it in the nick of time and put in an order with P.G. Curzon-Cross. I just met him outside and he told me I've made a hundred grand whilst I've been away.'

Huart nodded. 'You've a real nose for money matters, Lennie, though I don't know how you sniffed this one out. The stock market's been a dead body for years. Jardines really brought it to life.'

Cosgrove's grin touched both walls. 'They don't call me Lennie the Lucky Pig for nought. A parcel of overseas money came in.

P.G. handles all the taipans' investments, you know. He was good enough to tip me off.'

'Loretta'll be envious. Her boutiques are doing well, but they don't clear a profit of $100,000 in a month. Perhaps you . . .' His voice died as he saw that his partner's grin had evaporated. 'Whatever is the matter?'

'We're getting a divorce, John.' The words were almost lost in the din.

'Lennie . . . I'm so sorry. What can I say?'

'No need to say anything. It was a mistake from the start. Loretta's too full of her boutiques and, as you say, they're a big success. But I'm at fault, too. Marriage is for others. I've never really been cut out for it. I delight too much in variety. I love flying off all over the place on business or for a holiday. I seek variety in everything I do. It was inevitable we'd break up sooner or later. Besides, there's another man.'

'Do you know who it is?'

'No. I don't care much either. He's welcome to those knockers. I had the best years of 'em. God I'm dry! Where's my drink? Boy!' He jerked his head about in a futile search for the waiter. 'Know what I'm going to do with my stock market boodle, John? I'm going to buy another racehorse. This one I'll call "Strike Two". And I'll buy another car. Maybe a Nash Rambler or one of those E-Type Jags. Sorry, old salt, but I do need that drink.' And with his grin back in place, he elbowed his way to the bar.

Huart watched the crowd swallow him up with mixed feelings. Though unlucky in love, Lennie the Fifth had the Midas touch when it came to matters financial. Next morning he would avidly listen to those 'ideas'. Yes, Tony Ezuelo could take over marketing for the Textiles and Garments Division. And when Alexander Chiu Man-king was made production manager after his return from Cornell with a BSc in industrial engineering, funded by Cumberland China as some compensation for the loss of his father, Cosgrove could abandon textiles completely. He wanted variety? As far as Huart was concerned, Lennie the Lucky Pig could take his pick.

Circulating amongst the now thinning crowd, Huart engaged in a series of short conversations with utility heads, senior bankers, a taipan or two. He reintroduced himself to the Governor and Lady Black, then sought out his hosts, thanked them again for inviting him, and left.

Night had fallen. Statue Square was lit by the Christmas lights looped across the façades of the banks. Upon the Bank of China

[315]

was a huge portrait of Mao and a bilingual banner lauding the 'Great Leap Forward', despite the disastrous crop failures that had brought about its sudden end. Across the square the Mandarin had reached full height. Prince's Building had gone and Huart could see Union House under construction on the land that once had given rise to Union, York and King's Buildings. A solitary statue had come back to the square: that of Sir Thomas Jackson. Huart thought it something of an epitome of modern Hong Kong that it took the skills of a banker, a money man, to survive in Central District, whilst time had removed royalty to the sidelines.

As he turned into Ice House Street, he looked up and saw the lights were on in the penthouse eighteen storeys in the sky. Ah Keung, knowing the titbits on offer at cocktail receptions, would be preparing a light supper. The Christmas lights that adorned Cumberland House bathed the narrow thoroughfare in a warm, friendly glow, and Huart felt like Father Christmas as he ran up the steps of 'The Flagstaff'. His 'Flagstaff'.

4

1962 became the Year of the enterprising Water Tiger. It was as good as its reputation and brought Cumberland China's sixth division. The aim of the Imports Division was to cater to those seeking the good things in life. Lennie the Fifth set out on a world-wide search for agencies.

By May he had them: caviare from Iran; smoked salmon from Ireland; sausage from Italy; ice cream from Norway; chocolate from Belgium; nougat from Turkey; cheeses from Holland; plus herbal teas from America; triple malt scotch; and vintage wines and liqueurs from France; vodka from Finland, beer from Munich; and, naturally, finest Cuban and Mexican cigars.

'Only the top of the top shelf is good enough!' Cosgrove told the Long Table. 'We will bring world trends to Hong Kong. The local standard of living is rising fast. An elite class is being bred here. The Imports Division will market to it – and charge accordingly.'

'Flog to the snobs, eh, Leonard?' observed Adelaide drily. 'Will somebody please stop this man before he reintroduces the opium trade?'

'Not a bad idea at all, old girl,' Cosgrove fired back. 'But it would have to be finest Indian grade or I'm not interested.'

The new division did him proud. Its chic products were distributed to outlets in leading hotels and prime locations in Central District and Tsimshatsui. A home delivery service was subcontracted. Vans painted in gold and stencilled with CUMBERLAND CHINA IMPORTS DIVISION became a common sight on the roads of the Peak, Mid Levels, Jardine's Lookout and Repulse Bay on the Island, and Kowloon Tong and Beacon Hill across the harbour. Lennie the Fifth had done it again with his Midas touch.

Relaxing in his penthouse lounge one Sunday, Huart listened to a government spokesman on television announce that, despite the dictates of the General Agreement on Tariffs and Trade and the quota system that limited textile exports to the USA and the EEC, Hong Kong's foreign trade had passed $10,000,000,000 on an annual basis for the first time. He heard the man go on to reveal that foreign investment was starting to come into the colony because 'the harmonious relations that existed between Hong Kong, London and Peking were evident to the rest of the world'.

The next morning, he read in the *Hong Kong and Oriental Daily* of the Government's renewed concern with the overcrowding. The population had passed three million, helped by the 60,000-strong flotsam of the 'Great Leap Forward' that had been on the right side of the border when it had been closed again after a twenty-five day human flood tide from Kwangtung. The Low-Cost Housing Programme that had been hastened into being by the Shek Kip Mei fire eight Christmasses ago was already struggling.

The summer of the Year of the Water Tiger proved an ironic one considering its governing element. It failed to rain. The winter had been dry, as usual, and the reservoirs and catchments were perilously low. Water rationing was introduced, emergency supplies were negotiated from China and sent by tanker down the Pearl River. Hong Kong was hot, desperately waterless, overcrowded and pressure-cooked by humidity. And life became that much less bearable for those living away from the districts served by the golden vans stencilled: CUMBERLAND CHINA IMPORTS DIVISION.

The first day of September is arguably deemed the start of autumn, when the 'wet season' has done its time. But the Year of the Water Tiger, having been spiteful with its summer, proved itself to be contrary, too. In the small hours of September 1st, nature pulled a trick on Hong Kong, a place of natural and unnatural extremes. The trick was to prove tragic for the colony. And especially tragic for Cumberland China.

A window smashed. Huart jerked from a deep sleep. A mad howling penetrated his sleep-addled brain. Cumberland House was swaying from side to side, groaning from its core as one oscillation ended, the next began. Water was spraying about the bedroom, being syphoned in by some demonic force. It was dark; heavily dark. An alien ambience possessed the room.

Typhoon!

Huart sat bolt upright. 'Fooool!' he yelled at himself in the blackness.

Closeted in his office throughout the previous day with Thomas Buckley, who had now fully taken over from Francis Roboza, he had ignored the storm warning Imelda had tried to relay to him. He had closed out the world beyond the August trading reports he was studying with rare concern. The company was behind target for the first time in seven years.

The shortfall was but ten per cent and the year was not half over. But it supplemented other signs of an overheating economy. Land values, having risen steadily since 1956, were soaring. Huart's hankering to repeat his property coup was chronic, but the over-inflated prices repelled him. The boom was being fuelled by cheap loans from scores of newly-licensed banks, which, desperate for business, were waging an interest rate war that, strange but true, was benefiting borrower and lender alike.

The ten per cent had eaten at him. Were the 1962–63 targets over-ambitious? Had he been naive to expect a forty per cent growth for the seventh year running? The Engineering Division was the main problem. Despite Nigel Print's assurances, Byron Browning was not making out. The slippage had begun in June and Buckley had pointed it out then. The West Country man had proved himself a first rate financial watchdog.

Discontented, but mentally drained and ready for sleep, Huart had gone to bed at one. He had heard but not listened to the rain spattering at the windows, and the strength of the wind gusts driving water between the joints. The drawn curtains had hidden the puddles on the ledges and the rivulets running down the walls to form sodden patches on the carpet.

'Fool!' he reproached himself again as he reached for the bedside lamp. It was gone. A bullying gust hit the building. It swayed violently. A metallic rasping sound came from above and he saw the airconditioner sucked into the void, its severed power cable sparking. 'Ah Keung! Pull the main fuse switch! Ah Keung!' He searched about in vain for his robe; he had slept in the raw since Burma. He reached down with his toes to touch only water. The floor was awash. He had to get out! Once the level rose to the power sockets the room would be a death trap. 'Ah Keung!' The second window went. Now rain fired in from two directions. Squinting hard, he saw light under the hallway door. Where was Ah Keung? He saw, too, that water was pouring into the room faster than it could escape.

He tried to stand. His feet came down on broken glass and his legs jack-knifed. His arms flailed in the violent blackness as an airborne tide knocked him to his knees. The rain pummelled his face, stung his naked flesh, filled his ears and muffled the wind that would otherwise have deafened him. The mantle radio smashed into his head. Coloured flecks danced on his retina as he overbalanced. A vision of the worst injury imaginable to man assailed him. He clasped his vitals in one hand as he fell, punched the other out to break his fall and yelled into the storm as his palm sliced open like a bone ham on a butcher's bench. He lay in a lake on a lakebed of broken glass, his face a corkscrew of pain.

He pushed himself to his knees, then onto knuckles and toes like a great ape and picked his way to the door. Another gust dumped him on his side. By the time he got there he was cut all over. He tried to turn the knob, but his blood and water made it impossible. He screwed it with both hands. But the door would not budge. As he started putting expletives end to end he worked it out: the typhoon's vortex had created a vacuum effect!

A squall smashed in the third window. A mirror spun like a pinwheel from its hook to disintegrate against the ceiling, firing shards willy-nilly. With everything coming at him he decided to try for the 'en suite' bathroom. He put a sodden cushion over his head and held it there with his cut hand, and wound a sheet around his knees. He drew himself into a crawling position and, using his good hand for support, pushed his knees forward. Caterpillar fashion, it took minutes to reach the bathroom. He wrenched the handle down and shoved. The door flew outwards, breaking the vacuum, and a gust sent him sprawling headlong onto the tiled floor.

He kicked the sheet away and, ignoring his burning lungs and the stinging of the myriad cuts, put his shoulder to the door. He could only get it halfway. He wedged his feet against the bathtub, levered the door to within six inches of the lock, and held it there.

A screaming *kamikaze* squall ended and, mustering every last atom, he drove himself against the door, ramming it into the face of the storm. It closed millimetre by millimetre. There was a click and he threw the bolt. He leapt aside as a gust tested it, and heaved a sigh of relief as it held.

He hit the light switch. The glare blinded him. He focused on something in his shaving mirror that could not possibly be him. It was a drenched apparition that bled from a mosaic of cuts. The flesh of its palm hung in straight-edged lumps and its knees were criss-crossed with razor thin scores. Huart looked from whatever it was to the towels on the rack. He reached out to them, intending to use them as bandages.

But his hand never made contact.

The typhoon struck with a fury supernatural. A two hundred knot devil gust penetrated the broken windows on the eighteenth floor of Cumberland House and delivered itself in a meteoric ball of raw godless hate upon the inch and a half of teak that stood between it and the reprieved being of John Huart. The lock gave at once and the wooden slab was propelled inwards. In the fraction of a fraction of a second before it hit him, a number of thoughts juggled for priority in Huart's brain.

Foremost of these was the one that told him he was a dead man.

Tentative light penetrated the heavy cloak of anaesthesia. The silence was all-enveloping. He was inside a tomb. He was indeed dead. But his fingertips retained sensitivity. They were touching something hard and cold. Pain began to throb through his body as if sent by a motor restarting. It came from the back of his head. It spread to his ear, his shoulders, back, hips, knees, feet. In death there still is pain? He forced his eyes to open. He was still alive. He saw the shattered bulb hanging from its cord overhead. The grey light was from the bathroom window. An eerie stillness, an unnatural silence prevailed.

The typhoon had gone.

He felt a weight on his chest. He looked down. He was on his back in the bathtub. Half the door was lying on him. It had split in two as it hit the corner of the tub and had delivered him only a glancing blow. He recalled it all now: tumbling backwards into the tub, his head coming down upon the tap. It was the last thing he could remember.

He pushed the door off him and roared with pain. He looked at his hands. The palms were sliced like plates of chicken meat, the tendons white in the mess of soggy wrinkled flesh. Blood welled. He levered himself up with his elbows and saw the pink coating over the bottom of the tub. 'God almighty!' he cried. 'I must have lost pints!'

There came a hammering upon the bedroom door outside. 'Master! Are you die? Master! Are you die?' Ah Keung's voice was a hoarse whisper.

Huart's diver's watch had also survived and it told him it was 6:15. He must have been out for about four hours! He hauled himself out of the tub, biting down on the pain. He tucked a towel around his waist and found his slippers. It was like walking on nails as he hobbled into the bedroom, and beheld a ruinous scene. The paint on the walls was blistered and water-stained; not a thing was left upon any of them. Furniture was strewn about, draped with the shreds of whatever had been upon it. Not one door was left on the built-in wardrobes. His clothes were in sodden heaps along the walls. The bed was on its side against the door, the mattress on top of it. And Ah Keung continued to beat with his old fists as he croaked: 'Master! Are you die? Master! Are you die?'

The water had evacuated down the bathroom drain, leaving a jigsaw of broken glass and bits of everything. He groaned in dismay and picked his way to the door. 'Ah Keung! I'm safe! I was in the bathroom. The bed is blocking the door. I'll move it. I'm safe, Ah Keung!'

He heard the gurgle of relief. 'Oh, Master! I so happy you not die yet. *Da fung* so big! Hurry quick please. *Da fung* come back. Hurry quick!'

'Coming back, Ah Keung? What do you mean – coming back?'

The old servant let go a hoarse squeal of frustration. How could Master be so clever in business, but an ox-skin lantern in the ways of nature? '*Da fung* only half finish! Hurry quick! *Fai dee! Fai dee aaah!*'

It hit Huart like a kick in the crotch. The calm outside was false! They were in the eye of the typhoon. Their respite was only temporary. At any time the typhoon would be back – from the opposite direction.

Ignoring the pain that came from everywhere, he pulled the mattress from the door, shoved the bed aside and wrenched the doorknob. Still it would not give. 'It's warped, Ah Keung! Push the door! Push! Hard as you can!'

Ah Keung pushed as Huart pulled. The door gave a loud crack, then came open. The old servant gazed at his employer with eyes

[321]

that gradually went circular in disbelief like a camera aperture opening. 'Master . . . ?'

Huart could not help it. He hitched the towel higher and smiled. 'Good morning, Ah Keung. I think we'll dispense with breakfast this morning. Please get iodine and bandages and some old clothes from the laundry.'

Ah Keung departed shaking his head. Master was brave, but quite mad. All *gwailo* are mad. But I thank *Kwan Yin* that mine is at least cultured.

Huart limped into the living room. The floor-to-ceiling glass doors to the balcony were criss-crossed with packing tape. He saw the shutters stacked in a corner. Outside. The typhoon had also taken Ah Keung by surprise. He reached the balcony door just as the harbour was closed out by a wave of black cloud that tumbled down from the Nine Dragons and gathered speed as it headed for Central District. He froze. To go out onto the balcony was to invite certain death. 'Ah Keung! The typhoon's coming back! Help me push the furniture against the balcony door!'

Mesmerised, he watched the great storm rush at him. It had seen him and it howled in fury and sent in its point gust to smash him anew. The wave of wind slammed into the building. The chequered glass seemed to bend in at Huart and the air around him vibrated against his eardrums. The floor beneath his feet shifted as Cumberland House swayed backward, quivered, then pitched forward like an eighteen-storey bullwhip.

It needed only two gusts. The doors blew in with an explosion of glass that peppered the lounge. The typhoon screamed with glee and dived into the opening. Cumberland House cried out and rocked from side to side as the wind gusts and the rain squalls filled it like a rapine herd.

5

But, even at the second attempt, Typhoon Wanda did not kill John Huart.

She had been the typhoon of typhoons, and her timing had been grievous. She had smitten Hong Kong dead centre with her storm tide at its peak, blowing up a set of tidal waves, driving them over the New Territories fishing village of Tai Po and drowning hundreds. And then, with her diabolical duty done, she had dragged her tail into Kwangtung Province like a gargantuan bee delivered of its sting and there, as with lesser storms of her kind spawned on the Pacific Ocean, she had faded away.

Amidst the devastion she had wreaked so efficiently, Typhoon Wanda had made a special target of Cumberland China. Huart was hospitalised for days whilst his body was sewn up and his palm was restored with a skin graft. His penthouse was a wreck. Only the kitchen, where Ah Keung and he had taken refuge, was untouched. His office was a swamp; the spiral staircase had proved an effective sluice. Not one of the other sixteen floors was undamaged. 'The Flagstaff' had, of course, been designed and constructed to withstand the typhoons that paid brief unwelcome visits every 'wet season', but it had not been built for Typhoon Wanda. Repairs to it were estimated to require three months and reinforcement work six more. But Cumberland China's toll did not end with a thousand cuts to its taipan's flesh and extensive damage to its property.

For Typhoon Wanda had killed Clive Bedrix.

He had been touring the branch offices in Singapore, Manila and Taipei when the typhoon had been born and had grown to its full size in just a few days. Its first landfall had been the Philippines. The brand new Boeing 707, with Bedrix aboard, that had taken off from Manila two days after Wanda had passed had been the first flight out of the crippled airport. Somewhere between the coast of Luzon and Kaohsiung, the 707 had run into Wanda's tail – the storm's girth had defied estimate – and had disappeared without any sign that it had ever existed. Nor a soul aboard it.

The funeral service was held a week later. Remorse lived on Huart's face amidst the scars of Typhoon Wanda as he delivered the eulogy from the pulpit with his bandaged hands clasped before him. The chapel was packed in poignant regard for the man with whom nobody would talk business, do business, share a San Mig, swop a joke, nor ever see again.

Clive Bedrix, the Quiet Achiever, the most capable lieutenant, the efficient implementer of his plans, was gone. 'What will we do without such a man?' Huart enquired of the congregation and any superior being who might be listening. 'What will we do without a man who gave his arm for his country and got on with his life as if the limb had been but a loan in the first place? What will we do without a man who lived that life so selflessly – and no

[323]

doubt gave it up the same way – as if it, too, was only on loan to him. What will we do without Clive Bedrix?'

After the service, Huart grasped Glynn Bedrix's hand and saw in the young man's eyes the deep, deep agony of personal loss. He was drawn to the suddenly fatherless son, realising that he, himself, was only too well qualified to fathom those depths. 'Glynn, they're big shoes to fill. You'll have every assistance from everyone in the company – and from me in particular – to fill them. Just as soon as you're ready . . .'

'Thank you, sir. Mum wants to go home as soon as possible. I'll go with her and see her settled in Market Harborough. Then I'll be back. Dad was a confirmed traditionalist. I must be one, too. There's no company for me but Cumberland China – and no man I'll work for but you, sir.'

Huart was in temporary accommodation in the Mandarin Hotel. The luxury inn stood in pride of place upon the Central Praya, now Connaught Road, Central, a block inland from the new Star Ferry pier. It fronted the harbour that grew busier every day, and the long red coats of its large Sikh doormen were visible from Kowloon. In his room that night Glynn Bedrix's words stayed with him, tempering his grief with a pride that was humble – and guilty. For it had been he who had sent Glynn's father on the tour of the branches to find out why the Ensurete Suisse operation was off to such a sluggish start.

Death was to violate Huart's personal sanctum twice more before the Year of the Water Tiger was over. In November, Sinclair MacLurie passed away in his sleep in his cottage outside Edinburgh. He had been eighty-one. Huart flew by BOAC Comet to Heathrow, then took an express train north for the funeral. Then, in January, Adelaide Huart-Brent succumbed to a bout of pneumonia that had developed complications in a winter of capricious temperatures. At seventy-eight, though her will remained unbent, her body did not. She died the day after being admitted to the Hong Kong Sanatorium. 'Hospital's only a place for people my age to go and kick the bucket!' she had insisted in typical contentiousness, and then had been stubborn enough to prove it.

Of the matriarch's kin, only her second grand-daughter came to see her laid to rest. At sixteen, Suzanne's face and body was on schedule for the magnificence that was in her genes. She had matured early, despite her inheritance of the Huart-Brent characteristic with the modern euphemism: 'independence'. She stayed a week in a room in the Mandarin on Huart's floor, then took Pan Am back to her college in New Jersey. Had it not been for the presence of his favourite 'niece', the lunar new year of the emotional Water Rabbit would have been a low one for Huart.

The empty chairs at the Long Table still rendered the AGM for 1962–63 a subdued ritual. For twelve years Clive Bedrix's tonic voice had read the annual report. Now it was replaced by that of Thomas Buckley, who spoke in clipped tones, reporting without flourish, conveying figures and percentages prosaically. The caustic wit of Adelaide Huart-Brent had gone with her. Huart acknowledged that he missed it.

Cumberland China had fallen just short of its targets for the past two years. Accordingly, projections for 1963–64 were fixed according to a more conservative formula. Even so, the coming year would bring a record profit as rental from Cumberland House would make its first positive contribution now that the H and K loan was fully paid off. The shrunken board approved the new targets, and ratified the redistribution of the shares liquidated by Ruby Bedrix and the trustee of Adelaide's estate.

Huart's unhappiness now extended to the company stock. The holdings of Cosgrove and himself were too large; power was in the hands of too few. As Buckley proceeded from topic to topic, Huart reviewed his middle management – members of a future board: Tony Ezuelo – Marketing Manager, Textile and Garments Division; Daniel Vail – Manager, Property Department; Glynn Bedrix – Manager, Insurance Department; Alexander Chiu Man-king – Production Manager, Textile and Garments Division; Thomas Buckley – Chief Accountant, Accounts and Administration Division. Huart thought of Byron Browning – Trading Manager, Engineering Division, saw the frown on Nigel Print's downcast face and crossed the name off his mental list.

He glanced at the empty panel on the east wall. After his chance meeting with Elizabeth Huart – yes, he was still sure it had been her – he had reinstated the message in the English language press. But again nothing worthwhile had come of it. If only he knew her married name . . !

Buckley concluded the annual report. Huart's summing-up was the shortest ever. Lunch this year was in the grill room of the Victoria Hotel.

'Rain?' Cosgrove poked his nose into his snifter of armagnac. 'It's so long since there's been any, I've quite forgotten what it looks like.'

'There're rumours,' revealed Nigel Print, 'that if the rains don't come in ten days, water will be cut to four hours every fourth day.'

'I've heard the same rumour,' Landers confessed, sucking on his pipe.

Cosgrove made a disparaging noise. 'S'no coincidence the one public utility making a hash of it year after year is the only one not run by private enterprise. Denationalise the Waterworks! That's the answer to it!'

Huart thought of the old Shanghai panacea. *'Maskee,'* he sighed.

'It was never like this back home.' Print saw the quick frown traverse Huart's face. 'But . . . too much rain there,' he added lamely.

'It was never like a lot of things "back home".' Cosgrove lifted the snifter to his lips. 'Christine Keeler . . . Mandy Rice-Davies . . . Ah . . .' He took a tipple and swirled it in his mouth. 'My kind of girls.'

'How can Macmillan survive the scandal?' Landers had posed the question rhetorically. British politics was one of his favourite lunchtime subjects. 'This Profumo fellow just has to resign.'

'Too true,' Cosgrove agreed laconically. 'Anyone who breaks the Eleventh Commandment should be made to take the consequences.'

'The "Eleventh Commandment", Lennie?' Landers frowned. 'What's that?'

' "Thou shalt not be found out".' Cosgrove patted his coat pocket. 'Well, what d'you know – I've gone and found myself out. I'm out of cigars.' He turned in his chair and called: 'Lola! Cigar, please. Chop-chop!'

The Victoria Grill at lunchtime was for men only. It was a tradition strictly observed. But it was not the restaurant's only idiosyncrasy. The other was Lola Lau, the cigar girl. She came to the table in a black *cheongsam* and opened a tray to reveal an assortment of cigars, several of which originated from agencies held by the Imports Division. Cosgrove selected one and Lola proceeded to prepare it for him with a *tour de force* that climaxed with one foot on the arm of his chair and an over-exposure of a lissom thigh up and down which the cigar was warmed.

'What colour today, old chap?' Landers enquired when the performance was over and Lola had moved on to the next table. 'Red's my guess.'

'Black,' Print disagreed. 'Must be black to go with her dress.'

'You're half right, Nigel,' Cosgrove said as he rolled the cigar between his fingertips under his nose. 'Right colour, at least.' He rolled his eyes and grinned. 'Actually, she wasn't wearing any at all.'

'Oh, come on, Lennie!'

Huart joined in the laughter and the subsequent banter and called for his cigar in turn. Nobody saw fit to question the eyesight of Lennie the Fifth that afternoon. They sat and joked until three, and Huart found that it took his mind off unhappier things.

Outside in the other Hong Kong, summer tightened its grip and the temperature and humidity climbed as surely as did the value of land and the cost of everything else. In the crowded, cramped, incestuous concrete ghettos of Kowloon, lines of common folk formed at standpipes with plastic buckets in each hand, and groups of labourers congregated in tea-houses to complain to each other about the heat, the drought, the falling value of their hard-earned money. Without the Victoria Hotel and its contemporary Central District oases of luxury, Hong Kong simmered in more ways than one. And a corner of the plaster over the crack in the pressure-cooker began to come unstuck.

6

The British electrical industry had rewarded Sir Reynard Armstrong after a series of slick corporate takeovers and mergers with the natural sobriquet: 'The Fox'. Hong Kong was number one export market for the conglomerate known as the Anglo-Saxon Group and he, as its chairman, flew in often, taking his customary suite in the Mandarin each time. Just once did he break tradition to sample the new Hilton which had opened at the head of Queen's Road, Central, on land that had been the Victoria Barracks' parade ground. On Friday, August 1st, 1964, The Fox was blessed with another Double Happiness. He signed a contract with Sir Bartholomew Orr for six more 60 megawatt turbo-alternators, then sat beside Huart in the front row immediately before the podium set up in the plush hotel function room, wearing a smile that could not be shifted. For he knew in advance the content of Sir Bart's announcement to the assembled press.

'Last week Cathay Electric connected its 400,000th consumer,' the doyen of the Asian power industry opened. 'We have installed plant capable of generating 480 megawatts and have raised our transmission voltage to 66,000 volts – 66kV as we in the industry call it. That is quite fine for now, but what of the future? We estimate that by the end of the decade, to meet the rising demand for our power we must be able to generate 1,500 megawatts – more than a two hundred per cent increase!'

There came an expectant hush. Second guesses as to Sir Bart's impending revelation had ranged from plans for a new power station, to a takeover of the small utility on Cheung Chau that generated from one antiquated diesel set, to both at once. Reynard Armstrong luxuriated in a bath of self-satisfaction as he anticipated the phraseology to come. Cathay Electric's Letter of Intent to order the plant and equipment for Phase A of the hitherto top secret Jubilee Bay Power Station, addressed to the Turbine Division of the Anglo-Saxon Group with a carbon copy for the Engineering Division of Cumberland China, he knew was at this moment being typed by Patrick O'Harah's secretary.

'We cannot expect to meet such rapidly increasing demand from our existing generating facility,' Sir Bart continued, 'so we must build a bigger one. Gentlemen of the press, I am most proud to announce to you . . .'

Armstrong saw in his mind's eye his face on the front cover of the next edition of the *Economist* and read the heading of the lead story:

'THE FOX' SNARES HONG KONG POWER STATION FOR BRITAIN

He saw, too, the name of Anglo-Saxon at the top of the *Financial Times* list. If he had been a Persian cat, Sir Reynard Armstrong would have purred. But nobody would have deemed him an animal so domesticated. The businessman-knight was indeed 'The Fox'.

Huart saw instead the paper shaking in Sir Bart's feeble grip, the other hand pressing on the table for support. He saw, too, the face of Kingston Orr. It was stonier, more disaffected than ever as he sat on Sir Bart's left, having recently been appointed to the board. On the doyen's right, in the seat normally allocated to a trusted deputy, sat Patrick O'Harah. Huart saw no communication between the two, and it worried him.

' . . . Phase A of the station will be capable of generating 1,600 megawatts of electricity. It will be commissioned before 1969. The contract for supply of the plant is now being negotiated. The contenders are the Anglo-Saxon Group of the UK and the Matamoto Corporation of Japan. Tomorrow Mr O'Harah here will announce the successful manufacturer . . .'

Huart also thought of the Letter of Intent being typed for the order he had negotiated with O'Harah under Sir Bart's benign eye. He thought of Cumberland China's agency commission. It helped his concern depart.

'God bless private enterprise!' Sir Bart proclaimed. 'Happiness, prosperity and a long life to all who promote the perpetuity of Hong Kong. We at Cathay Electric subscribe to and endorse the *laissez faire* policy of our government. May God also bless all of you here today.'

He took his seat to prolonged applause. Hong Kong loved Sir Bart. The newsmen treated him respectfully with their questions and he answered each one fully, whilst remaining seated. When it was over, O'Harah assisted him from the podium to the corner where a bar had been set up and plates of small chow laid out. Kingston Orr tagged along.

The party that followed was a happy one. Everyone had something to celebrate. Sir Bart and his directors had a new power station. Armstrong was an hour away from confirmation that his group had landed the biggest export order ever placed with a British electrical manufacturer. Huart and his growing *hong* were going from success to success. The local press had a page one story and plenty to eat and drink.

But there were dampers, even if these were seen only by Huart, and they did not include the lack of water in the washrooms, where barrels were filled every fourth day and ran out on the third. The 'wet season' had again refused to open on time or since, completing a hat-trick of dry summers. The dehydrated expressions on the faces of Kingston Orr and Jeremy Parrot, now financial controller of Cathay Electric as well as its company secretary, could therefore have been considered in season.

Huart delved again into his memory. Where had he met that man before?

Sitting in the back of his Rolls-Royce Silver Ghost as it crossed the harbour on the vehicular ferry, Sir Bart ignored the deep-seated pain that grew in his chest until it was too late. Suddenly he clutched himself and pitched forward onto the floor, where he gasped and wheezed in a futile attempt to suck in life-preserving oxygen. His fingers clawed tufts from the carpet beneath his head. Blood pulsed from his mouth, his nostrils, his ears. His face turned a shade of blue, then purple.

Alone in the front, Kingston Orr gaped over the back of his seat at the convulsing tangle of arms and legs. Then he looked about. The slow, wading ferry was in mid harbour, fifteen minutes from the pier. In those minutes his stepfather could die. He was that close to owning the fastest growing power company in Asia.

The chauffeur was at the rail in the bow, engaged in conversation with a contemporary whom Kingston Orr recognised to be in the employ of Dr Martinez, a partner of a prominent Central medical practice. What a coincidence, he thought. The doctor must be in his car somewhere on the ferry. If I find him quickly, I may be able to save the old man's life.

Sir Bart gave out a horrible croak. Kingston looked back again and watched him trying to say something, his bulging eyes imploring, not understanding what was happening. And he made his decision. 'Father, Dr Martinez is on the ferry. I'll go get him.'

Sir Bart groaned his gratitude. He heard the door slam, then a murderous rocket of pain soared from his innards into his brain and his legs kicked in reckless, helpless frenzy.

Kingston Orr saw the Triumph 2000 near the bow with Dr Martinez in the rear reading the racing page of the *Hong Kong and Oriental Daily*. He looked up as the shadow fell on him through the open window and smiled in recognition. 'Why, good afternoon, Kingston. You look well. How is your father? Coming for his annual check up, soon? Can't be too prudent at his age, you know.'

Kingston Orr bent his head and said quietly: 'I am fine, thank you, Dr Martinez. And thank you for being concerned for my father. Actually – ' He looked back at the Rolls-Royce. 'He is fine also. Just fine.'

The heir to the largest power company in Asia strolled to the bow of the vehicular ferry where, to the chauffeur's complete surprise, he lit one Turf after the other and obliged the man to listen to a continuous flow of idle chatter that lasted fifteen minutes.

The day after Sir Bart's funeral the board of Cathay Electric confirmed Kingston Orr's appointment as chief executive. His first official duty was to dictate two directives that were effective immediately: one being the summary dismissal of Patrick O'Harah, the second the promotion of Jeremy Parrot to general manager.

The next day he joined Abraham Male aboard a JAL Boeing 707 destined for Haneda Airport, Tokyo. Upon landing they were informed that normal customs formalities had been waived by high order, and were escorted to the VIP lounge. There they were greeted by a hugely smiling Tetsuo Hondo, who introduced them to a dapper Japanese gentleman in a dark blue Savile Row suit. This was Kenjo Matamoto, Hondo's omnipotent president, and grandson of the founder of the Rising Sun's premier *zaibatsu*.

Kingston Orr's bow was the quintessence of Japanese etiquette. He handed over an envelope with an uncharacteristic smile of genuine pleasure. Hondo translated out loud to his president the retyped Letter of Intent addressed to Matamoto Electric Corporation. There was a copy for Male & Son, and Abraham Male was presented with a second envelope that contained it. 'It's taken a long time, Abraham. But better late than never.'

'All the sweeter for it, Kingston. All the sweeter.'

At precisely that instant, the telephone rang on Huart's desk. His eyes flicked to Sir Reynard Armstrong who was sitting before him, scratching his jaw, his nose, his ears with a developing anxiety. He picked up the receiver, unease slowing his hand. 'Yes, Imelda?'

'I have Mr Parrot of Cathay Electric for you, sir.' She had pronounced it Par-oh. Everyone did now.

'Thank you, Imelda. Put him through, please.' There was a click on the line. 'Hello? Mr Parrot? My congratulations on your promotion. I regret I have not yet had the pleasure of meeting you in person to – '

'Thank you, Mr Huart,' an antiseptic voice cut in. 'I, myself, regret that it has taken me too long getting back at you – I mean back to you. I see you've been calling me. I have several messages here.'

'You must be a busy man,' Huart conceded and swallowed the bile before it could rise further. Where in God's name had he met this individual before? 'However, I was calling about the – '

'Yes. About Jubilee Bay Phase A . . .'

Huart glanced at Armstrong, who was perched on the edge of his chair, leaning forward, his eyes beneath his bushy eyebrows very round and fearfully alert. All visions of future covers of the *Economist* had vanished from the mind's eye of The Fox.

The synthetic voice resumed. 'I have bad news for you, Mr Huart. Mr Orr is not available to meet with you today. In fact he's not in Hong Kong. He is at this very moment in Tokyo – giving the contract to your competitor. Better luck next time. That's if you decide to try it again. By the way, you do spell your name H-U-A-R-T, don't you?'

The buzz on the line seemed to echo off the walls. The receiver was a lead weight in Huart's hand. Where? he thought, his brain a tangled knot. Where have I met that bastard before?

<h1 style="text-align:center">7</h1>

The run on the Hongkong and Kwangtung Bank happened on a dull winter's business day in January, 1965, which was the last month of the Year of the Wood Dragon, and still a time to be watchful for fires and eruptions.

Huart and Glynn Bedrix were in the Mandarin Grill, fencing with Prince Gino Lugano Androne between mouthfuls of fresh asparagus tips and scallops *bonne femme* washed down with a Spatburgunder white. The charm of the founder of Ensurete Suisse did not hide his impatience with the pace at which his Asian venture was developing, and the business talk continued until the Swiss billionaire left for Kai Tak in a hotel limousine.

Bedrix put words to his ire as they crossed over Chater Road through the enclosed footbridge to the new Prince's Building. 'We started from scratch six years ago with nothing but Dad's personal experience and his contacts. Nobody had heard of Ensurete Suisse then, let alone wanted to buy insurance from them. Male & Son had the market in their pocket. Sir, wouldn't you agree that Lugano's expecting too much too soon?'

The youthful indignation brought a smile that could best be described as avuncular. 'Our prince has a mission in life, Glynn. He's determined to top Wagoner somewhere and he thinks "somewhere" can be Asia. Ultimately he wants Ensurete Suisse to be the world's largest underwriter. He won't rest until he's Number One . . .' Huart rubbed the knuckles of his right hand and felt the nostalgic impact of a Chicago cheekbone. 'And Wagoner is relegated to Number Two.' But as they passed the well-stocked windows of the shops of the Prince's Building arcade, both the nostalgia and the smile evaporated. 'We must be careful. The Swiss are objective businessmen and our prince is indelibly Swiss. If we don't get him what he wants soon, he'll open his own regional office and cut our exclusivity.'

'But what can we do?' the Manager, Insurance Division asked. 'Expanding the sales force would mean exceeding the expenditure budget. But – '

'But we have no choice. I believe we'll meet our target with the existing sales force, but Lugano considers that target is too conservative. It runs against my grain to increase overheads when I'm convinced we're heading into a bad patch, perhaps even a recession, but – ' He turned to Bedrix. 'Can you check what the effect will be if we increase our sales personnel by fifty per cent in Hong Kong and one third in Singapore and Taipei? Can you give me figures over the next three years by Friday?'

'You'll have them as soon as we get back to the office. I did them prior to our last monthly review meeting. They're on my file.'

'Good work, Glynn. Bring that file up to the seventeenth floor as soon as we get back. We'll go over your figures and, if we see eye to eye, I'll ask you to start recruiting immediately. And one more thing . . .'

'Sir?'

'Work hard on Lugano. Personally. Sleep with him if you have to.'

Bedrix looked back and up at the big man on the step above him as the escalator descended to Des Voeux Road, and gave an uncertain laugh.

'Joking, Glynn,' Huart chuckled, then: 'What on earth is that noise?'

'Noise? It's the jackhammers demolishing St George's Building.'

'No, not that. There's something else. Listen.'

'I hear it. It sounds like a riot. But it couldn't be. Not in Central!'

Des Voeux Road was clogged with cars. Drivers were pumping horns at the pedestrians swarming towards the sound echoing out of the concrete canyon that was Ice House Street. Huart led Bedrix through the crowd to the corner, where from his height he could see what was happening. What he did see was a wild mob outside Cumberland House, pushing to get in.

'It is a riot!' he called over his shoulder. 'And its either our building or the H and K that's the target for it. Come on!'

He led the way to the steps of Cumberland House, which were covered by pushing bodies, waving arms and flapping mouths shouting: 'Heung Gong Kwong Doong dai chaat! Bay faan ngaw cheen! Bay faan ngaw cheen!'

'They say the H and K are robbers!' Bedrix translated, though Huart had caught the gist of it. 'They're demanding their money

[333]

back. It's a bank run! Surely the H and K haven't over-speculated in the property market!'

There was no getting past the mob. There came a fresh burst of shouting, followed by a surge forward. A sharp crack split the air and a panel of the glass wall between the lobby and the banking hall splintered, then crashed down to a chorus of frightened screams and Cantonese curses.

'They're going to wreck the bank!' Huart shouted. 'We've got to stop it! We've got to get in there!' But he still could not see a way through or around the wall of bodies. 'Where's the police?'

The wail of the siren answered his entreaty in an instant. He turned to see a police van pull up on Queen's Road. A riot squad of Blue Berets sprang from it and quickly assembled in a bellicose formation. A British officer strode forward with a loud hailer. In Cantonese he made a first attempt to call the mob to order. It had no effect. He called again. The mob still paid no heed. It pressed harder into Cumberland House. Bodies were squashed against the glass wall. A second panel shattered.

'Gas masks on!'

Huart swore as the riot squad donned masks in a series of co-ordinated dark blue movements. 'It'll be tear gas next, Glynn. We'd best get away from here. Try to push your way along the wall into the lobby.' Employing their greater bulk plus the smooth-ness of the marble cladding on the wall, they shouldered and elbowed a passage and managed to reach the first elevator just as the warning tear gas canister was fired.

'It's stuck on the fourth floor!' Huart shouted through the handkerchief over his mouth and nose. The management of the H and K had their plush offices on that floor. 'Try for the stairs!' They pushed on.

The tear gas fell upon the mob. A sneezing and coughing erupted, and the first signs of panic. The mob about-turned. Those at the front became those at the rear and all pushed towards fresh air. The crush of bodies left the wall and Huart and Bedrix could see into the banking hall.

'Oh, my God!'

The mass of waving brown arms and hands clasping red and gold passbooks was like a bamboo crop in a typhoon. The booths of the tellers were obliterated by it. A wailing imploring chant could be heard through the breaks in the glass wall, punctuated by the cries of those cut by glass.

The European officer led his squad at the trot up the steps into the bank. He lifted the loud hailer and bellowed again in colloquial

Cantonese. Part of the crowd turned, their eyes transforming instantly to fearful orbs at the sight of the beefy Blue Beret *bong baan* and his specially trained men with visored helmets, perspex shields and raised truncheons that gave them the look of science fiction invaders. The curses and shouts of *Aiiieee yahhh!* died down until all that remained was a complete, contrasting silence. The mass of suddenly humble people, who seconds before had been a remorseless mob, melted back.

'*Choot hui!* Outside! Get outside and line up like good folk. *Hay yau chi lay ahh!* How dare you break this bank! I will tell this bank to keep your money to pay for it. Outside and line up! Don't run! I will tell the bank manager to serve you one at a time *Fai dee yook!* Move!'

Like children caught with their fingers in the *laisee* packets the day before the lunar new year feast, grown men and women crept sheepishly past the Blue Berets out to join the line that was being organised along the Queen's Road footpath. Wailing in weak protest, those who had led the assault on the teller booths were sternly directed to the rear.

An ambulance pulled up and dozens ran to it with cut faces, arms, legs.

The banking hall was cleared of people. A scene of overturned tables and chairs and paper forms scattered on a bed of broken glass was left in their wake. The tellers and clerks stared at the Blue Berets with faces drained of colour. Many of the girls were crying. European executives were taking charge, directing the cleaning up, preparing for the return, one-by-one, of the hundreds of depositors-turned-withdrawers. Bundles of banknotes were being carried in via the emergency exit – a passageway aptly named under the circumstances – and stacked behind each teller in piles that rose and rose until they almost touched the ceiling. The money – not all of which belonged to the H and K, the rest being on loan from the other Big Banks – quickly achieved its purpose, calming those at the head of the line on Queen's Road.

Huart went up to the Blue Beret officer. 'I recommend you check the fourth floor, Inspector. I fear there could be trouble there, too.'

'And who the hell are you?'

'John Huart. I own this building.'

The *bong baan* nodded. 'Right you are, sir. Sergeant Luk! Follow me!'

The Blue Berets disappeared up the stairs.

Huart cast his disbelieving eyes about the banking hall. 'What

[335]

sparked this off, Glynn?' And when Bedrix shrugged, he added: 'Let's go up to the fourth floor and make sure Percy Landers is alright, then ask him.'

They found the ex-credit manager, now General Manager, Corporate Finance, barricaded in his office.

'You can open up, Percy,' Huart called through the door. 'The police have got it all under control.'

'We've been a victim of mistaken identity!' Landers protested a minute later as he stood with something stronger than sherry in his hand. 'We have a delinquent account with an almost identical name: Hong Kong and Kwantung Realty. We lent to them in '62 and they built a block of flats next to the airport. Dashed loan should never have been approved – not my doing, you understand. They haven't sold hardly a flat, of course. Who in his right mind would want to live where the wheels of jetliners leave skid marks on your roof as they land, and take your washing right off the dashed line. We foreclosed after half a dozen extensions – well, perhaps two or three – and word's got out that we've gone bankrupt, not the penny-ante property company that's the cause of it. The result is what you saw . . .' He gestured with his hand in silent summation of what he considered an event too ridiculous on which to waste one more word.

'Confusion over the name of a bankrupt company brought on a run on the H and K?' Huart mused aloud. 'What's Hong Kong coming to?'

'God only knows!' Landers retorted. 'And why us instead of one of these local Chinese banks to whom the Government's been granting licences as if they were dashed lottery tickets? Ever since we – the Exchange Banks Association, that is – pegged interest rates and put an end to the war going on between them all, I've been expecting it to break. Borrowing short at rising rates, lending long at cut rates and surviving on dashed cash flow? How long could it go on? I've been waiting for the public to switch to the security of the bigger banks like us, then for the Chinese banks to try to meet the withdrawals by calling in loans. But the money isn't there because it's been lost in idiotic schemes like blocks of flats smack on the Kai Tak runway. So what happens next?' He looked at Huart, his face no longer that of a phlegmatic British banker.

'Bank runs,' Huart obliged.

'Yes, bank runs. But why this bank? Why the H and K?'

'Bank runs,' Huart repeated as if Landers had not spoken.

'Bankruptcies and unemployment in a society with no welfare. And trouble.'

8

'No jay-vee, John boy. No way. Silicon Valley says so,' Scott Overbeck repeated as he lounged bare-chested in a wicker chair on the sloping lawn of the Deep Water Bay villa leased for him by Shearman Electronics. 'And especially no jay-vee that leaves us under fifty per cent. Forget it. You're flogging a dead horse. We've just bought a site for a second factory. We're branching out, not cutting our stake. No disrespect, old buddy, but would an elephant jay-vee with a mouse?'

Huart cringed under the bombardment of clichés and personal idioms which habitually embellished the Californian's diction, but managed a smile.

Overbeck misread it as a sign of consensus. 'Stuff business!' he decreed with a wave of his hand. 'It's Saturday afternoon. The week's over. The sun's great. Take your shirt off and get a tan. Have another beer!'

'Thanks, Scott. I've time for just one more.' Glynn Bedrix's Cathay Pacific flight was due to land in an hour and Huart wanted to hear the insurance manager's report on the expanded Singapore office first-hand. He looked down at the Saturday afternoon golfers teeing off from the clubhouse below. Cars lined Island Road; they belonged to the Caucasian families sunbaking on the white sand of Deep Water Bay and bathing in its gentle surf. The Mid Autumn Festival was past, and the Chinese had stopped swimming in the ocean, believing its temperature to have fallen to an unhealthy degree. 'Land remains a costly item,' he pointed out. 'It's off the peak, and will fall further. Why don't you wait a while?'

'A decision taken and not implemented is no decision at all, John boy.'

'You must be very confident of recovering your investment.'

Overbeck drained his Budweiser. 'So long as Peking keeps on its side of the border, we'll be A-okay – all of us, including China. Peking benefits from Hong Kong as it is. Land values won't fall much. The problems with these tin pot family-owned banks are minor. Land'll soon start going up again and it'll keep on going.

China'll provide the foundation for it. In a few years our investment in the second factory will've proved a bargain. Then why not a third factory – and a fourth?'

The Californian heaved his 250 pounds of muscle from the chair, jogged over the expanse of lawn and disappeared into the house. He re-emerged with a half-dozen cans of beer and picked up his discourse where he had left off. Huart paid attention. It was said that Overbeck hobnobbed with men who held apocryphal business credentials consistent with inhabitants of the guarded building in Garden Road behind the American Consulate.

'Since the "Great Leap Forward", Mao has listened to Chou En-lai. The national economy has recovered to '58 levels under the management of Chou's protégés: Liu Shao-chi and his deputy, Teng Hsiao-ping, who lead the "New Right" movement. Capitalism is starting in Communist China, I kid you not. The wheel's almost come full circle. Chou wants a break in the wall China put up between itself and the West during the Korean War. We should see signs of it soon.' He paused to punch holes in the first can. 'I'll make a prediction, John boy. It'll rock you to your socks. Before this decade ends there'll be a Shearman factory in Shanghai – a jay-vee with the Communists – with me in charge. Now that's a jay-vee.' He pointed the can at Huart in emphasis, then drained it. 'Now you know my personal ambition. Some ambition, eh? I'll go down in history.'

'It's certainly a grand aim, Scott,' Huart agreed, wondering which partner Overbeck would consider the elephant and which the mouse. 'But how do you know this "New Right" isn't just a passing phase? The policy they promote cuts across Mao's most basic anti-capitalist ground rules.'

Overbeck nodded. 'It sure does. But Mao's on his way out. Liu Shao-chi's taking over – with Chou on the sidelines, watching and waiting like the old campaigner he is. John boy, last week at a national sports rally, Peking Stadium was wallpapered with pictures of Liu side by side with Mao and – goddamn significant this – of exactly equal size. And that's not all. October 1st – anniversary of the People's Republic – pictures of both were paraded outside the Great Hall of the People and all over Tien-anmen Square. They're even starting to call him "Chairman Liu". He'll be top dog in Peking very soon, John boy. I kid you not.'

'What advantage does Shearman see in setting up manufacture in China?'

The Californian grinned, proud of his inside knowledge and happy to let it out in measured doses. The big Brit was a nice guy, but out of touch. With funny business concepts, too. A jay-vee with Shearman? Who would credit it? Would a shark jay-vee with a sprat? He opened another can and replied: 'Cheap labour. Cheap raw materials. Hong Kong labour gets more expensive all the time. Nothing's indigenous – raw materials have to be shipped in. We're okay for five to ten years, then the place'll price itself out of the low-middle end of the consumer product market. Then places like Singapore, Taiwan – even Korea – will be churning out the basic products. And then comes China! From Shanghai we could service the Asian market. To start with, the Chinese'll make us export the end-products to realise our profit. And once we've proved the jay-vee works, there comes for Shearman the real prize. The Chinese domestic market! Nearly a billion consumers! Think of it, John boy.'

Huart had to protest. 'But, Scott, there's no money at grass roots level in China to produce a domestic market for electronic consumables – '

Overbeck laughed richly, as if he held the key to it all. 'Just you wait for China to start exporting its oil, John boy. Just you wait till then. Oil will be the gold of the new age. You wait and see. I kid you not.'

Ah Lam, Huart's newly recruited chauffeur, was off duty Saturday afternoons, so he drove the Wolseley himself through Wongneichong Gap back to Central District. His brain was fiercely active. Was Overbeck right? Was China changing as he had described? Could trade links, for which Andrew had given up so much to be first in line, be re-established? Would western manufacturers be admitted back to the Middle Kingdom? Would trading companies follow? Could Cumberland China regain its birthright?

Could the second pledge be fulfilled?

There was already so much to do in Hong Kong, and the Asian branch offices had to be expanded. Even so, Huart knew that if the hint of an opportunity presented itself from the north, he would snatch at it with both hands. He would take it, despite the limitations of his still developing management team headed by only three executive directors.

This took his thoughts off on a tangent. The board had to be expanded, but none of the managers was ready to join it. It would take two or three more years at least. And then what? Who was there to succeed him? Something very deep down told him none of the existing managers would ever qualify. He had to find Elizabeth Huart again and then . . .

And then what? Not until he had led the company back to China, not until there was again an office in Shanghai, would his task be done. He could never pass on his personal pledges to a successor, certainly not one whose blood was not Huart. The pledges given to Andrew in his last hour had been on behalf of the family. It behoved the family to fulfil them.

By the time the Wolseley slipped down Garden Road and around the curved frontage of the Hilton into Queen's Road, Central, and Huart saw Cumberland House top the skyline, he had made a decision. It had been galvanised by the dynamic information provided by Scott Overbeck. He would add a 'China Expert', a sinologist, to his personal staff. It was a decision that was to prove significant.

9

'Waaall, suck mah tooool,' crooned the negro in the psychedelic shirt as he nodded his head in admiration. 'So you's a real live millionaire man? So what you doin' hangin' out in this here place?'

Lennie the Fifth took up his double pink gin. He lovingly caressed the glass then downed it, attacking the thirst that had accumulated during the day. It was well into the night and he was, to use his favourite new expression, 'feeling no pain'. 'Otis, I come here to drink. I'm a professional drinker. The best drinking partner for a professional drinker is a perfect stranger. Tomorrow morning you'll be on that 707 back to Saigon and we'll never meet again. That makes you a perfect stranger.'

'Heyyy, Lennie – nobody's perfect, man.'

They looked to the door as two of Otis's white contemporaries in floral shirts and close-cropped haircuts entered the bar, ran their eyes over the girls at the tables, liked what they saw and called for beers in voices loud with derring-do. Inside a minute, two girls had joined them and two glasses of tea, each costing ten dollars, had been served up.

The Miami Bar in Cameron Road was but one of Cosgrove's 'watering holes' across the harbour in Tsimshatsui, distant from his Central District stamping ground and his bachelor apartment on the Peak. For hours he had been sitting at the bar amidst the raucous GIs half his age, incongruous in sports jacket and red bowtie, chain smoking Havanas, downing double pink gins one after the other and revelling in the sensation it produced of youth rekindled. And loving the flesh market that animated about him.

'But you are perfect, Otis,' Cosgrove added as an afterthought. 'You're a perfect idiot to be going back tomorrow and presenting your substantial backside for little yellow men to shoot full of holes.'

Otis's humour evaporated. 'They's not yellow, man – they's little brown slope-headed mother-fuckers. But they got no chance to shoot this here ass, 'cos it sits in a goddamn a.p.c. with armour plate all round it. You must think I'm as stupid as you look, man.' Snapping his fingers to the Beach Boys, he sauntered to the jukebox and began stabbing buttons.

Feeling a presence at his left elbow, Cosgrove looked down into a pair of cash-register eyes. 'Good evening, Mama-san. Care for a drink?'

She thumbed a melon seed between her teeth and chewed noisily. 'You buy one my girls drink first. That make me more happy. We got new girl start t'night. Nice girl. Sexy girl. *Meen Foot Hau Jaak* like her for sure.' She leaned closer and whispered: 'She cherry girl, too.'

He guffawed. 'A real live cherry girl in this ignoble establishment? Never happen. Never bloody happen!'

Her face transformed into a mask of theatrical insult. 'You be nice! I no bullshit. She cherry girl for sure. Maybe she like you. Maybe she let you take it. But you gotta buy her drink first.'

He feigned interest. 'Show me the cherry girl. Which one is she?'

The mama-san indicated a bargirl in a leather dress which, if it was an inch shorter, could have doubled as a belt. She was playing thirteen card poker with two of her sorority, her long-nailed fingers flicking the cards across the table with a dexterity born of regular practice. Cosgrove gave a sly smile and said: 'Her name's Mabel, right?'

'That right. How you know?'

'She was working in Gaslight last week. I bought her out Wednesday night and screwed her. Her cherry's grown back? Clever. But it doesn't look as if her tits've grown with it.'

'*Choi!*' She cuffed him on the shoulder in protest. Then, deciding he was not worth further effort, she walked off with her nose in the air.

Cosgrove called for his next drink as a slickly attired Chinese came in from Cameron Road. The whole place stiffened. This was the owner of the Miami Bar, and many many others. His eyes quickly summed up the scene, then rested on Cosgrove. 'Hullo, Lennie. You lookin' good t'night.'

'Good evening, Errol.' Cosgrove lifted his glass in salute. 'Business is booming again tonight. Half the girls've been bought out already, as you can see. I trust all your other establishments are doing as well. Your bank manager must be pleased. Want to sell me some shares?'

Errol Tu hated Hong Kong *gwailos*. But he just managed to tolerate the ones who chose to transfer cash from their wallets to his. Especially this one. 'Can't complain, Lennie. But not doin' good as you.'

'Haven't seen you here for a while. New bar? Or new mistress?'

'I been busy Macau. Make gamble legal there. Our casino open soon. I give you free ticket. Maybe not – too dang'rous for us. You so lucky. You be Lucky Pig for sure. Okay, Lennie, see you later.' He disappeared through a beaded curtain into the office at the rear of the bar.

By midnight Cosgrove's belly was tight with gin and his immediate desire had turned unequivocally carnal. He turned on his stool and assessed the remaining bargirls one by one, and rejected them all. The best, including Mabel, had been 'bought out' and were already, no doubt, supine on hotel or guest house beds beneath their ardent, thrusting hirers.

Flicking a tip to the bartender, he picked his way to the door. Along Cameron Road the neon signs beckoned him: 'Joe's Place', 'King's Lodge', 'Maydo Bar', 'Caron Night Club and Bar', 'Cherry Bar'. The girls called to him from the doorways: all young, all pretty, all available.

'Jesus H. Christ, what a town!' Lennie the Fifth ejaculated as he made a beeline for a halter top that hinted at something reasonable beneath.

10

The first of the Fire Horse's 383 days dawned on January 21st, 1966.

On the salient known as Jardine's Lookout, the grey Saturday morning was lanced with spitting drizzle. Tu Chien looked out at it whilst he spooned his swallow's nest soup. It was a good sign. Every lunar new year was timed to coincide with a spell of cold, wet weather that would otherwise be considered inhospitable. A wet start meant a money year. If the sages got it wrong and the first day was dry, Tu Chien would take heed and prescribe caution in his business deals to come.

The Wood Snake had swelled the coffers of Great Horse Enterprises from trade in gold and diamonds and rent from the Tu tenements crowding North Point, Quarry Bay and Shaukeiwan. The war in Vietnam had made Wai-tsun's 'entertainment' empire the star performer, and there was now legalised gambling in Macau. In addition, the Daima Bank and Great Horse Textiles, the family's respectable exterior, were themselves profitable.

It was Tu Chien's birthday, the end of his sixth decade on earth. In the Chinese order of things, completion of the cycle of sixty years was an event of significance. Tonight, a splendiferous banquet of twenty-four courses, comprising a cornucopia of speciality Shanghai dishes, would celebrate the arrival at the grand age of the Tu family patriarch. It was a day for rejoicing, a day on which to be proud. But deep down Tu Chien stored a trepidation, a submerged fear that today would be proved just or fallacious. It was all to do with his time of birth: during the Hour of the Rat on the very first day of the Year of the Fire Horse.

The legend decreed that whatever personal wealth, power or acclaim he might achieve, it risked total destruction by his own hand. It decreed also that the ruination of his family would follow. He knew the legend well. He knew, too, that he could do nothing to prevent it coming to pass, should it indeed be his destiny. He had lived his life in concert with a time bomb, not knowing whether it was alive or dead. And if it was alive, it would be set to explode in the Year of the Fire Horse. For Tu Chien, this year was most likely to prove the legend to be ill-fated.

He had tempted that fate once. And he still suffered for it.

He looked into the pigeon-blood red eyes of the Ch'in Dynasty horse on his desk. They burnt like the fire that had destroyed the original two centuries before. Were they mocking him because of his fate? Or were they transmitting to him the immortality they were meant to represent?

The office-study was quiet. Great Horse Villa was cocooned in expectant silence, shrouded by the rain clouds. It was as if the world about Tu Chien was looking over his shoulder, waiting with him for the verdict.

'*Aiii yahh!*' he breathed into the empty soup bowl. 'It is said that patience is a virtue – but virtue can be an unprofitable investment.'

His hip was paining him. His head was aching. Where was Number One Wife? How long did it take to collect the rice papers bearing the predictions of the ninety-nine sticks from the temple of the Ten Thousand Buddhas at Shatin? He had allowed her the new Rolls-Royce Silver Shadow for the journey. It was not as comfortable as the old Silver Wraith that she said she preferred, but it was faster. At three a.m., when she had left, the roads in Kowloon would have been empty. She should have been first in line at the temple. What was keeping her? It had to be a bad sign.

'*Aiii yahh!*' he repeated as he sipped the *bo lay* tea.

His thoughts switched briefly to his four *tsip* concubines still abed. He had given little time to them recently. Any thought of adding young blood to their ranks had remained stillborn. Was he aging so fast?

He stroked the long hairs that grew from his jaw, opened the drawer and saw it was almost 7:45. He took up the jar of 'Tiger Balm' and massaged the mentholated ointment into his temples with his fingertips. Gradually his head cleared and his unworthy impatience dissolved. He reached for the teapot and was rewarded by a noise at the door. '*Yap lay!* Come!'

Number One Wife entered, her head of silver hair slightly bowed. His eyes fell to the fingers that clutched the rolled yellow rice papers bearing the cryptic revelations for his year to come. Would they be propitious? Hope gave way to anxiety. He quelled it. By the Lord Buddha, he had given the woman enough red notes to influence a hundred parasite priests! His hope returned. But the fear accompanied it.

'Come, *Tai-tai*,' he summoned with an exaggerated austerity that was a lid on his emotions and his affection for this woman who had been his for forty years. 'Sit there.' He indicated the most comfortable chair.

'Thank you, Lord.' She shuffled slowly to it, her limbs stiff with the cold. 'My sorrow for being late. There were so many at the temple. All born in the Year of the Horse are fearful. There were many expectant mothers, and all were weeping. There will be many abortions this year.'

He nodded slowly. It was to be expected. His heart beat loudly in his breast. 'Now, tell me, *Tai-tai*,' he prompted when she was seated. 'What was the number of the first stick – your Lord's stick?'

'My sorrow – your number was indecisive, Lord,' she breathed tremulously as she unfolded the first rice paper and passed it across the desk.

He read the row of ideograms brush-stroked with the vermilion pigment once used by the emperors of China, his expression wooden. It told him that he must take care of his health. It was the same each year. But this time there was no hint of personal joy outside that earnt by hard work. The rice paper confirmed it: he was indeed aging too quickly. The joys of the body were but a memory, together with his youth now long gone. 'Take care of myself, it says, *Tai-tai*. I do not need a priest to instruct me so. But you did pay him well to pray for me, ah?'

'I gave him all the money I had, Lord. He will pray for you every day.'

'Good. And what has the year in store for our family?'

She gave him the second rice paper. 'The priest said it is a good number, Lord. My sorrow – not wonderful like last year, but good.'

The ideograms told him the family would be protected. But, again, not as well as last year. Precautions must be taken. He looked up. He held his breath. 'The last stick? The one for Great Horse Enterprises?'

'Here, Lord. Read it carefully. My sorrow – I do not understand it.'

Alarm paid him a visit as he took the last rice paper. Through narrowed lids he read each ideogram. His heart skipped a beat. Dread dropped into his gut like a lead weight. His great fear was proved valid! The bomb was live! He almost groaned aloud, then something cut it off. For in the reaction of reading the message again, he had seen something different. If he took an alternative meaning for the third ideogram, the portent of the message altered completely. It was no longer bad. It became good! Good, that is, for Great Horse Enterprises. But still bad, calamitous in fact, for others. The message told of an impending political disaster that would be misread by all. But anyone who interpreted it correctly would reap an untold fortune. In the Year of the Fire Horse, the rice paper message decreed, nothing should be accepted at face value.

'*Ho*,' he breathed. '*Tsui ho!*'

Number One Wife released a silent sigh of relief. 'As I said, Lord, I do not understand the message, but then I am quite stupid. I am overjoyed that my Lord can read it and that it pleases him. My sorrow – perhaps it has something to do with the strange phenomenon in the weather?'

'Weather, *Tai-tai?*' he was puzzled, intrigued. Number One Wife was old, but never a fool. 'Of what phenomenon do you speak?'

She leaned forward, her face and bearing humble. 'Around our house the clouds are low, and past the window the soft rain falls, Lord . . .'

'Yes, I can see that, woman. It is a good omen. But what . . ?'

'But down below – in the place where the foreigners work in their tall buildings and where all the banks are – it does not rain. The sun has risen early and shines brightly. My sorrow – it is a phenomenon, no?'

His eyes flamed. 'It is indeed, *Tai-tai!* The omen confirms the prediction for Great Horse Enterprises! You are clever to recognise it and mention it to me. It will influence my decisions this year.'

Number One Wife bowed, brimming with pride.

He sipped his tea and gloried in the sensation as his body relaxed. The year would be bad. There would be *mah faan*. Lots of it. But not for him and not for his family, provided he looked for the truth behind the misleading events that were foretold. Most importantly, his destiny as a Fire Horse was not to be ill-fated. He had been reprieved from the disaster that was beyond his control. And, compared to the risks of this year, those to come offered comparative benevolence. His longevity and the family's continued good fortune were virtually assured.

And what of the giant? Surely disaster was for him. Though pleasure was to be denied Tu Chien's flesh, was that most ultimate long-awaited joy of mind and soul to be granted him in the Year of the Fire Horse?

At seven a.m. on Chinese New Year's Day, or any other day, John Huart sat down eighteen storeys above Central District to a breakfast of bacon and eggs. The difference today was that he had to prepare the meal himself. Both servants were in China. Their thirteenth month salary packet tucked in their *saamfoo*, Ah Keung and the cook, Ah Kai, had boarded the train for Lo Wu the night before. Now they would be eating congee in Canton with their estranged families, and clutching the Re-entry Permits that ensured their passage back through the border checkpoint at the end of the festive period. Huart had come to accept their absence as an annual penance which renewed his appreciation of their services.

He put down yesterday's *Hong Kong and Oriental Daily* – local newspaper publishers liken the first two days of the lunar year to Christmas Day and Good Friday, and there are no editions – and took up Virginia's last letter. He re-read her account of the growing international success of her cosmetics operation under the brand name 'Virginia May A'dor', an adaptation from her maiden name, Adair, which she had resumed after her divorce. She planned to visit in April and offer the Imports Division an exclusive distributorship. Huart had smiled. Cosgrove's marketing flair and a range of women's cosmetics from the top New York shelf had to be a profitable combination. Would business usurp romance in his relationship with Virginia? Never. They would make time for both, come April.

As usual, he had allocated himself a work quota for the four-day holiday break. It was a truism that the staff knew he was on holiday when he came down to the seventeenth floor in a sports shirt. Now into the final quarter of financial year 1965–66, Cumberland China was heading yet again for a record profit. Concurrently, Huart's own wealth had grown to the point where, prompted by news that the taxation level was to be increased to fifteen per cent on April 1st, he had considered it necessary to commission a personal accountant cum taxation consultant.

The penthouse was lit by the sunburst. Should he accept Scott Overbeck's invitation to spend the day on his junk, after all? Huart asked himself. The sunshine was inviting, even if the air would be chilly. And a day with the Overbecks would be as much work as relaxation. He could start his review of the third-quarterly results tomorrow and still finish before Tuesday night. Any guilt thus assuaged, he went to the telephone.

Huart could not see it, but on Jardine's Lookout it was raining. Even if he had been aware of the anomaly in the weather, it would have meant as little to him as being informed of the legend of the Fire Horse. 'What a wonderful Chinese New Year's Day,' he proclaimed aloud as he dialled the Deep Water Bay number. 'It has to be a good omen for the year ahead.'

11

'You are quite beyond belief.' The approbation was rich in Huart's eyes as well as his voice as he gazed upon the face that regularly graced the covers of *Cosmopolitan*, *Vogue* and *Businesswoman*. 'Being merely a great beauty was not good enough for you, you had to go out and become a celebrity as well. Why on earth didn't I marry you?'

'Yes, why didn't you? It would have saved me from all this . . .' Virginia proffered the fussing waiter with her smile. ' . . . all this attention.'

'You don't like attention?'

'I love it.' She chuckled deep in her throat and Huart thought the sound was like a brook bubbling. 'What a lovely idea it was to come all the way out here for lunch. Darling, could I have some more wine, please.'

He poured the Pouilly-Fuisse. 'Virginia, I would've stifled you if we'd married. The real you would have been buried and the world would have been deprived of your contribution to fashion, and to beauty.'

'What a chauvinist thing to say. But maybe I would've liked you stifling me every night.' She appraised his rock-like features, skin still firm though crossed by wrinkles in concession to age, hair silvering at the temples. 'Do you still make love without a hair falling out of place?'

'I was unaware I did, and that it irked. But you'll find out later.' He gave the smile that she loved. 'Really – I would've frustrated you. One dominating businessman for a husband should be enough for one lifetime.'

Virginia glanced around the clubhouse restaurant, and reverted to business. 'So it's agreed that Cumberland China takes on exclusive distribution of "Virginia May A'dor" cosmetics? Do you really think you can fit "Sensuous *Septembre* – the Edible Lipstick", into your portfolio of smart shirts, insurance policies and big ugly power stations?'

This time Huart's smile was professional. 'Yes to all that. You'll like Lennie's plans to cater to Hong Kong's *beau monde* as well as its *bon vivant*.' His expression sobered. 'But power stations are a sore point. We're out and the Japs are in. Thanks to the spread of our operations, the worst it's done has been to make quite a dent in our growth curve.'

'You talk as if you're out permanently.'

'There's no reason for optimism. The client won't even talk to us. If I didn't know that Kingston Orr had inherited one of the largest fortunes in Asia, I'd swear there was monkey business between him and Matamoto. Perhaps it's that general manager of his. I'm getting old fast. I know I've met that man before, yet try as I might I can't remember where. It was before the war, I'm sure of that. It must have been in Shanghai . . .'

'Enough of business, you poor old English gentleman. Let's walk. I'm too sore to ride any more. You'd better not be too sore to ride me tonight.'

'Virginia!' Huart almost gagged on his coffee. 'Keep your voice down. The waiter will hear you. Jockey Club members have been black-balled for less. Only horses are permitted to talk sex at Beas River, you know.'

'You British are so stuffy. I'd turn it into Birds 'n' Beas River.'

They strolled the rustic New Territories retreat, talked until evening, then rode in Huart's new Rover to the Carlton Hotel on Tai Po Road. They dined on the balcony and watched Hong Kong Island light up across the harbour and the Peak fade into the night sky. Only the roar of the airliners coming in to land at Kai Tak broke into their easy, endless chat.

They left the Carlton at 9:40. 'Drive to the Peninsula Hotel, please, Ah Lam,' Huart instructed his chauffeur. The Rover slid through Kowloon to Nathan Road past the concrete housing blocks of Mongkok and the markets and shops of Yaumatei. Huart and Virginia held hands like adolescents. The airconditioner mixed her perfume with the scent of new upholstery and varnished woodwork. Tsimshatsui's neon lit the sky ahead.

They were into the crowd outside the Princess Theatre before Ah Lam knew it. '*Ai yahh*,' he breathed as he slowed the Rover to a crawl, then to a complete stop. He looked out in trepidation at the young men eyeing the Rover's paintwork. '*Fei tsai*.' Teddy boys. Then he read the ideograms on the banners they were holding and his heart beat faster.

'Something's up,' Huart said quietly. 'What do the banners say, Ah Lam?'

'Star F . . . Ferry give bad service. Should not be allow' rise fares.'

'It must be quite a fare increase to make Chinese demonstrate,' Virginia suggested. 'They're always so placid.'

'Five cents,' Huart told her. 'It's the Ferry's first fare rise in fifteen years. Someone's stirring things up. I don't like it. Some of these chaps look nasty. We'd best get out of here. Ah Lam, try to push on. Keep on that taxi's tail. The crowd should thin out past the theatre.'

A Mercedes cab in front was inching forward, sounding its horn. A Chinese couple was in its rear, looking fearfully about. Ah Lam divided his attention between keeping the Rover on its bumper and watching the angry faces and the raised fists. Then he saw a youth let go a *kung fu* kick at the rear door of the cab and he choked down on a squeal of fright.

Huart was puzzled to see the woman's face turn into a mask of pain. The kick could not have hurt her. 'Ah Lam, lock the doors,' he instructed as he punched the rear catches. After several minutes the crowd parted and the cab broke away. It accelerated south on Nathan Road, the Rover right on its tail. On the corner ahead they could see the square outline of the Peninsula and the lights of Hong Kong Island across the harbour. Ah Lam relaxed the muscles that had been clamped around his bladder.

'I'm glad we're out of that,' Virginia breathed.

The second crowd was outside Chungking Mansions. The place was a maze of guest houses cum brothels, shops and curry restaurants. A gathering at its entrance was normal, it being the Greenwich Village of Kowloon, but this was no normal congregation. Ah Lam braked behind the cab with reborn anxiety and blasted his horn in concert. Cantonese insults were thrown back. Fists were shaken. It registered with Huart that the distress of the couple in the rear of the cab was disproportionate to the threat the youthful belligerence was posing.

Then there came an awesome sound. It began as a dull roar. Then it grew. It was as if an angry football crowd was on the march. And coming their way. Huart recalled the run on the H and K six months before. But this was more ominous. He peered between the bodies. 'Just look at that . . !'

A phalanx of chanting, banner waving youths were rounding the Peninsula Hotel. It marched north and mixed with the crowd outside Chungking Mansions, swelling it to over a thousand. The shouting, chanting, swearing, and the stamping of feet combined into a lusty roar. In an instant the crowd had turned into a mob and the mob pressed in on the trapped cars – objects of foreign affluence – hurling jeers and insults. The cab was occupied by common folk of common blood, but was not spared. Tyres were kicked. Fists hammered on roofs, bonnets, boots, against windows.

The air inside the Rover had gone cold. Huart saw the back of Ah Lam's neck had turned white and his knuckles bulged as he gripped the wheel. Virginia looked out at the faces and grasped the big hand on her knee. Huart's adrenalin was flowing. 'We've got to get out of here!'

Virginia looked at him. 'A masterly observation, John, darling.'

The first brick fell. It bounced from the roof of the cab into the mob. Another followed. A bottle smashed on the Rover's bonnet and glass fragments splattered into the faces around it. Ah Lam released a yelp.

'Those things are coming from above!' Huart hissed.

It was true. Bricks, bottles, cans, balloons full of water were raining down indiscriminately from the roof of Chungking Mansions. The mob cried out in confusion, threw their arms across their faces and ducked for cover. Then, shrieking in pain and insult, it set upon the two cars. The Rover began to rock. It was being pushed from both sides. Huart and Virginia were thrown into each other. Ah Lam gripped the wheel for dear life. Through the front windscreen they could see the taxi receiving the same treatment. Unrestrained terror filled the faces of the couple. The woman was suddenly convulsed with pain and fell back out of sight.

'She's badly hurt . . !' Huart cried helplessly.

More bricks fell. The cab's windscreen shattered. An iron bar was rammed through the side window, taking the driver on the temple. Virginia gasped as she saw him disappear. Ah Lam sobbed and shook. It was his turn next. He lost the fight with his bladder muscles and his lap filled.

'God! God! God!' Huart's brain searched frantically for a way out. With the cab immobilised, their escape was completely blocked.

The roof of a double-decker bus appeared on the other carriageway. A section of the mob scaled the dividing fence and set about it with iron bars and bricks, smashing in its windows one by one. Huart watched it all through the gaps that had appeared in the human wall. And saw a way out. He leaned close to his chauffeur's ear. 'Ah Lam! Do you hear me?'

'Yes . . . Master.' It was weak, but there.

Speaking steadily, Huart said: 'I'm going to move that taxi. When you see me drive on, follow closely – just like before. Understand, Ah Lam?'

Ah Lam knew it was the last he would ever see of his master, but nodded.

Huart turned to Virginia. 'Lock the door behind me. Keep talking to Ah Lam. Keep him calm. When we get through this lot go straight to the Pen and wait for me there. I'm going to drive the taxi to Kowloon Hospital. The driver must be badly hurt and the woman looks in trouble, too.'

'John, be careful.' She squeezed his arm, then leaned forward. 'We'll be fine, Ah Lam. Master will get us out of here. We'll be fine.'

Ah Lam had never heard such a lie. The truth was they were all going to be killed! But why him? He never used the Star Ferry. Only to visit his wife's parents in Tokwawan and his brother in Kwun Tong and . . . *Gau meng ah!* Save Life! Where were the useless corruptible police?

A brace of bottles smashed on the Rover's roof, showering broken glass. The hammering and pushing ceased as hands pulled back to protect faces.

'Now!' Huart wrenched open the door, threw himself out and slammed it behind him for Virginia to snap the lock. He turned, his arms and fists raised like a boxer, to find that his weight and momentum had cleared a path. He forged through it and the cries of: '*Gwailo! Saat say koei!*' Kill the foreign devil! He made the cab as the fists found his back.

Its engine was still running. The driver was sprawled across the front seat, groaning, blood streaming from a head wound. Glass was all over the inside of the cab like Christmas tinsel. The woman in the rear was on her back, legs splayed, screaming in pain. Her partner lay over her, frozen with fear, eyes pressed shut. And comprehension hit Huart like a bayonet in the gut. The woman was in labour.

'*Saat say gwailo aaaah!*'

The mob surged at Huart. A bamboo pole smacked him squarely between the shoulder blades. A bottle from above just missed him and smashed at his feet. Punches buffeted him all over. Something crashed into his head and coloured lights exploded before his eyes. He bellowed like a wounded bull, swung his right fist in an arc to his rear and felt his forearm impact something that caved in with a sweet crunch. Bodies fell about as he got the door unlocked and tore it open. He pushed the driver to the passenger's side and drew his long legs under the wheel. His knee hit the dashboard and he winced. He hauled the door shut and locked it as a youth dived at him through the window. A sharp rock landed flush on his cheek and he felt his flesh gash. But there was no stopping him now.

Thank God I've driven a Mercedes before! he cried to himself as he rammed the shift into first, planted his palm on the horn and his foot on the accelerator. The cab lurched forward and the grasping hands tore half his shirt from his body. Brake-accelerator-brake-accelerator-brake. The mob read the raw resolution on his face. It hesitated. The wall cracked and he drove the cab at it. He glanced in the mirror to see the Rover right on his tail. The woman in the rear screamed and threw her torso into an arch. The man released a babble of rambling Cantonese. Huart smelt the sweat, the blood, the terror. It spurred him on.

A riot had taken Nathan Road. The police pagoda was aflame. So was the bus. In Peking Road cars were being overturned. The plate glass window of Shui Hing Department Store disintegrated as a rubbish bin was heaved into it. Figures leapt into the opening. Looting started. Furnishings were set afire. Smoke poured into the road. Youths ran about in a mad-crazy frenzy, smashing, kicking, screaming. The noise was deafening.

Huart's eyes smarted from the smoke. His chest heaved. Four youths timed his next braking and flung themselves on the cab. He accelerated hard. Two fell off but the others hung on. One threw himself across the shattered windscreen and Huart braked in reflex. In an instant the mob had the cab in its hands. It began to rock to a rhythmic chanting, bouncing higher and higher. Yelling in blind desperate rage, Huart rolled from one side to the other. He punched through the side window and a youth reeled backwards with a broken jaw, but there was another instantly in his place. The cab was on the verge of tipping over. One more push would do it. Then Huart smelled the tear gas.

So did his assailants. They hesitated for a vital half-second and missed the timing of what would have been the final bounce. The cab rocked back onto its four wheels and Huart planted his foot. With a screech of tyres it lurched forward, its momentum pinning the two youths to the bonnet. There was a crunch and the wheel jerked in Huart's hand. I've done someone in, he told himself. He slammed on the brake and the two youths flew from the bonnet. The cab was rammed from the rear and Huart glanced in the mirror and shouted in approval. It was Ah Lam and the Rover.

To his front, the Blue Berets were charging at him in a wall of perspex shields, lobbing tear gas canisters that hit the bitumen and rolled about giving out white clouds. The seething mob stilled, then scattered at the run. The Blue Berets charged on through the gas and the smoke, past the burning pagoda. The wall of shields parted and Huart took off through the gap with a screech of rubber. He threw the cab left at the carpark on the Salisbury Road corner and sped past Signal Hill into Chatham Road. In the mirror he saw the Rover U-turn into the Peninsula and released his breath. At least Virginia was safe. Now for this lot.

The woman pitched into a renting scream. The man had come about and was doing his best to pacify her, warbling in Cantonese. The slumped driver gave forth a protracted groan. A symphony of suffering filled the cab as Huart scorched over Jordan Road into Nairn Road, changed down at the Argyle Street intersection and swung into Waterloo Road. The casualty entrance of Kowloon Hospital was in front of him and he went straight for it, his arrival announced by the blasting horns and screeching tyres of the traffic across whose path he had scythed.

The eyes of the duty staff expanded into disbelieving orbs at the sight of a battered six foot five Englishman in a torn and bloodied shirt leaping from behind the wheel of a Mercedes cab. They went progressively larger as they watched him haul the unconscious driver from the other side, carry him up the steps, lower him onto a bench, gesticulate that he was now their charge, and shout: 'Who speaks English around here?'

'I do, sir!' A male orderly ran forward.

'A woman's giving birth in the taxi outside. Direct me to Maternity!'

The back seat was the scene of another prolonged contraction. The orderly climbed in and called: 'Straight ahead, sir, then turn right.'

'Hang on!' Huart floored the accelerator, tore past a sign specifying a ten mile an hour speed limit, cornered, and slammed to a halt outside the first building. He scooped up the woman in his arms, took the stairs three at a time and barged through a double door. The husband followed, his eyes fixed on the giant foreign devil as if somehow he was *Kwan Yin* incarnate, his brain telling him that his miserable *fung shui* had changed at last and surely he must this time be blessed with a son.

The orderly called out. Two nurses came running. Huart saw a mobile stretcher against a wall and laid the woman on it as another contraction took her. She screamed long, penetratingly into the air. Blood flowed over the white sheet. Huart's forearms and front ran red with it. 'Come on! Get your act together!' He shouted at everybody and everything.

'That's enough of that!' drilled an authoritative voice and he turned to see an English sister striding towards him. He smiled wearily and stepped aside. She glared at him as if he had turned up for dinner in the nude and swung on the nurses. 'Call Doctor Brennan at once!' Then it was the orderly's turn. 'Don't just stand there like a stale bottle, young man! Help nurse push the patient to the delivery room! Move!'

'But, I don't belong here, sis – '

'Move!'

The woman arched into a terminal contraction and the orderly

[354]

moved. When the stretcher had disappeared down the corridor, Huart found the washroom, bathed his cut cheek with warm water and pressed a paper towel to it. Then he found a telephone and rang Virginia at the Peninsula.

She let him finish, then summed it all up with: 'Well done, Clark Kent.'

He spend the next hour in the waiting room with a chain-smoking father-to-be, politely declining the pack of Viceroys that was proffered every few minutes. The man wore basic tradesman's garb and open-toed sandals. Huart had little doubt the new child would be one of several.

As if he had read his thoughts, the man held up four fingers. '*Say gaw lui.*' Huart recognised the Cantonese for 'female'. '*Ngaw hay mong nee gaw choot sai hai tsai!*' he went on, passionately to express his hope for a long-awaited son.

Before he could stop it, Huart's memory had rewound two dozen years to strip the covering off a long lost pain. Life could be so unequal: here was a father decrying his affliction of four live daughters! He recalled his last time in this hospital, twelve years ago. The coincidence registered: twelve years between trag-edies. Twelve since his cousin's death; twenty-four since the mass-acre of his family. Was it thirty-six since his mother . . .? Yes – 1930. And twelve years before that his father had died at Amiens. Coincidence indeed. Life was bizarre as well as unequal.

Then what would befall him this year? he wondered wearily. When he had faced disaster in the early fifties, he had believed he was living under a curse. Since then he had not the time nor the cause to think further on it. The last twelve years, on the whole, had been very good to him.

At midnight a nurse appeared. She spoke in Cantonese and the man's face lit up like an electric light. Huart went to him and pumped his hand. The new father of a first son looked up and said over and over: '*Daw jeh! Daw jeh! Daw jeh, Seen-saang! Cheng mun . . . Cheng mun nay-ge meng?*'

Huart cocked an eyebrow at the nurse. 'Mr Lee wants to know your name.'

'Huart. My name is Huart. My first name is John.'

The nurse translated. 'Mr Lee will name his son Yeok-hon. It is the equivalent of John. You are the baby's godfather – if you accept.'

'Accept? Of course I accept.'

'Then congratulations, Mr Huart. It is a real honour for a . . .'

'*Gwailo?*'

[355]

She gave a tight smile. 'If I were you, I'd have that cut treated. They will do it over at Casualty. But hurry. Ambulances are bringing in a lot of injured people. It seems there's some trouble in Nathan Road.'

'Just a little,' Huart conceded. He looked around for Mr Lee to bid him farewell and saw him standing apart with a mask of concern in place of the joy that had been there moments before. 'Whatever's wrong, nurse? Is there something wrong with the baby?'

She made an ironic gesture. 'How long have you lived in Hong Kong?'

'Seventeen years.'

The nurse nodded. 'You know about Chinese beliefs?'

'Some.'

'Mr Lee has just realised that his son is born in the Year of the Fire Horse. His blessing is mixed.'

12

The miniature Cantonese gentleman was a model of dress and decorum. He could pass for a valet to a British lord, Huart decided as he ran his eyes over the *curriculum vitae* upon his desk. He saw that the name typed at the top had been abbreviated to merely: Y.Y. Szeto.

'I am informed by Alexander Chiu Man-king that you were at Cornell with him, Mr Szeto,' Huart opened. But he did not wait for affirmation before going straight into the subject on which every other candidate had been found wanting. 'Could you kindly tell me, in as few words as possible, what you know about the Great Proletarian Cultural Revolution.'

There was no hesitation. 'It is a doctrine that comes from the contest between the aspirants to succeed Mao Tse-tung. It is the means by which the extreme left wing, supported by Mao and championed by Lin Piao, plan to overcome the "New Right" movement of Liu Shao-chi and Teng Hsiao-ping. But it has gone beyond its intended limits and become violent.'

'In what way?'

'The intelligentsia of China is now the target of the "revolution" as well as the "New Right". Recently, students were incited to assault the chancellors of Nanking and Wuhan universities. The latter attack was brutal and the learned scholar died from it. It seems the students overlooked that he was a founding member of the Chinese Communist Party.'

'Who are the Red Guards?'

'The term appeared in Peking newspapers for the first time on June 26th. It is another pseudonym for the Party's youth organisation, which Mao once called his "Little Revolutionary Generals". The Red Guards have just staged their first public appearance. It supplemented a rally of one million people that included tens of thousands of cadres brought to Peking from almost every city in China.'

'What is the future of Liu Shao-chi and Teng Hsiao-ping?'

'Not very bright.'

'And Chou En-lai?'

'He is surviving by means of a consummate exhibition of fence walking.'

'Thank you, Mr Szeto.' Huart closed the file on his desk. No further questions were necessary. He had found his sinologist.

'With land values and the stock market falling like they are, and a population that won't stop rising – it's gone past three and three-quarter million, you know – we've got to find ways of stimulating exports,' the Financial Secretary of the Hong Kong Government told Huart at a cocktail party the Friday night before his sixtieth birthday. 'We're doing what we can to achieve that. Forming the Trade Development Council and the Export Credit Insurance Corporation out of capital fully subscribed by the Government is an effective beginning.'

'The last thing we need right now is more civil unrest,' the Jardine taipan put in unnecessarily, referring to the Star Ferry Riots in April that had claimed Nathan Road for three nights and brought down a curfew in Kowloon. 'The Government's got to find more ways than that of getting all these people back to work in a hurry, old chap.'

'Don't the *hongs* share the responsibility?'

'And we meet it, Financial Secretary. We tell you what to do, don't we?'

The top civil servant frowned himself off to the washroom.

The Jardine taipan went on unabashed: 'It was a fine decision for the Government to put *laissez faire* aside and get on with that road tunnel under Lion Rock, and to seal off that place in Tolo Harbour . . .'

'Plover Cove,' Huart obliged.

'Plover Cove. Thanks, old chap. Of course, you don't have to ask where the idea came from. We can well do with 30,000 million gallons of water of our own. You can never be sure when China will get bloody-minded and refuse to sell us theirs. But, you know how things go – we'll build the reservoir and never need the water. Look at those June rainstorms.'

'I was out of the colony most of June,' Huart excused himself.

'Lucky you. Twelve inches in one day – four in an hour. Landslips everywhere, including the university. The Bowen Road Bridge came down and took the Peak Tram track with it. Needed eight days to rebuild it all. Peak Road went, too. I was trapped at home for days without a telephone. Wettest June on record, it was. The poor Chinese suffered. It dealt the rehousing programme a helluva blow. Where were you in June, old chap?'

'UK, the Continent, the States . . .'

'Bit game with all these airline disasters all over the shop, weren't you? Helluva year. Riots, rains and bloody heat like I've never known. And I've two more of these to attend before dinner. Cheerio, old chap.'

'Hi, John boy!' It was Scott Overbeck. 'Look, old buddy, I'm as sorry as I can be. I've just been called to Silicon Valley. I leave tomorrow and it means I can't make your birthday shindig tomorrow night. But Margot'll be there. She wouldn't miss it. When you're all diving into shark's fin and beggar's chicken, I'll be getting ready to face my *el supremo*. I can almost taste it – the food, that is. I love Chinese chow. So does Margot. Hey, I can trust you with her, can't I, buddy?'

'Of course not. You're giving me just the chance I've been waiting for. But an urgent meeting usually means an emergency, Scott.'

'Nahh.' Overbeck laughed a trifle too easily. 'No emergency at all. See you when I get back, John boy. And happy birthday from me.'

'Thanks, Scott. Have a good flight.' Huart was thoughtful as he watched the Californian's back go out the door. The sudden meeting had to have something to do with China.

The last course of the banquet being held in a private section of the Moon Yuet Restaurant of the Victoria Hotel was served at ten pm. By then Huart could classify it a success. Not an unqualified success, he thought as he looked across the head table at Billson

Hsu and his son, but still successful. They had yet to say a word, but they had attended.

Not content only to celebrate a personal milestone, Huart, as with most things he did now, had organised the banquet for maximum business advantage. Besides his directors and divisional managers, he had invited all captains of industry, senior commercial, financial and engineering executives, with wives, who were Cumberland China's 1966–67 targets. One stipulation had been for at least one third of his guests to be Chinese, and he had personally ensured the seating met the demands of status, of 'face'. Accordingly, Billson Hsu, billionaire head of the Unicorn Realty empire which owned the property next to Cumberland House, could only be put at the head table, and his son beside him.

Huart had been happily surprised at their acceptance. With land values declining, his real estate ambitions were being rekindled. Landers had warned him the company's cash reserves made it a plum target for one of the major *hongs* at this time of squeezed credit and had pressed him to put the funds to use. Huart had been non-committal. He knew exactly what he wanted to do with the cash. At the right time.

He had elected to mark his birthday Chinese style for three reasons. One was to respect that third of his guests, a second was to remind them all of the company's origins, and the last was further to remind himself of the pledge he had made to return to them. He had opted for five tables of twelve diners each, a total of sixty. It matched, so Imelda Roboza had told him, the lunar cycle with its twelve animals and five elements.

'Not only that,' Huart had added with a chuckle, 'it computes. Sixty years. Sixty guests. They can each bring a candle.'

But there were absentees: Percy and Maurine Landers who were on leave; Scott Overbeck, of course, and Lennie Cosgrove, who had missed his connection in Bangkok from where he had cabled his regrets. All European flights touched down in the Thai capital as the direct air corridor over Vietnam had been closed by the war. But the absentee Huart regretted most was Kingston Orr, who had declined through his secretary without bothering to have her manufacture any excuse on his behalf.

Huart had covered the gaps by putting Mr and Mrs Y.Y. Szeto, who had been invited subsequent to his appointment, at the head table with Johnson Sze Cho-lok, Deputy Manager of Hua Ting Company, the discreetly influential purchasing corporation for the People's Republic of China. Though his title suggested a senior, the deceptively affable Mr Sze was in fact the top local communist official outside the Bank of China and the Hsin Hua News Agency. Huart had put his sinologist straight to work.

As each course was served, the host's health and longevity was toasted by Caucasians with beer or French wine, by Chinese with *heung peen* jasmine tea or orange juice. All races complimented the chef as they consumed the minced pigeon with pine seeds and water chestnut, dipped chopsticks into the sliced whelk sautéed with duck's web, and spoons into bowls of double boiled superior shark's fin flavoured with red vinegar. Then came steamed fresh carp, followed by the host's favourite: stuffed crab claws flavoured with a sweet and sour sauce. When the choice of noodles or glutinous rice came, he, as usual, opted for the former, his taste for rice still scourged from his palate by his jungle ordeals. Dessert was sweetened sago cream with taro balls. And the last course, according to custom, was fruit: assorted melons and fresh oranges.

It was as the fruit was being served and conversation around the head table was threatening to flag, that Billson Hsu voluntarily opened his mouth for a purpose other than to receive food or drink for the first time and said in cautious, accented English: ''Scuse, Mr Huar', you really sixty year old t'day?'

'I am, Mr Hsu.' Huart gave a congenial smile in anticipation of the evening's hackneyed compliment concerning his youthful appearance.

'Is western calendar?'

'That's correct. My Chinese age is less flattering.'

Polite chuckles circled the table. The Chinese almanac added to western age by adjudging a person to be one year old at birth.

Billson Hsu's small, narrow head nodded slowly. 'Then you rare man,' he said softly, his eyes harbouring a deep oriental sagacity. A graduate of the old Chinese school, his only apparent condescensions to 'foreign' custom were his tailored suit and his English nickname of 'Billson'. He had derived it from 'Son of Bill' after hearing the tale of Buffalo Bill, and deciding the Wild West character epitomised all red-haired, crazy *gwailo*, who were either too ignorant or too lazy to master the correct tonal pronunciation of his full Shanghai name: Hsu Hsiao-hsieh.

Huart willed his prized guest to say more and was delighted when he did.

'We Chinese say you "Fire Horse", Mr Huar'. This Year of Horse, but is not ordin'ry Horse year. Ev'ry sixty year, fifth Year of Horse in cycle is rule' by fire. This fifth Horse year. So was year you born. Is 1906?'

'Yes,' Huart confirmed. He thought of the explanation given by

[360]

the nurse at Kowloon Hospital when Mr Lee's joy had turned to dismay. 'Is it bad?'

'Maybe.' Billson Hsu, fearing offence to his host, smiled carefully. The table had fallen into a respectful silence. 'But many great man born in Year of Fire Horse. Cicero . . . Rembran' . . .' The smile crinkled into a grin. 'Davy Crockett, and . . .' He almost giggled. 'Buff''lo Bill!'

'Oh, very good, Mr Hsu!' Sir Frederick Lloyd Oberon, Chairman of the Hongkong and Kwangtung Bank, joined in the laughter at the head table.

'But many bad man, too,' the senior Hsu went on. 'Like Lor' Haw Haw and Adol' Eichmann. And failure king, too . . . like Richard II. And also mos' unluckies' man in worl' t'day: poor Mr Pu Yi. He born in Year of Fire Horse – same year you, Mr Huar' – and be las' emp'ror of China after two thousan' years. Then he be made emp'ror again by Japanese. Emp'ror of Manchuria. But now he jus' *foki* in Peking for communis' master.'

Huart was wondering how, with all this in him, Billson Hsu could have stayed silent all evening. The voice of Johnson Sze provided the answer.

'So Mr Pu Yi is a reformed and privileged Fire Horse.'

The small Hsu eyes flashed, his face contorted into an expression that would have qualified as deadly lethal if looks could kill, and Huart looked on in helpless dismay as the prized guest fired back: 'You say he priv'lege to have so much broken promise jus' like you communis' make ev'ryone in Shanghai? You say he reform'? I say he blainwash'!'

'You seem to have done well out of our "broken promises", Mr Hsu.'

'Sure. I sure make my money quick in Hong Kong. We have so little time here till 1997 when you communis' come here, too. An' make more your broken promise. You bet my fam'ly be firs' gone then – '

Oberon just beat Huart to it. 'What a coincidental sequence, John! If this year is a Fire Horse year, and so was 1906 . . . then so was 1846.'

'I suppose so, Eric,' Huart responded, thankful but missing the point.

'According to my bank's research into the origins of Cumberland China – if I recall correctly – Charles Huart was born in 1846.'

'I wasn't aware of that,' Huart admitted. So what? he almost added.

'Charles Huart?' Margot Overbeck piped up. 'Who was he?'

'My third cousin's grandfather. He founded the company in Chungking in 1873, then moved its base to Shanghai.'

Billson Hsu's face, less flushed, had taken on an expression of wonder. 'Your comp'ny foun' by Fire Horse, Mr Huar'? An' you Fire Horse, too?'

'It looks like it, Mr Hsu.' Huart willed someone to change the subject.

'*Ha!* So rare thing! Never b'fore do I know any two Fire Horse in one comp'ny – in one dyn'sty. So rare thing! Mr Huar', in your life you ever have your fortune tol'?'

'Never, Mr Hsu.' How could he bring this to an end?

'Oh you should, John!' squealed Margot Overbeck.

He groaned inwardly as he remembered Scott's wife was a horoscope freak.

'It be mos' int'rest for you, Mr Huar',' Billson Hsu insisted. 'Your fortune have big contras'. Can be mos' good or can be mos' bad. But we Chinese b'lieve more bad thing than good thing happen this year. Like typhoon. Or big rain. Or earthquake. Or rev'lution. Or war. Or – '

'The San Francisco earthquake was in 1906,' Margot Overbeck reminded them all. 'Oh, isn't that so very interesting!'

Herbert Jarvis's wife, Mary, made her contribution: '1906 was a bad year for Hong Kong too.' She looked at her husband. 'I read it in Victoria Land's history, Bert. There was a string of big typhoons. One killed ten thousand. It wrecked all the ships in the harbour and wiped out all the boat people. And after that, the account that I read said, there was a five year recession – '

'Just like we have right now,' Victoria Land's newly promoted general manager observed drily.

'Five cycles of sixty years takes us back to 1666,' Oberon pointed out proudly, 'and the Great Fire of London.'

Mary Jarvis actually gasped. 'And ten cycles before that was 1066 and the Battle of Hastings. The Norman Invasion!'

'And what about this year?' Margot Overbeck enthused. 'Those rains in June! Awful they were, weren't they? And those terrible riots in Kowloon in April! John, you were caught up in one, remember? Isn't that absolute proof of what Mr Hsu says? Isn't it?'

'All that still not bad enough,' Billson Hsu disagreed, his small eyes fixed like lasers upon Johnson Sze. 'Mus' be worse than tha'. Like a . . . a Communis' Invasion!'

Margot Overbeck had not heard this and in her innocence

she aborted the communist official's acerbic response. 'John! Oh, John!'

'Yes, Margot?' Huart smiled through his embarrassment.

'John, you really must go and get your fortune told!'

'Why, Margot?'

'Because if you don't after everything Mr Hsu has been kind enough to tell you tonight, he'll be most offended. And quite right, too.'

That did it.

'Am I crazy?'

Huart wiped his brow with a handkerchief that gave sodden testimony to the heat of the morning; again the mercury was rising past 35 degrees Celsius. It was his eighteenth summer in Hong Kong, hottest of them all.

'Am I crazy?' he asked himself for the umpteenth time.

He had climbed from Queen's Road, Central, through the heat to the top of the Ladder Streets, an ascent of irregular stone and cement platforms laid upon the foot of the incline that escalated into the sheer face of the Peak. He was in the centre of old Hong Kong. Shoppers moved about, with gait measured in the heat, amongst the stalls that rendered the district a marketplace *extraordinaire*. Anything that walked, flew, sang, talked, cried; anything that could be eaten, worn, used or mounted could be purchased at bargain prices from the rows of wood-framed stalls.

Chattering *amahs* were out in white half-coats, black trousers, waxed hair glinting in the sunlight, hands grasping cane baskets, flicking bamboo fans. Caucasian *missees* browsed in sun hats for knick-knacks, faces stern lest they be mistaken as tourists and charged accordingly. The real tourists, wide-eyed and eager, foraged for memorabilia amongst the stalls. It was mid morning: shoppers' hour in the Ladder Streets.

Across the way Huart saw an ancient stone building with, above its door, the number that Imelda Roboza had given to him. He crossed to it and peered up a rickety wooden staircase, barely wide enough for him, rising almost perpendicularly into darkness. Again he analysed his mission. Did senility come so young? Or was he really only going crazy? In the end it was crass curiosity that sent him up the staircase.

The plaster was coated with fungus, dust and airborne filth off the street. The air was thick and damp and old. The staircase protested his weight at each step; he was likely the heaviest person ever to have climbed it and he fully expected it to collapse under him at any moment.

He came to a door hidden in shadow. It took many seconds for him to find the number that told him it was the right one. It opened outwards and he squeezed around it to find himself in a tiny cubicle that reeked with the fumes from the burning joss sticks crammed into a large earthenware bowl full of grey ash. It was noticeably cooler in here.

'Hello?' he called softly, ready to turn and leave. 'Anyone there?'

He saw a bamboo curtain drawn aside by a long transparent fingernail and an ancient oriental face appear around it. The eyes were opaque, sightless. He heard a whisper that ended with: ' . . . Mr John Huart?'

'Er, yes.'

'Your secretary called me. You are right on time. Please come through.'

The face withdrew. Huart, wondering how the blind man knew if he was on time or not, bent double and followed it through the curtain to find himself in another cubicle even more confined than the first. Here the smell of damp mixed with the joss, resulting in a unique stink. It was cool, even chilly compared with the temperature outside. Close up, he saw the face was an extension of a wizened body inside a yellow robe.

'Please sit.' The fortune teller pointed at a stool and squeezed himself behind a table crowded with books. Piles of more books reached from the floor to the low angled ceiling. Everything in the cubicle was old, the only concessions to modern technology being a metal-framed electric fan, which was not working despite the heat, a telephone of a design that could have made it the first ever installed in Hong Kong, and a naked electric light bulb hanging from a twisted wire, all of which was caked with insect excreta and dust.

Huart sat down with difficulty, his movements restricted by the angle of the ceiling, and looked into the bottomless eyes.

'You are a very large man, Mr Huart.'

The afflicted, Huart knew, compensate by developing their other senses. He replied: 'I'm six feet five inches in height and I weigh approximately two hundred and fifty pounds. I trust the floor can stand my weight?'

'This building has been here for one hundred years. It has survived many typhoons, rains and floods in that time. It will certainly survive you.'

Huart smiled to himself and relaxed. Imelda Roboza had told

him: 'He is a Doctor of Philosophy. It is said that he has become a millionaire from telling fortunes. He is very famous with the Chinese. Many of the most wealthy families go to him every lunar new year. No-one knows how old he is. There is a tale that the building was built around him as he sat.'

'When is your birthday, Mr Huart?'

'August 21st, 1906,' he answered, amused by the abruptness.

There was the merest quiver of the forehead. 'The hour of your birth?'

'Around two a.m., I think.'

'Can you be sure? It is very important.'

'Yes. Two o'clock in the morning. I remember my mother complaining – '

A skeletal hand lifted. 'Mr Huart, I have a full schedule today. My next appointment is in – ' His fingers slipped into the sleeve of his robe. '– fifteen minutes. I apologise for being rude, but to serve you well I must allow time for you to answer all my questions fully.'

'Er, sorry.' It had been a long time since John Huart had been chastised for time wasting. He folded his arms and waited, now highly amused.

'You were born in the Hour of the Ox. It explains why, within yourself, despite the scepticism you wear on your exterior at the moment, you do not consider this consultation a complete waste of time. The consistency and serious approach to life of the Ox has tempered the restlessness and impetuosity of the Horse, under whose auspices you were born, you have lived, and will continue to live.'

'I understand I am a "Fire Horse",' Huart said, risking further censure.

'You are. That can be very good for you and for those who depend on you, or it can be very bad. We shall see. Please bend your head forward.'

He did as he was told and for a full minute ten cold fingertips pressed every square millimetre of his skull.

'Thank you. You can sit up now.'

The quintet of flesh-covered bones that was the fortune teller's right hand snaked out to take up a small copper turtle, and the left pushed three coins into its mouth. Then both hands held it in front of the ancient face and shook it for another minute in tempo with a hummed incantation. All this time the dead eyes seemed to stay fixed on Huart and he shivered involuntarily. Finally the unnerving noise ended and the fortune teller tipped the coins onto the table. They rolled about before coming to rest one after another in a straight line, side by side. Huart could see they were engraved with the faces of mythological gods. With a fingertip the old man felt each one.

'Mr Huart . . . you have had a tragic life.'

Huart suppressed an intake of breath, more surprised than impressed. No, he was impressed. He waited for more. The cubicle rang with silence.

'The Year of the Horse has been very cruel to you. I can tell you have had four personal tragedies at equal intervals. You now expect a fifth.'

Huart gaped. He could not believe his ears.

'But there will be no fifth tragedy. In Cantonese the word for "death" is *say*. Consequently, disasters can have a sequence of four as the word for "four" is "*say*". You hear the slight difference in tone? In the case of yourself this convenient rule applies. You have had your four disasters. They have been terrible in the extreme, each befalling your immediate family. But do not fear, Mr Huart, the sequence is exhausted. There will be no fifth personal tragedy this year. The Year of the Fire Horse will not be your enemy in that way.'

The fortune teller paused, seeming to search for a deeper message, then continued. 'I sense you accept what I say to be accurate, so I choose to proceed. What of the future? You must wish to forget the past. Look at the coins and note how they have fallen in a row, touching each other to form a solid wall. This means there will be an obstacle placed in your path, something which will threaten your future. I see it as a huge wave of water endangering your fire element. It is coming towards you even as I speak. You note how the head of each figure points in the same direction? This means there is only one way through the wave. Choice is eliminated. What is this wave? I cannot describe it exactly as it is an intangible. It is a flow of events, dictated by public opinion or by a political force. It will force a great decision upon you and give you no time to make it. But you must make it, for not to do so will result in the wave overtaking you and drowning you in your indecision. Should you decide to turn and flee along with all around you, the wave will take you up – as big a man as you are – and wash you like a grain of sand onto the shore. There you will be one grain amongst countless billions. I can tell you were not born to be just a grain of sand, Mr Huart.'

The fortune teller fell silent. Without his engrossing discourse the cubicle adopted an eerie ambience, like a sacred precinct.

Huart stared into the blind eyes for long seconds, not knowing what to think. 'This obstacle. This wave. How will I recognise it?' Wonder and scepticism so competed in his voice he hardly recognised it as his own.

'You will know it. Your decision will also be obvious. But I warn you, Mr Huart, all your friends and associates will believe you to be mad. But you must take no notice. You are a Fire Horse. This is your year.'

That seemed to be all. Huart rose. 'How do I pay you?'

From the sleeve appeared a small square of paper with a dozen ideograms brush-stroked on it. 'Please sign it. At month's end it will be brought to your office for payment. You will not consider the fee exorbitant.'

Huart took it and signed. It was the old fashioned chit system, based on trust and integrity. The fortune teller's great age became manifest.

Leaving the building was like entering a sauna bath. The sunlight stung his eyes as he squinted at the unabated activity of the Ladder Streets. He descended slowly to Queen's Road, still not knowing what to think.

In the same time that it took John Huart to walk east on Queen's Road, Central to Cumberland House, twenty miles to the north a group of Hakka farmers crossed south over the Lo Wu Bridge. They were mostly women, as Hakka males shunned menial labour, and they were dressed in their clan garb of loose black tunics, baggy trousers and wide black and red lampshade headgear. Every day of their lives they came from Shum Chun in Kwangtung Province, the People's Republic of China, to work the fields in the New Territories of Hong Kong, British Crown Colony, that their families had owned for centuries, since long before 1898 when a border fence had been put up between their *heung ha* and their fields.

But on this day they did something different. They held aloft pictures of Mao Tse-tung and sang communist slogans to the police and immigration officers at the southern end of the bridge as they passed by.

It was not realised until later, but on this burning August day in the Year of the Fire Horse the Great Proletarian Cultural Revolution came to Hong Kong.

The corpse bobbed in the wash of the Star ferries that churned either side of it. Its spine arched out of the water like a handle to which its bound hands appeared to be attached. It had been dead a long time – long enough to float down the Pearl River all the way from Canton, and its silent message was horribly loud to Scott Overbeck.

'A single bullet in the back of the neck,' he muttered to Huart as they stood at the ferry rail looking down. 'That's the 1966 reward for being suspected of having enough intelligence to want to open the country up to the West. I would never have believed it – but there's the evidence.'

Huart could not believe it either. 'But there must be a significance in China agreeing to supply more water to Hong Kong until next June . . .'

Overbeck snorted. 'It needs the cash for guns for the goddamn Red Guards as well as the PLA. Better check out the water for dead bodies first.'

Huart said nothing more. The corpse had taken him back thirty years to his first sight of the Whangpoo River and its wretched human flotsam.

'And it's spreading to Macau!' Overbeck went on 'It's fanaticism! Pure mindlessness! Mao must've been desperate to hang on to power to have let Lin Piao even start it. Desperate? Insane! They'll have a lot to answer for in that big rice paddy in the sky, John boy. It can't go on. China will suffer for it. The country still hasn't fully recovered from the last disaster: Mao's "Great Leap Forward". Forward? Great Leap into the Shit Heap, more like. And now with the PLA and this variation on the Hitler Jugend behind them, Mao and Lin'll destroy China if it goes on.' He turned and looked at Huart, his face grave. 'And Hong Kong with it.'

Huart could not help it. 'What's Silicon Valley's policy now, Scott?'

It produced a wry expression. 'I'll give you one thing, John boy – you never give up. Hong Kong's sure not looking as safe as it was. Something's going to happen. And soon. Macau's on the boil. The Red Guards are just over the border. They're real, John boy, not the figment of someone's imagination. I've seen them myself through binoculars from Lok Ma Chau. They march through Shum Chun with their banners and pictures of Mao and their little red books like schoolyard bullies. Wait till they get those guns. Then it'll really be on. I kid you not.'

At a Bank of America cocktail party in November, Huart was introduced to Michael Rosselino, Executive Vice President of Orion Oil of Dallas, and found him also concerned with the future of Hong Kong, his anxiety stimulated by his company's considerable property assets in East Kowloon.

'We regard China and Hong Kong as homogenous. The longer this so-called "revolution" goes on the future of this place will be affected pro-rata. No disrespect to you British, you understand. You've done a great job of administration here. But there's nearly a billion people up there!'

Midnight that night found Huart standing on his balcony looking north. The air was warm. Summer was being greedy. It had started early and wet and was refusing to end, hanging on like the last party guest. From his perch above Central District, he looked at the shadowy peaks of the Nine Dragons silhouetted in the moonlight. Beyond them was the leased real estate of the New Territories. And beyond that was China – the Middle Kingdom. Great, sinister, mysterious. And, as far as Hong Kong was concerned, omnipotent.

He analysed every word spoken in his hearing by the guests of the Bank of America. Was the American community over-reacting? He thought of the dogmatic parochial stance his cousin had twice taken in Shanghai. Andrew Huart-Brent had been proved wrong, over-confident, even naive in hindsight. And at a fantastic cost. Would he, John Stanford Huart, fare any better now that he was chancellor of the future of Cumberland China?

What information, what intelligence did he possess? None. Not a thing, except the obscure pronouncement of an ancient fortune teller who sat like an emaciated phantom in a putrid cubicle somewhere atop the Ladder Streets. And something else: a nascent gut feeling that Hong Kong, this extraordinary place he had chosen as his home for the second half of his life – his third life – would survive any and all adversity.

Every day of the last fortnight of November and the first week of December, the newspapers reported the Macau riots on their front pages. The summer of 1966 extended into a warm autumn, setting another meteorological record: it was the hottest year ever. The Fire Horse was writing its reign into Asian history as one of unprecedented rainfall, heat and political turmoil. It had until February 8th, 1967, to really outdo itself.

Autumn ended at last. The temperature plummeted overnight as the first winter monsoon dispersed the humid haze that had preceded it. The street corner hawkers materialised with their blackened *woks*, and the warm tang of roasting chestnuts and corn on the cob wafted on the chill air.

Huart sat in his office wearing his waistcoat for the first time since March. Ah Keung had lit the fire in the penthouse hearth and the fragrance of wood smoke drifted down the stairs to render the office seemingly too cosy, too homely for a place of hard business. It was quiet, save for the whistle of the Mongolian wind that licked Cumberland House and the rustle of the *Hong Kong and Oriental Daily* in Huart's hands.

He looked up from the review of the deteriorating situation in the Portuguese enclave forty sea miles west. 'Eight Red Guards dead and thirty-five wounded,' he summarised to the man who sat like an alert praying mantis in the armchair opposite. 'What happens now?'

Y. Y. Szeto blinked. It was his only sign of life. He could not remember his last smile, and the information he had gathered gave no cause for him to remedy that. 'The Macau Government wishes to capitulate. The Governor has offered to return the colony to Peking. The offer has been refused.'

Huart frowned. 'What then . . . ?'

'The Red Guards seek a public apology for the deaths of their comrades at the hands of the Portuguese soldiers. They will get it. The Governor will officially apologise and accept all the Red Guards' demands.'

Huart shook his head in wonder. 'And what of Hong Kong? Business here is already hard hit. The stock market falls each day. Rents are plummeting. Lines outside the American Consulate stretch halfway up Garden Road. What price a US visa on the black market today, Mr Szeto?'

'One hundred thousand dollars.'

Huart kept his smile to himself. The man knew everything! Instead he sat back and looked at the ceiling and rearranged his thoughts. The silence was broken only by the ticking of the pendulum clock on the wall. Outside the greyness deepened. Pinheads of rain sprinkled on the windows.

'Give me all of the bad news, then,' he invited at length.

The man employed under the misnomer of 'company secretary' blinked once more. 'The news is indeed not encouraging. Peking is delighted with the success the Red Guards have had in Macau and believes that the Cultural Revolution has gained international face with the capitulation of the government there. The head of the Chinese Chamber of Commerce is now in a position to dictate policy on behalf of Peking. He will be the real governor of Macau in future. Peking wants the same for Hong Kong.'

'Go on, please,' Huart urged, his apprehension thinly covered.

'Peking will fund a campaign aimed at destroying our infrastructure. The fund will be controlled by local communists, plus Red Guard agents who will be spirited across the border. Blue collar workers will be incited to strike. The strikes will be escalated into riots. The objective of the campaign is to confront the Hong Kong Government, and the police in particular, with a huge crisis. Peking believes our administration will fold like Macau's. China will then gain effective control of Hong Kong without the need to resort to open invasion.'

'How can Peking so believe in this scenario?'

'The local communists have promised outright victory.'

'On what basis?'

'The Star Ferry riots in April. The police were severely tested, but for only three days. Peking has been promised that if the test is maintained over a longer term – weeks, even months – the police will lose control, the people will lose faith in the British administration, and Hong Kong will be China's for the taking.'

Huart drew a deep breath. The news was awful. He lifted both hands and pushed his fingers through his hair until they joined behind his head. The accuracy of Y. Y. Szeto's intelligence was undoubted. His credentials were as impeccable as his dress and his delivery. But the man was a living, breathing secret, incarcerated behind an impenetrable exterior that was as much a weapon as it was a trademark. Rumours that had reached Huart included the one that fingered him as a member of the local left wing movement that so featured in his report. At Cornell, according to Alexander Chiu, Y. Y. Szeto had produced acquaintances with connections behind the Bamboo Curtain one after the other, whilst simultaneously updating his personal capitalist philosophy. Huart had himself decided his sinologist was not just ambivalent, but 'omnivalent'.

He lowered his arms. 'When will this campaign begin, Mr Szeto?'

'Preparations are already under way. The target date is obvious.'

Huart's eyebrows lifted. It was not obvious to him.

'The "Workers' Day", sir,' Y. Y. Szeto obliged. 'The first of May.'

Fifteen minutes separated the 'company secretary' from Thomas Buckley, Financial Controller, and the monthly review of the company's performance in financial year 1966–67. Huart employed them in cogitation.

Could the Hong Kong administration and the police withstand an organised onslaught from within the territory greater, more determined than that which had overpowered Macau? Would the Wilson Government support its colony from its sanctuary in White-hall, half the globe away? Hong Kong's worth to Britain would be tested along with everything else. Would that worth be enough to have the British Army garrison deployed to support the police? Huart remembered August 1940, when his battalion was removed from Shanghai in a time of local challenge. Was it now Hong Kong's turn?

In what direction flowed the tide of local opinion? He thought of the falling stock market, the collapsing property values, the impatient lines leading up Garden Road from the American Consulate. He saw again the concern on the faces on Queen's Road, in the Hong Kong Club, in the private race boxes at Happy Valley, even around the Long Table. And he knew the answer. Tide? A chord of his memory was tugged and it went back three and a half months to a dark, dank cubicle. He tried to recall what the old fortune teller had predicted. Tide? Wave? Yes, wave. Only one way through it. Which way? But there was only one way to breach a wave: head-on! Deep in his core, he felt the gut feeling coalesce and the warmth of it rise up through him.

And then, with a Great Fire burning in his breast, John Stanford Huart decided he had no alternative but to buck the trend.

'Sir, with your approval, we must adjust downwards the 1966–67 targets,' Thomas Buckley opened after accepting the customary cup of jasmine tea.

' "Adjust downwards", Tom?' Huart's smile was almost cynical. 'If you mean "reduce", then say so. Reduce them by how much?'

Buckley cleared his throat and rechecked the figures on his pad. 'After analysing the half yearly results, it is recommended that Turnover and Net Profit targets be adjusted dow – er, reduced – by ten per cent to reflect the adverse economic situation and the political uncertainty – '

Huart's gaze was piercing and it soon made Buckley uncomfortable. He had never seen his chairman's eyes so clear, his brow so unmarked by lines of concentration, deliberation or tension. It was as if he had just witnessed the parting of the Dead Sea and been converted to the Faith. Or had the seriousness of the situation driven him to barbiturates? And his voice was different. It was youthful, and even more decisive than usual. 'You anticipate gross margins to fall, too, Tom?'

'Er, no. I have maintained them. Perhaps I also should cut them to – '

'Then, to maintain the targeted Net Profit percentage, as you state, you must have found ways to trim overheads by – ' Huart jabbed buttons on his Shearman electronic desk calculator. '2,800,000 dollars. Correct?'

The confidence returned to Buckley's pinched face. 'Yes, sir.'

'How, Tom?'

'Staff cuts, sir. Mainly in Manufacturing – in the Textiles and Garments Division. Our projected complement is 425. Last year it was 377. It is recommended to cut back to the '65–'66 level and hold there – '

'For how long?'

'At least until the end of this financial year, certainly. Probably even well into the next. Things look like getting worse before they get better. Did you hear the latest on Macau on the eleven o'clock news? A public apology by the Governor, no less. Who would have believed it?'

Huart's brows did not arch from surprise. He was even happy. Y. Y. Szeto had been spot on! He half listened as Buckley talked, though he knew the accountant was making basic economic sense. But, from what he now knew, lay-offs at Wai Wai Road would play into the hands of the communist agitators and guarantee strife. He knew of the discontent on the factory floor over the long hours that went with the two shift system common in Hong Kong. He had to remedy it before May Day, not exacerbate it.

He stood and walked to the window and looked out on the grey morning dressed with low cloud that spat persistent drizzle into the cold wind over Central District. He studied his reflection, nodded to himself in final confirmation, then turned to face his financial controller with a parade ground mien spontaneously resurrected from his military past. 'I hear what you say, Tom, but I want you to have a complete rethink.'

'Sir?'

'It is the policy of this company – based on my personal policy – not to break a single ricebowl. I will not sanction lay-offs.'

'But, sir – '

'I know, Tom. Hard times should beget hard measures. But we took account of the economic situation when we set this year's targets, did we not?'

'Yes . . . but the situation has become much worse than we antic – '

'Tom, we adhere to the original targets.' Huart looked down at the paper on his desk. 'Turnover of $245,000,000. Net Profit of $31,000,000.'

Buckley was speechless. He sat there. His lower lip fell. His face was aghast. The chairman had to be on barbiturates!

Undeterred, Huart continued. 'I am calling a meeting at nine tomorrow to confirm my decision. All divisional managers are to attend. We've less than four months before the end of the financial year. Less than four months in which to accelerate our performance, not decelerate. I'll need the full support of yourself and all the other senior managers, Tom. It will mean a lot of extra work for you. I apologise deeply for that.'

Buckley regained control of his face. 'Sir . . . it will be as you wish.'

'Thank you, Tom. I know I can count on you. I'll see you at nine, then. And could I have an updated report on our cash position before lunch?'

Buckley left tight-lipped, his keen financial brain already attacking the new task that had come out of nowhere. His concern over his chairman's health was not forgotten, merely filed for further consideration.

Huart telephoned Antonio Ezuelo and Alexander Chiu. Both confirmed their support for Buckley's plan for staff reductions, then listened in silent scepticism as he informed them of the meeting the next morning and the reason for it. He then called Nigel Print. If overheads were to be trimmed anywhere, he told himself, it should be the Engineering Division.

Ten minutes later Daniel Vail sat in front of Huart's desk. The Manager, Property Division, was reading from a typewritten report. ' . . . the oil storage depot is contained within a twenty-seven acre site on the waterfront in East Kowloon north of Kai Tak Airport. Reclamation, subject to government approval, would add nine acres to it. Valuation as at April 1st this year was $115,000,000. As requested in your memorandum dated November 25th, a new valuation was made this week by Johns Leung Pullen. They now estimate the thirty-six acres as worth $96,500,000.'

Huart tapped his calculator. 'Down sixteen per cent in eight months. What would you put the value of the site at come Chinese New Year, Dan?'

Vail pursed his lips as he did the sums in his head. 'Two more months with values continuing to fall? Maybe even as low as $85,000,000.'

'Are you certain Orion Oil will put the site on the market?' Huart asked in the clear, spirited voice that was his for the morning.

Vail nodded. 'Of that I'm now quite sure.'

'Why?' The question merely sought confirmation. Huart knew the reason.

'Orion considers any property north of Boundary Street to be potentially worthless. Their political advisers predict that within six months China will make a claim on Whitehall for premature termination of the lease on the New Territories, and they believe it will succeed. Considering post-war history, there is a precedent: Attlee's socialist government relinquished the other British colonies in Asia. If the conservatives were in power, the Americans would be more confident of the future of the New Territories. They think Wilson will hand it back to Mao on a plate.'

Huart was nodding and peering into space through narrowed lids. He said nothing. Vail took this as licence to continue.

'Orion have a back-up oil storage depot on Lamma Island which they feel has better longevity and they will transfer their tank farm there. The East Kowloon site should be on the market by Christmas.' The property manager looked up from the report in his hands and added rhetorically: 'But who in their right mind would purchase it?'

He was therefore puzzled when he thought he heard Huart say whilst still gazing off into space: 'We would, Dan.'

'Pardon, sir?'

Huart slowly lowered his eyes until they met Vail's. 'We would, Dan,' he repeated. 'Cumberland China is going to purchase the Orion Oil site. We are going to build apartments on it. Not small apartments, not big apartments, but middle-sized apartments for middle class people to buy from your Property Division at middle-of-the-road prices. My congratulations, Dan. You're about to expand. I want to build a middle class city on that site − after we buy it. And we'll buy it for − ' Again the calculator came into action. 'Sixty million dollars. Or less.'

Vail looked at Huart with every muscle in his body frozen in mild shock. 'Er ... yes, sir. If you say so, sir,' he mumbled at last.

Huart leaned forward, his eyes bright. 'Dan, I want you to go back to Johns Leung Pullen and tell them to give you a weekly valuation on that site. Then go to the best quantity surveyor in Hong Kong – Livingstone and Briley, perhaps. Get their estimate of how many apartments the site could accommodate – allowing reasonable living space – and the cost of development. I want no tenement philosophy. The theme is "middle class", don't forget. I want to see a preliminary draft before Christmas Eve.'

'But people are lining up for tickets out of Hong Kong. Who'll still be around with the cash to buy a new middle class apartment – or any sort of apartment? By the time we develop, the New Territories will be – '

'So you agree with Orion's political advisers, Dan?'

'Er, no, sir. Of course not. Well, not completely. But, I mean, taking such a big decision right now, of all times ... It's ...'

'It's unusual.' Huart smiled. 'Perhaps so. But we'll take it anyway.'

Huart watched Vail go, taking with him a face as clouded as the sky outside. The fortune teller had been so right. They all thought him mad.

The telephone rang. It was Scott Overbeck. 'Heard the eleven o'clock news, John boy? Macau is finished as a free society. And Radio Peking announced five minutes ago that Hong Kong's turn is next. I kid you not. What d'you think of that one?'

'A little strong, Scott. Just propaganda, I'm sure.'

'Sure. Sure. Ahh ... d'you still maybe want to buy our operation here?'

Huart kept his voice phlegmatic. 'Buy, Scott? Fifty-one per cent?'

'No, buddy, I – '

'Sorry – no soap, as you Americans would say.'

'Hey, let me finish. I mean one hundred per cent. Lock, stock and barrel. I've just been given the word. Silicon Valley had warning of the Radio Peking announcement. Shearman Electronics is pulling out of Hong Kong.'

Huart's nervous system sparked. 'I'll set up a meeting with my bankers and call you back at three.'

'I'll be waiting, John boy.'

Holding Thomas Buckley's cash position summary in one hand, Huart dialled Percy Landers' direct number with the other.

'Terribly sorry, old boy, but I'm tied up for lunch,' the deputy head of the Hongkong and Kwangtung Bank began.

'With whom, Percy? Sir David Trench?'

'Not today, John,' the banker laughed. 'Nor any day. The Governor and I are not that friendly yet. No, with my chairman.'

'Then cry off, Percy. I'm more important. Eric will understand when you tell him that I'm about to buy two electronics factories in Kwun Tong and thirty-six acres of East Kowloon. Am I right in thinking the H and K would be interested in talking to me about it?'

There came a brief silence. Then Landers' unruffled voice said: 'You are – if you're serious, John. Your cash position is healthy, and that's an understatement. But didn't you hear the eleven o'clock news?'

Was everyone in Central District sitting by their radio? 'I know what's happened in Macau. And what Radio Peking said.'

'Radio Peking? What have they said now?'

'It's Hong Kong's turn next.'

'Oh dear.'

'Are we on for lunch or not? Mandarin Grill?'

'You're serious? I mean, about buying . . . What was it you said?' Huart told him again. 'It's my turn to pay, John. So I choose. Jackson Room.'

'Uh-uh. It's mine. Too many ears in the Club.'

'You win.' Landers sighed lugubriously down the line. 'We could do with more like you just now. You wouldn't believe the money that's leaving the colony. It's a madhouse around here. What do you have up there with you? You can't quite see as far as Peking so it must be a crystal ball.'

'Nothing as scientific as that, Percy.'

Landers gave out another sigh. 'Alright, I'll see you in three quarters of an hour. That's if you haven't been committed by then.' He rang off.

Huart looked at the clock. 12:15. Cosgrove would be in the Bowling Alley Bar. He buzzed Imelda Roboza and asked her to have him paged.

'Cosgrove here.' Huart could hear the chink of ice in his partner's glass and the calls of his liar dice contemporaries in the background.

'Lennie, I've just made some important decisions.' He smiled at the size of his understatement. 'The company is to purchase twenty-seven acres of land and nine acres of seabed north of

Boundary Street, plus a couple of manufacturing plants in Kwun Tong.'

'Kwun Tong? Shearman?' Cosgrove gave laconically down the line.

'That's right. I'll give you the full details this afternoon after I've discussed the finance over lunch with Percy. I shall be seeking your approval before I commit. What time will you be free to – ?'

'Won't be back this afternoon, John,' Cosgrove cut in. 'Too cold outside. Big game on here. I've bloody P.G. nailed to the wall at last. Been waiting this chance for years. Why don't you go ahead without me?'

'But, Lennie – ' The line was already dead.

Huart slowly shook his head in wonderment. Here he was about to spend $300,000,000 of company and borrowed H and K cash, a large portion of which belonged to a man who was content to let him do it whilst he tossed liar dice and yarned by the fire in the Bowling Alley Bar. Success had not changed that man one iota from the live-for-today, fatalistic opportunist Huart had met by pure, marvellous chance nearly sixteen years before in that same bar. Lennie the Fifth. Lennie the Lucky Pig. How Huart loved him!

14

As the Fire Horse conceded tenure to its trusting, unsuspecting cousin, the Fire Goat, the Great Proletarian Cultural Revolution spread through China like a conflagration. As its threat to Hong Kong grew more ominous, businesses closed, money left, people followed, and hawkers, Hong Kong's human unemployment index, clogged the streets.

The executive committees of Shearman Electronics and Orion Oil found a certain sympathy with Huart for his procrastination. Nevertheless, as the weeks went by, the telegraphic triangle linking Hong Kong, Silicon Valley and Dallas began to run hot. It seemed that each time Huart took up his telephone it was to hear an American voice give him a new quote.

'Sixty-nine million, John,' Michael Rosselino sighed. 'It's as low as we can go. We do have others interested, you know.'

'I'll tell my experts, Mike,' Huart promised. 'But, you know, they gave me a new valuation just this morning. It was only sixty-six million.'

'Oh, shit. Here we go again.'

Huart knew he could afford to be patient; indeed he was affording it better with each new price. His target date was May 2nd, the day after Y. Y. Szeto had forecast the first industrial disputes would break out.

But in sight of the Workers' Day, the local communists lost patience. In the last week of April strikes brought production lines at three Kowloon factories to a sudden halt.

Huart had persuaded Alexander Chiu to eliminate the two-shift system at Wai Wai Road and a third had been added. It had not been a problem to find the extra staff; unemployed hands had been enquiring at the personnel office every day since the start of the recession. Salaries had not been cut, and on April 1st an incentive scheme was introduced based on higher production quotas. It quickly produced results. The fifty per cent increase in payroll was covered by an equal rise in output and Tony Ezuelo and his team were overseas locating the new accounts needed to absorb the expanded production. Rested, rewarded and content, the workers at Wai Wai Road sent packing every communist agitator that dared set foot on their factory floor.

'The men are too busy to think of a holiday right now,' Alexander Chiu affirmed to his relieved chairman. 'Particularly an unpaid one.'

Cumberland China had just fallen short of its 1966–67 targets. Huart kept his satisfaction private and urged his executive staff to greater effort. If any felt he had become unreasonable, none showed it. He was well aware of the danger of prolonging the pressure on them and upon himself. But his gut feeling was stronger than ever, even though he was blatantly going against the advice of all who dared give it.

'Are you sure you're doing the right thing, John?' asked Percy Landers who, like all bankers, only felt comfortable in situations which were devoid of even a modicum of risk.

'You're pissing into a headwind, John,' observed Cosgrove, who then went off to the Bowling Alley Bar to drown his anxieties in pink gin before they could take any definite shape.

'Am I right or am I mad?' Huart would ask himself, going into the boardroom and standing before the canvas faces. In Andrew's eyes he would see only approval and in those of the Great Man, whose likeness hung on the south-west wall, he would see encouragement. And he would come out again with the blood of the 'China Huarts' pulsating through his veins.

May Day came and went and in its wake a strike at a San Po Kong plastics factory exploded into the first riot. Kowloon streets became conduits for waving banners and little red books, and auditoria for Maoist songs and slogans. The police were fettered by orders to exercise restraint in the face of the intimidation they confronted. Radio Peking and local left-wing newspapers praised the uprising of the workers of Hong Kong.

On Tuesday, May 16th, John Huart and Michael Rosselino signed their contract. Orion Oil had sold their thirty-six acres of East Kowloon to Cumberland China for $56,500,000.

Next day the headlines of the *Hong Kong and Oriental Daily* read:

WHITEHALL PROTESTS CHINESE OUTRAGES

Red Guards had spent an hour roughing-up the British Counsellor in Canton, and in Shanghai the house of the British Diplomatic Representative had been ransacked by a Maoist mob.

Meanwhile, the *Business Daily* supplement announced:

ORION OIL SELLS EAST KOWLOON SITE

TRADING COMPANY, CUMBERLAND CHINA, PUTS NAME ON MAP

The following day's headlines related the next episode in Peking's war of words with London:

'GET OUT OF HONG KONG' WARNS RADIO PEKING

ONE MILLION MARCH PAST BRITISH MISSION IN PEKING

CHARGE D'AFFAIRES WALKS OUT ON CHEN YI ANTI-BRITISH
BANQUET SPEECH

Huart took out his Parker fountain pen again on Friday, May 19th. He put his signature to a very thick purchasing agreement, looked on as it was countersigned by Scott Overbeck, and was the owner of two fully operational, if presently dormant, electronics manufacturing and assembly plants in Kwun Tong, a block from the cargo handling terminal of Kai Tak International Airport.

The next morning he unfolded the *Hong Kong and Oriental Daily* over his bacon and eggs to read:

[380]

Chou En-lai, Marshall Chen Yi and Chen Po-ta had sat on the rostrum of the Peking Sports Stadium before one hundred thousand Red Guards and listened to them chant at burning effigies of Harold Wilson.

He flicked to the *Business Daily* and found a photograph of himself smiling back at him.

IT'S CUMBERLAND CHINA AGAIN –
GROWING *HONG* BUYS OUT SHEARMAN ELECTRONICS

There was an exposé on the company and himself under the heading:

WHO IS 'MAJOR-GENERAL' JOHN STANFORD HUART?

The Chinese language press gave prominence to Cumberland China and its lofty chief executive that day. The texts were studded with idioms which were to christen this new business phenomenon possessed with either a sure vision of a bright future, or a death wish. Most chose the latter.

The following weekend the Great Proletarian Cultural Revolution invited itself to Central District. Its focal point was the Bank of China.

The surroundings of the Supreme Court, the Hongkong and Shanghai Bank and the Hilton Hotel swarmed with 'revolutionaries', who set upon any European businessman, newsman or tourist who ventured near. Out of their midst reared the Bank of China, its façade draped with enormous red and yellow banners. From its roof, loudspeakers blared incessant progaganda across Central District.

A block to the west, Huart had no choice but to listen to the bombardment of metallic belligerence as he ate his Saturday lunch. 'Such flagrant discourtesy to one's hosts,' he muttered.

'Communist no good,' Ah Keung delivered sullenly as he brought in the salad bowl. 'Why they no stay China? Communist no damning good.'

Huart smiled to himself. It was the opinion of every local Chinese he had heard venture one. His gut feeling burned as he attacked his salad.

Suddenly he winced as a painfully familiar high-pitched wailing penetrated the penthouse window. 'Cantonese opera?' He laughed at the bewilderment on his houseboy's face. 'It's the loudspeakers on Beaconsfield House, Ah Keung. We're fighting back!'

The din was awful. It aptly represented the disharmony of the time.

Later that afternoon, Huart walked past the Bank of China on his way to the Hong Kong Club. The streets were empty. The loudspeakers were silent. He looked at the broken windows of the Hilton coffee shop, saw the 'blood' stains on Queen's Road that smelled like tomato sauce and felt the acrimony still hot in the air.

The mob had twice marched up Garden Road to intimidate the Governor in his residence. Finally the patience of the police had broken, whereupon the 'revolutionaries' had made themselves scarce. For the time being.

The next Monday the Government imposed a curfew and threatened the reintroduction of water rationing. After the dry winter of the Fire Horse, the 'wet season' of the Fire Goat was also proving a misnomer.

That evening the telephone rang in Huart's penthouse. 'It's me, buddy – Scott. Now that I'm out of a job here, I figure I ought to vacate this Garden of Eden I live in, even though the rent comes down every month. I spoke to the landlord about it today and just caught him in time. His visa's come through and he's off to the States, too. He's keen to sell the house in a hurry and asked me who might be interested. First person I thought of was you. Seems he knows you.'

'Who is it, Scott?'

'Billson Hsu.'

Huart's smile was loud and long. 'I'm interested, Scott. Deep Water Bay is perfect for getting away from Central on weekends. It's been a bit crowded around here on Saturdays of late.'

'That's great, John boy,' Overbeck chuckled. Crowded? There's a war on in Hong Kong and the guy just ignores it. Crazy Brit. 'Oh, by the way, congrats on getting Gene Browne to stay on at Kwun Tong. He's a good 'un. Silicon Valley is down on me for losing that Texan.'

'Sorry, Scott. I made him a fair offer. I need a good man in charge.'

Overbeck rang off and Huart went down the staircase to his office to do some paperwork whilst he waited for the call from Billson Hsu.

By the end of May, stoppages hit the utilities, ferries, buses.

Taxi drivers were paid from the special fund provided by Peking to leave their cabs at home. Army coxswains were seconded to operate the ferries and became the object of ridicule when they found the task of docking the bobbing swaying craft beyond them. The food suppliers and carriers were next to strike. The cost of daily victuals shot up. And every day the riots continued, more desperate, more violent.

In June China reneged on its 1966 water supply agreement and Hong Kong's taps were turned off, except for four hours every other day. Then Peking announced it had exploded its first hydrogen bomb. It was not until the second Saturday in July that the significance of it hit Hong Kong.

Of eight couples who had been sent the Huart invitation to dine in the penthouse on Saturday, July 8th, only four were in the colony to accept.

As cocktails were being taken in the lounge, a hand that must have been directed by fate or *fung shui* turned on the television. There was an immediate newsflash. The room was cast into suspended animation, with every face turned to the screen and imprinted with the apprehension of the time, which a familiar public school accent proceeded to justify.

'Tension on the Hong Kong-China border exploded into open conflict today at Shataukok when, without warning, the police post came under machine gun and sniper fire which, our sources confirm, came from the other side where armed units of the People's Liberation Army have been seen to be active in recent weeks. The post was under siege for several hours and it is reported that its eighty-six personnel have suffered heavy casualties. The toll is five police officers killed and thirteen wounded –'

'What!?' cried Alvin Bucks, senior partner of Jackson, Sloan and Butler.

'Oh, no . . .' gasped Kang Ho-sun, the man who was Kang Shipping.

'The bloody bastards're invading Hong Kong!' Joseph Arlott of the Godown Company heard the echo of his expletives. 'My apologies, ladies –'

'Quiet!' Huart exploded. 'Er, sorry, everybody . . .' he added as he leaned forward on the edge of his chair to listen to every plum, narcotic word.

' . . . sightings of armed PLA troops assembling near the border. One report has put their number at seven hundred. British Army units stationed in the New Territories have been mobilised

[383]

and are in defensive positions around Shataukok and along the border. All firing has now stopped and the police post has been evacuated. The British Government has protested to Peking via the Chinese Mission in London and a counter protest has been received by Whitehall alleging provocation by the Hong Kong Police which, Peking says, left the Chinese security forces with no choice but to open fire in self defence – '

'Self defence!?' cried Alvin Bucks.

'Bloody lying little bastards!' Arlott hissed. 'My apologies, ladies.'

"*Aii yah*'!' breathed Flora Kang, her eyes questing roundly in a face of otherwise sophisticated oriental composure. 'What happens now?'

'Is it invasion?' her husband entreated, looking from face to face.

That of Myron Greenfield, owner of Emerald and Dutton, was reflecting an afternoon invested in the confines of the Bowling Alley Bar. 'Let 'em come,' he gritted. 'We'll teach 'em a thing or two. Let 'em come.'

Huart's brain was racing madly in all directions. This had not been part of any of Y.Y. Szeto's intelligence reports! He was at a loss what to say or do next: pull a face, crack a joke, slash his wrists . . .

He was saved by the telephone in the hall.

He heard Ah Keung's muffled Cantonese, then the houseboy was whispering into his ear: 'It for you, Master. Man say very urgen'. I say you have dinner. But he say very very very urgen'. Sorry, Master . . .'

'Ah Keung, I'll take it,' Huart said at once. 'Excuse me, everyone.'

'It'll be the Commander, British Forces wanting you up at the border quick smart, John,' suggested Greenfield, but it brought no laughter.

'My . . . My name is Wilburforce Wing Junior. Our family owns a few commercial buildings – well, a lot, actually – in Tsimshatsui and Hung Hom. We wish to sell them. We are emigrating to Canada – er, nothing to do with the troubles here, you understand? A coincidence, actually. We applied for our visas last month – well, last year, actually. It's the weather you understand? The summers here are so hot and humid. Last year was so bad and this summer is badder – worse, I mean. My father can't take any more of it – the heat, I mean – the summer heat, you understand . . . ?'

[384]

For a full minute Huart listened to the rambling of the son of Wilberforce Wing Senior, OBE, JP, multi-millionaire, member of the Legislative Council, and property baron. As he stood there with the telephone to one ear and a finger rammed into the other, a singular undisputable fact gleamed like a diamond in the quagmire that had been his brain:

He was in water so deep he had no choice but to swim – or sink.

In his mind he heard the old fortune teller relate the conundrum and in his mind's eye he saw the tidal wave rise up ready to crash down on him. And he squared his large shoulders, took a deep breath. And dived in.

'Mister Wing!'

The sad diatribe of Wilberforce Wing Junior was severed in mid tangent.

'Yes!' Huart went on. 'I would be interested to talk with you, together with my property manager, Mr Vail. Can we meet in my office on Monday?'

'Monday? Oh, too late. We have just booked tickets – well, last month, actually – and we fly out tomorrow night for Vancouver, you understand? We must meet tomorrow. Tomorrow morning. Early. Is it possible . . . ?'

'Oh . . . very well, Mr Wing,' Huart said, counterfeiting a reluctance that he knew would lower the price. 'Tomorrow. In my office at nine.'

'Seven o'clock, Mr Huart. Seven o'clock, please . . .'

'It is Sunday tomorrow, Mr Wing . . .' In the silence of the tactical pause he could hear the desperate breathing of the man on the other end of the line. He could hear the throb of his own pulse against his eardrum. And it occurred to him that he had turned into an animal – a predator of the concrete jungle which he had helped to build. 'Very well. Seven o'clock. But I can't guarantee we'll come to any agreement –'

'Thank you, Mr Huart. Thank you so much! Our price will be reasonable. Very reasonable.'

'We'll see, Mr Wing. I'm on the seventeenth floor of Cumberland House. Take the end elevator. It's an express. You do know where it is . . . ?'

'Oh, yes, Mr Huart. Everyone in Hong Kong knows it. It is famous. The Flagstaff, yes? And you are famous, also. And so clever to buy land from the Americans when they are running away. Not like us, you understand? Running away, I mean. We're not running away. It's really the weather. And my father's health.

[385]

Yes, Mr Huart, you are famous. My father and I will come tomorrow at seven. We will bring our legal and our financial people, you understand? Thank you, Mr Huart. Thank you so much. You are famous. And clever. Mr Huart, you will keep this confidential, please?'

'You have my word on it, Mr Wing.'

'Oh, thank you, Mr Huart. Bye-bye now. You are so famous. And clever.'

Huart stared at the buzzing receiver. 'Clever?' he mused. 'Or mad?'

The call from Wilburforce Wing Junior was but the first he received that night. Thrice more he excused himself from the head of the dinner table to go into the hall and speak to anxious men he had never met before. On each occasion his guests looked at each other with eyebrows arched.

'Congratulations, John,' grinned Myron Greenfield after over-hearing part of the fourth conversation on his way to the bathroom, where pails of water signified the further curtailment of the water supply to four hours every fourth day. 'One day I'll be able to tell my grandchildren I knew the man who bought Hong Kong, the biggest ghost town in the East.'

On his return to the dining room, Huart picked up his glass of Cheval Blanc 1961, smiled around at his bemused guests, cried: 'Eat! Drink! Be merry! For tomorrow – I buy! *Maskee!*' And downed the full-blooded St-Emilion in one swallow as his guests looked at each other again, this time with expressions of undis-guised pity.

'Poor John,' Joseph Arlott said to his wife as they rode in the express elevator to Ice House Street. 'All this trouble has affected his mind.' He clicked his teeth, then added: 'Dear, I think you should call Jardine Airways first thing and book two seats to London. It might be an idea if we took some of that three months leave owing to me. Don't you agree?'

The days joined together one by one to become a week. Y. Y. Szeto was in and out of the seventeenth floor like a cuckoo clock stuck at noon.

Huart's gut feeling curdled and became a clot in his bowel.

The border was not just quiet, it was soundless. The security forces lay in their trenches with a round up the spout and watched for green uniforms coming at them through the heat haze and the rolls of barbed wire that glinted new in the broiling sun.

Whilst the army sweated and waited, the police changed their tactics and went onto the offensive. They raided the headquarters of the left-wing unions and their control centres set up in communist schools, offices and tenements. Campaign officials were arrested. Weapons and files were seized. And the riots stopped.

But then the bombings started.

Multifarious objects were left in crowded cinemas, on ferries, at bus or tram stops or pedestrian crossings, outside banks, in department stores and hotel lobbies. Many were instruments of hoax. Just as many were real. Many were defused by specialist police units. Many were duds. A lot went off.

And, meanwhile, the border remained an ominous place. But a quiet one.

Huart hated to be taken away from Hong Kong at a time like this. Only an invitation to his favourite 'niece''s twenty-first birthday party in New York could do it. He discovered Suzanne to have become a full-grown woman in body and mind, and with very definite plans.

'I'm going to take on Wall Street for a couple of years, Uncle John, to run other people's money through my fingers and get the feel of it. I've had offers, you know.'

He looked at her face, her figure, her legs streaming out of the mini skirt. 'I can believe it, Suzie,' he conceded.

'Then, one day, I'm coming to Hong Kong to play with my own money – now that it's all mine.'

'Yes, Suzie – it's all yours now.'

'Thanks for looking after it so well for me, Uncle John.' She stood on tiptoe to kiss his cheek. 'You're the best there is.'

'Do you really plan to come to Hong Kong?'

'You bet. You know, I think I know why you keep that panel empty on the boardroom wall. You're going to be stepping down one day and I plan to attend the ceremony as the respresentative of the next Huart generation. Maybe I'll even be the next taipan and keep it in the family. But I'll settle for a seat on the board to begin with.' She kissed him again.

'It's yours any time,' he promised, not sure how serious she really was.

She laughed. It was like a flash of light. Then she frowned. 'I read a lot about Hong Kong these days. I see it on TV, too. It looks like big trouble. I hear you're buying property like it's going out of style.'

'It is – in Hong Kong.' His smile was a wry one.

'I know you know what you're doing, Uncle John. From up

there where you are you can see what's going on in China. You have my vote, for one.'

'Thank you, Suzie.'

'You must be mad, John,' Virginia adjudged a week later. 'I saw that mob in Nathan Road, remember? And you say it's worse than that!'

'You're right, my dear sweet nagging lover. I am mad. Now drink up your martini, wish me a happy birthday – and show me you mean it.'

'Happy birthday, my mad, mad mountain of a man,' she sighed as she came to him. 'And this had better prove to you that I do mean it.'

Afterwards they showered and dressed, then took a cab to Broadway. He could not decide between *Fiddler on the Roof*, *Man of La Mancha* or *Cabaret*. She solved it by directing the driver to the theatre where a Eugene O'Neill play was being performed.

'But O'Neill didn't even write all of *More Stately Mansions*,' Huart protested. 'It was his dying wish for the unfinished manuscript to be destroyed.' After a moment he added: 'And a man's last request should be obeyed.' He was thinking of Andrew and his revelation of the existence of a half-aunt by the name of Elizabeth Jane Huart.

Virginia dug him in the ribs at four a.m., but he was wide awake. It was not jetlag. It was not the realisation that Suzanne had changed so much he could see her mother coming through. (Paulette, a taipan's widow awaiting her second divorce, was even more the unsatisfied woman.) It was not what his favourite 'niece' had said about succession.

It was the latest news from Hong Kong.

A crazed Red Guard mob had burnt down the British Mission in Peking. The diplomatic staff of eighteen men and five women had been prevented from escaping until PLA soldiers had improvised a belated rescue.

'Peking probably considers it compensation for the sacking of the Summer Palace a hundred years ago,' Huart commented to Virginia over breakfast, and then listened to the voice of Sinclair MacLurie inside his head as it quoted again to him the prediction of Sir Robert Hart: 'The day will come when China will repay with interest all the injuries and insults she has suffered at the hands of the European powers.'

And he told himself he would never fulfil the second pledge either.

Ah Lam met him at Kai Tak with the Rover and drove him

through Kowloon streets that were wrapped in apprehension. The vehicular ferry was late and slow. It did not occur to Huart until he was in the express elevator that they had not seen another vehicle all the way from the airport.

<h1 style="text-align:center">15</h1>

Beneath two inch banner headlines, the *Hong Kong and Oriental Daily* reported on the imminent certainty of Britain and China severing diplomatic relations. The furrows of Huart's forehead were etched deep as he peered over the top of the broadsheet and muttered: 'Well, Mr Szeto, bad news is big news and the news is getting badder and bigger.' He reached for his cup of jasmine tea and, with quickening pulse, ventured the question: 'What news from Canton, then?'

The sinologist blinked as he mentally constructed his answer. It was unnecessary for his employer to know that his mission across the border had been perilous in the extreme; that he had found his contacts in Canton living out each day in terror; that the Red Guards were acting as judge, jury and executioner; that the proletariat were being exhorted to inform on friends, neighbours, even family suspected of the slightest sympathy to capitalistic or anti-Maoist belief. It was only necessary to announce that, during the three weeks he had lived on the threshold of capture, interrogation and a bullet in the back of the neck, he had extracted an item of news that gave sight of a ray of hope.

When he spoke, despite his ordeal, the words came with habitual prosaic economy. 'Last month in Wuhan a battle was fought between the PLA area command and Red Guard units combined with Maoist factions.'

Huart nodded. 'There have been clashes between pro and anti-Mao factions all over China, Mr Szeto.'

Unperturbed by his employer's display of impatience, the sinologist went on at his own pace. 'The significance of this one is attested to by the fact that a mediation team headed by Chou En-lai went to Wuhan to negotiate a truce. This, however, failed. Chou was forced to call in paratroopers and gunboats and had the city surrounded. The PLA commander was arrested and taken to Peking for trial.'

'What it indicates to me,' Huart offered flatly, 'is that the Red Guards now hold sway over the PLA and that China is on the brink of civil war.'

Y.Y. Szeto blinked again. 'That appears to be true.'

'Only "appears"?'

'The battle in Wuhan was the first outbreak of open conflict between the Chinese army and the Red Guards. The revolt of the PLA – for that was what it was – has demonstrated that the Cultural Revolution no longer has its unequivocal support.' There was a pause and, for an instant, Huart thought Y. Y. Szeto was going to smile. 'This revolution within a revolution has repeated history: Wuhan was the scene of the first armed protest against the Manchus on "Double Tenth", 1911.'

Huart acknowledged the unprecedented aside with his eyebrows.

The sinologist bent his reed of a torso forward. 'The news comes from an impeccable source,' he emphasised. 'My informant was in Wuhan at the time and was present at the mediation negotiations and also at private meetings in which Chou En-lai spoke of a new direction to the campaign.'

'What "new direction", Mr Szeto?'

'A *volte face*. Chou has been waiting for an event which he can use against the fanatics in the Politburo. Now he has it. If the PLA and the Red Guards start fighting each other across every province of China, the country will be vulnerable to outside aggressors – '

'Russia?'

Y. Y. Szeto nodded and sat back. 'Since the beginning of the "Great Leap Forward", Peking has so alienated itself that its only friends are North Vietnam, North Korea and Albania. Russia can see that China is ripe for invasion and is reinforcing its border army. Chou En-lai considers that invasion will come soon. My informant heard him say as much.'

Huart almost whistled. 'Russia is poised on the border, and meanwhile the Chinese Army is engaged in a national fracas with the country's youth? It certainly is time for a new direction.'

'But Chou must first convince Mao. And neutralise his wife.'

'Chiang Ching?'

The sinologist nodded again. 'As I left Canton I was told that before the end of this month her four closest followers will have been purged.'

Huart put the question uppermost in his mind: 'And what of Hong Kong?'

'The riots ceased in July because Peking lost confidence in the promises of the local communists that they would still bring the police to their knees. Campaign funds were withdrawn. All that can be afforded now is what you see: home-made bombs going off in public places – '

'Killing innocent Chinese civilians,' Huart finished.

Y. Y. Szeto stood up. 'The conclusion is that the trouble here has not long to go. If you have any more purchases to make, my recommendation is for you to complete them quickly.'

'If I could, I would,' Huart laughed. 'Unfortunately, the bank refuses to lend me any more money.'

'Then go to another bank. A friend of mine is looking to lend. His family owns the Nam Yeung Commercial Bank.'

'But, Mr Szeto, if he knows what I know, it's a certainty his rate will be less than the best.' Huart rose from his chair and shook his 'company secretary' by the hand. 'You have thoroughly earned your retainer, sir. Our agreement expires at the end of this month. May I propose a two year extension – at a fifty per cent increase in remuneration?'

'I trust I would not be considered too much of a capitalist if I asked for double? The first two years have entailed a few unforeseen risks.'

'Agreed.' It was as Huart had anticipated. He took a deep breath. Relief flowed through him in a salving spasm. Was it really to be over at last? He felt an extra foot tall as he walked to the door and, consequently, Y. Y. Szeto seemed a foot shorter beside him. 'One last question . . .'

'Yes?'

'Will there be a signal to indicate the Cultural Revolution is over?'

'Over for Hong Kong? Yes. If Chou En-lai has succeeded, the first sign will come on National Day – October 1st – when China will agree to turn on the taps again, so to speak – '

'Thank God.'

' – and after that look out for the "Smile Campaign".' It had been said with the straightest of faces. 'You will recognise it when you see it,' the sinologist added as the big man's eyebrows arched in wonder.

At 11:00 am on the first Friday of the month, Nigel Print had a standing appointment on the seventeenth floor. For up to two hours he would review the Engineering Division's performance with his chairman, then go with him for lunch in the Hong Kong

Club, Jimmy's Kitchen, the Mandarin Grill or the Victoria Grill. On one occasion Thomas Buckley had accompanied them. Print had sat through that lunch thoroughly taciturn in the face of the financial controller's valid but overly direct questioning, and Huart had kept them apart ever since. The engineering director had been on time for every monthly meeting in the thirteen years he had been with the company. It was therefore an extraordinary thing when he showed up fifteen minutes late for the one on Friday, September 1st, 1967.

'Tea or coffee, Mr Print?' Imelda Roboza enquired as usual. She confined it to that. Pleasantries seemed inappropriate. And her station was not one to vouchsafe comment on his lateness, nor to draw attention to his ashen face, his uncombed hair, his staring eyes, nor his fingers that shook as they held the mid-morning edition of *The Register*. So, from just inside the door, she watched him walk with robotic gait to the chairman's desk and stand there with his mouth open whilst he tried in vain to eject a word or words. Then she returned to her typewriter without repeating her unanswered question, and sat and wondered.

Huart did not look up from the file in front of him as he greeted: 'Good morning, Nigel. Traffic bad, was it? Help yourself to a cup of jasmine tea.' He brimmed with *savoir vivre*. Neither Print's unprecedented lateness, nor the content of the file could fracture the quietude that had cloaked him for the past few days. 'I see that Byron Browning has reported bad news from Cathay Electric again. What can we do about it, Nigel? What – ' Now he lifted his head. 'Good God, man! Are you ill?'

Print was gripping the desk with one hand for support. The other grasped the folded newspaper and Huart could see the sweaty black smudges of newsprint on his fingers. 'It's this place, sir . . .' Notwithstanding his long service, Print had never addressed his chairman other than most formally, and his broken voice brought back memories of Andrew's down the landline from Shanghai all those years ago. ' . . . this awful place.'

'Whatever has happened, Nigel? You look like you've seen a ghost!'

Print shook his head, as much to clear it as to indicate the negative. 'Not a ghost. That'd be preferable to what I have seen. I've . . . I've just seen a little boy's leg blown off by a bomb. It was awful, sir. Simply awful. It was . . .' The voice fell away into nothing.

Huart went to him, placed both hands on his shoulders and gently pushed him into a chair. He sat mechanically and stared fixedly at the window behind the desk, unfocused on the deep blue-green of the harbour beyond. Huart went to the liquor cabinet that was there for special occasions: contract signings, festive observances, birthday toasts, and poured a shot of Chivas Regal into a crystal tumbler. Print accepted it meekly, sipped once, then swallowed the remainder in a single toss.

'That's fine whisky, sir.'

'Have another.'

'If I may. I realise it's early in the day, but I've had quite a shock.'

As he sipped the second, some of the colour returned to his face.

Parking his rear on the edge of his desk, Huart invited: 'Now, why don't you tell me what happened, Nigel.'

'An hour or so ago I was in Happy Valley. There wasn't a taxi anywhere. A big crowd was gathered outside the racecourse. There was an airline bag on the track. A tram had stopped a few yards from it and other trams were backed up all the way to Causeway Bay. Traffic was at a complete standstill. Everything was held up because of that bag. I was running late. I thought to myself I wasn't going to be late because of a stupid bag. I walked over to it. I was going to show everyone how silly they were. I was going to pick it up and put it in a rubbish bin. I was sure it was one of those hoaxes . . . you know?' He looked up. Huart nodded slowly, knowing what was coming. 'A Chinese boy – he must have been about ten – same as our Martin – jumped from the first tram and ran in front of me. He . . . He kicked the bag like it was a football. He was being a hero in front of his friends, I suppose. And the bag blew up. The boy blew up with it. Straight up in the air. His right leg . . . Gone. I kept thinking: "That could've been our Martin". Then I thought: "No. That could've been me." It could've been me with no leg. Or worse. Sir, I nearly killed myself today getting to this meeting on time. I've never been late in thirteen years, you know. At last I found a *pak pai* – '

Poor Nigel, Huart was thinking. He's been overdoing it. The past year's been a strain on us all. He should take his family on a holiday and get away from Hong Kong before he breaks completely.

' – and downstairs I saw this – ' Print lifted the folded copy of *The Register*, flicked it open and pointed at the headlines.

CHINESE DIPLOMATS BRAWL WITH POLICE OUTSIDE LONDON
MISSION

Huart could not prevent the grimace of disbelief. He grabbed the paper from Print's fingers and his eyes raced over the report that told how the Chinese employees of Peking's Legation Building in Langham Place had gone into the street and begun assaulting British civilians. 'Bobbies' had quickly come to the rescue and had been set upon with baseball bats and pick handles. Reasons put forward for the incident were obscure.

'This is just too much, sir,' Print breathed. 'This is just too damned stupid for words!' Here were more departures from the norm: never before had he raised his voice, nor had he been heard to swear. 'As if riots, bombings and threats of invasion are not enough! Now a mob of so-called "diplomats" go beserk in a London street! It's just too much! China is ruled by idiots. There's no future here. Hong Kong is doomed. I've had it, sir. I'm taking my family back to England.'

Huart's eyes were compassionate. 'Now, Nigel . . . Calm down. Take the rest of the day off. Take the week off. You need a holiday – a break from Hong Kong. It's been stressful lately. This morning you were witness to something awful. And this story is about one crazy incident – '

'One incident?' Print interrupted, something else he had hitherto never dared to do. 'There's been nothing but crazy incidents since the Star Ferry got a five cent fare rise and the place went potty. I still can't believe it. Over five darned cents! I tell you again, sir – this place is doomed!' He took a deep breath. 'Sir – I'm tendering my resignation.'

Huart stood up. It was his turn to inhale deeply. The action seemed to intimidate Print who shrank into his chair. A disappointment rose in Huart. Here was a director of his proposing what amounted to desertion under fire at a time when the end of the war was in sight. 'Nigel, you can't resign. The company needs you. I need you.'

Print shook his head. 'No, sir. This has been building up inside me for a long time. The children really should go to the UK for their schooling. The education system here isn't up to scratch. Anyway, Regina would hate to have them away at boarding school. And she hates the violence here. You do understand, sir, don't you? It's for my family – '

'What about the Engineering Division?' Huart's voice had turned cold.

'Byron Browning can take over – '

Huart snorted. 'Browning? I was going to ask you to put somebody over him. That report there – ' He indicated the file on his desk, ' – is an admission of inability, lack of initiative and – '

'No, sir. You're wrong about Byron. He'll rise to the challenge. He's been . . . well . . . hiding behind me. I hate to say it, but it's true. I'm sure he could handle the division on his own.'

Huart's eyelids tightened. 'You're serious then, Nigel. You wish to resign from Cumberland China?'

'Yes, sir.' It had come without hesitation. 'I do.'

A silence fell. Huart's jaw seemed fixed in concrete. Vexation burned in the back of his eyes. A new fact surfaced and beat him with its obviousness. He would be better off without the man. The Engineering Division was in need of a new leader. It had been the lame duck of the company for too long. Buckley had been right. Why had he not seen it earlier?

'Alright, Nigel,' he acquiesced in an slow expulsion of breath. 'But I insist you take the rest of the day off. Come and see me at 8:30 tomorrow morning. If you still feel the same way after a night's sleep, I'll accept your resignation.'

Print nodded slowly. He pushed himself out of the chair, murmured his thanks, and left the office. When he had gone, Huart stood looking down at the white scars on his palms. He resisted the urge to push his fingers through his hair, and instead forced them into two tight fists. It was not a disaster, he told himself. He would not allow it to be.

His eyes fell on the newspaper on his desk and focused on a secondary heading above a column labelled 'China Desk':

CHIANG CHING PROTEGES EXPELLED.

Calm returned to him. Y. Y. Szeto's information had proved reliable yet again. He went to the liquor cabinet and poured a Chivas for himself. No, Print's capitulation was not a disaster. Tomorrow, the man would either resign, or back down. Either way, he had to go.

He tossed down the scotch and growled with satisfaction as it burnt its way into his innards. And he realised with a stimulating rush that he was looking forward to the challenge. He would turn the Engineering Division around with his own hands if need be. Just like he had grasped what was left of Cumberland China eighteen years ago – when he had been blessed with good luck, and that very best type of good luck: Good Timing. All he needed now was for the rabid insanity that was running amok in China to come to an overdue end.

[395]

On the wall behind his desk was a relief map of Hong Kong. It was dotted with coloured marker pins, each representing a property that was now owned by Cumberland China. Huart knew the quantity, but he counted them anyway. There were thirty-six marker pins on the map.

He looked out the window over Central District, over the harbour across to the peaks of the Nine Dragons that were bathed in bright September sunshine. 'End it now!' he commanded the Middle Kingdom hidden beyond. 'End your bloody useless Great Proletarian Cultural Revolution now!'

16

But even when, on October 1st, the Kwangtung water authorities announced the resumption of supplies to Hong Kong, the end did not come. The bombs continued to kill and maim. But, gradually, the genuine incidents became less and the hoaxes became more. There even came a few weeks of relative calm. But was it a false crest? Was it just the calm before the return of the storm? Huart asked himself as 1967 came to a close.

Then, on a cool dull business morning in January, he was walking past the entrance of the Bank of China on Des Voeux Road, Central, when something made him look up. A knot of people were gathered on the top step between the stone mandarin lions. A bomb there? he asked himself. Surely not, there had not been a bombing for over a month. It was probably a hoax, but they were rare now, too. Intrigued, he halted in mid stride.

The men and women were all wearing the stereotyped communist grey cloth. They saw him standing there looking up at them, and they all turned to face him. He cringed in anticipation of a personal public harangue on the greatness of Chairman Mao, and made to walk off. He instantly aborted the impulse, and stood on Des Voeux Road and stared and stared.

'What . . ?'

As if a remote switch had been thrown, the faces that had carried the Draconian message of the Great Proletarian Cultural Revolution had exploded into a collective beaming smile. A dozen pairs of eyes sparkled; two dozen rows of teeth gleamed white and bright. Even the angry visage on the faces of the stone lions seemed to have melted in concert. Then everything including the grey skies turned brilliant as, in unison, the workers of the counting house of Mao bowed. And Huart bowed back, all the way down from his height. When he straightened, he was grinning from ear to ear. He waved his hand and called: 'Welcome back to the world, comrades!' And he spun on his heel and set off for Cumberland House, his elation brimming. He had to force himself not to break into a run.

He breezed past his secretary's desk and she looked up in surprise. 'Ask Mr Szeto to come up at once, please, Imelda!'

Outside, the 'Smile Campaign' was erupting across Hong Kong like azaleas in April, in the headquarters and branches of the Bank of China and its twelve sister banks, in the communist department stores, in the offices of the Hsin Hua News Agency and all the others of the left-wing fourth estate. The snap epidemic of good-will sent from Peking was a blatant abrogation of all that had gone before. Nevertheless, its genial façade was backed up by extreme courtesy, even obsequiousness, with foreign devils, of all people, singled out for special treatment.

'The fiasco outside the Legation Building in London was the nadir of the Cultural Revolution as far as Chou En-lai was concerned,' the sinologist explained, his hand lost inside his employer's great fist. 'He was able to convince the Politburo that it was a serious mistake, helped by the world press, which was merciless. That single attempt to export the revolution inter-nationally only succeeded in sounding the first ring of its death-knell. Chou is most grateful to the fanatics who thought it up.'

'Sir, you have proved my best investment by far,' Huart expounded. 'I would like to make that investment a long-term one. Would you do me the honour of accepting a permanent appointment to the company's management team? You have studied accountancy, I recall . . ?'

'A little in my spare time, Mr Huart. Only four years.'

'And business administration?'

'Two years.'

'The position of Company Secretary is created. Mr Szeto – you're it.'

'I humbly accept.'

As the Earth Monkey took over, the stock and property markets began to rise. They were the barometers of confidence returned. Trade recovered and passed $20,000,000,000 on an annual basis.

Every time Cosgrove entered the Bowling Alley Bar, he listened for the calls: 'Hey, Lennie! Come over here and touch me!' or: 'Have a drink, Lennie! Any friend of Mao's is a friend of mine!' or the one he loved the most: 'Here comes Lennie, the f – – Lucky Pig!'

Now when John Huart walked through a door into any restaurant, it fell silent in an instant. 'Your usual table is ready, Mr Huart,' bowed the *maître d'hîtel* of the Mandarin Grill. 'Follow me, please. Your host is here. In fact, he arrived several minutes early.'

'So nice to see you again, John.' The Jardine taipan rose from his chair. 'So glad you were able to make it. We've so much to talk about.'

As the first month of financial year 1968–69 began, the property assets of Cumberland China, backed up by its extensive manufacturing and trading operations, put it for the second time in history in the same league as Jardine Matheson, Butterfield and Swire and the other great *hongs*. Huart never showed the depths of his pride in having directed the company through prolonged crisis. Though he had always been too well aware that the precepts for the course he had so steadfastly pursued were totally uncorroborative, he now phlegmatically accepted the reality of the rewards it had brought. Indeed, the winnings from his magnificent gamble were incalculable. Cumberland China had recovered the crown it had worn without dispute in the halcyon days of Shanghai and, for himself, he had won such material wealth that only the expanded team of professionals he employed could begin to fathom the extent of it.

John Huart had become a man among businessmen.

He was the figurehead of the greatest Asian business phenomenon of the century. His picture and his personal comments featured regularly in the press. He epitomised the hugely successful man, modern Hong Kong style.

Nicknames were a natural consequence. The Chinese newspapers dubbed him *Dai Shu Cheung Kwan*: the General Under the Big Tree – a name earned by a leader who disclaims personal credit for his victories, and *Dai Yee Ngau*: literally the Large Eared Ox. It is a local belief that large ears are a manifestation of intelligence, of consequential prosperity, and a guarantee of longevity, whilst the Ox symbolises the empire builder. The English language press took it up and Huart became the Empire Rebuilder, and then the Altitudinal Taipan. It was *The Register* that first christened Cumberland China the Born Again *Hong*. The other papers quickly took it up.

Huart directed that all his employees receive a special payment from the Bonus Fund in April, 1968. But it was only one of the ways he intended to thank them.

At a twelve-course banquet on which no expense had been spared, and which required a complete deck of the Tai Pak Floating Restaurant in Aberdeen, he thanked them out loud as Imelda Roboza, dwarfed beside him at the microphone, simultaneously translated into Cantonese.

'Your individual contributions – your collective contribution – to the company have enabled it to fight its way through the most difficult and frightening year for Hong Kong since the end of the Second World War. The company has had to start its life over again. It has grown up again and we have grown with it. I trust you are as proud to belong to Cumberland China as Mr Cosgrove and I are to have you working with us. We are all, each of us, only single components of the company. We must all work together to keep it what it has become: The Born Again *Hong*.'

He resumed his seat to the accompaniment of applause too enthusiastic and stereophonic to be merely polite. He pushed his chopsticks into the dish of braised soft-bone chicken before him, dipped a portion into the snake sauce, and winked across at his partner.

Hosting number two table, Lennie the Fifth was feeling no pain. That afternoon he had laid out one of his newly won millions. The eighty-two foot cruiser yacht would be called *Midas Touch*. He lifted his double pink gin and winked back, loud and long. Hong Kong was on the brink of another boom. And Lennie the Lucky Pig had drawn pole position.

At the top tables, the senior managers and their wives sat by the dozen. Percy and Maurine Landers were on Huart's right, and on his left were Mr and Mrs Y. Y. Szeto. Also at his table were Thomas Buckley and his prim spouse, Gladys, and Glynn Bedrix, who had brought along his stunning fiancée, Patricia Curzon-Cross, the stockbroker's daughter. There was also the new head of the Engineering Division and his wife. Guy Knox had been headhunted from London. He had sound qualifications and proven experience, and had soon gained his taipan's confidence.

Huart counted the challenges ahead. He gave thanks to the spirit of the ancient soothsayer who had so predicted the future from a cubicle atop the Ladder Streets; Imelda Roboza had told him that morning the prophet had died.

He remembered yet again his pledges to Andrew, and had to

acknowledge their fulfilment to be as remote as ever. He studied the men about him and unconsciously began to select his successor.

But at no time during that night of celebration did the Altitudinal Taipan, head of the Born Again *Hong*, give any thought whatsoever to the legend of the Fire Horse.

17

'Every day richer!' proclaimed Tu Chien. 'Fortune has smiled on us and frowned on others. It told us to stay and buy, others to sell and go. It told them to sell to us, and now we own all North Point and half Causeway Bay and Wanchai. But I have not summoned you here to tell what you already know.' He looked up through the pavilion roof at the thick cumulus scudding across the sky. Blossoms and ripening fruit scented the breeze. It was the time of sweet plenty. 'But riches can be a burden – like an elephant's tusk in a forest fire. My son and nephews have inherited their ivory. They did not earn it from any personal inventiveness, special talent nor scholarly learning. I must decide for the future of the family. I cannot wait – lest the family reduces itself to internal squabbling and becomes like a dog pack biting on the same dogbone.'

Alain To Wai-kit listened intently to his great-uncle's diction. It was, as usual, rife with the traditional idioms of old China. Great Horse Mansion was the only place in Hong Kong where he heard such phraseology.

'I look for my successor amongst the family,' Tu Chien went on, 'but I do not see him. He is a strong man in mind and body, a pioneer, a leader. But he is not there. He must be ruthless, unbending in the typhoon, and a murderer if need be. Like that one.' He jabbed a bony finger at the newspaper on the stone floor beside his rattan chair.

The young man from the branch of the family called To looked down and saw a smiling European face he had seen often of late. 'The Large Eared Ox is a murderer, Great-uncle?'

The patriarch sipped his *bo lay* and expirated hard and it was obvious the crux of the audience was reached. Alain To's impatience with its formality and preamble dissolved and he leaned forward.

'The family has a vital task for you, Wai-kit. I have seen that you are different. You are one who does not wish the world to treat you like straw. You will not be a pearl lost in the sea. You wish to touch tin and turn it to gold. I have chosen you to be made even more different.'

Tu Chien shifted painfully in the chair. He was only sixty-one by Chinese age, but seemed to have gone well past it. Life had accelerated for him. It was a cruelty that tainted what fortune had bestowed. Yet his eyes gleamed as if to light the future so that only he could see and read it. He leaned to the low table with the stone inlay and topped up both cups with the pungent coal-black tea that was even older than he.

Alain To sipped it cautiously and thought the taste worsened every time.

'Wai-kit, I am sending you to the land of the foreign devils. England. I have arranged for you to attend university there for three years.'

Ai yah! The young man missed a breath. Three years! A lifetime!

'You will graduate as a Bachelor of Science in Engineering at Salford University in Manchester. We have family there. They own restaurants. In Hong Kong there will be built many hotels, office buildings, residential blocks. They will be tall and modern. They will require highly trained engineers to design and build them. An engineer who is also trained in business will be one with a difference. The university will make you an engineer. The family will make you a businessman.' Tu Chien looked up at the sky again. 'There is profit every time a book is opened, Wai-kit.'

Alain To was a product of the modern generation, and three years in a Manchester university did not fit with his plans at all. He had his own plan to start business for himself as a broker in mutual funds, shares, commodities, or anything that would turn a quick profit. Nevertheless, it did not occur to him to question his patriarch's decree. It was not blind acceptance of supreme authority, but fear of the consequences if he resisted. 'I am honoured to serve the family. I will work hard and qualify as an engineer. Thank you for the opportunity, Great-uncle.'

Tu Chien nodded and almost smiled. '*Tsui ho*, Wai-kit. The task will be a laborious one, but the rewards will be forever restful. *Yum boei.*'

They drank more of the tea and Alain To's eyes watered. 'I am

[401]

so proud to have been given this task that it has invoked my inner emotions.'

Tu Chien added: 'On your return, you will become part of a plan of vast scope. But first you must graduate from the foreign devil university.' He nodded again, this time to convey that the audience was concluded.

As the young man stood the patriarch appraised him. He was handsome and tall. He was slim, but with no hint of fragility. The Shanghai genes have cancelled out the structural flaws of his southern father, Tu Chien affirmed to himself. Yes, he had chosen the right one. 'You will hear the cock crow and you will know it is time for you to rise up,' he told his great-nephew. 'But first you must learn how to listen. Your education is about to begin, Wai-kit. Three years is but a thousand days.'

The young man from the branch of the family called To left the pavilion with his face set. Tu Chien watched him disappear around the rockery at the top of the garden, then dropped his eyes to the newspaper. 'You are not the only one to have profited from the misjudgement of others. So have I, but I do not crow about it as you do. You have been lucky. So have I. But your luck will change – when I choose it to.'

Almost fifteen years had passed since Chiang Kai-shek had ordered an end to the vendetta against the giant. The aged head-of-state would very likely have forgotten about Major-General John Stanford Huart by now, but Tu Chien could not be sure of this. The best-laid plans are subtle and not hurried, he told himself again. And the plan that was forming in his brain had to be subtle in the extreme. It had to deceive not only the giant himself, but also the whole of Hong Kong and, most of all, the President of the Republic of China and all his watchers. It had to be a plan so subtle that it would deceive the world. Until it was too late.

18

Braga Circuit, Kowloon Tong was heavily quiet, as if the whole street was in mourning. No birds sang in its shady trees, no insects hummed on its still air. At last the front door of the two-storey house at one end of it closed on the last condolence, leaving Elizabeth Zagan alone with her son, except for the servants. She went on his arm to the lounge. It was his favourite room. Decorated in Gothic Revival style, furnished in Kyushu cedarwood, it was an extension of his mother: elegantly Eurasian.

Matthew Zagan was weary, his senses dulled from hopping by air between Darwin, Port Moresby, Manila. The cable had given him three days to get from Arnhem Land to his father's funeral. He had just made it, changing into white shirt, black tie and dark blue suit in a Kai Tak toilet, then taking a taxi direct to the cemetry. He had slept few of those seventy-two hours, and now fatigue pressed in on him like a vice.

The Cantonese houseboy brought tea, then Elizabeth Zagan dismissed him. Her face was drawn, but her eyes were clear as she sat and watched her son throw off his coat, pull at his tie and tug open his collar. When he fell into his father's armchair and lit up a Marlboro, she frowned. 'How long have you been smoking, Matthew?'

'Six months or so.' He exhaled in a white stream. 'All the men smoked on the station. There wasn't much else to do nights but drink and smoke.'

'It killed your father,' she admonished indirectly.

He took the cigarette from his lips and looked at it, then put it back. Once he might have pretended she could control such things. But that was before his graduation with honours from the London School of Economics, before he had gone on to Harvard for his MBA, and before he had taken the past year off to work with his hands, arms and shoulders in the Outback in a sabbatical, of sorts, between his academic and business lives.

She saw that the time had come. 'I have something to tell you, Matthew.'

His pride stirred as he looked at her. In her fifties, she was still his perfect woman, retaining the qualities he admired most: intelligence, grace, loveliness. And a strength of character moulded by her struggle to advance in the Hong Kong business community despite the double handicap given her at birth: being female, and being of mixed blood. All his life he had felt as one with her, and he remembered the Croatian proverb his father had once passed on to him: 'A son inherits the mother, a daughter the father.' He fought off his weariness. 'What is it, Mother?'

She pressed her fingertips together as if in prayer, raised them to her pursed lips, then pushed her hands between her knees. It took several seconds for her to carry on with what she had started, and when she did speak, she kept her voice to a whisper. She did not want the servants to hear. 'Your father's dream was that you

[403]

would work at his side on *The Register* and inherit it on his death. That dream was all that kept him going over the last few years.'

He nodded readily. 'I have always accepted it as my ambition. I followed your guidance in my schooling and studied hard to qualify for it. Now that he's gone, I'm home to stay. I'm ready to join *The Register*.'

'I did not direct your education for you to run a newspaper, Matthew.'

He frowned. 'Mother . . ? Say that again, please.'

She did so.

'You don't want me to start with *The Register* right away? When, then?'

'Never. Not at all.'

He frowned again, harder. 'Mother – just what are you getting at?'

'What do you know of me? What do you know of your father?'

His features turned quizzical. His mother never joked nor wasted words. He chewed on the last question first and had to admit to himself that his recall of his father was indistinct. Jean-Baptiste Zagan had been a traveller. As Far East correspondent for *Le Monde*, *L'Express* and *Le Canard Enchaîné*, he had been at home only between assignments until 1960, when he had retired and started *The Register* and stayed put. But then it had been Matthew who had been away from home. Father and son had been together hardly a month each year of the last seven. He went back to the first question and said: 'I don't know what you're getting at.'

'What do you know of your heritage, Matthew?'

'Mother . . .' he began, then an explanation for the strange interrogation came to him. 'You're telling me that my father . . . was not my father?'

She recoiled. 'Of course he was your father! I refer to something before him. I refer to my mother and my father.'

His frown deepened. 'You've never spoken of them. Not once. I dared not ask. When I began to understand these things, I suspected that you – '

'That I was illegitimate?'

'Well . . . yes.'

'I was – according to some people's rules.'

His tired brain tried to grapple with the ramifications, but it was too much: the telegram delivered by helicopter, the dash to Hong Kong, the funeral. Now this. 'Mother, why don't you tell me the full story?'

She took the *Hong Kong and Oriental Daily* from the sideboard, spread it over the coffee table and pointed at a photograph on the front page. He leaned forward to read the caption. 'John Huart? Who's he?'

She flicked to the features page and pointed again. The heading read:

WHO WILL INHERIT THE GENERAL'S EMPIRE?

He read aloud: 'It is inevitable that the next taipan of the Born Again *Hong* will not be from the Huart clan. The reason is straightforward – there are no more Huarts. "Major-General" John Huart, the fourth family member to lead the *hong*, was tragically made a widower and childless when his whole family including his two infant sons died in the fall of Singapore in 1942. When recently asked about plans for remarriage, his reply was quick and definite. 'Too old and no time.' He has been seen often with New York cosmetics queen, Virginia May Adair but has repeatedly denied that the relationship is more than – '

Elizabeth Zagan's hand covered the text. 'You've read enough, Matthew.'

He lifted his eyes to hers and saw the raw intensity. It was a day for surprises. 'You're related to – ' He glanced down. ' – this man Huart?'

'Only distantly. My father and his great-grandfather were brothers.'

'How can that be? Such a difference in generations, I mean.'

'My father was a man called Charles Huart. He founded that company.' She nodded at the table. 'He was sixty-five when I was born in Shanghai. My mother was his legal concubine. Her name was Lin Ching-hsu.'

By now Matthew Zagan's mouth was open. 'I'm the grandson of the founder of this so-called Born Again *Hong*?'

She gave a fleeting smile. 'It was I who coined that name.'

He ignored this. 'I'm his – ' The common derogation flew to his lips and he clamped down on it. 'I'm his illegitimate grandson?'

'Grandson – yes. Illegitimate – no. Not by the law of the time. But I will return to that. I kept my parents' identity from you. I also kept it from your father. If it had become known, the consequences would have jeopardised your education and your life.' She saw his face pass from puzzlement to confusion. 'Let me explain – '

He stood up. 'First, I need a drink. Is there any beer in the house?' He walked through the swing door to the kitchen and came back with a dark brown bottle of San Miguel in his fist. He raised it to his lips.

'We drink from glasses in this house, Matthew.'

'We drink this way in the Outback, Mother,' he retorted, returning to his father's armchair. 'On with your story. Story? It's a fairy tale.'

She frowned. 'I'm serious, Matthew. I have the proof. My mother entered her concubinage according to Chinese law. Charles Huart was a widower. She lived with him in one of his villas whenever he was in Shanghai. He travelled all over China. All of the time. The company was very large. It had branch offices in all the treaty ports, including Hong Kong. My mother was a well-kept secret. Then I was born. My father loved me dearly. I still remember him as the strongest man I ever met, even in his seventies. He had just one disappointment in his life: he had no son – no heir to his company. His first marriage had been to a French-Canadian woman who died giving birth to his first daughter. When he died himself in 1930, the existence of my mother and myself was revealed in his will. I was eighteen at the time and studying at the Sorbonne – where I met your father. The will also decreed that any grandson born to either of his daughters would have claim to the company. His first daughter – my half-sister – contested it even though she had a son. My mother had no heart for the fight. She had been devoted to my father and had relied on him totally. When he died, half of her died, too. My half-sister had her packed off to Hong Kong and I got here in time to watch her die. Her last wish was for me to have a son. I promised her I would. And I did.'

'To be second in line? You had me so I could be second – ?'

'Wait, Matthew. In 1939 your father was posted to Hong Kong. We married. You were born. The Japanese came. We escaped to the Philippines, then Sydney, just in time.' She watched him take a mouthful of beer as he frowned on in disbelief. 'My son, through you the family can claim what it rightfully owns. You are Charles Huart's grandson – and his heir.'

His smile was cold. 'Second in line, Mother. With illegitimate lineage.'

'My mother's marriage was legal under Chinese law. The state of concubinage is still recognised in Hong Kong, Matthew.'

'By the Chinese, Mother. To Europeans – especially the British – it has the same stigma as any form of polygamy.' He saw that it had hurt.

'Matthew, why are you attacking me so?'

[406]

His face softened involuntarily. 'I'm sorry, Mother. I'm dead tired and my father was buried today. And now I'm finding out things that make me feel I don't know who I am any more.' He looked down at the picture of John Huart. 'Prove I'm the grandson of the founder of that company.'

From her handbag she took a key which she used to unlock a drawer in the sideboard. She returned with a small rosewood box inlaid with mother-of-pearl and fastened by a copper clasp. A second key opened it. She took out four folded squares of paper that were brown with age, opened and smoothed out each one with delicate fingers. Even so, one tore along a crease to confirm its antiquity. Three of the papers were official documents, one bi-lingual: the English written with a flowery quill pen and the Chinese in classical brush-stroked ideograms. The fourth was a newspaper clipping. 'Read them, Matthew,' she urged. 'Start with that one.'

She had indicated the document that was completely in Chinese. Though he spoke fluently the three main dialects: Cantonese, Mandarin and Shanghai, he had only a rudimentary knowledge of their common writing. Yet it was enough for him to know he was looking at a contract of concubinage in which one Lin Ching-hsu swore by her ancestors that she was giving her body and her soul to one Charles Roland Huart for him to do with as he pleased in the determination of her ability to bear him a son. It was endorsed by the imprints of two personal chops – his and hers – upon twin blobs of red wax. It was witnessed by a Chinese solicitor and was dated Monday, September 15th, 1908.

From the box Elizabeth Zagan extracted two small carved ivory pieces, their bases crusted and cracked with red. 'These are the chops that were applied to that contract. And to that. It is my birth certificate.' He was already looking at his mother's maiden name: Elizabeth Jane Huart.

A third document, consisting of two pages of English, was a certified copy titled: 'The Last Will and Testament of Charle-magne Roland Huart'. Matthew scanned the text and could see that it was exactly as she had told him. 'Charlemagne?'

'My father's full Christian name. He rarely used it.'

'Adelaide Huart-Brent?'

'My half-sister. She's dead now.'

'Andrew Huart-Brent?'

'Her son. Charles Huart's first grandson. Your half-cousin.'

'The first in line.'

'He died in 1954. You have been first in line for fourteen years.'

Very slowly, he lifted his eyes to hers.

'Now are you convinced as to your heritage, Matthew?'

He was lost for words, until: 'I seem to remember that when I was about fourteen, I read something somewhere – '

She was already pointing to the newspaper clipping. It was a classified message. One corner carried the date: Friday, June 2nd, 1961. 'The one you remember was in the press right after your half-cousin died. Seven years later, I met John Huart in Central by accident. How he recognised me, I don't know. That appeared two days later, and every day thereafter for months. My half-sister was still on the Cumberland China board then. She must have told him to seek me out and buy me off – just as she did to my mother in Shanghai. She died about five years ago.'

Matthew took up Charles Huart's chop between thumb and forefinger. 'How can we prove this to be authentic?'

'Check it against records, like agency agreements, in Cumberland House.'

He frowned at her. 'How can we possibly do that?'

'It will be simple when you are on the inside.'

'Mother, don't talk in riddles.'

'Listen to me, Matthew. If you attempt an outright claim on that company, you will fail. John Huart will produce a battery of lawyers to beat you down and we'll both be laughed out of Hong Kong. No, my son – you are going to have to earn your heritage the hard way. You were born Eurasian. You don't look Eurasian but you are. The only way you will succeed is to prove beyond doubt that you are better than everyone else in that company. You must show Hong Kong you are better than John Huart. Then, and only then, will the company become yours – both by birthright and by achievement.' She had finished. She sat back and watched him.

The grin began at the corners of his mouth. Gradually it spread over his face. The red-rimmed eyes sparkled. 'Instead of *The Register*, you want me to join Cumberland China and work my way right up to the top. Yes?'

She leaned forward. 'You will start out in the Engineering Division. My research has revealed that it is not doing well and has openings – '

'But I'm not an engineer!'

'It matters little. It's management ability and brains that are needed. Engineering is just part of the company's activities. If you really were an engineer you'd be restricted to it. You must have no restrictions on you if you're to be the next taipan of Cumberland China Limited.'

[408]

'Mother . . .' He recognised the futility of any protest. In any case, he was intrigued beyond himself. 'Who will help you with *The Register?*'

'The newspaper is not bankrupt. I will hire competent people. As for you – you have an interview in Cumberland House with the personnel manager next Monday at ten for the post of Engineering Trading Manager. I forged your signature on your application. You couldn't have prepared a better *curriculum vitae* yourself.'

'Mother . . .' Words failed him once more. He shook his head in disbelief. When he did ask the question that was aimed at drawing final confirmation, each word was pronounced with an individual emphasis. 'Am – I – really – the – grandson – of – Charles . . . Charlemagne – Roland – Huart?'

Elizabeth Zagan's smile drove from the room the lingering demons of grief. 'Yes, my son. You are his grandson. And you are his heir. The Born Again *Hong* belongs to you.'

'It's beyond belief,' said Matthew Zagan. 'It's like being born twice!'

Book IV

TIME OF RUSHING WATER

Hong Kong: 18 June 1972 – 27 March 1973

1

Rain!

The man with the title: Trading Manager, Engineering Division, Cumberland China Limited, looked out the window thirteen storeys over Mid Levels at it. It blanketed Central District, obscured the harbour and its brown border that testified to the alluvial destruction of the land above, and blotted Kowloon from view. It had rained through May, and non-stop for seventy-two hours up to Sunday evening, June 18th, 1972.

'Won't it ease up, even for five minutes?' Matthew Zagan said over his shoulder. He took out a pack and counted his last three Marlboros. 'I'll be out of cigarettes soon. Then I'll be no good to you or anyone else.'

Guy Knox, seated at his dining table amidst papers, graphs, reports, took his fingers away from the Golden Century electronic calculator and looked at his watch. It was almost six. Over an hour had passed since the British engineer from the Public Works Department had knocked on the door to inform him that the high-rises to the east were being evacuated, that their power and gas supplies would then be cut as a landslip from the garden terrace above was expected if the rain persisted. 'No need to fret, sir. It'll be minor. Shouldn't affect this building – if it comes. We've built a sandbag wall along the footpath outside to contain it.'

The 'wet season' had opened early, smothering the South China coast with heavy laden clouds that refused to shift. And then the Water Rat had set about indulging itself to the fullest. Subscribers to the correlation between water and money had rubbed thumb and forefinger together. The stock market had stirred. During May it had begun to agitate. The Hang Seng Index had risen to 421, twenty per cent up on the beginning of the year. In June it had lifted to 450.

The Knox apartment, leased by the Born Again *Hong* for its divisional director, was silent except for the *amah* preparing sandwiches in the kitchen, the tapping of calculator buttons and the rain outside. Knox's family had flown out to London the night before to begin their annual summer holiday. The engineer director was to join them in a week, after he and Zagan had moulded a strategy towards Cathay Electric. Some members of the utility's board had been pressing Kingston Orr to invite international tenders for Phase B of Jubliee Bay Power Station, which was to be twice the size of Phase A. John Huart had been lobbying those directors, aiming to pre-empt another clandestine negotiation with the consortium nicknamed 'Japan Incorporated', headed by the electrical arm of the biggest *zaibatsu:* Matamoto Corporation.

'It's going to be difficult,' Knox affirmed, lifting his head. 'Taking UK inflation over the past decade and comparing it with Japan, Anglo-Saxon are going to be well out on price – unless Reynard the Fox gives what the Japs would call a "por'itical discount".'

'Guy, you know that a competitive price, though essential, will not be the vital factor on the day.' Zagan returned to the chair opposite his director. 'That will be a man by the name of Kingston Orr.'

For two more hours they analysed the project from all angles as they bit into the ham and egg sandwiches. Zagan stubbed out his last Marlboro.

Knox sighed. 'I'm fuzzy in the head. A cold shower will clear it. But first – ' He turned on TVB's broadcast channel to catch the news report. On the screen came scenes of mountainsides that had shifted, squatter communities that had slid from already precarious perches, pre-war tenements that had collapsed, vehicles washed into nullahs. Dead bodies. 'Thirty-six inches in three days. A yard of water in seventy-two hours! Look – the rain's eased a bit. Why don't you dash down to Central and get some more of your infernal cigarettes? We'll resume in an hour.'

Zagan pulled out his car keys. 'I'll try the Hilton.'

Outside, the rain still fell, but more lightly. Night had taken hold. To the east it was as if Mid Levels was in blackout. The high-rises stood dark and empty. As he gunned the fine-tuned engine of his 1957 MGTF out of the car park, Zagan saw the double wall of sandbags. He waved to the PWD engineers who stood in a group: smoking, drinking *cha*, and looking up at the sheer slope that stretched high into the thick, heavy night.

Something caused him to look also, out through his rain spattered windscreen. It had been a noise: a metallic rasping like the groaning of the hawsers of a ship at anchor. Directly across the road there was a monstrous cavity. It was like a colossal mouth stretched open in a yawn, black and vulgar. It was a construction site, an excavation into the side of the Peak where another apartment block was scheduled to rise.

The MGTF's headlights glistened on the wet surface of the wall of sheet steel piles driven into the earth at the back of the site. The wall was holding back the Peak which, just there, had been cut into at an angle of eighty degrees. The raised arm of a diesel-operated pile-driver flicked starkly across the twin beams as Zagan accelerated away. His eyes diverted to squint ahead between the swishing windscreen wipers.

Had he left the Knox high-rise ten seconds later, his headlights would probably have picked up a movement in the wall, and he may have seen the water gush from a gap between two buckling lengths of sheet steel.

As Zagan piloted the MGTF down slippery Castle Road into Robinson Road and turned right towards Garden Road, up above the Knox high-rise the columns supporting the garden terrace broke like sodden candy bars. The structure collapsed with a roar, cascaded into a two-storey house and took it along. Packed with slabs of reinforced concrete, the mountain mud agglomerated into an avalanche that sought out the line of least resistance. Consequently, it did not travel perpendicularly to where the wall of sandbags waited to break its charge; it veered left into the yawning excavation. The wall of interlocked sheet steel gave way and the side of the Peak disgorged across the road in a roaring tumbling slithering hideous tide. It crashed into the thirteen-storey apartment block, smothered it from the ground to the fourth floor. And carried right on.

The lake around the Hilton Hotel was three feet deep. The tops of abandoned cars poked out of it like miniature offshore islands. Zagan parked the MGTF on the footpath outside St John's Cathedral, took off his shoes and socks, rolled up his trousers, and waded through the rain and the flood to the side entrance of the hotel. He took the escalator to the lobby and walked through it barefoot and sopping wet. He looked so much a component of the rainstorm that no-one paid him any heed. At the magazine stall he bought a carton of Marlboros, enough to last him through three more days of continuous rain, and the Sunday newspaper.

The drive back through the network of roads that tacked up the face of the Peak was achieved with extreme difficulty as the tyres slipped continuously on the mud-coated bitumen.

It was a hundred yards from the entrance of the Knox high-rise when the headlights blazed into something that should not have been there. Zagan slammed on his brakes and stared at the impassable barrier before him. It took seconds for him to accept that the black slithering morass of mud, uprooted trees and bushes, broken concrete beams, buckled piles, sections of brick wall and slabs of *chunam* cement was real. Massively, horrifically real.

'What in hell's name has happened!?'

He jumped out. The bitumen shivered beneath his feet. There came a deep rumbling, as if the Peak was suffering from flatulence. Then parts of it broke away and a wave of mud, on which rode maverick granite boulders the size of dump-trucks, flowed past him down the gigantic 'slippery dip' of ruin and disaster into the empty void below. From down there he could hear the screams rising into the Mid Levels night.

He looked up and squinted through the rain, his mouth agape. Where the lights of the thirteenth floor Knox apartment should have been, the moon shone insipidly through a crack in the bellicose rain clouds that tumbled across the sky. And then, like a criminal hand withdrawn after the perpetration of its felony, the killer rains of the Year of the Water Rat abruptly stopped.

2

Every business day the Noon Day Gun told the deputy chairman of Cumberland China that the time had come for him to sink his first gin. But he was as unpredictable as he was unfaithful to any and all discipline. His position at the top but one of the Born Again *Hong* afforded him privilege, which he exercised to the limit and beyond. It was just 8:30 when he barrelled into Huart's office with a 360 degree grin in what was a double departure from the norm: he would never usually be about at this hour, let alone imbibe at it. That it was a Special Occasion, which the pendulum clock on the wall seemed to proclaim with its proud chimes, conferred some licence. Even so, Monday, August 21st, 1972, had to be very special for Lennie the Fifth to start it so abnormally.

His white mop fell about his ruddy face, burnt brown by the sun and sea winds that weathered the deck of *Midas Touch*. His red bowtie was askew and his cream suit was sodden. His chauffeur had dropped him right at the Cumberland House entrance, but still he had fallen foul of Typhoon Betty, at last in her death throes west of Foochow. Without a word he produced a bottle of Beefeater's and a glass from his pockets, poured a shot and lifted it to his taipan in a toast. 'Here's to the new public *hong!*' he cried, then tossed back the gin and belched gloriously.

Confrontation with his partner's unmitigated disregard for convention crinkled Huart's face into a joyous mosaic. It had occasioned their first meeting on another rainy day twenty-one years before, and had brightened his life ever since. He crossed to the sideboard and poured himself a cup of jasmine tea from the pot that was topped up throughout the day by Imelda Roboza. '*Yum sing*, Lennie!' he reciprocated.

Cosgrove shook his head lugubriously. 'You never bloody well change, old salt, do you? What does it take to make you unwind just a little?'

Huart thought on it. 'A screw not yet invented?' he suggested, and they laughed at the *double entendre* like the old friends they were.

It was not that the Altitudinal Taipan had turned teetotal, nor that he disagreed with the occasion. It was just that, as much as the style of Cosgrove's entrance was his own, dedicated mental preparation for the board meeting starting at nine sharp was unabridged John Stanford Huart. It was to be no ordinary meeting, but the first sitting around the Long Table of the new board of Cumberland China, and its object was the ratification of the *hong*'s first ever public issue of shares. Then at ten, when trading on the four stock exchanges was to open, Huart would announce it at a press conference in the Connaught Room of the Mandarin.

'Many happy returns, John!' Cosgrove called as he extracted a Havana.

'Thank you, Lennie. Coinciding our little manifesto with my sixty-sixth birthday certainly gives Double Happiness. But we will celebrate later. There's much to do first. It's going to be a long day for us all.'

Huart turned to the window. The greyness outside cast his reflection, framed in the fluorescent lighting, back at him. He tried to pick out the harbour through the rain that spattered against the pane in large drops, but saw only the concrete foetus of Connaught Centre going up on the reclamation next to the Star Ferry pier. Thirty-five storeys and still rising, it already towered over all else in Central District.

'Look at it. The most expensive piece of real estate in the world. And reclaimed at that, all 53,000 square feet of it. Its superstructure only two-thirds built, and already the first seventeen floors are fully let and will be occupied before it's topped out.' He went to the sideboard to refill his cup. 'It's the sign of new times. We're driven faster and faster by an impatient world. Bigger and bigger. Better and better. That building is pioneering a new era. It's the first with a computerised control system linking its lighting, airconditioning, fire protection, security and elevators. In future all major buildings will have it. The Engineering Division – Cumberland Engineering Limited, I mean – should get its share of business with the Tomson Controls agency Matthew Zagan tied down. That fellow has your luck, Lennie. He's fortunate to be living. Not so Guy Knox – still trussed up in hospital with a broken back.'

Cosgrove blew smoke rings and kept his opinion of Zagan to himself.

Huart chuckled. 'Andrew once told me how a new business era began when they invented airmail and replies came in weeks instead of months. Now with telex we have it the same day. It is another new era. The Cross-Harbour Tunnel has opened, Kai Tak runway is 3,000 feet longer to take the new jumbo jets and the first berth at Kwai Chung is there for third generation container ships. The Goverment's talking of allocating six billion for an underground railway, trade is strong, our dollar's the third hardest currency in the world after the Swiss franc and the yen. Six months ago Nixon and Chou En-lai signed the "Shanghai Communiqué". And who can tell what opportunities will come from that!' He turned on Cosgrove, his eyes bright. 'Our timing is good, Lennie. Good timing is the best type of good luck – except perhaps in your case.' He chuckled again. 'Now's the time for growth and the public will finance it. The Chinese believe the Year of the Rat is the year to invest, you know. And it's the time for us to look north. To China.'

Cosgrove agreed with everything his taipan had said, except one: China. He was not convinced any opportunity lay over the border at all. This was the place for a fast fortune. The stock market was more active each day, the Hang Seng Index was nudging 500, and he was doing his damnedest to help it higher. A fourth exchange had opened, the third new bourse in as many years. It was true: the Chinese did believe, according to their absurd horoscope, that this was the year to invest. And the crystal ball of Lennie the Lucky Pig told him it was also the Year to Take Advantage.

And take advantage he had, using personal and some company

funds to play a market free of regulation under the official policy of 'positive non-interventionism', a modern pseudonym, for *laissez faire*. Others were beginning to catch on. Overseas money was flooding in. But he had been there first. And now Huart had agreed to bankroll a scheme for him to speculate on shares to his heart's content. 'So when's the ten million being transferred into the Cicero Investments account, John?'

Huart could not miss the unsubtlety of the change of subject. 'This morning, after the board meeting. You're in a hurry to hit the market?'

'Yes and no. It should start to fall as soon as our announcement hits the exchanges. I want the funds on hand to buy in at the bottom.'

Huart was astonished. 'Fall? But news of the issue should stimulate it.'

Cosgrove grinned. 'Old salt, you're the biggest taipan in Hong Kong in more ways than one. You weren't a bad soldier either, by all accounts. But where the stock market is concerned, you're a rank amateur.'

Huart could not disagree. The new fad had not interested him beyond his recognition of it as a casino worthy to test his partner's famous luck.

'Our issue will be many times over-subscribed,' Cosgrove asserted. 'It will probably break all records. But where will the cash come from to support the applications? The market, of course. Cash comes out – prices go down. Prices go down – Lennie buys in. When the shares are allocated and those that miss out put their returned cheques back in, the market will rise. Prices go up – Lennie cashes in. Cicero Investments will show a net profit within sixty days of incorporation. Like it?'

'You'll put the ten million straight in?'

'And send prices up? No. I'll buy over the fortnight between the issue and the selection of subscribers, then wait for prices to rise again before selling. Buy in September, sell in October. That's the plan.'

Huart nodded. 'Go to it. Charlemagne Enterprises is putting up the ten million dollars for Cicero Investments to use in this venture. You, Lennie, are Cicero Investments. Go to it. Make a million for us.'

'Nothing so small, John.' Cosgrove puffed on his Havana.

A quick frown visited Huart's face. 'But don't forget – under no circumstances is Cicero to trade in Cumberland China shares. I won't have us vulnerable to accusation of insider trading, rife though the practice is. By your own request, in the new capitalisation you have retained a personal ten per cent in the company, whereas I elected to place all my stock under Charlemagne Enterprises, where I have – to retain our equal partnership overall – a majority shareholding of sixty per cent to your forty per cent. Charlemagne holds fifty-one per cent of Cumberland China and one hundred per cent of Cicero Investments. I never planned it this way, Lennie, but it has come out on paper that I am your boss.'

Cosgrove came up with a lame expression. 'Thank you for the lesson in simple arithmetic, old salt. You've always been my boss and you know it. Have you once heard me complain about it?'

'My apologies, Lennie,' Huart murmured. 'I must have sounded boorish.'

'A little. Now you've got it out of your system, perhaps you'll get down from that big white horse. I always thought you were an infantryman.'

A wind gust chased itself around the building and Huart turned again to the window. The rain had stopped and he could see the glow of the welding torches flickering through Connaught Centre's circular apertures.

Cosgrove's cigar smoke curled before him. 'I see Buckley's persuaded you to recapitalise our property assets only by two hundred per cent,' he said with thinly veiled criticism. 'Three hundred would reflect current market value. Four hundred a year hence. The conservatives win again.'

'They do,' Huart confirmed. 'Tom and Y. Y. Szeto have put it all together very well. And with grand help from the H and K – '

'Landers ought to bloody well help!' Cosgrove's laugh was cynical. 'Five per cent of the new shares at a discount? He's made a nice juicy profit just by putting his signature on a few pieces of paper.'

'Icing on the cake, Lennie. We'll need more of the H and K's goodwill and their credit in the future, just as we've needed it in the past.'

'Take off your rose-tinted glasses, John. If things had ever gone wrong for us, the good old H and K would've been okay. In '66–'67 they had little choice. If Hong Kong had gone down the plughole, they would've gone with it. In '56 they would've snapped up Wai Wai Road. And as for '54 – look what it's left us: Bairstow and MacKittrick at the Long Table.' Cosgrove bit on his cigar. 'Landers' bloody bloodhounds!'

But Huart disagreed. He neither begrudged the H and K their

[420]

spoils, nor Percy Landers the personal success that had come from his nexus with the rocket that was Cumberland China. Backing Huart's scheme for Cumberland House had started the ascent which had peaked with the commencement of construction on the Orion Oil site of Gum Bak Leen Sun Chuen – or 'Golden Century New Town' – a city of seventy-five towers of apartments for 100,000 people. Stage I had been snapped up by eager buyers financed by H and K 'Golden Century' mortgages. Stages II and III, for which public applications would open in two days, were about to be topped out. Today the business card of The Honourable Percy Davenport Landers read: Chairman, Hongkong and Kwangtung Bank.

Cosgrove stubbed out his cigar. 'So all that's needed now is for the executive directors to agree to the package. Right?'

'Correct.'

'They'll be in like Rin Tin Tin. By offering each of them a half per cent of the company in a share option to be taken up over five years, you've made them instant millionaires. On paper, at least. The board meeting'll be all over in fifteen minutes. I'll put money on it.'

'You may be right,' Huart agreed. 'It's an offer they can't very well refuse. It's purposely generous as compensation for the time it's taken me to put the package together. But Tom Buckley thinks it would be in the company's interest to have each director sign a bond not to sell the shares on the open market during the five years.'

Cosgrove grunted. 'Buckley'd mortgage his John Thomas to please you.'

'I say the man's a jolly fine accountant, Lennie!' Huart retorted, leaping to the West Countryman's defence in a briny tone.

'He's an arse-licker,' Cosgrove persisted. 'A parasite. Just like all bloody accountants. That goes for bankers, too. They sit in their ivory towers like Caligula at the Colosseum. They take no part in real business. They take no risks. That's left to do-ers like you and me. If this "new era" means more accountants and more bankers – ' He looked sharply up at Huart as if an unsavoury possibility had just occurred to him. 'I suppose Buckley's managed to secure for himself the same deal as the working directors?' He had over-emphasised the penultimate word.

'He has.' Huart nodded. 'And deservedly so.'

Cosgrove decided to end it there. If the Great Man had a fault, it was myopia when looking at Tom Buckley. The number-cruncher was a plastic turd – not even a genuine shit! He would have to deal in his own way with the newly titled Director of Finance and Administration. 'But,' he went on more temperately, 'I'm pleased for young Glynn, Tony Ezuelo, Dan Vail, Gene Browne, Alex Chiu. But it's such foul luck for Guy Knox.'

'I've put his package into trust.' Huart drained his cup and grimaced. 'His luck was two-faced. It was good in that he was having a shower and came down inside the cast iron bath tub. The *amah* wasn't so fortunate, poor woman. But his luck – and ours – was bad in that it happened just as he was starting to make an impact. It's the first time since the early sixties that the Engineering Division has made a significant contribution. Now it's up to Knox's manager to carry on with it.'

'Hmmm. Zargon.'

'It's "Zay-gan". As in Fagan. French or Yugoslav lineage, I believe.'

'Chinese, too.'

'Where did you hear that?'

Cosgrove looked away. 'Gossip, you know.'

'Provided he does the job – and gets us back Cathay Electric on Jubilee Bay Phase B – his ancestors could have been Hottentots for all I care.' Huart strode over the carpet to refill his cup again. 'What of Imports and Exports, Lennie? What's your forecast?'

Cosgrove shrugged. 'Good and bad. With the Hong Kong dollar released from sterling and pegged to the greenback we're making a bonus exchange gain on every UK purchase. But its making exports less competitive.'

'One never wins all ways all the time. Europe is hard right now. When Britain joined the EEC we lost out. But not so the States whilst parity between the currencies is maintained. Tell Tony to concentrate there, will you?' Huart had rated Ezuelo more highly ever since the now titled Director of Imports and Exports had extracted the Textiles and Garments Division from the wig trade in the nick of time.

'Why Cicero?' Cosgrove digressed.

'Pardon, Lennie?'

'Why call it Cicero Investments? And why Charlemagne Enterprises, too?'

Huart turned and spoke to the window. 'Marcus Tullius Cicero is said to have written: "It is fortune, not wisdom, that rules man's life." An apt maxim for our investment enterprise, don't you think?'

Cosgrove cocked an eyebrow. 'Okay. But Charlemagne was illiterate. It was Charles Huart's full Christian name, wasn't it?'

[422]

'That's not all of it. There's a connection between Cicero and Charlemagne, and – ' Huart hesitated. ' – between Charles Huart and myself.'

'Sounds jolly intriguing.'

'It is – if you follow Chinese legend.'

'Chinese legend? What are you talking about?'

'All four were – are – Horses.'

'Horses?'

'Horses, Lennie. Every one of us was born in the Year of the Horse – all but Charlemagne in the Year of the Fire Horse.'

'Fire Horse?' Cosgrove's brow knitted. 'John . . ?'

'Sir Paul Catchick Chater, whose business descendants own half Central District, was a Fire Horse. So's Leonid Brezhnev. And King Faisal.'

Cosgrove laid a hand on Huart's arm. 'It's all that tea you drink, John. It waterlogs your brain – makes you think you're Chinese. I'd cut down on it if I were you.'

Huart chuckled. If his partner knew the truth behind those decisions he had taken in 1966 and followed through with in 1967 . . . If he knew they were not a product of brilliant insight and super-shrewdness, as everyone believed . . . If he knew they had been influenced by raw gut instinct and the abstract pronouncement of a blind Chinese soothsayer . . . If . . .

'So which of them is going to take my place, Lennie?' he asked suddenly.

'Eh? What're you talking about? You'll go on forever. So will I.'

Huart turned slowly from the window. 'No I won't. Which one, Lennie?'

'Luv-a-duck! I've had enough. I need a pee. So should you with all that bloody tea inside you. You must have hollow legs.' Cosgrove bundled off to the door connecting his own office. 'I'll see you at the Long Table in – ' He looked at his Omega. 'Eight minutes, or so.' Then he was gone.

Heavy nimbus was hurdling north over the Nine Dragons. Down below, Hong Kong was returning to normal after the typhoon. The murmur of traffic was intensifying and the sound reassured him, as the captain of an airliner draws confidence from the healthy hum of his engines. He watched the workmen swarming over the soaked concrete shell of Connaught Centre. The sheer size of the building-to-be fascinated him.

Today, his sixty-sixth birthday, he would tell the television cameras, the radio microphones and the local and world press that each division of the Born Again *Hong* had been registered as a separate subsidiary and that the holding company was offering twenty-five per cent of its shares to the public. It would be the proudest day of his business life. But his face and his thoughts stayed humble. He felt young. For the love of God he felt so young! But his body was no longer. It had betrayed him. He was incarcerated in the shell of an old man. The company needed at its helm a young man in a young man's body. The time was near for him to hand over to such a man. But which one?

He sighed. It was a manifestation that the borders of exhaustion had been reached. The Chinese believe that a sigh brought one a step closer to death. So be it, he decided. In recent weeks hardly a moment had been spared from the complicated, arduous task of putting together the recipe for recapitalisation and 'going public'. There had been endless legal, financial, personnel and administrative procedures to follow in the finest detail. And there had been the lobbying: with the H and K as the bank was underwriting the issue, but also with Cosgrove, with Buckley, with Suzanne Huart-Brent in New York, and with each member of the new board. In the end, the recipe had been just the way Huart had wanted it.

Suddenly, he found himself with a minute or two in which to reflect. It was a rare luxury and he embraced it. He found himself musing: we tumble through life, giving little or no time to think on it, nor to measure in real worth what we have done with it. Ah, there is value in reflection, in seeing through the mind's eye your own life story unfold, and picking the mistakes, reliving the failures and the triumphs, the anger and the elation, the grief and the conquest of grief. And above all, in noting that you have survived and, in surviving, that you have conquered life.

His introspection was disintegrated by a bellow of laughter from the boardroom. It was the deep Texan mirth of Gene Browne. Then Glynn Bedrix joined in. There came the voices of others. The newly constituted board of Cumberland China was gathering around the Long Table. There was excitement in the air. Something big was breaking. They were all part of it. Huart smiled to himself. It was even bigger than they knew. He must select one of them as his successor. Very soon.

The clock showed 8:55 as the fourth taipan of Cumberland China moved to the door of his en-suite bathroom. With his hand on the knob, he paused. The thought surfaced again of his eighteen year search for the illegitimate progeny of Charles Roland

Huart, the original taipan and Fire Horse. He grimaced and went into the bathroom to scrub the image of failure from his face.

The clear, respectful tap at the outside door preceded the entry of Y. Y. Szeto, a bundle of files under his arm. His eyes flicked to the coffee table, where the glass and bottle of Beefeater's had been abandoned in stark incongruity, then up to Huart. 'The members of the new board are assembled, sir,' he announced in his typical matter-of-fact tone.

'Thank you, Mr Szeto,' Huart acknowledged to his reflection in the wall mirror as he checked the set of his navy blue suit, hand-tailored from finest English worsted by Delano Choi of the Gloucester Building arcade. He adjusted his maroon Golden Century tie under the collar of his white 'Business Line 72' shirt, both made at Wai Wai Road, ran a comb through his silvering hair, then bent to cast a critical eye inculcated by his military years over the flawless leather skin of his black size-twelves from Bally of Switzerland. Satisfied, he nodded to his diminutive and equally well attired company secretary, strode to the door between his office and the boardroom, and pulled it open.

There were eight men present, all standing conversing in groups beside the Long Table, it was an unspoken but inviolate rule that nobody seated himself before the taipan. Boardroom rules, however, did not apply to the deputy chairman. Huart noted Cosgrove had, as usual, organised himself to be the last to arrive as he proceeded down the elongated pinewood table, shaking the hand of each new director in turn.

'Gregory, you're looking fit. When's the cricket season starting?'

'In four weeks, sir,' replied Gregory Bairstow, the first appointee from the H and K. He was also the colony opening bat.

'Good morning, sir. I trust you are well.' This came from Bairstow's colleague, Stuart MacKittrick, a popular and efficient Scot.

'Most well, Mac. Hello, Gene. How's the new line at Factory Senior?'

'Morning, John,' beamed Eugene T. Brown, Director of Electronics and chief executive of Cumberland Electronics Limited. The Texan was the only one to come close to the taipan in height and to address him by his first name, due more to natural American casualness than anything else. 'There're one or two teething problems, but nothing we can't get fixed after some trial and error and a coupla late nights.'

Huart nodded, his faith in Gene Browne as firm as the man's

grip. Next he came to the Director of Finance and Administration. 'Good morning, Tom. This seems to be an important day for us all.'

'Good morning, sir.' Thomas Buckley elevated his thin frame to its five feet ten inches. The skin on his pinched face crinkled like tissue paper before it could qualify as a smile. 'It certainly is an important day for the company. And I trust it's also a happy birthday for you.'

'Why, thank you, Tom.' It seemed that Buckley had the only accurate personal file on his taipan. It confirmed the top accountant was ambitious. Cosgrove was wary of him, but Huart sought ambition in every man at the Long Table, mixed with competence. But who owned the best combination?

In turn, he greeted Alexander Chiu Man-king, Director of Textiles and Garments; Daniel Vail, Director of Properties; Glynn Bedrix, Director of Insurance; Antonio Ezeulo, Director of Imports and Exports; and, finally, Raymond Clinton O'Young, his legal adviser. The solicitor was not a director, but had been invited as an 'observer'. He was Cantonese, but considered himself British enough to project an exaggerated Oxbridge accent and to have opted for an adulterated translation of his surname, which for others in his clan was written 'Auyeung'. Despite his pedantry, O'Young was an asset to Huart on company law and, being Chinese, was able to contribute to the taipan's demand for the interests of both East and West to be identified and served in all things.

Huart arrived at his high-backed leather chair before the south wall. Glancing at Cosgrove's empty place, he motioned for all to be seated. Buckley took the chair on his left. The others assumed their customary positions along both sides of the table with the two H and K men facing each other at the far end where Y. Y. Szeto, the last to sit, prepared to transcribe every word spoken onto his shorthand pad at 150 words per minute. Huart had yet to catch him out on even a trifling inaccuracy.

Giving Cosgrove time, he looked to the map of the world on the north wall. The *hong*'s logo, a large gold-plated round 'C' was affixed to the centre so that China appeared inside the circle. Then he swept his eyes along the east wall, his eyes meeting those of each of his precursor taipans, ending with himself. This circuit had become an impromptu ritual which concluded with him looking at the empty panel. Its evergreen pronouncement that he was mortal and seeking a worthy successor was particularly apt this morning. Which likeness was to occupy it?

[426]

The door in the east wall opened and Cosgrove entered. He greeted all simultaneously with a characteristic gesture, except Buckley whom he favoured with a scowl that was there, then not there. Huart recognised again the mannerisms of his dead cousin. It produced both amusement and alarm. Andrew had broken a golden rule of business: 'The object of business is profit; the enemy of profit is emotion; there are many forms of emotion: impatience, vanity, revenge.' Back in 1954 he had been new at the game and too green to subscribe to the rule. Now he kept emotion out of his business thoughts, and kept clear of those who did not. So what of Lennie the Fifth? he asked himself. Seeking refuge in the platitude that conceded one exception to every rule, he welcomed his partner with: 'Good morning, Mr Deputy Chairman – again.'

'Morning, Mr Chairman.' Cosgrove winked. 'Luv-a-duck! What a lovely morning. Lovely for ducks and for companies going public.' He took three gold-banded Havanas from a packet with the insignia of a competitive brand and quipped: 'Just checking out the opposition,' and laid them side-by-side upon the Long Table before the leather-bound folder with 'L.C.' in gold lettering in one corner. An initialled folder was before each director, but his was the only one that always remained closed.

Huart opened the first meeting of the new board of the Born Again *Hong* at 9:03. Cosgrove was proved correct. It was over at 9:18.

Prior to leaving the seventeenth floor of Cumberland House for the press conference at the Mandarin, Huart dictated a telex to New York.

FOR THE ATTENTION OF SUZANNE HUART-BRENT:

WITH YOUR PROXY, NEW BOARD TODAY RATIFIED RESTRUCTURE AND RECAPITALISATION. YOUR HOLDING NOW 5.5 PER CENT OF COMPANY STOCK.

PUBLIC ISSUE OF 25 PER CENT ALSO UNANIMOUSLY APPROVED.

SORRY YOU HAD TO MISS MEETING AT LAST MINUTE. PLEASE TELEX FLIGHT DETAILS SOONEST. LOOKING FORWARD VERY MUCH TO SEEING YOU.

LOVE FROM UNCLE JOHN.

Andrew's second daughter, already a very rich young woman of

[427]

twenty-six, was about to become richer. Huart was confident that the Hong Kong public would enthusiastically embrace the share issue and that Cumberland China stock would quickly climb to double its par value. Or even more.

As successful as he had been in business in the past, the Altitudinal Taipan was restricted to an educated guess at the immediate future. If he had possessed the ability actually to see what lay ahead, he would have recognised that his guess was a conservative one. In the extreme.

3

Atop the salient known as Jardine's Lookout, another pair of hands was mining the mother lodes that were the Hong Kong property and stock markets. Simultaneous with the colony's recovery, Overseas Chinese money had flowed back through accounts in the Daima Bank. Tu Chien had kept out of the public eye whilst he had, since 1968, multiplied the worth of Great Horse Enterprises tenfold and his personal wealth by double that.

At 7:10 a.m. on Tuesday, August 22nd, 1972, a black Rolls-Royce Silver Wraith, its licence plate bearing the digits 118, drew up at the gold-plated gates of Great Horse Mansion. Tu Chien had bought the number at an auction for $100,000 for its phonetic match in Cantonese to the maxim: 'Every day richer!' The gates opened electronically and the chauffeur drove the huge limousine forward over the one hundred yards of gravel that glistened in the early morning August sun. Tu Chien had the stones replaced each lunar new year. He loved fine automobiles, but detested their excrement. A servant helped him alight, but he insisted on pushing himself up the steps to the columned portico between the sentinel stone lions. Each day seemed to add to the climb. His time was passing like a mad stallion galloping over a crack. He had so little time left . . .

Great Horse Mansion had been constructed about a thick central column which dominated its foyer. Around it Tu Chien had built an aquarium out of specially reinforced glass that extended halfway to the lofty ceiling. It was the breeding ground of a thousand mouse garoupa, a fish the Cantonese called *baan yu*: the most prized, most exorbitantly priced seafood delicacy in

Hong Kong. Before each banquet guests were invited to select a fish, which the chef would then prepare with a unique magnificence. Being invited to dine at Great Horse Mansion had become a privilege rare and valued by those who knew. But today the mouse garoupa afforded Tu Chien fleeting interest.

Consumed by impatience, he took his private elevator to his bedchamber where he changed into a thick winter long-gown in defiance of the forecast for a maximum of 34 degrees Celsius. A chill was in his bones this morning. It had to have something to do with the endless rains.

At 7:30 Tu Chien entered his office-study, put himself gingerly into his chair, eased his feet out of his Florsheim slip-ons and began his breakfast. He took the *Hong Kong and Oriental Daily* from the top of the stack, opened at the *Business Daily* supplement and almost gagged on his swallow's nest soup. There it was! In bold black and white.

CUMBERLAND CHINA TO GO PUBLIC
'GENERAL' HUART OUTLINES HONG KONG'S BIGGEST NEW ISSUE
EVER

A story under the byline of Kym Marshall, Business Editor, appeared beside a photograph of the giant and his directors sitting behind a white-clothed table and a battery of microphones. He turned the page and saw the prospectus printed across a double broadsheet.

'*Ai yah!*' he breathed, nodding in sweet satisfaction. '*Ho yeh. Hoooo yeh!*' Good. It was so good! Wai-kit's information was accurate.

Now his plan could start.

He poured more *bo lay* tea and studied the prospectus, the edges of his eyes crinkling in concentration. The Born Again *Hong* was increasing its capitalisation to $500,000,000 and was offering a quarter of it to the public. The prospectus detailed the owners of the other seventy-five per cent and Tu Chien memorised each name, each percentage.

He devoured the reports in the other papers, but none added anything of significance to Kym Marshall's account. The 'Daily' business editor had expanded on his story with a history of 'Major-General' John Stanford Huart's incredibly dynamic rise to business prominence.

' "Insight and acumen"?' Tu Chien scoffed. 'The man has the luck of a peasant who digs for gold and finds silver. The fools were throwing their fortunes away and all he had to do was hold out his hand and catch one or two. But I must desist from wasting energy on useless jealousy. I had both my hands out that year, also.' He smiled to himself.

He studied the photographs of the press conference, concentrating on the man to the giant's right with the boyish grin under a mop of white hair. He noted the fat Havana between the man's fingers, two more on the table before him, and the extravagance of the bowtie. Even in the indistinct newsprint reproduction he saw the gleam of mischief in the eyes.

'*Wang chung cho pieh*,' he breathed. The time has come to catch the turtle in the jar.

He waited, unmoving, until he heard the squelch of tyres on gravel. He counted the three cars: Hoi-sang's Rolls-Royce Silver Wraith II – purchased to upstage his father, Wai-ming's Aston Martin, and Wai-tsun's Alpha Romeo – a film star's automobile. There came the slam of doors as Tu Chien checked the heavy Rolex wedged halfway up his forearm. He drew air into his lungs and willed his brain clear of the dregs of age. He looked into the pigeon-blood eyes of fire of the Ch'in horse upon his desk and he knew that this morning's meeting of the heads of the Tu family would be one of substance.

Just after eleven a.m. a telephone rang continuously in a Kowloon Tong apartment. Finally a woman's voice, husky and containing an undisguised petulance born of interrupted sleep, answered in Cantonese. '*Weiii? Been gaw aahh?*'

Errol Tu Wai-tsun's mouth quivered into a smirk as he recalled the luxurious grip of the famous lips speaking to him across Victoria Harbour. '*Ti-loei? Hay sun may?* Are you awake?' As the stunned silence prolonged, the smirk broadened into a leer.

'I am awake, *Tu Seen-sang*.' The tone was alert, respectful, fearful.

'*Ho*. Are you alone, *Ti-loei?*'

'Yes, I am alone.'

'*Ho*. I am in need of a small favour. Can you accommodate me?'

The famous woman at the end of the line checked an intake of breath. 'I am your servant, *Tu Seen-sang*. Do you want me today?'

'It is not I who wants you, *Ti-loei*.' Errol Tu laughed softly. 'I am much too busy even for you. No, there is another task I would have you perform for me. Now listen carefully to my instructions.' And he spoke for several minutes before hanging up. Next he dialled a number in Jardine's Lookout.

'*Wei?*' Tu Chien demanded.

'The lid of the jar is open, Uncle.'

Errol Tu Wai-tsun smirked again as he replaced the receiver. *Ai yah*. What an exquisite jar. What a lucky turtle.

4

'The wind that blows, the ship that goes – ' Lennie the Fifth called the age-old toast to the hot, still air of the harbour. 'And the lass that loves a sailor!'

He quaffed champagne from a chilled glass then, hands light on the helm, he piloted *Midas Touch* past the end of the Kellett Island breakwater, swung to starboard and pointed the bow of his beloved eighty-two foot cruiser yacht at the Lei Yue Mun Channel. 'A refill, *garçon*, if you please. Chop-chop!'

The uniformed Eurasian steward leant into the cockpit, pulled the magnum from the ice bucket at Cosgrove's feet, refilled his glass to the lip and proffered a tray of *petit-beurre* spread with Iranian caviare.

'*Merci, garçon.*'

'Welcome, Mr Cosglow.' The steward withdrew below to the galley.

The champagne and caviare, of course, were brands distributed by Cumberland Imports Limited, formerly the Imports Division. Although the latter was passable, the former was dull, and Cosgrove made a mental note to tell Tony Ezeulo to switch to a particular Avize variety he had in mind.

Both Chinese crew boys stood on deck, watching forward. There was little else for them to do. Not a breath of wind came off the water to prompt the unlashing of the sails from the main and mizzen masts. The harbour stretched between the island and the peninsula like a sheet of blue glass. Seagulls hovered just above it as if admiring their reflections.

As the 180 horsepower Perkins diesel drove the cruiser yacht smoothly eastwards at eight knots, Cosgrove sat at the helm in a Cardin casual ensemble: light blue vest, white slacks slightly flared, and matching Italian sneakers that did not mark the deeply varnished teak deck. He was hard and fit, broad of chest, forearms hairy and muscular, suntan deep and vital. At five in the afternoon the summer sun retained its noon strength; its unfiltered rays burned down on him through an atmosphere scoured temporarily pure by the winds and the rain of Typhoon Betty, but he did not feel it under the insulation of his white mop.

For Lennie the Lucky Pig life got better each day. He grinned all around at the world that he had by the vitals, and with the floating colony tucked behind the Causeway Bay typhoon shelter passing by to starboard, he lit up a Havana and burst with ribald gusto into a sea shanty.

And he reviewed in his mind the day that had thus far been superlative. But not perfect. Only a woman could make it so. But not just any woman.

As he had predicted, the stock market had fallen. Today, thirty minutes before close of trading, he had instructed P. G. Curzon-Cross to buy for Cicero Investments $2,500,000 worth of shares across a spectrum of blue chips: the H and K, Victoria Land, Cathay Electric, Shang Navigation, Wing Luen Kai Realty, China Rice Importers and the Godown Company. Then he had telephoned a stock exchange official to ask: 'Heard the rumour about us merging with Male & Son, Keith?'

'No, Lennie. can't say I – '

'Well, we've backed off. Thought I'd let you know before the wrong story got around and pushed our opening price too high for the man on the Shaukeiwan tram. You know. Confidentially, Abe Male's strapped for cash right now . . .'

Cosgrove laughed aloud at the recall. Of course the rumour was totally apocryphal. But it would be believed, despite the fact that any venture between John Huart and Abraham Male, whose cash shortage was real but temporary, was a pathological impossibility. Male & Son's stock would fall until Cosgrove took a big piece of it at a discount. He laughed again as he visualised Male's expression on learning his company had been the pawn in a neat quick profit for Cicero Investments.

As usual, the business day of Lennie the Fifth had finished at four. In accordance with his time-honoured Tuesday routine, his Daimler had dropped him at the Yacht Club at 4:30, and now the cruiser yacht bore him past the tip of the Kai Tak runway, a man-made finger stabbing into the harbour. The ship-breaking yards at Yau Tong and the squatter sprawl on the hillside above passed to port. Cosgrove steered into the narrow channel between the island promontory of Shaukeiwan and that of Lei Yue Mun on the peninsula and, once through, he adjusted the helm a few degrees to starboard and headed for Joss House Bay.

Away from the harbour proper, fewer craft were competing for sea room. A junk chugged out of the east, its engine designating it of local origin – only communist junks from the Pearl River still used sails and would today be lying becalmed. A tramp steamer, low in the water, headed in from the open sea, a Taiwanese flag at its mast. On the horizon a container ship powered west towards the Kwai Chung Terminal. To port in Junk Bay, speedboats towed weaving dodging water-skiers in and out and around anchored pleasure craft.

Then Cosgrove saw the powerboat stationary in the water dead ahead.

He stood and peered. The boat had one occupant, a woman. A young woman. She had long black Asian hair and was kneeling, pulling on the starter cord of an outboard motor. His first impression was that she was naked, then as *Midas Touch* drew closer he made out that she was wearing a pink bikini. It had to be the briefest he had ever seen.

He saw her throw the cord aside in disgust and stand, legs braced apart against the rocking of the powerboat, hands on hips. Too well built for a model, he assessed, his eyes fastened on the bosom which had to be all of thirty-eight inches. The bikini top was fighting to contain them all and the bottom pulled into her crotch. He started as a tingle of static electricity reminded him he was wearing nylon underpants.

She looked up, saw the big yacht approaching and waved.

'What a bloody bottler!' Cosgrove whistled to himself. 'Sammy! Where the bloody hell are you?' he called to his number one crew boy.

'Sir?' A tousled black head appeared from the forward hatch.

'Boat in distress ahead. We're stopping to lend a hand.'

The crew boys leapt on deck. Cosgrove throttled back the Perkins. The yacht eased to a stop ten feet from the boat and Sammy dropped anchor.

'Ahoy there!' Cosgrove called. 'Need help?'

Despite her fashionably large sunglasses, he could see she was a looker, too. Her long hair was tied with a pink ribbon that matched the bikini. The crew boys ogled over the deck rail. They seemed to know her.

'Oh, yes! Yes, please! I don't know what wrong with the engine. I been trying get it started a long time. Thank you so much!'

The English was accented. Japanese? No, legs too long. Korean? 'Sammy here's an expert on outboards. Sammy, throw the lady a

[433]

line chop-chop. Then get on down and fix the engine. There's a good lad.'

'Yessir!' Sammy was known to be the tardiest deckhand on Kellett Island, but for this task his enthusiasm was unbridled. 'Catch this, Miss Tze!'

A polypropylene cord snaked through the air to land on the stern of the powerboat. She reached out tentatively, and watched it slide into the water. 'I'll get it!' the second crew boy yelled, tore off his T-shirt and dived in. He surfaced with the cord and, treading water, tied it to the stern. Sammy hauled the boat in and secured the cord to a cleat.

'Why don't you come aboard while Sammy fixes the engine?' Cosgrove dropped the rope ladder over the side and reached out.

She came on deck like an uncoiling python and stood before him in bare feet, her eyes level with his. She smiled. Her teeth flashed in the setting sun. She pushed her sunglasses back to reveal a photogenic face: deep dark brown sloe eyes, long lashes, eyelids with a Caucasian double slit, nose high-bridged – perhaps the work of a clinic in Taipei or Tokyo. Her skin shone like tanned jade.

He grinned. 'I am Leonard Cosgrove. Most people call me Lennie.'

She offered her hand. 'I am Carla Tze Ti and I think I'm in your debt.'

'I'm happy to have the advantage, Miss Tze. Aren't you in films? Sing Company, isn't it?'

She smiled. 'Yes. That's me,' she purred. 'Have you seen any my movies?'

'Some.' It was an untruth. But he had seen publicity shots, magazine pictures, billboard likenesses, none of which did her justice. Carla Tze Ti was the most popular Taiwanese movie actress on the local screen. Reputedly in her mid twenties, she was perhaps older.

'How old are you, Mr Cosgrove?'

Knowing such a question was not considered gauche in Asia, where age is respected, he replied smoothly: 'Call me Lennie, my dear. "Mr Cosgrove" makes me sound older than I am. Actually, I'm forty-nine.' He grinned again. Lennie the Fifth had been forty-nine for eleven years.

'That's what I guessed,' she laughed. 'A perfect age for a man.'

'Would you like some champagne and caviare, Miss Tze?'

'Carla, please, Lennie. Yes, I'd love some.'

He called for a fresh magnum and dropped the awning over

the cockpit. She draped herself along the bench-seat and caught him looking.

'Sir!' Sammy called from the powerboat.

Cosgrove had forgotten all about him. 'What is it, Sammy? Have you found the trouble? I hope not.' He winked at Carla who smiled back.

'Plastic bag caught in propeller! Can't get it off!'

'Then make Miss Tze's boat fast to our stern. She's our guest for the rest of the cruise.' His eyebrows arched at her. There was no dissent.

'Yes, sir!'

Cosgrove poured champagne. 'Where would you like to be taken, Carla?'

'Oh, I don't mind,' she replied with indifference. 'It's a Sing Company boat. I was taking it out for a run. I had no plan. I been filming three days straight. I had to get away for a while. I was going crazy.'

'I know the feeling well.' He gestured to the north. 'I was planning to anchor off Pak Sha Wan for a dinner afloat of lobster and king prawns. All on my own. I'd be absolutely delighted if you would join me. I have a superb white burgundy on ice. That's if you enjoy a dry wine . . ?'

'Mmmm.' Carla stretched her arms into the air like a cat. Her breasts surged against the pink fabric. Cosgrove swallowed hard. She looked into the red sky that bespoke another hot day coming and purred: 'How come you know I love wine? I soooo happy to join you tonight. You very nice.'

'Super! Sammy! We're going on to Pak Sha Wan as planned. Up anchor!'

'Yes, sir!' The number one crew boy climbed aboard.

'And I love cheeses too. You have cheeses, Lennie?'

He nodded and managed to keep the delight off his face. It was unusual for a Chinese female to admit to a taste for wine and cheese. 'Camembert and Brie and Gruyère and Boursin and Emmenthaler and Edam and –' He stopped short of mentioning the Danish Blue and the Gorgonzola, all produce of Cumberland Imports Limited.

'Goody-goody! It will be lovely night, Lennie.'

Cosgrove checked that the anchor was in and the powerboat was secure and started the engine. The Perkins burst into life with a lusty bellow. He steered *Midas Touch* first south-east towards Joss House Bay, then swung the helm north-west around Fat Tong

Point into the sunset. Ahead was Port Shelter, and then Pak Sha Wan.

Carla Tze Ti gaily returned his chat whilst he feasted on the sight of her. 'This so lovely champagne,' she said as he topped her glass again.

'Yes, it is. My company imports it.'

'Oh, really? Your company must be very successful.'

'We do all right. Some more caviare, Carla?'

'Yes, please. This is so lovely boat. It is yours?'

'Yes. All mine.'

'How much it cost?'

'A million dollars.'

'US dollar? *Ai yah!* You must be very rich, Lennie.'

'I do all right,' he agreed, not bothering to correct her. 'Look, your glass is empty already. More champagne, Carla?'

Later, as *Midas Touch* rocked gently at anchor under a full moon, and a light breeze kissed the waters of Pak Sha Wan, Lennie Cosgrove and Carla Tze Ti ate dinner by candlelight. They tore the lobster tails in strips and picked the shells off the king prawns with their fingertips. They washed down the delicious seafood with Chevalier-Montrachet 1967.

They talked non-stop small talk. His was salted with innuendo and hers spiced with a light laughter that came easily but still kept him guessing. And all the time the groin of Lennie the Fifth was knotted in certain knowledge of exactly what form the perfect ending to his superlative day just had to take.

With the cheese the Eurasian steward brought slices of red juicy water melon, then coffee and two balloons half filled with forty-year vintage armagnac. 'You were very adventurous taking a speed-boat out on your own, Carla,' he pointed out. 'You do have a mariner's licence . . ?'

She shook her head.

'But that's very dangerous.'

'I like it dangerous.' She smiled into his eyes and took up her balloon. 'Skol!' The glass drained without leaving her lips. She reached up and pulled at the pink ribbon and a black shower fell over her shoulders.

Cosgrove could wait no longer. He reached out and took her hand, touching her for the first time since he had helped her aboard. 'And now, you would like a personal guided tour of my boat?'

'Will it be dangerous?'

'I guarantee it.'

Standing with her in the teak panelled master's cabin with its double berth, his senses reeled with the closeness of her bikini-clad body, the redolence of her flawless skin. His eyes fastened on the pink fabric of her bra, stretched taut against the bulging pressure within.

'Are those real?' It had been a hoarse whisper.

She looked at him with eyes of milk chocolate and smiled slowly, then reached behind and unclipped her bikini top. It fell to the deck.

He tried not to gape, but it was too much. Pointing at him were the two most splendid breasts he had ever seen, and he had seen plenty in the forty plus years he had been looking. Carla Tze Ti's were twin mounds of rounded smooth satin, slightly uplifting, curved, thrusting, the nipples pink and full and ringed by aureoles of flawless symmetry.

The Cardin slacks of the deputy chairman of the Born Again *Hong* were pushed from within by the most violent erection in the life of Lennie the Lucky Pig, and the perfect ending to his superlative day began as she moved to him, placed one hand over his bulging crotch. And squeezed. A groan of ecstatic pain was wrung from deep down inside him as, with her other hand, she reached behind his neck and pulled his head down.

He lifted his head just long enough to look into those milk chocolate eyes and moan: 'Ohh, Carlaaaa . . . !'

She breathed her hot forty-year vintage armagnac breath into his ear and invited licentiously: 'Call me *Ti-loei*, Lennie. All my lovers do.'

5

The Altitudinal Taipan settled into the plush leather upholstery of his maroon Jaguar XJ12. He closed his eyes and was instantly sorry he did, for a mantle of fatigue closed upon him like the lid of an undersized coffin. Before he could stop himself, he had already defied the Chinese superstition and issued a prolonged sigh.

'Home now, sir?'

Huart rallied a reply. 'Home, Ah Lam. And put on the *Peer Gynt*, please.'

Is it time for a holiday? he debated with himself as a cassette was pushed into the dashboard and the airconditioned saloon was caressed by the resonant chords of classical music. He had not had a break longer than a few days for as long as he could remember. No, he decided. It was not a holiday that he needed. Work was still the recreation he craved. All that was required was a good night's sleep.

The Jaguar slid east on Salisbury Road into Chatham Road, then glided into the flyover system that ended at the Kowloon entrance to the new Cross-Harbour Tunnel. Ah Lam embraced the freedom of being able to pilot the big automobile at forty miles per hour for a straight stretch of three quarters of a mile through the eastern of the twin tubes that sat upon the bed of Victoria Harbour.

Huart reviewed in his mind the speech he had delivered in the Peninsula ballroom. It had been the annual dinner of the Textile Exporters' Association. He had written it himself, and it had contained an appeal for increased investment in new machinery, production resources, personnel training; and for resistance to the increasing temptation presented by the escalating value of the land on which the colony's factories stood.

'It is said that only hindsight has 20:20 vision. But he who looks backwards will soon find he has walked into a wall. We must look forward and not use our land for the purpose of building walls that we will walk into some day in the future.' He had taken his seat to prolonged applause.

The dinner had been preceded by the usual string of cocktail parties in Central. At the last, hosted by the Belgian Bank, Huart had lingered ten minutes past his schedule, deep in conversation with the new Financial Secretary. He had left convinced the choice was a good one.

It was midnight when the Jaguar hummed up the incline out of the tunnel exit. Ah Lam sped west on Waterfront Road into Cotton Tree Drive, took the ramp into Queen's Road, Central, and sounded his horn at the Cumberland House gate. Huart alighted in the basement, bid goodnight to his chauffeur and the attendant who had admitted them – two of the five thousand plus now in his employ – and took the express elevator to the seventeenth floor, where he collected the file full of telexes from his desk before climbing the spiral staircase to his apartment.

The crate of *Corton Charlemagne* 1966 was waiting in the hall, tied in a red, white and blue ribbon. A card in familiar looping script read.

[438]

1966: YEAR OF GREAT WINE AND GREATER DECISIONS. NOW
WE SAVOUR THE FRUITS OF THAT YEAR, IN MORE WAYS
THAN ONE.

WITH WARMEST REGARDS FROM YOUR GREATEST FAN,

LENNIE

Huart smiled in admiration of his partner's good taste and feel
for the occasion. The white burgundy was famous for its aging
quality and its appellation and vintage were, likewise, most apt.
'Ah Keung! Come!'

'I coming, Master!' The houseboy appeared with cup of cocoa
in hand.

'Thank you, Ah Keung. We'll have six bottles of this wine on
ice for tomorrow night's dinner. Prince Lugano and his lady will
be coming. Also Lord Armstrong and Sir Leo Cheshunt, and Mr
Bedrix and Miss Patricia. And a new face – a Mr Matthew Zagan.'

'Yes, Master.'

Huart moved to the balcony door. 'And could you ask Ah Kai
to prepare Szechuan prawns. The Prince enjoys spicy food. Is my
bath ready?'

'Ready, Master.'

After Typhoon Wanda, the lounge had been refurnished in
Burmese teak and *Pandauk* redwood. Paintings of the Shwedagon,
the plains at Pagan, and of the Shanghai Bund adorned the walls.
On a mantelpiece stood a photograph of Jennifer, James and baby
Andrew John, taken in the bungalow in Singapore in October,
1940, just before he had left them for the last time. Upon a
bookcase opposite was a studio portrait of Virginia.

On the balcony the humidity hit his face like a hot towel. He
sipped his cocoa and looked across the tops of the buildings two
blocks north to Connaught Centre. Work continued inside its shell
under the arcs of site lights. The monstrous silhouette blotted out
half the harbour and the lights of Kowloon. It had come to annoy
him. He had designed the penthouse with the harbour as a mural
of perpetual motion for his enjoyment. Patience, he chided
himself. The imperfection was not to last long.

Later he sat in a cold bath, making notes on each telex. The
tub had been specially imported from the States to accommodate
the full stretch of his seventy-seven inches. He laid his head
back, slid the sponge beneath it and closed his eyes. A minibus
accelerated from the lights at the intersection of Ice House Street

and Queen's Road, Central, the pitch of its engine echoing off the buildings. But Huart did not hear it. He was elsewhere, locked in the arms of the angel of reflection.

The incessant honking of the minibus's horn penetrated the window. It overpowered the hum of the Cody wall airconditioner and hit Huart's eardrum. He awoke. The alarm clock told him it was only 5:25. A Cantonese monologue rose from Queen's Road, then a third, then a fourth. It occurred to him that the voices were the loudest of many. Then he heard car doors slam and another minibus roar in and screech to a halt. There was a succession of shouts. They rewound his memory to January, 1965.

Another bank run? Please, God – no! We've just gone public!

He sprang out of bed and showered-shaved-dressed. Ah Keung kept out of his way and was not surprised when he left without saying goodbye.

From inside the elevator as it neared the lobby he could hear more Cantonese voices. Many of them. It had to be another run on the H and K! The crowd had surrounded the building, just like '65. The elevator doors opened and he flew into the lobby, his eyes questing with alarm.

Stopping in his tracks, his fingers went to his tie and straightened it.

He looked at the line of Chinese that began at a desk against the north wall and went down the steps, around the corner into Ice House Street. They were all well-dressed, middle class and orderly. They looked back at him in curiosity. Some of the faces registered recognition.

'*Jo sun, Dai Yee Ngau*,' greeted the man at the head of the line.

Huart's anxiety left him in a flood as he realised the people were not there to remove their money from his bankers, but for just the opposite reason. The English half of the bilingual sign above the desk read:

GUM BAK LEEN SUN CHUEN – STAGES II & III
APPLICATIONS FOR APARTMENTS

'*Jo sun, Dai Yee Ngau!*' a woman called and, one after the other, the greeting echoed along the line: Good morning, Large Eared Ox!

Huart's smile lit the lobby of his building. 'Good morning, everybody!' he responded. 'I hope you will all be very happy with your new homes!'

[440]

Then he heard the sound of more people at his rear and he turned to see the second line. It started from the entrance to the H and K and led out to Queen's Road. He walked outside and his eyes widened in disbelief. Along the pavement elbow-to-elbow people stretched like a serpentine all the way to the Bank of China. There was bedding, cooking pots, porcelain bowls, bundles of chopsticks, radios, fantan boards. Some still slept, but most were awake: standing or squatting, cooking rice or eating it. A clan of fisherwomen conversed in a shouting match. It was they who had contributed to his awakening.

As he watched, more people arrived on foot or alighted from minibuses, taxis, cars. They were Cantonese, Tangar, Hoklo, Hakka, Chiuchow. They were men in suits, girls in frocks, *amahs* in white tops and black pants. They were taxi drivers, bus conductors, government workers, labourers, waiters, or *fokis* who had occupied a space overnight for 'tea money'.

Huart still could not believe it. Application forms to subscribe for shares in Cumberland China could be obtained from the H and K as of nine o'clock that morning. This was the queue for those forms.

The people saw Huart and waved and called: '*Dai Yee Ngau ho yeh! Gum Bak Leen ho yeh!*' The Large Eared Ox is great! Golden Century is great!

He smiled and waved back and wished them all good luck. Then he turned and walked to the Mandarin. He would be early for his breakfast appointment with Lord Armstrong and Sir Leo Cheshunt, but he needed a black coffee before his encounter with the top duo of the largest electrical and electronics conglomerate in the United Kingdom.

A hotel lobby at six a.m. ought to be deserted. Therefore his eyes were drawn to the threesome standing beside the concierge's desk. Two were Japanese, a middle-aged man in golfing attire and a young woman. The third, similarly dressed, was Kingston Orr.

'Good morning, Kingston! Off for a round at Fan Ling? The day starts early for the dedicated.' And the devious, he added to himself.

Orr appeared taken aback at first. Then he smiled thinly and introduced the couple. 'Mr Tetsuo Hondo and his daughter, Yumiko.'

'John Huart. I'm very pleased to meet you both.' He shook the man's limp hand, then smiled at the girl. She had the round kabuki mask face of the Japanese female and was wearing a thin summer dress that revealed short, nyloned legs. There seemed to be nothing outstanding about her. But her father was familiar. 'Have we met before, Mr Hondo?'

Tetsuo Hondo hesitated. 'No. Sank you, Mr Huart. We never meet before.'

But he knew he had heard the voice somewhere, years ago. He looked from face to face, but no-one appeared inclined to say more and the air was soon strained. It was apparent to Huart that he had interrupted a very private conversation. 'Well, time for my breakfast appointment. Goodbye, Kingston ... Mr Hondo ... Miss Hondo.'

They bowed as one, Kingston Orr included, his action a spontaneous one.

'Tetsuo Hondo?' Sir Leo Cheshunt's brow furrowed. He paused in the midst of his scrambled eggs, looked about the other tables in the Mandarin Grill and whispered: 'He's now the Vice President of Matamoto Electric. He's the brains behind their fantastic export growth in the Middle East, Africa, Indonesia and now here. If Kingston Orr is meeting him so early in the day you can bet they're not discussing *sukiyaki* – or just golf.'

The penny dropped for Huart. 'Now I remember where I met him!' He went on to outline the encounter in Patrick O'Harah's office in December, 1954 at which Hondo had so admirably mastered his humiliation.

'O'Harah did us no favour,' Lord Armstrong observed ruefully. 'Hondo has no doubt borne a grudge ever since. The Japs lost World War II, but there's a distinct danger they'll win the peace. What can we do, John? We must move quickly,' Cheshunt's smooth BBC vowels projected. 'We've lost every Cathay Electric contract since Sir Bart died. We can't let Matamoto walk off with Jubilee Bay Phase B without a fight.'

Huart seemed to weigh carefully his words to come. 'What does it take to organise a knighthood?' he eventually asked.

Armstrong's left eyebrow arched. 'What exactly do you mean, John?'

'If a colonial subject bought a 150 million pound power station from a British company, would that be enough to qualify for a knighthood?'

Cheshunt leaned forward. 'Would such a thing influence Kingston Orr?'

'Perhaps. Though he professes to hate the British and the class system, a psychiatrist might say that's because of an inferiority complex from being kept in his stepfather's shadow all his life. If we can elevate him in his own eyes, we may win in more ways than one. I feel it's a base solution, gentlemen – but we're confronted with a base problem.'

[442]

Both Armstrong and Cheshunt were nodding. They exchanged glances.

'It's worth considering,' said the peer. 'I'll see what I can stir up at Westminster. And with Ted Heath. He's in such a stew with the economy and hopelessly embarrassed over the latest unemployment figures. This is an opportunity for him to provide three years work for five hundred voters just by adding another name to the honours list. Of course, it could only become official, so to speak, after the order was placed, John.'

'Naturally. I suggest, Reynard, you start the ball rolling as soon as you get back to London. Such matters, I'm sure, take time. As it stands, Kingston Orr will either do a deal with Matamoto – as he did last time – or if he does go to international tender, he will merely use us as a club with which to beat the Japanese down in their price.'

'It will be done as you require,' Armstrong affirmed.

Cheshunt looked at his watch. 'Time to go. We'll see you tonight, John.'

'Indeed, Leo. Come to Cumberland House at eight. Take the end elevator. It goes directly to the penthouse. Reynard's an old hand at my dinners. Casual, gentlemen, please. And it's a Chinese menu tonight – Szechuan.'

'Jolly good.' Cheshunt signalled the waiter.

Huart touched his arm. 'It's already on my account, Leo. I've a standing arrangement here. When you're in Hong Kong, you're my guest.'

On Des Voeux Road, Huart saw that the two lines originating from Cumberland House had met up and intermingled. They were still growing. Police were out in force to keep them under control. He was a man most proud as he walked into Ice House Street. But he was not to know that one person in three in the line starting at the H and K was there by an instruction that originated from the man with the walking stick. And that man's aim was for the pride of the Altitudinal Taipan to precede a fall.

6

It was not only the jutting breasts beneath the clinging blouse with the Fifth Avenue motif that drew all eyes outside Kai Tak terminal building. It was not only the snow blonde hair cascading to the shoulders, nor the undeniably beautiful face, nor the ming vase hips and the legs that went on forever. It was all these put together, and then something else. For Suzanne Huart-Brent was every inch, every ounce her mother's daughter.

She stood with one hand clasping a Gucci handbag. The other was clamped upon a hip, the elbow thrust out at a ninety degree angle to semaphore her impatience, though she had been waiting for only three minutes. She had slept reasonably in the first-class TWA seat from Los Angeles. But now her skin felt grimed and her senses were dulled after the day-long night spent enclosed within the pressurised cabin thirty thousand feet above the Pacific. She thought of the hot foam bath that was waiting in the Mandarin suite and her patience broke, just as the sleek black Daimler with the tulip-shaped 'M' on each door oozed to a stop before her.

An hour and a half later the private telephone on Huart's desk rang. A glance at the pendulum clock told him it was 11:45.

'And how's the biggest taipan in the Big Lychee today?'

There was a quick silence, then: 'Suzie! So you're here! Why didn't you telex the flight number like I asked you to do? I would've come to Kai Tak to meet you. Still Miss Independence, aren't you – ?'

'Dear Uncle John, nobody but nobody is permitted to see me after I've slept in my clothes all the way from LA. I have strict rules about some things – particularly where my favourite men are concerned.'

' "Men", eh? So how was the flight? Tiring?'

She sighed. 'Long-long-long. Three stops. I was dead on my feet at the airport. I've just got out of the bath. It saved my life.'

'What are you planning to do now?'

'A light lunch in the room. Alone. Don't go breaking your schedule for me, Uncle John. I know what it must be like for you at the moment with the public issue and things. Exciting times, aren't they? After lunch I've some shopping to do at Lane Crawford. Women's things – you know.'

'Are you free for dinner?'

'I am – unless some tall dark handsome guy asks me out.'

'I'm asking instead. Join us in the penthouse. It's to be Chinese. And casual. I'm in need of a hostess and there'll be one or two interesting people for you to meet. Unaccompanied men, too – and not just myself.'

'Matchmaking, Uncle John?'

'No matchmaking, Suzie. I would like your opinion of one of my guests.'

'Which one?'

'A Matthew Zagan.'

'Interesting name. Sounds European.'

'The surname's Yugoslavian. The man himself is British, with rumours of French and Asian ancestry. And he's tall, dark and handsome, I guess – if you go for men who look like George Hamilton.'

'I go for. What time do you want me?'

'My guests are arriving at eight. Why don't you come around seven? Then we can have a private hour together. How does that sound?'

'Perfect, Uncle John. Just perfect. See you at seven.'

She replaced the ivory-white receiver in its cradle, then picked it up again and ordered a fruit juice and salad from room service. The gold Longines that was a twenty-first birthday present from her uncle announced it was bedtime in New York. But she was in Hong Kong, and it was lunch time here. She congratulated herself for eating sparingly on the plane.

She dug into her Gucci handbag with long platinum nails and extracted a pack of Benson and Hedges and a Cartier lighter. Inhaling the filtered smoke, she went to the window. The panorama of Victoria Harbour was broken by the bulk of Connaught Centre diagonally across Connaught Road, once the Central Praya, but she hardly noticed the obstruction. The scene reminded her of New York, the Big Apple, whose raw unabashed drive into the next century she was attuned to and loved with a passion.

She thought of 'Uncle John'. She loved him deeply, too. But his time as taipan was drawing to a close. Who was in line to take over the running of Cumberland China? Who were the candidates for fifth taipan?

Suzanne Huart-Brent had brought herself and her 5.5 per cent stockholding to Hong Kong to find that out.

7

'*Diu lay lo mo!* Screw your old mother!' ejaculated Alfred Tsang Ming yet again as he scooped boiled rice into his mouth with his chopsticks. 'But, *ging lay*, we have not the margin for the discount to Keung Fung that Younger Brother Law insists upon – ' Grains of *baak faan* showered from his mouth. ' – plus his personal kick-back and all the others!'

Alain To's patience was wearing thin. Though it was safer to conspire with a fool in preference to an intelligent man, it was also trying. The project engineer never questioned his manager's decision, but he had constantly to be reminded of fundamental rules of business. 'Of course there is not enough margin, Ah Ming,' he asserted. 'There never is, is there? Giving Keung Fung Holdings their twelve per cent discount will not only ensure we are awarded the contract, it will also ensure we lose money on it. There is nothing new in this. What did we do last time?'

The eyes brightened. 'We . . . We carried the loss over to the next job!'

'Well done, Ah Ming. Our books are only audited at the end of each contract, and the auditors are lazy. The Jade Court Hotel contract will not be finished until at least the end of 1974, probably later with all the usual variations and problems. Younger Brother Law's uncle is sure to change his mind ten thousand times before he decides whether the swimming pool is to go on the roof or in the podium.'

'*Foong tsou!*'

They looked up and signalled to a young girl pushing a trolley stacked with round bamboo *loong* containing boiled chicken feet.

Another trolley came by with beef patties and dishes of spiced spareribs chopped into small pieces. '*Ngau yook – pai gwut!*' this girl called, punctuating the dull roar from the throats of five hundred diners.

The Gloucester Restaurant was a complete floor of the out-dated building that had been converted from the Gloucester Hotel. It was now infamous for its ill designed offices, but famous for its restaurant, which was in turn renowned for its *dim sum*. Conse-quently, between 11:30 and 2:30, seven days a week, it was crammed with Central District Chinese and a sprinkling of Euro-pean businessmen and/or tourists: all talking, talking, talking; sipping tea from porcelain cups; nibbling on beef dumplings, *har gau* and *siu mai*, chicken pieces with skin roasted in honey to a unique crispness, dipping spoons into bowls of corn and crabmeat soup . . .

Alain To had a standing reservation at the Gloucester Restaurant, as he did at half a dozen others in Central. He was served quickly and with deference, something he accepted with consistent indifference. He snapped his fingers at a girl calling:

'*Ngau laam – ngau tsaap!*' and watched as a bowl with strips of ox belly lining and another with pieces of the intestines of a cow were placed before him.

'Ha!' he scoffed as he jabbed his chopsticks at the choicest piece. 'If the General Under the Big Tree knew what its branches concealed . . . If he knew that every engineering contract was a financial disaster and not the pot of gold depicted in the reports sent up to him by the Chicken Eye Buckley . . . If he knew that . . .'

'You are too smart for him to ever know,' Alfred Tsang Ming giggled as he poured *heung peen* tea into the cup of his manager, who tapped a forefinger on the tabletop in appreciation. The liquid blackened as the pot drained to the tealeaves. He placed the lid across the rim and in seconds a *foki* had brought a fresh pot. 'The General Under the Big Tree will never know because you are a genius, *ging lay*.'

'You think so, Ah Ming?' Alain To enjoyed few things in life more than having his ego massaged.

'*Jun ge!* Definitely. Soon you will surely be equal to Chiu Man-king, Y.Y. Szeto and the lawyer, O'Young.' He had pronounced it 'Auyeung'.

'Those bananas! You think I am like them: yellow and tough on the outside but white and soft – a *gwailo* stooge – inside? *Hay yau chi lay*. Never will I stoop to their level. And, *dai lo*, if you stay with me, neither will you. *Diu lay lo mo!* Screw your old mother!'

The project engineer nodded, both chastised and inspired. He transferred a helping of *baak choy* from its dish into his manager's bowl. A second round of boiled rice arrived and they finished their meal in silence.

In the crowded elevator, Ah Ming announced importantly: 'China Rice held steady, though the market fell this morning. I have a thousand of their profit-making shares. And I'll buy more tomorrow. And some of K.O. Shang as well. The market will go up tomorrow. It's been falling all week.' He looked around proudly at the expressionless faces in the elevator.

'Don't pick up a shoestring and lose a fortune, *dai lo*.' Alain To's warning was well-intended and, in issuing it, he acknowledged the idiom to be from his great-uncle's repertoire. Perhaps he was growing as wise.

The office girls in the rear of the elevator tittered and the back of Ah Ming's neck reddened. He had lost face in a crowd of strangers.

[447]

Alain To smiled to himself. The stock market was something he had chosen to avoid. Instead, he was impatient for the horse racing season to begin next month. He believed only in the corruption of people. Jockeys were human. Younger Brother Law was human. The sub-contractors he dealt with were human. Ah Ming was human. All of them could be corrupted and were therefore trustworthy. But share prices blew about like leaves in a typhoon. Yes, the typhoon could be summoned up by humans, but they were special humans: the omnipotent men whose circle he had yet to penetrate.

His great-uncle was one of them, probably even at its centre. Why else would he have received instructions from Great Horse Mansion to obtain application forms for 100,000 of the new shares in Cumberland China? Why else would the $500,000 needed to support the application have appeared in his account at the Daima Bank that morning?

'The twelve per cent discount for Keung Fung is decided, *ging lay?*' Ah Ming yawned as they parted outside the Gloucester Building. At his manager's behest he had spent the night on the pavement outside the H and K.

'It is decided.'

'And Younger Brother Law?'

'I will handle him. Go tell him of the discount. Nothing more.'

Alain To walked east on Des Voeux Road, Central, over a bed of roses that was fertilised by the kickback scheme he manipulated: his subcontractors and suppliers cut him in on their payments for every order he placed on them. And now there was the chance of something big. Keung Fung Holdings were building the 600-room Jade Court Hotel in Nathan Road, Tsimshatsui. He had set up Younger Brother Law, nephew of Law Shek-ho – Keung Fung's owner, to receive in cash via a bogus subcontractor five per cent of the value of the electrical and mechanical engineering contract for the hotel. But there were two conditions: firstly, Younger Brother Law had to persuade his uncle to award the contract to the Contracting Division of Cumberland Engineering Limited; and secondly, half the cash had to be kicked back to Alain To, its manager.

As he walked, he calculated again in his head two and a half per cent of $38,000,000 dollars. '*Aiiyahhh!*' he breathed to himself.

And he gave silent thanks to his great-uncle for sending him to Salford University, and for the telephone call on his return with his degree to the personnel manager of Gum Bak Leen, whose wife's cousin was surnamed Tu. It had been magical the way more experienced people above and around him had found themselves moved sideways or passed over for promotion.

As is normal after lunch, the Des Voeux Road pavement was crowded with men in suits with flared, cuffless strides and shoes with buckles and elevated heels, and with local office girls with slender legs exposed beneath mini-skirts and height enhanced by cork-heeled pumps. But Alain To ignored the females of his own race in favour of the European ladies heading for Lane Crawford or the shops in the Pedder Street arcades.

On the corner of Ice House Street he stopped short. *'Dui lay lo mo!'* he exclaimed under his breath as he stared at the vision of Suzanne Huart-Brent as she stepped from the pavement outside Prince's Building and came across Des Voeux Road in his direction. *'Diu lay lo moooo.'*

8

Confronted with two guests of honour who were not averse to a manifestation of temperament if they suspected their face was not being catered to, Huart took extra care over his seating plan. Despite an imbalance of six to three, he succeeded in positioning each male guest next to at least one female by sacrificing the pleasure for himself. On his right he put Prince Lugano and his current 'fiancée', Danielle. Lord Armstrong, who had as much an eye for a pretty face as for a pretty profit, was placed on the hostess's right with Patricia Curzon-Cross beside him.

Hemmed in by such pulchritude, the 'Fox' could not resist setting out to make an impression. 'Only in Hong Kong could such a thing happen!' he declared authoritatively, then took a half inch off his Corton Charlemagne 1966 with as much panache. 'Wonderful chablis, John – '

'Thank you, Reynard.'

'Indeed,' the peer carried on, 'it would be unheard-of elsewhere in the world. To tear down a building only fourteen years old! And one as architecturally striking as this – ' He gestured expansively with his hand.

Armstrong's outburst typified the reaction to Huart's noon announcement to the press. It had made headlines first in *The Register*.

The redevelopment would combine the adjacent site on Queen's Road, Central that Huart had purchased the day before Billson Hsu had fled Hong Kong in 1967, and was now part of the land bank under the aegis of Cumberland Properties Limited. A fifty-five storey office complex, to be named New Cumberland House, would rise in place of the two existing buildings. It was to be thirty feet higher than Connaught Centre.

'It's a matter of pure economics, Reynard,' Huart responded. 'This building is too small by today's standards. In 1955 when we designed it, it was fine. Plus we've done nothing with the site next door for five years except show it as an asset in our balance sheet. Rental from it is unexciting. Developing both sites together will result in a building that will generate eight times the revenue. In addition – ' It occurred to him that Victoria Land had tried to do the same thing in the mid-fifties, but had been foiled by Billson Hsu. Good timing, he reminded himself as he gestured to Ah Keung to open another bottle of wine, is the best type of good luck. ' – the H and K have just bought Harold House on the corner of Ice House Street and Des Voeux Road for their Central headquarters. Their decision to reduce their office in Cumberland House to a branch caused ours to be made that much sooner.'

'But such a fine edifice, John,' Sir Leo Cheshunt protested from Huart's left. 'Economics rules, but it's a great shame. Such a work of art.'

'Don't be too concerned, Leo,' Huart assured him. 'Come 1975 you'll see a virtual replica of Cumberland House standing on the ground beneath us. Bigger of course, but the same architecture, recessed angled windows, Roman arches, solid glass walls, marble lobby, bleached stone façade . . .'

'Where will you put your offices in the meantime?' Prince Lugano asked in his clipped Swiss accent as he stroked the thigh of Danielle, a Paris model with skeletal chassis, perpetual pout and haunting eyes. With the main course almost eaten, she had yet to venture a comment on anything.

Huart delayed his reply until he had selected a healthy Szechuan prawn from the dish before him and placed it in Lugano's bowl, then had done the same for each of the other guests within arm's reach. He looked to the foot of the table, met Suzanne's eyes and gave a quick frown.

She glanced to her left and rolled her eyes in exasperation.

Matthew Zagan's skin still ran with invisible sweat. He had

prayed the taipan would not seat him near her, but had found himself on her immediate left. Consequently, the meal was proving a bittersweet ordeal. He was rendered inert, inanimate. It was as if he were Superman and she was made from kryptonite. She had certainly been sculptured from something, he had adjudged at first sight, and by a hand that had attempted a mere imitation of beauty but had surpassed its objective. He had hardly spoken to her, though she had plied him with hostess-type questions. But if words were not flowing between them, something else was, and it was tying his emotions and his tongue in knots. She was the most desirable woman he had ever laid eyes upon. But she was also the most untouchable.

'The sales, administrative and engineering staff will move to temporary accommodation in buildings we own in East Point,' Huart advised. 'The executive staff will stay in Central. Today I signed a three year lease on a location that is rather elevated – to say the least – '

'And where would that be, Uncle John?' Suzanne interjected. 'You haven't struck a deal with God to redevelop Heaven, have you?'

'Not quite, Suzie.' Huart laughed with the others. 'The directors will be moving into offices at the top of Connaught Centre. So will the Long Table – and that will be something of an engineering feat.'

'Well . . !' Cheshunt was visibly impressed.

Armstrong laughed. 'I'll bet the rent up there'll be sky high, too, eh?'

The soaring edifice had captured the imagination of all. But none more than Huart, who had decided first to join it, then beat it. The joy of working from the loftiest point in the colony would indeed cost a premium, but would be worth every dollar. No-one was going to look down on Cumberland China. And when Connaught Centre was no longer the pinnacle, he would move to the top of the building that was: New Cumberland House.

'This is the week for announcements,' he continued. 'Prince Lugano is not in Hong Kong just because he promised Danielle a shopping spree.' He winked at the Paris model, but saw no reaction. 'Gino . . ?'

'It would be unlawful to let these prawns go cold.' Lugano spooned a fresh helping into his bowl. 'Why not let Glynn make the announcement? He deserves the honour. He's done most of the hard work, after all.'

'A grand suggestion. Glynn, you have the floor.'

With wine glass in hand, the Director of Insurance rose from the chair between Danielle and Zagan and smiled across at his fiancée, who glowed with affectionate pride. 'This is something of an undeserved honour . . .'

'Come now,' called Huart. 'No misplaced modesty, please.'

The young executive's smile broadened. 'I think a toast is in order. To add one more noteworthy achievement to the week, Cumberland China is to expand its financial activities beyond insurance into merchant banking. Today the Ensurete Cumberland Bank was registered in Hong Kong. Its shareholding will be forty per cent the Lugano Androne Bank, forty per cent Cumberland China and twenty per cent the Hongkong and Kwangtung Bank. It will occupy the ground and first two floors of New Cumberland House. I propose a toast to the new venture!'

Warm sentiments exploded: 'Hear, hear!' 'Wonderful news!' 'Congratulations, Glynn! Congratulations John! Congratulations Prince Lugano!'

'There is cause for another toast,' Huart declared as he also stood. 'As his reward for all this, Glynn will receive greater responsibility, more to worry about, less time to spend with Patricia, and no extra salary.' He waited for the laughter to subside before continuing. 'But to prove the Long Table is not attended by a collection of ingrates, I'm happy to announce that Glynn at least has a new title. He is no longer merely the Director of Insurance, he is henceforth to be known as the Director of Insurance . . . and Banking. Congratulations, Glynn!'

Armstrong gave a chortle. 'You'll go down in history as the Englishman who brought Swiss banking to Hong Kong, John. Novel! Admirably novel.'

They raised their glasses and Ah Keung hurried to open the last bottle of *Corton Charlemagne*, then carried in the steaming white almond bean curd that was Lugano's favourite local dessert. At eleven, the owner of the Lugano Androne Bank and Ensurete Suisse apologised on behalf of Danielle who, he said, had developed a headache. Glynn Bedrix and Patricia also made to leave. The prince and his 'fiancée' were their charges.

'Headache, my foot,' the newly titled Director of Insurance and Banking whispered to Huart as they walked to the door. 'We're all off to the new discotheque in the basement of the Hilton and we'll be there until it closes at two. Our prince is in his second childhood.'

'Sounds like good clean fun to me, Glynn,' Huart chuckled.

'Good luck to him. From the look of Danielle, she doesn't get much sleep.'

'Yes, sir. It is somewhat embarrassing . . .'

'Don't be so prudish, Glynn. Gino's been separated for years.'

Bedrix frowned. 'You mean you don't know, sir?'

'Know what, Glynn?'

'Oh, I thought you did. Actually . . . Danielle's no Paris model. She – er, he – is the most famous female impersonator in Pigalle.'

'No!' Huart quickly recovered himself, then gave a weak laugh. 'Do you mean to tell me I had the seating arrangement wrong after all?'

A balloon of cognac warming in his right palm, a cigar between the index and middle fingers of his left, the 'Fox' lounged in an armchair from which he continued to pontificate. 'It's because he's damned Eurasian! Kingston Orr wouldn't behave like this if he'd had a decent upbringing.'

In another armchair, Sir Leo Cheshunt wore an after-dinner expression as he studied the toes of his A Testoni casuals. Like his chairman, who now sat with his nose thrust over his cognac, he was ignorant of the gross error that had just been made.

Huart, in a third armchair, made to protest, then stopped and glanced across at Matthew Zagan, sitting impassively at one end of the sofa.

At the other end, Suzanne Huart-Brent lifted a fresh Benson and Hedges to her lips and ran the tip of her tongue around the filter tip. She crossed her legs and adjusted the midi so that it exposed maximum leg. She regretted the passing of the mini, not because Paris was going from one extreme to the other, but because she wished she was wearing one right now. But she saw that Zagan had reacted neither to Armstrong's gaffe nor to her flash of thigh, and pulled a private face. The man was an annoying enigma. A damn good looking one, but an enigma. She could bring out the man in men just by breathing in, but with this one she could hold her breath for a full minute and it would still fail.

Huart waited. The quality of Matthew Zagan's reaction, or the lack of one, would decide his future in Cumberland China.

Aware he was the litmus paper in a snap test, Zagan lit another Marlboro and sifted through the dozen lines he had ready to deliver in response to the Fox's witless observation. When the weight of silence had reached its limit, he selected one. 'I believe what you mean, Lord Armstrong, is this: If Kingston Orr was pure Chinese, it's unlikely that he would ever deign to acknowledge our

[453]

foreign existence. In that case, we're fortunate he is Eurasian. At least it gives us half a chance.'

'Uh?' The peer lifted his gaze, his eyes heavy under the effect of the supreme quality white burgundy and fine cognac. 'What's that you say?'

'How clever, Matthew – or is it Matt?' Suzanne gave a feminine chuckle. 'But aren't you Eurasian yourself?'

By now, helped by the cognac, he had come to terms with the reality of her. He smiled. 'Either will do, Miss Huart-Brent. Yes, my mother is Eurasian. My father was European. I, myself, am one quarter British, a quarter French, a quarter Yugoslav – and one quarter Shanghai Chinese.'

The Fox's lower lip fell half an inch. His ears reddened.

'Your father is dead?' Suzanne asked. 'I'm sorry . . . you did use the past tense. And please call me Suzie. Uncle John does.'

Zagan nodded. 'My father died four years ago. When he was a foreign correspondent he used three passports: French, Swiss and British. I chose British, as did my mother.'

'Shanghai Chinese?' Huart imparted. 'Do you speak the dialect?'

'Yes. And two others. I learnt Shanghai dialect from my mother, Cantonese in Hong Kong as a child, and I studied Mandarin at college.'

Huart's eyebrows lifted the merest fraction. 'You speak French?'

'I do.'

'Any other languages?'

'No others, I'm afraid.'

'Isn't five enough, Uncle John?' Suzanne reproved. 'I speak one. I rate anyone who can speak half a language other than their native tongue.'

'Then you'd admire my *amah*, Miss Huart-Brent . . . ah, Suzie,' Zagan put in with a half-smile. 'She speaks three: Cantonese, Hakka and English.'

She frowned, unsure if he was making fun of her.

Huart was amused. 'What does your mother do, Matthew?'

'She owns *The Register*.' He had made it sound unimportant.

'The afternoon newspaper?' Huart enquired.

'That's right.'

Leo Cheshunt stirred. 'Powerful organ, the press.'

'I've used it to advantage often.' Armstrong tried to smile away his embarrassment of minutes earlier, though his ears retained the evidence.

Zagan exhaled into the air above his head. 'I'm doing just that now.'

[454]

Huart looked at him. 'What do you mean?'

Seeing he was the centre of attention, Zagan leaned forward. 'I've spent hours, days – even weeks if you add it all together – in *The Register*'s morgue putting together a file on one Jeremy Parrot.'

Huart, Armstrong, Cheshunt all looked at each other.

'*The Register* came from the old *Shanghai Times*, back issues of which were in the morgue. I'd heard Jeremy Parrot was in Shanghai before the war, so I went through them and eventually found a photograph of him on a 1938 social page. It was his twenty-first birthday and at the time he was an assistant manager at East China Rice Exporters – '

'Now I remember the man!' All eyes flew to Huart.

'The old memory's on today, John,' Cheshunt observed. 'First Hondo, and now Parrot.'

Huart ignored it. 'Parrot's uncle owned East China Rice Exporters . . .'

'Then there's no love lost in that family,' Zagan said. 'The company dismissed him subsequently – for suspected embezzlement.'

Huart was sceptical. 'The *Shanghai Times* wouldn't print that!'

'In 1938 they might not have,' Zagan agreed. 'But in 1946 they certainly did. That was the year Jeremy Parrot stood trial in London – once again for embezzlement. His family got him off.'

'I had a run-in with the fellow in Shanghai,' Huart recalled. 'I was a company commander then. I caught him in action with a teenage prostitute in an alley. It was New Year's morning. I can see it like it was yesterday. He threatened me, I remember. I'll be . . . So he's held that grudge against me all this time. What a strange fellow.'

'What a charming fellow,' supplemented Cheshunt.

'A teenage prostitute in an alley, Uncle John?' Suzanne laughed. 'And you say you caught him red-handed?'

'It was actually the girl who had him in hand – in a manner of speaking. But he was more blue than red. It was the middle of winter.'

'Kingston Orr leaves all commercial negotiations in Parrot's hands,' Zagan pointed out, returning them all to the subject. 'He only involves himself at the beginning and at the very end when the contract documents are put before him to sign – at which time he invariably insists on a "face" discount.' He looked from one to the other, finishing with Armstrong. 'The point of it all is: It's not Kingston Orr and his ancestry that's our only problem. So is Jeremy Parrot – a true-blue Englishman.'

The 'Fox' gagged on his cognac.

'What do you suggest, Matthew?' Huart asked, thus far impressed.

Zagan shrugged. 'Nothing . . . yet.'

'How much more time do you need?'

'One month. Maybe two.'

'But negotiations for Jubilee Bay Phase B are to begin soon,' Armstrong protested. 'We have precious little time!'

'We have the time.'

'How can you be so certain?' Cheshunt asked.

Zagan looked at him. 'Parrot will only deal with Matamoto through Male & Son. He never, for various reasons – probably ethnic – deals direct with the Japanese. Abraham Male is his closest confidant, and Male told me himself today that geotechnical problems with the slope behind the site will delay the project until at least January next year – '

'Excuse me,' Huart interrupted in a flinty voice. 'Why should Abraham Male see fit to tell you this – or anything? You're his arch competitor. Any information he would give would be deliberately misleading.'

'Under normal circumstances that would be true,' Zagan agreed.

'What makes the current circumstances abnormal?' Huart persisted.

Zagan shrugged again. 'He says he's heard good things about me. This morning he offered me the position of Trading Director of Male & Son.'

'You turned him down flat, of course.'

'Of course not. An open door swings both ways.'

The council of war continued into the small hours. Suzanne fought off her jet-lag as she watched Matthew Zagan perform, all the time enjoying the pleasant twinge in her loins.

9

Lennie the Lucky Pig hooked a finger under the collar of his dress shirt and grimaced. It was after midnight, but still uncomfortably warm standing on the steps of the Peninsula Hotel inside a dinner jacket. All the gin, bordeaux and armagnac that had flowed into him at the intimate corner table in the *Chesa* was now flowing out again from every pore. Luv-a-duck, how had they survived in Hong Kong before airconditioning? What the hell had they done with his Daimler?

Carla Tze Ti massaged a pliant breast into his rib cage. She was cool, perspicuous, somehow inhabited within a pink skin-tight jumpsuit secured by a red zipper that ran from her throat to her crotch. Pink was her top colour, Cosgrove had decided. Pink bikini. Pink jumpsuit. Pink –

'Nipples.'

'Ha?'

'Pink nipples. You've got pink nipples.'

She giggled and pushed the breast harder into him.

He drank in her perfume. 'Where'll we go – if they find the damn car?'

'I know special place,' she purred. 'I know very special place.'

The Daimler drew up before them. 'Let's go, then.' He took her arm.

The doorman stood by the passenger door and the parking attendant eagerly held out the car keys. Each managed to keep their eyes all over her whilst pocketing a fifty dollar note. 'Thank you so much, Mr Cosglow.'

He got in behind the wheel and she slid across the seat to him and tucked her right breast under his armpit. He flattened the accelerator and powered the Daimler around the fountain into Salisbury Road.

The filial warmth of the Mid-Autumn Festival was in the air. It was the night parents let children stay up late to play with lighted lanterns, and families gathered on high ground to eat sweet *yuet bang* cakes and gaze at the moon which, in the Year of the Water Rat, traversed the night sky over Hong Kong full and bright in optimum auspicious glory.

In the airconditioned luxury of the Daimler, Lennie Cosgrove felt warmth of a different kind as the fingernails of Carla Tze Ti stroked the inside of his thigh, and he sped towards Kowloon Tong at a mile a minute. She directed him off Waterloo Road into a street he recognised. On one corner was the house of Sir Ignatius Tao, proprietor of the College of All Saints, and across from it stood the home of a supreme court judge.

'There.' She pointed at a neon sign that read: Red Phoenix Motel.

He drove into a paved courtyard and parked the Daimler

[457]

between a Rolls-Royce Corniche and a Mercedes Benz 500SE with white cloths draped over their licence plates. An attendant in a tuxedo appeared with alacrity, a cloth in each hand, and proceeded to safeguard the public reputation of the deputy chairman of Cumberland China, who climbed from airconditioning into humidity. 'Mid autumn? They sure have got it wrong this year.'

Carla led him through a glass door draped with chartreuse curtains into a reception area lit by spotlights shining through a floor-to-ceiling aquarium, whose fish cast moving shadows. Cosgrove felt as if he had entered an underground grotto. But the doors painted with 'Utopia Room', 'Nirvana Room' and 'Paradise Room' brought him down – or up – to earth.

'This place very popular with Sing Company starlets,' Carla told him.

'And with their horny boyfriends, I'll bet,' he added, with the palm of his hand moulded to the curve of the most famous derrière in Hong Kong.

The man in the tuxedo unlocked the Paradise Room. They followed him into a suite with a circular bed that was turned down in readiness and waited as he mechanically flicked switches on a control panel beside it. The lights dimmed, perfume flowed from the airconditioning diffusers and the chords of Paul Mauriat oozed from hidden stereo speakers. Then he left without having spoken a word nor made any gesture, and Cosgrove looked at Carla as if she was appetiser, entrée, main course and dessert all on one superbly arranged plate.

She lifted a hand to her throat, took the zipper between long-nailed thumb and index finger and drew it all the way down. Very slowly. She put her hands on her hips, squared her shoulders and rippled them like a showgirl. The jumpsuit sprang open. And there in front of his eyes was the *pièce de résistance:* the most famous breasts in Hong Kong.

He dived to the feast. Somehow, she managed to remove his dinner jacket, his bowtie, his dress shirt, and the rest of his clothing item by item without him feeling a thing. And on the circular bed, as she performed on him her personal variations to a familiar theme in time to the throb of *Je t'aime, Je t'aime*, Lennie the Lucky Pig discovered just how aptly named was the Paradise Room of the Red Phoenix Motel, Kowloon Tong.

Two hours and four climaxes later, he was lying naked and flat on his back grinning up at himself in the mirror on the ceiling. He stretched extravagantly in all directions and his finger contacted a button on the control panel. There came the whirring of the motor beneath the mattress and the central section of the bed began to lift under him. His grin became a mask of ecstasy as he retrieved from most recent memory the vision of her above him, riding him as his pelvis was rhythmically raised and lowered. Had that been the second time or the third? He plucked something from between his teeth and examined it in the suffused glow of the indirect lighting. It was a black pubic hair. 'I always dreamed of sixty-nining with a movie star,' he chuckled to himself.

He heard Carla in the bathroom, humming a Mandarin love song as water ran into the sunken tub, where he had taken her the third time or had it been the second? He punched the button and the bed ceased its movement. He twisted onto one elbow, pulled the magnum of Dom Perignon from the ice bucket on the side table and refilled first his glass, then the one smudged with lipstick, then relit his Havana with his Dunhill lighter.

Propping himself against the headboard, he watched his throbbing member withdraw upon itself like a disused opera glass to rehabilitate amongst the damp hair that matted his groin. The pacific tones of Paul Mauriat harmonised with the hum of the wall airconditioner. And sated, relaxed, happy, Lennie the Fifth ruminated on his circumstances.

Today the stock market had blown out of the doldrums it had been in for three weeks since the Index had fallen to 460 and stayed there. In that time, he had bought selected shares in half million dollar parcels until Cicero Investments' ten million dollar stake was fully employed. Then had come the phenomenal news that Cumberland China's public issue had been a record sixty-six times oversubscribed. Today, the money of the tens of thousands whose applications had been returned with letters of regret had been thrust back into the market. The Index had jumped. And he knew that on Monday it would jump again.

Next Wednesday, trading in Cumberland China shares was to open on the four stock exchanges. Fuelled by the announcements of New Cumberland House and the Ensurete Cumberland Bank, the opening price was sure to exceed the par value of five dollars. The question was: by how much?

But, happy as he was, Cosgrove was also impatient. Ten million dollars was a trifle. Cicero Investments was but a toy fashioned by the General to keep him occupied. He had played along with the plan. But it was not for reasons of 'tradition' he had asked to retain a personal holding of ten per cent in Cumberland China.

[459]

Oh, no. It was to give himself access to a real pot of gold – a fifty million dollar personal cash bank that would explode in value the instant the stock market opened on Wednesday.

Lennie the Fifth had developed an addiction for playing for big stakes. The rule prohibiting the others at the Long Table from trading in their own shares did not apply to him. He was above any restriction. 'Thou shalt not be found out!' he promised his image above him, and popped a sequence of smoke rings into the dusky light of the suite and watched them drift upon the chords of *Love in Every Room*.

Carla Tze Ti came out of the bathroom, once more inside the epidermic jumpsuit. She looked fresh, dynamic and gave not a hint that her body had just been subjected to a two hour bout of raw, repetitive sex.

'Why me?' he asked her.

She looked back at him in innocent surprise. 'Why you? Why you what?'

'I know I was born lucky. But tell me true – why have I been selected to receive all this wonderful treatment?'

'You don't like it?'

'You're not listening. I said it was wonderful. Sure I like it. What man wouldn't like it? I love it! Luv-a-duck, if I could find a way to put it in bottles I'd be the richest bloody man in the world.'

She studied him in puzzlement. 'Put it in bottles? How . . ?'

'Carla, why have you selected me for your sexual action?' he insisted.

She shrugged. 'I like you. You . . . You mature man. Mature man don't want to get involved. Mature man just like to screw. I like to screw – '

'I noticed.'

'And I like *gwailo* yo-yo. Chinese man too small. Your yo-yo just perfect.' She looked at it and pulled a face. 'But not perfect now. Now it *look deem boon*. It half past six.'

'It might be half past bloody six now. But it was midnight all night.'

She frowned. 'Lennie – something you said I don't understand . . .'

'What's that?'

'I thought you already richest bloody man in world. No?'

He laughed. 'Here, finish the champagne.'

At reception the man in the tuxedo presented Cosgrove with his bill. It came to $695.00: $120.00 for the room, $575.00 for the Dom Perignon, including service. He flicked two five hundred dollar notes out of his billfold onto the counter. 'Keep the change,' he winked. 'But how about a change of music next time? Two hours of Mauriat's a bit much.'

To his surprise the man produced an intelligent laugh. 'I promise we will have new music for you next time.' The English had been perfect.

Cosgrove turned back. 'You own this establishment . . ?'

'You're kidding. No. I only work here at nights.'

'Have you studied in England at all? I mean – your English is so good.'

'I went to medical college in London.' The man gave a sad expression. 'But I failed. I discovered I couldn't even dissect a frog.'

'Is this your only job?'

'No. By day I work as a stockbroker's clerk.'

'Really?' Cosgrove grinned. 'Have you a good tip for me, er . . ?'

'Waldo. Waldo Wu. Perhaps. Have you one for me first?'

'Actually, I have.' Cosgrove swelled his chest. 'Did you apply for any shares in Cumberland China?'

Waldo Wu nodded.

'Were you successful?'

'No, unfortunately.'

'Then buy up as many as you can when the market opens Wednesday and sit tight. The price'll double in a week. You can take that from me.'

'And who are you, sir?'

Cosgrove wagged a finger. 'The horse's mouth, of course.'

The man laughed again. 'Now would you like my tip?'

'Okay.' The chuckle was a little indulgent. 'Shoot, Waldo.'

Waldo Wu looked pointedly at Carla and said: 'Buy Sing Company.'

Cosgrove followed his gaze to the Sing Company starlet standing at his side. She shrugged indifferently and he saw the joke. 'Very good! Very funny!' He took her by the arm. 'Come, lover. Time for beddy-byes.'

Waldo Wu listened to the laughter until the door of the Daimler closed upon it. When the hum of the engine had faded towards Waterloo Road he went into the Paradise Room. He glanced at the rumpled sheets, the empty magnum, the glass with the lipstick on it. He sniffed the tangy aftermath of sex that spiced the air. And he smiled to himself. He went to the control panel and cut Paul Mauriat in mid track. Then he pressed a section of mirror which swung inwards to reveal the lens of a movie camera. He removed the cassette and pushed the mirror back into position.

He sat on the bed and dialled a Hong Kong number. As he listened to the repetitive rings, his fingers stroked the blade of the surgical scalpel in the pocket of his tuxedo. He had not failed medical college. He had passed. His tutor had told him he could slice a frog into little pieces with the artistry of a master surgeon.

There was a click on the line, then: '*Weiiii?*'

'*Tu Seen-sang?*'

'*Ngaw hai.*'

In a Cantonese devoid of the Kompo accent of his parents, the man in the tuxedo said simply: 'The turtle is in the jar.'

Across the harbour, in one of the seven bedrooms of his duplex apartment in Tin Hau Temple Road, Errol Tu Wai-tsun replaced his telephone and allowed the smirk to slowly envelop his face.

10

The annual visit of the *Dai Yee Ngau* delivered a godown-full of face upon the Lee family of Koon Wah Mansion, Mongkok. It rekindled their *fung shui* and it blessed them anew with *Fook, Luk, Shou:* Wealth, Happiness and Longevity. Again the neighbours would relate to each other for weeks to come how Yeok-hon's sex had changed in his mother's womb as the giant had carried her into the Kowloon Hospital. If not for him, they would say, poor Lee would have spurned his wife, possessed of so wretched a womb that it would spawn five female children; and hang his head in shame in the presence of his *mahjong* cronies; and visit the ballrooms more often. And rightly so.

Usually the *Dai Yee Ngau* would come on his godson's birthday. But if something prevented that, then he would show up at Dragon Boat Festival time on a rainy June day and sit and watch the races on the Lees' eleven inch black and white television set and cheer on the Mongkok team in a voice as loud as the whole family combined. But this year, because of the pressure of work associated with preparations for the restructuring of the Born Again *Hong* and the public issue, he had not been able to come until the time of the Mid-Autumn Festival, bringing with him tins of *yuet bang* mooncakes and a sixteen inch jade statue of *Kwan Yin*.

'It is lucky to be given a *Kwan Yin*,' Imelda Roboza had told him. 'A family should never buy the statue for itself as that invites bad luck. It should be received as a gift. The Lees will be very happy with it.'

Huart had to stoop inside the single-room tenement. It was an archetype of the thousands that made Mongkok into the world's most densely populated square mile. The open windows admitted the unremitting clamour of traffic, the noise of the hawker market below and the sidewalk artisans, of adults living on top of each other and children at play. The air was a living thing. It mixed the smells of fish, vegetables and fruit, the coalescence of exhaust fumes and the odour of overflowing people. Yet it was neutralised by the aroma of the midday meal simmering in a *wok* on the LP gas burner behind the blanket that partitioned off one corner into a kitchen. *Choy sum* green vegetables, *ngar choy* bean sprouts, bamboo shoots and fat juicy mushrooms simmered in sunflower oil. Eight chipped bowls of *baak faan*, eight tea cups and eight pairs of wooden chopsticks were arranged around a porcelain dish of *char siu* barbecued pork pieces upon the folding table in the centre of the tenement.

They were for Mr and Mrs Lee, his septuagenarian mother, the four Lee daughters and Yeok-hon, six years and five months, who held tight to his present as he looked up with unabashed wonderment at the tallest man on earth and wished to himself over and over that this day would never end.

The door to the tenement was hooked open to help the whirring pedestal fan dissipate the heat into the corridor, where the children of Koon Wah Mansion peered in through the iron grille at the spectacle of the seventy-seven inches of the *Dai Yee Ngau* looming twenty over his secretary.

The Jaguar had been held up in the Cross-Harbour Tunnel, which was proving excessively popular, and they had arrived too close to lunch. Mr Lee had come home for the meal from the Shanghai Street electrical shop where he worked seven days a week. He had his singlet rolled up over his navel, and his wife stood behind him in spotless *saamfoo*. The children were in a silent group, looking from their young brother up to his godfather and down again. The old lady was kneeling before the red-painted *sun ju pai* Buddhist shrine, pushing joss sticks into a brass pot upon the scuffed parquet floor. When the family ate, the gods ate too.

Mr Lee took off in rapid Cantonese. Huart waited for the translation.

[463]

'Mr Lee thanks you very much for the *Kwan Yin*. He says you have done so much for his family, but he has done nothing for you in return.'

Huart said: 'Tell Mr Lee that I must apologise for the low quality of the jade, but I hope nevertheless that it brings him and his family the good fortune and greater prosperity they deserve.'

She translated with barely concealed pride at her employer's faultless etiquette. Mr Lee was embarrassed to the limits of his humility and his diction, when it resumed, was effusive.

'He knows his jade. He can see the statue is of high quality. He doesn't know how to thank you sufficiently. He asked me to tell you he has successfully subscribed for some shares in *Gum Bak Leen*. Not many, just a few. He will give them to Yeok-hon when the boy comes of age. He says the shares will make his son very rich.'

It stirred Huart to learn that the family had invested their undoubtedly limited funds in his company. At best they would have received two or three blocks, each of a hundred five dollar shares. He said a prayer to the stock market god and asked him to fix the opening price on Wednesday far enough above par value to give all those in need, like the Lees, a worthwhile instant profit. Newspaper speculation had it as high as ten dollars. That morning the *Hong Kong and Oriental Daily* had printed Kym Marshall's personal estimate, one to be respected, at eight dollars.

'Tell Mr Lee his confidence in my company is a gift above all others. I am gratified. My company will not disappoint him – I promise.'

It took over half an hour for them to complete their goodbyes. They were implored to stay and join the family at lunch. But Huart, determined not to deprive the Lees of their hard-earned food, invented one excuse after another. Yeok-hon clung to his kneecap until he climbed into the rear of the Jaguar. The godson of the *Dai Yee Ngau* was still waving long after the big car was lost in the traffic on Boundary Street.

Imelda Roboza alighted in La Salle Road where she lived with her aging father. Lack of physical glamour and dedication to her job had rendered her a confirmed spinster. Huart acknowledged the extent to which he relied on her, and resolved never to take her for granted.

Ah Lam drove south on Nathan Road. At Gascoigne Road, Huart could see that the lunchtime traffic using the Cross-Harbour Tunnel was even thicker.

'Take the vehicular ferry, please, Ah Lam. I'm in no hurry.'

It was Saturday afternoon. The working week was ended. Huart
sank into the upholstery and let his mind wander. In the hour it
would take to reach his weekend villa in Deep Water Bay he had
much to think about. Foremost in his mind was that morning's
meeting with Y. Y. Szeto, who had just returned from two weeks
in Peking.

'The "Shanghai Communiqué" is the charter of the next
epoch,' the company secretary had told him. 'Not just for the
Americans – for the West. Britain will be invited to stage a technology exhibition in Peking.'

'We'll take a big part in it!' Huart had enthused. 'When is it to
be?'

'Early next year. I have already confirmed our participation.'

Huart had pressed his intercom. 'Imelda, please ask Mr Zagan
to come up.' He had dealt with the uncertainty on Y. Y. Szeto's
face by adding: 'He speaks fluent Mandarin, you know.'

The Jaguar turned off the ferry ramp into Connaught Road,
Central and nosed through the traffic past the P & O Building,
the GPO, Union House.

Huart studied the progress of Connaught Centre upon the
reclamation directly opposite the bronzed dignity of St George's
Building, domain of the fabulously rich Kadoories who, it was
said, had lost their bid for the site to the owners of the Mandarin,
then found the fifty-two storey colossus closing out their harbour
view. It was also said that, had the Kadoories won the site for
themselves, it would have been the guests of the Mandarin with
their panorama all but obliterated. Huart thought the rumour
exemplified the consequences of coming second in a Hong Kong
business confrontation, no matter who you were.

Ah Lam swung right around the hole in the ground where the
Furama Hotel was soon to rise, and powered the Jaguar up the
steep incline of Cotton Tree Drive onto the shoulder of the Peak.
Magazine Gap Road wound into Peak Road, then Stubbs Road,
all bored through stark rock faces fringed by the lush green tropical
shrubbery that thrived in the volcanic soil of the mountain-top
that was Hong Kong Island.

Up here above the weekday world of concrete and business, the
high-rises of the wealthy soared from foundations that had been
poured in seemingly impossible locations, so steep was the slope.
Piledrivers plunged, rose, plunged again. Jackhammers rattled.
Excavators clawed at the earth. It produced in Huart a mixture of

feelings. Cumberland Properties Limited owned a choice selection of the apartment blocks and the sites for more.

He took in the view through the heat haze across the harbour to Kowloon, down to Wanchai, Causeway Bay and Happy Valley, where the racecourse was a green glade in a forest of building-coloured buildings.

They circuited the roundabout into Wongneichong Gap Road, then dropped over the saddle into Repulse Bay Road. Small coves, indented like jewels along the island's south coast, winked through breaks in the foliage.

Huart felt the strain seep from his body. Weekends at Deep Water Bay had become delightful thirty-six hour watersheds between business weeks. They were periods of sanctuary, in which he could not only reflect, but also plan. And, most importantly, decide.

The Born Again *Hong* had at first been a demanding child, a product of his sweat, his daring, his astounding luck. It had grown to maturity, like a son growing into manhood. This train of thought delivered to his mind's eye a vision of his sons. James would be thirty-four and Andrew John thirty-two, had they lived. Would they have followed tradition into the British Army? If so, they might now be in Northern Ireland, and in danger. But they were not. They were dead; gone so early in life.

If not for that one Japanese torpedo on the first day of the Year of the Water Horse, Huart would not be in Hong Kong at all. That missile had been the tragic instrument of his life's redirection. Because of it he had returned to the East. Because of it he was a success. He was rich, respected and famous. How cruelly benevolent could life be!

But what was success? Someone had once told him: 'Look around a room of businessmen and pick out the successful ones. It's quite easy – they're the ones with the unhappy faces.'

After thirty years Huart had to admit he still grieved for what his sons might have been. As the Jaguar turned down into Island Road, the realisation came to him. Cumberland China had emerged to fill that aching void in his life. The company had taken the place of his sons!

Now he understood his pathological concern with the identity of the man who would take it all over. Now he knew what that vacant panel on the east wall of the boardroom actually represented: the non-existent image of his dead sons! He groaned out loud. If that was his criteria, then no mortal man could meet it.

Suddenly clear of mind, he ran through the three names once again:

Thomas Buckley.

Glynn Bedrix.

Matthew Zagan.

But which one of the three?

Driveways to terraced houses led off Island Road, which opened into the casual sweep of Deep Water Bay. Its white sand and rippling blue water was crowded with Chinese having their last dip of the year. A flotilla of pleasure craft bobbed at anchor around Middle Island. Speedboats towed water-skiers. Golfers teed off from the clubhouse, whilst sunbathers stretched out on loungers on the terrace before the Victoria Recreation Club tucked into the rocks at the western extremity of the bay.

In striking contrast to it all was Huart's sudden vision of Mr Lee in his rolled-up singlet hard at work every Saturday afternoon in that Shanghai Street electrical shop. He thought of the family's savings that had been entrusted with rigid faith to his company, and he was consumed first by a return of humility, then by a burning determination never to fail the Lees of Koon Wah Mansion, Mongkok, and all the others who had invested in him so.

The Jaguar stormed up the narrow path and halted before the front door of the villa. Huart stepped out and felt the breeze on his face, smelled the balmy scent of pointsettia and bauhinia flowers, heard the calls of the tropical birds and saw his houseboy's welcoming smile.

'Lunch is ready on the balcony, Master.'

'Thank you, Ah Chi. Did Ah Keung send over more of Mr Cosgrove's wine?'

The houseboy nodded. 'Would Master like some with lunch?'

'Just one glass, Ah Chi. No more. This afternoon I work.'

Ah Chi watched his employer walk tall into the house. 'It is good. He looks well again. The tiredness has gone. *Yu jook lay man maan soei.* May he live for ten thousand years!' It was the ancient salute to the emperors of China.

Ah Lam scratched an itch through his cap. '*Ngaam sai,*' he agreed, though he thought Ah Chi had overdone it. But only a little.

11

'Send Wai-kit to me.'

The servant finished pouring the *bo lay* into the two cups, then bowed and withdrew. Tu Chien sipped, expirated loudly and knew a Double Happiness as the invigorating tea enhanced the pleasure that had been his ever since the envelopes with the round gold logo of *Gum Bak Leen* had started appearing in letterboxes all over Hong Kong. For, as at mid-afternoon, Saturday, September 16th, 1972, the giant had unwittingly delivered to Tu Chien, via his network of nominees and agents, ownership of seven per cent of the Born Again *Hong*. And when the stock exchanges opened on Wednesday, he would commence his acquisition of the remaining eighteen per cent that would be in the fickle hands of 'the public'.

From the pavilion at the bottom of the garden of Great Horse Mansion, he could hear the laughter of the children playing hide-and-seek amongst the bushes, trees and rockeries, supervised by fan-waving *amahs*. On the verandah the Tu women were volubly playing *mahjong*, Number One Wife leading the gossip, with the *tsip* concubines keeping clear. The Tu men sat in an expensively-dressed group and talked business.

Tu Chien enjoyed the times of the festivals when the whole family came to visit. At such times he knew his life had been worthwhile; he could see for himself how well he had provided for his clan. And now he was embarked on a scheme to give the family something it lacked: complete public respectability. The Tus were little known in Hong Kong and until now he had preferred it that way. But he had been thinking ahead. 1997 was only a quarter of a century away. He would not be alive to see the Communists take over, but his offspring would, and they could not stay as they would inherit the death sentence that was still on his head. There would not be room for them in Taipei, where Tu Huang and his family ruled the roost. They would have to migrate to one of the foreign devil lands: England, the United States or Canada. Wai-kit had been educated overseas and was being groomed to take over under the patriarch's tutelage. But the family he inherited must be different from the family today. It had to be made 'internationally acceptable' in time for 1997.

So Tu Chien planned a Great Event that would bring a Double Happiness to top all Double Happinesses. His hatred for the giant had grown from a mere burning malignance into the core of a sleeping volcano. He would destroy him in every way other than

[468]

physically, and in the process he would secure for the family the greatest of the foreign devil *hongs*.

He touched the thick white jade ring he had placed on his middle finger that morning. He always wore it on festival days to protect his family from injury whilst they were at his home and under his responsibility. Any misfortune that was at large would first concentrate its force upon the ring and break it. Jade on the body was a proven sacrificial anode.

'You summoned me, Great-uncle?'

'Wai-kit, ten days ago I asked you to study closely the character of each of the directors of your company. You have completed the task?'

Alain To sipped the *bo lay* and stifled a grimace. 'Yes, Great-uncle.'

'Then tell me about them. Firstly, what of this man Bedrix?'

'He is well thought of by everyone. He is the one who has everything. His fiancée is the daughter of a rich stockbroker. He is a shooting star in the company and has been given the nickname of "Neil Armstrong".'

'Shooting stars fall to earth,' Tu Chien observed. 'What is this perfect one's weakness?'

'I know not – yet.'

'Then you have not completed the task at all, Wai-kit.' Tu Chien's lips drew into a thin line and Alain To swallowed. 'To what elevation does this "shooting star" aspire?'

'The very highest, Great-uncle.'

'Then he can be corrupted. Crows are black the world over.'

'I will find his weakness, Great-uncle. I am sorry for my failure.'

Tu Chien ignored the apology. 'What of the accountant, Buckley?'

This time Alain To smiled with confidence. 'The Chicken Eye's weakness is blatant. He is vain. He also aims for the top, and believes that to reach it he must show that he is more than just an accountant.'

'In which field of business does he show interest?'

'Property. His best friend is the man Vail. They are always together.'

'And this Vail is worthy?'

Alain To shrugged. 'He is not significant. All his major decisions have been taken by the General Under the Big Tree.'

Tu Chien's eyes flinted. 'Never call him that in my hearing, Wai-kit. It is too good a name for a murderer of small boys and young women.'

'I am sorry, Great-uncle.'

'Tell me of the American, Browne.'

'That one is really an American. The British discount him. He will not rise further. He is a specialist. If taken away from his electronics factories he would be as ineffective as a giraffe in a field of sweet potato. He is the one most loyal to the giant.'

Then Tu Chien asked about Antonio Ezuelo.

'He is the most corruptible of them all. A philanderer, and careless at it. He was the easiest to find out about. I am surprised the giant has not done so, too, but Ezuelo is protected by the *Meen Foot Hau Jaak* – Cosgrove the Pig. Great-uncle, that leaves Chiu Man-king – '

Tu Chien's hand flicked out of the sleeve of his long-gown. 'Talk not of Chiu. It is quite unnecessary. He will be easily dealt with – so long as he retains his very last memory of his father.'

Though puzzled, Alain To said nothing.

'Are there any others worthy of attention?'

'None, Great-uncle – ' Alain To paused as a thought came to him. 'There is one other. He is manager of the Trading Division in my company – Cumberland Engineering. His name is Matthew Zagan.' He gave a casual wave of his hand. 'But he can be discounted. He will never rise far.'

'How can you be so certain?'

'The man is Eurasian.'

Tu Chien nodded. 'A handicap indeed.'

Suzanne Huart-Brent went straight for the jugular. 'Matthew Zagan, why have you been avoiding me?'

He looked up from the menu into those eyes. They were like Venus fly-traps. They glowed and enticed, and once he allowed himself to come too close to them, he knew he would be trapped and helpless. 'I don't know,' he lied. 'I've been busy . . .' God, she was beautiful. Why had he come?

'Busy-busy-busy. Everyone's so busy. Uncle John's busy. You're busy. I'm busy.' She sipped her Chateauneuf du Pape 1967 and watched him.

He was glad to move to a different subject. 'You've been busy? I thought you came to Hong Kong for a holiday.'

She leaned forward. The venus fly-traps came near. He backed off and she frowned. 'I've been busy trying to get you to ask me to dinner.'

'But you invited me . . .'

'Suzie. My name is Suzie. As in Suzie Wong. Why don't you

use it?' She sighed. 'I'm sorry. Who asked who – whom? – is unimportant. You came and we're here and I'm glad.'

'You did say you had something to discuss with me.'

She smiled mysteriously. 'Yes. Some business. In the Big Lychee it's always business. Business is the honey that attracts the Hong Kong bee.'

Zagan thought again of Venus fly-traps and took refuge in a quick survey of the restaurant. Au Trou Normand in Hankow Road, Tsimshatsui was one of his favourites. Its low ceiling, smoked wood rafters, plaster walls, red and white checkered table-cloths and melting flickering candles constructed a romantic atmosphere. But for this dinner he had left romance at home. How ironic it was that every other man in the place, having mentally stripped Suzanne naked, was now furtively taking part in her gang rape. 'What business, Suzie?' he eventually had to ask.

She took out a Benson and Hedges. He lit it. 'They say smoking can kill you,' she side-stepped, exhaling to her left.

He smiled. She was so different. '*Au contraire*. It saved my life.'

'Oh, yeah?'

He told her of his lucky escape on Sunday, June 18th, concluding with: 'So now you understand why I say I'll never give up smoking.'

'Touch me. Maybe some of that luck'll rub off.' She put her hand on his.

He took his away. 'Suzie – what business?'

The mysterious smile returned. 'Have you ever slept with a taipan's daughter, Matt?' It was said so conversationally that he laughed as he asked her to repeat it. She laughed, too, as she obliged.

He seemed to relax. 'There aren't that many taipans' daughters around and I haven't slept with those that are.'

'Yet . . ?'

'I'm not likely to, either.'

'The way you're going, I completely agree,' she said, and when his only reaction was to toy with the stem of his wine glass, she was prompted to go further. 'You'd like to, wouldn't you?'

'I'd like to what?' Zagan knew he was stalling badly.

'Sleep with a taipan's daughter, Matt. Sleep with me, for instance.'

He frowned at last. 'Suzie, why pick on me for your shock tactics?'

'Don't answer a question with a question.'

[471]

'It's my question that's unanswered,' he countered. 'What business?'

'Okay . . .' This time when she leaned forward he did not back off. 'By my observation, there are several men jockeying to succeed Uncle John.'

'I suppose there are . . .'

'And your name's on the list.'

He took time out to light a fresh Marlboro. 'You can put anyone you like on your own list. But why me?'

'Matt . . . I've seen through you.'

'Who else have you seen through? What about Gene Browne, countryman?'

'Hmmm. The Texan Taipan. It does have a ring to it.' She laughed, then glanced up at the waiter. 'Come, Matt. Let's order first.'

She ordered ratatouille and venison, he jambon and boeuf bourgignon.

'Names, Suzie,' he pressed.

She drained her wine. 'Glynn Bedrix . . .'

'Which one? Neil Armstrong or the real Glynn Bedrix?'

'Tom Buckley . . .'

Zagan nodded. 'He's trying.'

She pulled a face at that one. 'You . . .'

'So you've said already.'

'And . . .' She drew on her cigarette. 'And me.'

'You?'

'Me and my five and a half per cent.' She tossed her head and added: 'But I'm not going on the hustings for myself alone.'

'What do you mean?'

'I'll be there to make a deal with the candidate I think Uncle John is going to select.' She inhaled deeply and he watched the smoke curl into her flared nostrils. 'I plan to put myself forward as his running mate.'

'Wife or mistress? Buckley's married and Bedrix is as good as.'

'Whichever way you want it, Matt.'

'What have my wishes to do with it?'

'Matt, cut the act and listen to me. I'm proposing a deal. It can be a business deal if you insist.'

He looked at her. 'And what do you have to bring to the table apart from your five point five per cent?'

'My influence with Uncle John.'

'Plus . . . ?'

'Plus myself.'

'As wife or mistress?'

'Whichever way you want it.'

He stared at her. 'You'd sacrifice yourself to become a taipan's woman?'

'It'd be no sacrifice, Matt.'

'What do you mean?'

'It'd be no sacrifice . . . because I've discovered that I love you.'

It knocked him completely off balance. He saw in her eyes that she spoke the truth and he wanted to take her and kiss her right then and there. But a lead weight in his gut pinned him to the chair and a voice in his head told him to laugh and say: 'Just what is this? Leap year? Sadie Hawkins Day? Is this how it's done in New York?'

Her eyes flashed fire. She jabbed her cigarette into shreds in the ashtray. 'I'm flying back to New York tomorrow. I came to Hong Kong on no holiday. I came on a personal mission – which I've just completed. But before I go I'll tell you something, Mister Matthew Zagan – ' She leaned forward and entrapped him with her eyes. He could not move. He was raped by her will, her directness, her ball-tearing beauty. 'Unless you accept my deal, I'll make goddamn certain Uncle John doesn't even consider you as a candidate to succeed him, let alone put the crown on your pig head. I suggest you think about that whilst I'm in New York, my darling Matt. Think about it, then call me. Here's my card. You'll see it has all my numbers.' She snapped her Gucci handbag shut, stood up. And left.

He watched her weave between the tables and through the crowded bar. Men moved aside to give her passage, then fixed upon the rear view of her as she stepped out into Hankow Road and hailed a taxi. The thick wooden door hung wide open on its hinges where she had flung it, and the last he saw of her through the rain that was falling again was a flash of two superlative legs as she swung them after her into the cab.

The dull boom of the Noon Day Gun carried from East Point to the ears of Lennie the Fifth as he bisected Statue Square with sprightly step. Ahead was the Bowling Alley Bar, his Monday string of double pink gins, his steak and kidney pie, his game of liar dice, and three hours of stimulating banter. By 12:15 his first drink was history, his lunch ordered by a nod to the captain, the liar dice rolling at the table surrounded by the six club regulars, and the banter in good voice.

'If you really can read the market like it's an open book like you tell us *ad nauseam*, Lennie, how d'you explain this pisspot film company?' P. G. Curzon-Cross demanded as he peered with exaggerated disgust at the score of his dice hidden under the lip of his upturned cup.

'Film company, P.G.?' Cosgrove retorted. 'What film company? Not into blue movies at your age, are you? Dirty old bleeder.'

'But of course, old bean.'

'Many a truth hidden in jest, P.G.,' Myron Greenfield pointed out.

'It's unbelievable what goes on these days,' Alvin Bucks interjected.

'What film company?' Cosgrove asked again.

'Such flea-bite organisations shouldn't be allowed to go public in the first place,' Greenfield declared. 'There should be a minimum size.'

'Quite right, Myron.' The senior partner of Jackson, Sloan and Butler quaffed a pint of San Miguel draught. 'Especially this flea-bite. We were asked to look at their prospectus back in June. We didn't think it was quite the done thing to list three hundred whores amongst their assets, exceedingly profitable though they might be. So they gave their business to the competition. Recognised a kindred spirit, I suppose.'

Cosgrove banged his fist on the table and the laughter aborted. 'What blasted film company? Damn you all!'

P. G. Curzon-Cross raised an eyebrow. 'Why, the Sing Company, Lennie. Their shares went mad this morning. Didn't you know?'

'Mad? What do you mean mad?'

'What's up with you, Cosgrove, old fellow?' Greenfield enquired with a wink around the table. 'Sold on Friday, did you? Too bad.'

'Too bad. Really too bad,' the stockbroker agreed, clicking his teeth. 'Had the book open at the wrong page, did you, old bean? Or perhaps you need glasses. You are getting on, you know.' He slapped his thigh in ostensible chagrin as he closed his cup over an excellent score.

'P.G.,' Cosgrove said in a voice that might have been adjudged threatening in other company, 'how'd you like these dice rammed up your nose?'

'Oh, don't do that, Lennie,' Alvin Bucks interjected. 'Then we'd never be able to guess your score. Besides, it's not in the rules.'

'What about the bloody Sing Company?' Cosgrove insisted. 'I tell you, I've never had any of their shares to sell.'

[474]

'Then you've missed out.' The stockbroker clicked his teeth again. 'The opening price was $1.90. By eleven it was three dollars. By 11:15 it was four. When the exchanges closed for lunch it was down again to three. The word is that it'll fall all the way back to two this afternoon.'

'Why the interest, Lennie?' asked Greenfield. 'Cumberland China planning a takeover of the Sing Company, eh? Is that why the price shot up? Not thinking of getting into the rebirth of Cantonese movies, eh, old frog?'

'More to the point: is Lennie getting into Cantonese movie starlets?' Alvin Bucks suggested.

But Cosgrove was not listening. He shook his head slowly from side to side. The legal man was not to know just how accurate his jest had been, but for one item: Carla Tze Ti was Taiwanese, not Cantonese. But Lennie the Fifth's brain dwelled not on trivia. 'A bloody pox on it!'

'A pox on what, Lennie?' P. G. Curzon-Cross enquired with exaggerated affront. 'Please keep your abominable bluffing until it's your turn, there's a good chap.'

'Ha-haaaa!' Cosgrove laughed, and they all looked at him strangely. But it had not been the stockbroker who had sparked his mirth. It had been the realisation that there was a bonus to be had in escorting Carla Tze Ti to the Red Phoenix Motel in Kowloon Tong in future.

12

Seven stock exchanges were incorporated under the Hong Kong Companies Ordinance, but only the four engaged in active trading were officially recognised as bourses. At ten o'clock on Wednesday, 20th September, Cumberland China shares opened on them all at $8.50. By close of trading at three p.m. the price had risen to $9.15. It ended the month at $11.00. The new share was popular. All 'sell' orders were quickly covered.

'It's to be expected,' Cosgrove explained to Huart. 'After all, our issue was sixty-six times oversubscribed. The public love us, John.'

In October the Hang Seng Index jumped in regular bounds, each peak surpassing the last. It reached 639, twenty-five per cent above the September high. The Born Again *Hong* finished October at $14.50.

A 100 point break in November brought the Index down from 750. It rebounded in December, hitting 843. Huart saw his company's price reach $17.50 before the November break, then pass this peak to end the year at $19.00. In three months and ten days Cumberland China shares had risen to almost four times par value. Huart thought of the Lees and felt good.

'He's not selling,' Imelda Roboza advised. 'I check with him every week, as you asked me to do. He insists he's keeping the shares for Yeok-hon.'

'Don't press him, then. But keep an eye on things, please, Imelda.'

The population passed four million, and it seemed every single one of them was playing the stock market. Life savings were taken from under floorboards and mattresses; jewellery and heirlooms were converted to cash; bank accounts were stripped bare. Then the borrowing started: from banks if collateral was had, from money-lenders at exorbitant rates of interest if it was not. Local banks began relaxing their definition of 'security' on loans intended for market speculation, and the people flocked in. Finance companies were spawned to solicit time deposits from the chary at favourable interest rates, then lend out to the punting masses. Money in circulation increased by over forty per cent.

'It smacks of *déjà vu*,' Huart warned. 'I recall too clearly the interest rate war of the early sixties. A recession followed that.'

'Stop worrying, John.' Cosgrove passed him the latest Cicero Investments profit statement. 'Read that and tell me you still feel like weeping.'

Huart mused: 'Forty billion dollars traded on the market in 1972. Three times 1971. Does it mean Hong Kong has arrived as a financial centre?'

The colony was gripped by a fever, the symptoms of which were wide eyes, laughing faces and a rubbing together of the thumb and forefinger. Small 'investors' flocked to stockbrokers and share dealers. They ranged from *fokis* to bamboo scaffolders, from *mafoos* to cab drivers, from watchmen to mutual funds salesmen, from *amahs* to nightclub hostesses. And all of them were so determined to get their hands on a block of shares.

Any share. It mattered not if it was issued by a *hong* or an unknown 'manufactory', so long as one of the one hundred newspapers or the new 'investment' rags recommended it, or the grapevine deemed it 'lucky', or the price of a block was within their

[476]

means. Or if it was a 'new issue': a chance to buy in at the ground floor and turn a quick profit.

There was a 'new issue' almost every day. They ranged from blue chips like Cumberland China, to companies registered 'yesterday' with assets of a few apartments, or a collection of barges, or a blueprint for a new indoor television antenna. They boasted their qualifications on a full page of newspaper, some displaying a local dignitary on the board to render unnecessary further study of the prospectus. Each new issue was many times oversubscribed by the super-speculative populace who camped all night outside whichever bank happened to be underwriting the issue.

The economy was skyrocketing and the value of land with it. Old buildings made way for new. Concrete was poured to the limits of the legislation. Designed and built in a hurry so as not to miss the boom, the skyscrapers sprung from the volcanic soil.

'The cost of buildings erected in 1972 is up by 42 per cent,' Huart told the Long Table in the last week of December at the last board meeting to be held in Cumberland House. 'Consequently, Cumberland Engineering is having a bumper year – both in Trading, run by Matthew Zagan, and in Contracting, run by – ' He looked to the foot of the table. 'Who manages the Contracting Division, Mr Szeto?'

'Alain To. He graduated from Salford and joined us eighteen months ago.'

'He's doing a grand job, then.' Huart swept the air with his hand. 'It's not only Engineering, gentlemen. All subsidiaries are enjoying a record year. Hong Kong's total foreign trade will exceed $40,000,000,000. It has doubled in five years. Next year it will pass $50,000,000,000.'

The Long Table moved to the fifty-second floor of Connaught Centre. Bamboo scaffolding and dark green netting went up over-night to conceal Cumberland House and its neighbour. In a matter of weeks both were gone.

As of January 1st, 1973, the Water Rat had a month and two days to live. As time ran out on the best animal of the twelve under whose auspices to invest, the market went mad. Daily turnover was between $400,000,000 and $500,000,000. Five years before, it had been one per cent of this.

In the midst of the dry season the rains returned. Dense nimbus hung over Hong Kong almost every day. Average rainfall was exceeded by eighty per cent. The people read into it nothing but good. The market surged.

Huart was torn in two. He knew that shares were overvalued, yet he was delighted with the profits flowing into the Cicero Investments account. Cosgrove seemed to have an uncanny knack for buying at the bottom and selling at the top as the Index fluctuated along its upward course. At times he 'sold short', borrowing selected shares through P. G. Curzon-Cross and cashing them in when the market was at a peak, then buying them back a few days later after the value had fallen, returning the shares and crediting the profits to Cicero Investments. On one occasion in mid January he even dared to 'sell short' some of his personal stock in Cumberland China. He was astounded at the difficulty his stockbroker experienced in covering his short position after the sharp break he had so accurately 'anticipated'. The share had not fallen in proportion to the market, and there were few 'sell' orders to seize upon.

'Cumberland China is extremely popular paper, Lennie,' P.G. told him. 'The unit value is now too high for the small local investor, so it has to be the institutions buying up, including London and New York. Your company is a blue chip investment in international opinion as well as local. You should consider offering more equity to the public.'

'I'll suggest it to John, P.G. Shall I quote you as the source? He might give you a seat at the Long Table for it. Now, will you be showing your ugly face at the Club today after the whipping I gave you yesterday?'

The stockbroker snorted. 'I'll be a bloody fool. You've got x-ray vision as well as a crystal ball. I always thought you were a little queer.'

'It takes one to know one, P.G.'

Cosgrove's clairvoyance continued to amaze. It was as if he had access at will to tomorrow's *Business Daily*. His market coups were becoming legend. His opinions were sought out. Kym Marshall called him regularly.

But Lennie the Lucky Pig alone knew his crystal ball had two arms and two legs, was named Waldo Wu, was dressed in a tuxedo and was alive and well after midnight in the Red Phoenix Motel, Kowloon Tong.

The Government was getting worried. It felt the economy overheating, saw the money supply burgeoning and the people distracted from industry into 'get rich quick' speculation. Warnings via the Government Information Services either went unheard or were ignored. The exponents of *laissez faire* and 'positive non-interventionism' began to criticise the bourses for laxity, then

[478]

moved to establish a Securities Commission and even threatened a Federation of Stock Exchanges to eliminate the shortcuts.

The public responded by sending the Hang Seng Index even higher.

Paperwork clogged up the office of every stockbroker in the colony. The Government ordered the exchanges closed on Monday, Wednesday and Friday afternoons to give them time to catch up. It had little positive effect, because the legitimate brokers were but one of the channels for the buying of shares. Countless unlicensed brokers had set themselves up to service 'exchanges' in small offices or apartments, each with its own makeshift counter-board and battery of telephones. And there were the lone-wolf share-pushers and hucksters operating amongst the illiterate in the outlying districts and in New Territories villages. Everyone but everyone wanted to be in on the stock market action. And was.

The pace quickened. The shortcuts became blatant. Shares began to change hands without being registered. Certificates began to be passed around like legal tender, the identity of each current 'owner' lost on a broker's floor in a pile of roneoed 'chits' that, bearing only the chop of some harassed clerk, were sole evidence of any transaction.

Concern in the corridors of the Colonial Secretariat turned to alarm. A way had to be found to arrest the public's mad-crazy plunge into the internecine whirlpool of instant paper profits. The heads of the stock exchanges were summoned to Lower Albert Road and asked to consider further restricting trading to half a day every day. Sir Percival Landers and the other chairmen of the Big Banks were called in to give their opinion on an increase in minimum lending rate to discourage borrowing.

'Crocodile tears!' Cosgrove held court in the Bowling Alley Bar. 'Bloody crocodile tears! The Government's estimated surplus for this financial year was $47,000,000. D'you know what it's going to be? Five billion is what. $700,000,000 from stamp duties and almost the same from the sale of crown land. Guess who's benefiting the most from the stock market and the property boom. That's right. The Hong Kong bloody Government!'

The Water Rat was sent scurrying into history with gold dust sprinkled on its tail. On Friday, February 2nd, 1973, the last day of the old lunar year, the Hang Seng Index soared through the 1,000 mark for the first time. It rose 128 points and closed the year at 1098.86.

Cumberland China shares were being traded at $37.50.

[479]

By custom, offices and factories closed early. Family heads took home tangerine bushes, peach blossoms for good fortune and red packets with newly minted *laisee* for the unmarried. The department stores did fast trade in red garments to be worn on the first two days of the new year.

That night families sat together for banquets. They wished each other *Kung Hei Fat Choy* over and over and prayed for the Water Ox to grant them more Wealth and greater Happiness, and guarantee their Longevity. Most of all they hoped for the continued rise of the magical Hang Seng Index, as the fortune tellers and the newspapers predicted.

The Water Ox did not set out to deceive. Its year dawned warm and dry.

The omen was ignored by all, except one. Tu Chien stood before a gap that had appeared in his bamboo and looked down on North Point. The view was clear and bright. The first day of the year should not be like this.

Number One Wife had returned from the Ten Thousand Buddha Temple in Shatin with disastrous news. The priest had died. The rice paper messages corresponding to the sticks cast by his replacement had been innocuous.

Back in his office-study he scanned again the previous day's newspapers. On the business pages were printed the sanguine predictions of the taipans for the Year of the Water Ox. The faces of the Great Men smiled back at him, the hated smile of the giant at the top of the column.

He shifted aggressively in his chair and a shaft of pain fired from his hip to rack his body. It was an agony of agonies, the worst one yet. He was barely conscious as he fought it down, and when at last his vision cleared he was looking into the eyes of the Ch'in horse on his desk. He waited for his strength to seep back and then he whispered: '*Kung Hei Fat Choy* to you, cat's excrement. They say you are a knowledgeable man, but there is one thing you do not know.'

Tu Chien was thinking of the vault in the Daima Bank where were stored enough share certificates to give him ownership of eleven per cent of the Born Again *Hong*.

Huart lazed in one of the deck chairs beside the deep end of his kidney-shaped pool. With Cumberland House being no more, he returned to Deep Water Bay each night as well as every weekend and holiday. The heat of the sun had produced beads of perspiration that dribbled down his bare white midriff. He lifted a *gunner* in a tall glass to his lips and took a sip. 'What an amazing Chinese New Year,' he repeated to Virginia as she applied a screening lotion to her shoulders. 'Here we are sunbathing in the first week of February. The Ox is smiling on us. What does he know that we don't, I wonder.'

'You tell me, John,' she replied abstractedly as she stretched her legs before her. 'The Chinese say you're closer to him than anybody else.'

'Superstition, darling. Just superstition. The Chinese are full of it.'

Nevertheless, he smiled to himself and lifted his face to the sun. It burnt his skin and warmed his core and he felt good. What indeed would the Ox bring his way? The British Industrial Technology Exhibition was on in Peking next month. Cumberland Engineering had taken a large stand and would be shipping several exhibits to the Chinese capital. It had to be the first step towards the fulfilment of his second pledge.

The first pledge had been stored in a compartment of his memory since his acceptance of the impossibility of it ever being discharged. His successor would be one of those available. He reviewed the names again.

Glynn Bedrix.

Matthew Zagan.

Thomas Buckley.

The crowd pushed and elbowed and craned its collective neck before the board on the wall outside Marina House. It spilled half onto Ice House Street and obstructed the traffic. It grew in size and volume, just like the stock market that provided the reason for its existence. The board carried the lunch-time prices of leading shares quoted on the Hong Kong Stock Exchange, which traded on a floor upstairs. Wednesday, February 7th, 1973, was the first trading day of the Year of the Water Ox, and the crowd was excited for good reason. The Hang Seng Index had picked up where it had left off. Another 48 points had been added to the peak.

Huart stood on the footpath before the great hole in the ground where Cumberland House had been. Soon the caissons of the building the press had dubbed in anticipation 'The Finest Tower in Asia' would be poured. He looked across Ice House Street at the crowd and shook his head at the scene. 'There has to be a limit,' he muttered. 'It has to break.'

Beside him Lennie the Fifth grinned to himself and scratched the itch in the centre of his right palm. It confirmed what the prices on the board across the street announced loud and clear: Big 'Bull' Market today. An itch in his left palm would have meant the opposite: a falling 'bear'. The crowd roared as new prices appeared on the board. Not just one bull, Cosgrove thought to himself. A whole herd of the bottlers.

'What's our price now, Lennie?' Huart asked. 'Can you see it?'

'It was up another ten dollars at one stage this morning. It must be close on $50.00 by now. Cicero's made another nine million – but not on our shares, of course.' He grinned up into his taipan's stern face.

The next day the Hang Seng Index rocketed to 1267 on record turnover of $705,000,000. Then on Friday, 9th February, the market was in pandemonium. The Index exploded 182 points to 1450. Amidst it all the price of Hongkong and Shanghai Bank shares was lifted from $426.00 to $675.00.

The Government decided completely to abandon both *laissez faire* and 'positive non-interventionism'. It ordered the suspension of afternoon trading on all exchanges until further notice.

Between ten and 12:45 on Monday, February 12th, the Index rose to 1503.

In the first four trading days of the Year of the Water Ox the market value of Hong Kong shares had increased on average by over thirty-six per cent. Cumberland China stood at $97.50.

The Government began to despair, and John Huart started losing sleep.

13

Beyond the windows of the JAL Boeing 707 as it tore down the runway, the world was lost in the grey-white omnipresence that had blanketed Kai Tak for three days. Its wheels lifted off the tarmac with a lurch and its engines strained up into the fog to the east over the harbour.

'R'adies and gentr'men, we have take off from Hong Kong. Our fr'ight to Tokyo Haneda Airport wir take four hour. Pr'ease keep seatber't fasten as we 'spect to 'counter turbur'ence for sev'rar minute.'

Kingston Orr sat in seat 2A of the first-class compartment, quite unperturbed by the dipping and the bumping and the swaying of the 707. He was studying the front page of the *Hong Kong and Oriental Daily* and the news was so good. He read with avidity Kym Marshall's comments on the Government's decision to proceed with the first four stages of the nine-stage underground Mass Transit Railway. By official decree had been conceived a consumer of electricity with an appetite to surpass all others. He turned to the financial page. The stock market was steady. Since the 71 point break ten days ago, the Hang Seng Index had fluctuated between 1430 and 1570. Marshall dubbed it a 'plateau of thankful consolidation'.

He tossed the broadsheet onto the seat beside him, pushed his recline button and closed his eyes. His thoughts glossed over the underground railway and the stock market. They fixed on tomorrow's contract signing with Tetsuo Hondo and his minions. It would be swift and uncomplicated, as usual. He would demand his personal discount; Hondo would grant it with ceremonial reluctance, then they both would sign. Jeremy Parrot had repeatedly assured him that it was all set up. There would be no delays.

Jubilee Bay Phase B had belonged to the Japanese all along. Matamoto had supplied Phase A on time, and Anglo-Saxon's bid for Phase B was ten per cent too high. He knew it would be. He had only agreed to invite tenders to prove the fact to those on his board who had not believed him. Never, but never, would he buy from the British.

His thoughts moved on to Yumiko Hondo. And lingered with reluctance. She had grown dumpy, unappetising. Her father seemed to expect him to ask for her hand each time they met. He grimaced at the prospect. What would Hong Kong society think of his taking a Japanese wife? Furthermore, what would they think if she was the daughter of the vice-president of Cathay Electric's largest supplier? He shuddered at the spectre of the scandal.

Suddenly he sat up and looked around the compartment, ignoring the wan face of his general manager in the seat behind. Abraham Male was not on board. That was good. He must be taking Cathay Pacific and would join them in the Imperial Hotel after they had checked in. Having Matamoto's agent on the same flight risked raised eyebrows, particularly when his award of the Jubilee Bay Phase B contract to them was announced. The head of the biggest power utility in Asia had become more and more paranoid about his public image. He sat back and closed his eyes again.

In seat 3A, Jeremy Parrot was dangling over a precipice of panic. He was quailing at the reality of his life depending on the ability of the JAL captain, a man whose nationality he privately despised, to fly solely by instruments. He cursed Kingston Orr to hell and gone. What was his hurry to sign with Matamoto? Couldn't it have waited for the fog to lift? What job is this that has me risking my life for no personal gain? If there was something in the Matamoto deal for me, it would be different. And a little word in Tetsuo Hondo's ear would soon fix that.

He gripped the armrests with sweaty palms and white knuckles, and closed his eyes so tight that it hurt as he prayed to the superior being whose existence he had rejected since his youth. The 707 hit an air pocket, dropped ten feet and Jeremy Parrot made a grab for the airsickness bag.

The telephone on the desk of the temporary East Point office of the Manager, Trading Division, Cumberland Engineering Limited, interrupted his meeting with his three Cantonese sales managers. 'Zagan speaking.'

'This is Abraham Male returning your call, Matthew. You have good news for me, I trust.'

'Yes, I have good news . . .'

'Wonderful, Matthew!'

' . . . and no, I also have bad news.'

'Whatever do you mean?'

Zagan gestured apologetically to his sales managers and they stood as one and left the office, leaving their files on their chairs for later. 'The bad news is that I must turn down your offer to join the board of Male & Son. I'm sorry it's taken so long for me to make up my mind.'

The silence was weighted. Then: 'Yes, you have procrastinated. Perhaps it shows you're not right for us in any case. Perhaps I'd be advised to keep you as a competitor. I need men that are assertive, decisive – '

'I feel the least I can do for you under the circumstances, Mr Male, is to give you the good news I mentioned.'

'And what might that be?'

'My congratulations on Jubilee Bay Phase B.'

'That's rather premature – '

'It's not premature at all, Mr Male. You see, we've given up. Lord Armstrong and Sir Leo Cheshunt flew back to London last night. It's obvious to them that Matamoto's offer is unbeatable.

You have a clear shot at the contract. Cathay Electric is yours for the taking.'

'Hmmm. So you're a quitter as well as a procrastinator, young man. Well, thank you, anyway. Sorry I can't chat on. I'm off to the airport.'

Zagan's intelligence had been accurate on that, too. 'Oh, Mr Male – '

'Yes?'

'You know, it's always easy to get the contract when your price is ten per cent below the competition. I don't see that it takes many smarts to do business that way. Perhaps that's why I've turned you down.'

In this silence Zagan listened to Male's resentment rising, and timed his disconnection a split second before it boiled over into words.

He recalled his managers and concluded the sales meeting, all the time keeping his fingers crossed under his desk. What he had told Abraham Male had been no lie. At about this time Armstrong and Cheshunt would indeed be landing at Heathrow. Their appointment with the prime minister was at noon, London time – seven p.m., Hong Kong time.

'And now, to business!' Kingston Orr demanded.

Backs straightened around the table on the tenth floor of the Matamoto Building in Minato-ku, Tokyo. The customary pleasantries were ended, the first sips from the ornate cups of green tea taken. It was Saturday, a holiday in Japan. But it was a day of work for the executive management of the electrical arm of the biggest *zaibatsu*, Matamoto Corporation.

For Kingston Orr was in town.

Abraham Male met the eyes of Tetsuo Hondo across the table. The vice-president of Matamoto Electric dropped his head a quarter of an inch.

All eyes were upon Kingston Orr as he opened the bound file before him. 'Hondo-san, I acknowledge Matamoto's fine effort to supply, install and commission on time the nine units 120 megawatt for Jubilee Bay Phase A. I understand we have agreed on a price for the ten units of 200 megawatt for Phase B. The capacity of my new power station, at 3,080 megawatts, will be the largest single generating installation in Asia. I do thank you, but I have one request to make before we sign the new contract.'

Hondo smiled and said without hesitation: 'Of course, Orr-san.'

Kingston Orr nodded. 'Good. My request is a simple one. I wish the price of the contract to be converted from yen into US dollars . . .'

Hondo looked to his lieutenants. They were stereotyped in grey business suits, white shirts, blue ties, and round faces that carried no dissent. 'That is no probr'em, Orr-san.'

' . . . at the rate of exchange that applied on February 12th.'

A stereophonic frown almost came from the Japanese side of the table. Orr-san was getting more devious. This was the first time he had not asked for his 'face' discount straight out.

'That same as ten per cent price reduction!' Hondo protested in his now almost fluent English. 'US dorr'ar was devar 'ued on Febr'ary 13th!'

'I'm well aware of that, Hondo-san,' Orr replied coolly. And it could devalue further, too, he thought, requiring fewer and fewer Hong Kong dollars as progress payments were made against a US dollar contract.

'So sorry, regret is impossibr'e,' Hondo stated flatly. 'We have no objection to price in US dorr'ar – if it at current rate of exchange.'

'I also regret, Hondo-san. I regret that the current rate of exchange is quite unacceptable.' Kingston Orr spoke softly, appreciating the other's performance. 'I could not sign the contract under such circumstances.'

Hondo glanced first at Male, and saw the minute gesture of reassurance. Then he flicked his eyes to Parrot and saw the same there. When he looked back to Orr his eyes were hard, so hard they did not interpret the frown they saw. 'As I said, Orr-san, contract in US dorr'ar is okay. But big risk US dorr'ar may devar'ue again – ' He glanced around the table, saw only blank faces and went on confidently. 'So we want ten per cent increase in price, not ten per cent reduction. So sorry – '

'Noooo!'

All eyes went to Abraham Male, who was staring at Hondo in total dismay. This was no part of the strategy he had put across the previous night in his room in the Imperial Hotel when he had announced Anglo-Saxon's withdrawal. 'You don't have to give Kingston his discount this time,' he had counselled. 'I know you've costed it into the contract sum, so save half of it for Matamoto and give half to Male & Son as extra commission in payment for the information.' Hondo had catechized him before agreeing. There had been no talk of demanding a price increase. So what had happened to change the strategy? Then Male remembered

Hondo had left him to meet Parrot for a drink. He looked sideways at the general manager, and saw the answer to his question written all over the smug, rat-like face.

In the meantime, an ominous silence had deposited itself upon the table.

Kingston Orr, his face like armour-plate, had fixed his glacial stare a foot above Tetsuo Hondo's head. When he spoke his voice cut the air like a lancet. 'Anybody who tries to take advantage of me discovers to his terminal regret just how much I do not appreciate such things. My father discovered it – and now so shall you.' He looked deliberately from face to face, finishing on that of his general manager. 'I mean every single one of you.' He stood and kicked back his chair with his heel. 'This negotiation is ended.' And he strode from the room.

At nine a.m. on Monday, February 26th, 1973, Kingston Orr stepped into the Heathrow Airport VIP lounge. He was totally alone. Eight hours ahead in Hong Kong, Jeremy Parrot, his desk cleared, was leaving the office with GENERAL MANAGER on the door for the last time.

A quartet of men of bearing came forward, their frames squared by business suits of British thread, Burberrys overcoats thrown across their arms. Orr waited for them to come to him, then extended his hand first to Matthew Zagan.

'Good morning, Matthew. How pleasantly unusual to meet you over here in London after so long. I hope your mother is well. She's a woman I have always respected. She's done such a wonderful job with *The Register* and virtually single handed. I regret I haven't seen either of you since your father's funeral. How many years ago was that . . ?'

'Almost five, Kingston.' Zagan introduced Lord Armstrong and Sir Leo Cheshunt, then the Secretary for Trade of Her Majesty's Government.

The five men left through a guarded exit and climbed into a black Rolls-Royce that was antiseptic clean. They drove into London along cold grey roads beneath a sky laden with nimbus and pulled up in Downing Street outside a door wearing number 10.

Kingston Orr's habitually metallic expression melted as he recognised the tall, white haired man who appeared in the doorway then came forward to shake his hand as he alighted from the limousine.

'It is indeed a pleasure to meet you, Mr Orr. Do come in out of this freezing weather. How I wish I had the seats in the House to have this country moved to the tropics . . .' On Ted Heath's face glowed one of his rare smiles. 'And Northern Ireland to the Arctic Circle.'

Kingston Orr reciprocated with an exceptional laugh of his own. Then he followed the prime minister into his residence.

14

Thomas Buckley, B.Com., FCA, FCIS, MBIM, Director of Finance and Administration, Cumberland China Limited, was as sharp-edged as a mint fresh five hundred dollar bill. His staff said of him that he had an electronic calculator for a heart, and the only thing he had yet to master in matters financial was the secret of the abacus.

At 3:45 on Friday, March 9th, the top money man of the Born Again *Hong* was at his desk in his office on the fiftieth floor of, Connaught Centre. The desk was surrounded on three sides by shelves that were jammed floor to ceiling with fat tomes on accounting, audit, economics, etcetera, the gold lettering on their spines glinting like pixy dust in the fluorescent light. The ambience of the office was scholarly, like that of some venerable library, though the great building it was in was brand new.

Over his pince-nez spectacles Buckley squinted at the document tied with a red ribbon fixed with a wax seal. He looked up at Daniel Vail. 'You say they signed it without any question at all?'

'Not a one,' the Director of Properties affirmed. 'Like I told you yesterday, they're in a cash bind. There's not enough money in tenements, even with the rent spiral. I could've talked them down to – '

Buckley raised his hand. 'This obsession with bargaining all of you seem to have in Hong Kong gives me a pain. All it does is slow things down for a gain that is insignificant. I'm glad to top the market price for a quick settlement. Next week there'll be a new market price. A higher one. And then we'll have created our own bargain – all for ourselves.'

He opened the document to the signature page and checked the three typewritten rectangles, headed 'The Property', 'The Purchaser' and 'The Seller'. He smiled, his cadaverous face folding into a network of deep-tracked creases. That he was a financial wizard had always been undisputed. And now he had shown his adeptness in that other plum sphere of modern business: the magic realm of Property.

'I hope you know what you're doing, Tom,' Vail cautioned. 'This has been too easy. Are you sure we were right not to tell the General?'

Buckley sighed. 'Vail, why don't you stick with the game you're best at: "follow the leader". In '66–'67 you tagged along after the General as he bought up half of Hong Kong. Now kindly do the same for me.'

The Director of Properties shut his mouth. He dropped his eyes to the file on Buckley's desk. 'Property Developments Associated with the Hong Kong Mass Transit Railway' had been typed on a label on its cover. He knew the contents, for he had written them himself based on information he had personally gleaned from contacts in the Colonial Secretariat and in the corporation being formed to build and operate the railway, which was already commonly known as the 'MTR'. He was awed by the scope of the project to connect underground the extremities of urban Hong Kong and Kowloon. It was to be financed largely by capital generated by the sale by tender of the prime residential and commercial air-space above most of the station concourses. He had suggested that Cumberland Properties prequalify as a tenderer, but Buckley had gone one better. He had decided that the real estate subsidiary should buy up buildings that already stood on land earmarked for the stations. Who but the existing owner, he had reasoned, would be better positioned to negotiate with the MTR Corporation for the right to develop the prime air-space?

'I just hope those drawings I got from that manager in Engineering stay accurate, Tom,' Vail persisted in a tone salted with concern. 'Lucky he had a relative in the MTRC draughting office who could run us off extra copies of some of the stations on the Island. Very lucky – '

'Of course we've been lucky! Luck's the ingredient that turns a near miss into a bullseye. It was luck that auction notice in the paper was face-up on your desk this morning! It was luck the site was bang on top of North Point station! Without luck we're nowhere. We had to move fast to deny anyone else a piece of ours. It was luck the sellers could negotiate with us at the first meeting and give up their plan to sell by auction. We've been lucky all along, haven't we? Didn't you say these people own more tenements in Quarry Bay – on top of the station there?'

'Yes, Tom. But they're not keen to sell – '

'Persuade them, man. Make them an offer they can't turn down.'

'They need cash,' Vail conceded. 'They said so. For the stock market.'

'Of course! Damn blasted gamblers, these Chinese. Fancy selling off prime real estate just so they can gamble away the proceeds. Fools.'

Buckley tried to imagine John Huart's face when, ten minutes hence, he announced the property coup. He could hear the Great Man's words: 'I couldn't have done it slicker myself, Tom! Congratulations! Finance and Administration is obviously too confining for a man of your talents.'

He pushed his pince-nez into the bridge of his nose and studied the contract in his hands. 'The Property' was six blocks of tenements in Hang On Street, North Point, 'The Purchaser' was Cumberland Properties Limited, and 'The Seller' was some organisation called Great Horse Realty Company. He looked at the ideogram signature of Tu Hoi-sang and Tu Wai-ming: the autographs of two of a family of fools. What other fool said that only a Chinese could outsmart another Chinese? 'Come on, Vail,' he commanded as he took his suit coat from the wardrobe. 'It's time to go and tell the General all about it.'

They were due on the fifty-second floor at four. In eleven years, Buckley had not caused a meeting with his taipan to be delayed so much as a second through his own tardiness. And he would ensure his directors gave him identical respect when he was selected to be the next taipan.

'The market hit a new peak today and Cicero Investments is in it right up to its gilt-edged testicles.' Lennie the Fifth sat back, crossed his legs and puffed harder on his cigar.

Huart's frown was hidden in shadow. His new office was a replica of the one in Cumberland House, except there was no spiral staircase and the windows were circular. The afternoon sun streamed through them. Beyond, the Nine Dragons were clear and stark. The view from the highest man-made point in Hong Kong was one worthy of the Altitudinal Taipan. 'You mean we have every single dollar invested?' he queried. 'All our profits as well as the original stake of ten million?'

Cosgrove nodded. 'At close of trading today the Index was at 1775 – a new record. It's heading for 2000. And it'll get there by the end of next week. End of the month at the latest.'

Huart thought on this. 'Lennie, so far you have been infallible.

But all this can't go on much longer. The price:earnings ratio of some of the blue chips is as high as 200. Ours, too. What did we close at today?'

'One hundred and seventy seven dollars.'

Huart shook his head. 'The Government's doing its damnedest to deflate the market. The banks are to be told to lift the minimum lending rate again. The third time this month. And it's only the ninth day! The Financial Secretary privately admits he's certain a crash is inevitable. Any one of a number of things could spark it: civil unrest over the rent spiral, or the death of Mao or Chou En-Lai . . .'

Cosgrove nodded again. 'This is true. But the current momentum is such that it will take the Index to 2000. There's no need to bail out yet. John, you shouldn't worry. It's me talking.'

'I do worry, you know that.'

'What's the worst that can happen to us?' Cosgrove leaned forward and jabbed his cigar at his audience for emphasis. 'Even if the Index falls to half what it is now before we bail out, we'll still be over a hundred million ahead.'

'That's fine for Cicero Investments, but whatever happens to Hong Kong in a stock market crash affects the company – and the two of us – just like it does the hawker in the street. We're not immune, you know – ' The intercom buzzed. 'Yes, Imelda?'

'Mr Buckley and Mr Vail are here to see you, sir.'

The pendulum clock chimed four. 'Ask them to give me a minute. Fix them up with a cup of jasmine tea each, will you, please?'

Cosgrove stood with alacrity. 'Buckley comes. I go.'

With regret Huart watched his partner quit the office through the door to his own. The gap between the two was wider than ever.

On his desk lay his passport, containing a full-page visa stamped with a five-pointed red star, and his air ticket for Peking. The British Industrial Technology Exhibition was to open on Monday, March 26th – seventeen days hence. By an amazing coincidence, it would be one hundred years to the day since Charles Huart had registered Cumberland China's first office in Chungking. The centenary was to be celebrated on the day, despite the exhibition, with a banquet of one hundred tables in the Dynasty Ballroom of the Victoria Hotel. Invitations to the 1,200 that would fill the tables had gone out over a month ago.

Huart would take a Cathay Pacific charter flight to Peking the afternoon following the centenary banquet, and he was looking forward to it with an impatience he found hard to conceal. He owed it all to two people: Y. Y. Szeto – who seemed to have been commuting between Peking and Hong Kong on essential liaison work, and Matthew Zagan – who had extracted fantastic support from the British engineering companies who had agreed to invest in participating on the Cumberland China stand.

The thought of Zagan had him taking up the carbon copy of the Letter of Intent with the masthead of Cathay Electric Corporation and Kingston Orr's underscored signature. He re-read it paragraph by paragraph, word by word. How had the man pulled it off? How had he been able to do what had appeared over the years to have become Impossible? Zagan had parried all his questions with the philosophy: 'Determine your enemy's weakness before he knows he has one, then exploit it point blank.'

Huart had accepted he would get no more than that. 'My niece told me you were an aggravating enigma,' he had said. 'But I didn't believe it until now. I'll bet the competition are even more in the dark.'

Next he picked up the telex that had just come in from Glynn Bedrix in Zurich, confirming Prince Lugano's support for the Director of Insurance and Banking's next venture: Cumberland Insurance Limited was to expand into the field of group policies and corporate provident funds.

The outer door opened and Thomas Buckley entered, a document tied in a red ribbon under his arm and Daniel Vail in trail. The top accountant was wearing a new face, and Huart read on it confidence, pride and other good things.

There may be no male progeny of Charles Huart on hand to become fifth taipan, he rationalised to himself, but neither was there any lack of substitute candidates of the highest quality.

Had the Director of Finance and Administration and the Director of Properties not come in just then, Huart would have proceeded to the next item on his desk: a copy of the *Hong Kong and Oriental Daily*'s annual *Economic Review* supplement. But it remained unread as, around the rosewood coffee table, the debate on the merits of the purchase of six blocks of tenements in Hang On Street, North Point gathered pace.

Even the Altitudinal Taipan was not to know, on that afternoon when the Hang Seng Index had hit its peak of peaks, that Kym Marshall's page 16 article would prove to be the spark that was to explode into the greatest financial crisis in Asian history.

[492]

In a rat-visited cockloft over the machine floor of the Magnificent Dragon Printing Company in Healthy Street, North Point, a man sat at a steel desk looking ten years past his five decades. One corner of his mouth held the butt of a Good Companion filter tip, the other a twisted grimace of rank anxiety, and in between the two he sighed: '*Aiiiyahh*,' as his hand reached out to the volume control of a transistor radio. The voice of the announcer jumped an octave and staccato Cantonese echoed through the cockloft and down to the machine floor where his son worked at an out-dated letter-press that was blackened with years of ink.

The man's name was Kwong Sum. He was a master printer. He operated the rows of presses of the *Hong Kong and Oriental Daily* after midnight, and his own solitary machine before that. He had been with the newspaper for thirty-eight years, starting out as the lowest-paid *foki* on the printing floor. He had taught himself the language that the presses churned out, and he had worked hard. He had saved assiduously until, four years ago, he had accumulated enough to buy the old letter-press, register the Magnificent Dragon Printing Company, pay three months' rent on the 180 square feet of ground floor in Healthy Street and build the cockloft as his office. He had run the press on his own until recently, when his son had found some time in between his studies to assist.

Now the master printer worked twice as hard, day and night. He saved ten times as hard, for his time was running out. And he kept alert for the opportunity that every worker deserves: the one to make him rich quick. Eight days ago, Kwong Sum had looked at page 16 of the *Economic Review* supplement going through the presses. And had seen his Main Chance.

He squinted at it again now, open on his desk. Under the heading 'The Great Paper Chase', Kym Marshall, in what had been intended as a journalistic warning to the authorities, told the world how easy it would be for any master printer to forge a Hong Kong style share certificate.

He prayed to *Kwan Yin* as the announcer ran off in alphabetical order the closing prices of companies listed on the Hong Kong Stock Exchange. It sounded as if most were up, but it was not until after the price of Zung Li Jones Garments that the Hang Seng Index was requoted, and Kwong Sum knew that the market had reversed direction. It had risen 64 points.

'*Aiiiyahh!*' he cried gleefully and gave mental thanks to *Kwan*

Yin for his salvation. The four day break had come to an end! The previous day the Index had closed at 1595, 180 points off last Friday's record peak. Some newspapers had said The Crash was on and he had panicked. The plates were not finished! He had worked feverishly through the night to complete the first one. And at last it was ready.

The voice on the radio went back to 'A' to begin running through prices on the Kam Ngan Stock Exchange, and then the Far East. The fourth and newest bourse, the Kowloon, was too small to rate a mention.

The creaking of the wooden ladder preceded the arrival in the cockloft of Kwong Siu-cheong. The master printer turned and saw the document in his son's hand. 'It is finished, Siu-cheong?' he asked. 'Let me see it.'

The youth handed his father the crisp rectangular sheet that was pungent with fresh ink, and watched as he switched on the table lamp, took up a magnifying glass and scrutinised the document. Then the master printer opened a drawer and took out a second document which looked identical to the first except for its creases and dog-eared corners. The glass was taken up again and the examination resumed.

At last Kwong Sum raised his head and smiled at his son. 'It is perfect, Ah Cheong. I cannot tell the two apart and I am a master printer. Now, go quickly and fix the wax seal to this one, apply the stockbroker's chop on the back as I showed you, then type in a name from the Dollar Directory. Then bring it back and let me examine it again. At the same time run off a trial batch. *Fai dee!* We have no time to waste.'

Kwong Siu-cheong flew down the ladder. He was a month shy of twenty-one. He was impecunious and a virgin, and chronically aware of both states.

Kwong Sum pulled the butt from his lower lip, reached into the bottom drawer and lifted out a half-empty bottle of Martell. 'I say that a worker should be allowed a vice or two,' he excused himself, extracting the cork. 'Forgery is not a vice – it is an art. It is an ancient art.'

He lifted the bottle to his lips, took a swig and felt the cognac burn deep into his stomach. He took a fresh cigarette from his crushed pack, lit it off the smouldering butt and inhaled deeply. From the floor below came the clacking of a typewriter, followed by a metallic rumbling as the letter-press started up. Kwong Sum grinned to himself, took a second swig, then slapped the cork into the neck and shut the bottle away.

[494]

He took up the creased dog-eared document that had served as the control from which he had produced the first plate. At that moment the piece of paper he held between his fingers was worth just under $18,000.00, more than he could expect to earn legitimately in six long months. He looked at the logo in the top right-hand corner that had so tested his skill as a master printer. It was not the round gold 'C' that had proved so difficult, but the miniature map of China in its centre.

16

Even at the western age of sixty-seven Tu Chien was learning new things.

I know now, he mused as he surveyed his male kin seated before him, why Cantonese millionaires elect not to abandon their tenements for plush apartments, why Tangar die amongst their gold aboard their junks, and why Hakka compradores thrive on dirt floors in New Territories cottages. Spartan surroundings breed tough offspring and ensure a family's perpetuity. So what of mine? Hoi-sang, my son, sits in American and French finery and owns no more resilience than a cabbage. Neither is the local ginger hot enough for third nephew. Sixth nephew has what it takes, but he is tainted by the business he does so well. So it shall fall to my great-nephew, even though southern blood runs in his veins. He looked at Wai-kit and noted the mature composure. Yes, this one learns fast. It is good that he missed the pampered upbringing of Bubbling Well Road.

In Shanghai dialect to a spot on the ceiling the patriarch said without seeming to discriminate: 'You seem displeased to have risen this early on a Sunday morning. Can this really be so?'

'But it is not so, Father,'

'I, for one, am not displeased, Uncle.'

The second protest had been Wai-ming's. Errol Tu said nothing, for his three a.m. telephone call had initiated the unscheduled meeting.

Knowing his great-uncle had not included him in his rebuke, Alain To had likewise said nothing.

'That is good,' Tu Chien allowed. 'For this meeting is with no mundane intent.' He took up the teapot, raised himself through a chrysalis of pain and shuffled around the desk to pour the black liquid into each of the four cups held up to receive it. None of the younger men of the family offered polite protestation at the superfluity of the ceremony, for they knew it revealed the depth of their patriarch's excitement.

Tu Chien resumed his seat and chose to cut short any further preamble. 'I tell you that the fortune of the family is suddenly at great risk.'

'How, Father – ?'

'Listen, and do not interrupt. I repeat: our fortune, and those of our patrons, are at risk. But we have been given a warning of it before anyone else. Because of this warning, we can save our fortunes – and at the same time remove the giant's testicles without him feeling a thing.'

He took three documents from a drawer and gave one to each, except Errol Tu, as it had been he who had brought them. 'Tell me what those papers represent.' The tone told that the answer was not obvious. 'Hoi-sang?'

'Why, it is a *Gum Bak Leen* share certificate, Father – such as we have been buying on the market. Now we own half the – '

'Look past the end of your nose, my son, or you are of less use to the family than a blind beggar. Look at the name of the registered owner.'

Chastened, Tu Hoi-sang looked down again, and squinted. 'Pope Paul VI?'

'Indeed. And the others?'

'The Duke of Edinburgh,' said Wai-ming in a puzzled tone.

'Richard M. Nixon,' followed Alain To with almost a smile. 'Forgeries, Great-uncle? But they are perfect. Where did they come from?'

'Wai-tsun will tell the story.'

Errol Tu took a deep breath. 'At midnight the night before last, a boy surnamed Kwong visited the House of Ecstatic Joy in North Point to give up his virginity. He had no cash to pay for the girl's services so he offered one of these. The *lo baan* noticed the name typed on it and was suspicious. He questioned the boy for twenty-four hours until, late last night he revealed his father was a master printer who had forged several thousand *Gum Bak Leen* share certificates, just like these. The boy had run off extra copies for himself, but then took names at random from the newspaper and typed them in as the "registered owners" contrary to his father's instruction to use local names from the Dollar Directory. The *lo baan* knew of our interest in *Gum Bak Leen* and called me. He will be appropriately rewarded.'

'Where is the boy, now?' Alain To enquired.

'In a back room at the House of Ecstatic Joy, pending my instructions.'

'You have, of course, seized the father.'

'The father is dead.'

'Dead?'

Errol Tu nodded. 'My men found him at dawn with a hole in his head.'

Alain To's eyes narrowed. 'And, of course, there were no forgeries.'

'And no printing plates,' Errol Tu affirmed.

'You suspect the son?' Alain To asked.

'No. The father tried to sell to the wrong people.'

'Does the son know of his father's associates? Has he given names and addresses of other workers in the factory?'

'There are no other workers. The boy knows nothing. He is not bright. He is but a horny simpleton.'

Tu Chien hawked and spat into the spittoon at the foot of his desk. 'We ought to thank the gods he was in the phase of mustard green of the tenth moon. If he wasn't so keen to do something with his *lun* besides pee through it, we would be aware of none of this.' He looked to sixth nephew. 'Will you be able to find the forgeries and the plates before the stock market opens tomorrow?'

Errol Tu spread his hands. 'I cannot say. A thousand of our people are looking already. We could alert ten thousand and still not find them in time. It could take a day – or a week. But by then . . .'

'By then it will be too late!' Alain To inserted and the patriarch's eyes flicked to him. 'The ones who have the forgeries will sell them quickly. The Central Registry will pick them up and alert the police. The newspapers will be on to it. The public will panic and sell their shares for fear they are all forged. And the stock market will crash . . .'

With that dire prediction a silence dropped upon the office-study. Tu Chien's hand rose to the twelve strands of waxed hair on his jaw and his eyes glazed over as he withdrew into a cocoon of cogitation. They watched his hand rising and falling and knew that in his brain tabloids of logic and experience were being shuffled into order.

In addition to the family fortune, Great Horse Enterprises was trustee for billions of dollars of Overseas Chinese money invested in the stock market. Tu Chien had picked 2000 as the Hang Seng Index's psychological pinnacle at which the big local and overseas investors would look to cash in. He had planned to be out by then, having liquidated all stock piecemeal and transferred into fixed deposit. Banks, the Daima included, were steadily lifting interest rates. The cash would stay on deposit whilst the stock market fell and brought property values down with it. When land became a bargain once again, Tu Chien would buy up. He knew that business was merely a reading of cycles, and that the current one was at its peak. Now was the time to unload any property not in a prime location – like six blocks of tenements in Hang On Street, North Point.

But what of the stock market? The murderers of the master printer would likely be callow fools who did not know nor care that they must ruin the very market they aimed to exploit. The Index would not reach 1700 again, let alone 2000. The moment the first forgery was detected, it would be like a basket of crabs tipped on the floors of the exchanges. He visualised the panic. It would be stereophonic! Epidemic! If it did not happen tomorrow, or the next day, then it would be the day after that. But Tu Chien's *fung shui* was magnificently benign. He knew of it today!

He would use the forgeries as a scalpel with a double cutting edge. He would withdraw from the market all that he had invested on behalf of the family and its patrons and by the same act he would precipitate the fall from grace of the giant. His eyes cleared, and when he spoke it was in a voice that belied his sixty-seven years by western reckoning and his deteriorating health. 'All of you – listen to my decision and confirm that you will follow my instructions!'

The four voices replied in unison: 'We confirm.'

'Listen well then. The selling of all our investments is to commence fifteen minutes after trading opens tomorrow. During those first fifteen minutes we will buy – just enough to set the market moving up. Then for the rest of the Hour of the Snake we will sell . . .'

Alain To racked his brain until he remembered that the Hour of the Snake started at nine a.m. and ended at eleven.

' . . . with caution, for we do not want alarm to spread too soon. In the next hour the selling can be more aggressive – in large blocks simultaneously on all four exchanges. Our aim must be to liquidate fifty per cent of all our stock by the close of trading tomorrow.'

He looked at each of the four in turn, they nodded in sequence, and he went on. 'On Tuesday we will follow the same pattern. We will buy for the first fifteen minutes to reverse the fall of the Index. It should not be difficult to achieve. Small investors will not sell tomorrow as they are the slowest to react. They will resume purchasing on Tuesday when they see our money going back in. Then, during Tuesday's Hour of the Horse we must sell at the going price every last share – except, of course . . .' He raised what was left of his sparse eyebrows.

'*Gum Bak Leen*,' Alain To inserted.

'*Ngaam la!*' Tu Chien kept private his pleasure at his great-nephew's ability to keep up. '*Gum Bak Leen* we do not sell. *Gum Bak Leen* we buy! All shares will be for sale. The prices will plummet. There will be no buyers except us. And we will only be interested in *Gum Bak Leen.*'

He drained his cup and looked through his eyebrows at Errol Tu. 'Wai-tsun, I have a special task for you. The man they call the *Meen Foot Hau Jaak* and the Lucky Pig . . .'

'Yes, Uncle?'

'Tonight he is to go to the Red Phoenix Motel. He is to learn there will be a major break in the market, lasting exactly two days. He is to be advised to sell short as soon as trading opens tomorrow. He is to be convinced this is a great opportunity. The greatest yet. Never to be repeated. He is to be further advised to cover himself in the last hour of trading on Tuesday. Not before, not after. It is clear?'

'Clear, Uncle.'

Tu Chien lifted his hand six inches and the meeting was over.

The patriarch looked at the empty chairs. 'Every day richer!' he said to them. The family would gain. And gain again. And not only that, by the end of the second month of the Year of the Water Ox, *Gum Bak Leen* would belong to him, and to the family. The giant would be dead. Still alive, but quite dead. And it was all to take place before a backdrop of chaos: the Crash of the Hong Kong stock market.

17

Without two of its regulars, the game of liar dice in the Bowling Alley Bar was unusually subdued. Though the clock showed that Tuesday, March 20th had reached 12:30, neither Lennie

Cosgrove nor P.G. Curzon-Cross had appeared. For at that moment they were at opposite ends of a Central District telephone line that was running hot.

'Luv-a-duck, P.G.! Here I am short ten million of my own company's paper and you say you can't cover a single solitary block? Not even on a falling market? What're your bloody clerks doing? They must be running round the floors of the exchange with their bloody eyes shut! What – ?'

The stockbroker cut in with an angry snort. 'Now come on, Lennie! That's damn unfair! In the last half hour we've been able to buy back all the shares we sold for Cicero Investments on your instructions first thing yesterday. But we just can't recover your Cumberland for you. Don't ask me why. I don't know what's going on. Every time a parcel comes onto any of the exchanges someone outbids us. Every time! I've told you before I think someone's buying up Cumberland China stock . . !'

'Then increase your bloody bids, P.G.! I've got to get those ten million shares back chop-bloody-chop! Or . . . or I'm a dead mackerel!'

'We're trying, but the counter-bid is always too quick and the price is always too far up on us. I tell you, Lennie . . . I tell you there's somebody out there staging a takeover bid for your company!'

'Ah, come on, P.G. Don't talk such bloody tommy-rot – !'

'Now who's got his eyes closed? I've suspected something for some time. Your price has never fallen with the market. It's always held up – even on a sharp break. And it's always risen ahead of the Index. Somebody has been shopping for your shares ever since you went public. Now you've gone and put your personal ten million slap bang into their hands! I'm not joking, Lennie – it's just damn impossible to cover for you!'

'Luv-a-bloody-duck!' Cosgrove's brain reeled. 'What's the market doing now? Where's the Index at?'

'It's levelled off in the last ten minutes. It was dropping like a rock, but your repurchases have helped steady it. Just a moment –' There was a muffled exchange, then the stockbroker's voice returned. 'At 12:30 the Index was 1557. Down 63 points today. It was at 1550 at one stage.'

Cosgrove's face folded upon itself into a prolonged grimace. Finally he sighed. 'Okay . . . Okay, P.G. Keep trying to cover for me, will you? Call me back as soon as you do. There's a good chap.'

'I'll do my best, Lennie. But I can't promise anything.'

[500]

Cosgrove replaced the receiver and dropped his head into his hands.

Luv-a-duck! Had he done the right thing? But Waldo Wu had been spot on with the forty-eight hour break. The Index had dropped over a hundred points in two days before the market had bottomed out. He lifted his head. Of course he had done right! Waldo Wu had never failed him. But where, he asked himself for the thousandth time, did the 'gopher' of a Kowloon Tong knocking shop get such dynamite inside information? He had never really asked. He had been happy to get the tips and pay well for them. And this had been the biggest and best of them all. This had been It. This had been the Big One! This had been what he was looking for a year ago when he had insisted on keeping ten per cent in Cumberland China instead of taking up a full half share in Charlemagne Enterprises.

Of course he had done it right! He had sold with the market at 1680 and had instructed P.G. to cover his position at 1550. He had made millions in a little over twenty-four hours. It had been a classic example of 'selling short'. But that only applied to Cicero Investments. For he had simultaneously 'sold short' his entire personal shareholding in the Born Again *Hong*. And now P.G. couldn't cover! Not one single solitary block of shares! It was incredible! No, it was impossible! It was absolutely impossible! Luv-a-bloody-duck!

Lennie the Lucky Pig felt the first skewer of panic stab at his innards.

He sat at his desk and sweated. He looked at the telephone: mute, dumb, useless. He looked at the clock on the wall. 12:35 . . . 12:36 . . . 12:37 . . . The telephone remained mute, dumb, useless. No way could he tear himself from it. He could not take those ten simple steps to the sideboard and pour the double gin that he craved. His stomach burned. His throat rasped. His face ran with sweat. He yanked out a handkerchief and mopped it.

12:40.

A quarter to one: closing time on the exchanges.

It was thirty seconds more before the telephone rang. Cosgrove lunged at it like a shipwrecked tourist grabbing for a lifeline.

'It's P.G., Lennie. No luck, I'm afraid. We have no option but to keep trying for you tomorrow.'

Cosgrove was speechless. His tongue curled into the back of his mouth.

'Lennie? Are you there, Lennie?'

It was a full half minute before Lennie the Fifth could produce a sound. 'How . . . How did the . . . Index end up?' It was a series of croaks.

'Pardon, old bean? What'd you say?'

Cosgrove cleared his throat. 'The Index. How did it end up?'

'1514. It fell 106 points on the day. 43 in the last fifteen minutes.'

'Ehhhhhh?' Cosgrove gagged in disbelief. '43 points in fifteen minutes? No! I don't believe you! It was supposed to have gone up, P.G. Not down! Up, you hear? Up! What the hell's going on down there – ?'

'A new rumour's doing the rounds, Lennie. Wait for it . . . Forgeries. Forged share certificates have been found at the Central Share Registry. Like I said, it's just a rumour at present. But a damn strong one.'

Cosgrove shook his head. His vision blurred. He shook his head again and mouthed the word as if he had never heard it before: 'Forgeries . . ?'

As the deputy chairman of Cumberland China dropped his receiver into its cradle with numbed fingers, in the adjoining office the Altitudinal Taipan picked up his own on the third ring. Imelda Roboza always switched the outside line through if she went to lunch with him still working.

'John Huart here.'

'Kym Marshall, *Business Daily*. Afternoon, General Huart. Remember me?'

Both the name and the Australian accent were indeed familiar. Marshall had interviewed him more than once. The business editor of the *Hong Kong and Oriental Daily* was the only man in the colony to address him to his face by his anachronistic army rank. Marshall had explained that, as they were not personal friends, Christian names were inappropriate, and in Australia nobody called anybody 'Mister' or 'Sir'.

'Then what, in Australia, do they call people who have had no military rank, Mr Marshall?' Huart had enquired.

'We call them "mate", of course, General Huart.'

It had been his first exposure to Australian humour and he had decided that it was distinctly of low humidity.

'I've been trying to reach your people,' the journalist went on quickly, 'but they all seem to have taken early lunches.'

'I'm late for lunch myself,' Huart threw in, impatient to get away to Jimmy's Kitchen. 'What can I do for you?'

Marshall went for the jugular. 'Is it true that trading in Cumberland China shares will be suspended before ten a.m. tomorrow?'

In the subsequent silence, Huart could hear a familiar background noise on the line. 'What did you say?'

Marshall repeated the question, word by word, his voice raised against the clamour around him. Huart frowned. The Australian was a professional and had never been known to make joke calls to Hong Kong taipans.

'Where are you calling from?'

'The observation gallery of the Kam Ngan Stock Exchange. This is where the rumours pop up first, General Huart – not fifty-two storeys in the sky. Only this one's no rumour any longer, and I'm calling you to have that confirmed. I've spoken to the Central Share Registry – '

'Central Share Registry? What've they to do with anything?'

There came an uncertain pause. 'You mean you don't know?'

'Just what am I supposed to know? Look, I'm sorry, but I am running late for my lunch appointment and I must – '

'General Huart – one hour ago a clerk at the Central Share Registry was processing three certificates of one hundred Cumberland China shares. They aroused his suspicion. He checked them out. Guess what he found.'

Huart sighed. 'I hate guessing games. Tell me.'

'Each of the certificates was forged.'

'Forged?'

'That's right. Forged. Now – I repeat my question. Will trading in your company's shares be suspended on all stock exchanges before ten o' – ?'

'No comment!' Huart fired down the line and hung up.

The Governor's entrance at the annual spring H and K cocktail party in the Victoria Hotel's Dynasty Ballroom set off a stir amongst a stir. Tension, mixed with the normal animation of the occasion, hung over the mingling throng like an inhospitable vapour. The lofty Scot, the Tall Big Man of the local commonfolk who thought the world of him, appeared with his wife at the entrance at six, ringed by aides who, like the viceregal couple, had honoured the occasion in their best evening wear.

Sir Percival Landers, improving with age like a vintage claret, was at the door with the Lady Maurine at the head of a line of the bank's directors and their spouses. Time permitted them each a one-liner to the Governor, likely the identical one to that delivered the year before.

[503]

The crowd in the Dynasty Ballroom was five-hundred strong. It was a cross-section of Hong Kong elite, and it included the entire complement of the Long Table, plus Matthew Zagan, whose attendance in the capacity of 'observer' had been requested by Huart at all future board meetings.

And at nine the next morning, he would sit at the Long Table for the first time. The reason behind the emergency meeting of the board of the Born Again *Hong* was known to every hawker in every street. It was blazened across the front page of *The Register:*

105.61 BREAK AS FORGED *GUM BAK LEEN* SHARES FOUND!

John Huart did not linger after the Governor's arrival. The two men, the tallest in the room and indeed the colony, exchanged perfunctory good wishes, then Huart left to join Y.Y. Szeto and Raymond Clinton O'Young who were at that time sitting down to a meeting with the chairmen of the four stock exchanges. He paused at the door to press a point with the man tipped to be the first Securities Commissioner, pumped Landers' hand, kissed the cheek of the Lady Maurine, and left.

Zagan watched him go, then drained his Carlsberg and cast an eye over the throng. If the walls caved in upon every person present, he reflected, Hong Kong would be instantly bankrupt. Thought of the day's uproar on the exchanges had him metaphorically checking the walls for cracks.

The *personae gratae* of the H and K stood in groups, holding napkins to glasses that were regularly replaced by an alert coterie of waiters. The room was abuzz with a topic of conversation that was unitary.

Along one complete wall East met West on a trestle table that supported a cornucopia of chow supplied by Cumberland Imports. A chef cut hickory cured Virginia ham, roast Tom turkey, leg of New Zealand lamb or side of Texas beef. There were dishes of smoked salmon, Sydney rock oysters, Belgian mussels, baby tartare steak and boneless chicken ... And steaming *loongs* of pork, mushroom or shrimp dumplings, plus *satay* on skewers, dishes of papaya, cantelope, honeydew melon, mango, lychees ...

Zagan's gaze ran into that of Abraham Male, who stood in a group with Sir Ken-on Shang and Ebenezer Au of China Rice Importers. Cheryl Male, the most striking woman present – as an ex-Channel Ten personality might expect to be – held the audience to her with her Sydney accent as her husband glared askance.

And the glare was not unfounded. In the wake of Jubilee Bay Phase B, Tetsuo Hondo had made two decisions. The first was to purchase for Yumiko a Japanese husband, the second was to place his *zaibatsu*'s Hong Kong activities in the hands of Matamoto (Hong Kong) Limited, which had been established to compete for the turn-key contract to build the MTR. The agency with Male & Son had been terminated.

'*C'est la guerre*,' Zagan said to himself as he took a fresh Carlsberg off the tray of a passing waiter.

Smeared with drooping *sang-froid*, Lennie the Fifth propped up the wall by the bar and made love to his tenth double pink gin. His face was flushed and his heartbeat had still to return to normal. He stopped biting his nails and fiddling with his bowtie when he saw Thomas Buckley sliding sideways through the crowd in his direction, and looked about for an escape route. But by the time he had seen one, it was too late. Pulling a face as if he had just discovered his tenth gin had been 'pinked' with castor oil instead of bitters, he hailed: 'Well, if it isn't our Director of Noughts and Crosses.'

Buckley reciprocated with a face of his own. 'Seeing that you've brought up the subject of games – what about yours?'

'Waffle, Buckley. As usual, you sprout waffle. Pray elucidate.'

'I'm referring to Cicero Investments. Are you out of the market?'

'And why, pray tell, should I be out of the jolly old market?'

'Do I really have to answer that?'

'Pretty please.'

Buckley clicked his teeth as if Cosgrove was nothing more than an *enfant terrible*. 'The crash is on, man. Surely you unloaded today?'

'You listen to too many rumours, my old toilet tissue.'

For five seconds the two set about each other with their eyes.

'You've given me my answer,' Buckley said, breaking the silence. 'You've still got Cicero Investments in up to its armpits, haven't you?'

'Up to its sperm bags, old bowel motion.'

Buckley drew his thin frame to its full height. 'Then I'll have some embarrassing questions for you at the Long Table tomorrow morning – after we vote for suspension of trading.'

Despite himself, Cosgrove swallowed hard. 'What's Cicero Investments got to do with you – and the board? It's owned by John and myself – '

'I'm a director of both Charlemagne and Cicero, if not a shareholder. And I take my responsibilities as a director quite seriously. Therefore, it's plenty to do with me – and the board.'

But instead Cosgrove asked: 'Why should the board vote for suspension?'

'Are you serious, man? It's the correct course of action. It's the only course. We're committed to protecting the interests of our shareholders. We have to give them the opportunity to have their paper verified.'

Cosgrove snorted. 'What happens to the shareholders you're "committed to protecting" while the arse falls out of the market and they're prevented from selling their shares, eh? They'll be beating your door down with baseball bats. Then they'll be into you – and I'll be there cheering 'em on. Protect the interests of our shareholders by suspending trading over three bloody pisspot forgeries? Luv-a-duck, what a load of tommy-rot!'

The force of Cosgrove's delivery had slammed a cover on the real reason for his opposition to the suspension. Before nine in the morning he had to successfully lobby enough directors to have it overruled. Suspension in trading would render the recovery of his own shares an impossibility.

He made to move off, then turned back. 'Here's one for you now, Number Cruncher. That property you and Vail went off on your own and bought in North Point the other day – those tenements in Hang On Street – '

Recall of victory set Buckley's small eyes alight. 'What about it? Not jealous of somebody else's success, are you?'

Cosgrove snorted again. 'You've gone and bought the company an orchard full of lemons there, Button Boy.'

'What do you mean "lemons"? The MTRC is building a station slap bang underneath. It's a real coup. Not for me personally, of course. For the company. I do believe you're jealous, man.'

'Luv-a-bloody-duck. Look, Christopher Wren, the first four stages of the MTR do not include North Point. Not for ten years will they build a line out there. And when they do it won't go anywhere near Hang On Street. There's Robertson-Ikin of the MTRC over there. Why don't you ask him? He'll tell you what he told me ten minutes ago, and that I've just passed on to you. But you seem to have your head stuck so far up your arse the only voice you can hear is your own. And pretty muffled it must be. You're a freak. I'd already picked you for a shit-stirrer and an arse-licker, but now I see you're a contortionist, too. You must be the only white man in the world with brown arms, brown tongue – and brown ears!'

The top accountant bristled. 'You're an uncouth so-and-so. How you got where you are I'll never know. Damn blasted luck, I'm sure – '

'Get off it, Number Cruncher. Go on, go and check with Robertson-Ikin. You obviously don't believe me.'

'Only a village idiot would believe you! I certainly will ask him. It'll teach you to try your childish jokes on me – '

'Good, Button Boy. Off you go. And when I see from your face that you've accepted the truth, then I'll do a deal with you.'

'Deal? What deal?'

Jabbing his finger into Buckley's chest, Cosgrove hissed: 'Just this. You don't go bringing up Cicero Investments at the Long Table tomorrow morning – and I won't mention your lemon orchard in North Point.'

As the top accountant moved towards the MTRC man with an expression no less self-assured, Cosgrove made a beeline for Bedrix, who was standing in a threesome with Ezuelo and Vail. He knew he could always rely on Tony and, as for the Director of Properties, he had the look about him that suggested he might have chanced his shareholding in the market despite having signed a pledge to the contrary.

But what about Bedrix? The man's footfall on the carpet of the boardroom was as uncontroversial as the real Neil Armstrong's upon the surface of the moon had been spectacular. Cosgrove looked at his watch. He had an hour to work a miracle.

He obliterated his tenth double pink gin and signalled to the bar for his eleventh as he passed by. The alcohol poured a soothing coating over his worries, and he called: 'Hi, Glynn. Hi Tony. Hi Dan. Have you heard about the Irishman who thought a bogus share certificate was a licence to swap his *de facto* wife . . ?'

18

His taipan hands flat upon the luxurious pinewood of the Long Table, Huart peered north along its patrician surface. Eyes turned south. Some held his gaze, others broke from it. Some hearts missed a beat, others did not falter. Feet shifted on the Tientsin carpet and chairs creaked under some of the most valuable buttocks in Hong Kong. He read the eyes that held steel this morning. He knew whose feet had shifted and which posteriors had moved. That was why he was the Altitudinal Taipan.

To his right, Lennie the Fifth seemed to be smiling and frowning at the same time, as if he was thinking hard in several directions at once. It made his face seem lopsided and gave his eyes a weird disharmony. He had defied self-established custom by being at the Long Table five minutes before nine and, in so doing, had broadcast that the subject to be covered at the emergency meeting was of vital personal importance.

Huart felt the two dimensional eyes of the first taipan and original Fire Horse over his left shoulder. To his right the empty panel on the east wall prodded him, as it always did. But no longer did it engender in him an impatience to decide; instead it produced a rare indecision.

Which of the three?

He glanced at Glynn Bedrix. The Director of Insurance and Banking sat easy, arms resting on the table, coat sleeves drawn back to reveal two inches of Italian cotton fixed with red jade cufflinks. Glynn is taller than his father, he assessed paternally, and recalled the black day when he had delivered the eulogy on a man whose life had terminated in the gross indignity of death without trace. But Clive Bedrix's legacy had perpetuated his memory in style. His son was proving a worthy member of the Long Table. And he was the closest to 'family' of all present.

To Huart's left Thomas Buckley drew the tip of a skeletal finger around his collar. Fourteen hours, none of them in sleep, had passed since the MTRC man had killed the top accountant's new self-confidence with a single guffaw. A pallor stained his face and his small eyes, the whites tracked with red, darted between three points: across at Cosgrove – then at Huart – down at the table before him – across at Cosgrove –

Matthew Zagan sat one chair in from the H and K directors who, like him, had no voting power and would be onlookers. With Guy Knox in England on extended convalescence, Huart had decided that this restriction should be lifted from the man who had restored Cathay Electric to him. Thus, on April 1st, Zagan would be conferred with the title of director.

The Rococo clock in the corner struck nine.

'Gentlemen, I thank you for attending at short notice. We all know why we are here and I trust the proceedings will not detain us long. Last evening, together with Mr Szeto and Raymond O'Young – who is available to speak on any legal point – I discussed the situation with the chairman of the stock exchanges.

I promised them our decision on suspension of trading in our shares would reach them by ten o'clock this morning. Your views, please. Does any director object to immediate suspension?'

The board had been constituted with eight voting directors, a four:four deadlock bringing in the chairman's casting vote. But with Knox missing, it had never been needed – though it was made *de facto* at every meeting. It was unknown for any director to vote against the taipan's will, which he made known with a subtle authority; the board had just received an example. What made the system work was Huart's virtual infallibility.

Gene Browne, almost casually dressed in beige suit and checked shirt, broke the silence with: 'What's the purpose of suspension anyhow?'

Huart cocked an eye to his left. 'Tom?'

Buckley bent his reed-like trunk to look down the table at the Director of Electronics. 'To place a moratorium on trading in our shares for a period in which holders present their certificates for verification.'

'How is this to be done?' asked Bedrix.

'How long will that take?' came simultaneously back from Browne.

'Announcements in the press, over the radio – '

'Both English and Chinese?' Bedrix injected.

'Of course,' Buckley said tersely. Interruptions hit a nerve with him. 'Plus television. A desk will be provided in the concourse for it.' He looked back to Browne. 'I estimate it will take one week to ten days.'

At this point Cosgrove decided to bring his spanner out of his pocket. He was seeing it all so clearly now. Through the night he had analysed the situation from front to back and back to front. With the dawn had come his decision not to unload Cicero Investments. Two factors had influenced it: one corroborative, the other just the opposite.

Waldo Wu's track record was a fact. He had been off this time, but only due to an accident. The market had turned at noon, just as he had said it would, hadn't it? But then these bloody forgeries had turned up! Whoever tipped Waldo off had to be someone with his fingertip right on the pulse: a Mr Big. And Mr Big would have backed off when he saw that the break was sharper than he had foreseen. But Mr Big would return to the market today. Buying! The Index was going up today. There was no doubt about that. It had to. Cosgrove had it all worked out.

And to confirm all this, his right palm was itching like mad!

He hunched his shoulders towards the Director of Finance and Administration and tossed his spanner across the table. 'It won't work,' he said.

Buckley looked back, his bloodshot eyes burning. 'Eh?'

'I said it won't work.'

'Why . . . ?'

Cosgrove picked up one of the three Havanas before him and took time out to light it. The effect was magical. All the eyes of the Long Table were drawn to him. 'It won't work because the names of people holding our share certificates – or any other company's for that matter – will not match with the names printed on the certificates themselves. Right?'

Buckley's smile was indulgent, even insolent. 'In every announcement we will advise those who come in to take the opportunity to register their shares. A strong recommendation – '

'It won't work,' repeated Cosgrove, shaking his head slowly from side to side and scoring a bullseye on Buckley's exposed nerve.

'Why, Lennie?' Huart inserted, seeing his top accountant lost for words and on the verge of losing his temper as well.

'Because registration freezes paper for three weeks. Who in his right mind is going to voluntarily lock up his shares while – ' He cast his eyes along the table, then back to Buckley. ' – while the market crashes about his ears? I tell you, Mr Buckley sir, your plan won't work!'

Cosgrove had himself deduced the crash was fantasy, but it suited his purpose to project a contrary opinion. He examined each face for its reaction to his statement, and saw Vail, at Buckley's side, nodding as he toyed with a tar guard. Yes, that one had surely sold short on his own paper. Was it the day the number-cruncher's stooge would turn? He saw Ezuelo sitting expressionless beneath black lotioned hair, a floral tie bisecting his narrow chest. But Cosgrove knew that he was against suspension, too. Hadn't he invested in his first breakfast for as long as he could remember to make certain of it? He needed one more on his side to kill the vote four: three. Who was it to be? He searched the other faces as Buckley found his voice.

'Whether people elect to register or not is up to them. We must do the right thing and give the public the opportunity to protect itself. The Government has been clamouring for stricter control of shares. And the police need time to apprehend the forgers and clear the forgeries from the system. They have asked us to suspend trading to assist in this – '

'Assist?' Cosgrove interrupted again. 'If there's no trading in the shares that are forged, it's logical to assume there'll be no more duff shares passed around. Suspension'll make the police's job harder, not easier. Even your village idiot can see that – '

'It seems to me the crux of the matter is not so much the three forged share certificates,' came from Alexander Chiu, 'but whether there will be more.' The Director of Textiles and Garments sat erect on Bedrix's right. He was tall for a Chinese, as his Shanghai-born father had been. Neatly attired in a fawn safari suit, he was the only one to shun the customary coat and tie. He drew on a 'More Menthol' as he watched and waited for the first reaction to his matter-of-fact statement.

Not unexpectedly, it came from Cosgrove. 'Exactly!' Bringing his fist down upon the table with more force than he had intended, he declared: 'Here we are sitting and talking about three scraps of paper! Trivia! We must be the highest paid mothers' club in the world! Think what this meeting is costing the company and its shareholders!'

The jarring under his elbows had knocked Buckley's thoughts into order. Why was Cosgrove so set to undermine the suspension of trading? he asked himself. Then it hit him: the malignant wart must have his own shares tied up in the stock market, as well as those of Cicero Investments! The more he considered it, the more he convinced himself it was not just a possibility. If he's done that, I'll nail him, he promised. I'll check the shareholders' roll. Of ten million shares in his name some must be submitted for re-registration, especially if we suspend trading. That's what the gangrenous little microbe has done! He's sold his shares in violation of the General's instructions. And if he doesn't bail Cicero Investments out today, I'll nail him on two points. But first the board has to vote for suspension. He looked across at Chiu and urged him on.

'What self-respecting forger would stop at three certificates?' the textile director obliged. 'There could be a thousand phoneys out there.'

'That's speculation!' Cosgrove cried.

'There's plenty of that going on in Hong Kong,' chuckled Gene Browne.

Nobody laughed.

'Not so,' Chiu retorted. 'It's logic.'

Cosgrove bit his lip. This one was not on his side.

One for me, Buckley counted.

'It sure is logic, Alex,' Browne threw in. 'There's no two ways about it – this share business has got hairs on it. I don't need to hear any more. We've got to suspend trading pronto. My mind's made up.'

Cosgrove swore to himself. It was three:three. Vail, Ezuelo and himself against, and Buckley, Chiu and Browne in favour. He glanced sideways at Bedrix. The Director of Insurance and Banking held the wild card.

Buckley had done his own sums and come up with a different score. Chiu and Browne were with him and Vail could be taken for granted. That was four for suspension. The votes of Bedrix and Ezuelo were therefore academic. Cosgrove was caught in the trap like the rodent he was. He would have to resign! Buckley visualised himself sitting in the seat on the General's right, one away from the taipan's chair. In his mind's eye he began to read the printing on his new business card: 'Deputy Ch – '

Then Vail opened his mouth for the first time and blew the dream apart.

'Couldn't we, er . . . delay our decision for twenty-four hours?'

Buckley swung on the Director of Properties and mentally strangled him.

Cosgrove could have leaned across the Long Table and kissed him.

'I'm afraid not, Dan,' Huart injected. 'I won't sanction another meeting tomorrow morning. Gregory and Mac have plenty to do at the bank and Matthew's not getting our stand for Peking organised by sitting here. As Lennie has so colourfully informed us, our time is money.' He glanced at the clock and stifled a grimace. It was taking longer than expected. 'We have thirty minutes before the stock exchanges open. Glynn?'

'What about PR?'

Cosgrove was onto it like a rabid dog on a paraplegic cat. 'Great point, Glynn! We had bad press this morning. Even Marshall was hard on us – '

'Hard?' Buckley cut in. 'I thought his report was quite factual and – '

'Too factual!' Cosgrove fired back. 'Where'd the facts come from, eh?'

'Now look here, you little – '

Cosgrove cut him and proceeded to expound in all directions: 'Bad press ought to be taken very seriously, gents! I say suspension of trading is against the free enterprise system. It shackles the free movement of money. It's the very opposite to *laissez faire*.'

Bedrix grimaced, turned to the foot of the table and asked: 'What's the opinion of the Chinese press, Mr Szeto?'

A question to the company secretary was rare. The diminutive gentleman lifted his eyes from the pad before him and looked at Bedrix as if to confirm that there had actually been a query. Then his fingers went to his gold tie pin as he directed his eyes up the Long Table.

Zagan was in a position to see the barely perceptible nod from the head. Y. Y. Szeto intrigued him greatly. The man was an oriental mystery, too articulate by far to be just a company secretary.

'The Chinese press is polarised.' As always, the words were picked with precision from the Cantonese scholar's phenomenal vocabulary. 'The business dailies insist that we suspend trading immediately. The more speculative newspapers – and the left wing publications – urge us to consider the plight of the small investor. Some editorials have even forecast the possibility of civil unrest if we should remove the freedom of the man in the street to trade in our shares with the market falling as it is.'

'My God,' breathed Vail.

'Hmmmmm.' This came from Bedrix.

'That's a bit much,' Buckley muttered.

'Is it?' Vail retorted. 'What about 1966? There were riots then over a measly five cents! Today we're talking about billions! Today we're faced with the crash of the entire Hong Kong stock market. My God!'

'Come now, Dan,' Buckley said soothingly, certain Vail could be won over. 'The 1966 riots weren't the result of a five cent fare increase. They came after a series of bank failures, bankruptcies and – '

'And at the end of a period of gross property escalation and a rent spiral,' Bedrix added. 'Exactly what we have right now.'

Buckley opened his mouth, then closed it again.

Cosgrove was watching Bedrix out of the corner of his eye. He saw the man was on the pivot of decision. A dose of the wisdom of self-preservation could just turn it, he thought. He peered across at Buckley with eyes suddenly soft and compassionate. The accountant stared back nonplussed – like an inebriated cobra confronted by a frisky mongoose.

'Tom, old turnip, for the first time this morning I agree with you. Hong Kong has always been an emotional place. China sits twenty miles away, waiting for something to go awry here. If there is civil unrest, what'll China do? I don't know. But there is one thing I do know. We're taking one hell of a risk here today. If we vote in favour of suspension, could that precipitate the crash of the stock market? Could the crash induce civil unrest, riots, wholesale disorder, mobs amok in the streets? In other words – '66 and '67 all over again? Or worse? Could Hong Kong survive it all this time? Would it end in the demise of this Crown Colony as we know it and, consequentially, the end of us? In this case, do we want history to show that those of us here today – sitting at this Long Table of ours – voted to commit tacit wholesale suicide?'

He sat back and took up the last Havana. The silence waited for him to prepare it, light up and take a puff. He peered through the smoke at Buckley and took heart at what he saw drawn on the pinched face. Luv-a-duck, had he even convinced the shit-for-brains number-cruncher?

'I interpret the silence as the end of discussion,' Huart said, looking again at the clock. It was 9:53. 'Am I right?'

The absence of response verified his assumption.

'Please note,' he went on, 'according to Raymond O'Young, we are under no legal obligation to suspend trading this morning, or at any time.' He gave this time to sink in. 'Ten o'clock is near. The question of suspension has drawn more diverse comment than I expected. All of it has been relevant, some more than other. It's a shame we have had to spend an hour on such a worthless subject as forgeries.' The unintentional pun brought a few smiles. 'It is my wish that this board be seen to act professionally. We have, first and foremost, an obligation to our shareholders. How would they expect us to vote? We should, at the outset, define "shareholder". Do we have an obligation to the speculators and gamblers who own our shares for a matter of hours before selling and pocketing the difference? Or do we have a greater obligation to those who supported us when we went public and subscribed for long-term gain? You may justly feel the former vastly outnumber the latter. That is yours to decide. Lennie has spoken of the political gravity of this board's decision this morning. Whilst endorsing his sentiments, I will add just one comment to them – and I emphasise it is a personal comment – ' The pause brought all eyes back to him. 'Suspension of trading in our shares may be an act of the very sanity many believe the Hong Kong stock market is lacking.' His point made, he breathed audibly in through his nose, then looked down the Long Table. 'Time to vote, Mr Szeto, please.'

'Yes, sir.' The voice of the company secretary, its timbre thin in comparison to its predecessor, took over. 'All those in favour

[514]

of suspension in trading in Cumberland China shares on the four stock exchanges being imposed forthwith, kindly signify by the raising of hands.'

Three arms went up immediately. They belonged to Thomas Buckley, Gene Browne and Alexander Chiu. There were no others.

Cosgrove glanced to his right, hope firing his eyes. Had he really won?

Buckley stared across at the man in the chair on Cosgrove's right. He couldn't have lost! Raise your hand, Neil Armstrong, damn blast you!

The Director of Insurance and Banking brought his left hand into view and laid it deliberately upon the table before him. From the corner of his eye Cosgrove saw the red jade cuff link flash in the fluorescent light and his heart missed a beat. Buckley's small eyes were fixed upon the limb as if he was mesmerized by it.

Bedrix's fingers flexed. Cosgrove held his breath. Buckley blinked; his raised arm was starting to ache. Bedrix's hand flattened on the pinewood. All eyes watched it. The fingers bunched into a fist, then opened, then drummed an obligato that boomed through the hanging silence. Long moments went by. Huart was prolonging the vote, disbelieving the result. He had not been surprised at his deputy chairman's disapproval of the proposed restrictions on share trading. It was in character. He had been surprised, however, at the little man's tenacity. Never before had his partner been able to influence the board more than he. But this time?

He could not help his frown as he looked at Glynn Bedrix peering into the grain of the Long Table, his handsome face marred by lines of concentration. But that left hand stayed where it was.

Cosgrove's facial muscles began to relax. His heartbeat slowed.

Buckley's diaphragm muscles bunched to hold on to his groan of dismay.

Huart, his bottom lip tucked over the top and his eyebrows hooded, sent another nod that was not a nod down the table.

Cosgrove drew on his Havana and tried hard not to grin as Y. Y. Szeto said: 'Gentlemen, if there are no more than three directors in favour of the immediate suspension of trading . . .'

The mechanism of the Rococo long-case clock began to whirr from the corner of the boardroom.

19

As the last few minutes before ten o'clock went by, the air in the Kam Ngan Stock Exchange on the seventh floor of Connaught Centre possessed the heat and the tang of a cauldron of boiling snake soup. Excitement, apprehension and raw fear all contributed their spice to the atmosphere.

From the mezzanine observation gallery, Kym Marshall divided his attention between the trading floor below, spreading from west wall to east, and the row of television screens overhead. He was uncomfortable, wedged as he was between bodies that sweated with the tension, but he was an inured member of the fourth estate. He had many times witnessed history in the making, and he had a strong hunch he was about to do so again.

Like the great building whose entire seventh floor was leased to it, the Kam Ngan Stock Exchange was fitted out with the latest technology. Each of the seven hundred trading desks was installed with six telephones, a nine inch television screen and a panel to focus upon any part of the wyteboard, which covered the north wall from east to west and from floor to ceiling. The board was illuminated by spotlights and was divided into vertical sections, one for each company listed on the exchange. Fifty ceiling-mounted cameras transmitted its image by closed circuit through the exchange and out into the greater gallery of Hong Kong, itself.

Only members of the exchange and their staff, and employees of the Kam Ngan were permitted on the floor, where the seven hundred desks were arranged in straight rows evocative of a university examination hall.

But instead of a reverent academic hush, there existed babel.

Seven hundred broking clerks shouted Cantonese into telephones or yelled it to floor brokers, who called to more clerks at the ten trading posts. Every other telephone was ringing. Every other pair of heels came down on the parquet floor as everyone took their place for the commencement of trading. Anything above walking pace was expressly forbidden on the floor, so the army of white shirts and green armbands had perfected a scurry that was not a run, but was certainly no walk either.

Eyes went to wristwatches or the clock over the midst of the wyteboard or to television screens as the last seconds to ten o'clock ticked away.

Marshall held his breath with the rest of Hong Kong. His ears rang, his spine protested at the angle it was forced into by the crush about him.

The second hand passed the hour hand. The noise fell. Ten seconds. Five. An electric silence gripped the exchange. No-one moved. All eyes were upon the impersonal face of the clock on the north wall. The second hand approached vertical, disappeared behind the minute hand. A bell rang.

And trading opened with a gut-wrenching roar.

The floor burst into frenetic motion. Broking clerks, telephones pressed to ears, scribbled on slips of paper, flicked them to floor brokers who hustled to trading posts where loud bargaining took place. Deals done, clerks crossed to the wyteboard to dab prices with chinagraph pencils under the names of the companies whose shares had been exchanged. A plus or a minus beside the figure indicated a rise or a fall.

Marshall looked down on a scene of cacophonous noise and apparent chaos. But it was all quite normal. The norm had been established on the first trading day of the Year of the Water Ox and emulated every day since.

He searched the screens for the 'C' section of the wyteboard. He saw it, then squinted until his eyes hurt. He could not believe what was there.

Under 'Cumberland China' there were figures: 185.00+. It was the closing price of the day before. For the last two days it had held steady, which was a phenomenon in itself considering the Hang Seng Index had lost 145 points. Even in yesterday's final crazy quarter hour, it had held ground whilst all others, under-mined by the forgeries, plummeted about it. That the forgeries were of Cumberland China paper made it more illogical.

But why was the price still showing? Marshall knew the *hong*'s board had met at nine, forty-five storeys above, to vote on an immediate suspension of trading. Surely General Huart was not keeping his shares on the market? Hadn't that morning's editorial been damning enough for him?

Around Marshall fingers pointed at the screen. Amongst the chatter that filled the gallery the words *Gum Bak Leen* were repeti-tive, ubiquitous. Several cameras had traversed to the 'C' section of the wyteboard.

What's going to happen next? he asked himself.

The answer appeared on the screen as if by remote control.

A clerk from the trading post in front of the Cumberland China counter pushed his way to the board, lifted his pencil towards the figures 185.00+ and wrote others immediately below. It was a new price: 190.00+

A hush settled over that section of the floor. Then, like a ripple diverging across the surface of a pond, it spread through the exchange.

A second clerk stepped up to take the place of the first. His pencil added a third row of figures. The price had jumped to 195.00+.

Seconds later Cumberland China hit $200.00 and a roar lifted from the floor. Everyone in the gallery was talking in rapid guttural Cantonese. Down below, it seemed all four thousand telephones were in use at once. Every television screen was showing the 'C' section. It was as if no other company existed. *Gum Bak Leen* was still trading! And its price was going up! Someone was buying! Heads were nodding, eyes were gleaming, hands were gesticulating, people were talking babbling yelling.

The cameras panned to the right. Clerks were stepping up to the wyteboard all across the north wall. Figures were being scribbled under two dozen counters at once. Beside every new price a plus sign was added.

In the corner of the screen above Marshall's head a six digit number appeared. It changed every few seconds in response to the impulses of a computer. It was the Hang Seng Index. It was rising fast.

1519.35 . . . 1521.11 . . . 1522.57 . . .

His mouth hung open. What was the General up to? By refusing to suspend trading he had turned a plummeting 'bear' market into a raging 'bull'. Small investors, unwilling to be diverted by three scraps of paper, were interpreting non-suspension as a divine gesture of supreme confidence in the stock market – a deliverance of great good *fung shui!*

As if to confirm this, a wave of excitement swept through the gallery. Eyes were round and happy and lusting. Mouths were flapping.

Marshall looked back up at the screen. The Index was accelerating.

1526.07 . . . 1529.19 . . . 1532.90 . . .

Who was behind it? It must be Cosgrove. It had the stamp of that chancer of chancers. He must have influenced the Cumberland China board. Marshall could not believe it. He heard the calls from every direction: '*Gum Bak Leen! Dai Yee Ngau! Gum Bak Leen! Dai Yee Ngau!*'

1534.88 . . . 1537.44 . . . 1540.73 . . .

The clock read 10:10. The Index had risen 26 points in ten minutes.

Marshall swore aloud. I've seen enough, he told himself. It's another 'bull' market sucking the fools in deeper. But as he turned to push his way out his ears detected something. The hubbub below was reducing. He looked up at the screen and saw a clerk writing in the Cumberland China section. It was not a new price. He was writing something in capitals. He squinted hard. The clerk backed away. The words leapt out at him:

TRADING SUSPENDED

A chilling silence gripped the Kam Ngan Stock Exchange.

Then the commotion was reborn. Tenfold.

Marshall swore again as he attempted to pull his notebook from his hip pocket to record the scene, but the press of bodies pinned his arms to his sides as everyone craned towards the awful words on the screen.

On the trading floor, clerks were leaping back to the board. New prices were appearing across it in rapid succession, just like before. But with one difference: all the new prices had minus signs beside them.

Marshall glanced up at the Index. It had turned. It was slipping. 1539.89 . . . 1538.33 . . . 1537.61 . . .

For the next forty minutes the Hang Seng Index steadily, inexorably fell back to its opening level of 1514. There it lingered for five minutes whilst the reaction to Cumberland China's suspension mellowed. Small investors, now uncertain, asked themselves what it all meant. Then, at eleven o'clock the Index moved back up a point. The faces in the gallery lit up with rekindled hope.

But sixty seconds later any and all optimism was proved fatal.

Pockets of abnormal agitation suddenly developed simultaneously at all trading posts. Then clerks began scurrying up to the board at a faster and faster pace. In their wake a sequence of minus signs appeared across the north wall. The seven hundred clerks at the seven hundred desks were shouting louder into the seven hundred telephones.

'Ai yah!' a man beside Marshall keened. 'Ai yah! Ai yah! Ai yah!'

The journalist grabbed him by the shoulder. 'What's happening? I'm from the newspaper. Bo jee yan! What's happening?'

'More forgeries!' the man shouted.

'Cumberland China? Gum Bak Leen?'

'Yes! Yes! Gum Bak Leen!'

'How many?'

The man's eyes were very round. 'Ohh, many! Very many!'

'Five? Ten? A dozen?'

'No. More. Many more. At least fifty! A hundred!'

'Are you sure?'

'Yes! Guard outside hear radio. Look! Look! *Chee seen! Chee seen!*'

Crazy! Crazy!

Marshall followed the line of the jabbing finger down to the trading floor. And could not believe what he saw there. The exchange was in complete uproar. It was as if the end of the world had been declared and everybody believed it. In violation of the rule, everyone was running in every direction. Jostling yelling arm-waving scrimmages were swamping the trading posts. Millions of dollars were being lost in the time it took for clerks to elbow their way through with their clients' 'sell' orders held aloft. Marshall swore again and peered up at the screen.

1507.69 . . . 1503.05 . . . 1499.36 . . .

He extricated his notebook and his pack of Winstons and began to write: 'Though close kin by breeding, no love is lost between the Ox and the Bull. Today I watched as the one put paid to the other. It was *fung shui* at its worst. The fratricide was perpetrated upon the floors of Hong Kong's stock exchanges which resembled more a quartet of abattoirs than the proud financial institutions they purport to be . . .'

He glanced up at the screen again.

1491.74 . . . 1488.11 . . . 1485.15 . . .

He carried on writing.

'By executing so close a relative in its own year, the Ox has revealed its hospitality to be less than zero. The small investors of Hong Kong would vouch for this. Hospitality has been a commodity not granted to them, but confined to the awe-inspiring institutions in which they have blindly invested, and to the army of foreign creditors who have visited and now seem to have departed, richer by much for their sojourn.

'With the Year of the Ox only forty-seven days old, there is more than enough time for him to make things so much worse . . .'

Pushed from all sides, Kym Marshall carried on to write the best editorial of his journalistic career on the back of a cigarette packet.

At 12:45 sharp the closing bell rang out. The wholesale bedlam stopped dead. The trading floor was like a battlefield on which both sides had lost. The white shirts and green armbands stood

[520]

amongst it and looked at each other, and blinked. Then everyone looked up at the screens.

1386.82.

Kym Marshall stuffed his pack of Winstons and his notebook back into his hip pocket. He pulled out his handkerchief and wiped the sweat from his brow. He had seen it made again: History. He had witnessed the end of the Great Hong Kong Stock Market Boom, the most fantastic event ever in the annals of Asian business.

20

It was at some point near dawn the next day when Lennie the Fifth decided to throw his personal fortune into the stock market. He was unaware of the exact time. In fact, he was unaware of anything except the Crash, Cicero Investments and his lost ten million Cumberland China shares. They possessed his thoughts, and prohibited him from the respite of even a moment's sleep. Beyond them, the rest of the world no longer existed.

Their common denominator was the stock market. For it he was ready to sacrifice himself, body and soul; he was quite prepared for it to be his sepulchre. He wondered if the governors of the exchanges would put up a plaque to his memory and what the epitaph upon it would be. He seemed to remember Kipling had once written something apt.

' . . . And the end of the fight . . . Is a tombstone white . . .'

The rest of the poem eluded him. He repeated the two lines over and over in his brain, but he could get no further. Suddenly he slammed his right fist into his palm with such force that it bruised.

'This bloody fight's not over yet! Not by a country mile.'

Recent events had clobbered his brain into an erratic organ. At times he was uplifted: like the morning before at the Long Table when he had almost – almost! – induced Glynn Bedrix to break a strict personal code. Y. Y. Szeto had the chairman of the Hong Kong Stock Exchange on the line when the Director of Insurance and Banking had raised that left arm.

But most times he witnessed life as if through a telescope, with its images floating on a lens. This restricted vision served to tranquillise him, so that three facts could push their way to the forefront, then dovetail into one overriding fact: The market had to be made to rise!

The lesser facts that had combined in this were as follows:

One: Whoever had collared his shares had done so for profit. He rejected P.G.'s theory that a takeover of the Born Again *Hong* was in progress. The most that any one entity could accumulate piecemeal on the exchanges was, he guessed, ten per cent, and his personal holding was a secret. Any organisation cash rich enough to buy it all would be wholly conspicuous. The price was $200.00. He had sold at $185.00. The buyer had a potential profit of $150,000,000; himself an equal loss. He discounted it. He must get his shares back! When suspension was lifted in a week, for the buyer to cash the shares and take his profit, the market must be made to rise.

Two: Every Cicero dollar was in the market. Even if he sold now he would still make a handsome profit. But then what? Cicero had been formed for him to play the market. No market – no play. No play – no fun. No fun – he would die! Therefore, to save his own life he had to preserve Cicero Investments, and the only way to do that was to make the market rise.

Three: He was a Very Rich Man. He had enough money to manipulate the market. If he threw it all in at once – it had to rise.

Ergo, by playing the Cosgrove millions, all his problems were solved.

It was exactly ten o'clock when he called P.G. Curzon-Cross. The stockbroker took over a minute to come on the line and then listened whilst Cosgrove talked non-stop for the next minute, concluding with: 'Now tell me you understand my instructions clearly, P.G.'

'Understand? I understand you've gone insane! Buy up big, you say? Look, old bean, we've been friends for too long. You're not just a client. The market's just opened and – ' There came a pause. ' – and, guess what, it's gone straight down. Shouldn't you – ?'

'D'you want the bloody business or not, P.G.? There're other brokers – '

The tone stung. 'Very well. Suit yourself. You're over twenty-one – I think. But I'm afraid the amount involved is well over the limit for the transaction to be on a verbal basis. I'm afraid we must ask you – '

'I'll put it in bloody writing, then!' Cosgrove shouted down the

[522]

line. 'I mean business, P.G.! Buy up big! Starting right now!' And he hung up on his old friend for the first time in his life.

With his hand still on the receiver, the thought came to him: 'What happens if my money alone is not enough to sustain a fresh "bull" run?' It was then and there that Lennie the Fifth decided he had to find Mr Big.

If the two of them joined forces, poured money into the market, bought up shares at what had become bargain basement prices, the result would be a foregone conclusion. The Index had to rise. Rise? It would take off like a polaris missile! With the Cosgrove millions going in today, and Mr Big's tomorrow, the Index would not stop even at 2000!

They would make millions – no, billions – together!

His next call was to an apartment in Kowloon Tong. Carla Tze Ti answered reluctantly, dreamily on the twenty-seventh ring.

'That's absolutely impossible! I refuse to believe it!' Thomas Buckley retorted. 'What d'you mean the number of share certificates presented for examination totals only two per cent?'

At the other end of the line Y. Y. Szeto winced. 'Two per cent, Mr Buckley, and most of that belongs to a Mr Lee Wing-tak of Koon Wah Mansion, Mongkok. He came in with his son, who he said is Mr Huart's god – '

'You're doing something wrong, man! You've got the Chinese on the sign in the concourse wrong. Or you've got it facing the wrong way. Or – Or something . . .'

'The Chinese is quite explicit and pointed in all directions, Mr Buckley. It is a four-sided sign.' The company secretary was absorbing the bluster of the Director of Finance and Administration like a lightning arrester. 'Perhaps you would like to check it for yourself?'

'That's just what I intend to do. I'm on my way down.'

'Very well. I'll meet you outside the – '

But Buckley had already hung up.

Then, wariness of coming off second best in a public confrontation with the super-efficient Mr Y. Y. Szeto caused him to hesitate. Perhaps it was too soon in the day for people to be coming in. He checked the time. It was almost noon. Had the wrong date been given out? No, he'd checked the text of the press, radio, television announcements himself. He had been so careful. He was going to get that septic dwarf! He just knew he had sold short on his ten per cent. He just knew it! All he had to do was watch the shareholders' roll. And then –

'Then I'll have him by his damn blasted short and curlies!'

He relived his victory of the day before. How sweet it had been. But Bedrix had almost given him a coronary in the process. And the sweetest was still to come: when he tipped his *bête noire* out of his seat at the Long Table and took his place. Then it would be just one more move to the left. But first he had to unload those damn blasted tenements!

He had shoved his chair back on its castors and taken one step on his way to carrying out his threat to Y. Y. Szeto when the intercom buzzed. It was his Cantonese secretary. 'Yes? What is it, Priscilla?'

'Mr Vail is here, Mr Buckley.'

He heaved a silent sigh of relief. 'Send him in.'

The Director of Properties slid sideways through the door and Buckley saw at once he had come to report failure.

'They're not interested.' The tone was lugubrious.

'Damn blast it, why?'

'I spoke to Bert Jarvis himself. He told me Hang On Street is too far from the harbour for prime residential development.'

'What about less-than-prime, or whatever it's called?'

'Middle class? Like Gum Bak Leen Sun Chuen? Jarvis said Victoria Land aren't the least bit interested in anything down market. That's more our speciality, he said. Cheeky sod. But, Tom, the site's too expensive for middle class development. We picked a good one. Wrong location, wrong price. We paid over the market and now the market's falling like a rock. We're out on a limb . . .' Vail spread his hands and bit his lip.

'Damn blast it!' Buckley ran off a litany of expletives.

Though he had heard better in church, Vail winced. It was all Buckley's fault. Why had he let the man trespass on territory outside his ledgers?

The Director of Finance and Administration advanced on Vail, who backtracked. 'It's all your fault!' he accused. 'You're supposed to be the property expert! Didn't you check the authenticity of those route drawings? Didn't you check on that chap in Engineering? What was his name?'

'Al – Alain To,' Vail stammered. 'No, I didn't. I thought you had.'

Buckley had left mercy at home. 'You're next to useless. You're losing your marbles. Where do you get off voting against suspension yesterday?'

'But – ' Vail gasped. 'Don't you see? I've sold – I've sold my shares.'

'Your shares? Your half per cent? You bloody fool. Wait till the General finds out. You'll be out on your ear!'

'But I needed the cash for a few days, Tom! Carole put a deposit down on this super manor in Surrey without telling me. She saw it and she liked it. You know how impulsive she is. Look, it'll be alright. I sold at 185. The market's in a nosedive, isn't it? I'll buy the shares back as soon as the suspension is lifted. The price'll be under 170. I'll have covered the deposit, and made one hell of a killing to boot.'

'You could end up losing your jock strap, man. The price was 200 at suspension. It could go even higher next week – even if everything else does go the other way. It's uncanny. The General's influence on the Chinese is so strong. They think his Clark Gable ears are dragon's wings – '

'Oh, God!' The skin on Vail's face went the colour of chalk.

'What now? What's wrong, man?' Buckley bullied.

'Bert Jarvis – '

'What of him?'

'He's a close personal friend of the General's! He'll tell him we tried to unload the Hang On Street tenements!'

The top accountant's pigmentation instantly matched Vail's. He had overlooked it.

The intercom buzzed again.

'Yes?' Buckley's voice was a defensive whine. 'What is it?'

'There's a Mr Alain To here to see you and Mr Vail – '

'Eh? Is there indeed!' He looked up, his eyebrows arched. Vail spread his hands again, equally surprised. 'Send him in.' Buckley looked to the door and ground his teeth. 'I'll have the tricky yellow termite for lunch – after we find out what his little game is.'

Alain To wore a cocktail party smile. His eyes flicked from one director to the other. Great-uncle had been right. The Chicken Eye and his dog were desperate, and therefore vulnerable.

'Good morning, Mr Buckley. And Mr Vail. Or is it afternoon?' His eyes dropped to his Rolex. 'How time flies. I trust you are both well.'

'Are your ears burning, man?' Buckley hissed, nicety a luxury thoroughly dispensed with. 'We were just talking about you.'

'Oh, really?' Alain To's composure was designed to unsettle further.

'We certainly were – ' Buckley advanced around his desk with his fists clenched. Vail took another step backwards. 'You've some questions to answer, Mister To. And very likely a fraud charge at the end of them.'

Alain To laughed disconcertingly and Buckley stopped in his tracks. He stood three feet from his adversary, unsure what to do next.

'Your situation is more dangerous than mine, Mr Buckley.'

'What d'you mean?'

'Come . . .' Alain To indicated the armchairs before the accountant's desk. 'Why don't we sit down and discuss this like businessmen. I'm sure you both wish to stay on as directors of this company, don't you?'

'What – What do you mean?' This came from Vail.

'I have a proposition to make to you. To both of you.'

They looked at him, totally flummoxed, their pupils dilated.

Alain To smiled once more. 'Perhaps it was unethical for my family to sell you those tenements in Hang On Street.'

'Your family?'

'Perhaps they would agree to buy them back – at the price you paid.'

Thomas Buckley and Daniel Vail looked at each other, their eyes widening with incredulous hope.

'But,' Alain To went on, 'before this can be agreed, there are certain conditions that you gentlemen must accept . . .'

The telephone on the desk of the Director of Imports and Exports rang for the first time that morning as the clock above the Star Ferry pier, fifty-one storeys below, struck 12.30.

'Ezuelo.'

'You don't know me,' opened a voice in Cantonese, 'but I know you.'

'I've no time for games,' Ezuelo cut in, using the same dialect and wondering who had given out his direct number. 'Call back later.'

'Wait!'

The force of it froze Ezuelo's hand in the act of hanging up. 'What?'

'I believe you know a Chiuchow lady called Bobo. Very beautiful. She has a daughter aged five. Very pretty. Looks a lot like you.'

Ezuelo could not prevent the stunned silence. He had been fearing a call like this. 'What do you want?'

'Bobo works in the Club Takara. You go there often. You seem to be a generous man. Sometimes you buy her out. She needs the commission – '

'*Diu la ma!*' Ezuelo swore. 'Get to the point!'

[526]

'If you insist. Many people know about Bobo and her daughter who looks a lot like you. Many do not. Your wife is in the latter category. And so is your boss. For the time being.'

Ezuelo capitulated with a sigh. 'Where do we meet?'

'Club Takara. Midnight. Don't be late. Yours is not my last appointment. Come to the manager's office. Ask for me. My name is Errol Tu.'

Four telephones were on the desk of the Director of Electronics in his office in 'Factory Senior' in Hoi Yuen Road, Kwun Tong. Two were connected to internal lines: one to each of the seven production floors below, the other to 'Factory Junior' around the corner in Wai Yip Street.

At 3:33, Thursday, March 22nd, both internal telephones rang at once.

'Sheet!' Gene Browne's Texan cadence went through the plasterboard wall to hit the inured ears of his Cantonese secretary. He grabbed a phone in each fist. 'Wait one!' he fired into his left hand at Ronson Sinn, Production Manager, Factory Junior. 'What's up?' he threw to his right. Factory Senior got priority. It was larger and more profitable.

'Big trouble, boss!' It was the assistant production manager.

'So what's new? Where's your ramrod?'

'Mr Ma at meeting – '

'Meeting? What goddamn meeting?'

'With union – '

'Union? What goddamn union? We don't have any union.'

'Have now.'

'Waddaya mean? Is this a joke?'

'No joke, boss. Got union now. Just call strike. All lines stop.'

'God – damn! That's got hairs all over it! Wait a second.' A metallic voice was drilling into the Texan's left ear. 'What is it Ronson? Don't tell me Factory Junior's on strike, too.'

'Strike? No, boss. We're on fire!'

'Whaaat?'

'Yes! Fire! All the production floors're on fire! All four of them! It started all at once. A fire on each floor. Gotta be arson! But why . . . ?'

Browne looked at both receivers as if they had spat in each ear. Then he heard the sirens come along Hoi Yeun Road and make the turn into Wai Yip Street. He looked up through the glass panel to see his secretary and the office staff crowded at the window, pointing. He looked too and saw the thick black smoke

[527]

billowing from the building two blocks away, partly obscuring the thick gold letters painted on its roof that read:

CUMBERLAND ELECTRONICS LIMITED

'Sheeeeeet!'

The spinning and weaving machines in Wai Wai Road suffered from age more each day, and maintenance costs were rising. Alexander Chiu Man-king had finally come to the decision that money would be saved if every single machine was scrapped and replaced with a brand new production line incorporating the advantages to manufacture of modern technology.

The Director of Textiles and Garments stood at the end of one of the thirty rows of spinners that extended over two hundred feet across the factory floor in a continuous succession of bobbins, spools, rocker arms and cradles that reached to the far wall. Not a one was moving.

If he had not been Chinese, if he had been in the privacy of his office, Alexander Chiu would have cursed aloud. But, as he was Chinese, and as he was standing with his chief engineer, he merely turned to his right-hand man of long standing and favoured him with a tired smile.

'I exceedingly regret you will have to work overnight to repair it, *dai lo*,' he pointed out. 'That is unless you have more luck in finding the fault than you have had with the stock market. We cannot have this one idle tomorrow. We are far enough behind as it is.'

The Cantonese engineer drew the back of his hand across his oil-streaked forehead. Afflicted at birth with a hare lip that had been half repaired by shoddy outpatient surgery, his smile and his sneer appeared as one. 'I may as well stay here, *Chiu Seen-sang*,' he groaned. 'I no longer have a home to return to. The bank took possession today.'

'But the market has turned around again. It went up 67 points.'

'Not enough. I put my borrowed money in two weeks ago when the Index was over 1700. It will bankrupt me if I sell now. *Diu lay lo mo!*'

'Worry not, *dai lo*. Perhaps the market will rise again tomorrow – and next week, also. You'll recover your money. Whatever you do, do not look worried. Remember the proverb: "If your face is swollen from a beating pretend to be a fat man".'

[528]

'I remember a different proverb: "He who has not a smiling face should not open a shop". I will be a tinker until I die.'

Alexander Chiu returned to his office, his face a mask of stone. His loyal chief engineer's plight was, he was certain, not unique.

He saw the plain white envelope propped up on his desk. He sliced it open, reached in, extracted the single sheet of paper and unfolded it. He saw the four ideograms drawn in what he assumed was dark red ink. His eyes narrowed. He had seen that message before. Twenty years ago.

In Shanghai dialect he read aloud to himself the four words.

'*Sze ... Yiu ... Yu ... Gu.*'

'Alain To? I don't know the gentleman, Amy. Who is he?'

'His card says Cumberland Engineering, Mr Bedrix. He is the manager of the Contracting Division.'

'I see. And he wants to see me on a business matter at this hour of the day without an appointment? Is it about contract insurance? He should see Moses Liang, then. In-house policies are his responsibility.'

'He says it's about business, but not about insurance.'

'Oh, very well. Ask Mr To to come in. Then you can go home. You have really been very efficient, considering it's only your second week working for me. I've nothing more for you today. Is there anything for me?'

'Your squash match with Mr Bairstow. Six o'clock. Yacht Club. Court 2.'

'I haven't forgotten, Amy. Thank you. See you tomorrow. Just a minute ... Alain To? Is he a relative of yours, by any chance?'

'My family name is Tu, Mr Bedrix. Not To. Goodnight.'

The Alpha Romeo parked in the courtyard of the Red Phoenix Motel in Kowloon Tong meant nothing to Cosgrove until he and Carla Tze Ti were shown into the Paradise Room and he saw the familiar face.

'Errol! So it's you! So you are Mr Big! Well, I'm not surprised, you know. I always thought you must be rolling in it with all those bars and clubs and knocking shops all over town. Business not so good now is it, eh? Not with Nixon pulling the GIs out of Vietnam. So you switched to the market chop-chop, eh? Smart fellow! But then I always knew – '

'Shut up.'

' – that you liked to gamble for big stakes. Casino in Macau

[529]

too small, eh? I go in for things big, too. You and me, Errol, we're two of a – '

'I say shut up already!'

This time Cosgrove shut up. Mouth open, he stared at Errol Tu sitting in the armchair beside the large circular bed in his blue sports jacket, a cigarette between his fingers, his eyes cold and unfriendly.

Waldo Wu stood to one side and just behind the chair. He had on his customary tuxedo, and his right hand was resting in a coat pocket and seemed to be toying with something. His expression duplicated Errol Tu's.

Cosgrove turned to Carla standing by the open door in a micro mini, her legs extending to the floor in all their glory, and spread his hands in mute query. Her blink told him it was as much a mystery to her.

'*Saan mun!*' Waldo Wu commanded.

She obediently closed the door.

'You sit there.' Errol Tu pointed at Cosgrove, then the bed.

Lennie the Fifth did as he was told, his round face folded in confusion.

Then a smirk broke Errol Tu's inhospitable mien. Cosgrove grinned back as his disquiet left him in a flood. 'Errol, you bloody kidder!'

'Champagne, Lennie?'

'You know me.'

Waldo Wu lifted the magnum of Dom Perignon from the ice bucket. It was a standing accessory whenever the Paradise Room was reserved for Lennie the Lucky Pig and the most famous body in Hong Kong. Cosgrove took the filled glass. It was the only one. 'You should know I don't like to drink alone,' he said, trying to sound casual.

'Tonight maybe there be many things you not like, Lennie.' The hardness was back in Errol Tu's voice.

Cosgrove frowned again, but nevertheless tossed down the champagne. He gestured to Waldo Wu for a refill, but the man in the tuxedo looked back woodenly, the fingers of his right hand fiddling incessantly inside his coat pocket. When he accepted that nobody was going to refill his glass, he leaned over and put it on the floor. They watched him as if he was a cockroach. Not since his internment in Stanley had his skin crawled so.

'Why you look for me?'

Cosgrove looked up at Errol Tu. 'I . . . I have a deal for you.'

'Deal? Deal 'bout what?'

'About the stock market.'

Errol Tu gave a barren laugh. 'I no longer int'rest in stock market.'

'But you don't know the all of it!' Cosgrove shifted his bottom along the bed closer to Errol Tu and rattled on breathlessly: 'Together we can make the market go up! Those forgeries were just a bad break. Maybe they were even a good break. Don't you see? Prices are down to bedrock. I put 600,000,000 into the market today – and look what it did! It went up, didn't it? I tell you, Errol, if you buy up tomorrow, everyone will jump back in. The market'll take off again all the way to 2000. We'll do it together! We'll save the market together and – '

'Shut up.'

'Errol, I know you got burnt on Tuesday. But, luv-a-duck, so did I – '

'I say shut up already.'

Cosgrove felt the talons of something sinister grip his insides. The Dom Perignon burnt like acid into the back of his throat. He coughed.

Errol Tu laughed. 'You one-piece stupid Pig! You think you come here see me, but that not so. I come here see you! Stock market not int'rest me. You hear that? This what I want talk 'bout – '

He pointed to the television set in the corner. Waldo Wu bent and threw a switch on the control panel. Horizontal lines jumped upon the screen as a video tape was set in motion. Then a picture flashed onto it. Carla promptly gasped and clasped a hand over her mouth.

Cosgrove twisted his torso around to peer at the moving images on the screen. He watched for almost a full minute, not saying a thing. Then he laughed. 'He's not at all bad for an old fucker, eh?' He winked at Carla, who groaned and covered her eyes with both hands. 'Now I get it,' he laughed, looking at Errol Tu. 'The lady's your wife, right? Gee, I'm sorry Errol. Now I know why you're upset. But I'd keep her on a leash at night, if I were you. And get her a mariner's licence, too. She – '

'Shut up.'

'You say that a lot.'

'Listen you one-piece stupid Pig! We have many copy that tape.'

'So it's a new business for you, Errol, eh? Blue movies, eh? You should do okay at the box office with that one, I reckon.'

Errol Tu's laugh was even more barren. 'That one for private

[531]

sale. To you. Price is all share in company call Char'magne Ent'prise.'

Cosgrove's jaw fell. He stared. He blinked. It all fell into place in an instant and he knew that in Hong Kong he was financially, morally dead.

'Nahh!' He shook his head and twisted around to look back at the screen. 'That tape there's not even worth half that much. Look at the male lead. Just look at him. Pretty fit for his age alright, but too much hair on his arse. And you can even see his bloody corns! The bird's not bad, though. She'll do okay in movies.' He burst into hysterical laughter.

Errol Tu's eyes narrowed. He had not expected this.

'If you not sign your share in Char'magne Ent'prise over to us – one copy that tape send to man with big ears. Your boss.'

But Cosgrove's wild laughter carried right on. 'Old John, you mean? Go on, send it. He'll love it! He's a closet voyeur . . . didn't you know? He'll be over here in a flash – oh, forgive the pun – asking you to do a tape with . . . him in it! Oh, luv-a-bloody-duck . . . I've got the stitch.'

Errol Tu glanced uncertainly up at Waldo Wu. 'We send copy to newspaper also,' he tried. 'To police also – '

'The Governor!' Tears were streaming down Cosgrove's face. 'Don't miss out the Governor! He'll never . . . forgive you. Oh . . . you're killing me!' He held his ribcage and swayed from side to side. 'The stitch! Oh . . . !'

Errol Tu stood up and looked down at Cosgrove, his face a mask of bewildered disgust. *Gwailos* were impossible! He strode to the door. Carla still leaned against it with her hands clamped over her face in gross embarrassment. He shoved her aside. With his hand on the knob, he turned and looked back at Waldo Wu, gave a single decisive nod. And was gone. The door swung back on its closer and shut behind him with a loud click.

Cosgrove's laughter died away. He pulled out a handkerchief and wiped his eyes. Luv-a-duck, he thought. The bluff worked!

'*Chaw do!*'

He looked up. Waldo Wu was glaring at Carla and pointing at the bed with his left hand. His right stayed in his coat pocket.

'*Chaw do aah!*'

Tentatively she came and sat beside Cosgrove. He took her hand. 'Don't worry, lover. As soon as friend Waldo goes back outside and starts writing up our chit like he's supposed to do, we'll have ourselves a fucking good time here. How does that sound? Hullo . . . Who's this, then?'

[532]

The door opened wide. Two men came in. They were big men, but they had to bend double to carry between them whatever it was that was covered by the wet hessian bag that dripped water across the carpet. They dropped it with a thump before the floor-to-ceiling mirror, and pulled off the hessian bag. Cosgrove sat and frowned at a solid block of ice.

The men glanced at Waldo Wu, who inclined his head towards the bed.

'Hey! What's all this *aaarghh* – !'

A karate chop to the throat sent him sprawling backwards, gagging and retching, both hands grasping at his adam's apple.

The men turned on Carla and pulled her to her feet. Whilst one pinned her arms behind her back, the other reached up and tore her blouse and her bra from her body. The famous breasts vibrated like twin sponge cakes, the nipples projecting like maras-chino cherries. But the man in front of her ignored them and reached for the belt of her micro mini. She screamed at the top of her voice and rammed her knee up at him. He ignored that too, and in seconds she was being carried stark naked kicking and struggling towards the block of ice in front of the mirror.

Waldo Wu spun a knob on the control panel and *Love is Blue* ejaculated from the overhead speakers at maximum volume. And then he withdrew his right hand from his coat pocket.

Carla Tze Ti's beautiful oriental eyes bulged in ugly terror. Her twin rows of perfect teeth flashed white as she screamed anew. And kept on screaming. She had acted out many scenes just like this on Sing Company sets. But this was part of no script.

Lennie the Fifth regained consciousness to the end-to-end screams that at first came from far away, then from somewhere closer, then seemed to be in the room with him and all around him, competing with the music that blared from above his head. He opened his eyes and saw in the mirror the face that once had been famous and photogenic, but was now a mask of hideous abandon. Gradually his brain acknowleged the horror taking place a few feet away. He could see every part of it, front and back. Then his eyes were drawn to the smooth silver thing in Waldo Wu's right hand that was flashing in the suffused light of the Paradise Room.

And the deputy chairman of Cumberland China keeled off the bed onto the floor in a dead faint.

21

'Murder, Wai-kit. Do you remember me telling you before you went to the foreign devil country that to be a worthy leader a man must be able to commit it if it proves part of a plan?'

Alain To nodded. 'I remember, Great-uncle. A leader must stand upright and not worry if his shadow is crooked.'

Tu Chien looked pleased. 'Good, Wai-kit. There are only two good men: one is dead and the other not yet born.' He seemed to study his great-nephew with a purpose, then added: 'Murder could be the final test.'

Though Alain To wondered what his great-uncle meant by this, he had no time to enquire before the patriarch went into his limited routine of *tai chi chuen*. Instead, he looked on as his mentor lifted one arm upwards and outwards in that timeless slow motion, replaced the hand for the other on the walking stick, then repeated the procedure with the other arm, bending his torso as far as his diseased hip would permit. He saw Tu Chien's eyes flicker as the vile pain surged within him, then saw the lines disappear from his forehead as it was conquered.

The patriarch was pure Shanghai in a land of southerners. His body was like bamboo, his bald head with its sloping brow as smooth as ivory. His age seemed great, but was enigmatic. And he carried both his body and his age with an extrinsic dignity worthy of the richest man in Hong Kong. For, Alain To knew, that was indeed who his great-uncle was.

Pure Shanghai he might be, but Tu Chien's time in the colony had touched him in superficial ways. His cotton long-gown reached the uppers of his black Florshiem slip-ons and on one skeletal wrist he carried, rather than wore, a solid gold Rolex Oyster Perpetual. Balance was achieved by the jade bracelet on his other wrist: almost colourless in testimony to its antiquity, and quite priceless. It provided his personal protection.

He had become a component part of the dawn of every business day. He materialised before sunrise Monday to Saturday, preceded by one Kompo bodyguard and shadowed by another, at the fountain in the Botanical Gardens. He had started his day in this oasis of sorts upon the instep of the Peak, demarcating the concrete jungle of Mid Levels above and Central District below, since the day in 1959 the giant had moved into Cumberland House. Now he looked down at Connaught Centre to issue his matutinal curse. It had become part of the ritual, together with his dawn exercises, which he could no longer force himself to extend beyond ten minutes.

He looked down at the building through the grey light of dawn. His chest heaved as his lungs took in the morning air that rose off the harbour. It was marinated with a humidity that would turn basting when the sun ascended, adding another to the sequence of warm March days that was rendering the Year of the Water Ox devoid of spring.

'The woman with the hair like white jade,' Tu Chien asked without warning. 'She will get in the way of the plan?'

Alain To imperceptibly drew breath. So that was the reason he had been invited into the patriarch's presence in this place, at this time. His memory conjured up the picture of her. 'I am told she is a very determined female.' And a prize for a man to own, he added to himself.

Tu Chien pursed his lips. 'You avoid the question.'

'Yes, Great-uncle – she will get in the way.'

'She is coming back to Hong Kong?'

'Yes.'

'Then she becomes part of the plan. You know what you must do, Wai-kit.'

Alain To held the patriarch's gaze as he locked his desires away. He indeed knew what he had to do. He had known it since that day he had watched her cross Des Voeux Road, Central, and pass by a foot from him. He had known it the moment he had sniffed her perfume and had turned and followed her with his eyes that day, and had never seen such a wonderful sight. Then he had followed with the rest of him, keeping a discreet distance. But not too discreet.

Suzanne Huart-Brent would be the key to his international acceptance after the family had seized the Born Again *Hong*, and after he had been made the first Chinese taipan. Alain To had broad vision, broader even than his mentor's, he now believed.

'Yes, Great-uncle,' he affirmed. 'I know very well what I must do.'

22

Where was Lennie the Fifth?

By the firing of the Noon Day Gun on Friday, March 23rd, his absence began to be noticed around Central District.

[535]

'Do you know where Mr Cosgrove is, Imelda?'

'No, Mr Huart. He doesn't answer at his home nor at any of his usual places, including the Club. No-one's seen him. No-one knows where he might be. He's left no messages with anyone. Mr Ezuelo and Mr Szeto are also looking for him on urgent matters.'

Huart frowned. He had not laid eyes on his partner since the suspension meeting had broken up on Wednesday morning, forty-eight hours ago. Surely he hadn't taken his defeat so much to heart.

'Shall I keep trying to reach him?'

'Yes. Yes, please, Imelda. Keep trying.'

Huart returned to his office and went to the window. He looked out over the harbour, a blue waterscape of industry with a backdrop of grey concrete and deep green mountains. It all looked normal But was it?

Who was out there flush with Cumberland China stock and keeping it a secret? He had suspected it for some time. He had seen the price hold up when it should have gone down and, when it did drop, how it had fallen so little. He had taken note of the reducing daily volume of shares traded up to last Monday. He had been prepared to believe the public coveted *Gum Bak Leen* paper, were holding it for long-term gain and releasing it only for a premium. Gradually he had come to suspect that, whilst his supposition was correct, his definition of 'public' had been much too broad.

The call for shareholders to present their paper for verification had been the event, or non-event, that had finally convinced him.

But it had brought him a pleasant surprise: one which made him reassess the real value of modern day materialism. It had come when Mr Lee of Koon Wah Mansion, Mongkok had deferentially handed over his 200,000 shares and autographed his receipt with a crude wooden chop. Mr Lee, the humble man of the one-room tenement, rolled-up singlet and seven-day week in a Shanghai Street electrical shop, had been all along a millionaire. He was now, on paper, a multi-millionaire.

The fire in Factory Junior that had gutted two floors and a month's output of merchandise had been highly suspicious. But the simultaneous strike in Factory Senior that had rendered idle four out of the seven production floors was beyond the remotest frontiers of coincidence.

And Wai Wai Road was a month behind schedule. Could he really trust Alex Chiu? Was the man nursing a twenty-year resentment over the death of his father at the hands of men whose real prey had been Huart himself?

And now, on top of everything else, his partner had disappeared. Where was he? Huart had an endless list of questions to put to

[536]

him, only one of which concerned Cicero Investments. He also had something important to tell him. But where on earth was Lennie the Fifth?

'Where is he?' Tony Ezuelo entreated into the air of his office. He consulted Cosgrove on every problem. And he sure had a problem now.

'Still no message from him, Miss Roboza?' asked Y. Y. Szeto. 'No? Thank you.' The expression on the company secretary's face as he hung up was as close to an emotion as its muscles had ever been able to muster. By his calculation, Cicero Investments had shed over a hundred million dollars of its profit this week.

'Where the hell is Lennie?' P. G. Curzon-Cross asked of the liar dice regulars at the table in the corner of the Bowling Alley Bar. Cosgrove had never missed a Friday. It was the prime session of the week. 'I've been living on nothing but ham sandwiches since this town started going mad,' the stockbroker went on with a grimace. 'I just know it's given me an ulcer. But not even the market could keep me in today.'

He felt a deep concern for his old friend, for only he knew Cosgrove was still locked into the market, both for Cicero and on his own account. That morning the fall of the Index had wiped out half the 67 point rise that had been purchased by him, and him alone, the day before.

And it would have fallen further, faster if the Central Share Registry had announced the new forgeries before noon. By 12:45, trading in the shares of the Godown Company, Shang Navigation, China Rice Importers, Wing Luen Kai Realty and the Boilincold Bottle Company had been suspended on all four stock exchanges.

'Why is the obnoxious little spunk bubble still there!?' Buckley cried, his small eyes boring into the computer print-out of the roll of shareholders. 'I was certain he'd sold his shares. I was certain I had him. Damn blast the leprous pygmy! I'd strangle him with my bare hands if I could only find him . . . !'

23

At one o'clock on Saturday, March 24th, as Hong Kong headed home for a weekend in which to prepare for the complete desertion of the stock market come ten a.m. Monday, Matthew Zagan's East Point telephone rang.

The voice on the line repelled him and aroused him, both at once.

'Guess who's back in the Big Lychee.'

'Either that or you're calling from New York again, Suzie.'

'As you make a habit of not returning my calls, I figure I've no choice but to check in person how my selection in the "Taipan Derby" is shaping up in the trials. I understand there's a new chair at the Long Table. Your odds are shortening. Congratulations, Matt, darling.'

Zagan kept his voice neutral. 'Thank you.'

'You've timed your run to perfection. You must be a thoroughbred.' She paused, but there had been no sarcasm. 'Not much time left before Uncle John announces the winner, you know. Only hours to go now.'

As she had intended, he reacted: 'Hours?'

'He thinks the reason I came to Hong Kong is in response to his invitation to the centenary banquet on Monday night. Poor Uncle John. He seems to have so much on his mind at present . . .'

That's something of an understatement, Zagan agreed to himself.

' . . . I did come for that, of course. But you know the real reason, Matt.'

'Tell me.'

'Uncle John let it slip. He tells me little things. After all, I do have a chair at the Long Table –'

'Complete with modesty panel, no doubt.'

She laughed with such spontaneity that he had to chuckle with her.

'Oh, Matt. Your one-liners are one of the things I love most about you. That and your damn sexual aggressiveness.'

'Suzie . . .'

'Okay, darling.' She laughed again. 'Hours? About fifty-six left now. You must know Uncle John is a sucker for the big occasion.'

'The centenary banquet?'

'Go to the top of the class. He's going to announce his choice for fifth taipan during his speech.'

Zagan frowned. It could be true at that.

Her voice took on a sudden urgency. 'Matt, I thought of a wonderful idea on the plane. How about dinner tonight? I want to make up for walking out on you last time. Let's go back to Au Trou Normand and finish the meal. I do love ratatouille. Okay, darling?'

'Oh, don't apologise, Suzie. I remember I enjoyed myself last time – after you left, I mean – and stuck me with the bill. It was your shout, as they call it Down Under. You did invite me, remember?'

'Chauvinist Aussie pig.'

'But I regret I have a dinner engagement tonight. Thanks anyway.'

Her voice lost its casualness. 'Afterwards, then.'

'Is that an order?'

She hesitated, then attacked. 'Damn right, buster. Don't forget what I told you last time. Nobody's closer to Uncle John than me.'

'Than I,' Zagan corrected.

'Hey, buster – '

'Don't threaten, Suzie. I get rather unhappy when anyone threatens me.'

'Matt – I'm in suite 901 of the Victoria Hotel. The Victoria, got it? Uncle John has the Mandarin and the Hilton booked out for all his overseas guests. Be there at midnight. Suite 901. It's very important.'

'Suzie, I can't. I'm flying to Peking on Tuesday. Tomorrow is all the time I have left to prepare. It's an important mission. I'm sure you know that. Tonight has to be an early one for me. I'm sorry, but – '

'Matt, please. Peking's important to you, but this is important to me.'

'Look, I'm sor – '

'Please-Please-Please!'

The line went dead. Zagan looked at the receiver, then slowly replaced it in its cradle. There were a great many places he might be at midnight tonight. But Suite 901 of the Victoria Hotel would not be one.

'Want a sneak preview of what the winner gets, Matt?'

Suzanne Huart-Brent turned and faced him. Her hair had been clipped in a fashionable Vidal Sassoon style. Her lovely face was composed. Her large brown eyes glinted. Her lips were pursed in determination.

Her platinum nailed fingers flicked down the front of the knee-length snow-white Siberian fur coat. Button by button.

'The winner gets Cumberland China . . .' She parted the coat slowly, then flung it open. 'And all this with it.'

Underneath she was completely, blatantly, magnificently naked.

Air sucked into Zagan's lungs at the sight of the sculptured majesty before him: his for the taking. He could not move. He

[539]

wanted her. He had to go to her. But half of him, the half that was related to her, held him fast to the spot. He decided to back away and walk out of the suite. But half of him, the half that was free, urged him forward.

He let her come to him over the Tientsin rug. He let her come right to him and still he could not move. Her arms encircled him and her cool breasts squashed against his chest. She reached up and pulled his head down to her. And he let her do it. Her mouth was over his, her tongue darting between his teeth, its tip writing her passion upon his throat.

Something surged in his core. He reached inside the coat and crushed her in both arms. Her body bent backwards, supple and willing. He devoured her with his mouth. His hands sought her body, every softly moulded talcumed part of it. He took her up as if she was a sheaf of feathers. She let her arms drop and the coat slipped to the rug like a snowfall in miniature. He carried her to the bed, his mouth still upon hers, searching deeper . . . deeper . . .

Then the voice that had been calling plaintively from inside the back of his head grew with sudden power.

He dropped her on the bed and stood back. His manhood bulged before him, a stark affidavit to the genuineness of his arousal.

She looked down at it, then up at him. The passion and victory on her face transformed into bafflement when she saw the multitude of emotions that competed for space on his. 'Matt . . ?'

'Suzie, I – I'm so sorry . . .'

'Sorry? Matt, what's wrong?'

He turned and strode to the door.

'Matt!?'

He reached the door, then turned to face her. 'I've got to go.'

'Go?' She sprang off the bed onto her feet like a puma. 'Go and leave me like this? What the hell did you come here for? What did you expect?'

'Suzie . . .'

'Why did you come?' It rose to almost a shriek.

A defiance, a cover over his inability to find the answer, rose within him. 'Why'd I come? Well, miss, you did say "please".'

It was a mistake.

'Get out.' Her voice was now very quiet, very clear.

He turned at the door. 'Suzie, there's something I can't tell you yet.'

She was unimpressed. 'Oh? And when will you feel like telling me?'

[540]

He smiled in a way she had not seen before, and she saw in it more of the man that lived within the body of Matthew Zagan. 'When I'm taipan.'

She stared at him. When she set her sights on a target she went for it with unequivocal determination. It had been that way with her studies, then with Wall Street, and now with Matthew Zagan. She knew she loved him, but now she knew he was not for her. And it hurt. Rejection was something she had dished out all her life. Being on the receiving end produced a destructive, yet unstoppable emotive force that came, her mother had told her, from her father's genes.

'Take something from me, Mister Zagan,' she affirmed in a voice like burnt sugar. 'You're not going to be taipan.'

Standing upon the fur coat in the centre of the rug, legs apart, arms akimbo, she reminded him of a naked warrior queen. But still he dismissed her with a shrug, and walked out of suite 901.

Suzanne Huart-Brent stared at the closed door for long, acrimonious seconds. Then she kicked the coat into the corner, strode purposefully to the telephone and dialled a number in Deep Water Bay.

'Uncle John? It's Suzie . . . Yes, I know it's late and you've a million other problems . . . Yes, there is something wrong. That man, Matthew Zagan was here tonight. Yes, in my room. He asked to see me about something to do with the company. It was a lie. He tried to . . . Uncle John, you must do something about him. Why? Because that man just tried to rape me!'

Zagan recognised the Cantonese voice as he stepped out of the elevator. The lobby was virtually deserted this late and the words carried easily to his ears, though quietly uttered. He paused behind a pillar and lit up a Marlboro. He saw the red note passed across the counter to the night clerk, and he heard spoken the numbers: '901'.

He gave Alain To ten seconds, then followed him out of the lobby onto Queen's Road, Central.

24

Incubus and John Huart had been soulmates for the entire weekend. Not a minute, awake or asleep, had passed in which he did not search each nook and cranny of his brain for the piece missing from the jigsaw puzzle that was scattered across it. He did not find it until ten minutes after dawn on Monday, March 26th Even then he would not have done so but for his trusty British Army issue binoculars, and the unseasonal light so early in the day, so early in the year. But when he did see it, he knew for certain the Born Again *Hong* was under attack. And he knew why.

He had been beating the dawn, and the Repulse Bay Road traffic, to Central District since the appearance of the first forgeries. But despite this pre-emptive start, the business day still proved too short to find solutions to the problems that seemed to spring out of the woodwork at each ring of the telephone. He was vouchsafed no respite from Problems, not even when abed after midnight on Saturday.

And there were the vital preparations for Peking.

On impulse, he took up the binoculars to admire the sunrise over Mount Parker. He swept the Peak, grimacing at the triangular concrete scab covering the great gouge taken out by the June 18th landslip. He lowered his line of sight to Mid Levels and inspected the Cumberland high-rises. Then he studied the flamingoes in the Botanical Gardens, then the devotees to *tai chi chuen* around the fountain. He was absorbing the tranquillity of their movements into his own tense body when he saw . . .

Tu Chien.

Age had conferred on the man an unkind camouflage. He was bald and bent and it may have been nineteen years, but Huart knew it was Tu Chien in the flesh. He would know that walking stick made from ebony anywhere.

And the hitherto disjointed pieces of the jigsaw puzzle flew into place upon the screen of his mind's eye.

Hong Kong is called a village with good reason. Nevertheless, Huart had not seen Tu Chien since that May day in 1954 at Kai Tak: the day Andrew Huart-Brent had died. After that he had shut him away in a crypt somewhere in his subconscious. Then, imbued with such confidence after his audience with Chiang Kai-shek in October, 1953, and absorbed in the omnifarious commission of running the Born Again *Hong*, he had been only too prepared to let time seal tight the lid on the crypt. Chiang's veto was to stand for life. And, though now a less prominent head of state at the great age of eighty-five, the President of the Republic of China, Huart's benefactor and indeed his saviour, was still very much alive. But he should have known a man like Tu Chien would not rest with that.

*

'Imelda, let me know at ten if there's still no news of Mr Cosgrove.'

'Yes, Mr Huart.'

He flicked off the intercom. At ten he would ask her to start calling the hospitals, the police, the Immigration Department. He put it aside until then and ran his eye over the first two entries in his desk diary.

8:00 – Zagan / Y. Y. Szeto – Peking briefing.

9:00 – Zagan / Bedrix / Buckley – Decision!

Then he dropped it to the bottom line.

19:00 – Centenary Banquet, Dynasty Ballroom.

The pendulum clock showed 8:05. He rejoined Zagan and Y. Y. Szeto, who were seated in the armchairs around the coffee table where he held his meetings, sipping jasmine tea.

'Mr Szeto, your news is a moonbeam on a black night,' he opened, taking up his cup and blowing the tealeaves from the near edge. 'There is so much going wrong in Hong Kong of late that the law of averages, as far as China is concerned, must be in our favour.'

The sinologist cum company secretary blinked. 'One consequence of President Nixon's visit last year is the re-emergence of the policies of Liu Shao-chi under a new nomenclature. Teng Hsiao-ping has appeared at an official function for the first time since the Cultural Revolution.'

'That sounds significant,' Huart suggested. 'How much so?'

'Very, and in several ways. Peking is showing to the world it does not execute its fallen leaders as Moscow does. Teng's experience and way of thinking are regarded by some influential Politburo members as rediscovered assets. He is an indefatigable man – a protégé of Chou En-lai in addition to being a disciple of Liu Shao-chi. It does appear that he is being repositioned to feature in the leadership after Mao and Chou pass on. He has already been given the nominal title of "Deputy Chairman".'

'It does sound good,' Huart agreed. 'How is Chou's health?'

'He is under constant treatment for the cancer.'

'And Mao?'

'Not encouraging. He is rarely seen in public now.'

Huart nodded, then looked at Zagan. 'Your first visit to China?'

'No, sir. I have visited the Canton Trade Fair with my father.'

[543]

'Yes. . . . You did say he was a foreign correspondent. Well, your first visit to Peking, then. Is everything arranged?'

Zagan deferred to Y.Y. Szeto, who nodded. 'Our Cathay Pacific charter takes off at 1600 hours tomorrow. We have had our rooms confirmed in the Peking Hotel. The Chinese are keen for the British Industrial Technology Exhibition to be a great success. My contacts have been able to arrange audiences with some reasonably important people for you.'

'Grand!' Huart beamed. 'My thanks to you, Mr Szeto.' He leaned forward. 'And Shanghai? Can we return via Shanghai? I would so much like to visit the old Cumberland Building on the Bund.'

The sinologist's eyes dropped a fraction. 'We must be careful there. I will do my best, but do not hold out too much hope. The Chinese are still sensitive about Shanghai's capitalist past. And it's no longer "The Bund" – it's now *Chong Shan Dong Lu*: Chung Shan Road East.'

Huart cancelled a sigh. The past is dead. Look to the future. The future for Cumberland China is north. And it's a whole new north up there. 'I understand,' he affirmed. 'Matthew, show me the updated exhibition programme, please, and the layout for the Cumberland Engineering stand.'

Zagan opened a file on the coffee table and began his report.

After half an hour the briefing ended and Y.Y. Szeto left.

Then Huart said: 'Matthew, before Glynn Bedrix and Tom Buckley arrive, I feel I should discuss something with you. It's about Suzie . . .'

Zagan's frown was quick.

'She's a spoiled, headstrong young woman, but with solid gold beneath. She called me late Saturday night and said you'd been to her room . . .'

Zagan's frown returned and this time stayed put.

'She called me again the following morning to tell me that whatever had happened – which was nothing – was all her doing. You've made a deep impression on her, Matthew.' He gave an avuncular smile. 'I'll say no more on the subject, and leave it to the two of you to work it out.'

The frown dissolved, leaving Zagan's face impassive. 'Thank you.'

The intercom buzzed.

'Yes, Imelda?'

'Mr Buckley and Mr Bedrix are here.'

*

[544]

'Today is a rare day – one in one hundred years.' Huart looked in turn at the three men seated with him around the coffee table.

The finalists.

He looked at Glynn Bedrix, the one closest to 'family', and liked what he saw. But Glynn, he thought, your father would never have been as indecisive over the suspension vote – and at the Long Table, no less.

He looked at Thomas Buckley and saw the stress lines. But the Director of Finance and Administration had proven himself as a dedicated workaholic who required no more than a vacation to recharge his batteries.

He looked again at Matthew Zagan. Something steered his eyes away from the impassive mien, across the office to the smaller portrait of Charles Huart behind his desk. He looked back. It was uncanny, he acknowledged.

He went on: 'On this day a century ago, that man on the wall over there founded Cumberland China in Chungking. A century later we have arguably the largest, most profitable company in Hong Kong, with branches in many countries . . .' He paused. 'But if I go on like that, you'll be right in accusing me of poaching from the speech I intend to make tonight.'

Buckley and Bedrix smiled in return. Zagan kept his face expressionless.

'No day is more appropriate than this for taking a great decision – one which has been in my mind and on my mind for a long time – and for its announcement.' Huart paused again. 'Gentlemen, today I will decide which one of you will take over from me as chief executive of this company. One of you is to be the fifth taipan of Cumberland China. I shall take my decision today, and announce it at the centenary banquet tonight.'

Buckley looked at Bedrix, and together they looked at Zagan. They seemed more surprised that he had been grouped with them than with the significance of the pronouncement that had just been made. Zagan ignored them.

Huart stood up and said: 'There is an important question I must put to the two who will not become fifth taipan . . .' He again looked at each of them. 'Will you fully support the new taipan, body and soul? Will you work for him, and with him? Will you continue to afford him the same true devotion and selfless endeavour that you have always afforded me?' He began with the Director of Finance and Administration. 'Tom?'

'Of course, sir!'

Then he looked at the Director of Insurance and Banking. 'Glynn?'

Bedrix squared his shoulders, glanced again at Buckley and Zagan. And hid well the surge of confidence. 'Sir, my devotion will always be to the company and to its taipan – whoever that man may be.'

'Matthew?'

Zagan looked up into the large sober face, the steady eyes and recalled an old Chinese proverb: 'He who rides a tiger will find it difficult to dismount'. Holding fast to the tiger's mane with both hands and digging his knees and ankles into its flanks, he gave his answer. 'If I am not taipan by midnight, you can expect my letter of resignation by eight tomorrow.'

The Altitudinal Taipan nodded. His Great Decision was taken.

25

Dead.

Lennie Cosgrove was dead.

Lennie the Fifth: deputy chairman of Cumberland China, multi-millionaire man-about-town, gourmet and connoisseur of wine, women, automobiles, cruiser yachts and racehorses, was dead.

The *Meen Foot Hau Jaak* of the Cantonese punting masses was dead, too.

And Lennie the Lucky Pig: that chancer of chancers, the man with the Midas touch, was especially dead.

At four p.m. on that dire March Monday, the ghost of them all sat curled up in one of the leather armchairs in the Bowling Alley Bar. Being mid-afternoon, the place was deserted. The beaten down, unshaven apparition that could have resembled Cosgrove, given enough imagination, was drinking double pink gin straight – one straight after the other – and was company for the real ghosts that hid in the shadowy corners. It made no sound except to call 'Boy!' when its glass was empty, then it moved only its shaking right hand to scribble an autograph and membership number on the chit and lift the refill to its bloodless lips as its eyes stared sightlessly into the knots in the ancient floorboards. But inside its dishevelled white head its brain was running wild.

Dead! I am dead! I have died and gone back to the womb, the Club, where I can wrap myself up like a foetus and float in a uterine bath of pink gin. And nobody can see me. And nobody can find me. And the world can go its own sweet bloody way. Without me.

'Boy! Double pink gin chop-chop! And make it pink! The last one looked like you pissed in it. Tasted like it, too. *Humbalaang yum!* Everybody drink up! Drink the bloody place dry and put it on my chit. Won't matter t'me, y'know. When the bloody bill comes next month – I'll be dead!'

Dead and gone. He was dead every-which-way.

He had signed his own death warrant in the Paradise Room of the Red Phoenix Motel. Two of them had held his wrist whilst he did it. If he had refused to sign the Deed of Sale of his forty per cent of Charlemagne Enterprises to some organisation called Great Horse Something, he would be dead already. Dead? He would be worse than dead – with his body in one place and his head in another. A great shudder went through him.

'Boy! Luv-a-duck, where the bloody hell are you?'

They had kept him in the Paradise Room for three and a half days, staring at the spot on the floor where the block of ice had been, at the thick, sticky pool that had changed from bright red to dark red to purple to black at the edges before it had started to stink. He had stared at it, recoiling from the flashbacks of what he had seen in the mirror in the spells of consciousness in between the longer breaks of merciful blackness. Then, knowing he was dead, knowing he was of no more use to them than a used condom that they could flush down the toilet at any time they chose, they let him out on the fourth day. Today.

He looked down at the competing headlines on the copy of *The Register* on the floor at his feet and saw he was dead there too. Dead twice over.

EXCHANGE CARNAGE! INDEX FALLS ANOTHER 188.70

Cicero Investments was still in the market. He couldn't pull it out. It was like the market was quicksand and he was in it up to his shrivelling vitals. He hadn't called P.G. He couldn't do that either. He couldn't face him. Why did the Index fall 189 points today, P.G.? How the hell do I know! How the hell could I know? I'm dead!

REGISTER EXCLUSIVE:
WHERE IS CARLA?

[547]

And there he was, deader than dead. If he kept quiet the guilt would put an end to him. But if he went to the police and told them about it the Tus would kill him. Or they would put the video tape in the mail, and Hong Kong would look at his hairy arse pumping up and down, and batter him to death with stones of condemnation.

In the Hong Kong he loved, in the one heaven on earth in which he could live, he had managed to die. Cause of death? Asphyxiation. Suffocation from falling face down in the excrement upon his own doorstep and being unable, or unwilling, to pull his stupid head out.

Even so, he might still be able to survive all that had gone so wrong if not for what would happen when the Tus registered his shares and his name was taken off the roll of shareholders. For then John Huart would disown him. And that would kill him most of all.

'Boy! Luv-a-bloody-duck! Where the hell are you all? Get here chop-chop!'

But the waiters of the Bowling Alley Bar were not listening to him. They were slaves to another voice, the one on the radio, that was telling them they were poor, that their syndicate money had evaporated into thin air.

'Boy! Boy! Luv-a-blood – Who the hell are you?'

A pair of black leather shoes had come within the apparition's limited field of vision.

'Where have you been, Mr Cosgrove?'

The accent was familiar. West Country? Oh no. Not Noughts and Crosses!

'Fuck off, hairy legs. Let me die in peace.'

'Decorum, Mr Cosgrove.'

The ghost looked up. It squinted, focusing with effort. 'Oh, it's you. Where'd you get that accent?'

'I spent a year in the Outback.'

'Outback? Out back of what?'

'It's in Australia, Mr Cosgrove. Arnhem Land. I worked on a station there for a time.'

'And they still made you a member here?'

'No.'

'Keep trying then.' The eyes glazed over and the body made as if to curl up and withdraw back into its foetal state.

'Mr Cosgrove, I think we should talk.'

The grey face contorted. 'Talk about what? The stock market? Talk to the 'boys' over there. They know all about it now. Boy!'

'No, Mr Cosgrove, not the stock market.'

'What then?'

'I think we should go somewhere private and talk about Carla Tze Ti.'

The ghost opened its mouth, but no sound came. Confusion, fear, recall of horror amalgamated in its red and white eyes. 'What do you – ? Where do you – ? Why – ?'

Matthew Zagan bent close to the apparition's ear and answered all. 'The police have found an unlisted Peak telephone number in her flat and a note that reads: "Lennie. Dinner. 8 o'clock. Shatin Heights Hotel." A *Register* reporter traced the number to you. The police will too. You were seen in the hotel restaurant. The lady was quite conspicuous. You left together after midnight. You haven't been to the office since Thursday morning. Why? I look at you and I can guess. Carla Tze Ti was a Sing Company starlet and good time girl. Errol Tu owns Sing Company. His nephew is rising high in Cumberland Engineering and has been tailing the taipan's niece since she arrived in Hong Kong. His brother and cousin sold Cumberland Properties six blocks of worthless North Point tenements at an inflated price. We have a torched factory, a strike at another and our shares seem to be all stitched up. Something's going on. I'm trying to find out what. I believe you can help me in that. I'd like you to come with me now. My mother is waiting for us in the car. Our solicitor is with her. Come, Mr Cosgrove.'

Zagan reached down, took his deputy chairman by the arm, and lifted him out of the chair like a rag doll. The ghost of Lennie the Fifth shuffled to the door on the arm of the tall dark young man with the big ears as if it had no volition of its own.

26

Like a noble sculpture of the great God of Business who is all-seeing, all-hearing, all-knowing, John Huart stood before the microphone on the rostrum. Seventy-seven inches of smooth-fitting black tuxedo and godlike head, he looked out over the one hundred tables that filled the Dynasty Ballroom of the Victoria Hotel like a sea of circles. One hundred tables it had to be. For that was the age of the Born Again *Hong*.

'Today, Monday, March 26th, 1973, the fifty-second day of this Year of the Ox, closed the first one hundred years in the life of Cumberland China. It has certainly been a Golden Century, through which, like the ever-fluctuating price of gold, the company's fortunes have risen, have fallen back, and have risen again . . .'

The 1,200 faces looked up at him. Though intent on his speech, each one wore an underlay of shock and after-shock. The reason was five digits. 188.70. They were branded into every brain in Hong Kong. For it was a chilling fact that the centenary of the Born Again *Hong* had been a day of all-consuming disaster. It had been the day on which corporate paper had devalued by 13.3 per cent in 165 minutes. And what would tomorrow bring?

Huart was approaching the climax of his speech. His audience awaited it with collectively bated breath as if the secret had leaked out. At no table was a side comment risked, nor was there a lapse in attention to light a cigarette, sip from a glass, nor even scratch an itch.

All night the hubbub that was an integral part of so grand a banquet had sustained itself. It was an uproar of conversation, of chopsticks clicking against porcelain, of lids scraping on copper tureens full of steaming birds' nests – one of the three soups amongst the fifteen courses, of the banging of the doors hidden by the ornamental screens as the dishes were delivered into the care of the three hundred serving staff under the eye of the twenty captains on duty for the great occasion.

But when the Altitudinal Taipan had stepped to the rostrum before the serving of the Peking duck, the din had been put to death.

The assemblage that was his audience was national and international. It included every person in the world who had a connection with the Born Again *Hong*, either historical or current. His most difficult task had been the seating arrangement – in particular, who should join him at the head table besides the guest of honour. The Governor sat directly before the rostrum looking up at it with calm shrewd visage that was proving an exemplar for all. Huart had eventually solved the problem by allocating the other seats at his table to his favourite neutrals.

Amongst these, the identity of the elegant lady on the Governor's right had everybody speculating. Virginia May Adair had a very familiar face and was obviously a woman of status. But who was she?

More a puzzle were the humble, grinning, chain-smoking Chinese man in an ill-fitting suit, crushed collar and twisted tie, and the small boy at his side. Mr Lee Wing-tak of Koon Wah Mansion, Mongkok, doubly staked his claim to a seat at the head table by being the Born Again *Hong*'s biggest 'small' shareholder, and the father of the taipan's godson.

And Francis Roboza had come out of reclusiveness to sit beside his daughter.

Each member of the Long Table, including Suzanne Huart-Brent and Matthew Zagan, and each member of the H and K board, was hosting a table in the first semi-circle before the rostrum where, with wives, sat directors of government departments and trade promotion bodies, members of the Executive and Legislative Councils, trade commissioners and consul-generals of three dozen nations, the chief managers of the H and K's competitor Big Banks, heads of public utilities and leading industrial, transportation and engineering corporations, and the taipan of every rival *hong*.

And there were the managers of the Cumberland China branch offices in Tokyo, Singapore, Kuala Lumpur, Djakarta, Manila, Seoul and Sydney, and the international offices in London, New York, San Francisco, Zurich and Brussels. But not Taipei. Huart had ordered its closure in the wake of Nixon's visit to China, whose senior local officials were in attendance.

A special thrill for him was the presence of those retired veterans Chuck Kreitzer, Hugh Dunlop and Angus Grey. Scott and Margot Overbeck had flown in from San Francisco. Lord Armstrong and Sir Leo Cheshunt had come straight from Kai Tak, their faces still aglow with victory. The heads and chief executives of every prime international agency held by each of the subsidiary companies had been invited. All had accepted.

Cumberland China was enthusiastically picking up the tab for it all.

But there had been sad news, too. Huart had learnt that Gilbert Dole had died in England, and that Billson Hsu's *fung shui* had deserted him in Toronto where he had succumbed to cancer of the back of the nose.

No invitation had been sent to Rex Wagoner. Nor to Hector Harrisford-House, who was sharing retirement in Cornwall with his rhododendrons. Nor to Jeremy Parrot, whose whereabouts were, in any case, unknown. Refusals had come in from Suzanne's mother, from Nigel and Regina Print, and from Abraham and Cheryl Male, who had flown south for a holiday on the Great Barrier Reef rather than attend.

As he orated, Huart's gaze fell upon his partner, who had arrived half an hour late – dressed to kill, bright-eyed, bushy-tailed: Lennie the Fifth of old. Enquiries into his four-day truancy had been shrugged off with characteristic insouciance. Huart had smiled away his misgivings. His questions would have to wait until after the banquet, and after the announcement, to which events had prevented Cosgrove from contributing.

Through a second microphone, Imelda Roboza translated into Cantonese. At a table in the first semi-circle, Y. Y. Szeto interpreted for the Peking officials seated around him, taking care with any historical item, however obliquely put, that risked offence. But there was no problem putting Huart's next words into Mandarin verbatim.

'It is not because of myself or because of any individual that the company has prospered. We owe our original debt of gratitude to China,' he nodded to Y. Y. Szeto's table, 'which gave Charles Huart his opportunity exactly one century ago. The Chinese place great store in having just one opportunity in life. I will now risk being considered greedy. I wish a second opportunity, and I fly to Peking tomorrow to ask in person.'

He bent and picked a glass of cognac off a tray held up by a waiter.

'Ladies and gentlemen – Lennie Cosgrove, our directors and I offer you a centenary toast. We apologise for not observing custom and coming to each table. We'd be dead drunk before we managed to get half way – '

An appreciative ripple provided the appropriate acknowledgement.

' – So I will ask the directors to rise and drink with me our toast to you all. I am very happy to have you here tonight. Some of you have come far to set the seal with us on the first one hundred years of Cumberland China. For each of you we have a memento of the occasion – '

He raised an arm and two hundred waiters, each carrying half a dozen parcels wrapped in gold paper, moved amongst the tables, handing out one to each guest. Huart watched Suzanne open hers and hold up a full-length robe of Shantung silk hand embroidered in golden thread with the *Gum Bak Leen* logo. She stood and tried it on to Caucasian kudos.

At his table in the second semi-circle, Alain To listened to

Cantonese disapproval. He would have to teach her, amongst many other things, how Chinese regarded the opening of presents in public to be a gauche act.

'And now . . .' Huart waited for silence to return. ' . . . we toast you all, and we thank you all. Gentlemen – '

The members of the Long Table rose, glasses of cognac in hand.

Alain To saw Zagan on his feet, and his eyebrows elevated.

'*Yum boei!*' Huart called out the traditional local toast.

'*Yum boei!*' the directors echoed.

'*Yum boei!*' the rest of the 1,200 throats returned.

The toast of one hundred years was made.

Huart set down his glass and cleared his throat. The 1,200 faces turned back to the rostrum and up at him. There was an interpretative silence. The climax was now.

Huart looked at Matthew Zagan. Beside him Kingston Orr sat open-faced, a changed man. His objective all along had been plain ordinary 'face'. He had tried to foster it in Tokyo at the expense of his prestige in Hong Kong, where his pro-Japanese motives had been misinterpreted. Kingston Orr, CBE, now had the 'face' he had been seeking. 'Couldn't get the chap a knighthood,' Lord Armstrong had apologised. 'Still, we have something for encores, don't we. There'll be more power stations in Hong Kong.' Huart looked back at Zagan. The new director had done grand work.

He next sought out Glynn Bedrix, who was hosting Prince Lugano, *sans* Danielle, in customary polished fashion with Patricia an efficient supplement at the Swiss tycoon's right elbow. The engagement was becoming protracted, Huart decided. Glynn should squeeze some pleasure out of life instead of devoting it all so selflessly to the company.

Thomas Buckley sat proudly at twelve o'clock in a circle of the colony's top money men and their wives. The Director of Finance and Administration preened noticeably under his taipan's direct and meaningful gaze.

'I am indeed a proud man tonight. With the fortunes of the company at their peak, I have selected this time to make an important announcement. And that is my retirement as chief executive – taipan as we like to call the job here – of Cumberland China – '

The silence was smashed like a wrecking ball hitting a plate glass window. Every mouth opened and gave forth a stereophonic gasp, then posed the same unbelieving question.

'But why . . . ?'

Every mouth, that is, except four.

Matthew Zagan sat stone-faced.

Wearing a preoccupied expression that was patently manufactured, Glynn Bedrix studied the chandelier above his head.

If they listened hard, all at Thomas Buckley's table could have heard the drumming of the top accountant's heart against his ribcage.

From the corner of her eye, Suzanne watched Zagan across three tables, her face a beautiful microcosm of the emotions that lived within her.

Gradually, silence resumed tenancy of the Dynasty Ballroom. Huart waited with impassive composure until it was completed.

'The man who will replace me as chief executive . . . The man who is to be the fifth taipan of Cumberland China. . . . The man who is to lead the Born Again *Hong* into its second "Golden Century" . . . This man's name is – '

It is a fact that the God of Business is all-seeing, all-hearing, all-knowing. But John Stanford Huart was only human. Accordingly, he had not seen the uninvited guest enter the ballroom. Neither had he heard the whispers as the man had wound his way through the tables on his way to the rostrum, his traditional cotton long-gown and determined painful gait with the aid of a walking stick drawing automatic comment. He did not know that Tu Chien was there until he lowered his gaze in the act of connecting with the man whom he was about to make a taipan . . .

And then he looked directly into those same godless Shanghai eyes that had sentenced him to death on the Bund nearly thirty-three years before.

And he knew they had returned out of history to carry out the sentence before a hundred tables filled with his peers, contemporaries, clients, shareholders, staff. And his lover. And the Governor of Hong Kong.

Tu Chien leaned on his walking stick, looking up. 'It is indeed time for you to relinquish your company!' The words had carried limited power, yet their pronunciation had been clear and only slightly accented. 'But it is I who will decide who will be its next taipan!'

Huart heard but did not absorb. It was the eyes that did it. They tranquillised, paralysed. He stood as if struck twice by lightning, like a great oak rigid in its final moments before it crashed to earth.

'Mr John Huart, I summon you and your directors to a meeting in your boardroom at ten o'clock tomorrow morning!'

Huart dug his voice out of the time-warp. 'Who are you to summon anybody anywhere? On what errand do you interrupt these proceedings?'

Tu Chien lifted his free hand and pointed the bone that was his index finger like an assassin's dagger. Huart could not stop himself watching the outsized Rolex slide down the insignificant forearm. 'At your Long Table tomorrow morning, I will prove that I and my company, Great Horse Enterprises, have taken Cumberland China from you. Within my rights as a major shareholder, I call an extraordinary board meeting! You cannot deny my right – in front of all these witnesses and your Lord Governor! Mr John Huart, prepare for your last business meeting!'

An unspoken suffix of four monosyllables rose out of Huart's memory like a vapour from a coffin.

Sze . . . Yu . . . Yiu . . . Gu!

Another silence gripped the Dynasty Ballroom. This one was a silence of crisis. The sea of faces staring up at Huart was a mosaic of shock upon shock. This was too much! As if the havoc on the stock exchanges was not enough for one day, now the Born Again *Hong* – the pillar of the very Establishment of Hong Kong, and of Shanghai before that – had just been challenged in the face of the Governor!

Even a taipan was tested at a time like this. Even the Altitudinal Taipan. Sixteen hours had passed since he had seen Tu Chien that morning. He had not had the time to fathom the direction, the size nor the mode of the attack he knew was coming. He knew it was imminent, but he had not anticipated its immediacy. Underneath his public suit of armour, he was shaken to the core. But only those who knew him intimately would have had any chance of detecting it. And there were few such people.

Lee Yeok-hon detected it. Seven years of age less eleven days, he made a mature resolution: It was his filial duty to kill this impudent old man who walked with a black stick.

The solitary white-haired Caucasian sat pensively at a table before the rostrum with his fingers around a double pink gin, watching the army of waiters dismantling the one hundred tables. The aftermath of the banquet of one hundred years was a ballroom of stained tablecloths, pyramids of orange and apple peel, and disarranged plates, bowls and chopsticks.

The deputy chairman of Cumberland China had uttered not a word since he had heard that aborted announcement with abject disbelief. Up to then he had been alive, his eyes alight with Lennie the Fifth mischief, his chatter endless. He had been rejecting alcohol, even for the toasts, and his senses had been more alive than he could remember. It had been as if he could see all through a wide-angle lens, recognising things that he had taken for granted in a life that had become a post-noon haze in which each day accelerated into the next and the next and the next . . .

He had the Zagans and their family solicitor to thank for leading him back to the path that was straight and narrow, if only for three short hours. Seated in the living room of the house in Braga Circuit and sobering under a double assault of questions and black coffee, he had cleansed himself by confessing his all. That had also taken three hours.

But then the Great Man had proclaimed to the world that the life of Lennie the Fifth was at its end. For, if he abdicated, so must his partner. They were a deuce. Castor and Pollux. The Siamese twins of Hong Kong business. And one had cut himself free without consulting the other.

After Tu Chien had levered himself from the Dynasty Ballroom and Huart had returned to the head table to go through the motions of the last five courses, Cosgrove had called for a double pink gin. It had been only the first.

The Governor and his Lady had left a minute after the fruit was served. Taking Y. Y. Szeto by the arm, Huart had followed, blocking the questions of Kym Marshall, an invited guest but a professional to the end. Within ten minutes every table had been empty. It was the local custom, and sharply observed this night. Today the stock market had met with bloody death and it would be bad form to prolong festivity. But, a man scorned, Lennie the Fifth was of a mind to reject custom outright.

With his parcel wrapped in gold under his arm, he left the Victoria Hotel with the determination of one on a mission, and on Queen's Road, Central came face to face with Thomas and Gladys Buckley as they were about to climb into the back of their Austin Princess.

'And where've you been for the last four days?' Buckley accused.

Cosgrove stopped in his tracks. 'So what's it to you, Button Boy?'

'A great deal. And more so tomorrow.'

'Tomorrow? Tell me, what happens tomorrow?'

Buckley actually threw out his chest. 'Tomorrow, I'll be the taipan and you'll be history, my little man.'

Cosgrove snorted. 'Taipan? You? You don't have Buckley's chance, Buckley. You'd finish fourth in a field of three. Look, a taipan's business is real business. You couldn't cope. Your business is bullshit!'

Buckley moved in front of his spouse as if to shield her from an impending physical assault. 'Cosgrove, my wife . . .'

'Yes, we've met. Good evening, Gladys.' She glared at him, though it was all beyond her, and he decided he was wasting precious time. 'Nighty-night, Button Boy.' He made to go, then turned back. 'D'you know, Tom, there's one thing I've always wanted to do . . .'

'Enrol in a course on good manners, I should hope.'

'That might be one way to make an impression on you. Here's another.' He lifted his foot and brought his heel down hard on Buckley's instep. The accountant let go a bellow and danced about the pavement of Queen's Road on one leg, whilst his wife looked on wide-eyed. 'You bubonic gnome . . . !'

'You've tried stepping on my toes once too often, mister. Now you know how it feels. You can sue me in the morning.' And before Buckley could say anything more, he had scurried off into the night.

Ten minutes later he was speeding skywards to the fifty-second floor in one of the twenty-four Connaught Centre elevators. The security guard saluted, produced a ring of keys and let him into his office. 'Misser Huar' work now too.' The guard knew something was up.

Cosgrove put his finger to his lips. 'No rest for the wicked, you know.'

Visibility was just possible in the light cast under the door adjoining Huart's office. He tiptoed to his desk and turned the lamp on low.

An hour later he was stepping into the Cockpit Bar on the top floor of the Victoria Hotel, where he thought he was not so well known. He swept the place with a discerning eye and settled on a brunette sitting alone at the bar. American divorcee, he adjudged as he crossed to the adjacent stool, where he promptly did something else he had always wanted to do. 'Madam, would you sleep with me for a million dollars?'

She took the cigarette from her mouth, turned slowly and looked him up and down. He sat there with his grin on, congratulating himself on his selection, and heard her ask: 'Do you have a million dollars?' It had come with a Boston accent.

Tucking both thumbs into the lapels of his dinner jacket, he replied with a broad wink: 'Madam, do I look like a pauper?'

'As a matter of fact, you don't. And you sound like fun. You're

British, aren't you? Sure, why not. I always fancied a night with David Niven.'

'Oh, good. Now, would you sleep with me for ten dollars?'

She recoiled. 'What d'you take me for? A hooker?'

'I've just ascertained that, madam. I am now seeking a discount. It's the way we do things in Hong Kong, you know. No disrespect intended.'

She hesitated, then laughed richly. 'Okay, Silver Tongue. Don't just sit there licking your eyebrows – let's go. And just so there's no misunderstanding between us, this night's on me.'

'Madam, you've been reading my mind.'

She took up the room key with the label that read 801 and slipped off the stool. Nodding at the parcel under his arm, she asked: 'What've you got there, Dave? Fish 'n' chips?'

He steered her to the elevator. 'My dressing gown, madam. What else?'

In the elevator he told the operator: 'Room 801, my good man. If I'm to go off tonight, it's to be with one helluva bang!'

'Double occupancy in 801? You're sure it's the *Meen Foot Hau Jaak*?'

The elevator operator nodded. 'The foreign woman will be rich tomorrow.'

The night clerk waited until the other was out of earshot, then dialled the number he had been given not thirty minutes before by the man who had said he was from CID.

27

Midnight.

From his command post high in the sky over Central District, the General Under the Big Tree was shoring up his defences. The second Fire Horse to build or rebuild an Asian business empire was fighting back.

On the floor below, Y. Y. Szeto was talking to New York. It was noon in the Big Apple, and he had been talking to it for over an hour. The West Coast would hear from him next. From four p.m. until the European business day had ended he had called London, Zurich and Frankfurt. Before that, since leaving Huart's office at 8:45 a.m., he had placed continuous calls to Sydney, Tokyo and Singapore. His cultured voice was hoarse. Both ears were afire from the constant press of the receiver. He had resigned himself to getting no sleep tonight.

Huart was likewise determined the day was not to end until he said so. He dialled the number again, counted the rings to ten again, and hung up again. It was no surprise that Cosgrove was not at home. It was too early. But he had so much to explain to his partner.

He took up the telephone once more and made the first of three identical calls. Ten minutes later he replaced the receiver and sat back.

'I apologise,' he had thrice said, 'for the unexpected interruption to my announcement tonight. Could you come to my office at seven sharp. The early hour is necessary for me to tell you which of you I have chosen to be fifth taipan – and which of you I expect to work with him, and with me, through this crisis that has been sprung on us.'

Thomas Buckley had hesitated, as if he was waiting to hear more, before he had confirmed. Huart had thought of calling him in to take over the project that Y. Y. Szeto was engaged upon so that the company secretary could get some sleep, but had decided against it. The top accountant's keen financial brain would be needed fresh the next day. It could prove to be the vital weapon in the battle.

Glynn Bedrix had responded with characteristic equilibrium. 'I shall be there, sir,' he had affirmed. 'Is there anything you require of me tonight? Anything at all?'

'Just one thing, Glynn. I want you to make sure you get a good night's sleep. Clear heads will be the order of the day tomorrow.'

He had called Matthew Zagan last, despite him having made his position quite clear that morning, and it being after midnight. But Zagan had merely muttered: 'Seven o'clock it is.' And hung up.

At 12:15 Huart called the Victoria Hotel and asked for suite 901.

'Suzie? How are you? Is everything alright? Look, I'm a little concerned about you. Why don't you go spend the rest of the night out at Deep Water Bay? I'll send my car to collect you . . . Are you sure then? Are you sure you'll be fine? Yes, I know you're a big girl now . . .'

He chatted with his favourite 'niece' for a quarter of an hour. At 12:30 she went to bed, and he returned to his battle plan.

In his 3,500 square foot townhouse in Mount Kellett Road,

Thomas Buckley replaced his telephone on the hallstand and studied his face in the mirror. He nodded to himself. It was all following the plan he had mapped out twelve years before. He could remember clearly what Gladys' words had been when he had told her they were leaving London.

'Hong Kong? It's in Japan, isn't it, dear?'

'No, dear. It's a crown colony on the south coast of China.'

'China? Why on earth do you want to go out there? You're an associate of Pedder, Dewe and Mottram. In five years you'll be a partner. You're not thinking of giving up eleven years of hard work – to go to China . . ?'

'Hong Kong is quite British, dear. I've researched it a great deal these last few weeks – ever since that first interview with John Huart. I told you about him. A fine man. A major-general in the British Army, he was. And decorated. Cumberland China is a well-established company. Excellent financial growth. Wonderful historical record. And I've been offered the post of chief accountant. That'll be just the beginning . . .'

A gust of frigid February wind had blown down Finchley Road and spattered white flecks against the window of the semi-detached brick house.

' . . . And the weather out there is sub-tropical, dear. It'll be so much better for your arthritis. Much better than in Dorset.'

'Yes, Thomas, but – '

'Dear, in Hong Kong there are Chinese to do the menial work. We British make the decisions. And the profits. I've researched it all. Mr Huart says we will live on top of a mountain called Victoria Peak. There, you see how British it all is? And we'll be much better off financially. We'll be able to send Archie to Eton. Huart went to Eton, you know, but only on a scholarship. At Eton Archie'll be able to lift his sights and seek out decent girls and drop that floozy from the record shop.'

That had done it. Thomas and Gladys Buckley had come to Hong Kong. And tomorrow, John Huart would step down in his protégé's favour. Yes, it was all going exactly according to plan.

He limped along the hall to his bedroom, sat on the bed and inspected again the red-black bruise that throbbed on his instep.

'I'll kill that malodorous midget! No I won't – I'll pay somebody else to do it. When I'm taipan, I'll put out a contract on him. I'll put his face in the dirt as well as his bum. I'll – '

'Thomas, do stop mumbling obscenities and get into bed. I think I'll be a lot happier if Mr Huart picks someone else and we can go back home. Life in Dorset was never so complicated.'

*

'Who was that calling you at this hour, my Glynn?'

Bedrix looked up from the telephone and grinned. It turned his handsome thirty-five year old face into that of a little boy.

He walked out onto the balcony of his Magazine Gap Road bachelor apartment. The lights of Kowloon glittered like a mint of gemstones scattered upon a nocturnal carpet. The neon advertising signs atop the Ocean Terminal danced upon the surface of the harbour. It was the most beautiful man-made sight in the world. It inspired him every time he looked at it.

A taxi churned up the steep gradient of the access road seventeen floors below and the revving of its badly tuned engine broke the spell.

'It was the taipan,' he called over his shoulder. Then he sniffed his Hennessy XXXO and grinned again. 'Or should I say the ex-taipan.'

'And what did he want with my Glynn?'

'He wants to see me at seven.'

'Seven in the morning? Oh, poor boy. No beauty sleep for you tonight.'

Bedrix laughed. 'I couldn't sleep anyway. I really can't believe it. I'm in an impregnable position. I can't lose! Whatever happens – whichever way it goes tomorrow – I can't lose. It's all falling for me. It's making my head spin. There's no way I could sleep tonight.'

'Then we will both stay up together. Here, my Glynn, make your beautiful head spin even more with this. I have prepared it with my very own hands especially for you.'

Bedrix took the joint and grinned again. 'You do look after me, Gino.'

The grandson of Charles Huart could not sleep either. Matthew Zagan was sharing his bed with knowledge that burned through his consciousness like a hot coal. And only part of it was his certainty that Suzanne was in great danger. He had tried to tell her after the banquet, but she had snubbed him. When he had looked for her again, she had gone.

He threw the bedsheet aside. The luminous hands on his watch both pointed to one. He twisted his naked body, switched on the bedside lamp and reached for the telephone, knocking the anonymous brown envelope off the table. He leaned down and picked it up. He checked the seal then, satisfied, tucked the envelope under the pillow and dialled the Victoria.

'Hello?' She was wide awake.

'Suzie? It's Matt.'

Silence. Then: 'What do you want? Didn't you get the message tonight? I thought I made it pretty clear.'

'Suzie, I'm sorry about Saturday night. I said I'd explain it all later and I will. Right now I have to warn you. I've reason to believe you may be in danger from – '

'Danger?' she cut in. 'No danger from you, buster. There's no need for you to explain anything to me. I've got it all worked out. You're a fag, Zagan. You're an honest-to-goodness genuine fag.'

'Suzie!' he protested. 'I'm serious! Look, I'll come over and – '

'No you won't. I'm serious, too. Keep away from me! To think I told you I loved you! To think I once thought you would be the next taipan. Some joke! No way in the world! No way in the world a fag could ever be taipan. Not in this town! So long, fag.'

The line went dead.

As Zagan stared into the mouthpiece the hot coal burst into flame. He took the telephone in both hands and threw it across the room. Then he leapt to his feet, pulled on a tracksuit and swept up his car keys. He was halfway across his lounge when he stopped. He returned to the bedroom, pulled the envelope from under the pillow and zipped it into a pocket of his tracksuit.

He spiralled the MGTF down the driveway and out onto Kennedy Road. In a few minutes he was burning up Stubbs Road. The Michelin radials screamed through a half circuit of the roundabout into Wongneichong Gap Road, and screamed again at every bend along the coast road all the way to Shek O at the eastern extremity of Hong Kong Island.

Running barefoot through the moonbeams cast upon the sand through the cracks in the thick cloud bank, Zagan covered the beach from one end to the other, then back again. It took an hour before the anger, the frustration, the gross insult had been worked out of his system.

'Fag – am – I?' he snorted in time with his breathing. 'Fag – am – I? Who's – a – fag? I'll – show – who's – a – fuck – ing – fag!'

On the fifty-second floor of Connaught Centre a desk lamp burned long. The office of the Altitudinal Taipan was wrapped in the rank stillness of the small hours as he lifted his telephone a final time. With index finger he deliberately, unhurriedly dialled a number for the second time since midnight. He swivelled in his chair and looked out through the circular window in the south wall at the darkened high-rises anchored into the Peak: some

[562]

halfway up in the belt known as Mid Levels, the rest clustered upon the spurs about its summit. In one of those high-rises a telephone was ringing.

'Hello . . ?'

Huart paused a half-second as he anticipated the effect his words were about to have on the man at the other end of the line.

'I'm sorry to get you up. But I feel it's unfair to keep you waiting a second longer. You deserve better treatment than that. I don't want you at seven. I want you at 6:30. Just you. You are my successor.'

The intake of breath was just audible on the line.

'But before you come, I want you to think very hard. I believe we have a traitor amongst us. I fear a fifth columnist will be sitting with us at the Long Table tomorrow. Think very hard. And in the morning, when you see me, give me the bastard's name.'

28

The Filipino band in the Club Takara in a basement off Peking Road, Tsimshatsui packed away its instruments at three a.m. The last hostesses changed out of ankle-length sequined *cheongsams* into street clothes and, their 'escort charge' paid, climbed the carpeted steps on the arms of their men for the night, or what was left of it.

Alain To checked his watch yet again. He touched his pocket to ensure the key to room 903 of the Victoria Hotel had not fallen out somewhere inside the VIP room where he had spent the last two hours in company with the girl from Tai Shan, who followed him to the exit with her heart beating hard against her ribs. She was the pick of the club's extensive harem. Being a member of the family that owned the Takara and most others in Tsimshatsui, Alain To could take his pick at any time, and often did.

On Peking Road the Sikh opened the door of the white Ferrari. As yet, no-one in Cumberland China had seen fit to query how the manager of the Contracting Division could afford such magnificent machinery.

He drove it fast, as he always did. In the light of the high-mast sodium lamps that illuminated the entrance to the Cross-Harbour Tunnel he made a fast re-inspection of the girl's legs, the swell of her bosom, the outline of her face. She felt his eyes using her as she stared ahead.

The digits on the dashboard read 3:17. There was no time left for Alain To to sleep. But, he promised himself, at least he would not be bored.

The clock above the Star Ferry pier on Hong Kong Island struck the hour. The sequence of chimes carried on the night air across Central District. On the steps of the Victoria Hotel, Waldo Wu counted them, then checked his wristwatch. It was five o'clock by that also.

He slipped through the dimly lit, deserted lobby like a wraith. To any casual eye his tuxedo would have made him a first-class guest returning from a night on the town. All the elevators were at the ground floor, doors open, unattended. He chose the middle car and pressed the button of the floor he had been told was the one. The doors closed and met in the middle. The elevator rose, lifting slowly from the lobby.

As Waldo Wu watched the indicators change: 1 ... 2 ... 3 ... 4 ... 5 ... his right hand rested in his coat pocket and his fingers fiddled incessantly with whatever he had concealed there.

In room 801, Lennie the Fifth, employing the very technique that had brought about his downfall, was taking the brunette again, this time from behind, as if it was the last coital milestone of his life.

'Take it ... easy, Dave ... You'll start ... a fire ... that way ...'

Suzanne Huart-Brent had abandoned her losing tussle with jet-lag. She was wide awake. The two telephone calls had not helped. Why was everybody so concerned with her welfare tonight? What was going on? First that weird little old monk gate-crashing Uncle John's speech just as he was about to tell the world who was to succeed him. (Her bet was still on Matt, though it hurt to admit it.) Then had come the telephone calls. It was all so – so really weird!

The room lights were on. She was sitting on the edge of her bed, experiencing the minor thrill of the freedom of nudity. The drapes rippled as a breeze came off the harbour through the balcony door. It was too hot to close it, too cool to switch on the airconditioning.

Suite 901 was a mess. She looked around at it dispassionately.

[564]

She had undressed with abandon. The urge to dance had taken her. Roberta Flack had come on the radio and she had turned up the volume, kicked off her shoes and spun about the room. She had unzipped her evening gown and let it fall to the carpet. There had been nothing more. The 'niece' of the Altitudinal Taipan had attended the centenary banquet in a new Dior gown minus the underwear that might have flawed it.

She took up her travelling clock and peered at it. It was 5:04, and she was still not tired. She groaned and visualised herself turning up at the Long Table in five hours with red-rimmed eyes.

She went to the mirror. Sassoon was great, but short hair made her look too boyish, she decided. It would take months to grow back. Years. She pulled at her hair as if that would make it lengthen. She groaned again.

The knock at the door interrupted her discontent.

'Who is it?'

There was no reply.

She looked around again and saw the gold paper parcel on a chair. She shook out the Shantung silk robe. It fitted perfectly.

She went to the door. 'Who is it?' she repeated.

'Room service, Miss Huart-Brent.'

'Okay.'

She unlatched the door and pulled it open.

The bellboy entered with a tray balanced on his fingertips. Her Bloody Mary stood upon it, red and cool in a long glass. He stumbled as his eyes skimmed involuntarily over the silhouette beneath the thin silk.

She pulled the garment tightly about herself and smiled. 'Twenty-four hour room service is a godsend for people with jet-lag,' she remarked conversationally.

'Yes, miss. Thank you, miss.'

He accepted the tip and let himself out, catching a last glimpse of her as she lifted the glass to her lips. He took the first elevator down to the kitchen. He could not wait to tell them all about it.

The middle car was on its way up from the lobby.

Waldo Wu stepped out of the elevator into the dark, still corridor and stood motionless, his right hand at rest in his coat pocket.

He listened in all directions for a full minute.

Outside, from inside a bamboo coop somewhere above the Ladder Streets, a cock crowed.

There were arrows on the wall. Rooms numbered from 01 to 20 were to the right. Waldo Wu set off silently in that direction.

[565]

29

Dawn.

It was the inevitable coming of the dreaded day. It painted a grey upon the night, which had hovered above the city-country that was Hong Kong like a mantle of potential energy. The ozone of the South China coast had been rendered vapid. And, with the Hang Seng Index having retreated a third from its record peak in just two weeks and a day, that other and more novel indigenous smell had been killed off once and for all.

That smell of Mammon.

In harmony with the ambience, the body in the Shantung silk robe fell quietly from a balcony of the Victoria Hotel. It hit Queen's Road, Central head first and bounced once, coming to rest face down. It lay unnoticed in the gloom for a full minute, spread half on the pavement, half on the bitumen, its limbs thrust out like the points of some gruesome compass. The gutter that bisected it ran with its red blood. One by one, a crowd gathered: coolies, newspaper vendors, watchmen, street sleepers in putrid black rags. They gawked at the corpse, their normally eliptical eyes quite circular.

Two blocks east, Matthew Zagan sat at the wheel of his MGTF waiting on the dilatory red light in front of the Hilton. He was more than merely impatient. He was apprehensive. There had been no answer from her room.

On the bucket seat beside him sat the plain brown envelope.

The sirens came from the right, the banshee wail of dire emergency rupturing the early morning sterility of Central District. An ambulance and a police landrover rocketed out of Queensway. And Zagan went cold. A sixth sense told him he was already too late as he accelerated through the red light, spun around the curved frontage of the Hilton and gave chase on Queen's Road past the Big Banks, past the golden hoardings painted with NEW CUMBERLAND HOUSE, across the Ice House Street intersection. The sirens ended at the bizarre crowd outside the Victoria. He ran the MGTF into the kerb and leapt out.

'Let me through!'

The knot of people unravelled at the sound of his voice and he was able to look down at the thing at their feet. But his eyes refused to focus. His senses would not function. Nothing about the corpse would register, except – gradually, awfully – two things just as the red blanket was drawn completely over it: the round gold logo in the centre of its back, and the short blonde hair spattered with blood and matter.

Something made him look up. And he saw directly above, peering over a balcony that was surely on the ninth floor, a face he recognised. The eyes intersected with his for an instant, then the face was withdrawn.

It provided the final, terrible confirmation.

'Oh no, no, no, no! Suzie!'

It was then that Matthew Zagan knew, despite everything that rendered it pathologically impossible, despite all that had driven him to scour the reality of it from him, he had loved Suzanne Huart-Brent.

The first light through the gap in the drapes of room 903 outlined the naked shapes upon the bed.

Alain To pushed his arms straight, arched his spine, and threw back his head. In this position he waited while his mounting climax ebbed. After a minute of immobility, still raised over the girl from Tai Shan, he resumed steady piston-like thrusts. She lay motionless, her arms and legs thrown out. But though she appeared inert, the secret muscles in contact with him were working lasciviously: gripping, releasing ... gripping, releasing ... Her long hair was spread over the pillow, her eyelids were pressed shut, her goldfish lips were pursed. But the wrinkles at the corners of her eyes betrayed the strain and tension that had been her lot for the past two hours.

Alain To's wristwatch bleeped. He gathered himself and thrust deeply. His whole body quivered. The hot flow over her innards signalled the end at last, and she groaned in a professional facsimile of ecstasy.

He withdrew from her and sat with his back turned. She waited, alert and fearful, for he could destroy her future with a single criticism.

'You have had too many men lately, I think.'

She gasped and fled to the bathroom, her hand at her mouth, teeth biting through the flesh. The perspiration on her satin skin glistened as she bisected the strips of dawn light.

He wiped himself with the bedsheet, smiling to himself. He had been told correctly. The girl from Tai Shan had certainly been a special screw.

He slipped on the towelling bathrobe and took the key from its pocket. At the door that connected with 901, he listened. He could hear nothing. Suzanne Huart-Brent was sleeping soundly.

Ho! He smiled again. Soon she would be sleeping like the dead.

He inserted the key noiselessly into the lock, and nudged the door open, as he had practised the afternoon before. 901 was in gloom, its drapes drawn. His fingers closed on the chloroform soaked cloth in the other pocket. He moved to the bed with stealth. And reached out.

The rumpled sheet was cold to his touch.

It took ten seconds for him to accept that the bed was empty. The alarm that welled in him as those seconds ticked by exploded into panic. His head swivelled to the bathroom door. It was ajar, a telltale black void beyond. He went about throwing open wardrobes and drawers. All were full of the garments, lingerie and cosmetics of a rich young American woman. The gilt-edged monogram on a Gucci handbag read: 'S H-B'.

'Aiiiiyahhh!' he cursed. With whom had she spent the night?

He sat on the bed – where she had slept – with his head in his hands. He had failed. His self-contrived master-stroke had misfired!

The wail of twin sirens grew rapidly louder and stopped directly below.

He went to the drapes and parted them. The door was open, the balcony empty. He peered over the railing at the circle of people on the Queen's Road pavement nine storeys below. He focused on the object in its centre. He saw the robe and the Cumberland China motif. He picked out the speckled blonde hair. A white face looked up at him. It bore the grief-stricken features of Matthew Zagan. He pulled his head back fast.

Zagan! *Gaw-gaw chow gau!* That foul-smelling reproductive organ!

With his hand over the knob of the connecting door he stopped to listen to the cogs of his brain as they meshed. He understood! Great-uncle had invoked a plan more brutal, more ruthless by far than the one he himself had concocted. It had been decided that not only would the woman with the hair of white jade be absent from the Long Table this morning, she was never to sit at it again! How had he given himself away? Great-uncle had known what was in his heart. *Aiiiyahhh!* The man was not mortal!

Zagan had seen him! The family would have to deal with that one, too.

Using the cloth, he wiped all the surfaces he could remember touching, then slipped into 903 and locked the door. He lay on his back on the bed as his breathing eased and his pulse slowed. But his thoughts returned to the woman he had most desired and now would never have. A familiar fire had him looking down at the erection rising out of his robe like a miniature cobra preparing to strike.

The girl came out of the bathroom, a towel wrapped about her. She looked at him, smiled in relief at her second chance and dropped the towel. She climbed onto the bed, extended experienced fingers, bent her head. And it was not long before Alain To was climaxing a second time with the dawn of the fifty-third day of the Year of the Water Ox.

The Kompo bodyguards wore dark suits and Paris ties. Their boyish faces belied the ruthlessness for which they were employed. But for their eyes that darted amongst the flora and fauna, they could have been lifesize bookends. They were a legacy of pre-1949 Shanghai that Tu Chien would dare not tempt fate by forgoing.

They had looked out for their *dai lo baan* through his *tai chi chuen*. Now he was resting on a wrought-iron bench and inspecting Government House, a hybrid of colonial and oriental architecture from alterations made during the Japanese occupation. Ribbed tiles and pagoda style towers blended with white stucco walls, square windows and Roman arches. Nestling in languid grandeur in the March dawn, it epitomised the meeting of east and west. But to Tu Chien it was just another building.

He saw the Union Jack being raised on one tower. The flag hung limply. Above it a hawk circled, seeking prey amongst the greenery. This meant much more to him. It was a double omen, and a light came to his eyes.

The viceregal slumber of the Tall Big Man from Scotland had surely been rent by nightmares. Last night all foreign devil heads would have tossed on stone pillows. And before the end of this day their red faces would be redder from the furnace blast of the wind of change. Today the Born Again *Hong* would belong to him. Tomorrow Hong Kong would be different.

He looked down upon it: upstart place of concrete, loose change, itinerant foreigners and second-class sawn-off Cantonese, none of whom knew who or what really controlled it all. It was not the Governor, nor the Big Banks, nor the Born Again *Hong*, Jardines, Butterfield and Swire. Nor even Peking. None of them had caused the Hang Seng Index to fall like a demented Tangar fisherwoman cast from the top of the Peak. None of them had orchestrated the suicidal sell-off that had converted the floors of the exchanges into arenas of fiscal death. None of them.

It had been he. And he alone.

And none of them knew who he was. His appearance before them last night had been brief. It had been a pleasure not to be delegated. Today, none of them knew of the family called Tu from Bubbling Well Road, Shanghai.

But that was about to change.

The sun sent its maiden rays over the South China Sea to stain the cloud above North Point and Hong Kong was revealed in soft focus. The vertical concrete of Central District poked through its nocturnal coverlet. Then Kowloon emerged by phases, doused in a balmy mixture of seasonal haze and residual pollution from the factories. Patches of fog rested upon the surface of the harbour like smudges on a seascape.

Tu Chien watched the land materialise before him and felt sad. Hoi-nam was not at his side to see it with him. The memories came rushing back.

Did Chiang Kai-shek remember? At the great age of eighty-five, no man, not even the president of a country had a right to. Thirty-three years is enough. Twelve thousand days! But then, he rationalised to himself, are not great armies maintained for years to be used on a single day?

He saw his prize emerge. Connaught Centre. It stood there, its circular windows like polka dots in the half light. There was the teak, leather, crystal lair of the giant – the Double Murderer.

'Sze . . . Yiu . . . Yu . . . Gu!'

The curse reinforced, it was time for the day to begin. Tu Chien pushed himself from the bench and the Kompo men came to attention. He waited for his bones to settle in their joints, then led the climb to Robinson Road and the black Rolls-Royce Silver Wraith with the licence number showing the digits 118.

The pain soared from his hip, worse at each step.

A wail of sirens rose from Central District, grew louder, then stopped abruptly somewhere below. Tu Chien gave no outward sign that it meant anything, but it did. It told him the last obstacle had been removed.

The seventy-seven inches of the Altitudinal Taipan were standing at the circular window, amplified by a parade ground erectness that he maintained despite the sixty-six years which were leaning on him this morning. Like thousands of others, he had not slept. Nevertheless, his dark blue hand-tailored suit displayed not a crease, his maroon tie was knotted with precision, and each cuff of his white 'Golden Century' business shirt protruded evenly.

Behind him the Long Table stretched into darkness. In a few hours it would be a corporate killing field, twenty-eight feet by six feet.

Through the binoculars he watched the black Rolls-Royce and the tailing Mercedes with its Kompo cargo accelerate east on Robinson Road, skirt the roundabout atop Garden Road and disappear behind Estoril Court.

And he muttered: 'Keep your fucking hands off my company . . . sir.'

A singular shaft of sunlight split the cloud above Wongneichong Gap and splashed upon the crown of Connaught Centre. The window glass was tinted, but Huart still had to squint as he looked down at the concrete and steel phalanxes of Central District, rising out of shadow.

'Good morning, Hong Kong,' he greeted it all. 'You magnificent harlot.'

With the binoculars he studied the lions of the Big Banks. The visage on the stone faces before the Bank of China was as ironic as it was fierce, being directed unpatriotically north – the direction he would be taking that afternoon. There, he had long ago decided, was the essence of Hong Kong: capitalist bronze side-by-side with communist stone, each ostensibly ignoring the other in their competing symbolism.

He saw the sun glint from the tip of the multi-storey gantry crane that pinpointed the site of New Cumberland House. With its caissons only just poured, the 'Finest Tower in Asia', was already fully let. He savoured the rush of pride, then turned away and looked up into the founder's two dimensional eyes. He wondered how the first taipan would have prepared for today's battle, a century and a day from the time he had fought alone, with a second-hand field gun and nothing but nerve and good timing for ammunition, to win the contract that had started everything.

Turning to his cousin's portrait, he said: 'It's for certain we're to face a determined attack, Andrew. But we have our defences well manned. And Suzie is here to support us. Don't worry, we'll carry the day.'

He glanced at the vacant panel on the east wall. It had rendered the boardroom asymetric, defied the laws of *fung shui* and tempted fate for fifteen years. But for only a few hours more, he assured himself.

The Rococo long-case clock struck 6:30. He went into his

office, stood by his desk and waited with his eyes lowered, tracing the grain until the outer door opened.

He did not look up as he demanded: 'It's true then? Do we have a fifth columnist in our ranks or don't we?'

The silence forced him to lift his head. He frowned at the young, handsome face that was strangely ashen, and did not notice immediately that his successor was standing with one hand hidden behind his back.

'It's true.'

Huart's eyes flashed with a mixture of apprehension and grit. 'Tell me, then! Who is it? Give me the bastard's name!'

The hand came slowly into view. Huart's eyes narrowed when he saw the envelope. He tore at it with fingers numbed by budding alarm, and flicked open the hand-written note, instantly recognising the looping script. He read it through once at speed, then again in horrified disbelief.

His hands flew to his head. His fingers raked backwards through his hair in a spontaneous reaction to disaster which he had not been able to eradicate in an environment that considered such gestures a weakness.

'Whyyyy . . !?' The voice of power was reduced to an anguished croak.

The years tumbled through a fissure in his memory as if it was the last moment of his life. He looked out and down at Central District. But he did not see it. He looked up to the looming backdrop of the Peak framed against the lightening sky. But neither did he see that. He opened his mouth. But no words came.

It was then, from out of the past, that John Stanford Huart remembered the legend of the Fire Horse. His great frame shuddered. Was the worst of it actually coming true?

Book V

BATTLE OF THE LONG TABLE

Hong Kong, Central District: 27 March 1973

1

After he had read the note into the mouthpiece twice and hung up, Huart asked: 'Where did you find it?'

Glynn Bedrix spread his hands apologetically. 'It was on Imelda's desk. There was something about it. I couldn't stop myself...'

Huart shook his head sadly. 'We must keep it strictly between the two of us. If the news should get out that the deputy chairman has sold his entire holding in Cumberland China and in Charlemagne Enterprises...' The big face was like grey stone. 'And...'

Bedrix nodded.

Heaving a sigh, Huart looked up to heaven. He blamed himself for committing the sin of taking too much for granted. Then he mustered a weary smile. It signalled that the intial tidal wave blown up by the terrible news had been breached, that a path had been espied leading out of the mire.

He went to his desk and placed his hand upon the stack of telexes. They were *de facto* proxies pledging support for him. They were the fruit of Y. Y. Szeto's twenty-four hour telephone marathon, and had come in through the night from international banks, investment houses, superannuation funds, insurance companies, building societies, treasuries...

'If it's Tu Chien he's sold to – and it has to be – that's 30.4 per cent of the company gone. If the snake has acquired more than 19.6 per cent from the public – we're finished. We shall have lost the company.'

Could he have that much? The question peeled away another layer of his sang-froid. No, it would be impossible! Wouldn't it?

'It's a stroke of luck that Suzanne's in town, John,' Bedrix reminded him. 'All the directors and the H and K will back you. And there's the half per cent in trust. Altogether that's fourteen per cent. Plus your 30.6 per cent via Charlemagne Enterprises... What do the proxies total?'

[575]

'Just over five.'

'Not quite fifty per cent.' Bedrix grimaced. 'We need one more percent to be certain of absolute control.'

Huart discussed the day ahead with the man he had chosen to succeed him until the pendulum clock began to chime seven o'clock and a knock came at the outer door.

'Enter!'

The smile on Thomas Buckley's face preceded him, broadcasting his conviction that this was the last time he was crossing this threshold as a mere guest. When he saw Bedrix already there, he stopped in his tracks. His face fell as realisation of the truth hit him between the eyes. But his recovery was fast and he stripped most of the outrage from his face and stored it for later use.

The tan seemed bleached from Matthew Zagan's skin. He stood like a zombie, as if his heart had been amputated without the aid of anaesthetic. Then he forced a smile. 'Good morning, Glynn. It appears that congratulations are in order. It also looks as though your first day as taipan is going to be the hardest.'

'That's exceedingly sporting of you, Zagan,' Bedrix acknowledged warily.

What an unusual young man, Huart was thinking. First he threatens me with resignation if I select somebody over him, then he acts the perfect loser when I do just that. His eyes were drawn again to the portrait of Charles Huart and he frowned in fleeting perplexity. It's uncanny, he told himself. The resemblance is absolutely uncanny.

'I know you will both give Glynn your fullest support.' Was he still taking too much for granted? 'As, of course, shall I. And our first chance to do just that will take place next door in about three hours.'

There was another knock at the door and a tired looking Y. Y. Szeto came in with a file in his hand. He whispered hoarsely: 'Sir, here is Mr Lee Wing-tak's proxy. He was just in my office to chop it.'

'Is he still there? I'll go out and thank him.'

'He's gone looking for Yeok-hon who seems to have lost himself in one of the elevators.' When Huart smiled knowingly, he held out a telex copy. 'And this just came in. Peking gave its sanction late last night.'

Huart read it at a glance. 'Grand work, Mr Szeto.' He passed the telex to Bedrix. 'You didn't know that China has owned half a million shares in our company ever since we went public, did you? A most discreet man is Johnson Sze. It's even nicer to know they're supporting me – and you, Glynn – today. That gives us fifty per cent.'

'But it's only just fifty percent,' Bedrix pointed out. 'It's too dicey. We need another half a million shares to be quite certain of our victory before we go into that meeting at ten.'

With a glance at Buckley, Zagan said: 'One look at the shareholder's roll will show that *The Register* Newspaper Limited hold enough stock to more than cover that.'

The Director of Finance and Administration looked as if he wished he was able to dispute it.

Huart asked: 'Do we have *The Register*'s support?'

Zagan's nod was calculated. 'Confirmation will be on telex by ten.'

'Thank you, Matthew,' Huart breathed. 'You have saved the day.'

2

There was room for two chairs at the head of the Long Table. One minute before ten, Huart took the one on the left, Bedrix the other. They sat side-by-side, like father and son, and waited in tight-lipped silence.

The twenty-eight foot slab of pinewood was fully employed. Nine chairs were arranged along each side: six to the head – the Cumberland China end, and three to the foot – where the challengers were to sit. Between the camps was a 'no man's land' a yard wide.

The two chairs to Bedrix's right were empty. Cosgrove's habitual lateness explained the first, but the non-appearance of Suzanne Huart-Brent was the subject of muffled conjecture. Huart glanced at the clock, then the door in the east wall. What was keeping Suzie and her 5.5 per cent?

Somehow Zagan had managed to purge her from his mind. He had confided in no-one, deciding that release too soon of such dire news could do no good.

Tu Chien waited five full minutes to show his disrespect, then led his execution squad through the reception area past the security guard, who would have drawn his pistol had he not been forewarned, and into the boardroom. His team of six followed in trail: his son, his nephews, his great-nephew – who engendered individual recognition – and Tu Chien's financial and legal advisers. They took their seats around the foot of the table, the patriarch in its centre where Y. Y. Szeto usually sat.

In the electric hush, each face in the crescent of twelve at the Cumberland China end wore its own expression: Huart's was granitic, Bedrix's wooden, Zagan's neutral. Bitterness had resurfaced on Buckley, supplemented by an obvious resolve. Vail seemed disoriented. Ezuelo looked lost. Alexander Chiu wore a mask of inscrutability made in Shanghai. Gene Browne looked as if he had forgone sleep for five days, which he had. The brows of the two H and K directors were furrowed, whilst the mien of Y. Y. Szeto and of Raymond Clinton O'Young was 'professional'.

From the corner, the ticking of the Rococo clock rapped upon the walls.

'I waste no further time!' Tu Chien called twenty-eight feet to Huart, ignoring the pretender at the giant's side. 'I will have you out of here within the hour!' His financial man pulled a bundle of papers bound with cloth tape from a briefcase and threw it on the table. The top document was a share certificate imprinted with a round gold logo. 'They are all genuine, and represent but a sample of the shares I control. We will produce the rest for re-registration in due course. You can believe me when I say that I have possession of 17.85 per cent of the shares you so kindly issued to the public. I thank you for that.' He sent his eyes to the third chair to Huart's left. The occupant began visibly to crumble. His fingers shook so much that the tar guard fell from between them. 'I also have half a million shares in the name of Mr Daniel Vail . . .'

Huart pivoted to his left, a look of speechless murder on his face. The ex-Director of Properties groaned as he slumped in his chair.

' . . . and another ten million shares in the name of Mr Leonard Cosgrove. Is that gentleman here to confirm the sale?'

Huart and Bedrix stared dead ahead. Zagan studied the grain in the Long Table. Every other eye darted to the first vacant chair, and every other mouth fell open. Tu Chien observed it all in amusement.

'Mr Cosgrove has a penchant for unpunctuality,' Huart said evenly. 'But his confirmation is unnecessary at this time. Is that all you have?'

'By no means.' Tu Chien took a document from his gown. 'This is a Deed of Sale of forty per cent of the stock of a company

[578]

called Charlemagne Enterprises. I believe it owns fifty-one per cent of *Gum Bak Leen*. The seller is, once again, Mr Cosgrove. The purchaser is my own company. The deed has been properly witnessed and notarised. It is quite legal.'

This time a chorus of gasps came from either side of the head of the Long Table. Tu Chien was pleased with their quality and their quantity.

'Is that all?' repeated Huart.

Tu Chien frowned. 'All? That is 48.75 per cent of your company!'

'It's not half. You don't have control.' Huart's tone remained even.

'I do – if you cannot better it. Right now!'

Huart looked at the two H and K directors. 'Do I have the bank's vote?'

Bairstow said: 'Our five per cent is right behind you, sir.'

Huart looked next at his company secretary. 'Mr Szeto?'

'We have proxies totalling 7.15 per cent, and the trustee automatically votes his half per cent with the chair.'

'Thank you, Mr Szeto. And I vote my 30.6 per cent through Charlemagne Enterprises in accordance with the constitution.'

He glanced to the second empty chair, then again to the door and fought down the urge to check the clock. Where in God's name was she? He recalled her resistance to his suggestion that she spend the night at Deep Water Bay. Had they actually got to her? He suddenly felt cold.

Zagan appeared lifeless. But inside his head a war was being waged. He would not let her control him dead when he had resisted her alive!

The Tu financial man was passing around his calculator. It produced half a dozen smiles around the foot of the table.

'43.25 per cent!' Tu Chien cried in triumph. 'The majority is mine by 5.5 per cent! I claim ownership of *Gum Bak Leen!* You cannot deny me . . . !'

Huart sat like a hunk of volcanic rock that was shattering from within. He willed the pieces to hold together a while longer, and threw his gaze in a last desperate hope towards the door.

It opened.

'Good morning everybody! I see you've gone and started without me.'

Nineteen heads swivelled to the unorthodox figure standing just into the boardroom. The fluorescent light shone white upon the tousled hair.

Unobtrusive in the crowd that thronged the lobby of Connaught Centre, Lee Yeok-hon waited impatiently for his chance. He had seen the old man in the long-gown who walked with the black stick enter the last of the bank of elevators that served the highest floors. He had watched the six men follow him like oxen, then gather around him as the aluminium-clad doors closed together in the middle.

Yeok-hon saw the security guard coming towards him, and he dived around a corner. After a minute the guard went back to his post and the boy circled back, just as the doors of another elevator opened and a dozen passengers discharged into the lobby.

He scurried in amongst the legs, burrowed his way to a corner and squatted like a wary rabbit. The doors closed and he was lifted up the core of the building, past the seventh floor where once again the Kam Ngan Stock Exchange was in uproar as it was inundated with 'sell' orders.

Nobody had pressed '52'. The highest button illuminated was '49', so he followed a man out on that floor to find himself in an alien world of corridors and glass doors through which pretty receptionists looked out at him and frowned.

Recognising the ideograms for 'exit', he put his shoulder to a wooden fire door and pushed with all his infant strength. It swung away from him and he squeezed around it, to be confronted by a second door which he had to pull open. He ran up several flights of stairs, gulping in the air that was laden with the smell of fresh concrete, until he saw '52' painted on the wall. He pushed through another fire door, and rested a while in the space between it and what he knew had to be the last door. He pulled it open enough to get his head around. Across a marble foyer he saw a glass wall upon which was the round gold symbol that he knew. Out loud he read the three ideograms fixed vertically beneath it in bronze that had been buffed to a gleam: 'Gum Bak Leen.'

Then he saw the security guard. And the black butt protruding from the holster on the man's hip. It presented an obstacle for which Lee Yeok-hon, seven years of age less ten days, had no immediate solution.

Huart exhaled long and hard in abject relief.

Tu Chien's usually dull oriental eyes were glistening marbles. He turned on his great-nephew and saw his own shock reflected there. 'I gave to you the task of –' Off balance, he had used Shanghai dialect.

'But I saw . . . I saw . . .' Alain To gasped. 'I thought you –'

Zagan's jaw fell to the table and his heart leapt into his mouth. Then an automatic muscle spasm clamped a vice on his emotions.

Nineteen pairs of male eyes fixed on the figure in the white knee-length fur coat and high heels. As Suzanne Huart-Brent placed her hands upon her hips, the front of the coat opened.

There came a subdued yet stereophonic gasp.

In the hallowed boardroom in the sky, before the altarstone of the Born Again *Hong*, she stood there in a tiger-skin bikini framed in white fur. She tracked with her deep brown eyes the twin rows of faces that admired her and, very slowly, she smiled.

'Please carry on. I apologise for my unconventional dress. I couldn't sleep. It took your advice, Uncle John, and went for a swim at Deep Water Bay. It was lovely. I fell asleep on the sand. Now, which is my chair?'

Huart indicated with his right hand. 'I suggest you take it quickly, Suzie, before we forget what we're here for.'

She met Zagan's eyes and saw the change there. She took the seat beside him, drawing the coat across her legs. He slipped his hand beneath it and squeezed the inside of her thigh. She did not resist.

'I'm – no – fag!' he issued out of the corner of his mouth.

'Prove it then,' she whispered. She looked at Glynn Bedrix occupying the seat of the fifth taipan and added: 'And do it damn quick.'

Huart's face had reconstructed itself into the professional mask he wore when in control. 'How do you pledge your shares, Suzie? To them – ?' He nodded to the foot of the table. 'Or to me? If you vote against me, the family loses the company. And if you vote with me, then they – ' Another nod. ' – and I and my supporters hold exactly equal stock. I repeat: exactly equal. It will then be up to the directors.'

She drew a pack of Benson and Hedges out of her coat. Zagan's lighter flared. She inhaled slowly.

Tu Chien's brain was racing as he recalculated the odds.

'Blood is thicker than "Tiger Balm", Uncle John.'

'Thank you, Suzie.'

It was a draw. 48.75 per cent each.

Now it was the turn of the men Huart had hand-picked, had trained, had worked with closely for more than a decade, had made rich. Now they had their chance to make a small repayment by seeing him through.

He sat back and felt the tension flow gloriously from him.

*

Behind the fire door across the foyer of the lift lobby on the fifty-second floor, Lee Yeok-hon waited, his resolve burning hot in his little boy's brain. His seventh birthday was only ten days away and he was to have his very first party. The *Dai Yee Ngau* had promised to come and to bring him a special present.

Absolutely nobody was permitted to make his godfather lose face in public. It was the duty of a godson to do something about it. How could he ever grow into a man if he did not take retribution? The Little Dragon would be proud of him. The Little Dragon would agree with his plan.

But Yeok-hon had never killed a real live bad man before. He had killed a million in his games and in his dreams. He wondered what it would feel like. He looked at the butt in the security guard's holster, and a great disdain filled his small lungs. The Little Dragon did not need a gun to kill his enemies. And neither did Lee Yeok-hon.

Thomas Buckley was first to announce his betrayal. He did so with an unforgiving leer. 'I pledge my stock to Great Horse Enterprises.'

Huart was thunderstruck. Before he could give voice, he was hit again.

'So do I,' declared Antonio Ezuelo.

A Texan fist smashed down upon the Long Table. 'Goddamn varmints!' Gene Browne swore hard. 'You've got hairs all over the goddamn lot o' you!'

Even the ghost of Charles Huart cringed.

The Director of Electronics drilled the traitors with bloodshot eyes. 'I support John Huart – come hell or high water!'

Huart looked to Alexander Chiu, and felt his breathing falter. Tu Chien had to have the power over that one. The Born Again *Hong* was lost.

But the Director of Textiles and Garments said softly: 'I also pledge my support for John Huart. Without hesitation. Without doubt.'

Thinking he had dreamt it, Huart stared dumbly at Alex Chiu until the man turned to him with a look a loyal student reserves for his teacher. Only then did he accept that he had been thrown a reprieve.

It was a draw again. 49.75 per cent each.

Only Glynn Bedrix was left to vote. The fifth taipan had the power of decision over the company that was already his.

Huart relaxed in his chair again: numbed, shaken.

[582]

Saved.

He looked sideways at Bedrix and the famous avuncular smile came inevitably to his big face. But his successor did not look back at him as he sat with his left arm extended, his fingertips tapping the pinewood, his red jade cufflinks shining in the fluorescent light. He was looking down the Long Table. He was looking at the death in Tu Chien's eyes.

The tapping grew louder.

Zagan's eyes traced the grain patterns as he waited.

Then Alain To made up for flunking his test. He pulled the switch on Bedrix. It was done quickly, but the pretender saw it. And the skin on his face drained of colour as if an internal sluice had been opened.

'I . . .' he began. 'I pledge my . . .'

He stopped again, and looked about the row of faces in confusion.

'Come on, Neil Armstrong,' Suzanne urged. 'Out with it!'

From the foot of the table, Alain To repeated the gesture. Again it had been quick. And silent. But to Glynn Bedrix it had been deafening, even though it had been merely an effeminate flick of the wrist.

The fifth taipan looked as if his gut was gripped by amoebic dysentery.

'I pledge my stock in Cumberland China to – '

The reception area that served the executive offices of Cumberland China was getting crowded. First the Eurasian woman had arrived to take a seat on the leather sofa. She had sat unmoving, her face stern, her knees together, her handbag perched upon them. She had looked repeatedly at her wristwatch, and when the receptionist had asked if she desired a cup of tea or coffee, she had shaken her head. It had seemed that she was too nervous, too intense, to risk a spoken word.

Then the police had come. There had been three of them: a burly European *bong baan* in civilian clothes, a uniformed sergeant and a constable. The inspector had introduced himself to the Eurasian woman, who had nodded her head. Then they had stood together in a group. And waited.

They were still waiting.

From across the lift lobby Lee Yeok-hon, peering around the fire door, had seen it all. He, too, continued to wait, and to watch. He knew that his task had been made more difficult. But he was no less determined.

*

' – to Great . . . to Great Horse Enterprises and . . . and the Tu family.'

Silence.

In it, Zagan could hear the fibres of the Long Table pulling asunder.

'What . . . What was that you said, Glynn?' Huart's voice was nothing more than a stunned whisper. 'I thought . . . I thought you said . . . I think that you're a little mixed up – '

Bedrix snarled: 'I said I pledge my shares to Great Horse Enterprises and the Tu family. That's clear enough, isn't it?'

Each word had driven a shaft an inch deeper under Huart's ribcage. He stiffened as he felt a crack opening along his core. His breath was rammed from his lungs. Then, like a sudden wind, it was sucked back. His chest heaved. He rose to his feet. Gripping the edge of the table for support, he blanketed the grinning faces at the foot with a look of thunder. His mouth opened to cry out, but his brain was not ready. It was still searching for the words.

Bedrix lowered his head and willed the ordeal to end, and the new life to begin for him. He knew he should hate himself, but he did not. Confronted with a choice between personal scandal – prison, even – and rank betrayal, he had with little compunction opted for the latter. That his choice would cost him nothing would soon be confirmed, he rationalised.

Suzanne's eyes glistened with angry tears as she looked at him. She drew breath to curse the Judas as she had never cursed a man before. But a restraining hand on her knee aborted her outburst.

Zagan lifted his head to look at her with a strange surety in his eyes.

Huart stood there, his eyes burning with a dull flame, his chest heaving. He was a beaten man. He was a destroyed man.

He was a deposed taipan!

He looked down the twenty-eight feet which now seemed like twenty-eight miles. He looked at the wizened old man in the long-gown who had nurtured thirty-three years of hatred and had released it all today. He looked at the man who had taken the Born Again *Hong* from him.

Tu Chien also rose, leaning on his walking stick. His face was the face of a general who has fought a protracted campaign and won through. 'It appears, Mr John Huart, that 50.25 per cent of *Gum Bak Leen* stock is now committed to me. Therefore it follows that we are standing at the wrong ends of this table.' He looked deliberately at Bedrix, then at Buckley, and said: 'And now I will choose *my* taipan.' He placed his hand on his great-nephew's shoulder. 'Wai-kit! Stand up! Let them see you!'

A chair tumbled to the floor. Buckley was on his feet, his arm jabbing, his finger pointing accusingly. 'But you promised me! You said I'd be taipan if I voted my stock with you! You double crossing – '

Bedrix was just behind him. 'Me! You said it would be me!'

Tu Chien's laugh sliced through the protesting cries like a chopper through fresh liver. 'You? Both of you? Either of you? How could any one of you be a taipan? An incompetent bighead? A homosexual?'

It was the moment Glynn Bedrix had been dreading for years. It reared up in front of him like the Creature from the Black Lagoon. It fell upon him and began to eat him whole. He whimpered and covered his face with his hands. He felt every single eye upon him and he withered under their weight. He did not consider simply denying the accusation for a moment. That would have done no good. In any case, he had pronounced the maximum sentence upon himself long ago.

'Do either of you want to change your vote?' Tu Chien was merciless. 'Go on! Both of you are finished in Hong Kong, whichever way you go now.'

Huart's body was shuddering as if it was a boiler about to burst. 'In God's name, what is this?' he roared like a wounded lion. 'Am I in a boardroom or a psychiatric ward? Am I amongst sane men or spoiled brats of children? Can I trust no-one? Of my board of directors – to whom I gave a piece of my company only to have it turned against me – have I but two men with me? Two? God bless them . . . !'

And there the last taipan to bear the name of Huart froze rigid as the curse reared out of memory to pinion him. And as the legend of the Fire Horse came back to him. He felt the double chill go through him like an Arctic winter. No! Not again! His father. His mother. His wife and sons. Then Andrew. And now. Now he had lost his *hong*: the family heritage that had been entrusted to him. He had lost Everything!

And by his own hand!

But he was damned if he was going down alone! With his fists clenched, he moved around the head of the table. Tu Chien made a signal, but Errol Tu's hand was already inside his jacket.

'Don't do it!'

The voice had been clear and strong. Huart stopped in his tracks.

'Don't do it!' Zagan repeated. 'You are not beaten yet.'

The boardroom fell into a new, expectant silence as all eyes went to the enigmatic young man who had thus far participated not at all.

Tu Chien laughed a contemptuous, confident laugh. 'And who can you be to so grandly to make so ridiculous an announcement?'

Turning his head in deliberate slow motion, Zagan proceeded to stare the patriarch down. In so doing, he delivered into the room an authority that gradually, thoroughly, neutralised everything. By some innate force he took the stage and swept it of all opposition.

'Who am I? Apart from myself, there is only one person alive who knows who I really am.' He flicked his eyes to the portrait of Charles Huart. 'And one dead.'

Huart looked up at the founder, and a dawn that had been a long time coming began to break. 'You mean . . . ?'

Zagan nodded. 'Charles Huart was my grandfather.'

He turned on his heel and walked from the room, returning immediately with his hand under the elbow of a well-dressed Eurasian woman, whose expression was stern. He brought her to the head of the Long Table.

'This is my mother: Elizabeth Jane Zagan. Her maiden name was Huart. As is yours. As was his – ' He nodded to the portrait. 'Her father.'

Huart had recognised her at once. She had changed little since that midsummer evening under the banyan at the foot of Battery Path. Indeed he had failed to find Charles Huart's offspring – they had found him!

But it was too late.

Matthew Zagan almost smiled as he read Huart's mind. He took a brown envelope from the inside pocket of his coat, extracted two documents and proffered one. Huart took it with a look of thorough mystification.

'That is the original of a Deed of Sale – exactly like the one we saw earlier – of Lennie Cosgrove's forty per cent holding in Charlemagne Enterprises. In it I am the purchaser. The date and time – witnessed and notarised by a Queen's Council, you will see – is in advance of the deed shown to us earlier – which is, consequently, invalid.'

With measured step, he walked the length of the Long Table. All eyes followed him. He handed Tu Chien the second document, a photostat copy. The patriarch nodded to the legal man, who took it tentatively.

'Mr Cosgrove did not own the shares he transferred to you, Mr

[586]

Tu, because he had already sold them to me. For one Hong Kong dollar. On my deed you will see that the time and date is 10:30 a.m., Friday, March 23rd, 1973. That is three days earlier than the time and date on yours.'

Errol Tu gave voice. 'It a fake! What you say impossible! Friday morning the *Meen Foot Hau Jaak* was in Red Phoenix Motel! I know it – '

'That's extremely interesting,' Zagan said softly. 'The police are outside. They're keen to talk with anyone who knows anything of Mr Cosgrove's movements between midnight last Thursday and when he turned up in the Hong Kong Club yesterday afternoon. I know exactly where he was during that time. He told me. Not only that, he signed a statement in front of witnesses, one of whom was myself. The police now have it. It gives an eyewitness account of how Carla Tze Ti was murdered.'

The challengers' camp was reduced to stunned speechlessness. Tu Chien frowned at Errol Tu, who removed his hand from the inside of his jacket.

Satisfied, Zagan walked back to the head of the table. He looked sadly at Huart and said: 'Lennie Cosgrove is dead, isn't he.'

Huart nodded slowly.

So Lennie the Fifth had been unable to face up to it after all. It had been his body on Queen's Road. 'Suicide,' Zagan muttered.

Again Huart nodded. 'He left a note. I dictated it to the police.'

But Elizabeth Zagan was shaking her head. 'It was murder. The police think he was hit with the barrel of a pistol and his body was thrown off the balcony to make it look like suicide.' She nodded to the foot of the table. 'They were tipped off that he had made a statement and tried to shut his mouth forever. But there was a witness: the woman he spent the night with. She was in the bathroom with the door locked when it happened. She heard the struggle, and heard him call out the man's name. When she thought it was safe, she called the police on the bathroom phone. They're now looking for a Mr Waldo Wu.'

Matthew Zagan looked from Huart to Tu Chien, then back to Huart. 'Lennie Cosgrove's forty per cent of Charlemagne Enterprises is mine. The 20.4 per cent of Cumberland China that it gives me is pledged in your support – giving you the majority you seek.' He paused. 'But on one condition.'

Huart groaned inwardly. What trick now? 'And that is?'

Tu Chien, seeking a miracle, hesitated in his move to quit the fight.

'This: Cumberland China gets a new board of directors,

consisting of men with their balls between their legs and not in somebody else's fist.'

'Matthew!' His mother was aghast.

'Seconded!' Suzanne cried enthusiastically.

Huart threw back his head and laughed. The dam on his tension broke, and it left him in a flood. He fell into his chair, drawing himself to the left, away from the shell of the man who had most betrayed him.

The four whose time in the sun had ended, who would pay the supreme business penalty for their betrayal, cringed in their chairs. Bedrix, Buckley, Vail and Ezuelo looked furtively at each other, partners in ruin.

The Long Table had been the field of a great corporate battle. It was strewn with its debris: shattered careers, broken dreams, and skeletons wrenched from tightly locked closets.

As one, the vanquished stood and formed ranks.

'You may have won this battle,' Tu Chien declared, pointing his walking stick first at Zagan, then at Huart. 'But the war goes on. It seems I have exposed my hand too soon, that is all. Double murderer, your time is still to come. And it will come very soon.'

Though most who were listening wondered what he had meant, it would have been too anticlimactic for any to query it.

'I think not, old man,' Huart returned. 'Now, every one of you, kindly get out of my boardroom.'

At the door, Tu Chien turned to look back at Huart with eyes that were bottomless. He switched them to Zagan, and fired his parting shot.

'*Sze... Yu... Yiu... Gu!*'

With that, the Battle of the Long Table was over.

'You are Tu Wai-tsun, alias Errol Tu?'

The *bong baan* from CID had pronounced the Cantonese tones abominably, all but destroying them in their competition with a pronounced Scots brogue. Even so, Tu Chien stopped in his tracks and brought his entourage to a halt behind him. Errol Tu's face had turned white.

The Tu solicitor came forward. 'I represent Mr Tu. What do you want?'

'We want 'im to assist us wi' our enquiries.'

'Enquiries into what?'

'Disappearance an' possible murder o' one Miss Soon Ti-liang, alias Miss Tze Ti, alias Miss Carla Tze Ti.'

[588]

'You no find body yet, ha?' Errol Tu scoffed. 'So you have no case – '

The solicitor's glare cut him off. 'Is it your intention to arrest my client at this time?'

The *bong baan* shook his head. 'But after questionin', who knows?'

'But you no find body yet!' Errol Tu protested.

The curious security guard moved away from the entrance.

Everyone was so intent on the solicitor's arguments in favour of his client's rights, that nobody saw the fire door on the far side of the lift lobby open twelve inches and a small figure scurry across the marble floor. Nobody saw the glass door of the reception area swing open and a little boy drop into a crouch.

'*Aaaahhhh yeeeeaaaahhhh!*'

The *kung fu* cry had them all turning. But it was already too late. Lee Yeok-hon had launched himself, his right leg extended horizontally in an attack kick of which his namesake idol, Bruce Lee Siu-lung – the Little Dragon himself – would have been proud. He was only forty-five pounds, but his momentum compensated. His foot took the walking stick, and Tu Chien had started to fall when Yeok-hon's heel carried through and impacted dead centre upon the hip joint.

'*Aaaaiiiiiyaaaahhhh!*'

Tu Chien screamed with his face contorted in all-consuming agony as the cancer he had kept preserved exploded through his body. His legs buckled as if they had broken in two and he hit the floor hard. A black vapour rose before his eyes, then fell to cover him like a shroud.

The bullet fired by the giant thirty-three years before had finally found its mark.

The last thought that flashed through Tu Chien's brain was a question: Who is this mad-crazy child who has killed me?

Lee Yeok-hon, born April 6th, 1966, the time of Clearness and Brightness in the Year of the Fire Horse, stood over the old man in the long-gown dying at his feet, and did not know whether to laugh or to cry.

'Call a doctor!' ordered the *bong baan*. 'Call a fookin' ambulance!'

Huart came running out of the boardroom. He strode to his godson and picked him up. Yeok-hon threw his arms around his godfather's neck and hung on tight. Together, in concert with everyone else standing about them, they looked down at the lifeless body upon the carpet.

The scattered jade fragments that had once been a bracelet so antique that it had been colourless and therefore priceless, went unnoticed until later.

3

'What I understand least, Matthew,' said Huart, 'is why you threatened me. You must have known that I never succumb to threats. There is no room for them in business.'

Zagan replaced his cup of jasmine tea on the coffee table. He took out his pack of Marlboros and offered it to Suzanne, who had changed into more conventional attire. She extracted one between varnished nails and the twin clouds of exhaled smoke softened the afternoon sunshine that streamed in through the circular windows.

'I knew that. And I made use of the knowledge. It was too soon for me to expose myself and be a target for the Tus like all the others. So I did the opposite and eliminated myself, knowing that it would be only a temporary elimination.'

'How could you be so sure?' Huart queried. 'You took an awful risk.'

Zagan shook his head. 'The Hang On Street fiasco ruled Buckley out . . .'

'It did.'

' . . . and Glynn Bedrix had to prove unsuitable.'

The thick skin over Huart's eyebrows bunched. 'But how did you know he was a. . . . How did you know about him? I worked so closely with him for thirteen years and at no time did I suspect anything like that.'

'With respect, you were looking at him up too close. Perhaps you were judging him by his father's example. Times have changed. I began to suspect it that night in your penthouse last August. After that I did some checking. There was an incident when he was at Oxford. The Tus must have done their own research.'

Huart's frown deepened. It had been such a day. To be sixty-six, and yet discover there was so much still to learn. . . . Times had indeed changed. The company needed someone like Matthew Zagan today, but it had all been so distasteful, so sordid, so Machiavellian.

Today, for several minutes, Huart had lost the Born Again *Hong*. For him, Cumberland China had been pronounced clinically dead before being revived by the production of a single document. It had been neat and not so clean. And its architect had been the very person he had been seeking for almost two decades: the grandson of Charles Huart. The man had been in his very employ, and was about to be admitted to his very Long Table, having claimed his seat in his own right. Yet he himself, the so-called Altitudinal Taipan, had been chronically unaware of it all. The time had indeed come for him to step down. Huart was almost glad.

He broke from his rumination. 'Was Tu Chien's Deed of Sale legal?'

Zagan shrugged. 'Yes and no. It was drawn up under duress, but it would have been Cosgrove's word against the Tus'. It was witnessed and notarised by a member of the Hong Kong Bar, don't forget.'

'How did you overcome that? How did you have your deed predated?'

'Some legal men are human. My mother and I engaged one who, when he heard Cosgrove's story, decided to serve justice by bending its rules.'

'Who is this man? I'll keep it confidential, of course, but I owe him.'

'I want him on the new board. His name is Raymond Clinton O'Young.'

There was another Huart had underestimated. 'So your deed is illegal?'

Again Zagan shrugged. 'Yes and no. It's every bit as legal or illegal as the Tus'. In any case, it served its purpose. But I should tell you that it is only one of two Deeds of Sale.' He took the brown envelope from his coat as Huart's eyebrows arched. 'Here is the second.'

Huart studied what appeared to be a duplicate of the first deed, except that it legalised the transfer of forty per cent of Charlemagne Enterprises from Matthew Zagan back to Leonard Cosgrove for one Hong Kong dollar. 'So Tu Chien owned the shares after all? I don't follow . . .'

'Look at the date.'

Huart did so. 'Tuesday, March 27th, 1973. Today?'

'For obvious reasons we decided to post-date the second deed a full day after the one we knew the Tus would present. Lennie Cosgrove's intention was not, of course, to transfer his share of

Charlemagne Enterprises to me at all, just to invalidate the deed he had been forced to sign. But early this morning, on the day of the reversal, he died. Therefore he couldn't have signed the second deed, and his forty per cent in Charlemagne consequently remains mine. Somehow I don't think the Tus – or anyone else – will challenge it. They've had enough.'

'I'm sure they have. The head of the family gone, a nephew in jail . . . And what's to be done with our Alain To?'

'I have a suggestion. The Contracting Division of Cumberland Engineering is rife with inefficiency and corruption. Every project is making a loss everywhere except on the balance sheet. Losses are being carried over to new projects. It's a cycle which will only end, and end rudely, when an audit is done on all projects simultaneously. Alain To has been the mastermind behind it. I suggest we sell the division to Great Horse Enterprises and give him to them to "manage" it – for an acceptable price.'

'Lennie's ten per cent in Cumberland China,' Huart agreed.

'If they refuse, we hand Alain To over to the Anti-Corruption Branch. The police are looking for a juicy commercial case to take the pressure off themselves and forestall the establishment of this independent commission that everyone's talking about.'

'They'll accept,' Huart predicted. 'They've lost enough menfolk for one day. And so have we. We have five chairs at the Long Table to fill. We had a case of potentially terminal cancer exposed today. It's been cut out, but it's left one hell of a hole to fill. The company will have to rehabilitate for a short while – then we'll emerge leaner, healthier, stronger. Five empty chairs. I really only regret one . . .'

Huart thought sadly how the Midas touch of Lennie the Fifth had turned septic. Cicero Investments had run its course; P. G. Curzon-Cross would unload all its shares on the market tomorrow. Though prices were heavily discounted from the peak, a healthy profit would still result, and the cash derived would be used to buy up the Cumberland China stock the Tus would dump when suspension was lifted at ten the next day. Cicero would then possess most of the public shares and, as its co-owners, he and Zagan would control nearly seventy per cent of the Born Again *Hong* between them. Today, after all that had happened, he liked it that way.

Aware of the cyclic inevitability of Cicero's demise, Huart had kept in reserve an alternative 'project' for his partner. Hong Kong's third largest money-spinner was tourism. Cumberland China was to diversify into the hotel industry, and the deputy chairman was to have led it. It would have suited him right down to his hand-made Italian calf-skin casuals.

He thought of the note that Lennie the Fifth had left for him, in which he had let Kipling do most of the explaining:

> 'And the end of the fight is a tombstone white
>   with the name of the late deceased,
> And the epitaph drear: "A fool lies here
>   Who tried to hustle the East." '

He sighed out loud. 'I always thought I was looking out for him. But this time, when he needed me most, I shut him out . . .'

'You couldn't even find him!' Suzanne retorted. 'Right up to the bitter end he was shacked up with some female I'll bet he'd hardly introduced himself to. He was a big boy, Uncle John. Don't you dare blame yourself for what happened to him. What he did to you was unforgivable.'

That avuncular smile reappeared. 'You're much more than "some female", Suzie. You might even comply with the anatomical criteria Matthew has laid down for members of the new board.'

Her return smile was decidedly feline. 'Oh, I think he knows better than that, Uncle John. You do remember, don't you Matt?'

Huart was quite certain the young man had blushed momentarily.

Then, with the intention of putting an end to it before it started up all over again, Zagan said to her: 'Hasn't it registered with you yet? Your great-grandfather was my grandfather. We have common blood, and what blood it is! Now do you see why I can't – ?'

It was the wholesomeness of her laughter that had stopped him. He looked to Huart for help, and saw him smiling too. 'What's so funny?'

'Charles Huart was many things, but being Suzie's great-grand-father was not one of them. Andrew Huart-Brent, Charles' grandson and your half-cousin, was not her father.'

'Say that again.'

Suzanne leaned forward. 'My real father was a Chicago insurance tycoon called Rex Wagoner. My mother revealed this to me after Andrew, the man I thought of as my father – and still do if the truth be known – died. She married Wagoner and wanted me to accept him. Under those circumstances it was natural for her to tell me he was, in fact, my father.'

Amazement, confusion, then relief each paid a visit to Zagan's face. 'Do you mean I've been torturing myself for nothing all this time?'

Suzanne's deep brown eyes looked on as he fought down the rough seas that had risen inside. Gradually, he succeeded, and then he looked back at her, but before he could say anything the door opened and his mother was there with a copy of *The Register*'s special edition. She held up the headlines for all to see.

NEW TAIPAN FOR *GUM BAK LEEN*
FIVE VACANCIES AT THE LONG TABLE

'I hope you will forgive my intrusion and my self-indulgence, but it's not often that the proprietor gets to write the lead story from personal observation. And about her very own son.'

Huart went to her and shook her hand. 'Mrs Zagan, I have much to thank you for. I will sum it up by thanking you for having your son . . .'

'Seconded,' Suzanne inserted.

' . . . but not for running away from me that evening on Queen's Road.'

'What would have happened if I hadn't, Mr Huart?'

'I would have asked you to dinner that night.'

She smiled. For her son it was a rare sight. 'Well, I happen to be free tonight, Mr Huart. But unfortunately, you're not. Your secretary asked me to remind both of you that your charter for Peking takes off at four. You have just forty minutes to make it to Kai Tak before the flight closes. Your car is waiting downstairs and all your luggage has been packed. I suggest you get moving. Gentlemen, China awaits you.'

Matthew Zagan took his mother in his arms and hugged her. It was an ingenuous act, but it was the thrill of her life. Through her son, triumph and justice had come to Elizabeth Jane Zagan, née Huart, at last. The events of this day of days had served to discharge her father's will.

Suzanne watched mother and son exchange a type of love she had never known. Her eyes followed him as they walked arm-in-arm to the door. They passed through it without him even turning to say goodbye.

After a moment, Elizabeth Zagan put her head back into the office and looked from John Huart, a man she had misjudged so, to his 'niece', the woman she now knew her son loved. 'So what are you both waiting for?'

Suzanne blinked away the film that had formed over her eyes. 'Both?'

Elizabeth nodded. 'Actually, there is a spare ticket for Peking and it has your name on it. Matthew said that Mr Szeto will be waiting for you at the airport with your visa. You'll both miss the flight if you don't get a move on.'

Though she carried the name, the blood of Suzanne Huart-Brent was not that of the Fire Horse. But she reacted as if it was. 'Mrs Zagan, if your son wants me to go to Peking, then tell him to come back here and ask me himself. Who does he think he is? The Fifth Taipan?'

Huart gave a chuckle as he walked past her. 'He should, Suzie. Because that's exactly what he is. Now, my sweet thing, are you coming to Peking with us or not?'

EPILOGUE

Peking: 31 March 1973

Epilogue

The balcony outside the window of room 421 of the Peking Hotel was wide enough to accommodate Huart and Zagan standing, but nothing more. Below, the *Chiang An Lu*, the Avenue of Everlasting Peace, extended in both directions as far as the eye could see. Upon it flowed a two-way flood tide of bicycles, heads of black hair and shoulders padded with blue Mao jackets. A symphony of bells carried up to the two men, who looked down and observed it all with avidity.

The Peking Hotel was an anachronism left over from the time when foreign presence intimidated the Manchu throne. Nevertheless, it was the best hotel in the city. Indeed, it was almost the only hotel, and its rooms were in such demand that Huart, Zagan and Suzanne had been lucky to get two between the three of them, despite possessing a 'confirmation'.

Suzanne had the luxury of a room to herself. Even so, her privacy was a myth as she had twice been caught *au naturel* by roomboys who neither knocked nor averted their gaze. Today she had gone off to climb the Great Wall and to look out over the plains of North China, rich and heady with tragic history.

A short walk away was the concrete agoraphobia of the square in front of Tienanmen, the Gate of Heavenly Peace. Not quite seven years before, a million 'Little Revolutionary Generals' had assembled there. A million hands had held aloft little red books and a million throats had called encouragement to the author, the Great Helmsman – whose giant portrait dominated from above the gate, and whose hand upon the helm had strayed too far to port.

In a corner of the square stood the Great Hall of the People, a building whose architecture did justice to its name in a country of one billion. There, on the third day of the British Industrial Technology Exhibition, in a reception room with walls of pastel green, floors with their thick hand-woven rugs and porcelain spittoons, and chairs covered in brown and draped with white lace antimacassars, Huart had been personally introduced to one of Y. Y. Szeto's 'reasonably important people': Chou En-lai.

'I thank you for granting my grand-nephew employment, Mr Huart,' the premier had opened. 'I trust that he has proved himself to be worthy. As a boy he always did try to seize an opportunity with both hands.'

Huart's company secretary had been standing behind his 'grand-uncle', wearing the first emotion anyone had ever seen on him: embarrassment.

'Mister Premier, "worthy" is quite an understatement. But your nephew's greatest ability of so many abilities has to be how to keep a secret.'

Chou En-lai had proffered that famous shrewd half-smile. 'Then he has not told you of the special present we have for you. That is good.'

'A present? But, Mister Premier, I'm the guest.'

Chou En-lai had left him to walk over to the side table and the puzzling wooden crate that had been standing amongst tea cups, thermos flasks and ashtrays. He had reached inside and carefully lifted out what appeared to Huart to be a ceramic statue of an ancient oriental horse.

'It is the only one of its kind ever made,' the premier had explained. 'It is a perfect replica of a chariot horse in the Ch'in Dynasty of two centuries ago. The previous caretaker had the eyes replaced with these Burmese rubies that shine like fire. It seems they represented something important to him. We would like you to receive it as a memento of your first visit to Peking. I hope that your second will follow soon.'

'Mister Premier, I . . . I'm not usually lost for words, but . . .'

'You may keep the statue for yourself,' Chou En-lai had continued, 'or you may make a gift of it to your godson on his seventh birthday.'

Something that Huart had been thinking as being very mysterious had suddenly taken on a very definite shape. He had nodded with the revelation and said softly: 'Mr Lee Wing-tak of Koon Wah Mansion, Mongkok.'

The premier had smiled again. 'We are an extremely large "family".' He had handed the statue to Huart, saying: 'And we never forget those who do right by us. Neither do we forget those who cross us. You see, Mr Huart, a long time ago – 1927, in fact – I made a pledge, too.'

Matthew Zagan lifted the brown bottle of Tsingtao beer and Huart touched his own against it in toast. He had left his Chivas in Hong Kong, the Peking Hotel had gin but no tonic, and there had been no champagne in China since 1949. Even so, the beer that was brewed with the natural spring water of Lao Shan tasted better than the finest Dom Perignon.

From inside room 421 the clack-clack-clack-clack of an old China-made typewriter punctuated the sibilant cadence of several voices speaking simultaneous Mandarin, amongst them that of Cumberland Engineering's interpreter. Each was making its excited contribution to the preparation of the twelve copies of the purchase contract bearing the masthead of the China National Machinery Import and Export Corporation.

All the machinery for the production of garments and the fabrication of modern elevators, the sample electro-mechanical telephone exchange, and the civil construction equipment that had been displayed on the Cumberland Engineering stand at the exhibition had been sold. The Chinese had pressed for a heavily discounted price, knowing exhibitors would be keen to sell 'off the stand' on the last day to save the expense of shipping their exhibits back to the United Kingdom via Hong Kong. They had not quite got their asking price, but the deal had nevertheless been struck.

It was a modest beginning for Cumberland China. But, most importantly, it was a beginning.

A New Beginning.

Zagan looked over the iron railing as a black limousine made in Shanghai to Russian specifications drew up at the hotel entrance. A rear door with a curtained window opened and Suzanne stepped out. As she climbed the steps into the Peking Hotel, she drew to her the masks that were the faces of the ubiquitous guards in green uniforms with crimson flashes.

She also drew the eyes of Matthew Zagan.

When she had disappeared inside, he cast his eyes again over the massed bicycles, blue boiler suits, round pink faces along the Avenue of Everlasting Peace. And saw the way ahead.

And he saw, too, that it had room for two.

John Huart had been following Zagan's gaze. And, inside the large head behind the avuncular smile, were ringing the words of curses now expurgated, of pledges long outstanding and now fulfilled.

And of a legend that had come to pass.